CW00764939

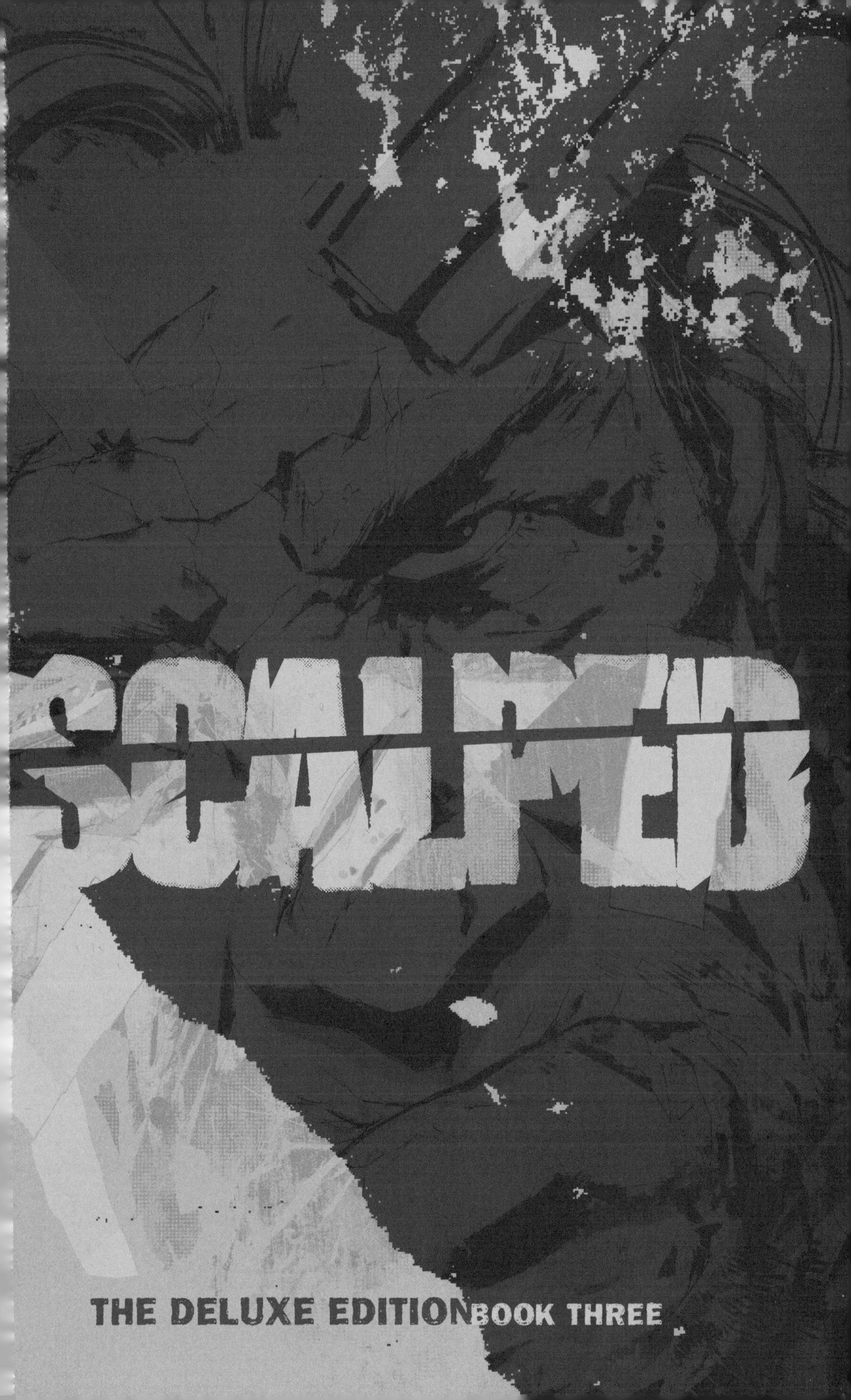
SCALPED
THE DELUXE EDITION BOOK THREE

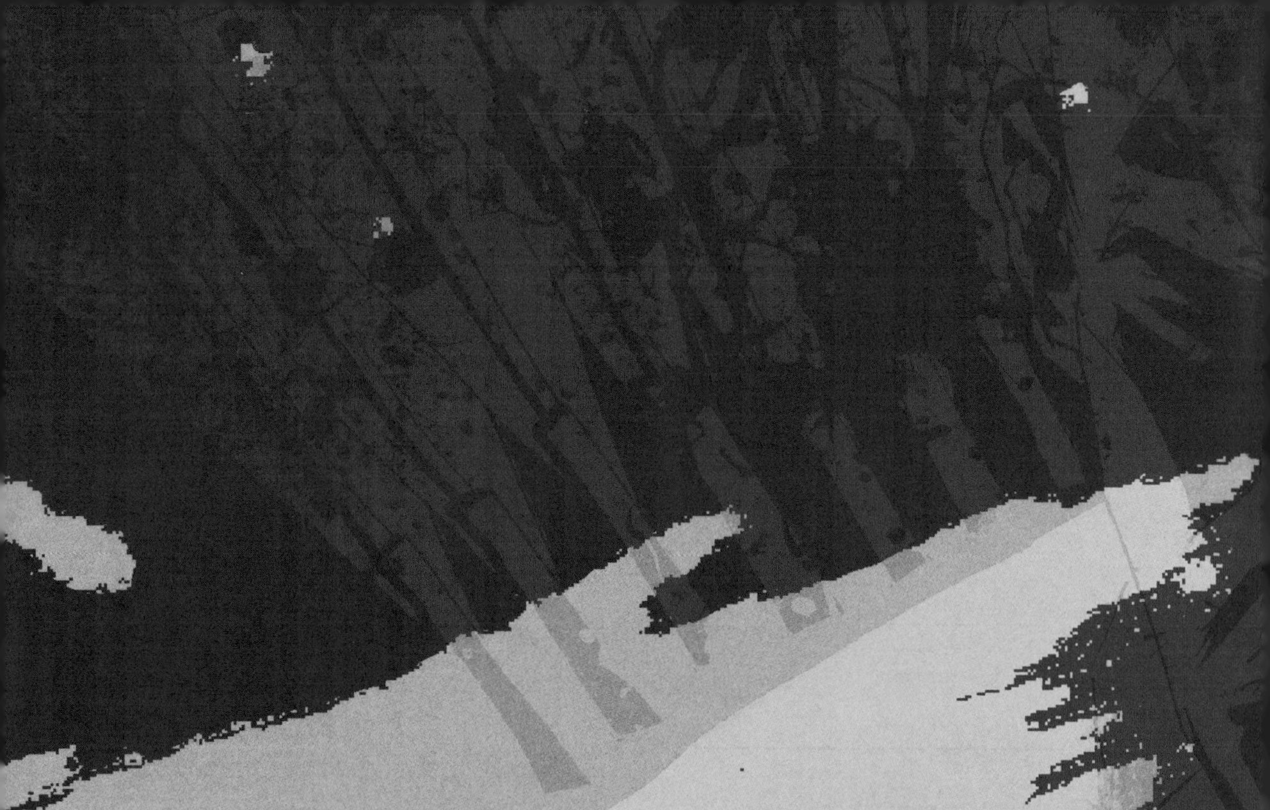

**JASON AARON**
Writer

**R. M. GUÉRA**
**DAVIDE FURNÒ** (ISSUE #26)
**FRANCESCO FRANCAVILLA** (ISSUE #27)
Artists

**GIULIA BRUSCO** WITH
**PATRICIA MULVIHILL (ISSUE #31)**
Colorists

**STEVE WANDS**
Letterer

**R.M. GUÉRA**
Cover Art

Original series covers by
**JOCK**

Introduction by **JASON STARR**

**SCALPED** created by
**JASON AARON** and **R. M. GUÉRA**

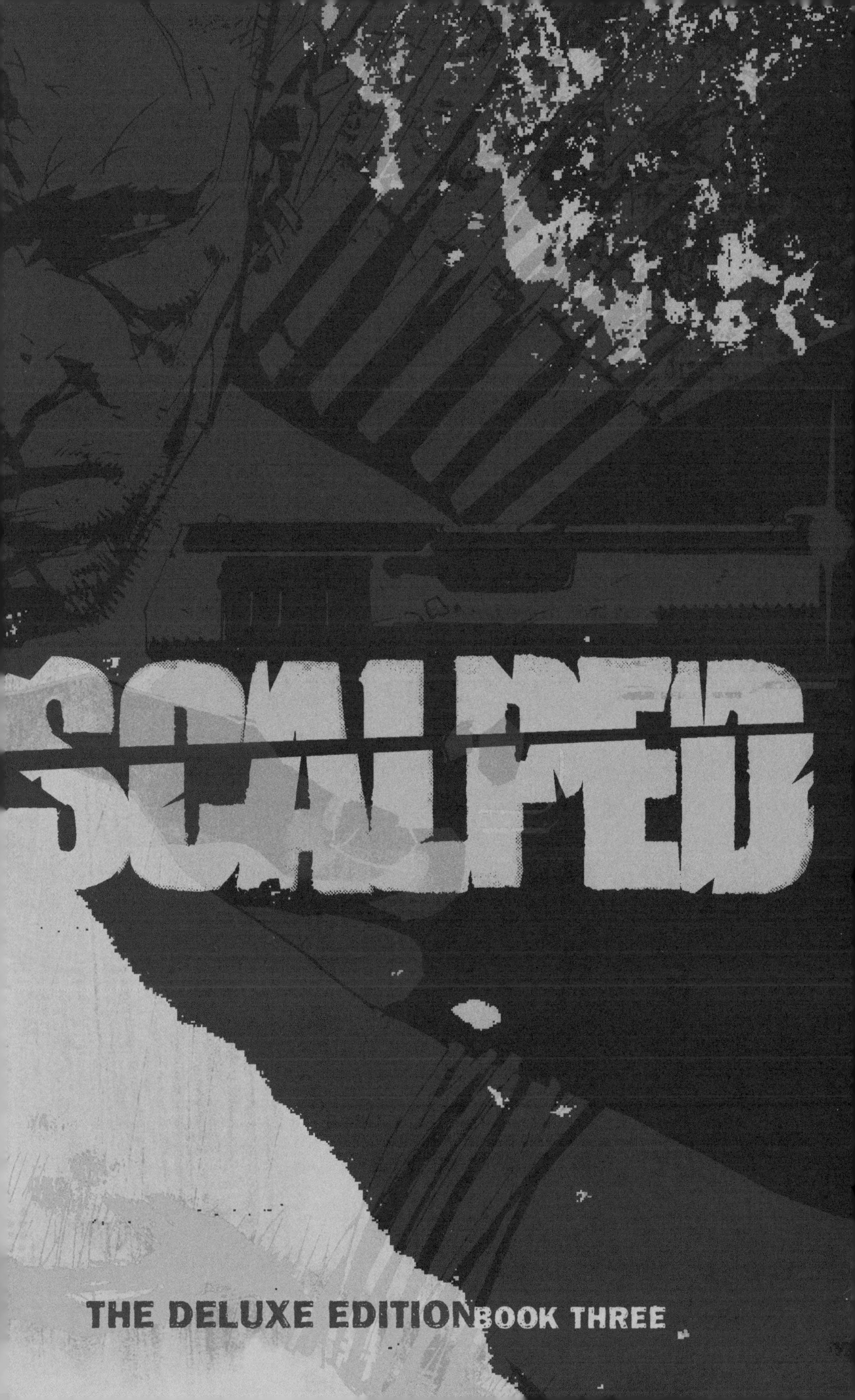
SCALPED
THE DELUXE EDITION BOOK THREE

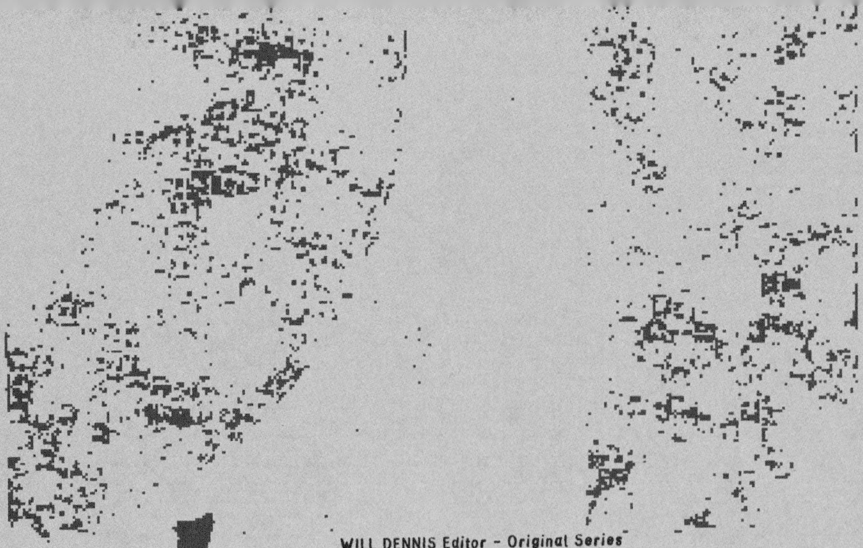

WILL DENNIS Editor - Original Series
MARK DOYLE Assistant Editor - Original Series
JEB WOODARD Group Editor - Collected Editions
SCOTT NYBAKKEN Editor - Collected Edition
DAMIAN RYLAND Publication Design

SHELLY BOND VP & Executive Editor - Vertigo

DIANE NELSON President
DAN DIDIO and JIM LEE Co-Publishers
GEOFF JOHNS Chief Creative Officer
AMIT DESAI Senior VP - Marketing & Global Franchise Management
NAIRI GARDINER Senior VP - Finance
SAM ADES VP - Digital Marketing
BOBBIE CHASE VP - Talent Development
MARK CHIARELLO Senior VP - Art, Design & Collected Editions
JOHN CUNNINGHAM VP - Content Strategy
ANNE DEPIES VP - Strategy Planning & Reporting
DON FALLETTI VP - Manufacturing Operations
LAWRENCE GANEM VP - Editorial Administration & Talent Relations
ALISON GILL Senior VP - Manufacturing & Operations
HANK KANALZ Senior VP - Editorial Strategy & Administration
JAY KOGAN VP - Legal Affairs
DEREK MADDALENA Senior VP - Sales & Business Development
JACK MAHAN VP - Business Affairs
DAN MIRON VP - Sales Planning & Trade Development
NICK NAPOLITANO VP - Manufacturing Administration
CAROL ROEDER VP - Marketing
EDDIE SCANNELL VP - Mass Account & Digital Sales
COURTNEY SIMMONS Senior VP - Publicity & Communications
JIM (SKI) SOKOLOWSKI VP - Comic Book Specialty & Newsstand Sales
SANDY YI Senior VP - Global Franchise Management

Logo design by JOCK

SCALPED: THE DELUXE EDITION BOOK THREE



DC Comics, 2900 West Alameda Avenue, Burbank, CA 91505.
Printed in Canada. First Printing.
ISBN: 978-1-4012-5858-0.

Library of Congress Cataloging-in-Publication Data

Aaron, Jason.
Scalped deluxe edition. Book three / Jason Aaron, writer ; R.M. Guéra, Davide Furnò, artists.
pages cm
ISBN 978-1-4012-5858-0 (hardback)
1. Indian reservations—Comic books, strips, etc. 2. Organized crime—Comic books, strips, etc. 3. Graphic novels.
I. Guéra, R. M., illustrator. II. Furnò, Davide, illustrator. III. Title.
PN6727.A22S287 2015
741.5'973—dc23
2015031189

PEFC Certified
Printed on paper from sustainably managed forests and controlled sources
PEFC
PEFC/01-31-106
www.pefc.org

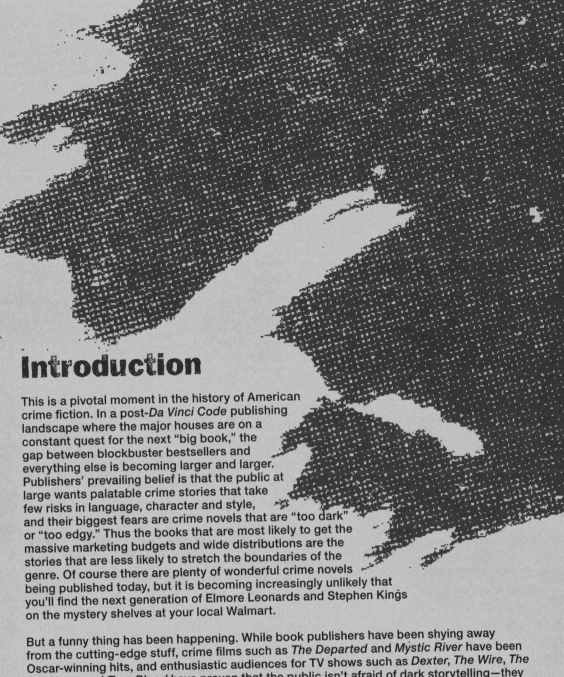

# Introduction

This is a pivotal moment in the history of American crime fiction. In a post-*Da Vinci Code* publishing landscape where the major houses are on a constant quest for the next "big book," the gap between blockbuster bestsellers and everything else is becoming larger and larger. Publishers' prevailing belief is that the public at large wants palatable crime stories that take few risks in language, character and style, and their biggest fears are crime novels that are "too dark" or "too edgy." Thus the books that are most likely to get the massive marketing budgets and wide distributions are the stories that are less likely to stretch the boundaries of the genre. Of course there are plenty of wonderful crime novels being published today, but it is becoming increasingly unlikely that you'll find the next generation of Elmore Leonards and Stephen Kings on the mystery shelves at your local Walmart.

But a funny thing has been happening. While book publishers have been shying away from the cutting-edge stuff, crime films such as *The Departed* and *Mystic River* have been Oscar-winning hits, and enthusiastic audiences for TV shows such as *Dexter*, *The Wire*, *The Sopranos* and *True Blood* have proven that the public isn't afraid of dark storytelling—they actually crave it. Showtime even recently boasted in a massive ad campaign that they have "the edgiest shows" on television. It's hard to imagine a major publishing house in the United States boasting that it publishes the edgiest crime fiction.

Sagely recognizing the public's appetite for groundbreaking storytelling, the comics industry has been ahead of the curve for years. Working almost exclusively in comics, writers such as Brian Azzarello, Garth Ennis and Ed Brubaker would make any shortlist of the finest crime writers of this generation. The latest crime master to emerge in comics is Jason Aaron.

Aaron's work—in SCALPED, in particular—is up there with the best of Elmore Leonard and George V. Higgins. It's everything great crime fiction should be—raw, honest, ironic, in-your-face and dark as hell. And why shouldn't it be dark? Crime by definition is dark, and Aaron refuses to give it to us any other way. He takes risks that few novelists would dare to take and fewer book publishers would dare to publish. He understands that to hook us and to get us to keep turning pages, we don't have to like his characters—actually making a character ultra-likable is a very good way to bore readers to tears—but we have to understand them. In "High Lonesome"—the best SCALPED story arc yet—he gives us some of the biggest assholes imaginable, and yet we can't get enough of them because they are so compelling and memorable and real. Plot-wise, Aaron uses structural techniques that, frankly, have never been used before, easing between past and present and multiple storylines, and it all comes together brilliantly in the end.

Just as William Faulkner brought his fictional Yoknapatawpha County to life, in a few pages of SCALPED you'll be immersed in a world—the Prairie Rose Indian Reservation—which is wholly and uniquely Aaron's own. Of course, none of this would be possible without the pitch-perfect, haunting artwork of R.M. Guéra, Davide Furnò and Francesco Francavilla.

Like a shark, the crime genre has to keep moving forward and innovating or it will die. Hopefully the book publishing industry will wake up to the public's appetite for risk-taking storytelling and the modern crime novel will have a new heyday. In the meantime, read SCALPED and discover a prime example of why some of the best crime fiction today is in comics.

## Jason Starr
### July 2009

*Jason Starr is the international best-selling author of many crime novels and thrillers, including* Savage Lane, Cold Caller, Nothing Personal, Hard Feelings, Tough Luck, Twisted City *and* Lights Out. *He has won the Anthony Award twice, as well as the Barry Award, and his books are published in more than a dozen languages. He has written comics and graphic novels for Vertigo (*THE CHILL*), DC (*DOC SAVAGE*) and Marvel (*Punisher Max, Wolverine Max *and the original novel* Ant-Man: Natural Enemy*). He has also cowritten four novels with Ken Bruen—*Bust, Slide, The Max *and* Pimp—*and co-edited* Bloodlines, *an anthology of horse racing stories for Vintage Books. He lives in Manhattan.*

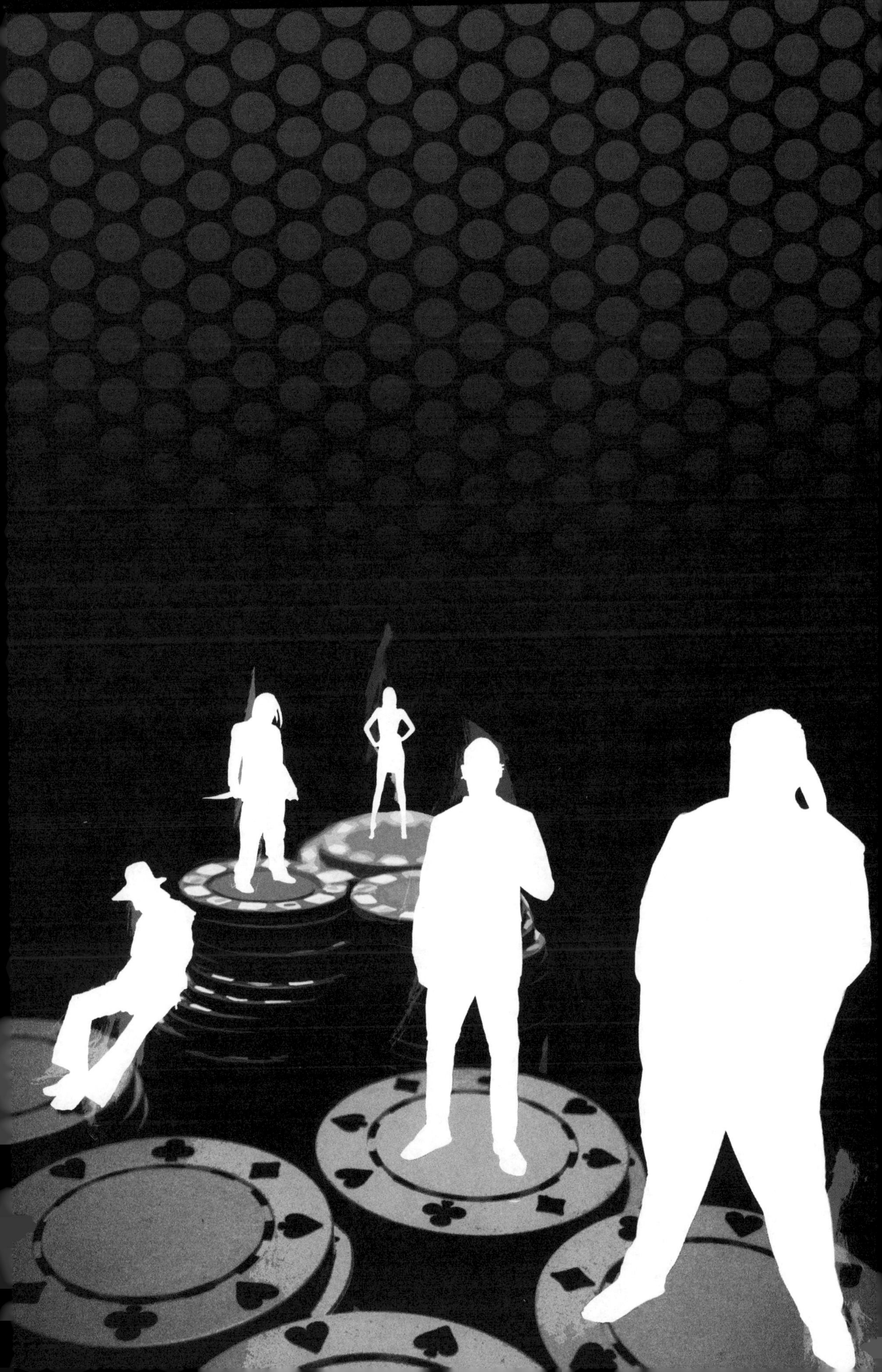

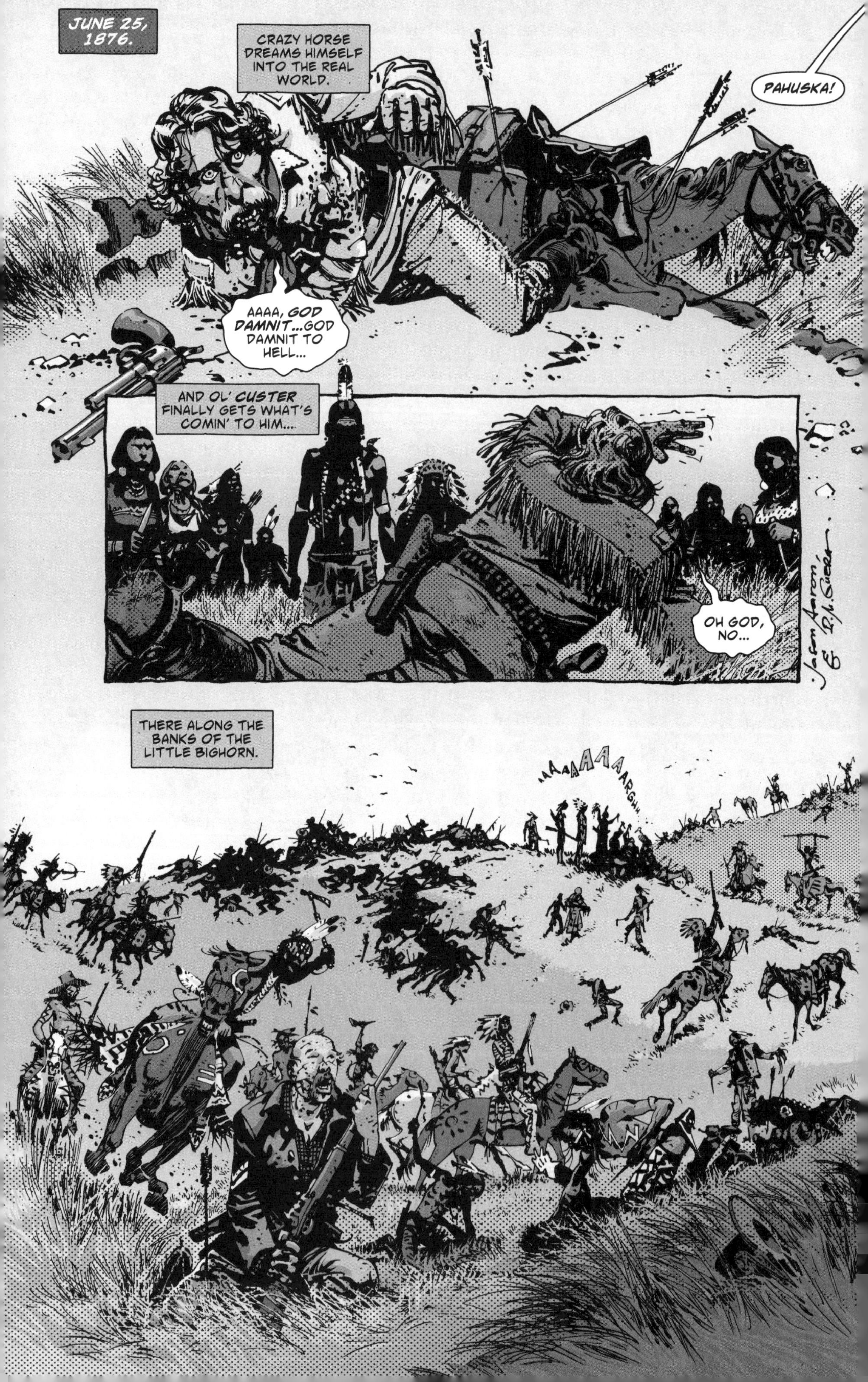

JUNE 25, 1876.
CRAZY HORSE DREAMS HIMSELF INTO THE REAL WORLD.
PAHUSKA!
AAAA, *GOD DAMNIT*...GOD DAMNIT TO HELL...
AND OL' *CUSTER* FINALLY GETS WHAT'S COMIN' TO HIM...
OH GOD, NO...
THERE ALONG THE BANKS OF THE LITTLE BIGHORN.
AAAAAAAARGHH

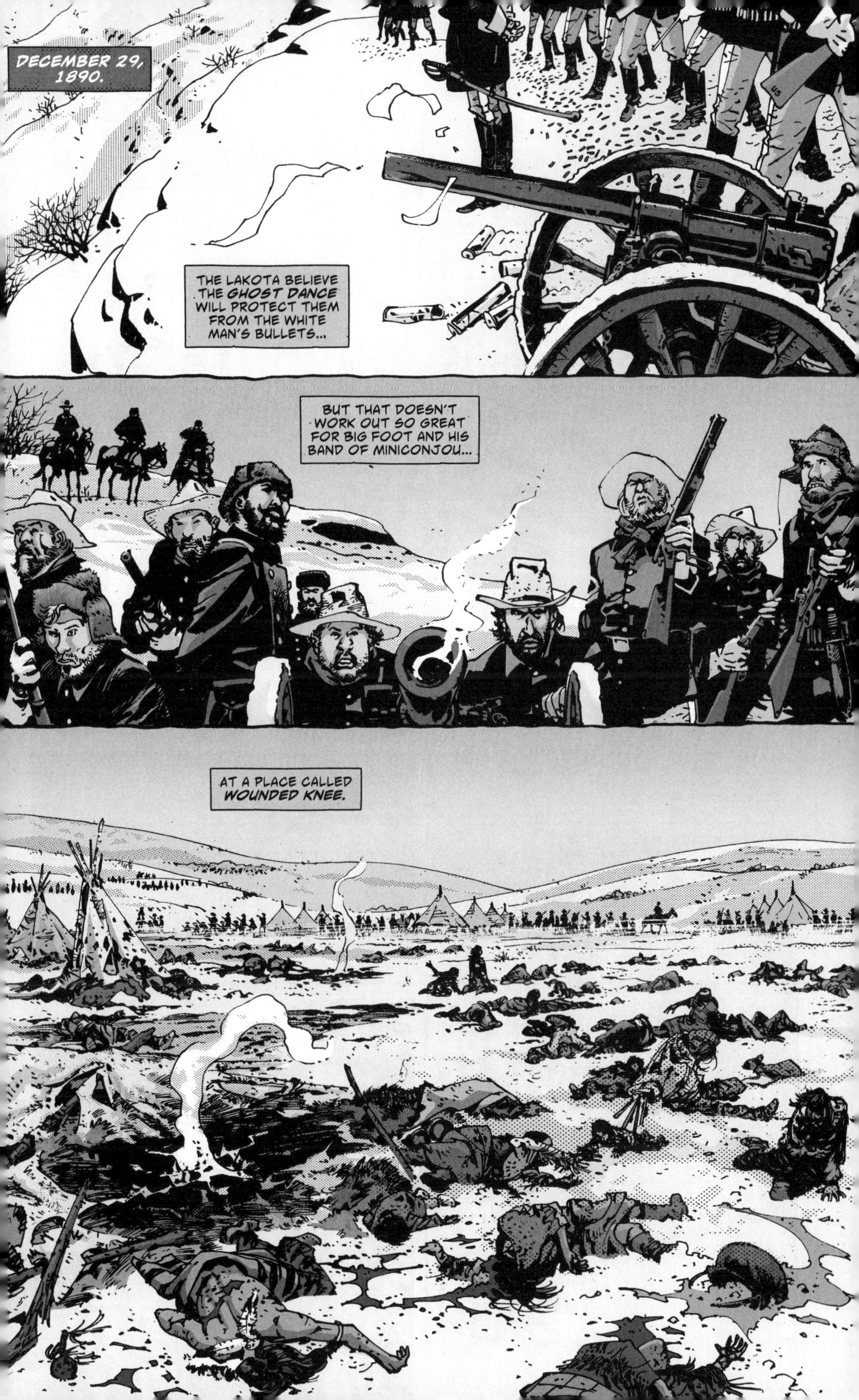
DECEMBER 29, 1890.
THE LAKOTA BELIEVE THE GHOST DANCE WILL PROTECT THEM FROM THE WHITE MAN'S BULLETS...
BUT THAT DOESN'T WORK OUT SO GREAT FOR BIG FOOT AND HIS BAND OF MINICONJOU...
AT A PLACE CALLED WOUNDED KNEE.

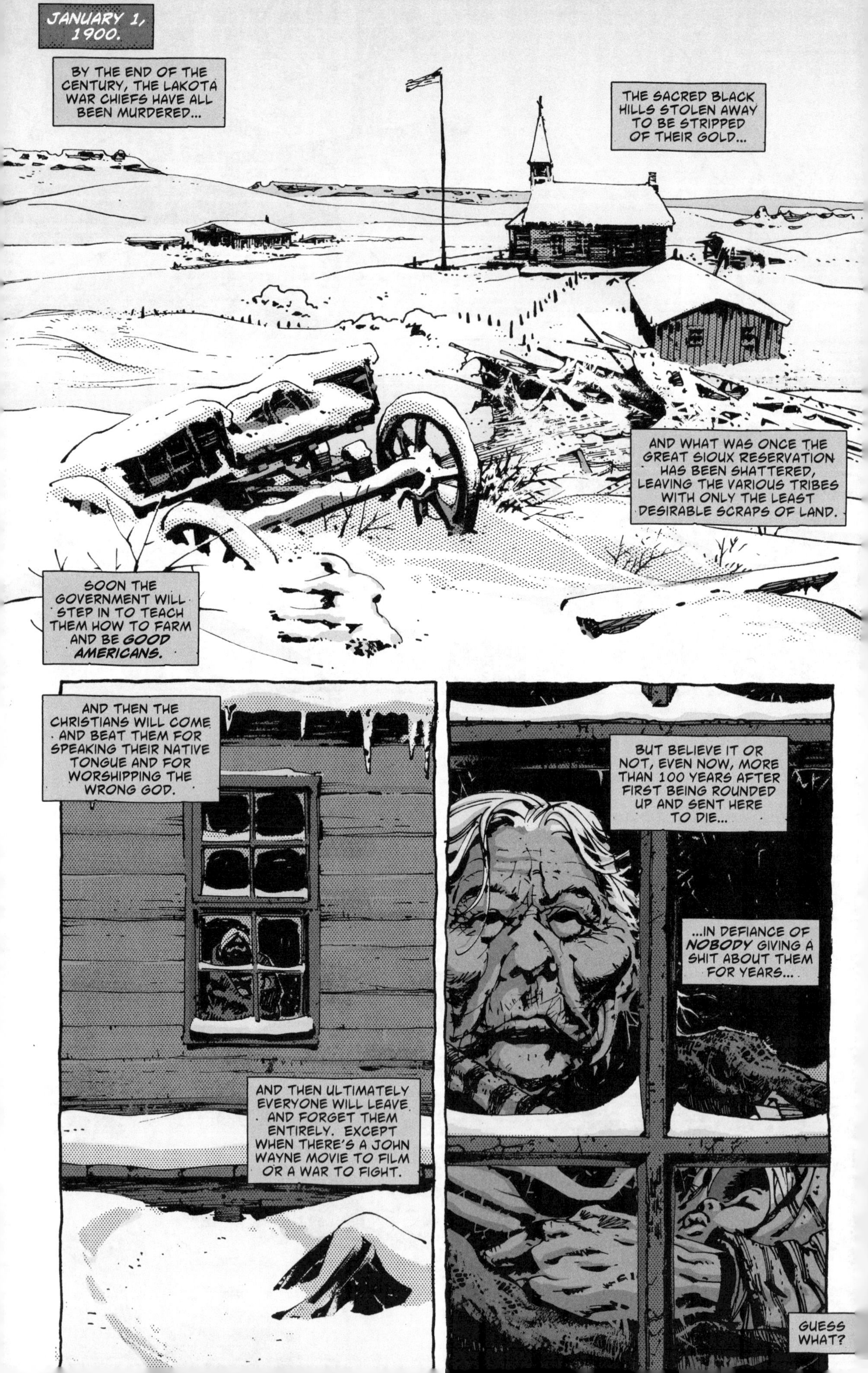
JANUARY 1, 1900.
BY THE END OF THE CENTURY, THE LAKOTA WAR CHIEFS HAVE ALL BEEN MURDERED...
THE SACRED BLACK HILLS STOLEN AWAY TO BE STRIPPED OF THEIR GOLD...
AND WHAT WAS ONCE THE GREAT SIOUX RESERVATION HAS BEEN SHATTERED, LEAVING THE VARIOUS TRIBES WITH ONLY THE LEAST DESIRABLE SCRAPS OF LAND.
SOON THE GOVERNMENT WILL STEP IN TO TEACH THEM HOW TO FARM AND BE *GOOD AMERICANS.*
AND THEN THE CHRISTIANS WILL COME AND BEAT THEM FOR SPEAKING THEIR NATIVE TONGUE AND FOR WORSHIPPING THE WRONG GOD.
AND THEN ULTIMATELY EVERYONE WILL LEAVE AND FORGET THEM ENTIRELY. EXCEPT WHEN THERE'S A JOHN WAYNE MOVIE TO FILM OR A WAR TO FIGHT.
BUT BELIEVE IT OR NOT, EVEN NOW, MORE THAN 100 YEARS AFTER FIRST BEING ROUNDED UP AND SENT HERE TO DIE...
...IN DEFIANCE OF *NOBODY* GIVING A SHIT ABOUT THEM FOR YEARS...
GUESS WHAT?

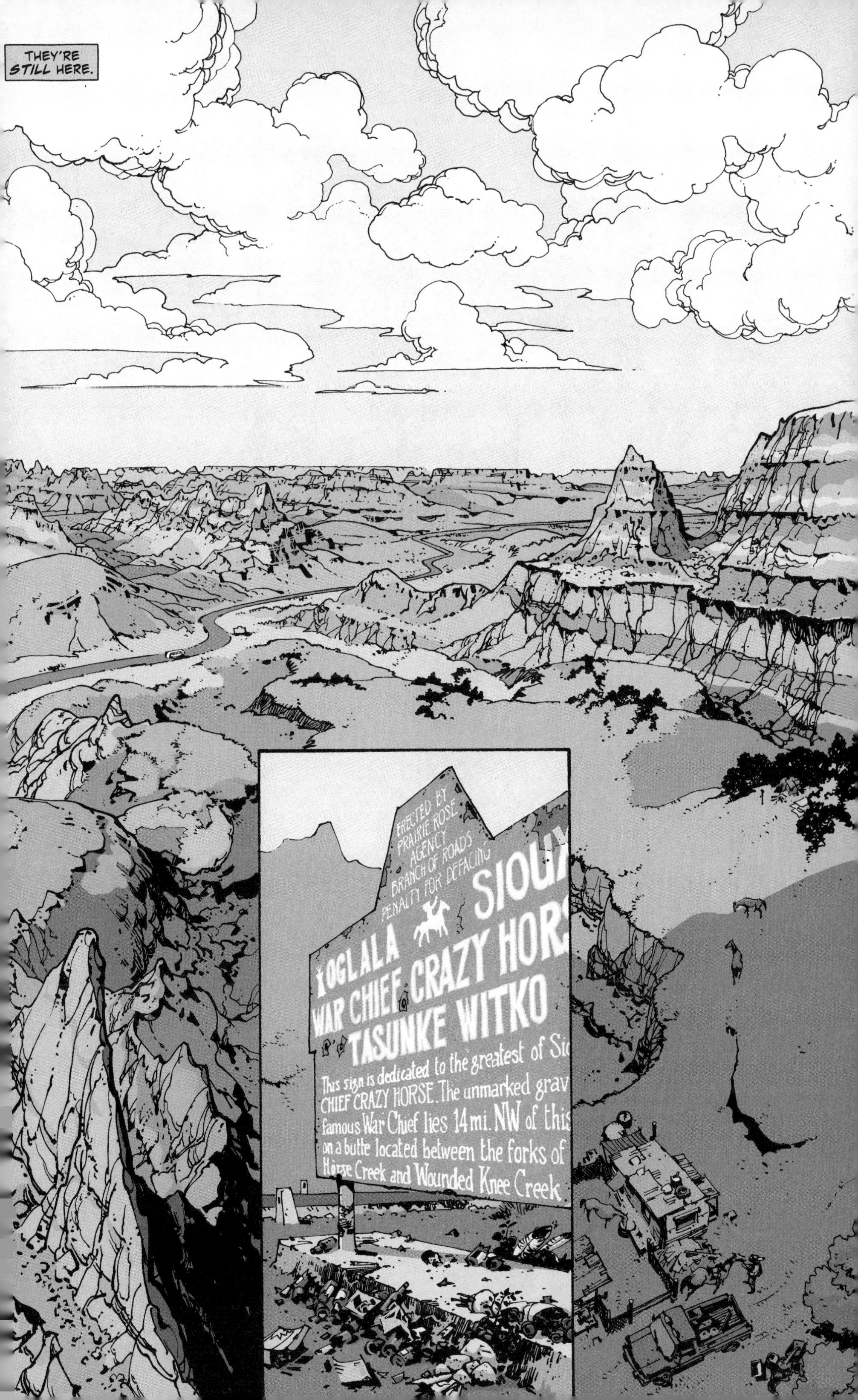
THEY'RE STILL HERE.
ERECTED BY
PRAIRIE ROSE
AGENCY
BRANCH OF ROADS
PENALTY FOR DEFACING
OGLALA
WAR CHIEF CRAZY HORS
TASUNKE WITKO
This sign is dedicated to the greatest of Si
CHIEF CRAZY HORSE. The unmarked grav
famous War Chief lies 14 mi. NW of this
on a butte located between the forks of
Horse Creek and Wounded Knee Creek

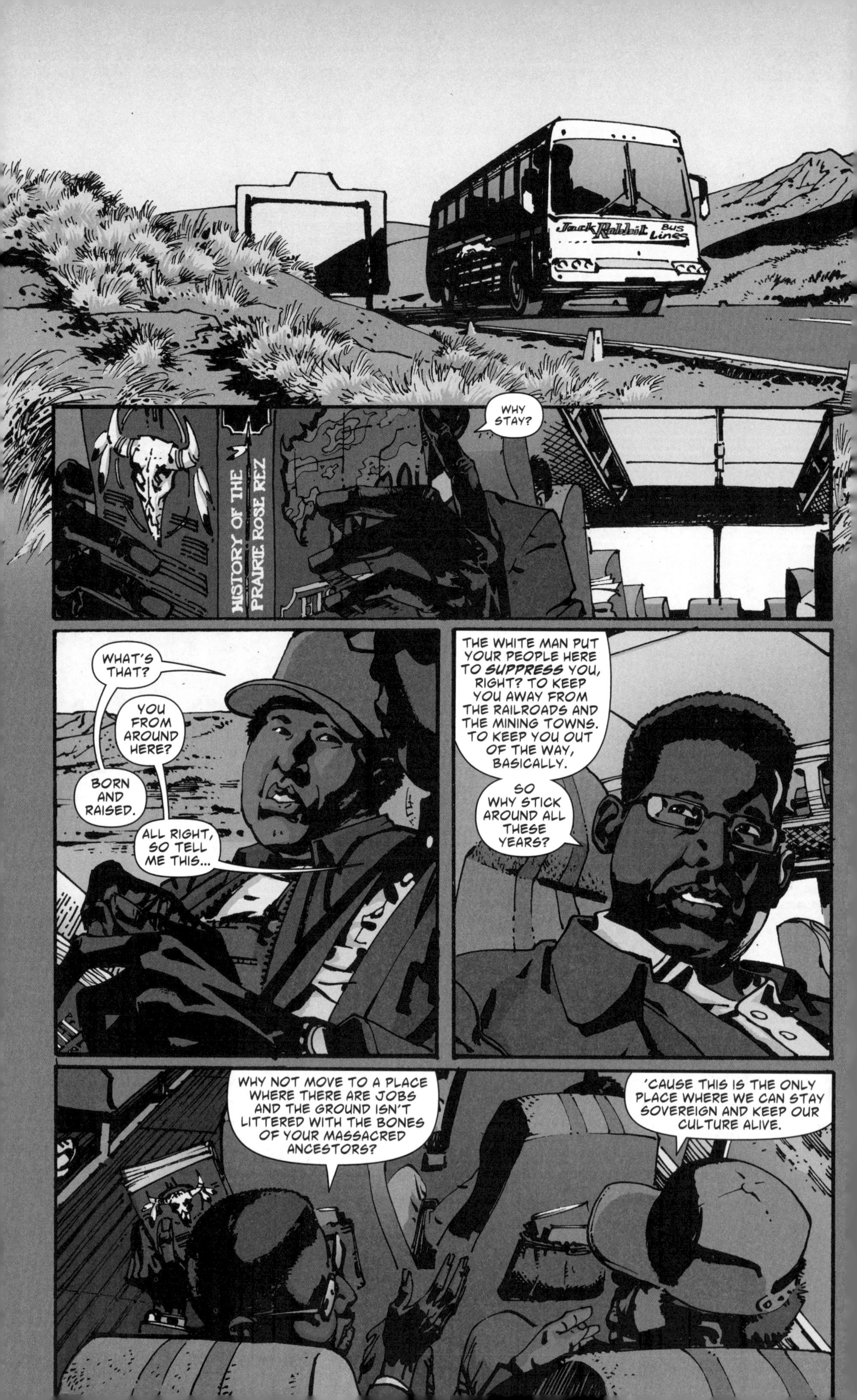
Jack Rabbit Bus Lines
HISTORY OF THE PRAIRIE ROSE REZ
WHY STAY?
WHAT'S THAT?
YOU FROM AROUND HERE?
BORN AND RAISED.
ALL RIGHT, SO TELL ME THIS...
THE WHITE MAN PUT YOUR PEOPLE HERE TO *SUPPRESS* YOU, RIGHT? TO KEEP YOU AWAY FROM THE RAILROADS AND THE MINING TOWNS. TO KEEP YOU OUT OF THE WAY, BASICALLY.
SO WHY STICK AROUND ALL THESE YEARS?
WHY NOT MOVE TO A PLACE WHERE THERE ARE JOBS AND THE GROUND ISN'T LITTERED WITH THE BONES OF YOUR MASSACRED ANCESTORS?
'CAUSE THIS IS THE ONLY PLACE WHERE WE CAN STAY SOVEREIGN AND KEEP OUR CULTURE ALIVE.

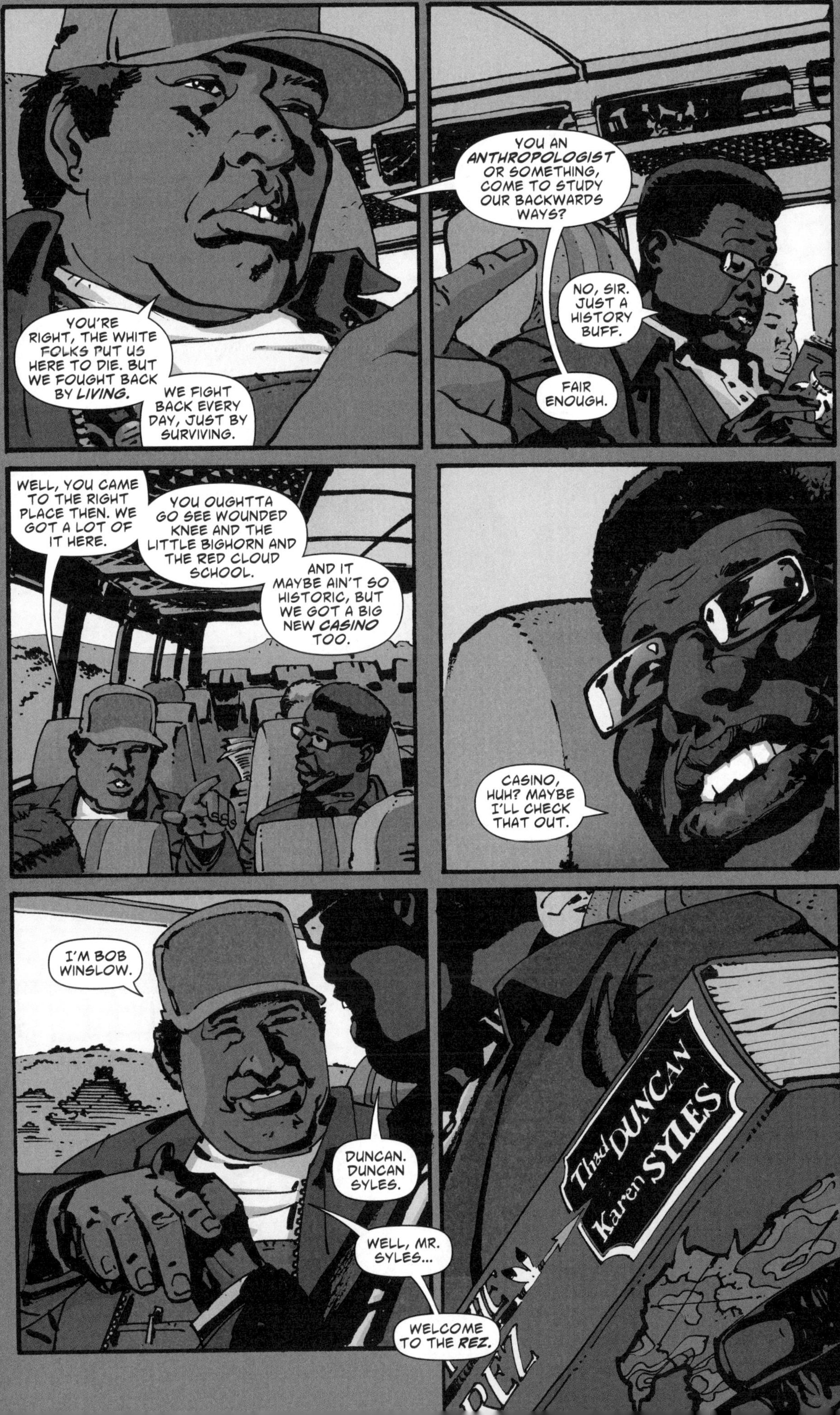

YOU AN ANTHROPOLOGIST OR SOMETHING, COME TO STUDY OUR BACKWARDS WAYS?
NO, SIR. JUST A HISTORY BUFF.
FAIR ENOUGH.
YOU'RE RIGHT, THE WHITE FOLKS PUT US HERE TO DIE. BUT WE FOUGHT BACK BY LIVING.
WE FIGHT BACK EVERY DAY, JUST BY SURVIVING.
WELL, YOU CAME TO THE RIGHT PLACE THEN. WE GOT A LOT OF IT HERE.
YOU OUGHTTA GO SEE WOUNDED KNEE AND THE LITTLE BIGHORN AND THE RED CLOUD SCHOOL.
AND IT MAYBE AIN'T SO HISTORIC, BUT WE GOT A BIG NEW CASINO TOO.
CASINO, HUH? MAYBE I'LL CHECK THAT OUT.
I'M BOB WINSLOW.
DUNCAN. DUNCAN SYLES.
WELL, MR. SYLES...
WELCOME TO THE REZ.
Thad DUNCAN
Karen SYLES

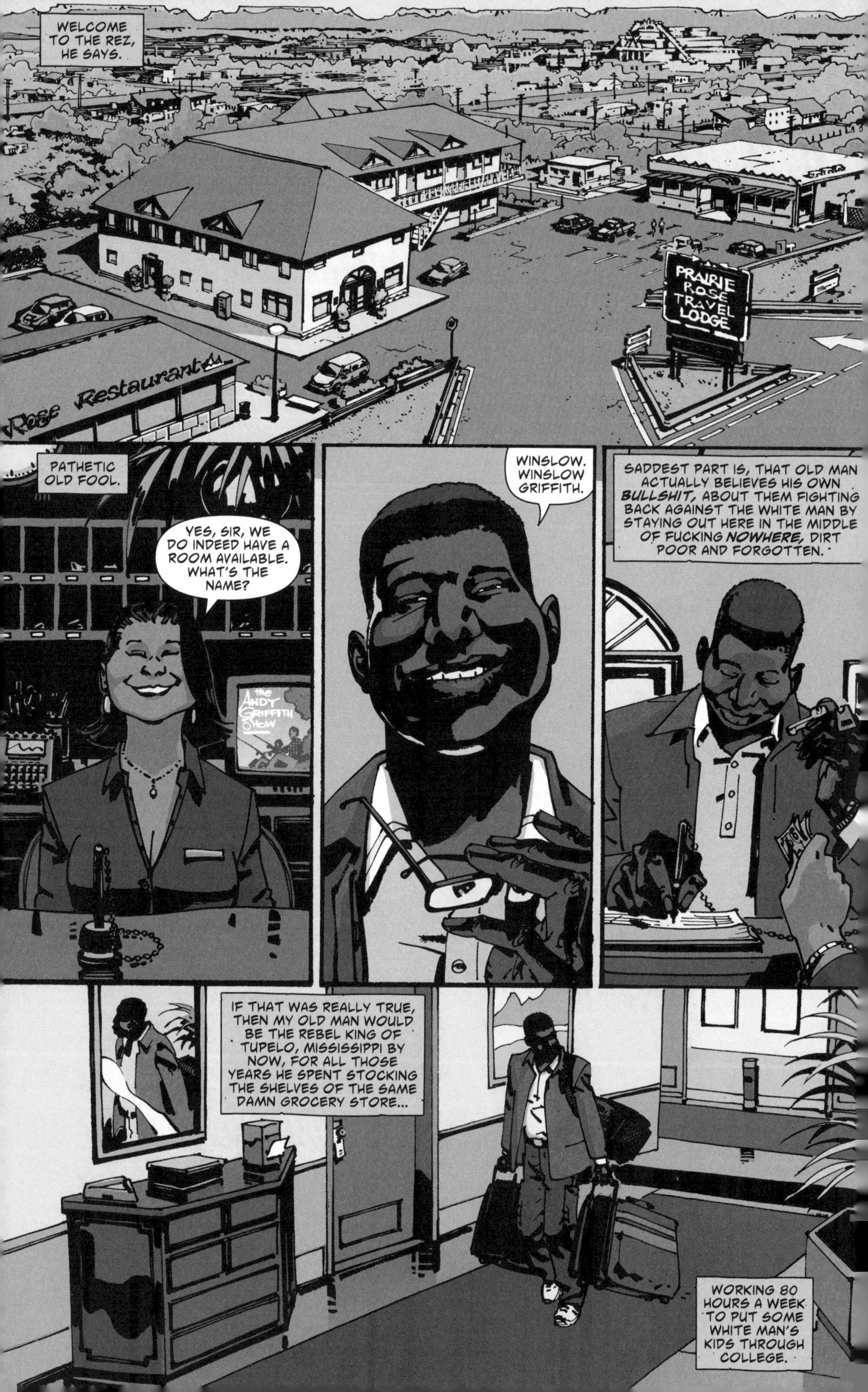
WELCOME TO THE REZ, HE SAYS.
PRAIRIE ROSE TRAVEL LODGE
Rose Restaurant
PATHETIC OLD FOOL.
YES, SIR, WE DO INDEED HAVE A ROOM AVAILABLE. WHAT'S THE NAME?
the ANDY GRIFFITH SHOW
WINSLOW. WINSLOW GRIFFITH.
SADDEST PART IS, THAT OLD MAN ACTUALLY BELIEVES HIS OWN BULLSHIT, ABOUT THEM FIGHTING BACK AGAINST THE WHITE MAN BY STAYING OUT HERE IN THE MIDDLE OF FUCKING NOWHERE, DIRT POOR AND FORGOTTEN.
IF THAT WAS REALLY TRUE, THEN MY OLD MAN WOULD BE THE REBEL KING OF TUPELO, MISSISSIPPI BY NOW, FOR ALL THOSE YEARS HE SPENT STOCKING THE SHELVES OF THE SAME DAMN GROCERY STORE...
WORKING 80 HOURS A WEEK TO PUT SOME WHITE MAN'S KIDS THROUGH COLLEGE.

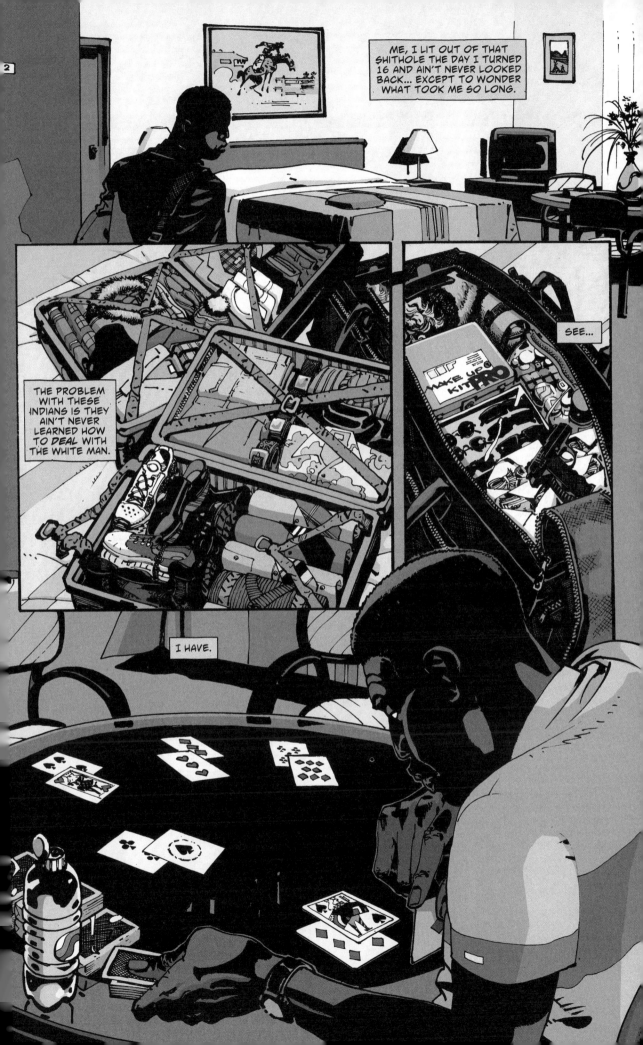

ME, I LIT OUT OF THAT SHITHOLE THE DAY I TURNED 16 AND AIN'T NEVER LOOKED BACK... EXCEPT TO WONDER WHAT TOOK ME SO LONG.

SEE...

THE PROBLEM WITH THESE INDIANS IS THEY AIN'T NEVER LEARNED HOW TO DEAL WITH THE WHITE MAN.

I HAVE.

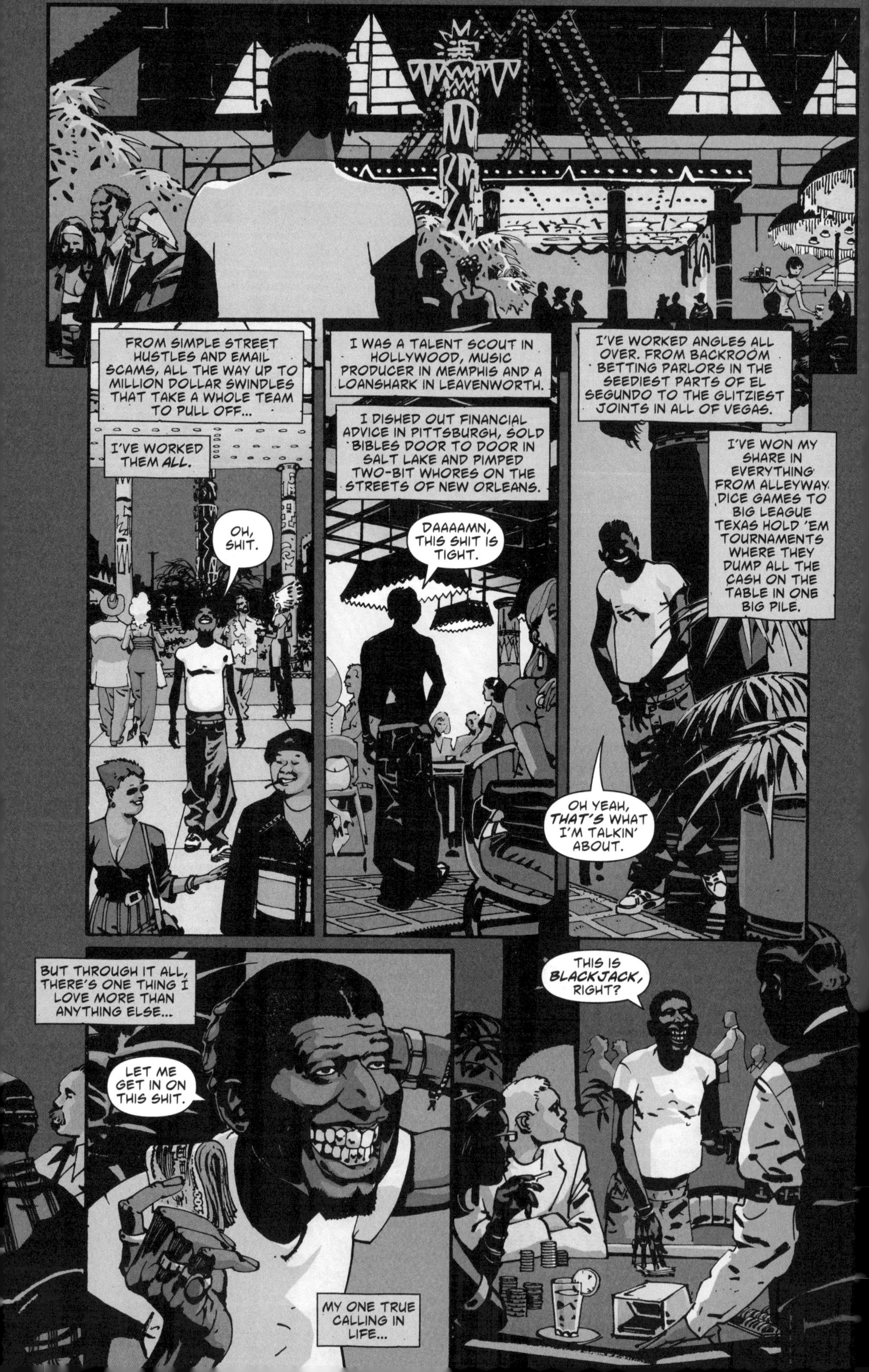
FROM SIMPLE STREET HUSTLES AND EMAIL SCAMS, ALL THE WAY UP TO MILLION DOLLAR SWINDLES THAT TAKE A WHOLE TEAM TO PULL OFF...
I'VE WORKED THEM ALL.
OH, SHIT.
I WAS A TALENT SCOUT IN HOLLYWOOD, MUSIC PRODUCER IN MEMPHIS AND A LOANSHARK IN LEAVENWORTH.
I DISHED OUT FINANCIAL ADVICE IN PITTSBURGH, SOLD BIBLES DOOR TO DOOR IN SALT LAKE AND PIMPED TWO-BIT WHORES ON THE STREETS OF NEW ORLEANS.
DAAAAMN, THIS SHIT IS TIGHT.
I'VE WORKED ANGLES ALL OVER. FROM BACKROOM BETTING PARLORS IN THE SEEDIEST PARTS OF EL SEGUNDO TO THE GLITZIEST JOINTS IN ALL OF VEGAS.
I'VE WON MY SHARE IN EVERYTHING FROM ALLEYWAY DICE GAMES TO BIG LEAGUE TEXAS HOLD 'EM TOURNAMENTS WHERE THEY DUMP ALL THE CASH ON THE TABLE IN ONE BIG PILE.
OH YEAH, THAT'S WHAT I'M TALKIN' ABOUT.
BUT THROUGH IT ALL, THERE'S ONE THING I LOVE MORE THAN ANYTHING ELSE...
LET ME GET IN ON THIS SHIT.
MY ONE TRUE CALLING IN LIFE...
THIS IS BLACKJACK, RIGHT?

CASHING IN $2000.

PEOPLE THINK YOU GOTTA BE SOME KINDA *RAIN MAN* TO COUNT CARDS.

NOT TRUE.

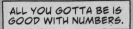

ALL YOU GOTTA BE IS GOOD WITH NUMBERS.

YEAH, LET ME GET A CUTTY AND ORANGE JUICE, WITH A COKE ON THE SIDE.

IT AIN'T MAGIC. IT'S JUST A *SYSTEM*. LETS YOU KNOW WHEN THE ODDS ARE IN YOUR FAVOR, AND WHEN YOU SHOULD RAISE YOUR BET.

KEEPING THE COUNT AND WORKING THE ODDS IS THE EASY PART. IT'S NOT GETTING *CAUGHT* THAT'S THE REAL CHALLENGE.

AND THAT ALL COMES DOWN TO ACTING.

OH YEAH, HERE WE GO...

LOOK AT ME. I'M THE JACK FUCKING NICHOLSON OF CARD COUNTERS. I'M WINNING OSCARS LEFT AND RIGHT OVER HERE.

AND I AIN'T DOING IT ON NO SEALED-OFF SOUNDSTAGE WITH JUST A FEW CAMERAS AND CREW AROUND. YOU MESS UP THERE, YOU CAN ALWAYS JUST DO ANOTHER TAKE, NO SWEAT.

I'M DOING THIS SHIT ON THE STAGE OF REAL LIFE, SURROUNDED BY THUGS AND KILLERS. I SLIP UP, I GET BEAT TO A FUCKING PULP...

HIT ME.

OR *WORSE*.

BUSTED.

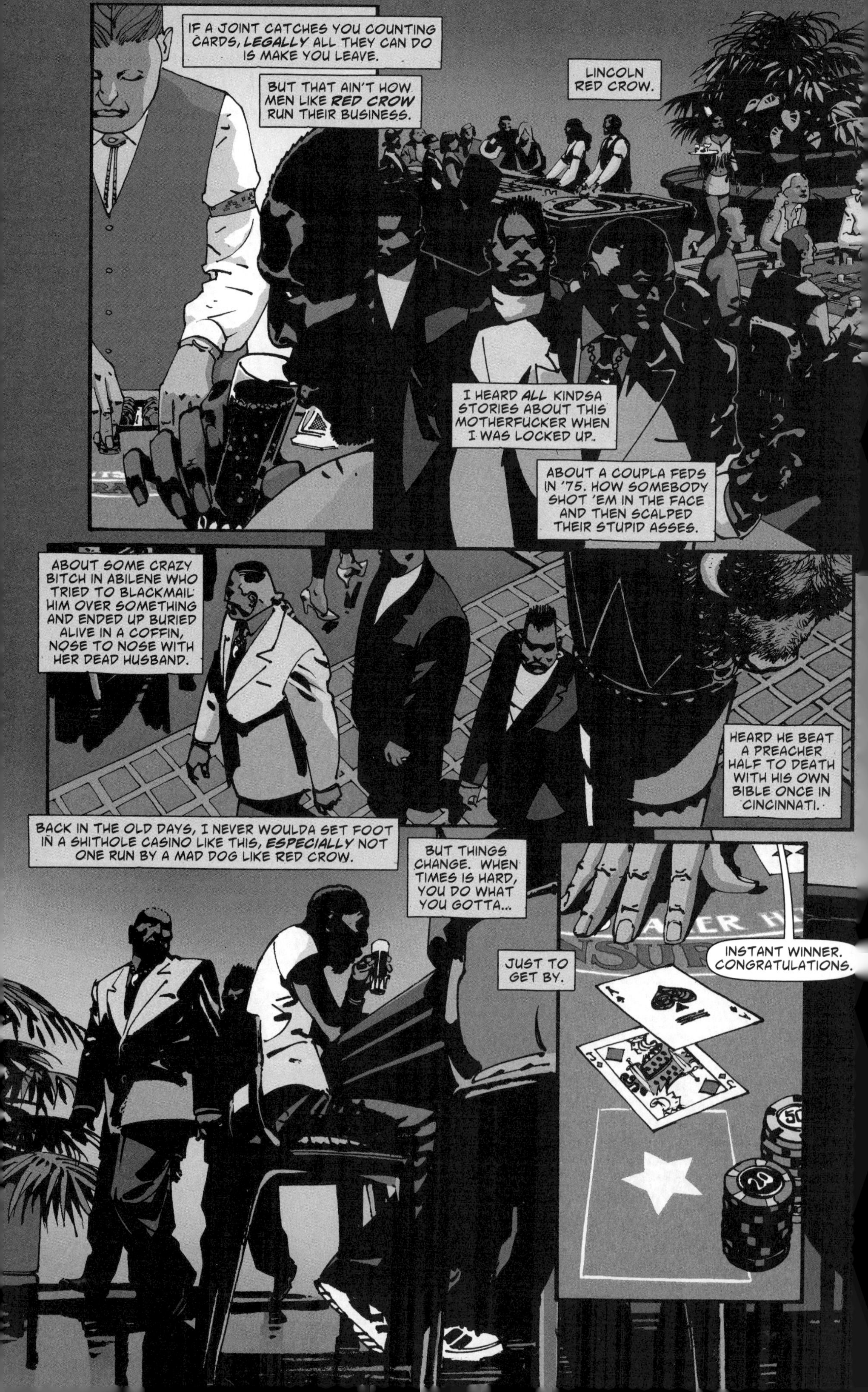

IF A JOINT CATCHES YOU COUNTING CARDS, LEGALLY ALL THEY CAN DO IS MAKE YOU LEAVE.
BUT THAT AIN'T HOW MEN LIKE RED CROW RUN THEIR BUSINESS.
LINCOLN RED CROW.
I HEARD ALL KINDSA STORIES ABOUT THIS MOTHERFUCKER WHEN I WAS LOCKED UP.
ABOUT A COUPLA FEDS IN '75. HOW SOMEBODY SHOT 'EM IN THE FACE AND THEN SCALPED THEIR STUPID ASSES.
ABOUT SOME CRAZY BITCH IN ABILENE WHO TRIED TO BLACKMAIL HIM OVER SOMETHING AND ENDED UP BURIED ALIVE IN A COFFIN, NOSE TO NOSE WITH HER DEAD HUSBAND.
HEARD HE BEAT A PREACHER HALF TO DEATH WITH HIS OWN BIBLE ONCE IN CINCINNATI.
BACK IN THE OLD DAYS, I NEVER WOULDA SET FOOT IN A SHITHOLE CASINO LIKE THIS, ESPECIALLY NOT ONE RUN BY A MAD DOG LIKE RED CROW.
BUT THINGS CHANGE. WHEN TIMES IS HARD, YOU DO WHAT YOU GOTTA...
JUST TO GET BY.
INSTANT WINNER. CONGRATULATIONS.

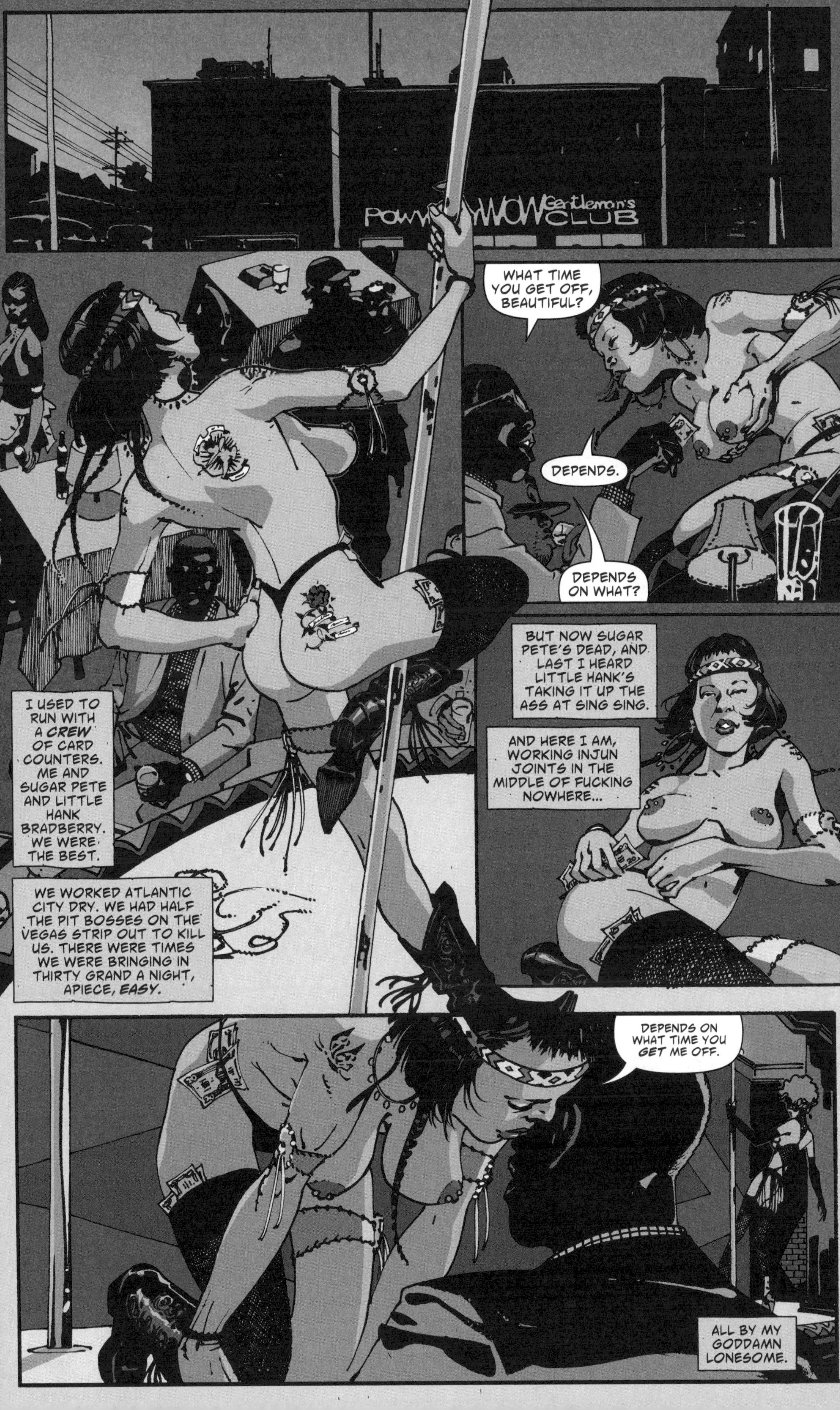
POW WOW Gentleman's CLUB
WHAT TIME YOU GET OFF, BEAUTIFUL?
DEPENDS.
DEPENDS ON WHAT?
I USED TO RUN WITH A *CREW* OF CARD COUNTERS. ME AND SUGAR PETE AND LITTLE HANK BRADBERRY. WE WERE THE BEST.
WE WORKED ATLANTIC CITY DRY. WE HAD HALF THE PIT BOSSES ON THE VEGAS STRIP OUT TO KILL US. THERE WERE TIMES WE WERE BRINGING IN THIRTY GRAND A NIGHT, APIECE, *EASY*.
BUT NOW SUGAR PETE'S DEAD, AND LAST I HEARD LITTLE HANK'S TAKING IT UP THE ASS AT SING SING.
AND HERE I AM, WORKING INJUN JOINTS IN THE MIDDLE OF FUCKING NOWHERE...
DEPENDS ON WHAT TIME YOU GET ME OFF.
ALL BY MY GODDAMN LONESOME.

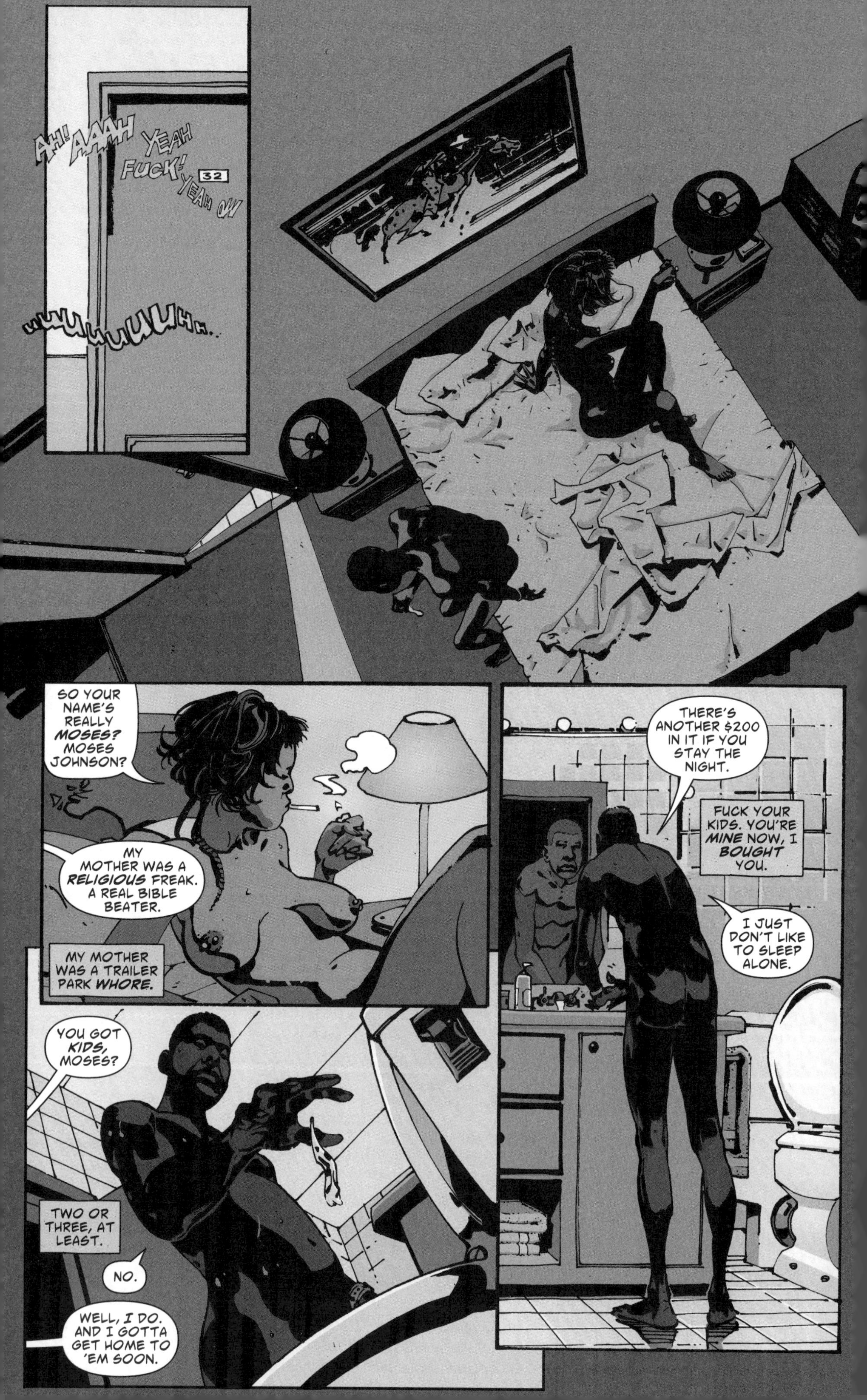
AH! AAAH YEAH
FUCK! YEAH OW
32
UUUUUUUUUHH..
SO YOUR NAME'S REALLY MOSES? MOSES JOHNSON?
MY MOTHER WAS A RELIGIOUS FREAK. A REAL BIBLE BEATER.
MY MOTHER WAS A TRAILER PARK WHORE.
YOU GOT KIDS, MOSES?
TWO OR THREE, AT LEAST.
NO.
WELL, I DO. AND I GOTTA GET HOME TO 'EM SOON.
THERE'S ANOTHER $200 IN IT IF YOU STAY THE NIGHT.
FUCK YOUR KIDS. YOU'RE MINE NOW, I BOUGHT YOU.
I JUST DON'T LIKE TO SLEEP ALONE.

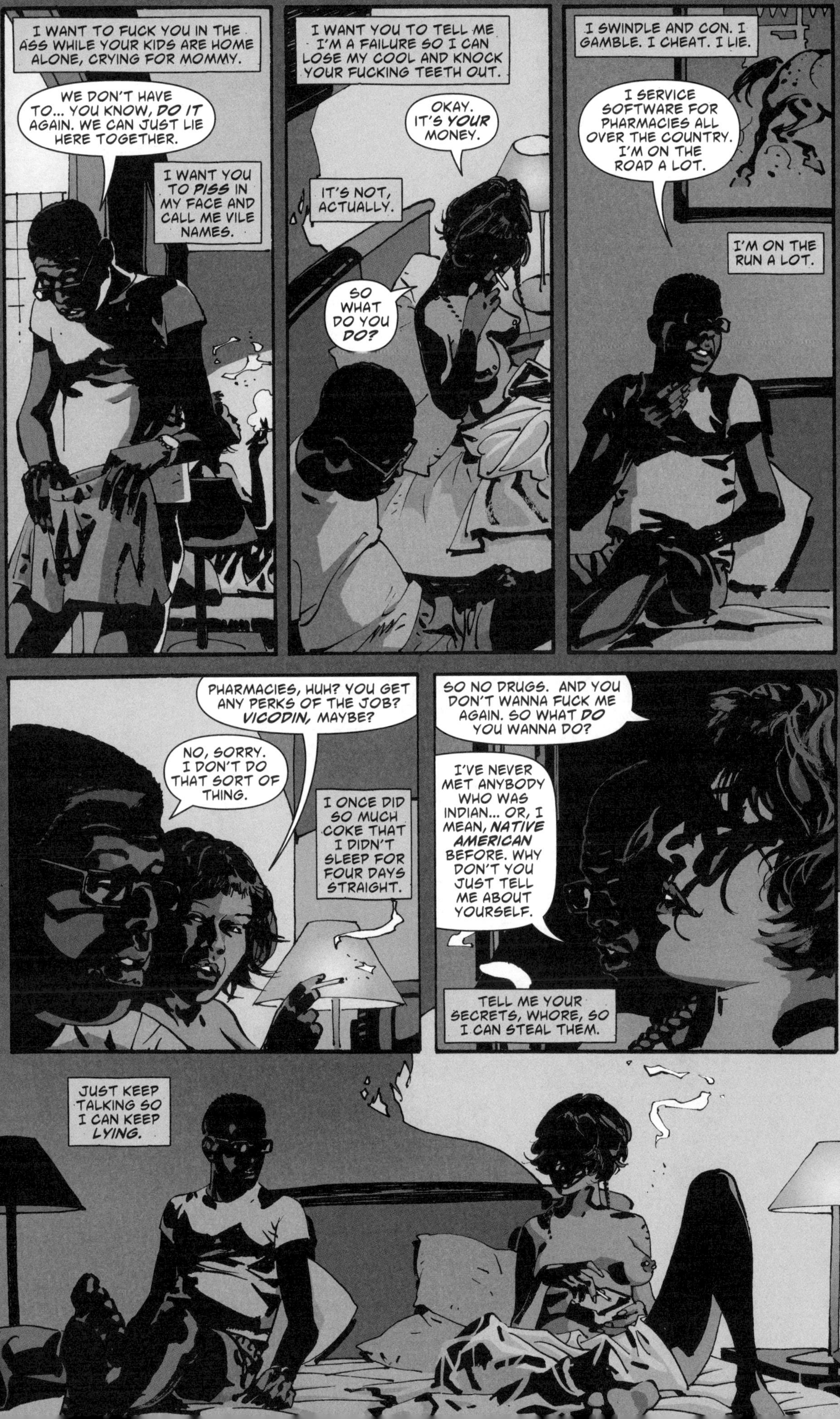
I WANT TO FUCK YOU IN THE ASS WHILE YOUR KIDS ARE HOME ALONE, CRYING FOR MOMMY.
WE DON'T HAVE TO... YOU KNOW, *DO IT* AGAIN. WE CAN JUST LIE HERE TOGETHER.
I WANT YOU TO *PISS* IN MY FACE AND CALL ME VILE NAMES.
I WANT YOU TO TELL ME I'M A FAILURE SO I CAN LOSE MY COOL AND KNOCK YOUR FUCKING TEETH OUT.
OKAY. IT'S *YOUR* MONEY.
IT'S NOT, ACTUALLY.
SO WHAT DO YOU *DO?*
I SWINDLE AND CON. I GAMBLE. I CHEAT. I LIE.
I SERVICE SOFTWARE FOR PHARMACIES ALL OVER THE COUNTRY. I'M ON THE ROAD A LOT.
I'M ON THE RUN A LOT.
PHARMACIES, HUH? YOU GET ANY PERKS OF THE JOB? *VICODIN,* MAYBE?
NO, SORRY. I DON'T DO THAT SORT OF THING.
I ONCE DID SO MUCH COKE THAT I DIDN'T SLEEP FOR FOUR DAYS STRAIGHT.
SO NO DRUGS. AND YOU DON'T WANNA FUCK ME AGAIN. SO WHAT *DO* YOU WANNA DO?
I'VE NEVER MET ANYBODY WHO WAS INDIAN... OR, I MEAN, *NATIVE AMERICAN* BEFORE. WHY DON'T YOU JUST TELL ME ABOUT YOURSELF.
TELL ME YOUR SECRETS, WHORE, SO I CAN STEAL THEM.
JUST KEEP TALKING SO I CAN KEEP *LYING.*

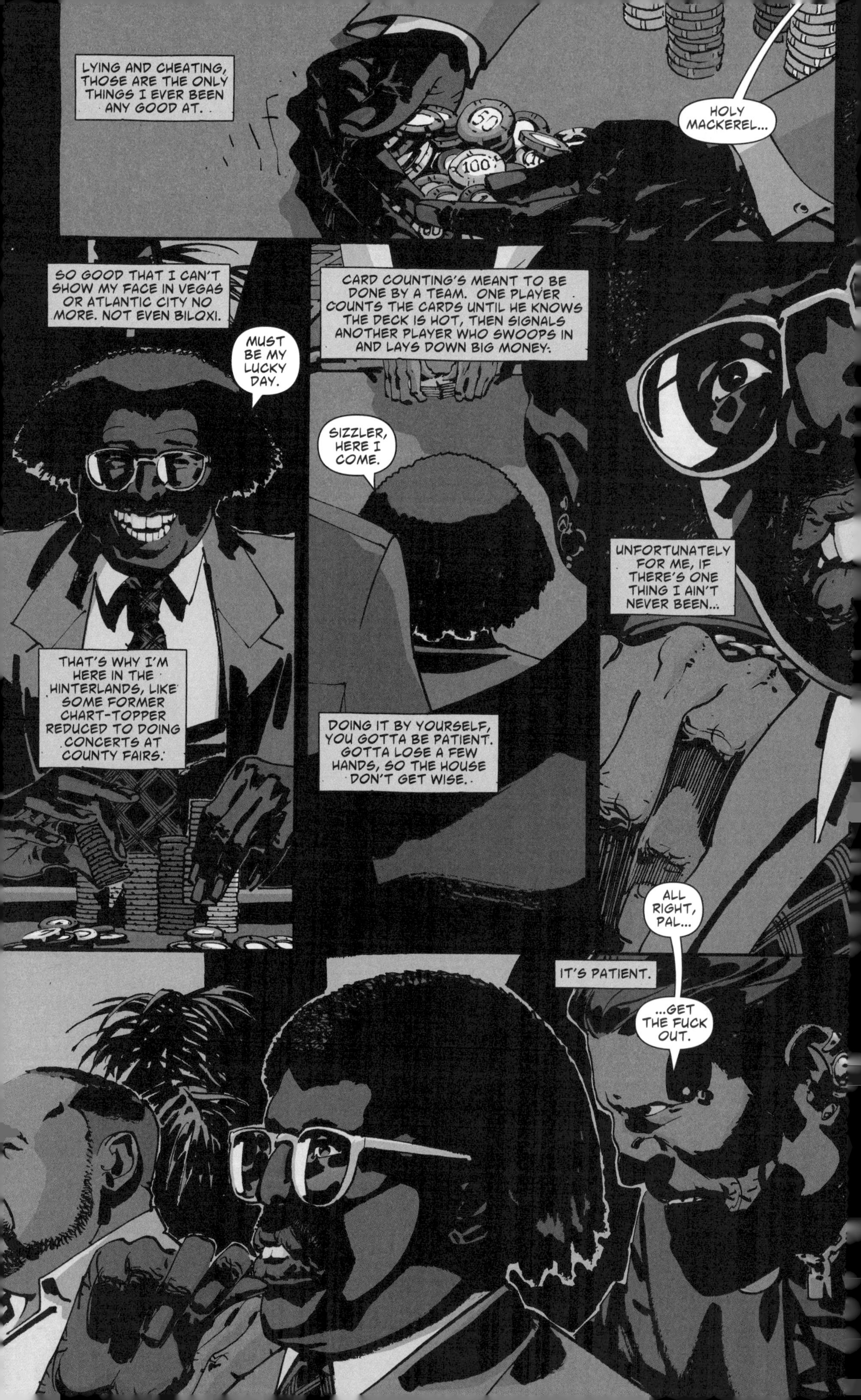
LYING AND CHEATING, THOSE ARE THE ONLY THINGS I EVER BEEN ANY GOOD AT.
50
100
HOLY MACKEREL...
SO GOOD THAT I CAN'T SHOW MY FACE IN VEGAS OR ATLANTIC CITY NO MORE. NOT EVEN BILOXI.
MUST BE MY LUCKY DAY.
THAT'S WHY I'M HERE IN THE HINTERLANDS, LIKE SOME FORMER CHART-TOPPER REDUCED TO DOING CONCERTS AT COUNTY FAIRS.
CARD COUNTING'S MEANT TO BE DONE BY A TEAM. ONE PLAYER COUNTS THE CARDS UNTIL HE KNOWS THE DECK IS HOT, THEN SIGNALS ANOTHER PLAYER WHO SWOOPS IN AND LAYS DOWN BIG MONEY.
SIZZLER, HERE I COME.
DOING IT BY YOURSELF, YOU GOTTA BE PATIENT. GOTTA LOSE A FEW HANDS, SO THE HOUSE DON'T GET WISE.
UNFORTUNATELY FOR ME, IF THERE'S ONE THING I AIN'T NEVER BEEN...
ALL RIGHT, PAL...
IT'S PATIENT.
...GET THE FUCK OUT.

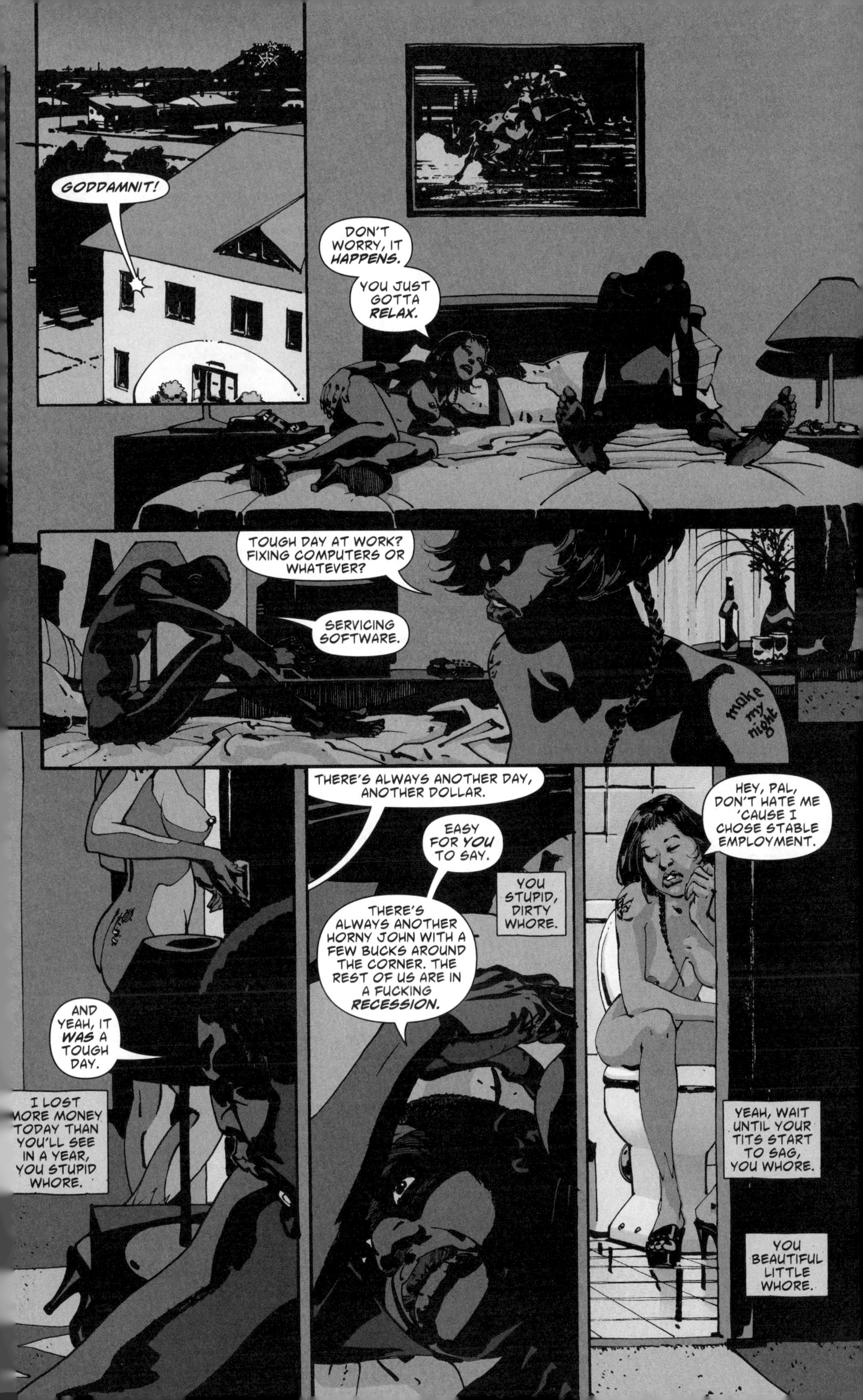
GODDAMNIT!
DON'T WORRY, IT HAPPENS.
YOU JUST GOTTA RELAX.
TOUGH DAY AT WORK? FIXING COMPUTERS OR WHATEVER?
SERVICING SOFTWARE.
make my night
THERE'S ALWAYS ANOTHER DAY, ANOTHER DOLLAR.
EASY FOR YOU TO SAY.
THERE'S ALWAYS ANOTHER HORNY JOHN WITH A FEW BUCKS AROUND THE CORNER. THE REST OF US ARE IN A FUCKING RECESSION.
YOU STUPID, DIRTY WHORE.
AND YEAH, IT WAS A TOUGH DAY.
I LOST MORE MONEY TODAY THAN YOU'LL SEE IN A YEAR, YOU STUPID WHORE.
HEY, PAL, DON'T HATE ME 'CAUSE I CHOSE STABLE EMPLOYMENT.
YEAH, WAIT UNTIL YOUR TITS START TO SAG, YOU WHORE.
YOU BEAUTIFUL LITTLE WHORE.

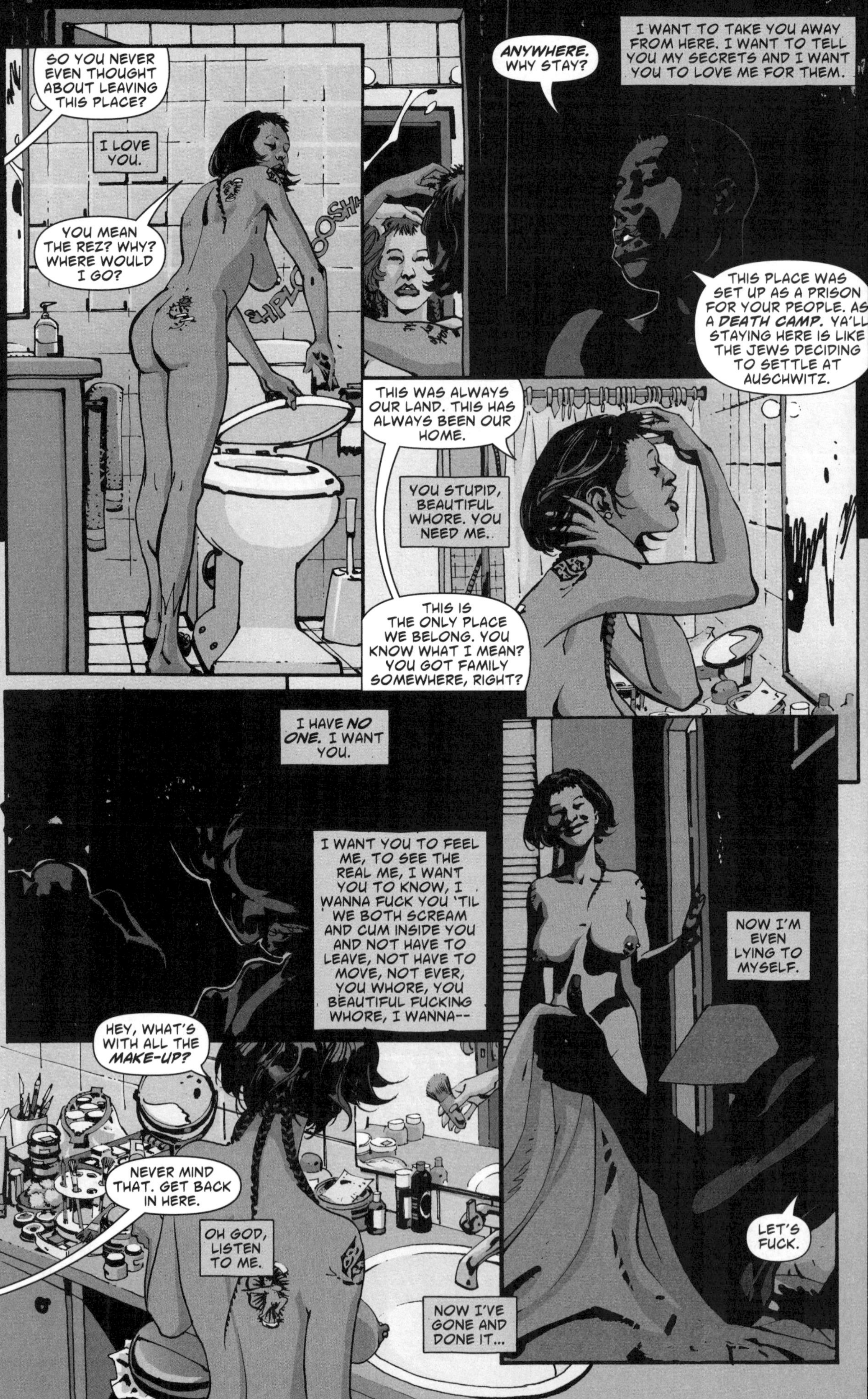
SO YOU NEVER EVEN THOUGHT ABOUT LEAVING THIS PLACE?
I LOVE YOU.
YOU MEAN THE REZ? WHY? WHERE WOULD I GO?
ANYWHERE. WHY STAY?
I WANT TO TAKE YOU AWAY FROM HERE. I WANT TO TELL YOU MY SECRETS AND I WANT YOU TO LOVE ME FOR THEM.
THIS PLACE WAS SET UP AS A PRISON FOR YOUR PEOPLE. AS A DEATH CAMP. YA'LL STAYING HERE IS LIKE THE JEWS DECIDING TO SETTLE AT AUSCHWITZ.
THIS WAS ALWAYS OUR LAND. THIS HAS ALWAYS BEEN OUR HOME.
YOU STUPID, BEAUTIFUL WHORE. YOU NEED ME.
THIS IS THE ONLY PLACE WE BELONG. YOU KNOW WHAT I MEAN? YOU GOT FAMILY SOMEWHERE, RIGHT?
I HAVE NO ONE. I WANT YOU.
I WANT YOU TO FEEL ME, TO SEE THE REAL ME, I WANT YOU TO KNOW, I WANNA FUCK YOU 'TIL WE BOTH SCREAM AND CUM INSIDE YOU AND NOT HAVE TO LEAVE, NOT HAVE TO MOVE, NOT EVER, YOU WHORE, YOU BEAUTIFUL FUCKING WHORE, I WANNA--
HEY, WHAT'S WITH ALL THE MAKE-UP?
NEVER MIND THAT. GET BACK IN HERE.
OH GOD, LISTEN TO ME.
NOW I'VE GONE AND DONE IT...
NOW I'M EVEN LYING TO MYSELF.
LET'S FUCK.

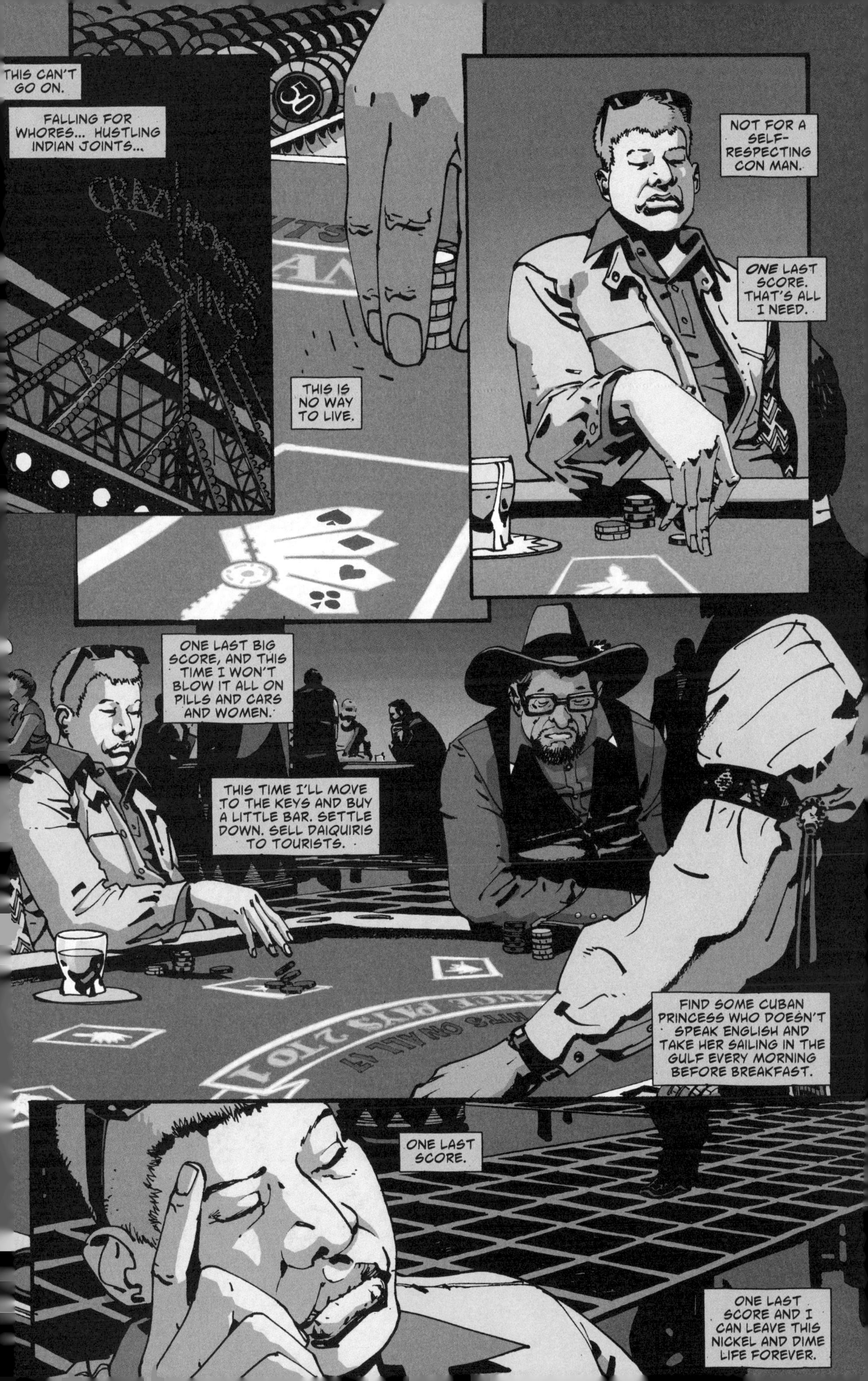
THIS CAN'T GO ON.
FALLING FOR WHORES... HUSTLING INDIAN JOINTS...
THIS IS NO WAY TO LIVE.
NOT FOR A SELF-RESPECTING CON MAN.
ONE LAST SCORE. THAT'S ALL I NEED.
ONE LAST BIG SCORE, AND THIS TIME I WON'T BLOW IT ALL ON PILLS AND CARS AND WOMEN.
THIS TIME I'LL MOVE TO THE KEYS AND BUY A LITTLE BAR. SETTLE DOWN. SELL DAIQUIRIS TO TOURISTS.
FIND SOME CUBAN PRINCESS WHO DOESN'T SPEAK ENGLISH AND TAKE HER SAILING IN THE GULF EVERY MORNING BEFORE BREAKFAST.
ONE LAST SCORE.
ONE LAST SCORE AND I CAN LEAVE THIS NICKEL AND DIME LIFE FOREVER.

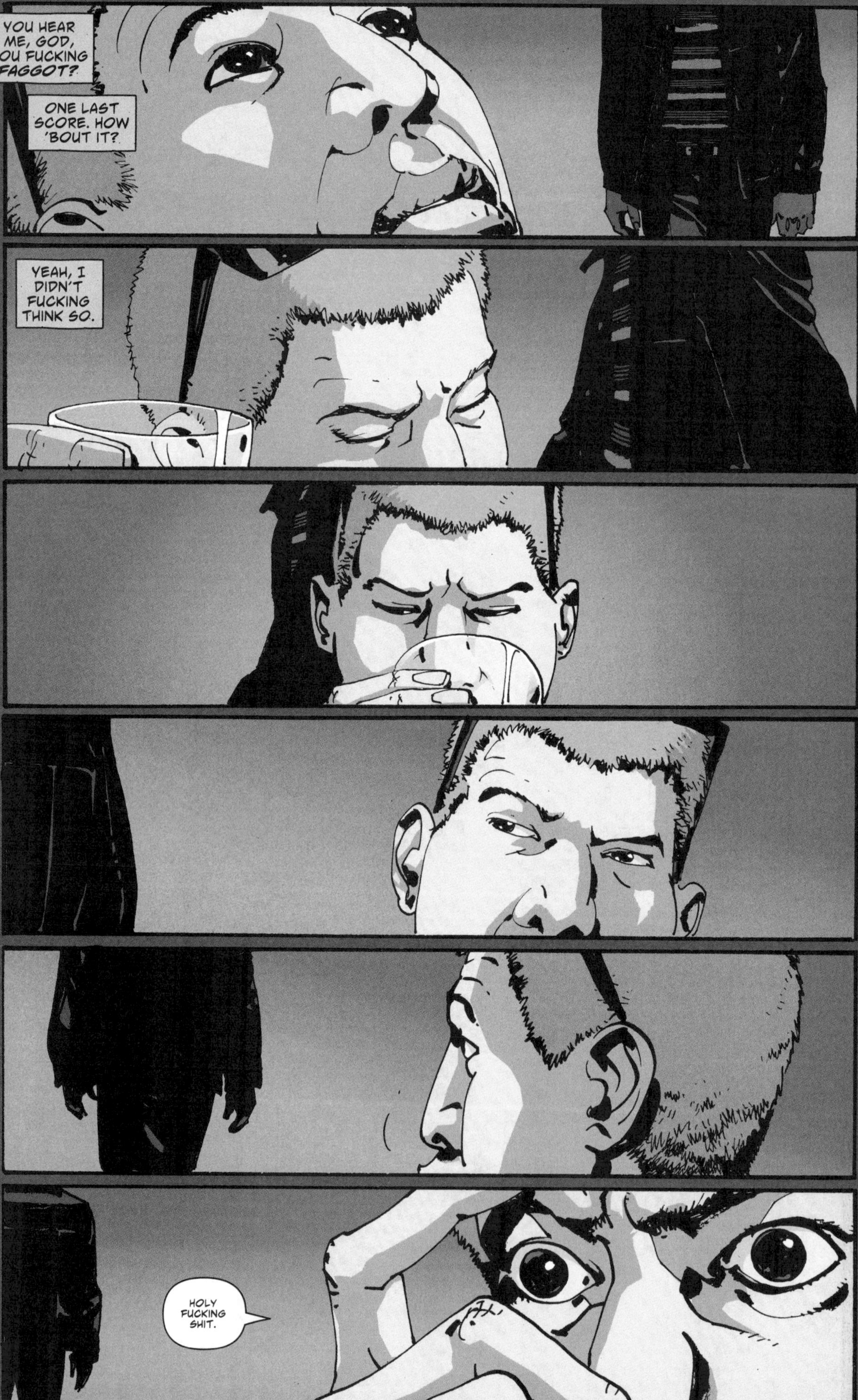
YOU HEAR ME, GOD, YOU FUCKING *FAGGOT?*
ONE LAST SCORE. HOW 'BOUT IT?
YEAH, I DIDN'T FUCKING THINK SO.
HOLY FUCKING SHIT.

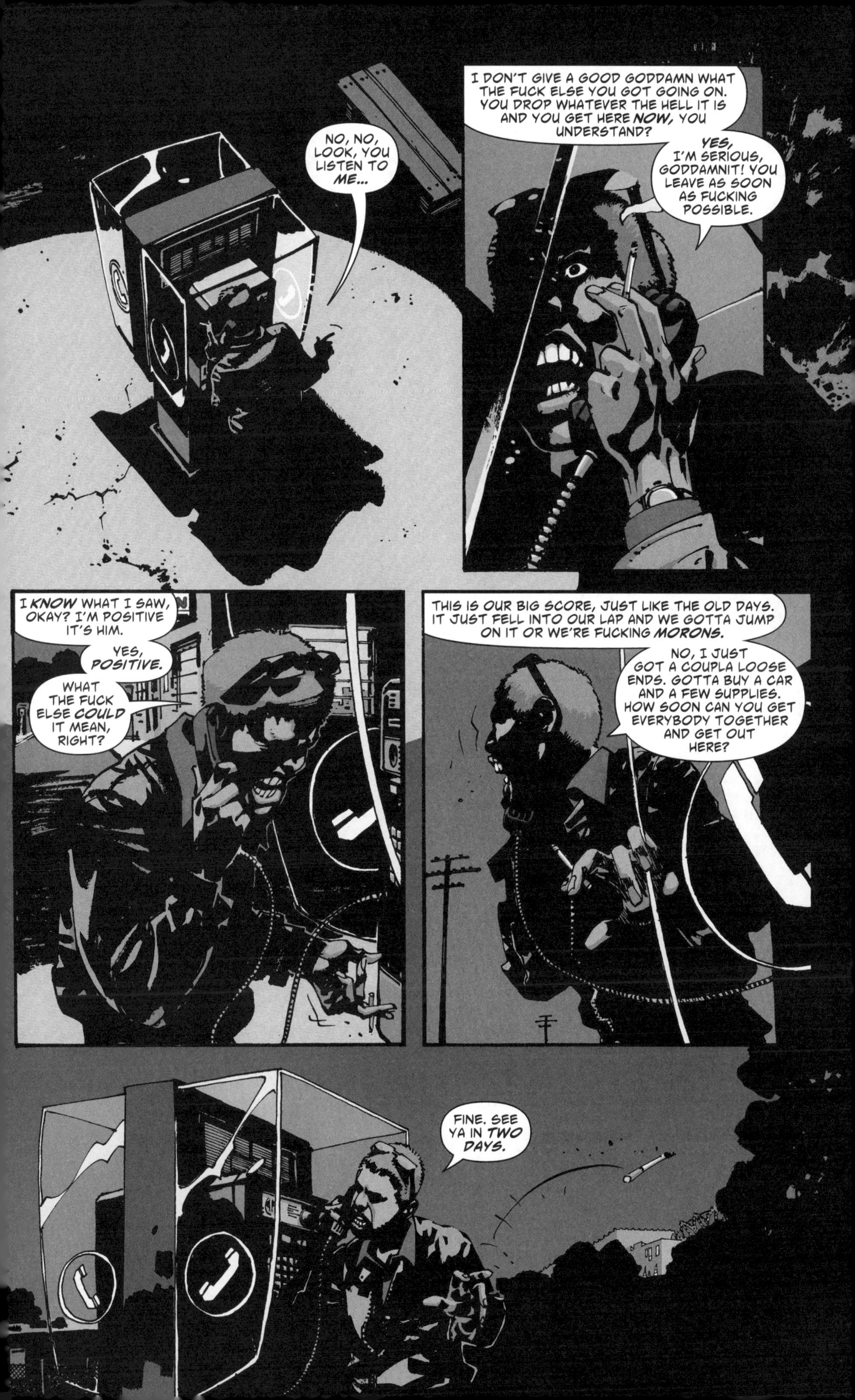
NO, NO, LOOK, YOU LISTEN TO ME...
I DON'T GIVE A GOOD GODDAMN WHAT THE FUCK ELSE YOU GOT GOING ON. YOU DROP WHATEVER THE HELL IT IS AND YOU GET HERE NOW, YOU UNDERSTAND?
YES, I'M SERIOUS, GODDAMNIT! YOU LEAVE AS SOON AS FUCKING POSSIBLE.
I KNOW WHAT I SAW, OKAY? I'M POSITIVE IT'S HIM.
YES, POSITIVE.
WHAT THE FUCK ELSE COULD IT MEAN, RIGHT?
THIS IS OUR BIG SCORE, JUST LIKE THE OLD DAYS. IT JUST FELL INTO OUR LAP AND WE GOTTA JUMP ON IT OR WE'RE FUCKING MORONS.
NO, I JUST GOT A COUPLA LOOSE ENDS. GOTTA BUY A CAR AND A FEW SUPPLIES. HOW SOON CAN YOU GET EVERYBODY TOGETHER AND GET OUT HERE?
FINE. SEE YA IN TWO DAYS.

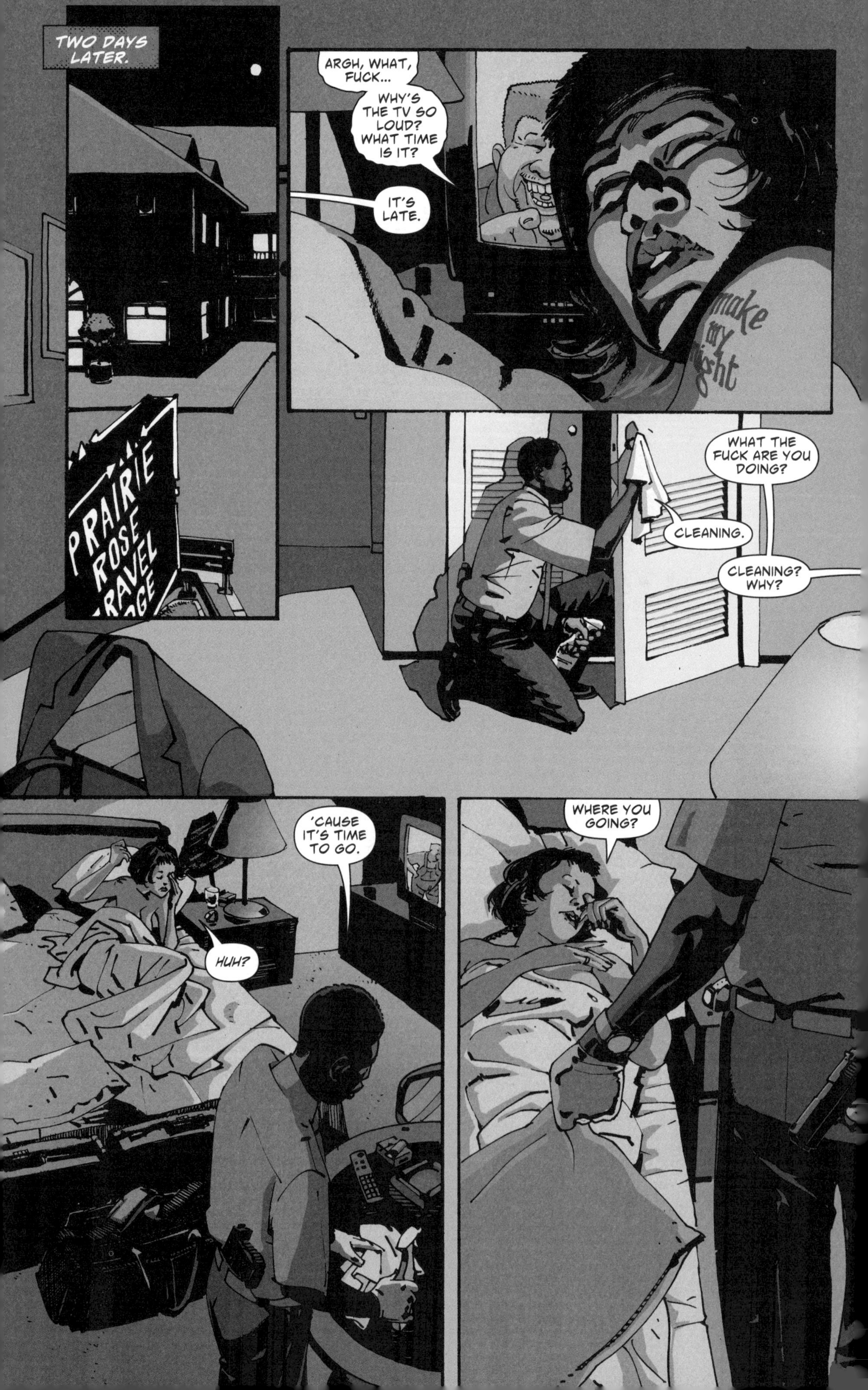
TWO DAYS LATER.
ARGH, WHAT, FUCK...
WHY'S THE TV SO LOUD? WHAT TIME IS IT?
IT'S LATE.
make my night
PRAIRIE ROSE
WHAT THE FUCK ARE YOU DOING?
CLEANING.
CLEANING? WHY?
'CAUSE IT'S TIME TO GO.
HUH?
WHERE YOU GOING?

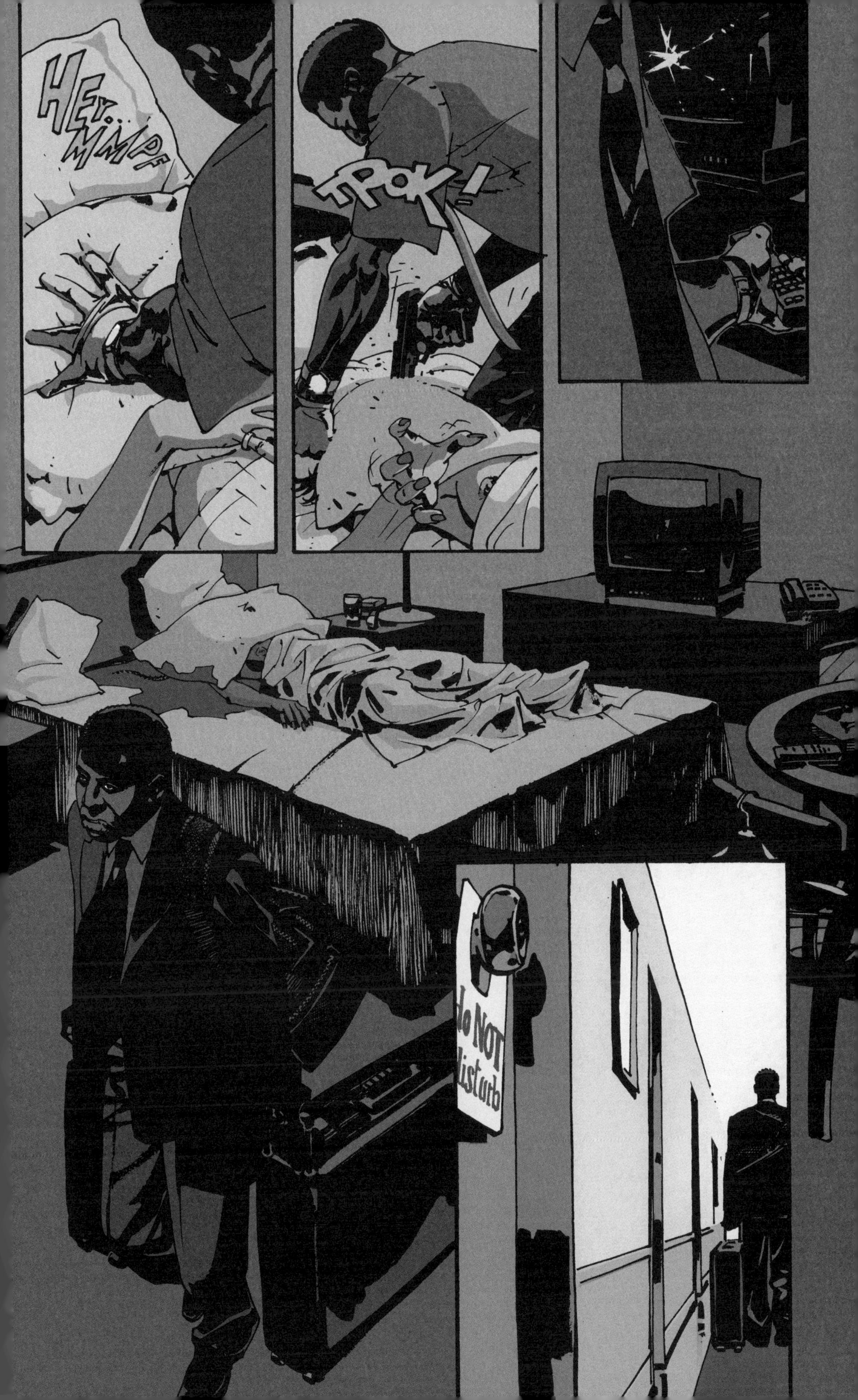
HEY... MMPF
FPOK!
Do NOT Disturb

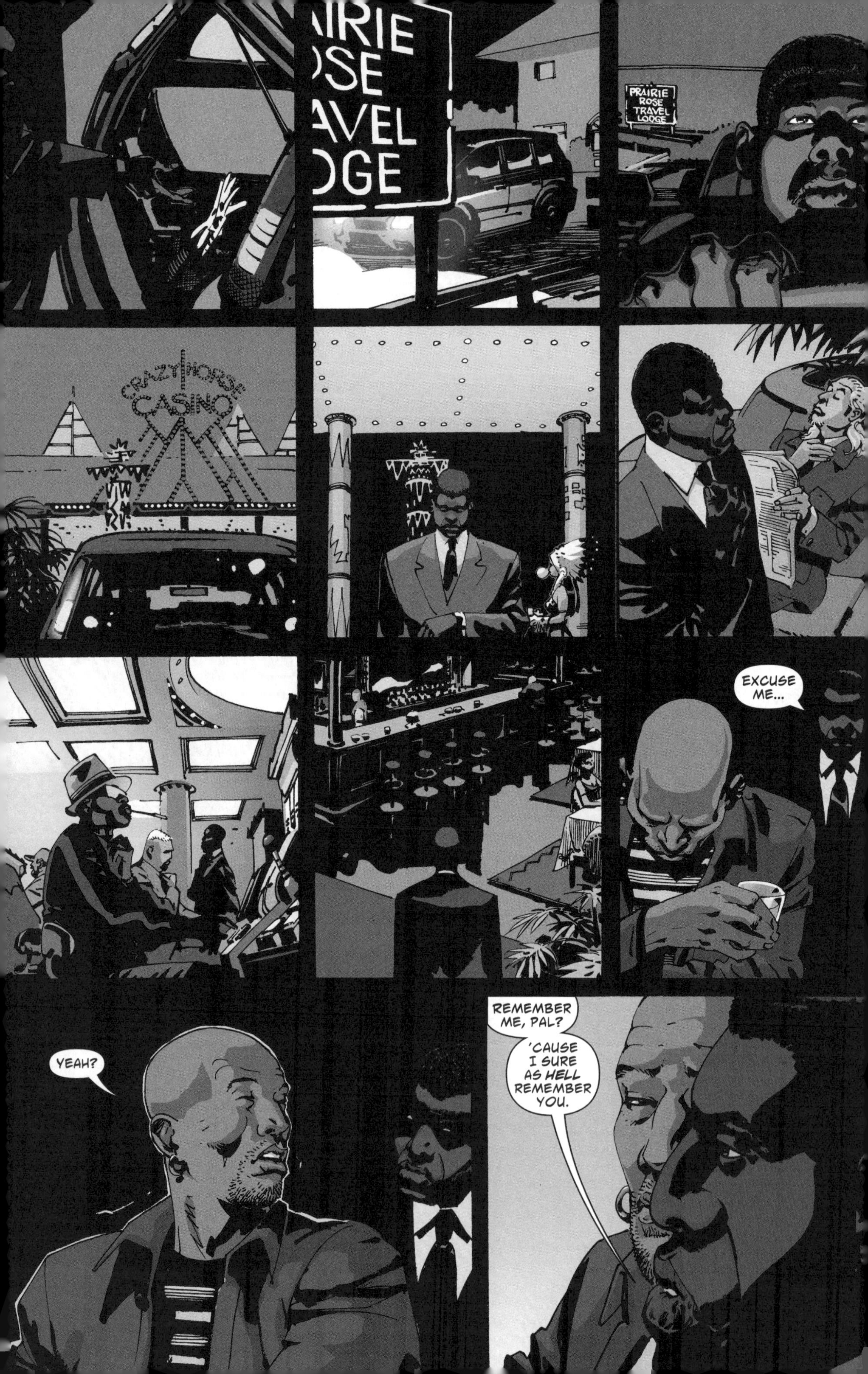
AIRIE
OSE
AVEL
OGE
PRAIRIE ROSE TRAVEL LODGE
CRAZY HORSE CASINO
EXCUSE ME...
YEAH?
REMEMBER ME, PAL?
'CAUSE I SURE AS HELL REMEMBER YOU.

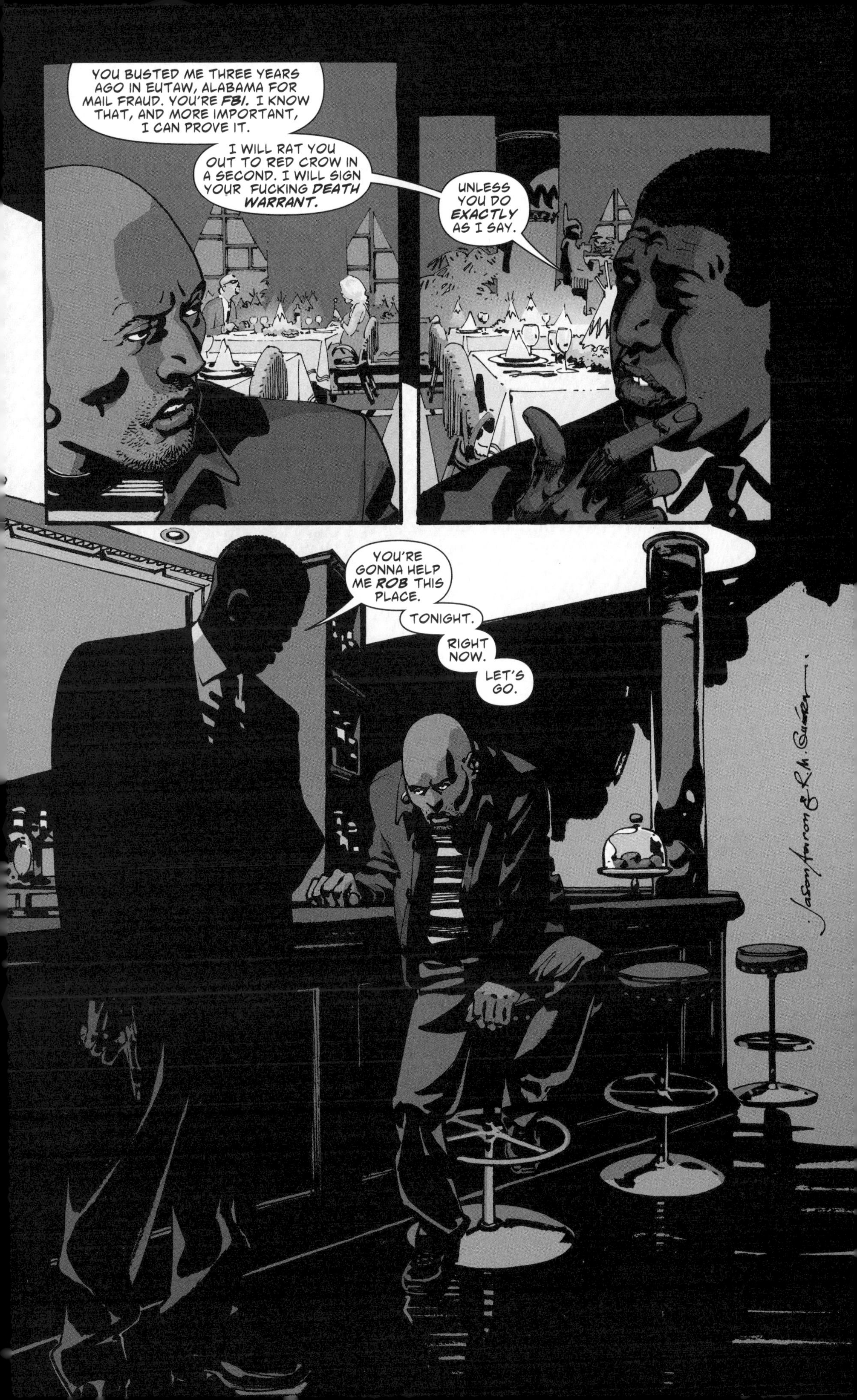
YOU BUSTED ME THREE YEARS AGO IN EUTAW, ALABAMA FOR MAIL FRAUD. YOU'RE FBI. I KNOW THAT, AND MORE IMPORTANT, I CAN PROVE IT.
I WILL RAT YOU OUT TO RED CROW IN A SECOND. I WILL SIGN YOUR FUCKING DEATH WARRANT.
UNLESS YOU DO EXACTLY AS I SAY.
YOU'RE GONNA HELP ME ROB THIS PLACE.
TONIGHT.
RIGHT NOW.
LET'S GO.

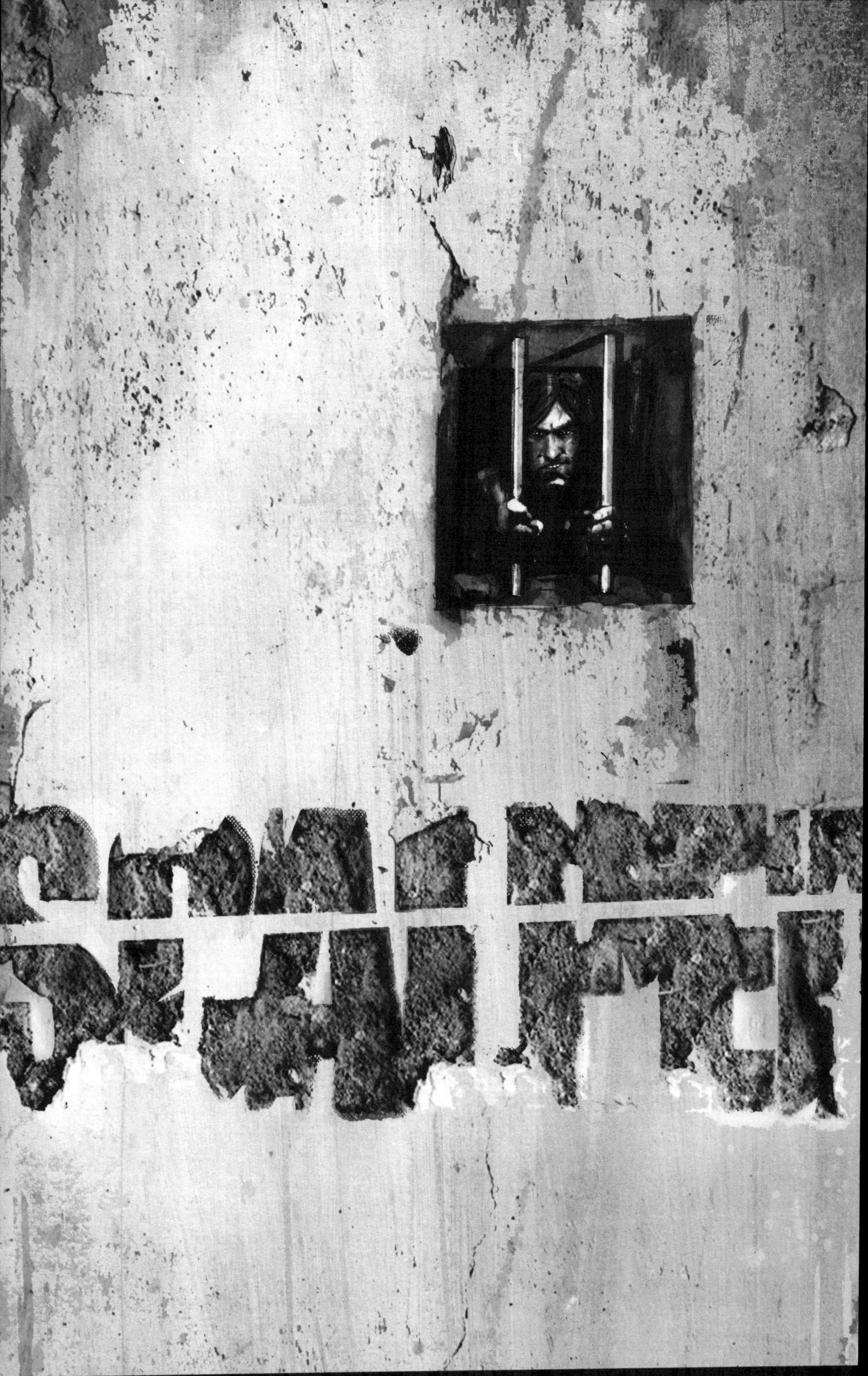

BEEN DOWN SO GODDAMN LONG THAT IT LOOKS LIKE UP TO ME

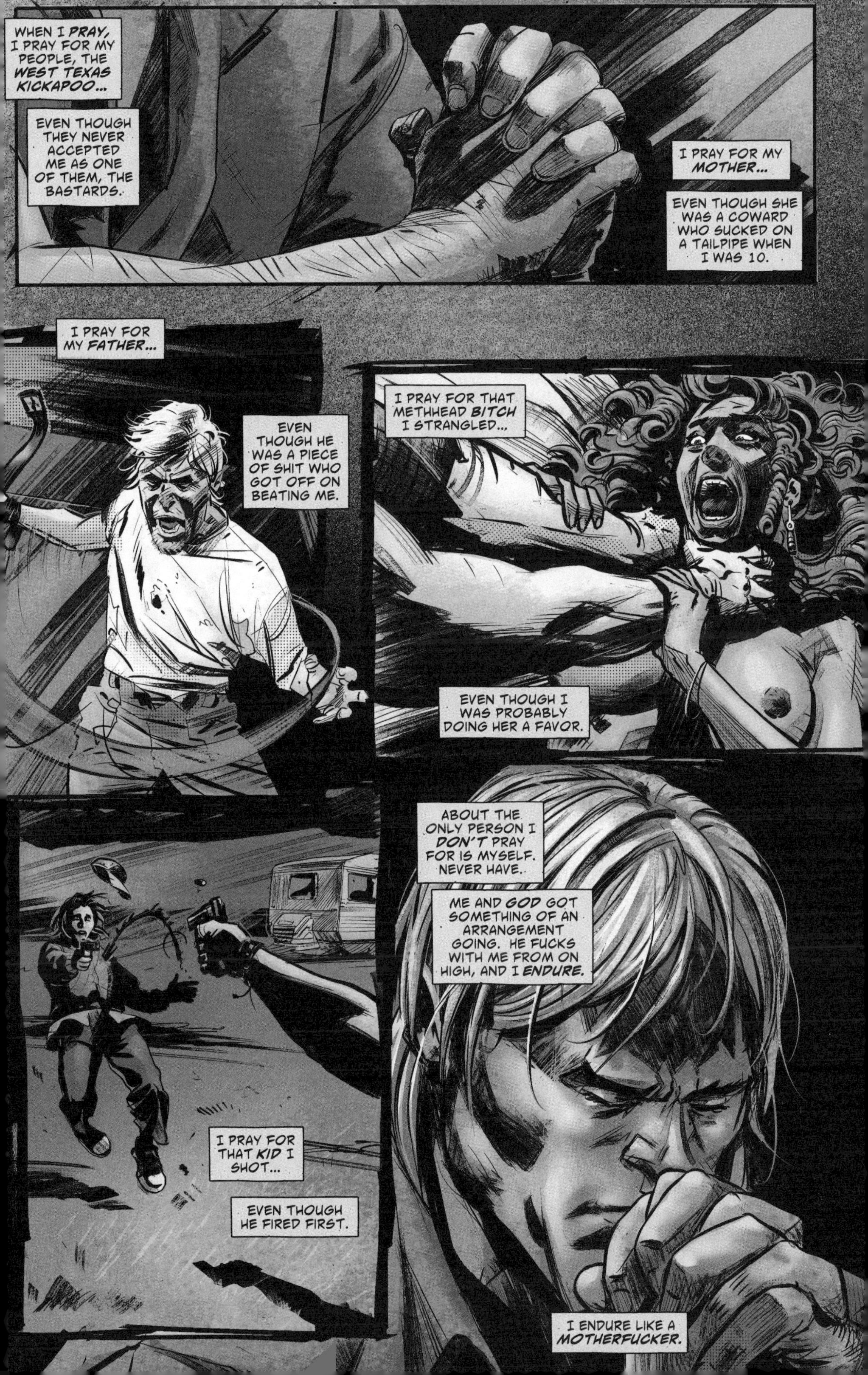
WHEN I PRAY, I PRAY FOR MY PEOPLE, THE WEST TEXAS KICKAPOO...
EVEN THOUGH THEY NEVER ACCEPTED ME AS ONE OF THEM, THE BASTARDS.
I PRAY FOR MY MOTHER...
EVEN THOUGH SHE WAS A COWARD WHO SUCKED ON A TAILPIPE WHEN I WAS 10.
I PRAY FOR MY FATHER...
EVEN THOUGH HE WAS A PIECE OF SHIT WHO GOT OFF ON BEATING ME.
I PRAY FOR THAT METHHEAD BITCH I STRANGLED...
EVEN THOUGH I WAS PROBABLY DOING HER A FAVOR.
I PRAY FOR THAT KID I SHOT...
EVEN THOUGH HE FIRED FIRST.
ABOUT THE ONLY PERSON I DON'T PRAY FOR IS MYSELF. NEVER HAVE.
ME AND GOD GOT SOMETHING OF AN ARRANGEMENT GOING. HE FUCKS WITH ME FROM ON HIGH, AND I ENDURE.
I ENDURE LIKE A MOTHERFUCKER.

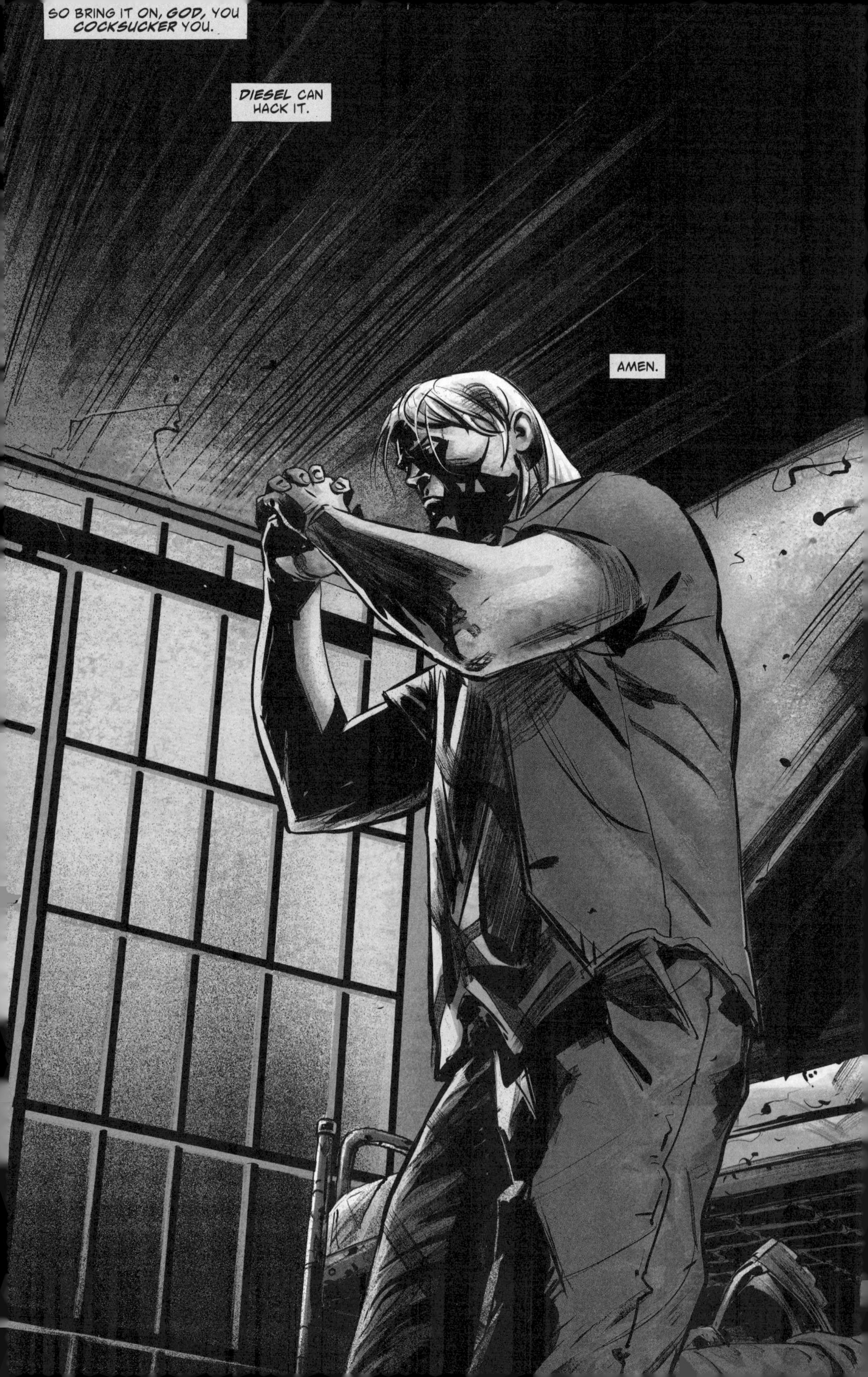
SO BRING IT ON, GOD, YOU COCKSUCKER YOU.
DIESEL CAN HACK IT.
AMEN.

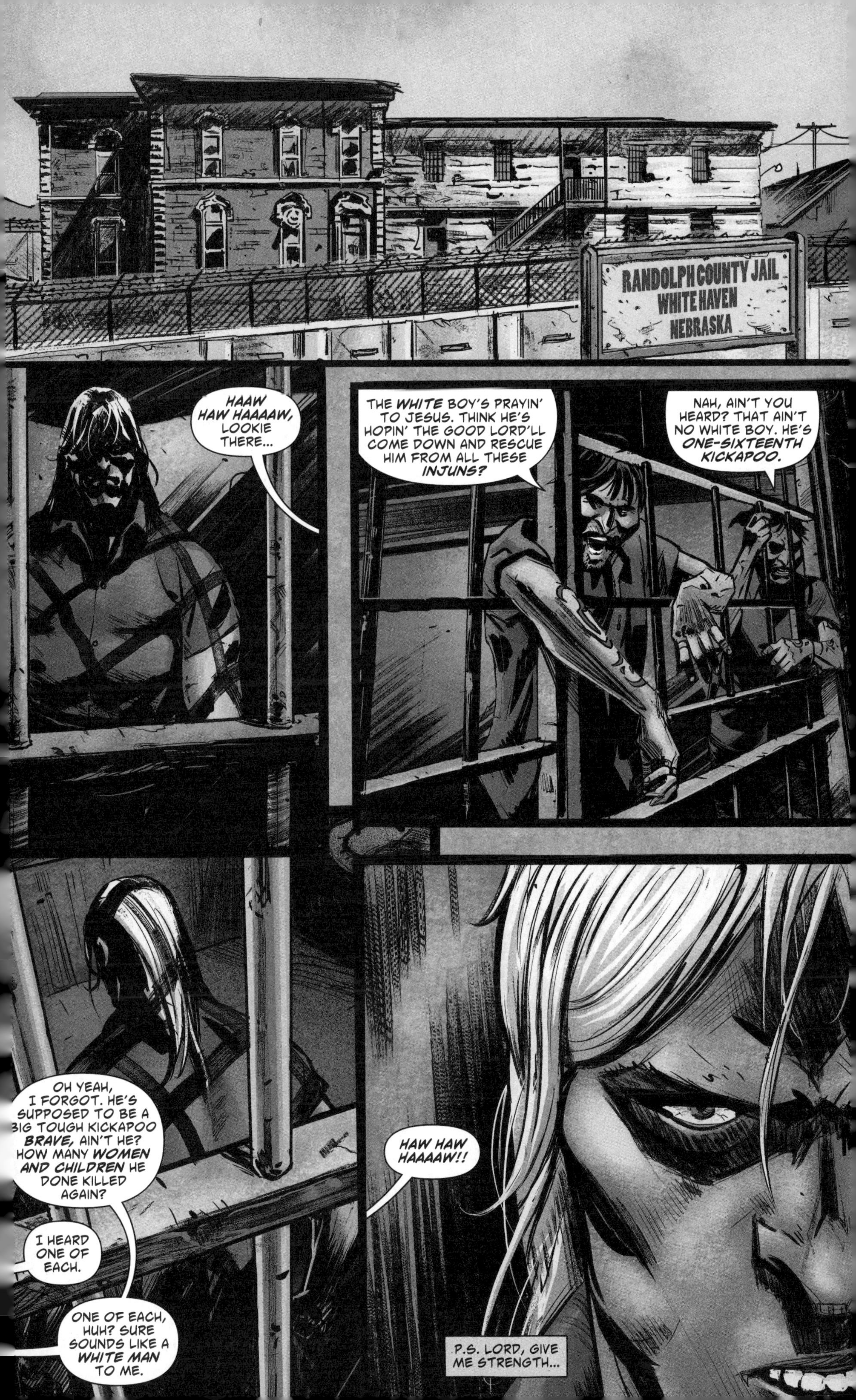
RANDOLPH COUNTY JAIL
WHITE HAVEN
NEBRASKA
HAAW HAW HAAAAW, LOOKIE THERE...
THE WHITE BOY'S PRAYIN' TO JESUS. THINK HE'S HOPIN' THE GOOD LORD'LL COME DOWN AND RESCUE HIM FROM ALL THESE INJUNS?
NAH, AIN'T YOU HEARD? THAT AIN'T NO WHITE BOY. HE'S ONE-SIXTEENTH KICKAPOO.
OH YEAH, I FORGOT. HE'S SUPPOSED TO BE A BIG TOUGH KICKAPOO BRAVE, AIN'T HE? HOW MANY WOMEN AND CHILDREN HE DONE KILLED AGAIN?
I HEARD ONE OF EACH.
ONE OF EACH, HUH? SURE SOUNDS LIKE A WHITE MAN TO ME.
HAW HAW HAAAAW!!
P.S. LORD, GIVE ME STRENGTH...

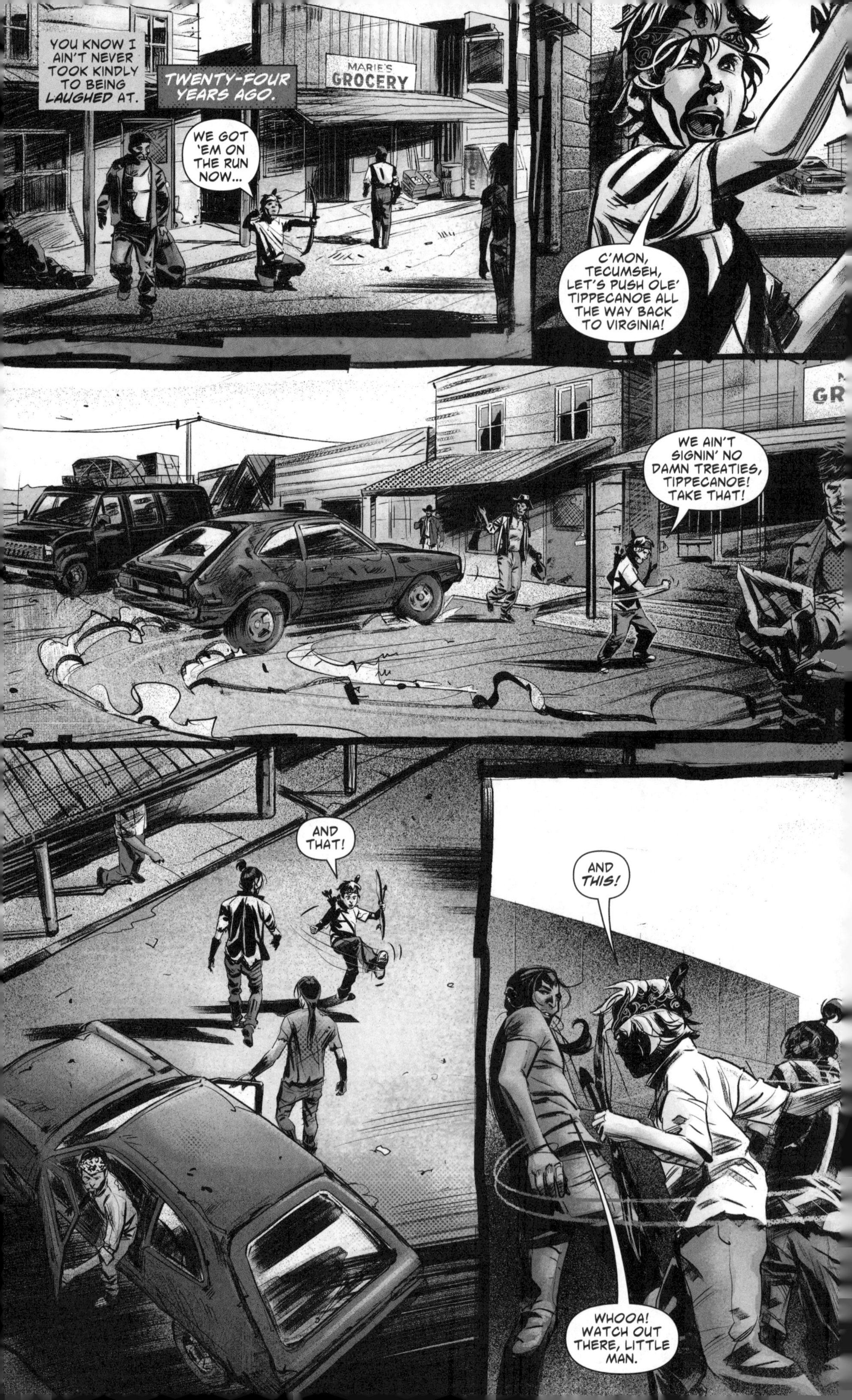

YOU KNOW I AIN'T NEVER TOOK KINDLY TO BEING *LAUGHED* AT.
TWENTY-FOUR YEARS AGO.
MARIE'S GROCERY
WE GOT 'EM ON THE RUN NOW...
C'MON, TECUMSEH, LET'S PUSH OLE' TIPPECANOE ALL THE WAY BACK TO VIRGINIA!
WE AIN'T SIGNIN' NO DAMN TREATIES, TIPPECANOE! TAKE THAT!
AND THAT!
AND *THIS!*
WHOOA! WATCH OUT THERE, LITTLE MAN.

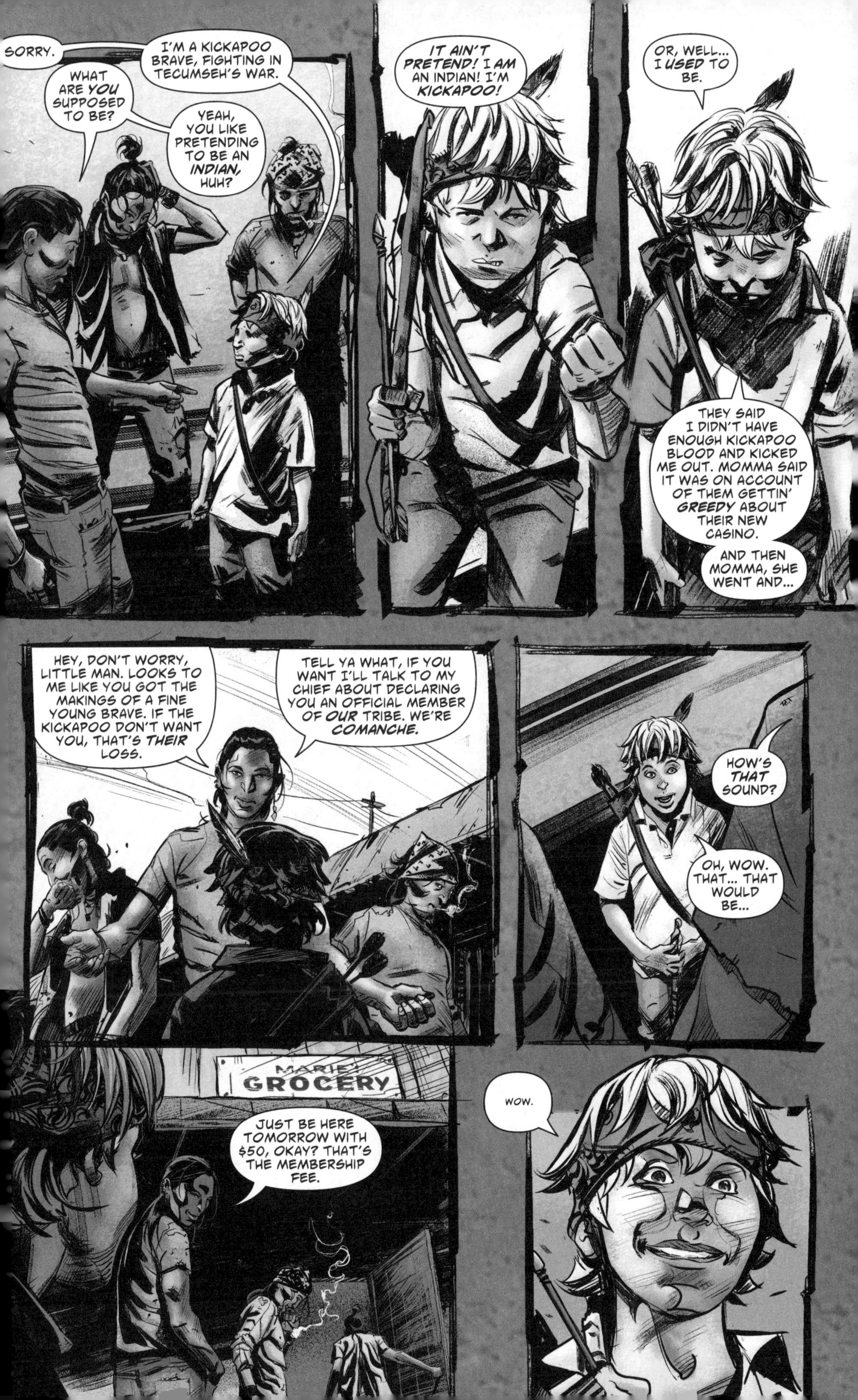
SORRY.
WHAT ARE YOU SUPPOSED TO BE?
I'M A KICKAPOO BRAVE, FIGHTING IN TECUMSEH'S WAR.
YEAH, YOU LIKE PRETENDING TO BE AN INDIAN, HUH?
IT AIN'T PRETEND! I AM AN INDIAN! I'M KICKAPOO!
OR, WELL... I USED TO BE.
THEY SAID I DIDN'T HAVE ENOUGH KICKAPOO BLOOD AND KICKED ME OUT. MOMMA SAID IT WAS ON ACCOUNT OF THEM GETTIN' GREEDY ABOUT THEIR NEW CASINO.
AND THEN MOMMA, SHE WENT AND...
HEY, DON'T WORRY, LITTLE MAN. LOOKS TO ME LIKE YOU GOT THE MAKINGS OF A FINE YOUNG BRAVE. IF THE KICKAPOO DON'T WANT YOU, THAT'S THEIR LOSS.
TELL YA WHAT, IF YOU WANT I'LL TALK TO MY CHIEF ABOUT DECLARING YOU AN OFFICIAL MEMBER OF OUR TRIBE. WE'RE COMANCHE.
HOW'S THAT SOUND?
OH, WOW. THAT... THAT WOULD BE...
GROCERY
JUST BE HERE TOMORROW WITH $50, OKAY? THAT'S THE MEMBERSHIP FEE.
WOW.

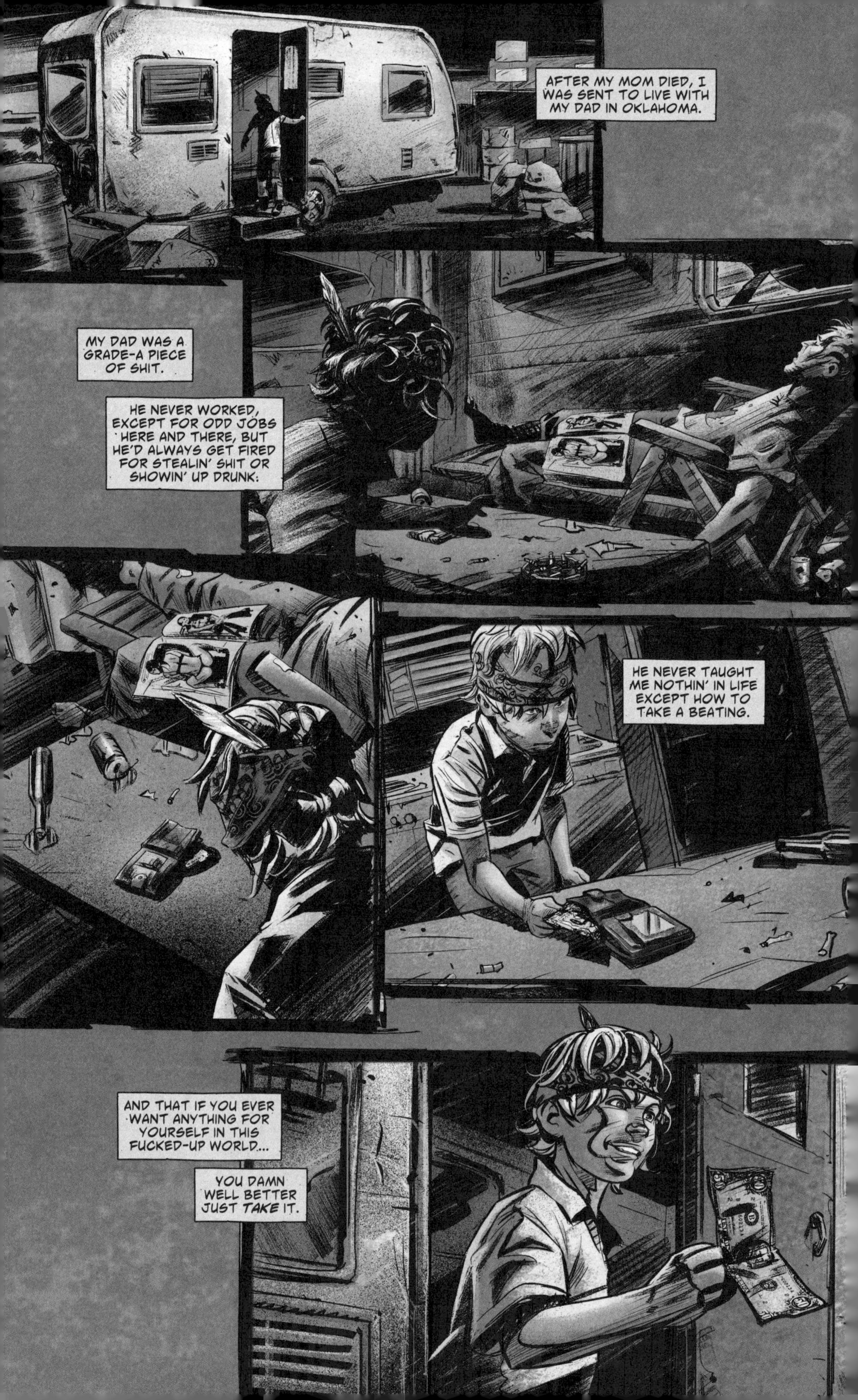
AFTER MY MOM DIED, I WAS SENT TO LIVE WITH MY DAD IN OKLAHOMA.
MY DAD WAS A GRADE-A PIECE OF SHIT.
HE NEVER WORKED, EXCEPT FOR ODD JOBS HERE AND THERE, BUT HE'D ALWAYS GET FIRED FOR STEALIN' SHIT OR SHOWIN' UP DRUNK.
HE NEVER TAUGHT ME NOTHIN' IN LIFE EXCEPT HOW TO TAKE A BEATING.
AND THAT IF YOU EVER WANT ANYTHING FOR YOURSELF IN THIS FUCKED-UP WORLD...
YOU DAMN WELL BETTER JUST *TAKE* IT.

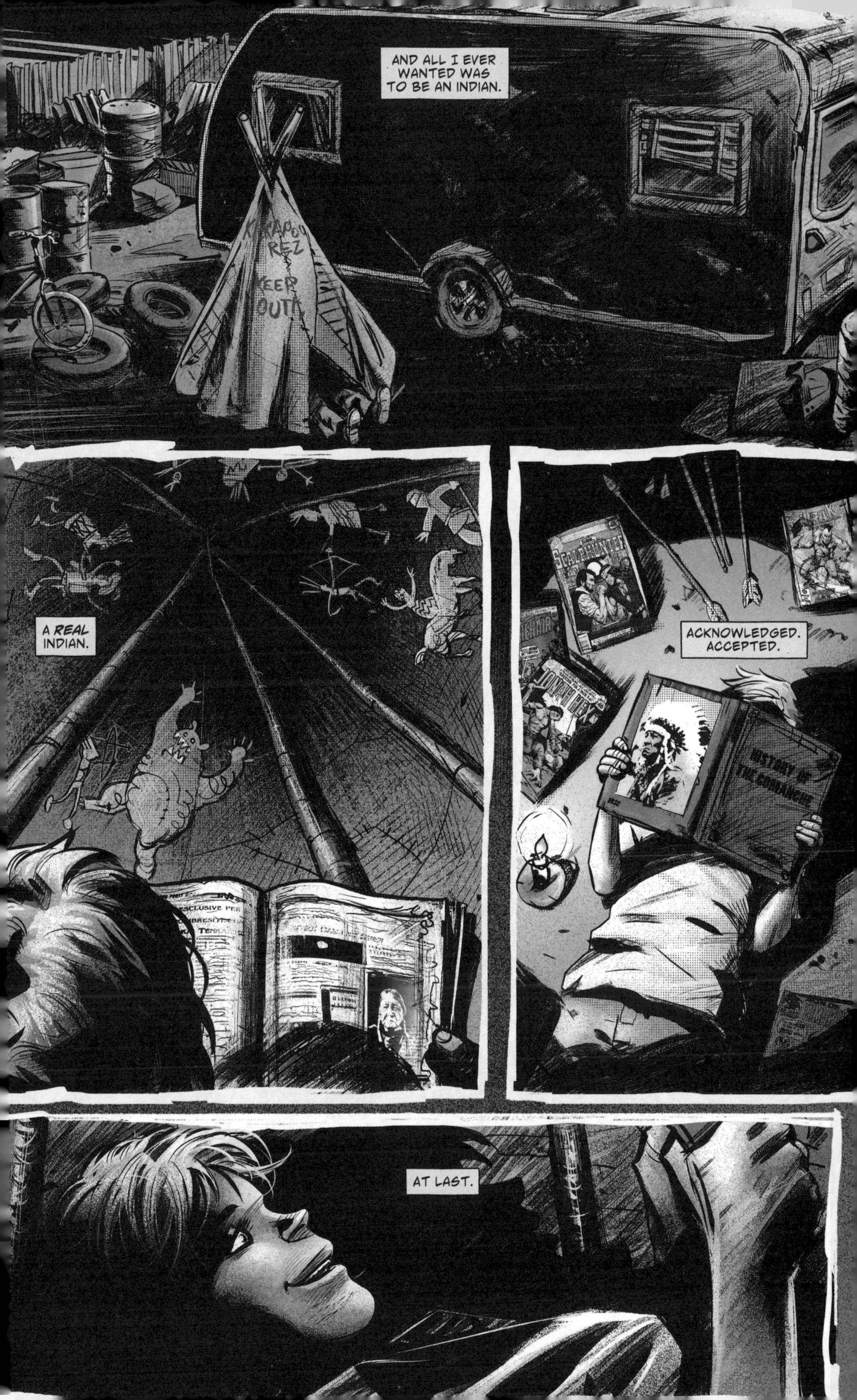
AND ALL I EVER WANTED WAS TO BE AN INDIAN.
REZ
KEEP OUT
A REAL INDIAN.
ACKNOWLEDGED. ACCEPTED.
JONAH HEX
HISTORY OF THE COMANCHE
AT LAST.

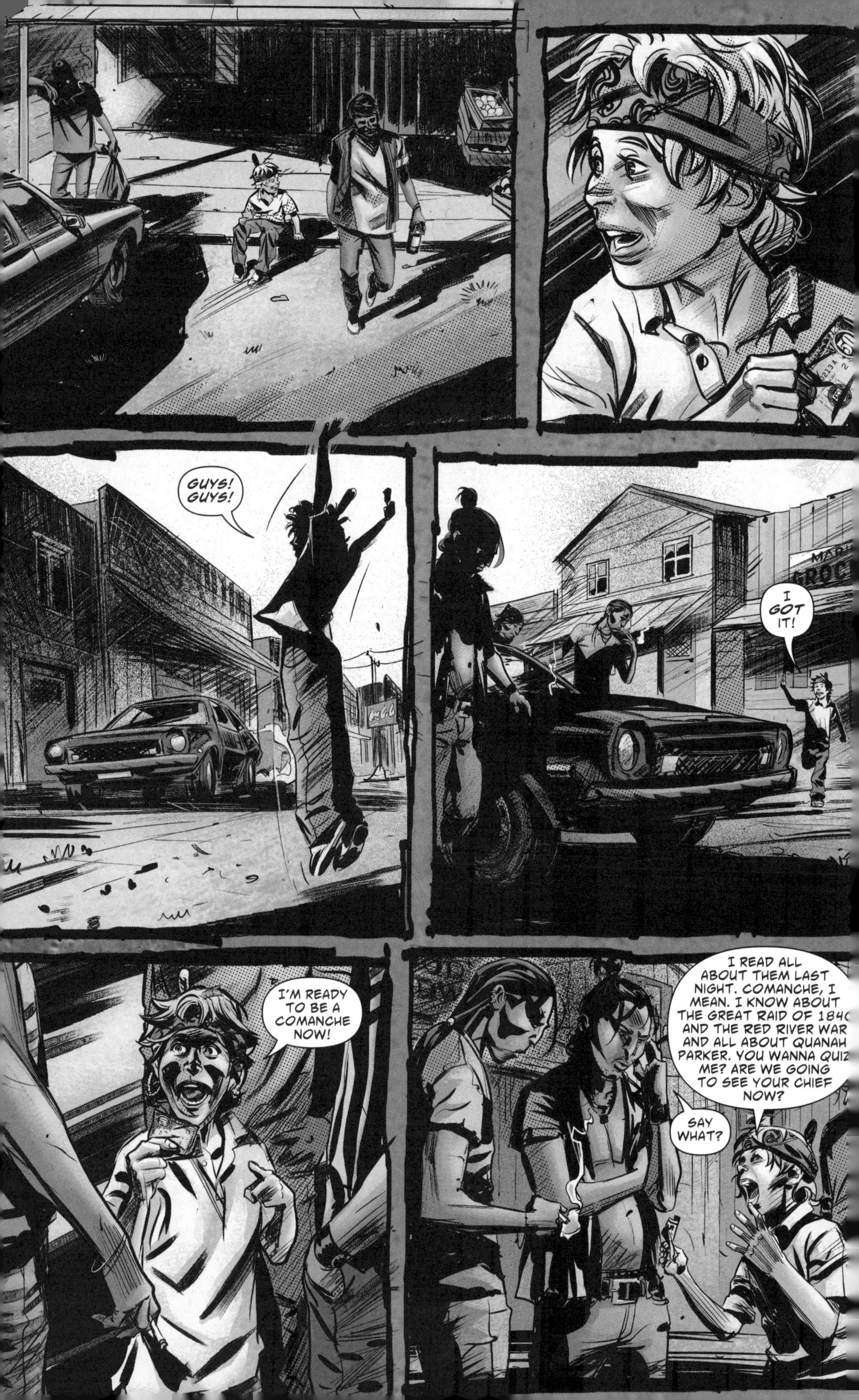
GUYS!
GUYS!
I GOT IT!
I'M READY TO BE A COMANCHE NOW!
I READ ALL ABOUT THEM LAST NIGHT. COMANCHE, I MEAN. I KNOW ABOUT THE GREAT RAID OF 1840 AND THE RED RIVER WAR AND ALL ABOUT QUANAH PARKER. YOU WANNA QUIZ ME? ARE WE GOING TO SEE YOUR CHIEF NOW?
SAY WHAT?

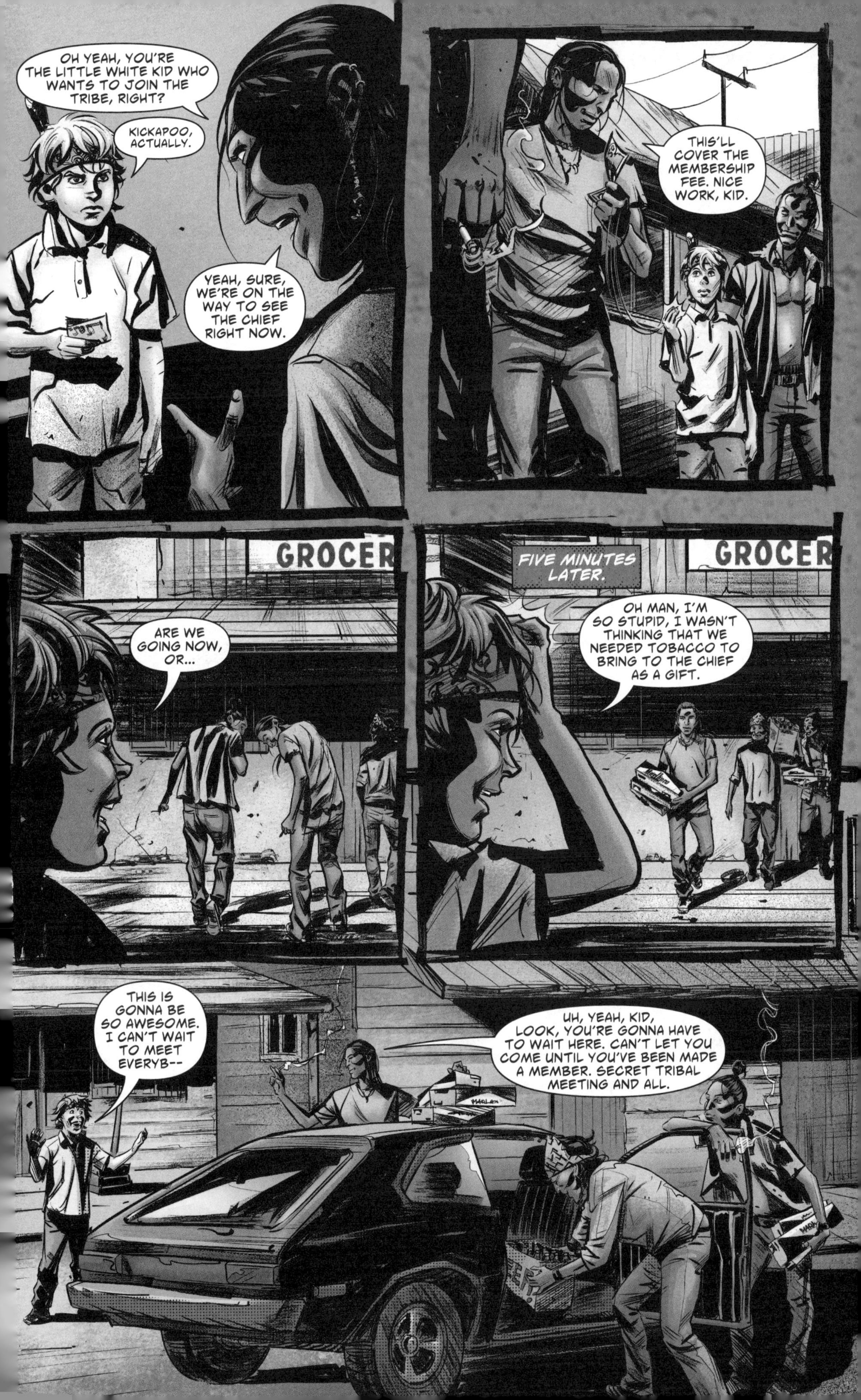
OH YEAH, YOU'RE THE LITTLE WHITE KID WHO WANTS TO JOIN THE TRIBE, RIGHT?
KICKAPOO, ACTUALLY.
YEAH, SURE, WE'RE ON THE WAY TO SEE THE CHIEF RIGHT NOW.
THIS'LL COVER THE MEMBERSHIP FEE. NICE WORK, KID.
GROCER
ARE WE GOING NOW, OR...
GROCER
FIVE MINUTES LATER.
OH MAN, I'M SO STUPID, I WASN'T THINKING THAT WE NEEDED TOBACCO TO BRING TO THE CHIEF AS A GIFT.
THIS IS GONNA BE SO AWESOME. I CAN'T WAIT TO MEET EVERYB--
UH, YEAH, KID, LOOK, YOU'RE GONNA HAVE TO WAIT HERE. CAN'T LET YOU COME UNTIL YOU'VE BEEN MADE A MEMBER. SECRET TRIBAL MEETING AND ALL.

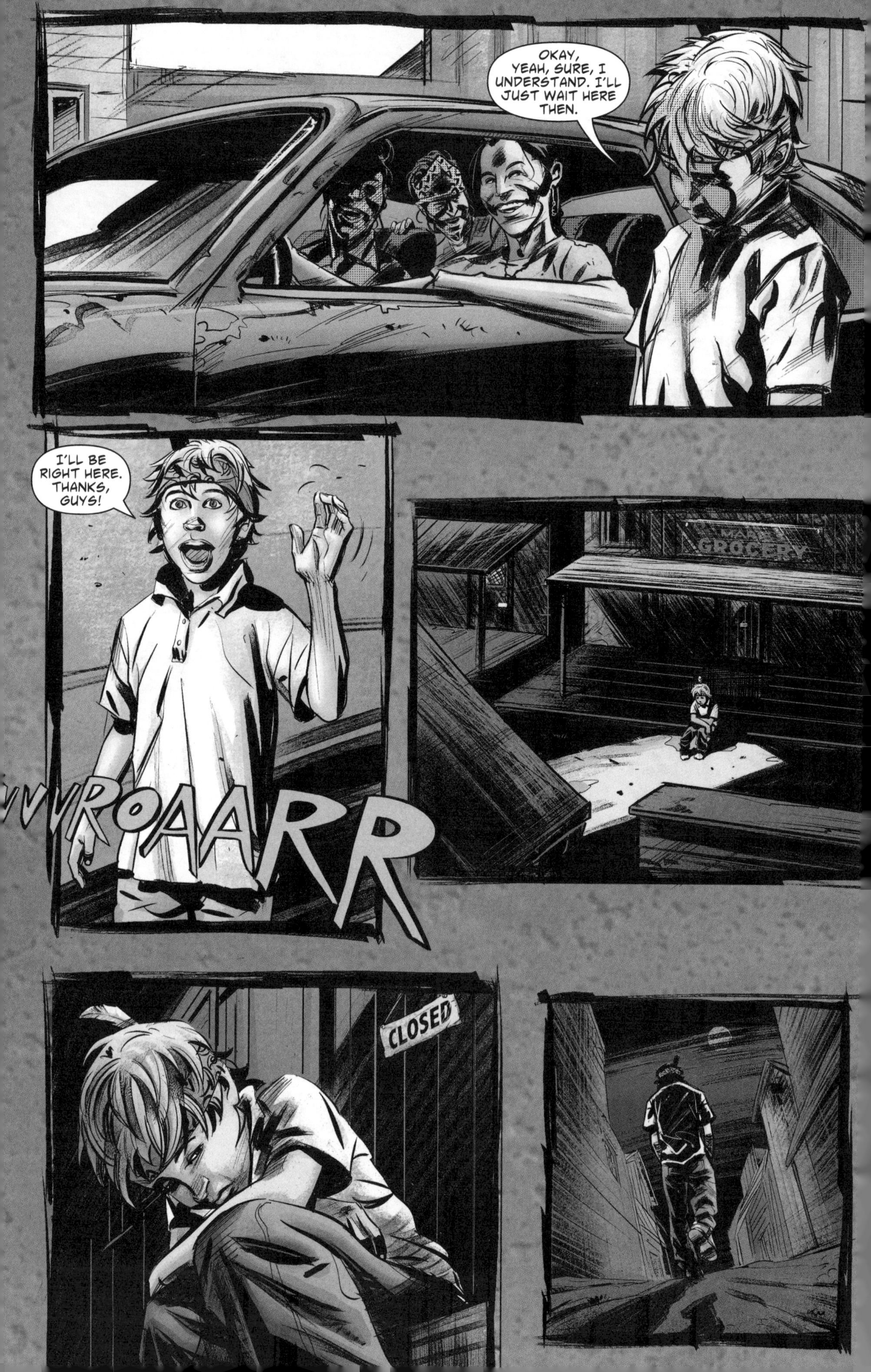
OKAY, YEAH, SURE, I UNDERSTAND. I'LL JUST WAIT HERE THEN.
I'LL BE RIGHT HERE. THANKS, GUYS!
VVVROAARR
GROCERY
CLOSED

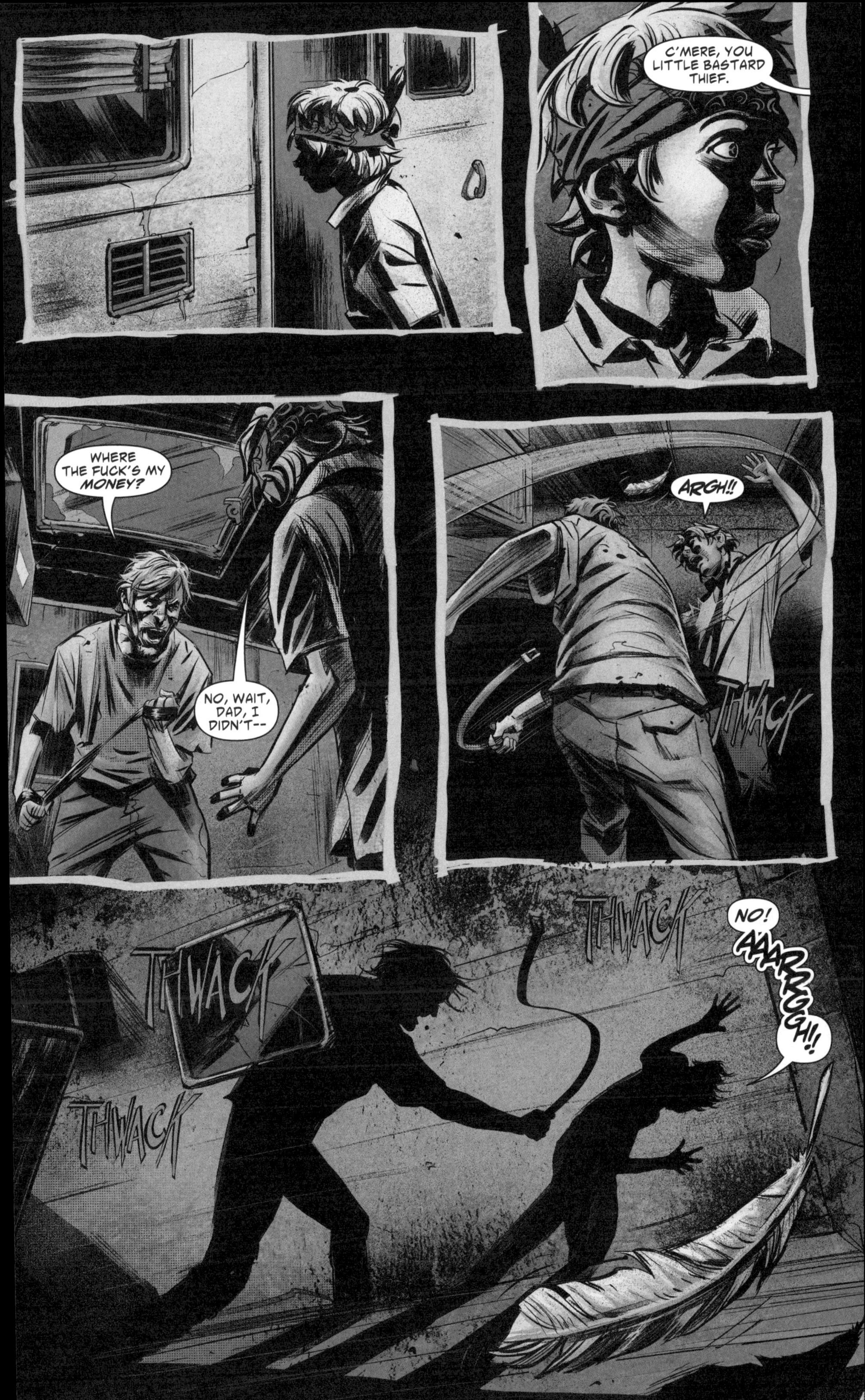
C'MERE, YOU LITTLE BASTARD THIEF.
WHERE THE FUCK'S MY MONEY?
NO, WAIT, DAD, I DIDN'T--
ARGH!!
THWACK
THWACK
THWACK
THWACK
NO! AAARRGGH!!

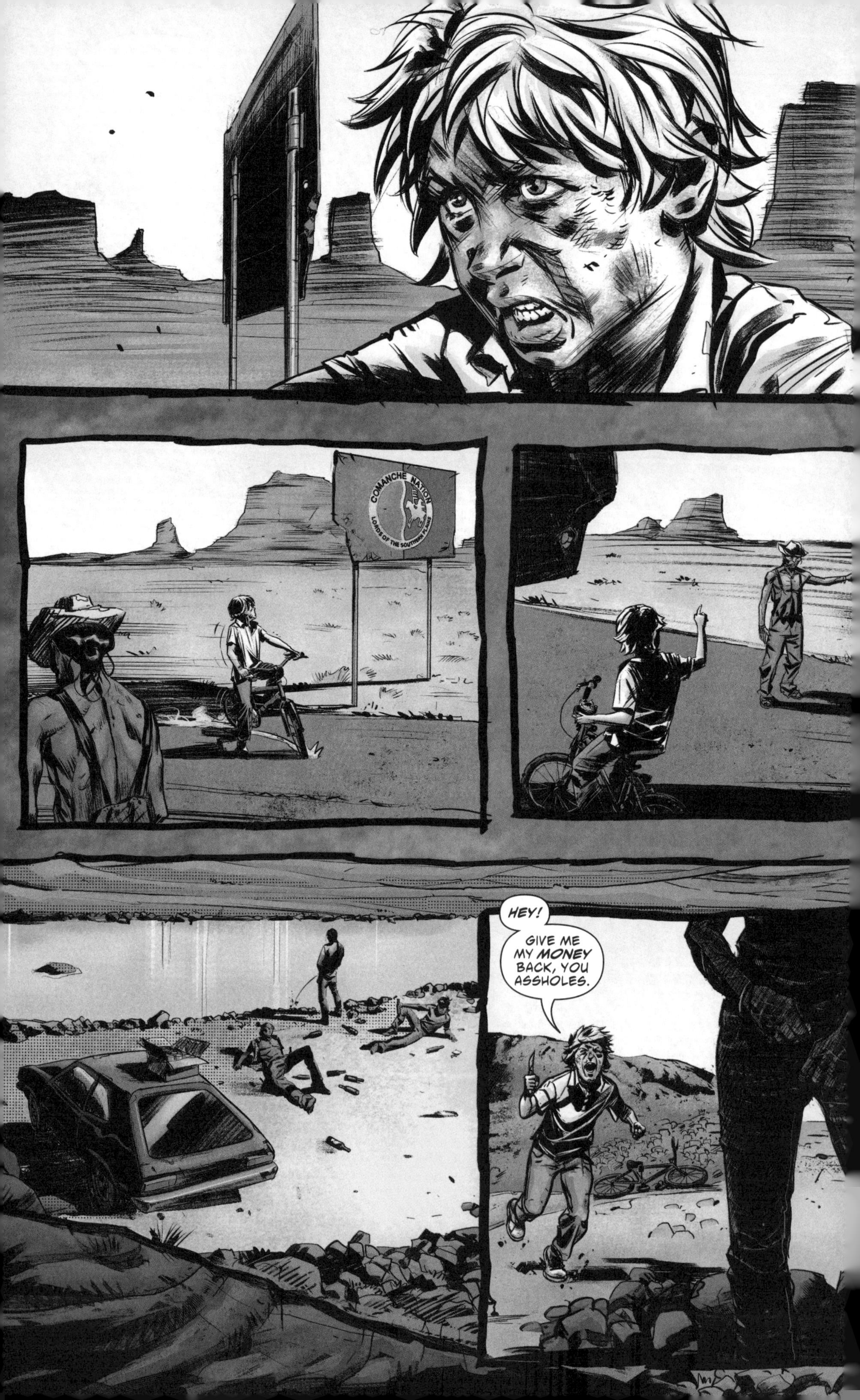
COMANCHE NATION
LORDS OF THE SOUTHERN PLAINS
HEY!
GIVE ME MY MONEY BACK, YOU ASSHOLES.

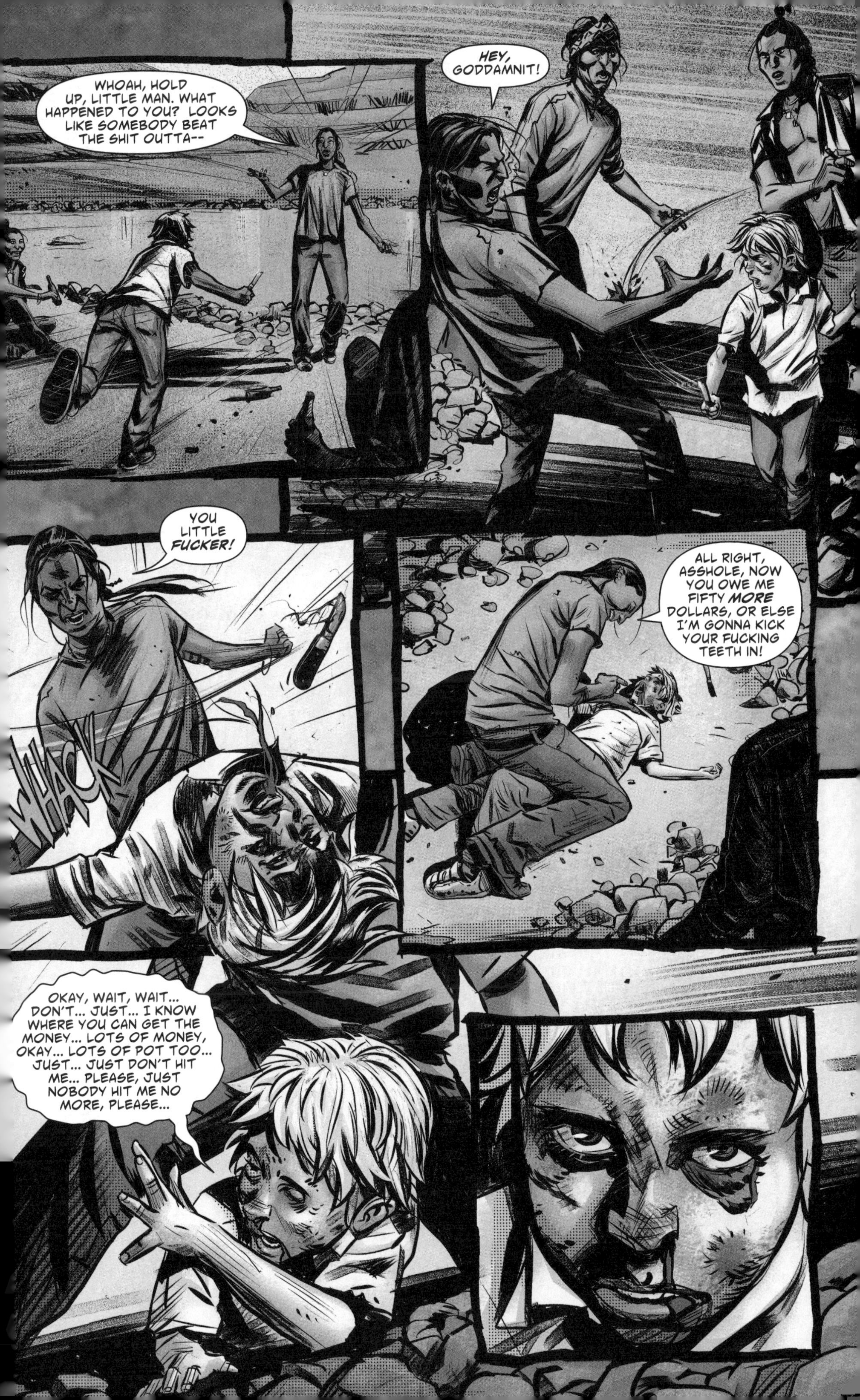
WHOAH, HOLD UP, LITTLE MAN. WHAT HAPPENED TO YOU? LOOKS LIKE SOMEBODY BEAT THE SHIT OUTTA--
HEY, GODDAMNIT!
YOU LITTLE FUCKER!
WHACK
ALL RIGHT, ASSHOLE, NOW YOU OWE ME FIFTY MORE DOLLARS, OR ELSE I'M GONNA KICK YOUR FUCKING TEETH IN!
OKAY, WAIT, WAIT... DON'T... JUST... I KNOW WHERE YOU CAN GET THE MONEY... LOTS OF MONEY, OKAY... LOTS OF POT TOO... JUST... JUST DON'T HIT ME... PLEASE, JUST NOBODY HIT ME NO MORE, PLEASE...

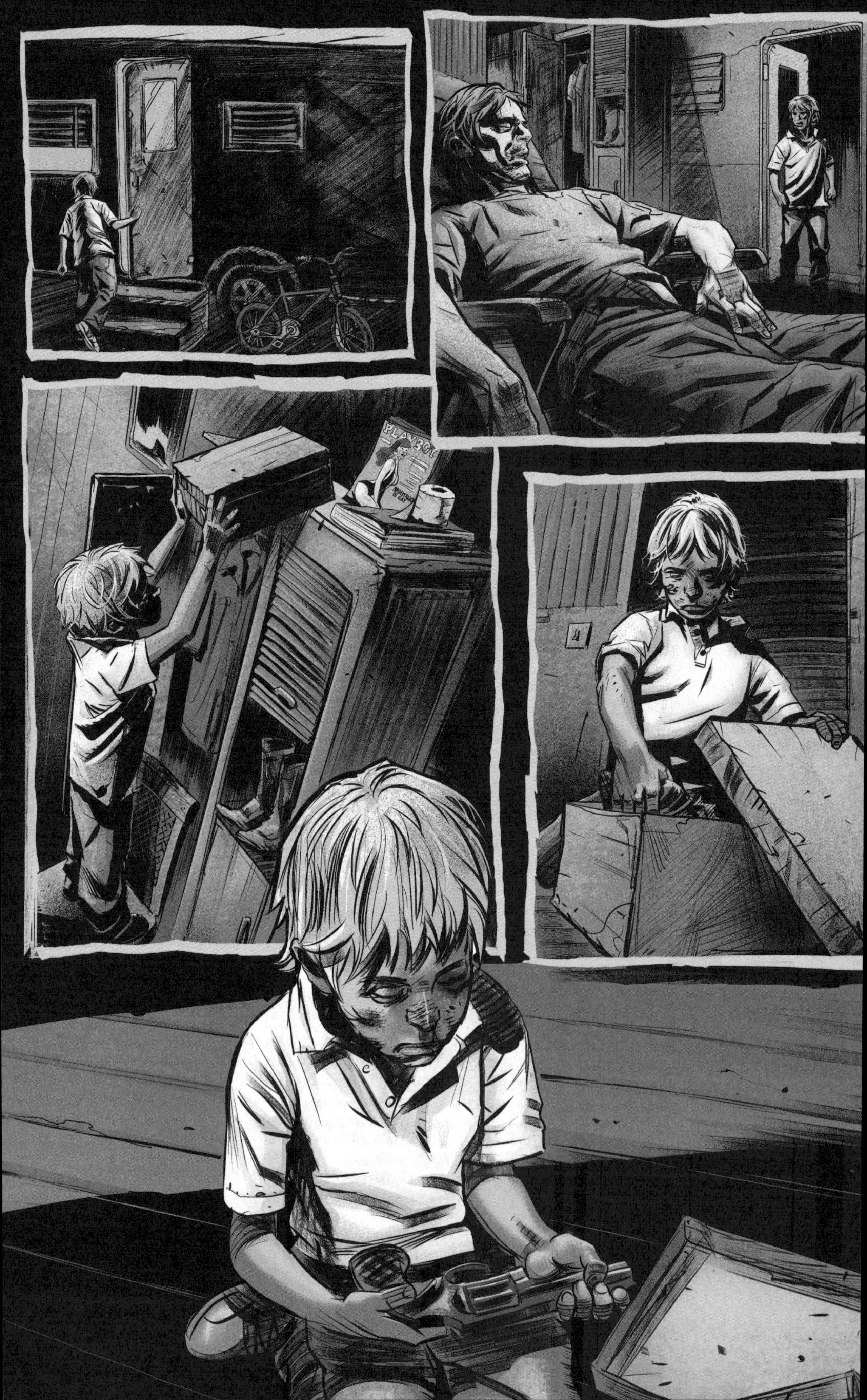

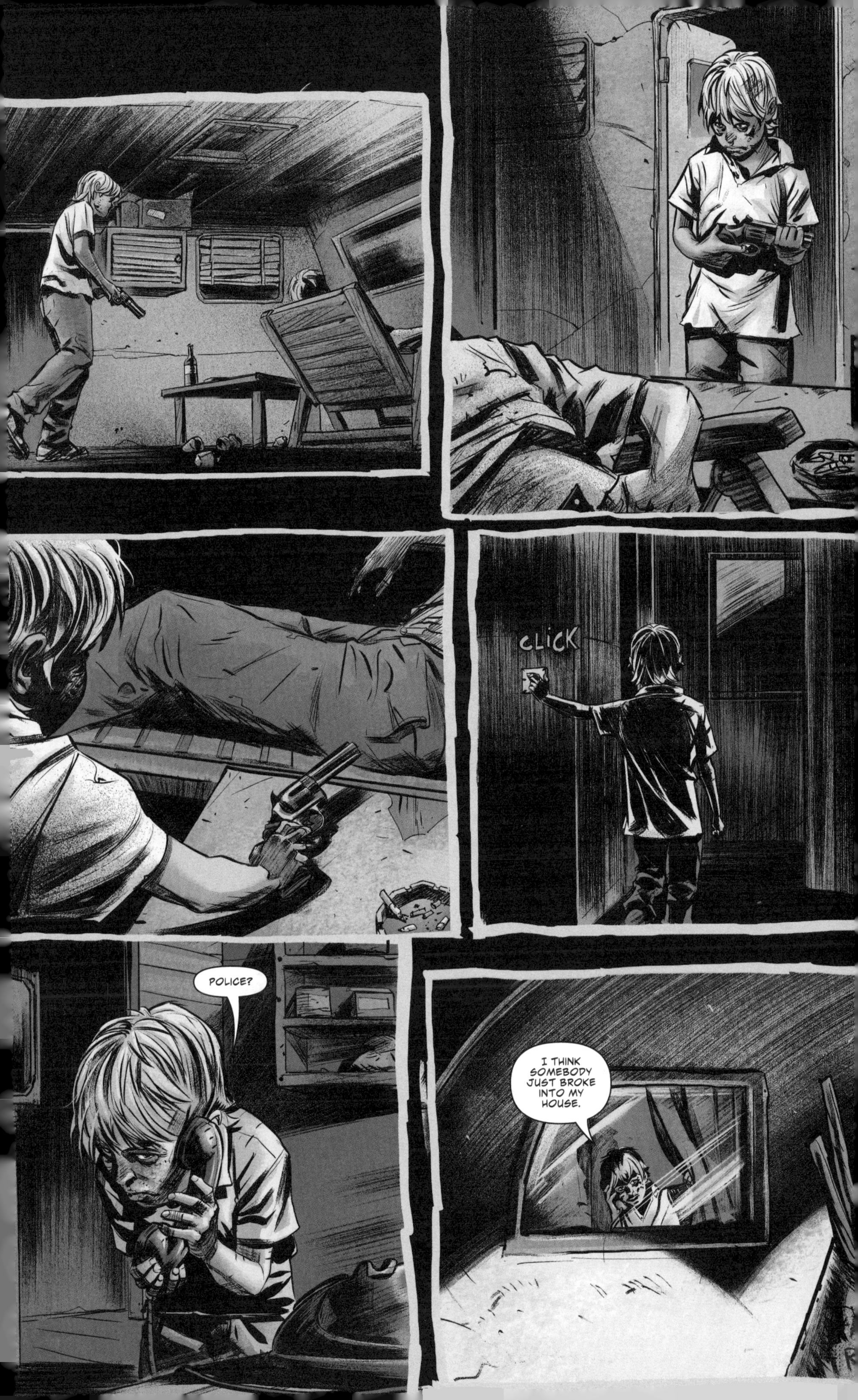
CLICK
POLICE?
I THINK SOMEBODY JUST BROKE INTO MY HOUSE.

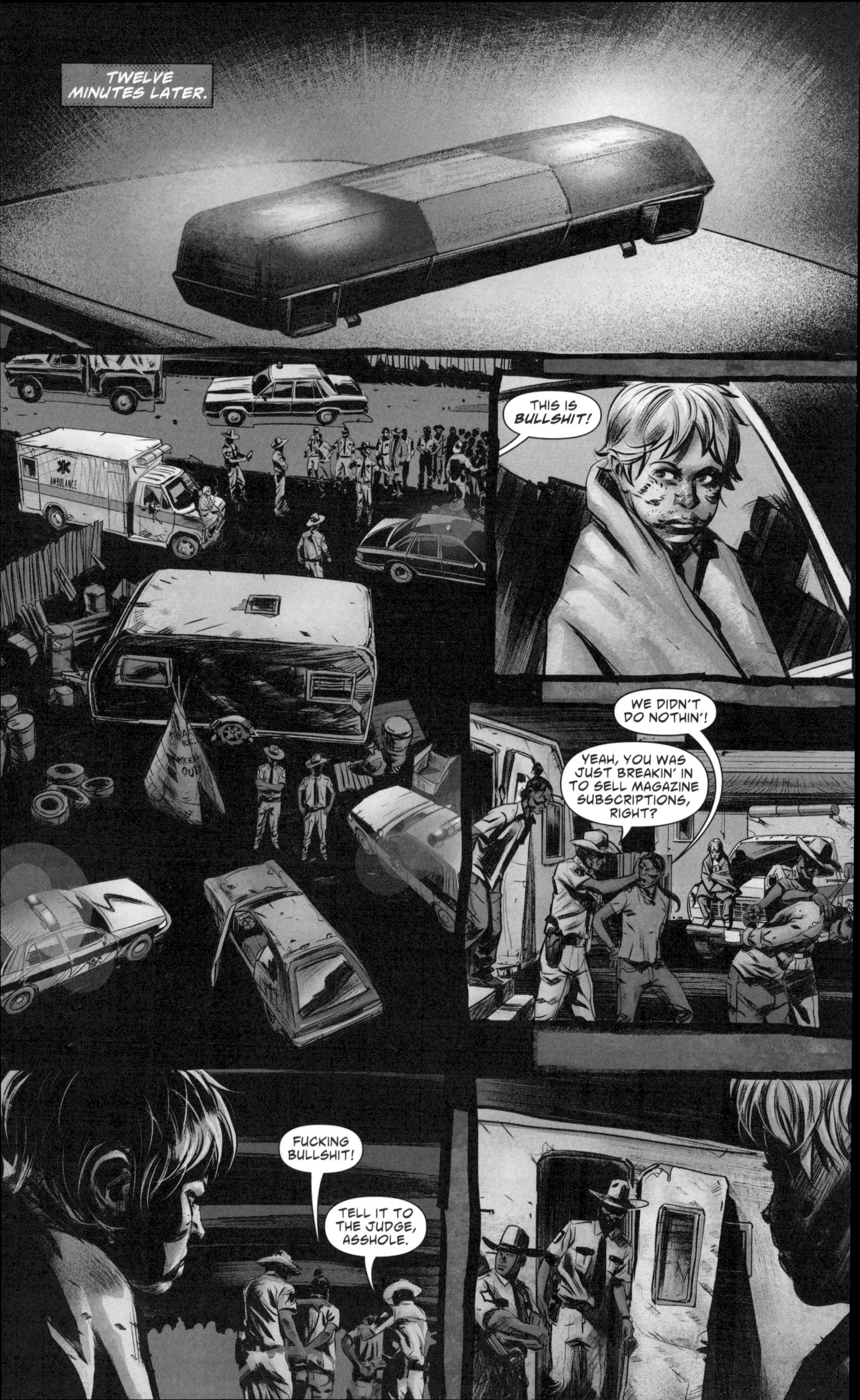
TWELVE MINUTES LATER.
THIS IS BULLSHIT!
WE DIDN'T DO NOTHIN'!
YEAH, YOU WAS JUST BREAKIN' IN TO SELL MAGAZINE SUBSCRIPTIONS, RIGHT?
FUCKING BULLSHIT!
TELL IT TO THE JUDGE, ASSHOLE.

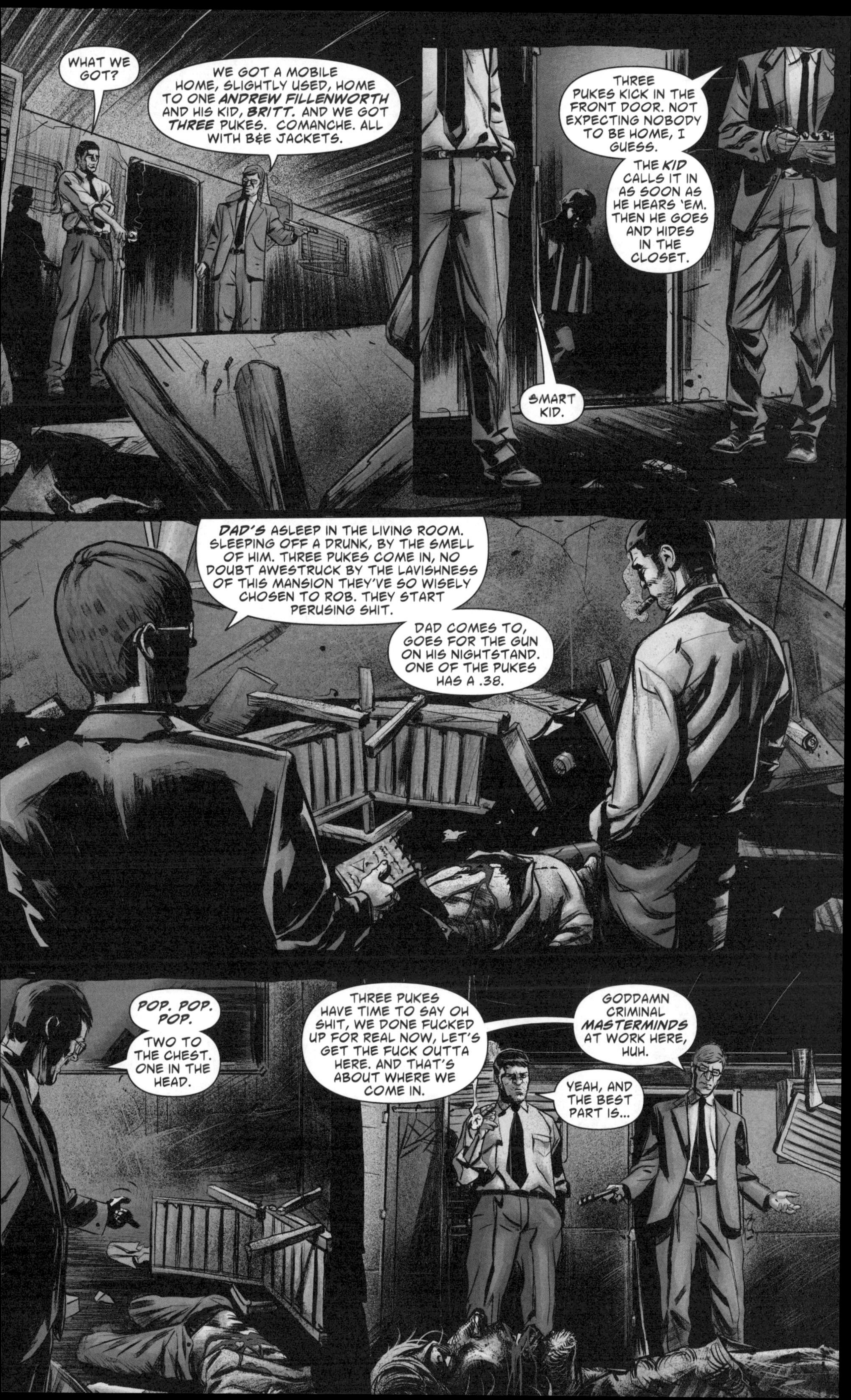
WHAT WE GOT?
WE GOT A MOBILE HOME, SLIGHTLY USED, HOME TO ONE ANDREW FILLENWORTH AND HIS KID, BRITT. AND WE GOT THREE PUKES. COMANCHE. ALL WITH B&E JACKETS.
THREE PUKES KICK IN THE FRONT DOOR. NOT EXPECTING NOBODY TO BE HOME, I GUESS.
THE KID CALLS IT IN AS SOON AS HE HEARS 'EM. THEN HE GOES AND HIDES IN THE CLOSET.
SMART KID.
DAD'S ASLEEP IN THE LIVING ROOM. SLEEPING OFF A DRUNK, BY THE SMELL OF HIM. THREE PUKES COME IN, NO DOUBT AWESTRUCK BY THE LAVISHNESS OF THIS MANSION THEY'VE SO WISELY CHOSEN TO ROB. THEY START PERUSING SHIT.
DAD COMES TO, GOES FOR THE GUN ON HIS NIGHTSTAND. ONE OF THE PUKES HAS A .38.
POP. POP. POP.
TWO TO THE CHEST. ONE IN THE HEAD.
THREE PUKES HAVE TIME TO SAY OH SHIT, WE DONE FUCKED UP FOR REAL NOW, LET'S GET THE FUCK OUTTA HERE. AND THAT'S ABOUT WHERE WE COME IN.
GODDAMN CRIMINAL MASTERMINDS AT WORK HERE, HUH.
YEAH, AND THE BEST PART IS...

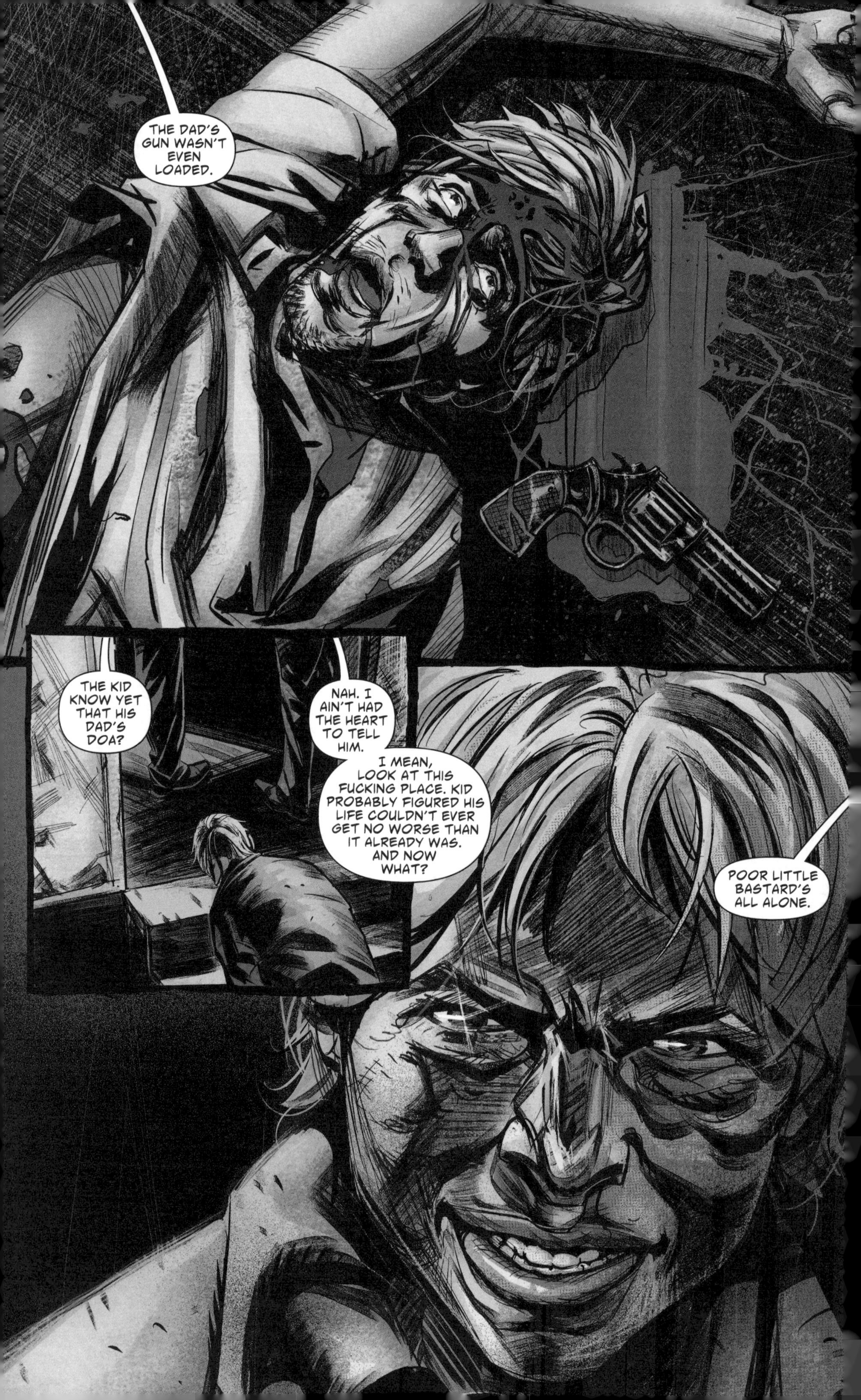
THE DAD'S GUN WASN'T EVEN LOADED.
THE KID KNOW YET THAT HIS DAD'S DOA?
NAH. I AIN'T HAD THE HEART TO TELL HIM.
I MEAN, LOOK AT THIS FUCKING PLACE. KID PROBABLY FIGURED HIS LIFE COULDN'T EVER GET NO WORSE THAN IT ALREADY WAS. AND NOW WHAT?
POOR LITTLE BASTARD'S ALL ALONE.

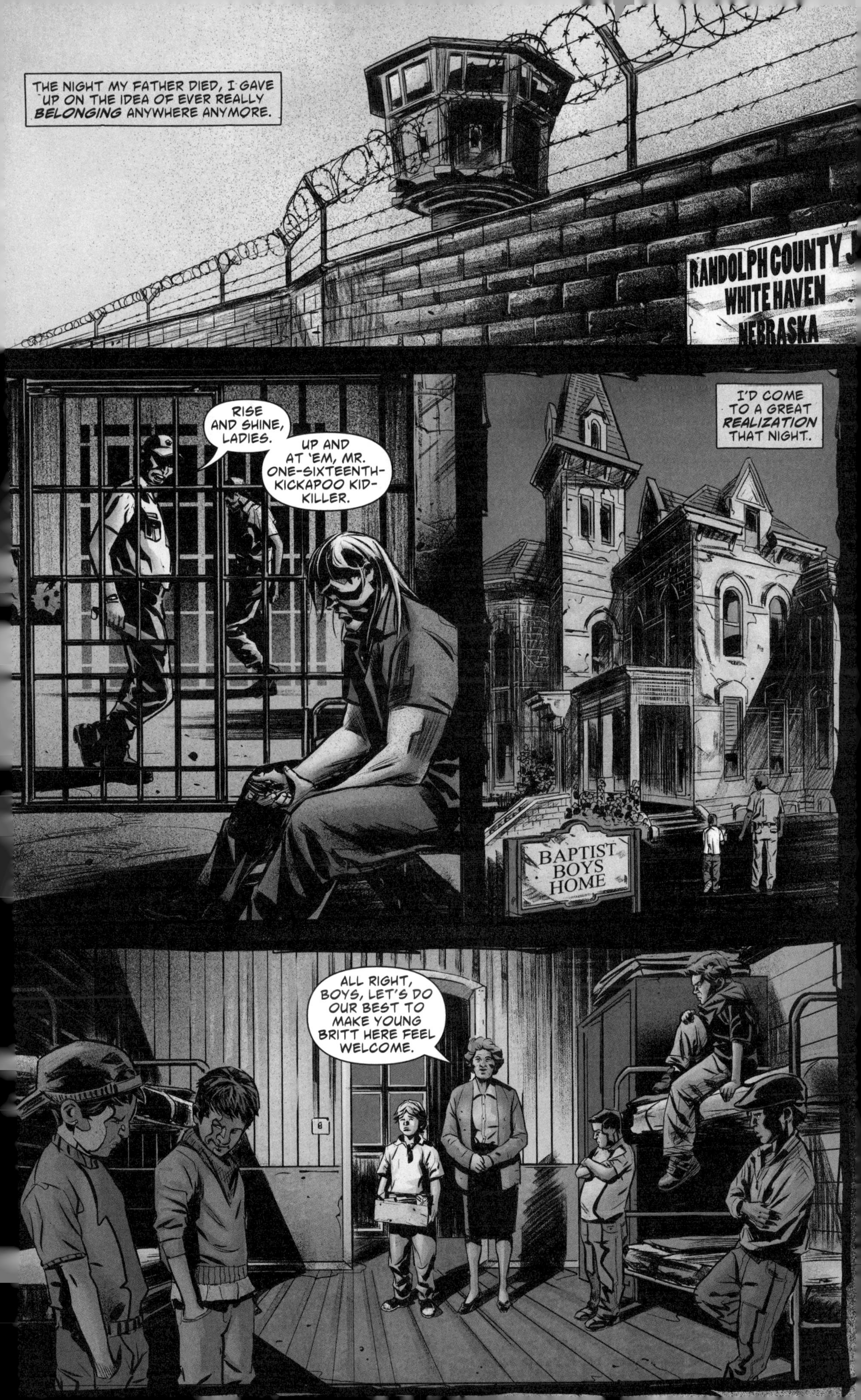
THE NIGHT MY FATHER DIED, I GAVE UP ON THE IDEA OF EVER REALLY *BELONGING* ANYWHERE ANYMORE.
RANDOLPH COUNTY J
WHITE HAVEN
NEBRASKA
RISE AND SHINE, LADIES.
UP AND AT 'EM, MR. ONE-SIXTEENTH-KICKAPOO KID-KILLER.
I'D COME TO A GREAT *REALIZATION* THAT NIGHT.
BAPTIST BOYS HOME
ALL RIGHT, BOYS, LET'S DO OUR BEST TO MAKE YOUNG BRITT HERE FEEL WELCOME.

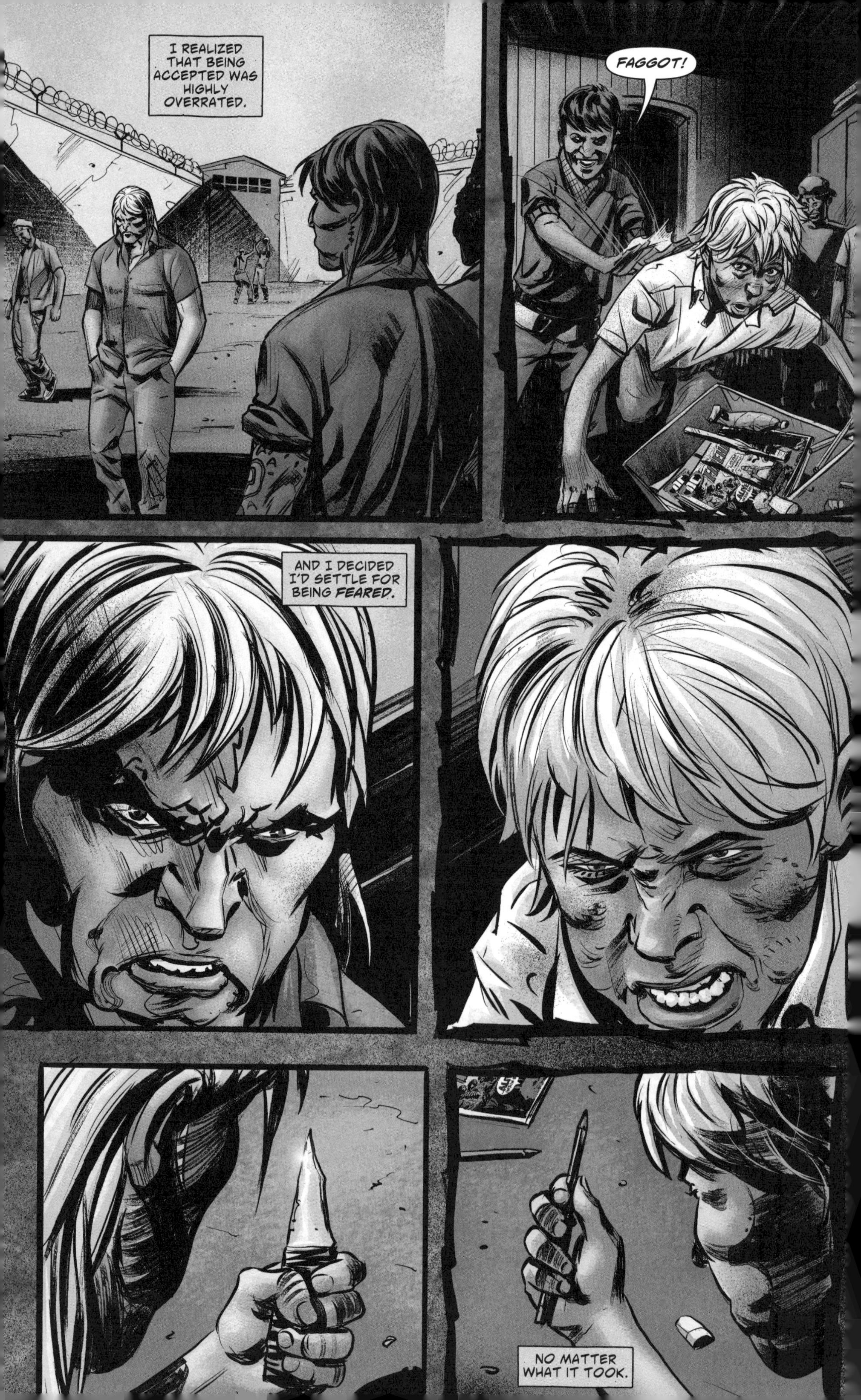
I REALIZED THAT BEING ACCEPTED WAS HIGHLY OVERRATED.
FAGGOT!
AND I DECIDED I'D SETTLE FOR BEING FEARED.
NO MATTER WHAT IT TOOK.

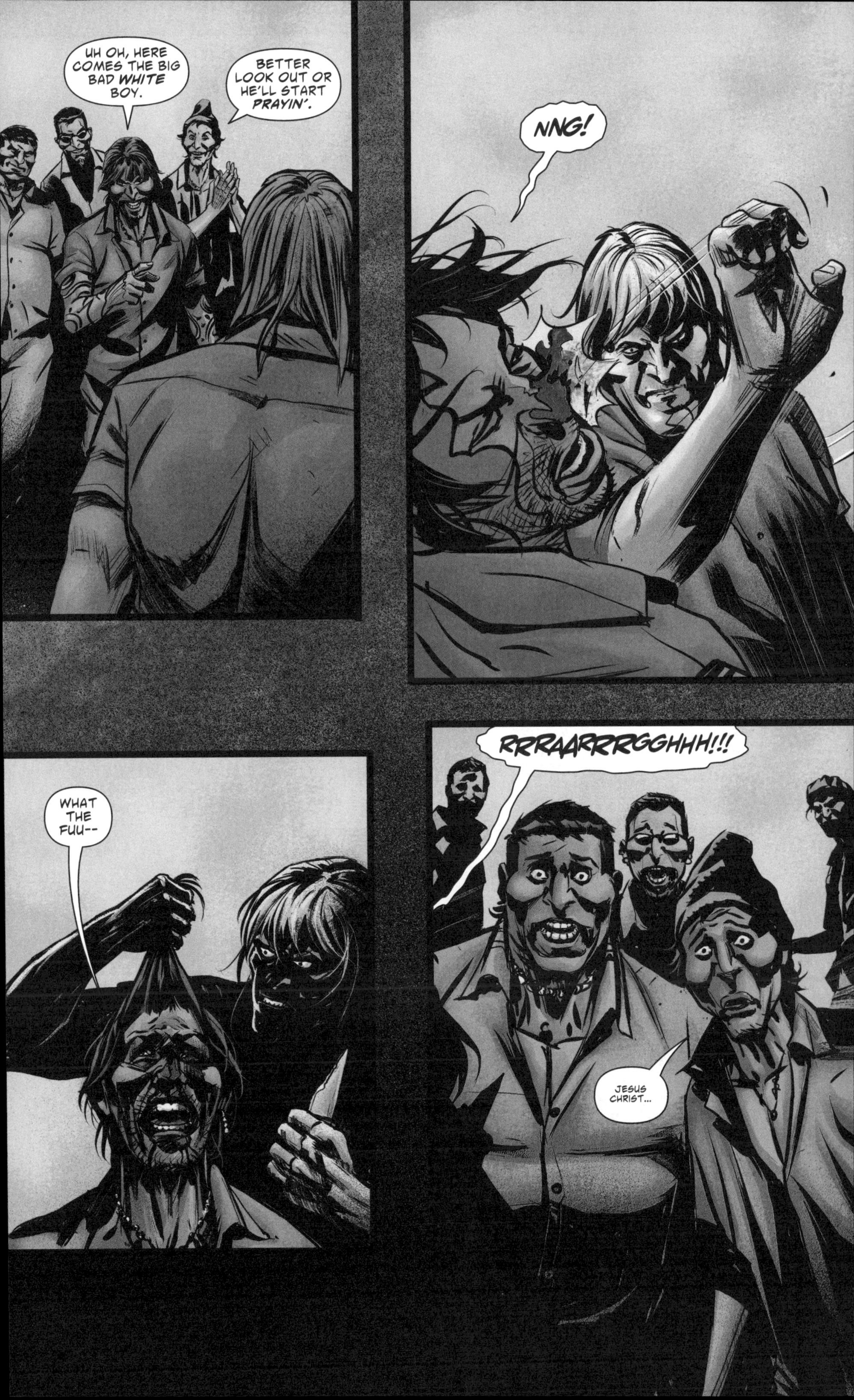
UH OH, HERE COMES THE BIG BAD *WHITE* BOY.
BETTER LOOK OUT OR HE'LL START *PRAYIN'*.
NNG!
WHAT THE FUU--
RRRAARRRGGHHH!!!
JESUS CHRIST...

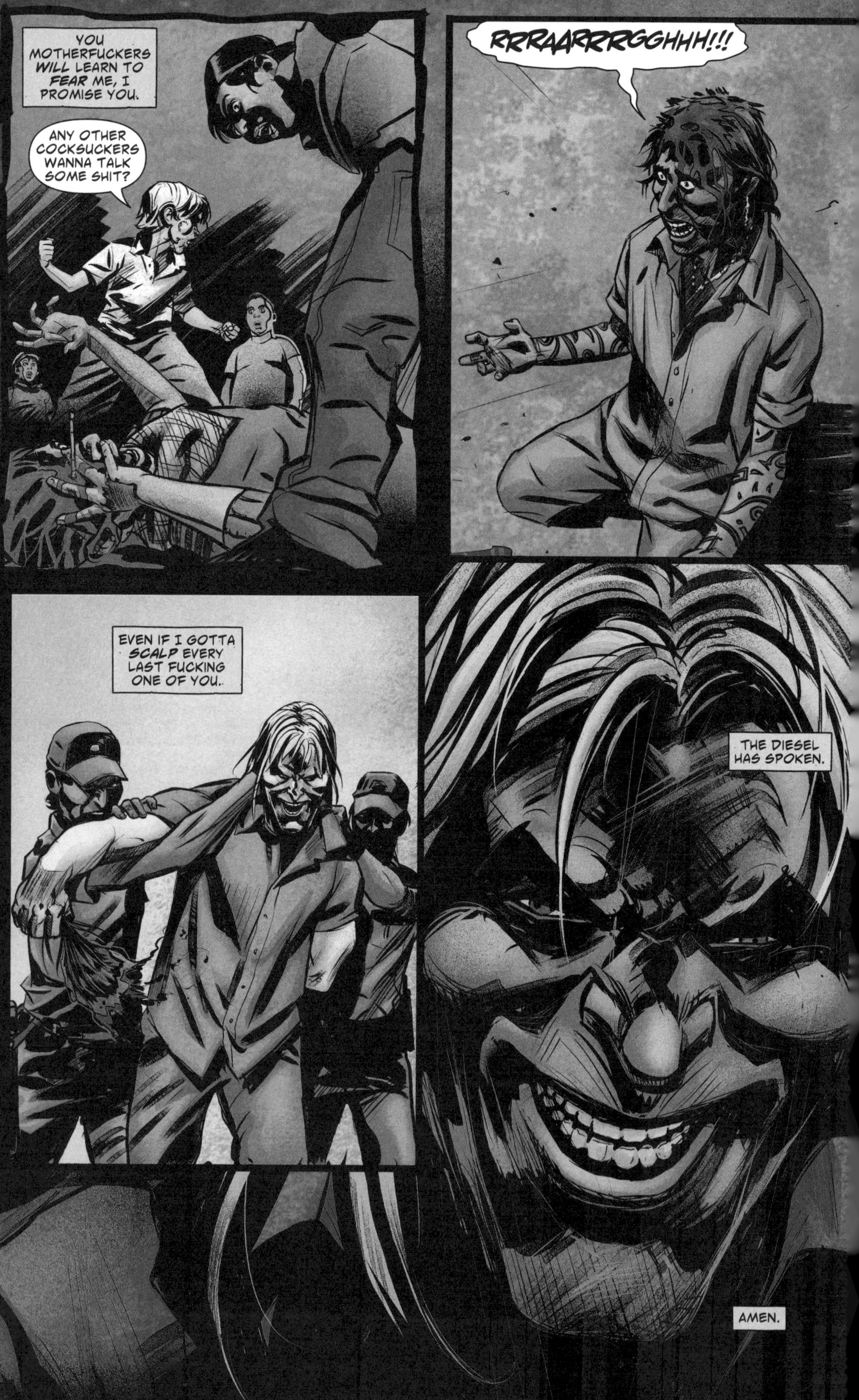
YOU MOTHERFUCKERS WILL LEARN TO FEAR ME, I PROMISE YOU.
ANY OTHER COCKSUCKERS WANNA TALK SOME SHIT?
RRRAARRRGGHHH!!!
EVEN IF I GOTTA SCALP EVERY LAST FUCKING ONE OF YOU..
THE DIESEL HAS SPOKEN.
AMEN.

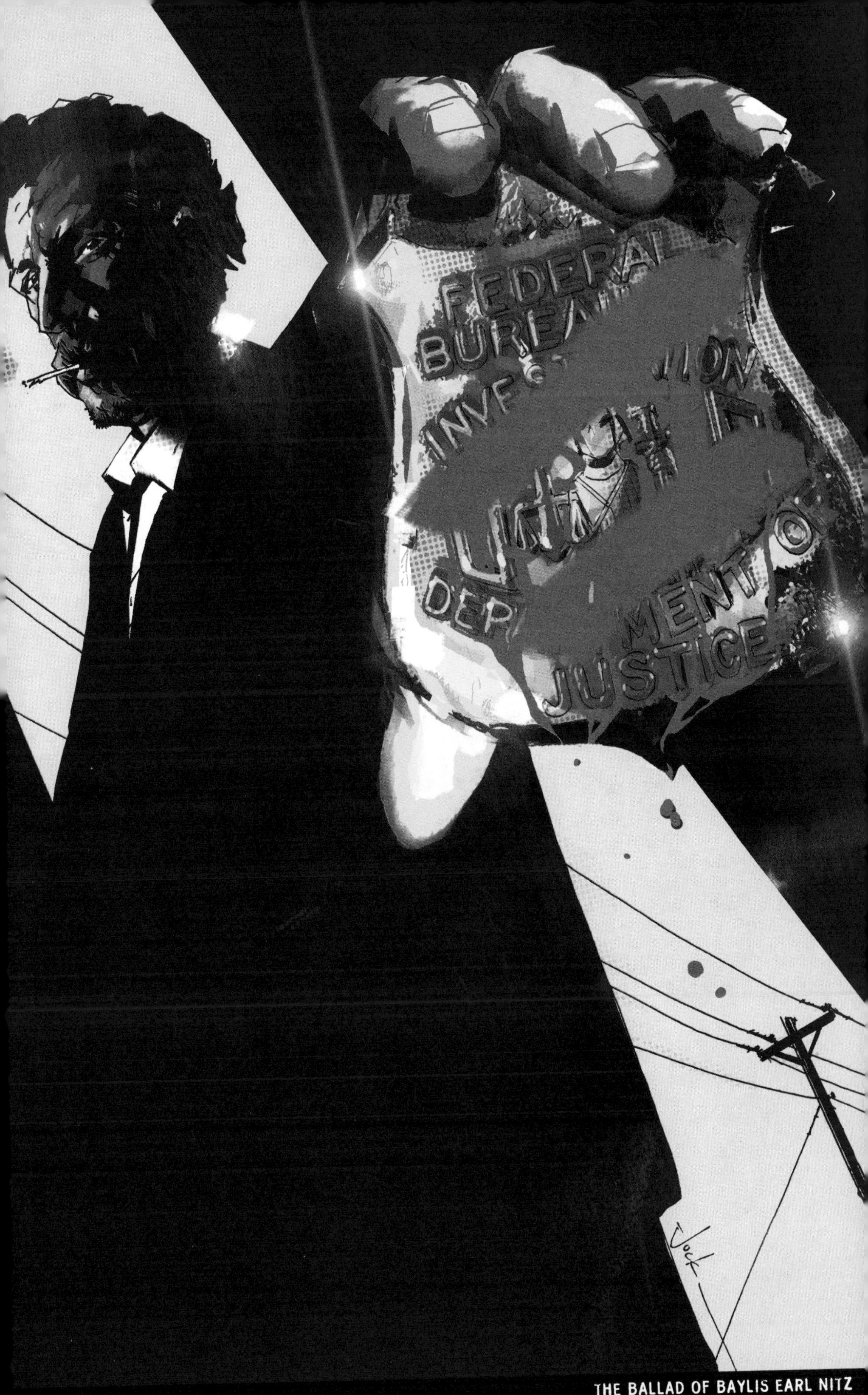
FEDERAL
JUSTICE

THE BALLAD OF BAYLIS EARL NITZ

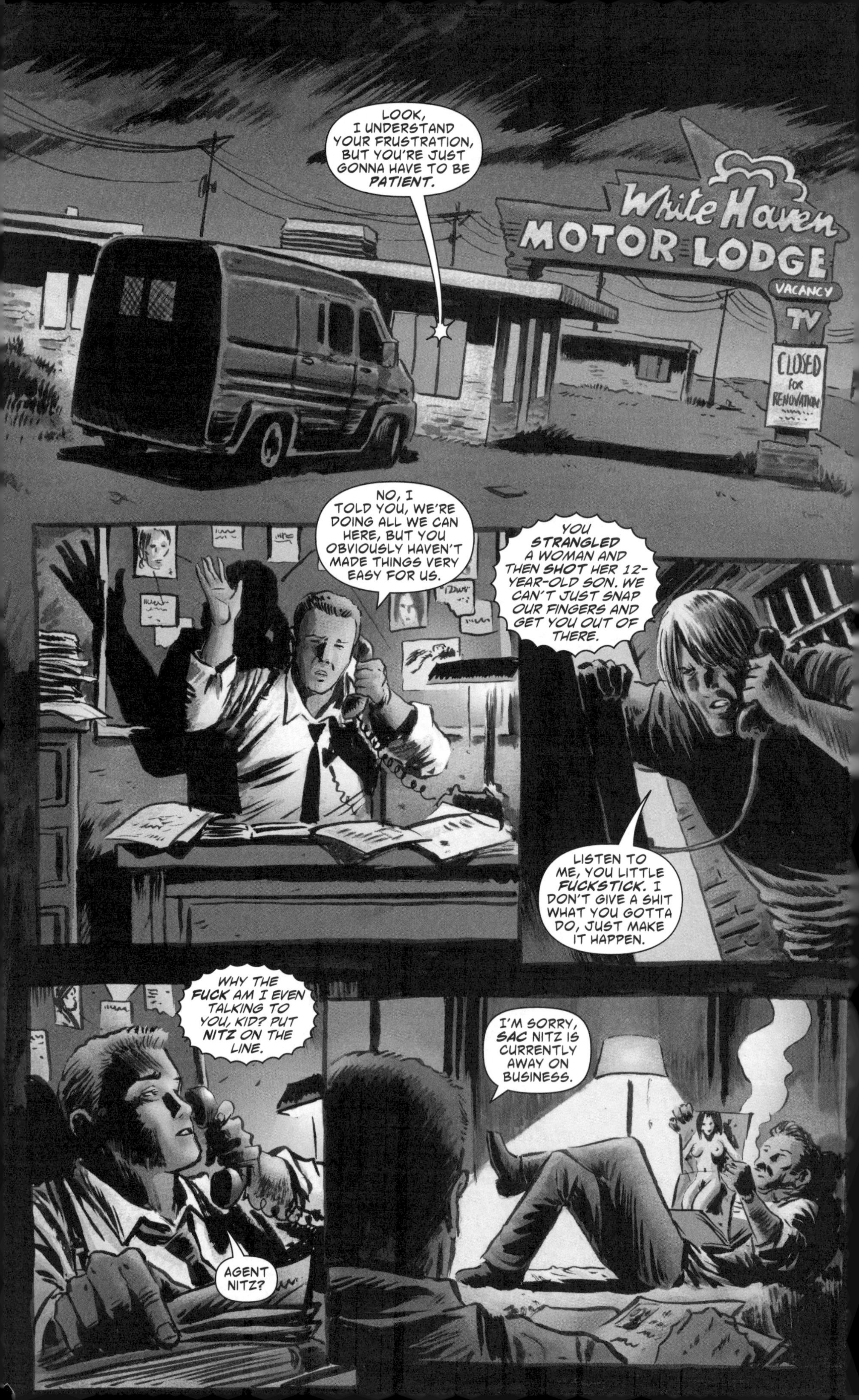
LOOK, I UNDERSTAND YOUR FRUSTRATION, BUT YOU'RE JUST GONNA HAVE TO BE PATIENT.
White Haven MOTOR LODGE
VACANCY
TV
CLOSED FOR RENOVATION
NO, I TOLD YOU, WE'RE DOING ALL WE CAN HERE, BUT YOU OBVIOUSLY HAVEN'T MADE THINGS VERY EASY FOR US.
YOU STRANGLED A WOMAN AND THEN SHOT HER 12-YEAR-OLD SON. WE CAN'T JUST SNAP OUR FINGERS AND GET YOU OUT OF THERE.
LISTEN TO ME, YOU LITTLE FUCKSTICK. I DON'T GIVE A SHIT WHAT YOU GOTTA DO, JUST MAKE IT HAPPEN.
WHY THE FUCK AM I EVEN TALKING TO YOU, KID? PUT NITZ ON THE LINE.
AGENT NITZ?
I'M SORRY, SAC NITZ IS CURRENTLY AWAY ON BUSINESS.

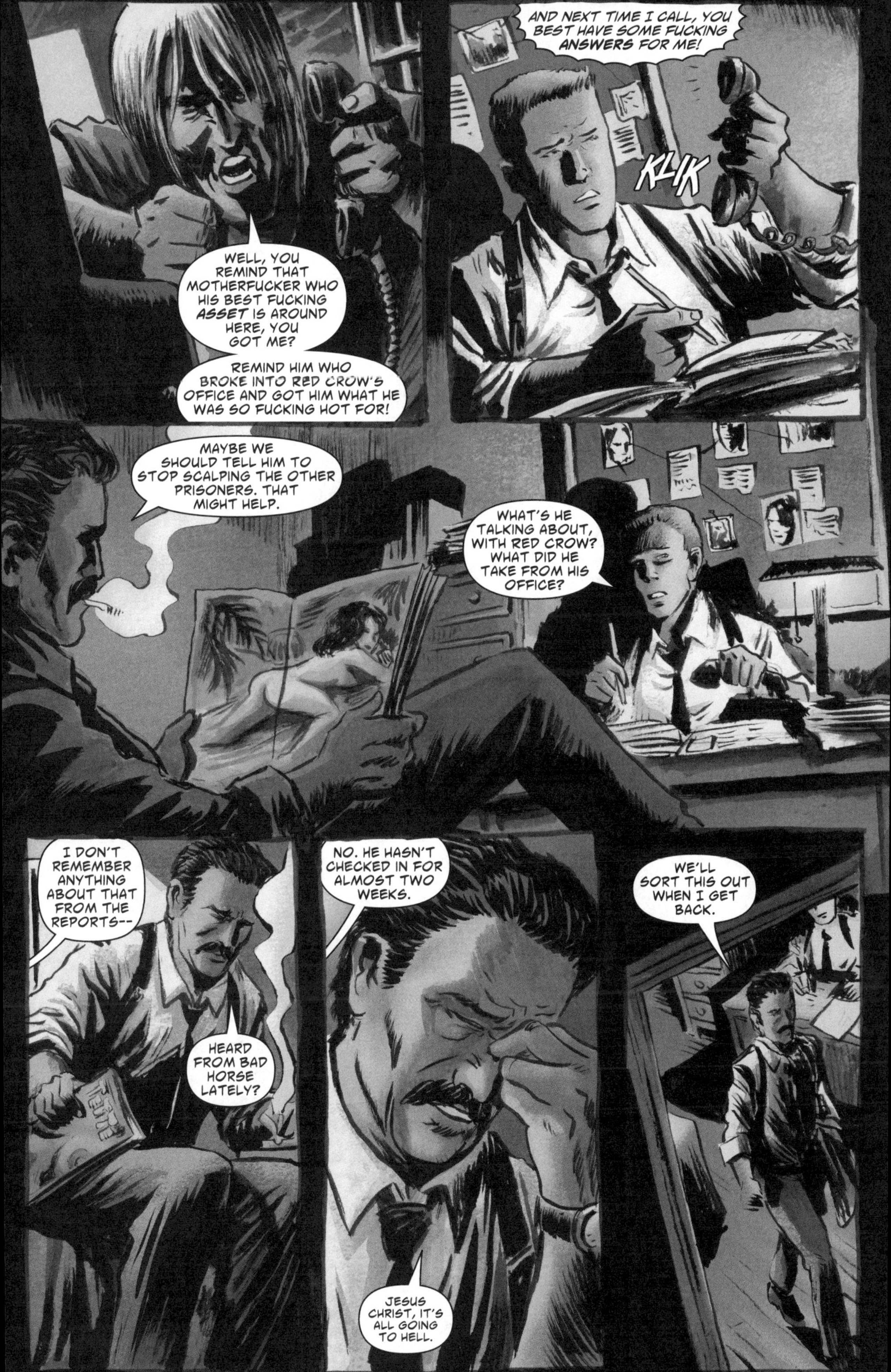
WELL, YOU REMIND THAT MOTHERFUCKER WHO HIS BEST FUCKING ASSET IS AROUND HERE, YOU GOT ME?
REMIND HIM WHO BROKE INTO RED CROW'S OFFICE AND GOT HIM WHAT HE WAS SO FUCKING HOT FOR!
AND NEXT TIME I CALL, YOU BEST HAVE SOME FUCKING ANSWERS FOR ME!
KLIK
MAYBE WE SHOULD TELL HIM TO STOP SCALPING THE OTHER PRISONERS. THAT MIGHT HELP.
WHAT'S HE TALKING ABOUT, WITH RED CROW? WHAT DID HE TAKE FROM HIS OFFICE?
I DON'T REMEMBER ANYTHING ABOUT THAT FROM THE REPORTS--
HEARD FROM BAD HORSE LATELY?
NO. HE HASN'T CHECKED IN FOR ALMOST TWO WEEKS.
JESUS CHRIST, IT'S ALL GOING TO HELL.
WE'LL SORT THIS OUT WHEN I GET BACK.

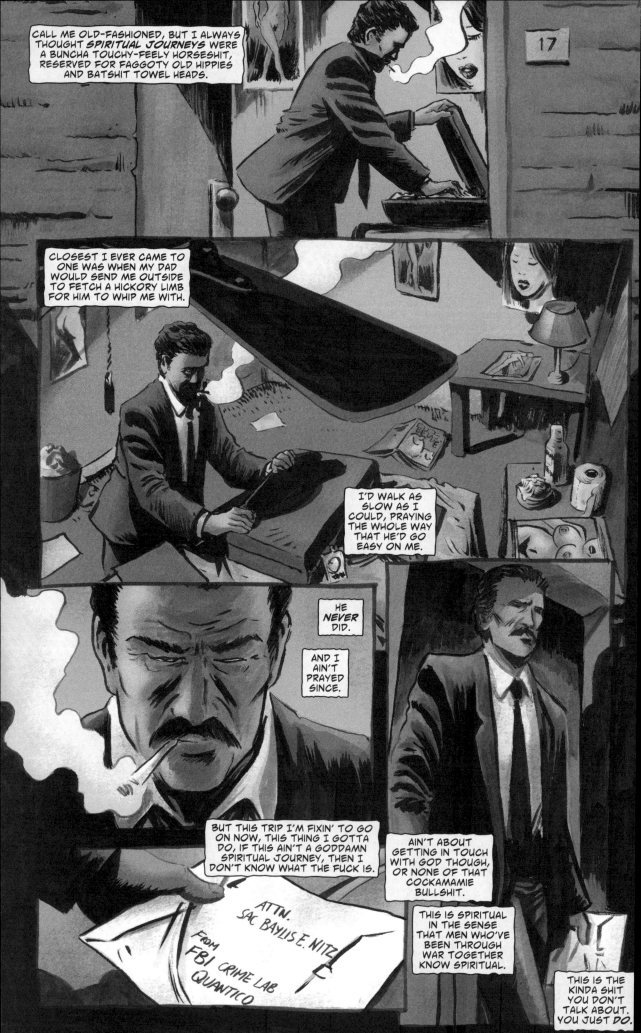

CALL ME OLD-FASHIONED, BUT I ALWAYS THOUGHT *SPIRITUAL JOURNEYS* WERE A BUNCHA TOUCHY-FEELY HORSESHIT, RESERVED FOR FAGGOTY OLD HIPPIES AND BATSHIT TOWEL HEADS.

CLOSEST I EVER CAME TO ONE WAS WHEN MY DAD WOULD SEND ME OUTSIDE TO FETCH A HICKORY LIMB FOR HIM TO WHIP ME WITH.

I'D WALK AS SLOW AS I COULD, PRAYING THE WHOLE WAY THAT HE'D GO EASY ON ME.

HE *NEVER* DID.

AND I AIN'T PRAYED SINCE.

BUT THIS TRIP I'M FIXIN' TO GO ON NOW, THIS THING I GOTTA DO, IF THIS AIN'T A GODDAMN SPIRITUAL JOURNEY, THEN I DON'T KNOW WHAT THE FUCK IS.

AIN'T ABOUT GETTING IN TOUCH WITH GOD THOUGH, OR NONE OF THAT COCKAMAMIE BULLSHIT.

THIS IS SPIRITUAL IN THE SENSE THAT MEN WHO'VE BEEN THROUGH WAR TOGETHER KNOW SPIRITUAL.

THIS IS THE KINDA SHIT YOU DON'T TALK ABOUT. YOU JUST DO.

ATTN. SAC BAYLIS E. NITZ

FROM FBI CRIME LAB QUANTICO

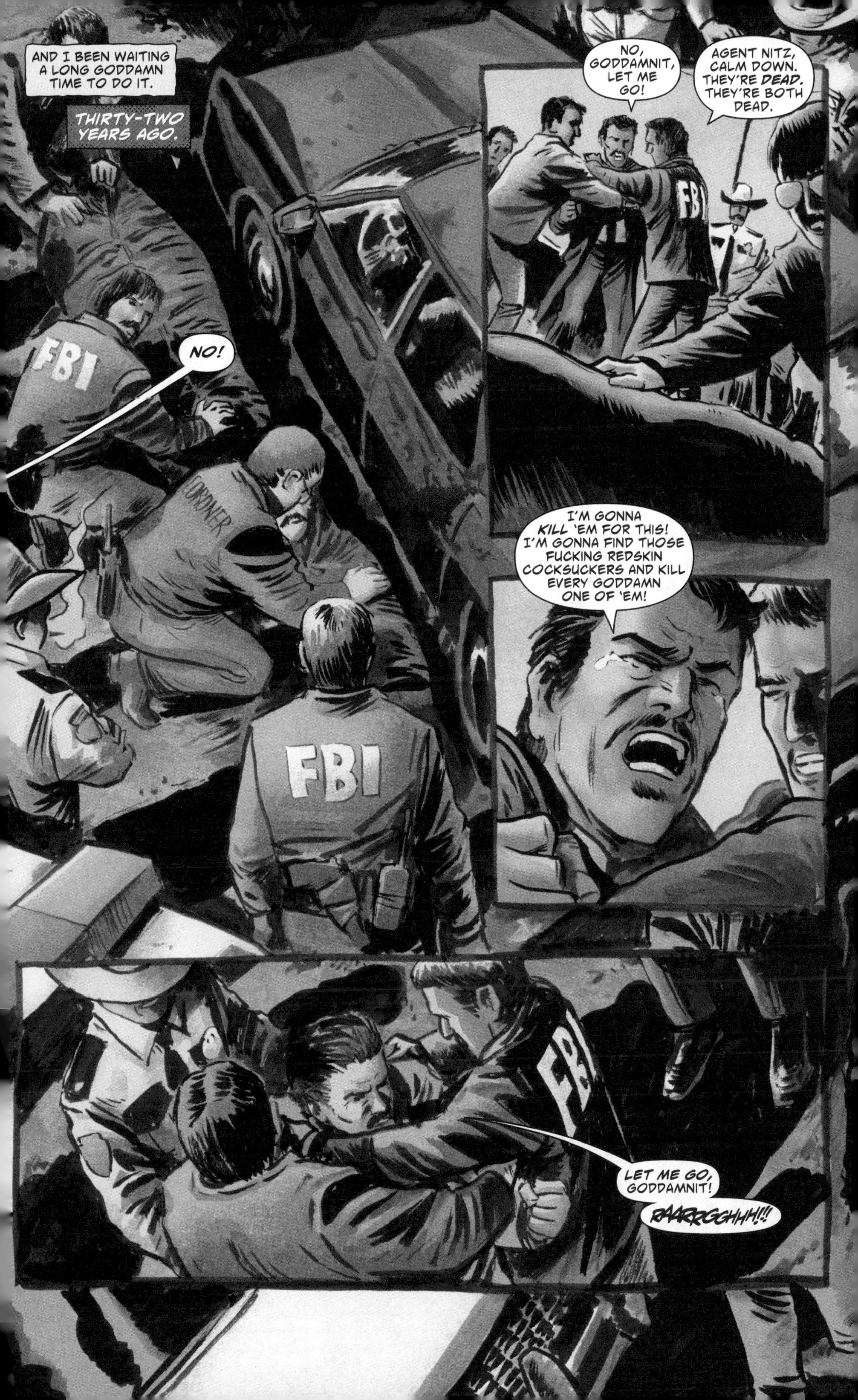
AND I BEEN WAITING A LONG GODDAMN TIME TO DO IT.
THIRTY-TWO YEARS AGO.
NO!
NO, GODDAMNIT, LET ME GO!
AGENT NITZ, CALM DOWN. THEY'RE DEAD. THEY'RE BOTH DEAD.
I'M GONNA KILL 'EM FOR THIS! I'M GONNA FIND THOSE FUCKING REDSKIN COCKSUCKERS AND KILL EVERY GODDAMN ONE OF 'EM!
LET ME GO, GODDAMNIT!
RAARRGGHHH!!!

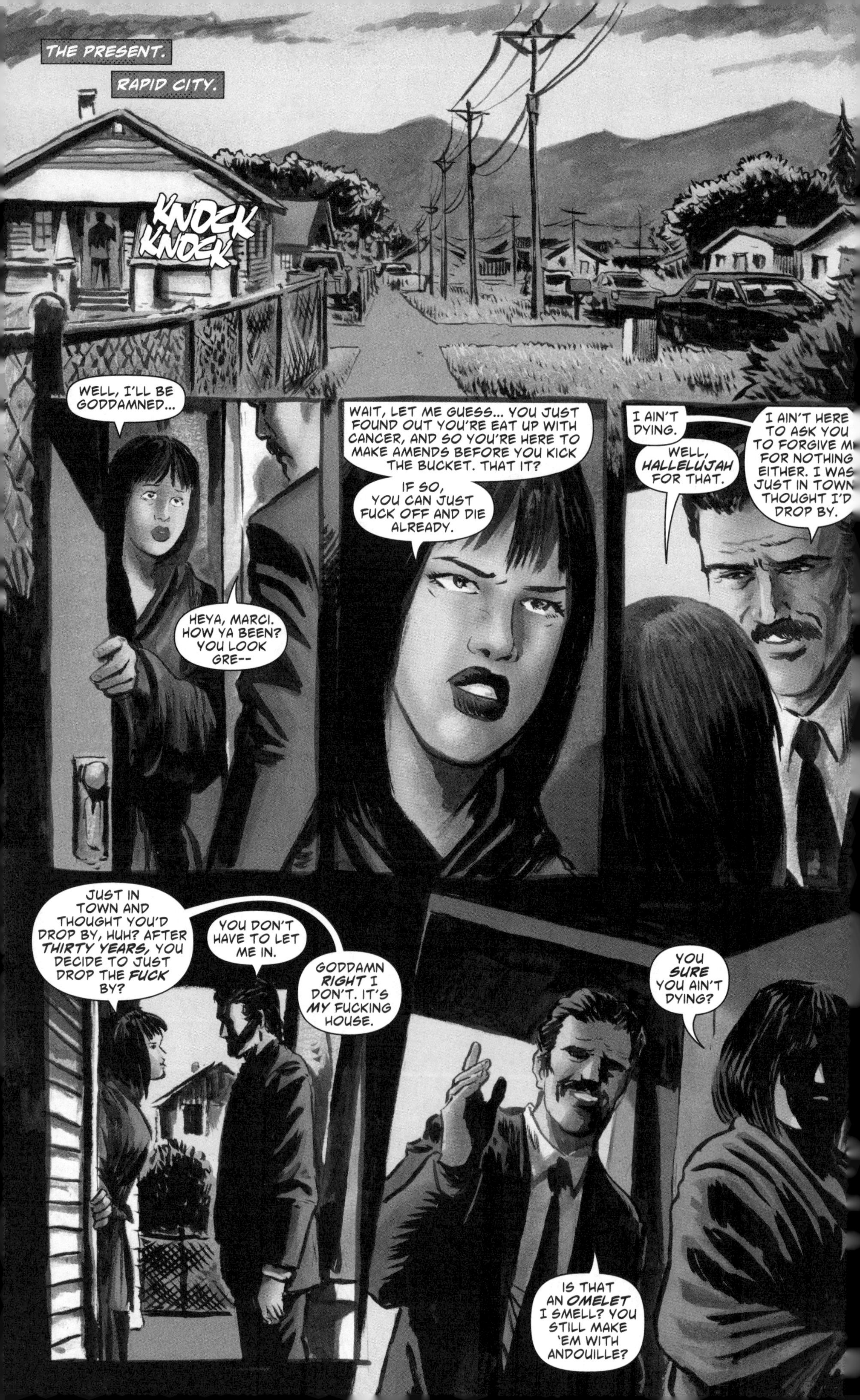
THE PRESENT.
RAPID CITY.
KNOCK KNOCK
WELL, I'LL BE GODDAMNED...
HEYA, MARCI. HOW YA BEEN? YOU LOOK GRE--
WAIT, LET ME GUESS... YOU JUST FOUND OUT YOU'RE EAT UP WITH CANCER, AND SO YOU'RE HERE TO MAKE AMENDS BEFORE YOU KICK THE BUCKET. THAT IT?
IF SO, YOU CAN JUST FUCK OFF AND DIE ALREADY.
I AIN'T DYING.
WELL, HALLELUJAH FOR THAT.
I AIN'T HERE TO ASK YOU TO FORGIVE M FOR NOTHING EITHER. I WAS JUST IN TOWN THOUGHT I'D DROP BY.
JUST IN TOWN AND THOUGHT YOU'D DROP BY, HUH? AFTER THIRTY YEARS, YOU DECIDE TO JUST DROP THE FUCK BY?
YOU DON'T HAVE TO LET ME IN.
GODDAMN RIGHT I DON'T. IT'S MY FUCKING HOUSE.
YOU SURE YOU AIN'T DYING?
IS THAT AN OMELET I SMELL? YOU STILL MAKE 'EM WITH ANDOUILLE?

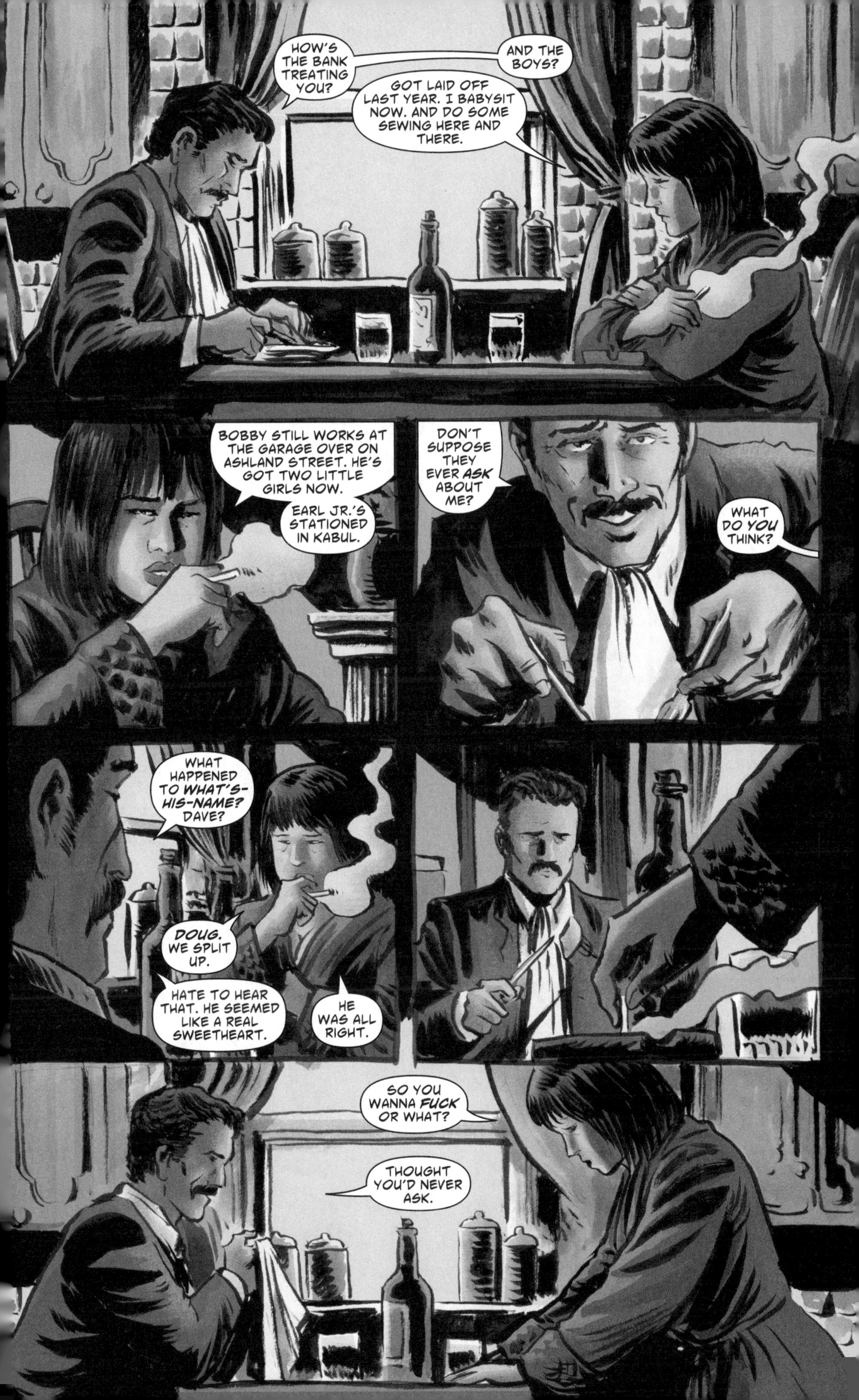

HOW'S THE BANK TREATING YOU?
AND THE BOYS?
GOT LAID OFF LAST YEAR. I BABYSIT NOW. AND DO SOME SEWING HERE AND THERE.
BOBBY STILL WORKS AT THE GARAGE OVER ON ASHLAND STREET. HE'S GOT TWO LITTLE GIRLS NOW.
EARL JR.'S STATIONED IN KABUL.
DON'T SUPPOSE THEY EVER ASK ABOUT ME?
WHAT DO YOU THINK?
WHAT HAPPENED TO WHAT'S-HIS-NAME? DAVE?
DOUG. WE SPLIT UP.
HATE TO HEAR THAT. HE SEEMED LIKE A REAL SWEETHEART.
HE WAS ALL RIGHT.
SO YOU WANNA FUCK OR WHAT?
THOUGHT YOU'D NEVER ASK.

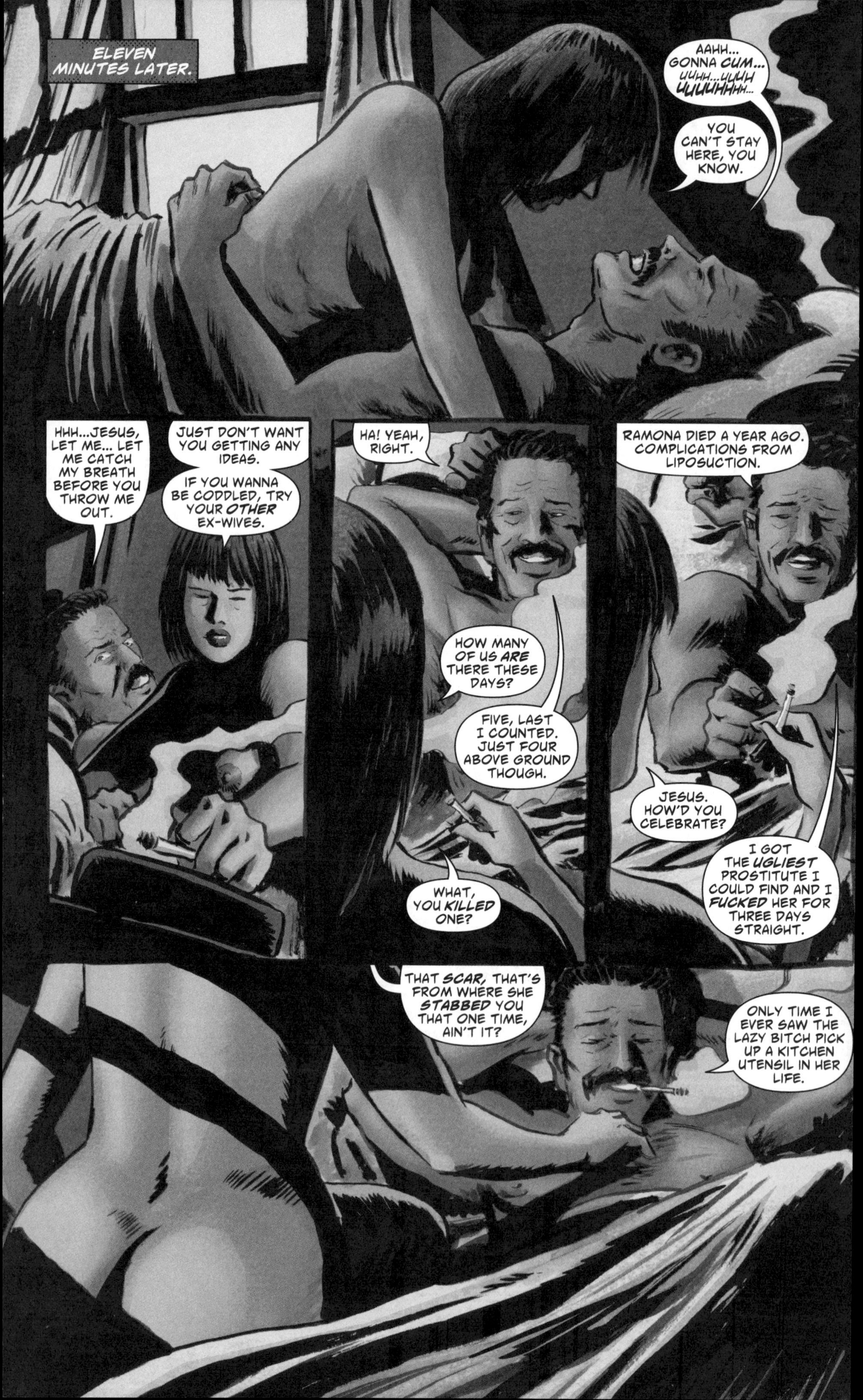
ELEVEN MINUTES LATER.
AAHH... GONNA CUM... UUHH...UUHH UUUUHHHH...
YOU CAN'T STAY HERE, YOU KNOW.
HHH...JESUS, LET ME... LET ME CATCH MY BREATH BEFORE YOU THROW ME OUT.
JUST DON'T WANT YOU GETTING ANY IDEAS.
IF YOU WANNA BE CODDLED, TRY YOUR OTHER EX-WIVES.
HA! YEAH, RIGHT.
HOW MANY OF US ARE THERE THESE DAYS?
FIVE, LAST I COUNTED. JUST FOUR ABOVE GROUND THOUGH.
WHAT, YOU KILLED ONE?
RAMONA DIED A YEAR AGO. COMPLICATIONS FROM LIPOSUCTION.
JESUS. HOW'D YOU CELEBRATE?
I GOT THE UGLIEST PROSTITUTE I COULD FIND AND I FUCKED HER FOR THREE DAYS STRAIGHT.
THAT SCAR, THAT'S FROM WHERE SHE STABBED YOU THAT ONE TIME, AIN'T IT?
ONLY TIME I EVER SAW THE LAZY BITCH PICK UP A KITCHEN UTENSIL IN HER LIFE.

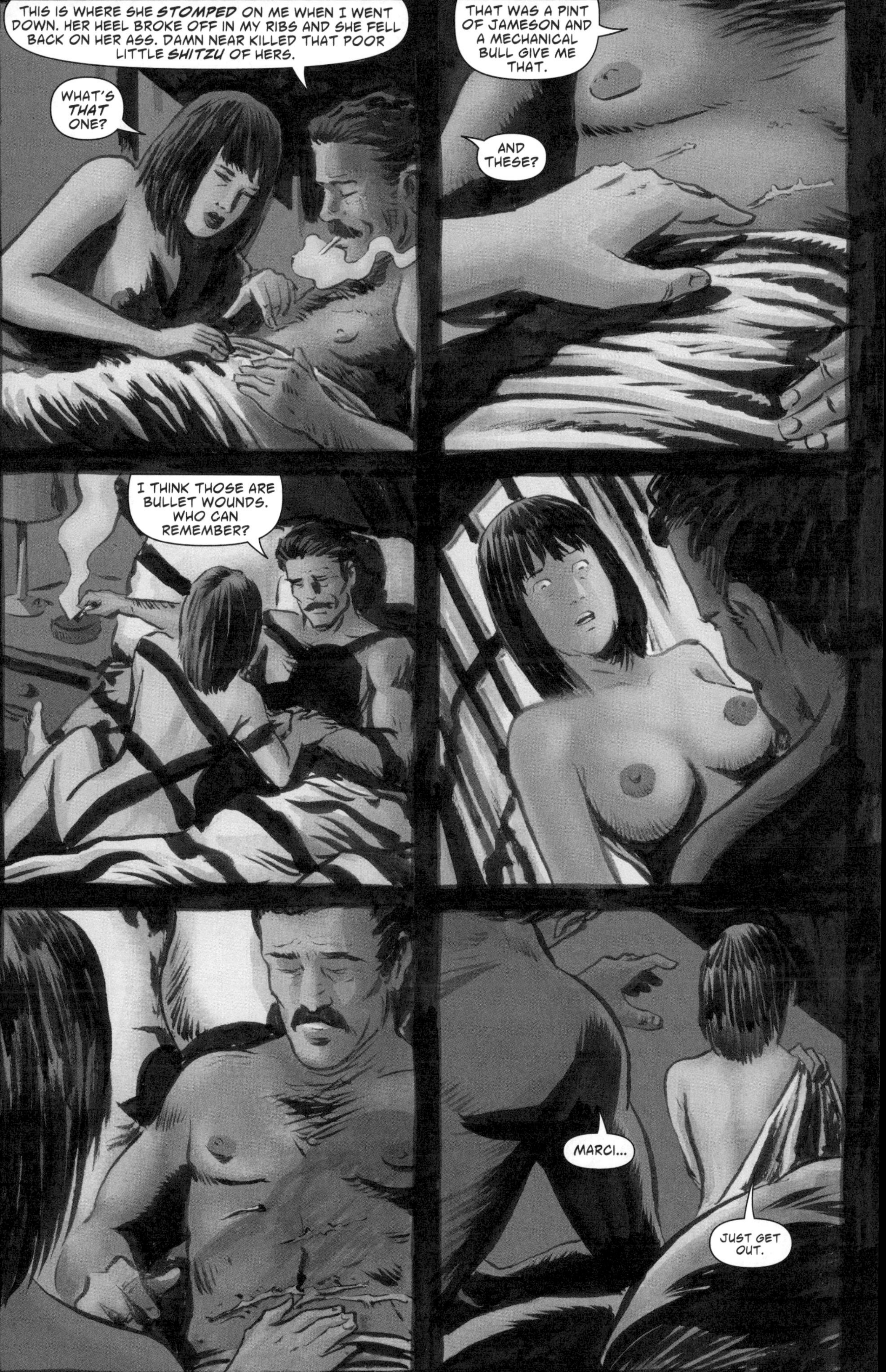
THIS IS WHERE SHE STOMPED ON ME WHEN I WENT DOWN. HER HEEL BROKE OFF IN MY RIBS AND SHE FELL BACK ON HER ASS. DAMN NEAR KILLED THAT POOR LITTLE SHITZU OF HERS.
WHAT'S THAT ONE?
THAT WAS A PINT OF JAMESON AND A MECHANICAL BULL GIVE ME THAT.
AND THESE?
I THINK THOSE ARE BULLET WOUNDS. WHO CAN REMEMBER?
MARCI...
JUST GET OUT.

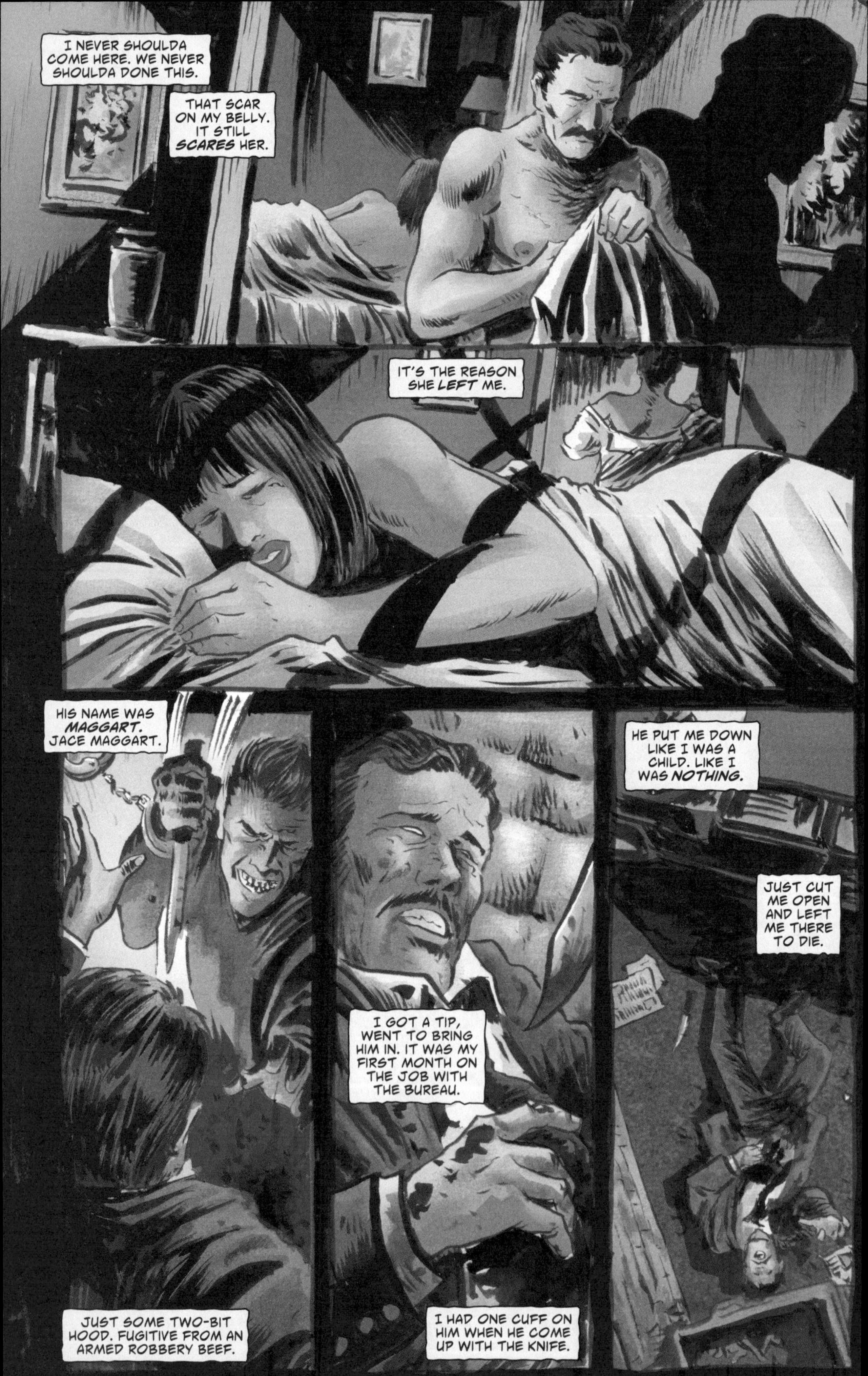

I NEVER SHOULDA COME HERE. WE NEVER SHOULDA DONE THIS.
THAT SCAR ON MY BELLY. IT STILL *SCARES* HER.
IT'S THE REASON SHE *LEFT* ME.
HIS NAME WAS *MAGGART*. JACE MAGGART.
JUST SOME TWO-BIT HOOD. FUGITIVE FROM AN ARMED ROBBERY BEEF.
I GOT A TIP, WENT TO BRING HIM IN. IT WAS MY FIRST MONTH ON THE JOB WITH THE BUREAU.
I HAD ONE CUFF ON HIM WHEN HE COME UP WITH THE KNIFE.
HE PUT ME DOWN LIKE I WAS A CHILD. LIKE I WAS *NOTHING*.
JUST CUT ME OPEN AND LEFT ME THERE TO DIE.

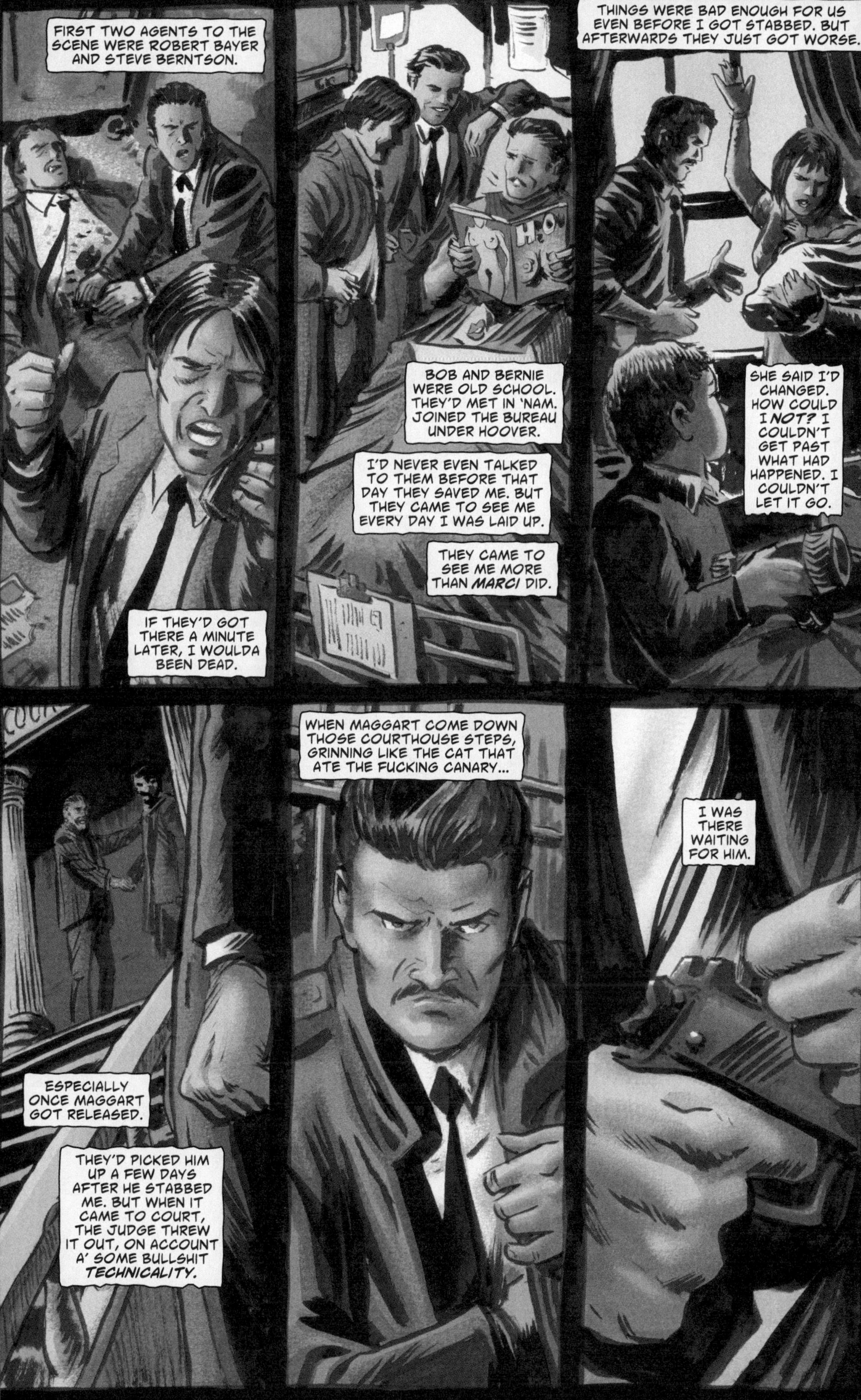
FIRST TWO AGENTS TO THE SCENE WERE ROBERT BAYER AND STEVE BERNTSON.
IF THEY'D GOT THERE A MINUTE LATER, I WOULDA BEEN DEAD.
BOB AND BERNIE WERE OLD SCHOOL. THEY'D MET IN 'NAM. JOINED THE BUREAU UNDER HOOVER.
I'D NEVER EVEN TALKED TO THEM BEFORE THAT DAY THEY SAVED ME. BUT THEY CAME TO SEE ME EVERY DAY I WAS LAID UP.
THEY CAME TO SEE ME MORE THAN *MARCI* DID.
THINGS WERE BAD ENOUGH FOR US EVEN BEFORE I GOT STABBED. BUT AFTERWARDS THEY JUST GOT WORSE.
SHE SAID I'D CHANGED. HOW COULD I *NOT?* I COULDN'T GET PAST WHAT HAD HAPPENED. I COULDN'T LET IT GO.
ESPECIALLY ONCE MAGGART GOT RELEASED.
THEY'D PICKED HIM UP A FEW DAYS AFTER HE STABBED ME. BUT WHEN IT CAME TO COURT, THE JUDGE THREW IT OUT, ON ACCOUNT A' SOME BULLSHIT *TECHNICALITY.*
WHEN MAGGART COME DOWN THOSE COURTHOUSE STEPS, GRINNING LIKE THE CAT THAT ATE THE FUCKING CANARY...
I WAS THERE WAITING FOR HIM.

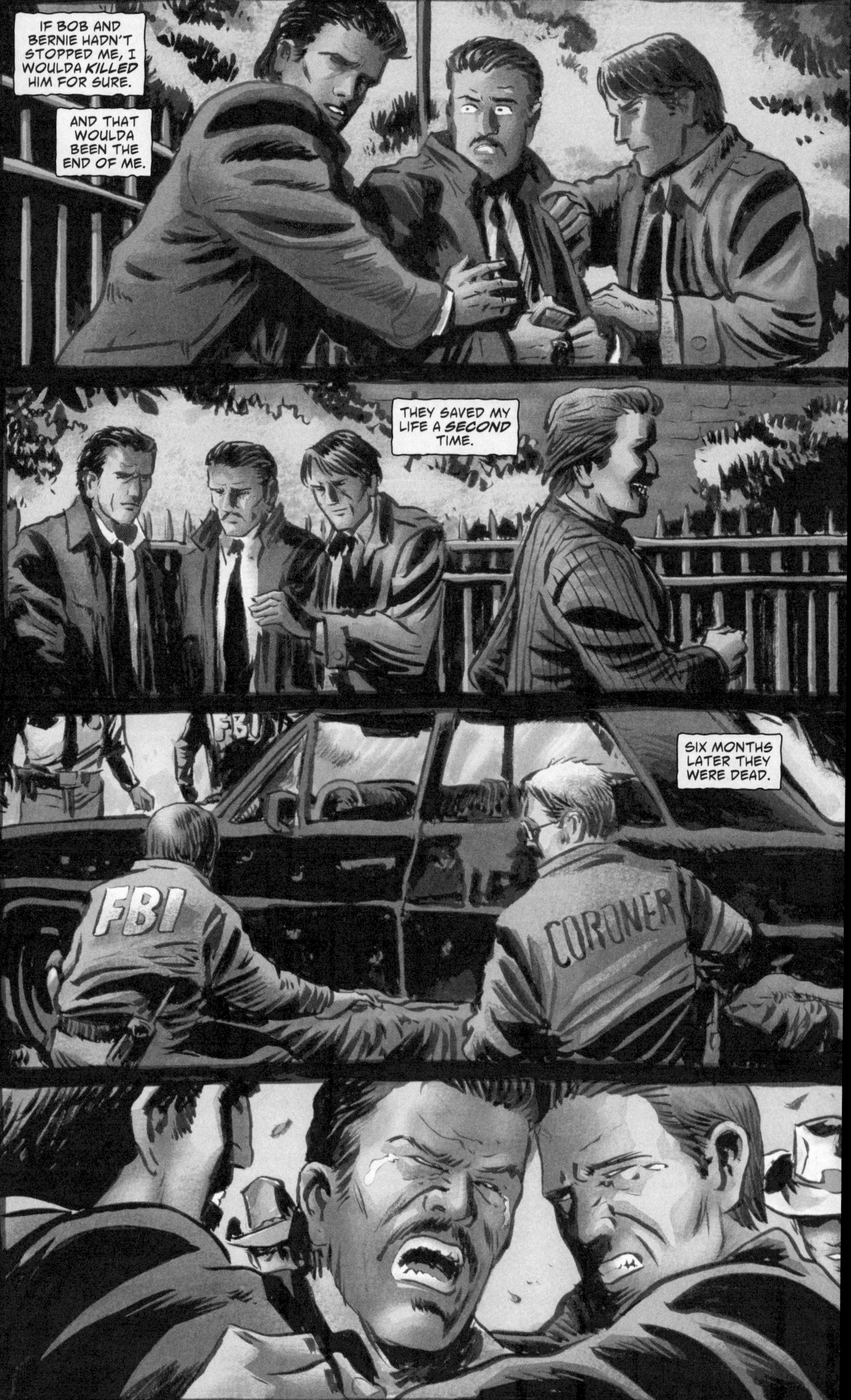
IF BOB AND BERNIE HADN'T STOPPED ME, I WOULDA KILLED HIM FOR SURE.
AND THAT WOULDA BEEN THE END OF ME.
THEY SAVED MY LIFE A SECOND TIME.
SIX MONTHS LATER THEY WERE DEAD.
FBI
FBI
CORONER

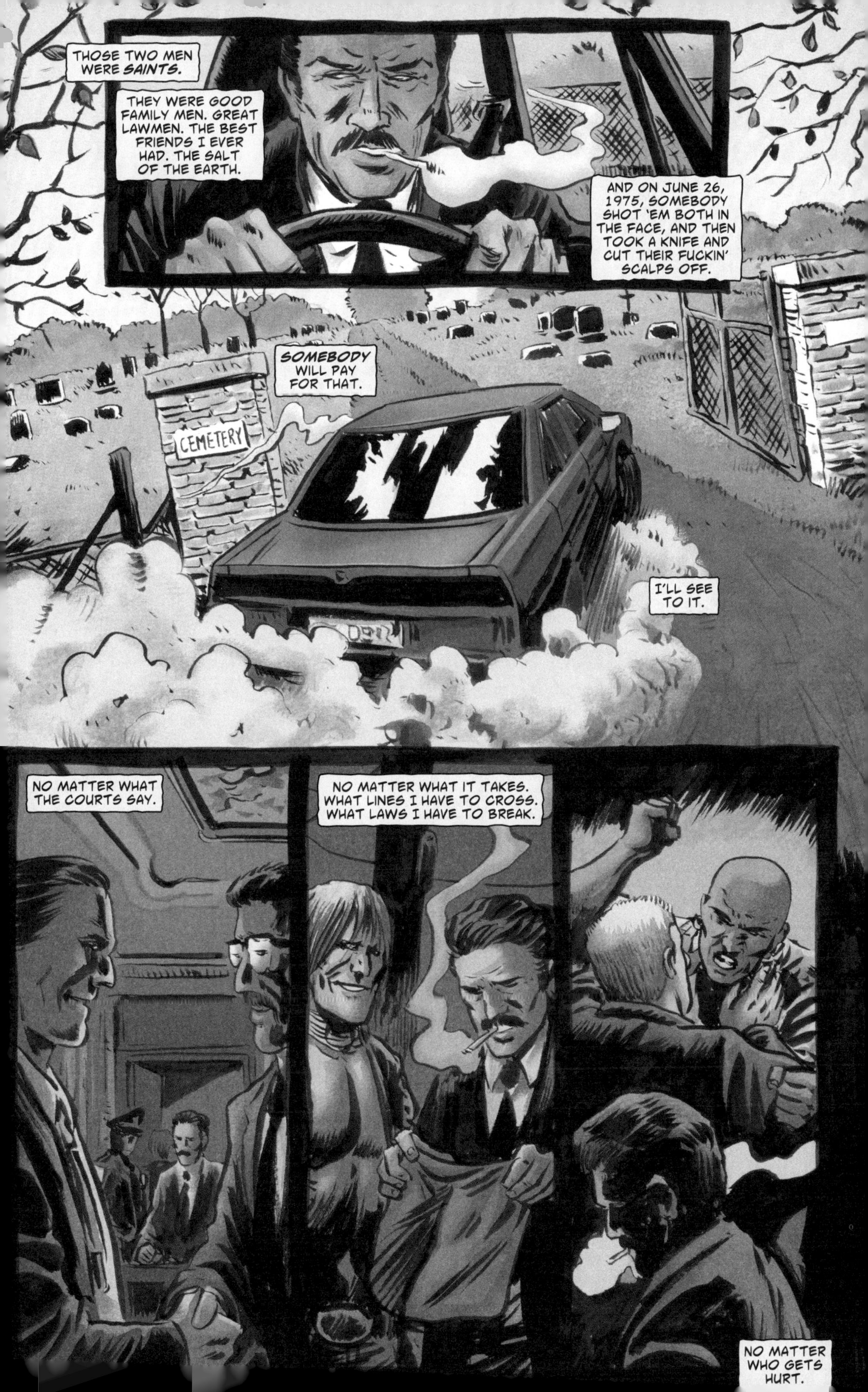
THOSE TWO MEN WERE SAINTS.
THEY WERE GOOD FAMILY MEN. GREAT LAWMEN. THE BEST FRIENDS I EVER HAD. THE SALT OF THE EARTH.
AND ON JUNE 26, 1975, SOMEBODY SHOT 'EM BOTH IN THE FACE, AND THEN TOOK A KNIFE AND CUT THEIR FUCKIN' SCALPS OFF.
SOMEBODY WILL PAY FOR THAT.
CEMETERY
I'LL SEE TO IT.
NO MATTER WHAT THE COURTS SAY.
NO MATTER WHAT IT TAKES. WHAT LINES I HAVE TO CROSS. WHAT LAWS I HAVE TO BREAK.
NO MATTER WHO GETS HURT.

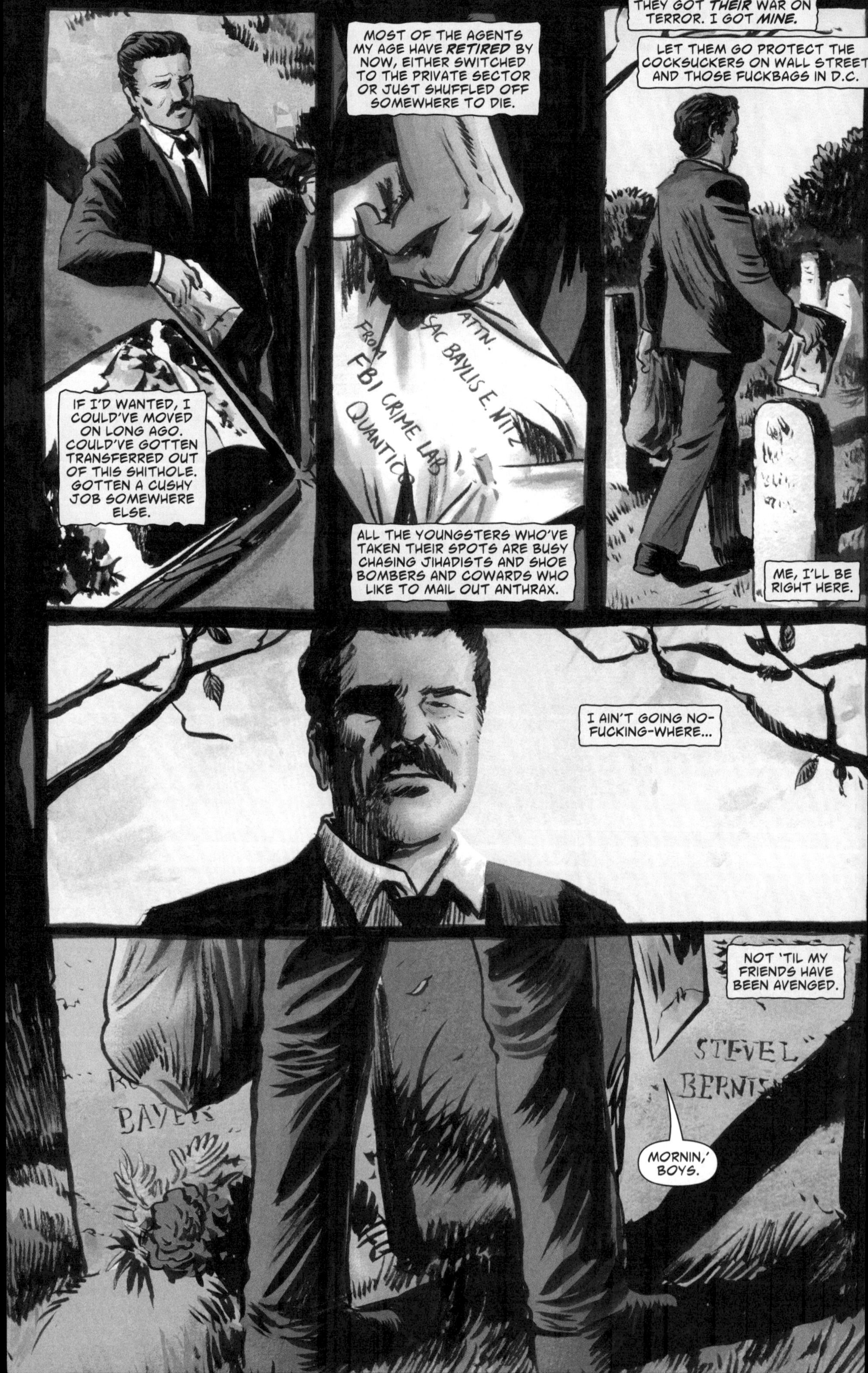
IF I'D WANTED, I COULD'VE MOVED ON LONG AGO. COULD'VE GOTTEN TRANSFERRED OUT OF THIS SHITHOLE. GOTTEN A CUSHY JOB SOMEWHERE ELSE.
MOST OF THE AGENTS MY AGE HAVE RETIRED BY NOW, EITHER SWITCHED TO THE PRIVATE SECTOR OR JUST SHUFFLED OFF SOMEWHERE TO DIE.
ATTN. SAC BAYLIS E. KITZ
FROM FBI CRIME LAB QUANTICO
ALL THE YOUNGSTERS WHO'VE TAKEN THEIR SPOTS ARE BUSY CHASING JIHADISTS AND SHOE BOMBERS AND COWARDS WHO LIKE TO MAIL OUT ANTHRAX.
THEY GOT THEIR WAR ON TERROR. I GOT MINE.
LET THEM GO PROTECT THE COCKSUCKERS ON WALL STREET AND THOSE FUCKBAGS IN D.C.
ME, I'LL BE RIGHT HERE.
I AIN'T GOING NO-FUCKING-WHERE...
NOT 'TIL MY FRIENDS HAVE BEEN AVENGED.
STEVE L. BERNIS
BAYERS
MORNIN,' BOYS.

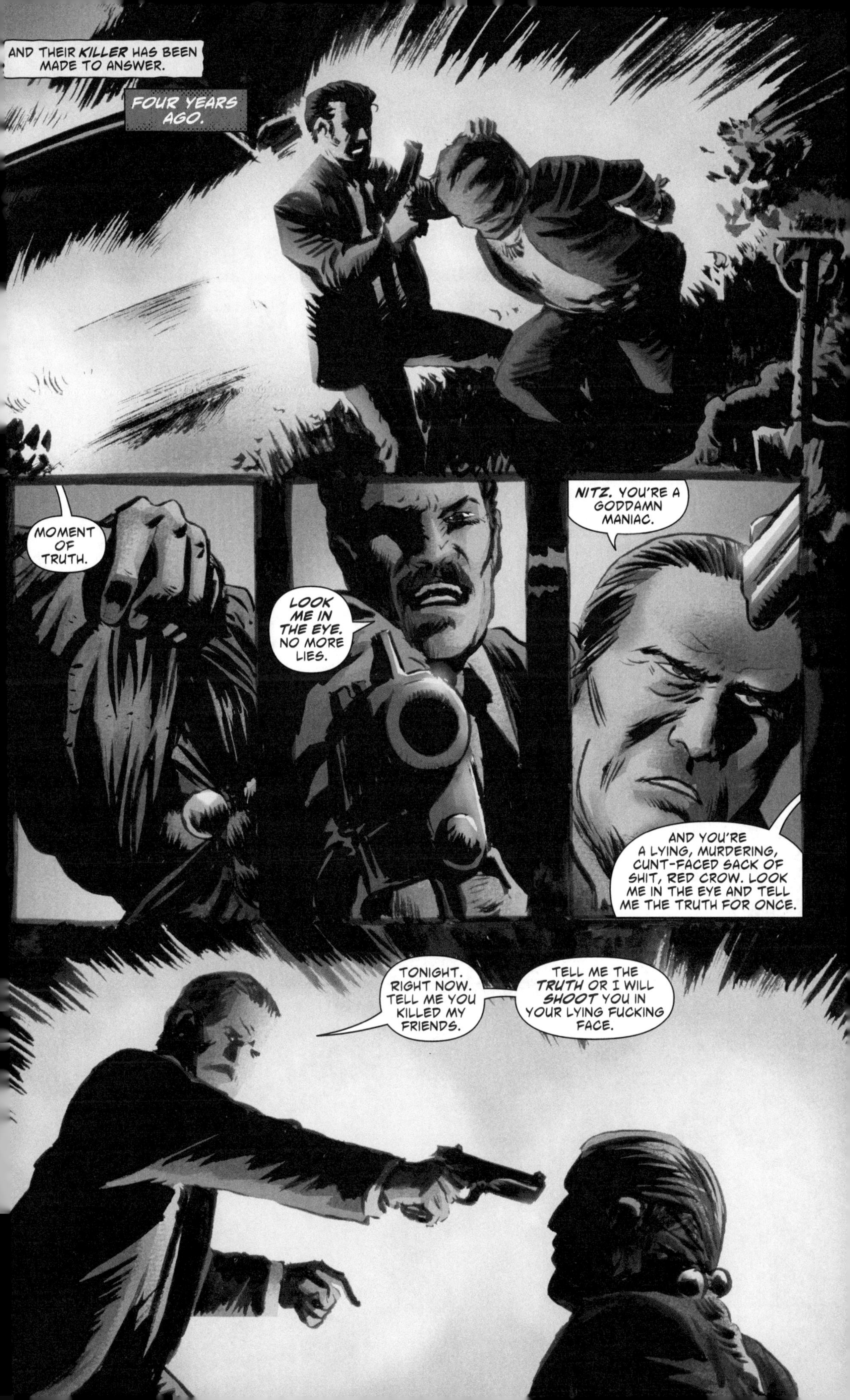
AND THEIR KILLER HAS BEEN MADE TO ANSWER.
FOUR YEARS AGO.
MOMENT OF TRUTH.
LOOK ME IN THE EYE. NO MORE LIES.
NITZ. YOU'RE A GODDAMN MANIAC.
AND YOU'RE A LYING, MURDERING, CUNT-FACED SACK OF SHIT, RED CROW. LOOK ME IN THE EYE AND TELL ME THE TRUTH FOR ONCE.
TONIGHT. RIGHT NOW. TELL ME YOU KILLED MY FRIENDS.
TELL ME THE TRUTH OR I WILL SHOOT YOU IN YOUR LYING FUCKING FACE.

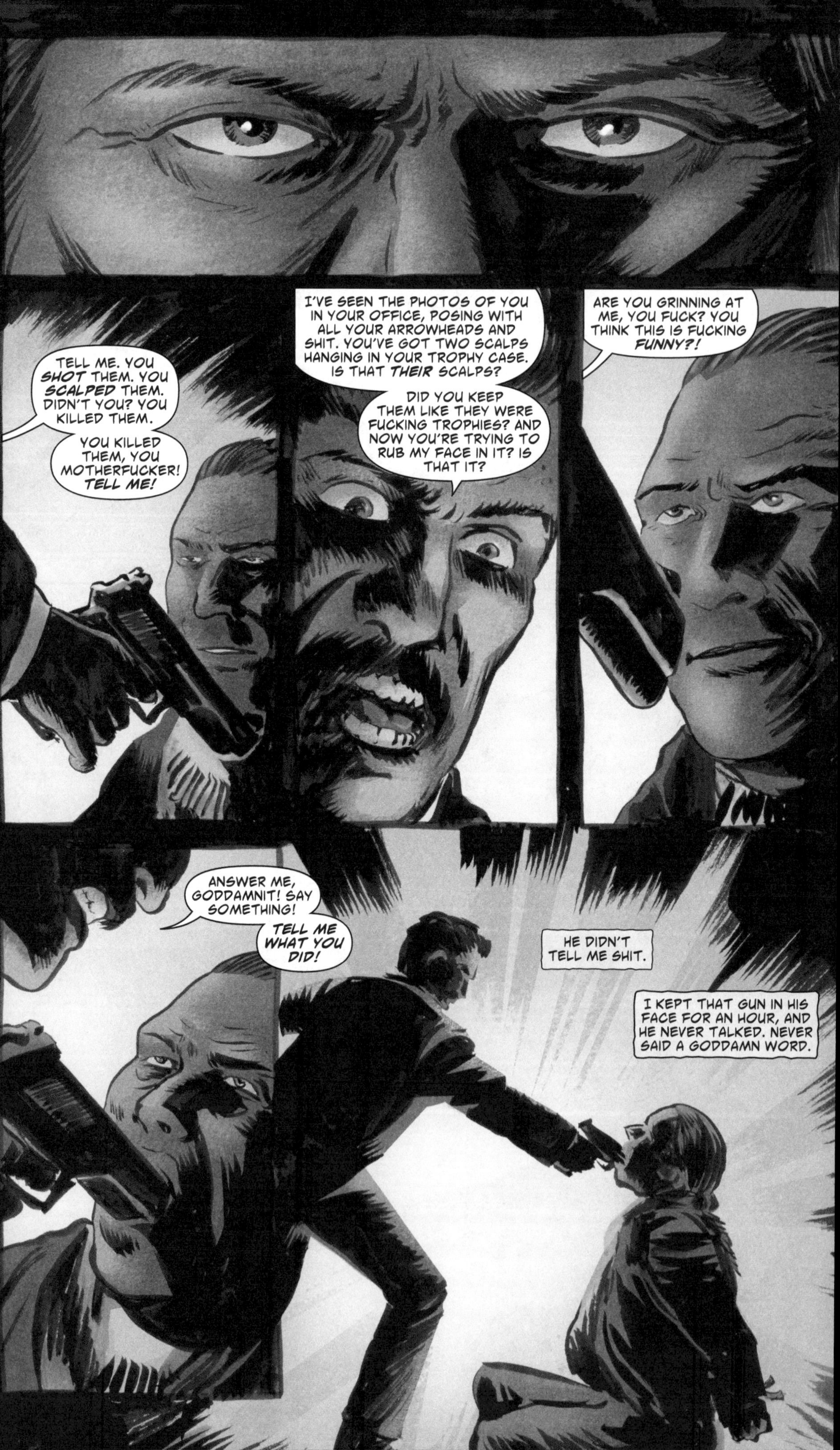
TELL ME. YOU SHOT THEM. YOU SCALPED THEM. DIDN'T YOU? YOU KILLED THEM.
YOU KILLED THEM, YOU MOTHERFUCKER! TELL ME!
I'VE SEEN THE PHOTOS OF YOU IN YOUR OFFICE, POSING WITH ALL YOUR ARROWHEADS AND SHIT. YOU'VE GOT TWO SCALPS HANGING IN YOUR TROPHY CASE. IS THAT THEIR SCALPS?
DID YOU KEEP THEM LIKE THEY WERE FUCKING TROPHIES? AND NOW YOU'RE TRYING TO RUB MY FACE IN IT? IS THAT IT?
ARE YOU GRINNING AT ME, YOU FUCK? YOU THINK THIS IS FUCKING FUNNY?!
ANSWER ME, GODDAMNIT! SAY SOMETHING!
TELL ME WHAT YOU DID!
HE DIDN'T TELL ME SHIT.
I KEPT THAT GUN IN HIS FACE FOR AN HOUR, AND HE NEVER TALKED. NEVER SAID A GODDAMN WORD.

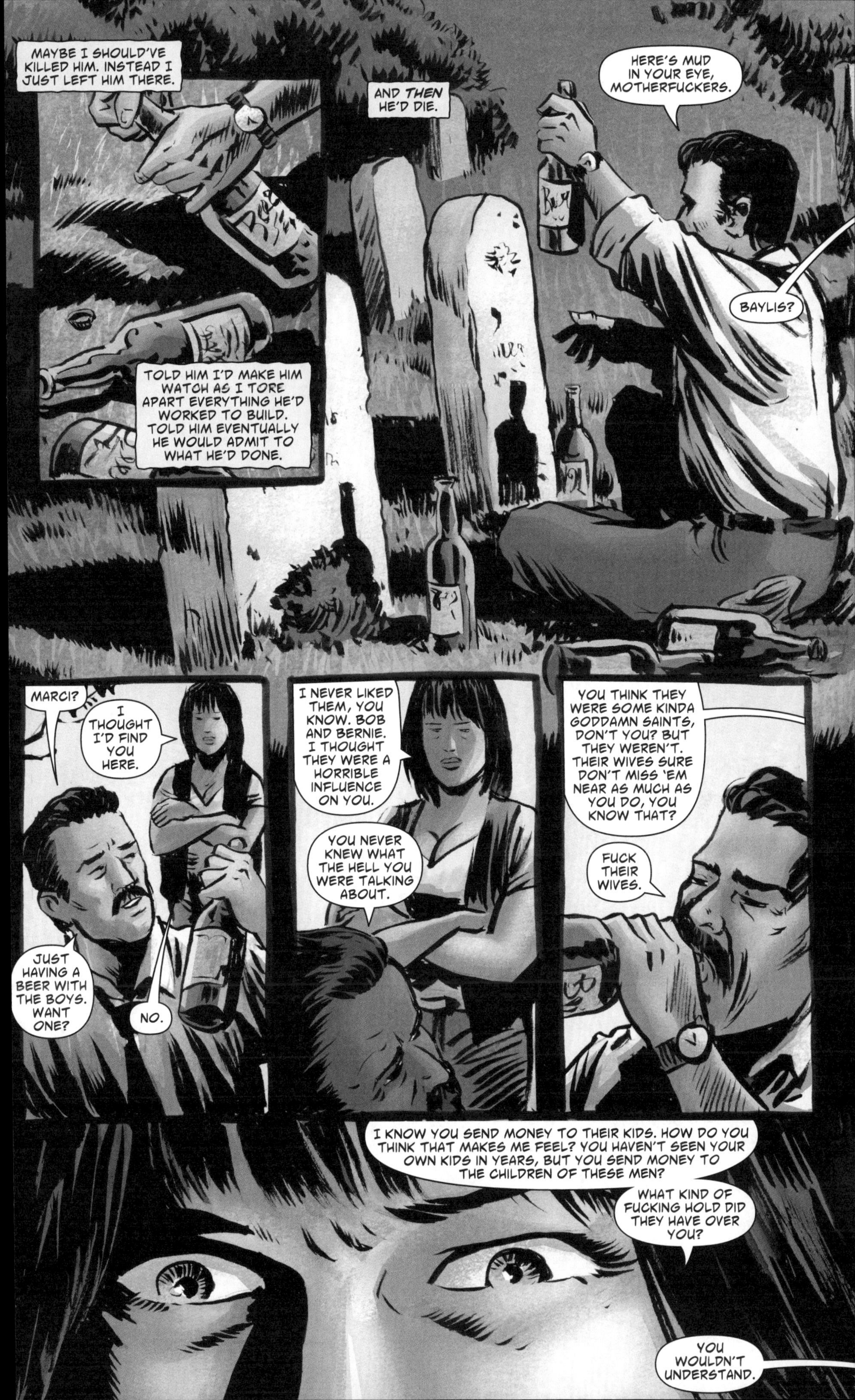
MAYBE I SHOULD'VE KILLED HIM. INSTEAD I JUST LEFT HIM THERE.
TOLD HIM I'D MAKE HIM WATCH AS I TORE APART EVERYTHING HE'D WORKED TO BUILD. TOLD HIM EVENTUALLY HE WOULD ADMIT TO WHAT HE'D DONE.
AND *THEN* HE'D DIE.
HERE'S MUD IN YOUR EYE, MOTHERFUCKERS.
BAYLIS?
MARCI?
I THOUGHT I'D FIND YOU HERE.
JUST HAVING A BEER WITH THE BOYS. WANT ONE?
NO.
I NEVER LIKED THEM, YOU KNOW. BOB AND BERNIE. I THOUGHT THEY WERE A HORRIBLE INFLUENCE ON YOU.
YOU NEVER KNEW WHAT THE HELL YOU WERE TALKING ABOUT.
YOU THINK THEY WERE SOME KINDA GODDAMN SAINTS, DON'T YOU? BUT THEY WEREN'T. THEIR WIVES SURE DON'T MISS 'EM NEAR AS MUCH AS YOU DO, YOU KNOW THAT?
FUCK THEIR WIVES.
I KNOW YOU SEND MONEY TO THEIR KIDS. HOW DO YOU THINK THAT MAKES ME FEEL? YOU HAVEN'T SEEN YOUR OWN KIDS IN YEARS, BUT YOU SEND MONEY TO THE CHILDREN OF THESE MEN?
WHAT KIND OF FUCKING HOLD DID THEY HAVE OVER YOU?
YOU WOULDN'T UNDERSTAND.

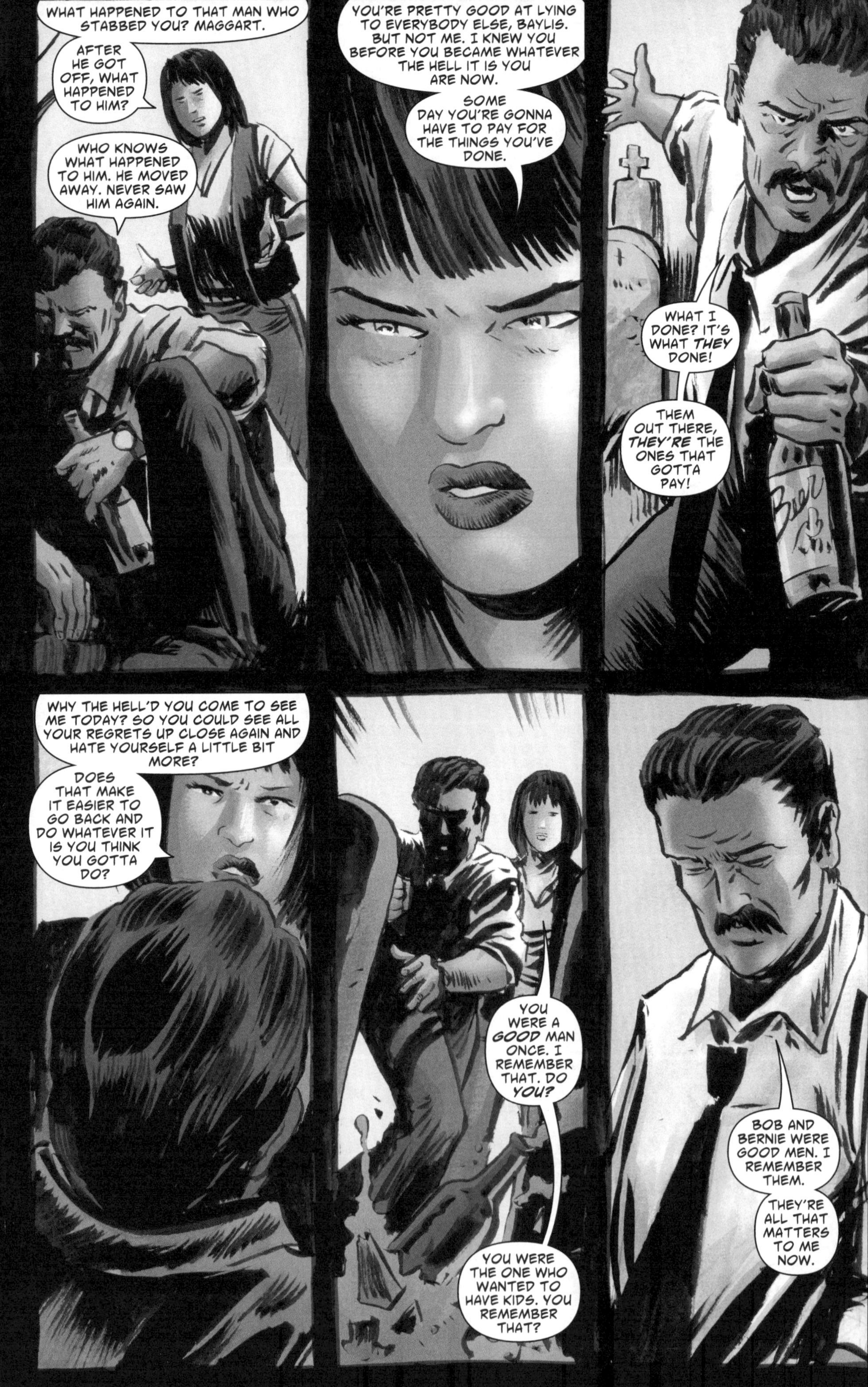
WHAT HAPPENED TO THAT MAN WHO STABBED YOU? MAGGART.
AFTER HE GOT OFF, WHAT HAPPENED TO HIM?
WHO KNOWS WHAT HAPPENED TO HIM. HE MOVED AWAY. NEVER SAW HIM AGAIN.
YOU'RE PRETTY GOOD AT LYING TO EVERYBODY ELSE, BAYLIS. BUT NOT ME. I KNEW YOU BEFORE YOU BECAME WHATEVER THE HELL IT IS YOU ARE NOW.
SOME DAY YOU'RE GONNA HAVE TO PAY FOR THE THINGS YOU'VE DONE.
WHAT I DONE? IT'S WHAT *THEY* DONE!
THEM OUT THERE, *THEY'RE* THE ONES THAT GOTTA PAY!
Beer
WHY THE HELL'D YOU COME TO SEE ME TODAY? SO YOU COULD SEE ALL YOUR REGRETS UP CLOSE AGAIN AND HATE YOURSELF A LITTLE BIT MORE?
DOES THAT MAKE IT EASIER TO GO BACK AND DO WHATEVER IT IS YOU THINK YOU GOTTA DO?
YOU WERE A *GOOD* MAN ONCE. I REMEMBER THAT. DO *YOU?*
YOU WERE THE ONE WHO WANTED TO HAVE KIDS. YOU REMEMBER THAT?
BOB AND BERNIE WERE GOOD MEN. I REMEMBER THEM.
THEY'RE ALL THAT MATTERS TO ME NOW.

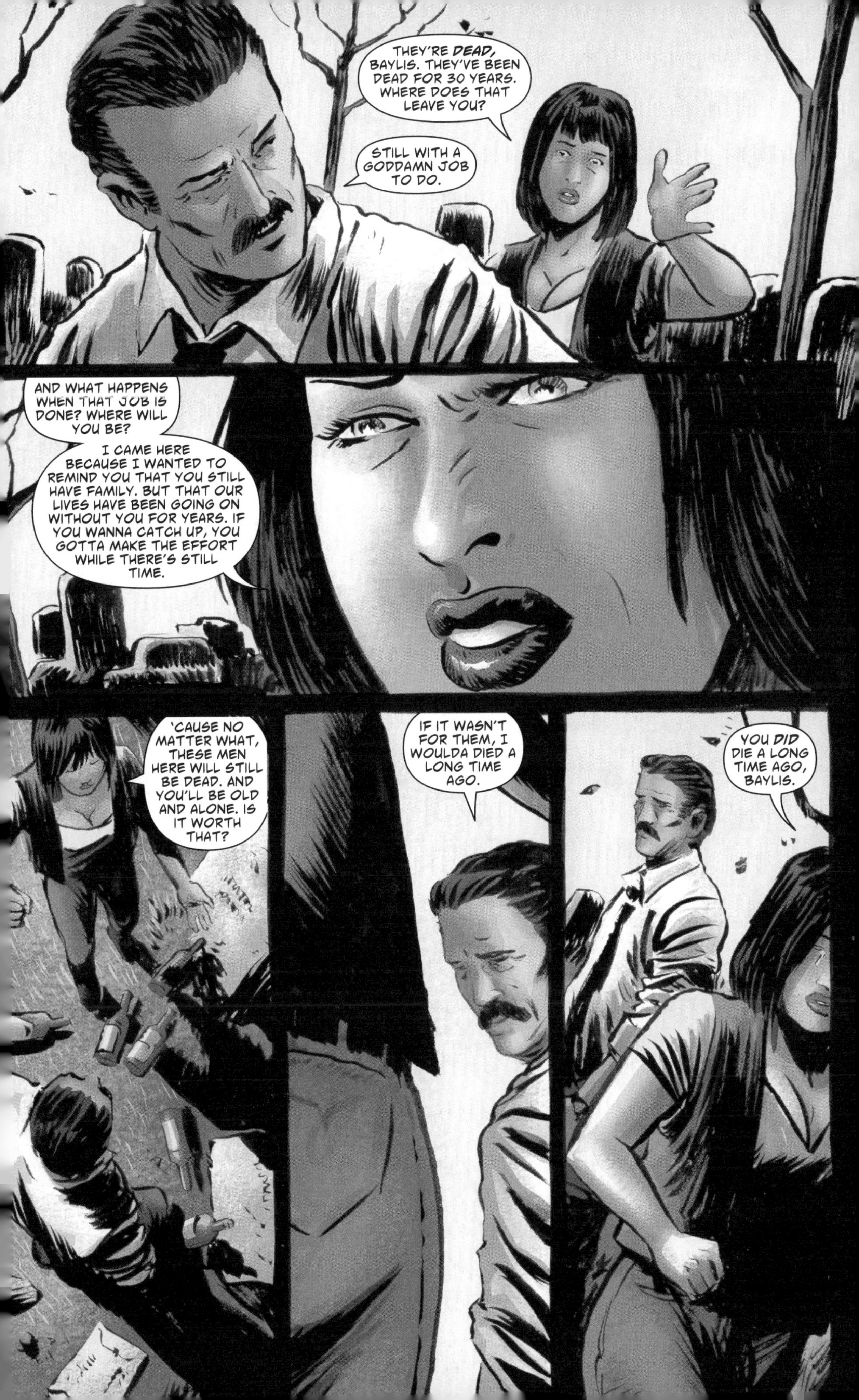
THEY'RE *DEAD*, BAYLIS. THEY'VE BEEN DEAD FOR 30 YEARS. WHERE DOES THAT LEAVE YOU?
STILL WITH A GODDAMN JOB TO DO.
AND WHAT HAPPENS WHEN THAT JOB IS DONE? WHERE WILL YOU BE?
I CAME HERE BECAUSE I WANTED TO REMIND YOU THAT YOU STILL HAVE FAMILY. BUT THAT OUR LIVES HAVE BEEN GOING ON WITHOUT YOU FOR YEARS. IF YOU WANNA CATCH UP, YOU GOTTA MAKE THE EFFORT WHILE THERE'S STILL TIME.
'CAUSE NO MATTER WHAT, THESE MEN HERE WILL STILL BE DEAD. AND YOU'LL BE OLD AND ALONE. IS IT WORTH THAT?
IF IT WASN'T FOR THEM, I WOULDA DIED A LONG TIME AGO.
YOU *DID* DIE A LONG TIME AGO, BAYLIS.

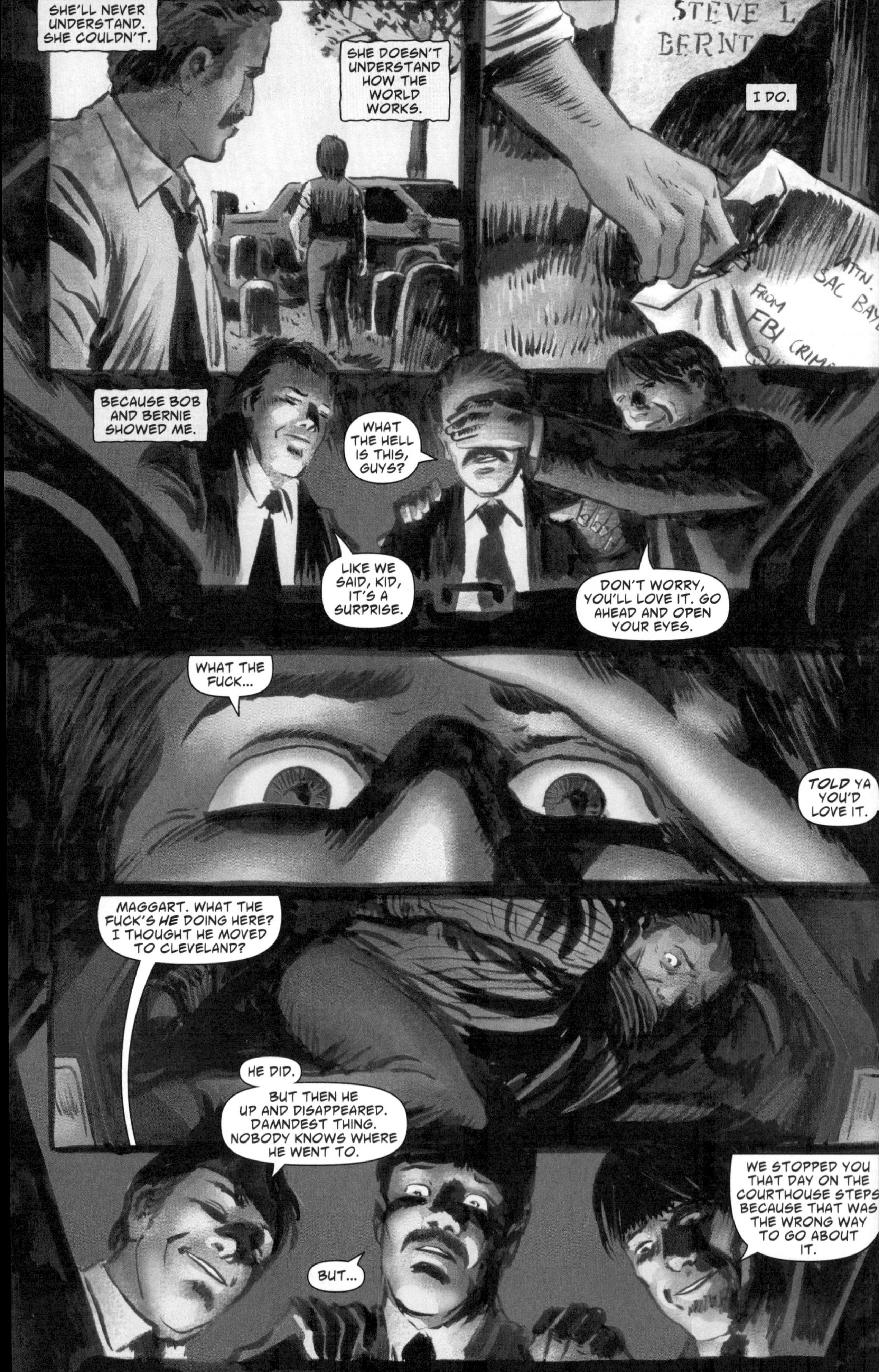
SHE'LL NEVER UNDERSTAND. SHE COULDN'T.
SHE DOESN'T UNDERSTAND HOW THE WORLD WORKS.
STEVE L
BERNT
I DO.
ATTN. SAC BAY
FROM FBI CRIM
BECAUSE BOB AND BERNIE SHOWED ME.
WHAT THE HELL IS THIS, GUYS?
LIKE WE SAID, KID, IT'S A SURPRISE.
DON'T WORRY, YOU'LL LOVE IT. GO AHEAD AND OPEN YOUR EYES.
WHAT THE FUCK...
*TOLD* YA YOU'D LOVE IT.
MAGGART. WHAT THE FUCK'S *HE* DOING HERE? I THOUGHT HE MOVED TO CLEVELAND?
HE DID.
BUT THEN HE UP AND DISAPPEARED. DAMNDEST THING. NOBODY KNOWS WHERE HE WENT TO.
BUT...
WE STOPPED YOU THAT DAY ON THE COURTHOUSE STEPS BECAUSE THAT WAS THE WRONG WAY TO GO ABOUT IT.

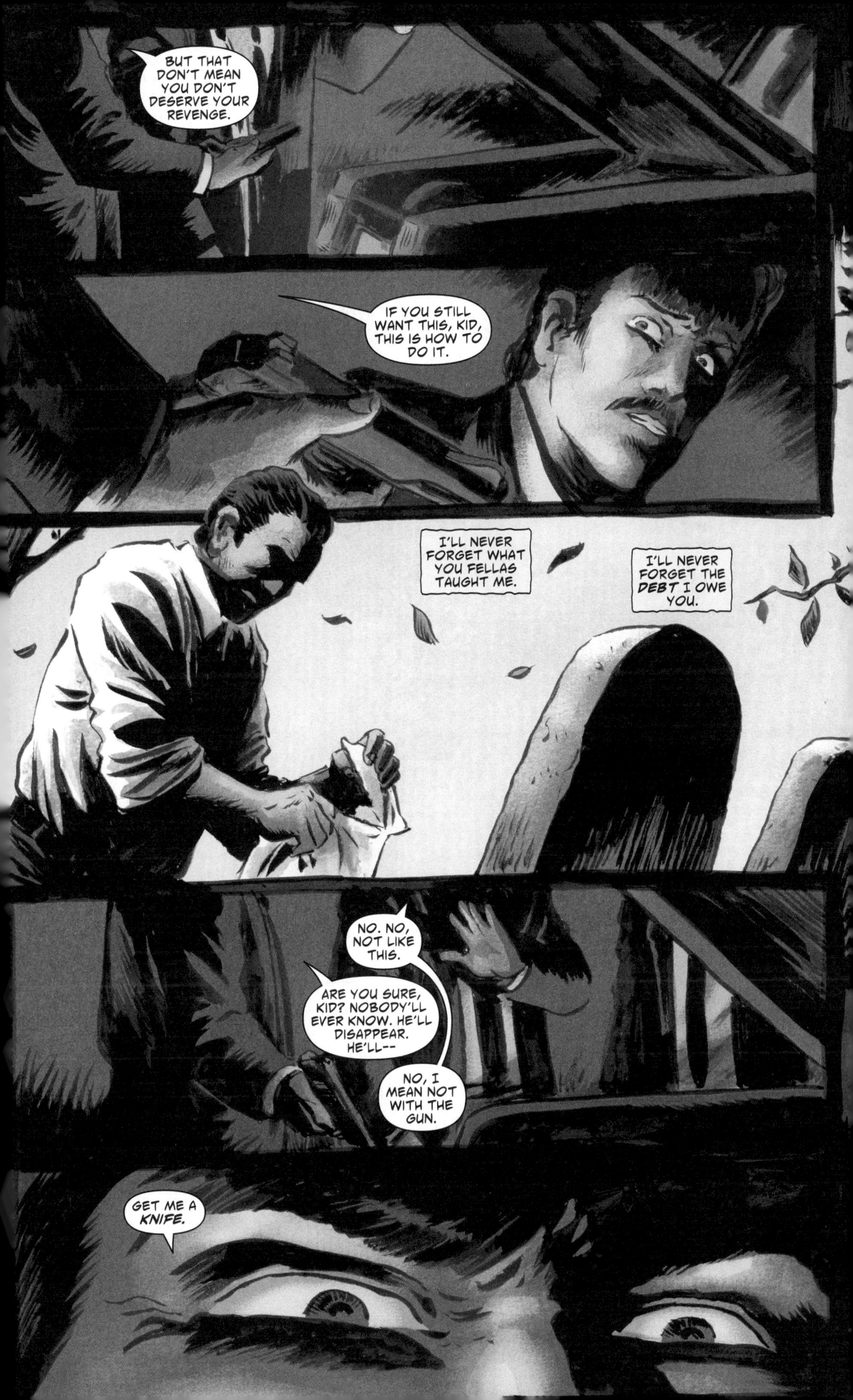
BUT THAT DON'T MEAN YOU DON'T DESERVE YOUR REVENGE.
IF YOU STILL WANT THIS, KID, THIS IS HOW TO DO IT.
I'LL NEVER FORGET WHAT YOU FELLAS TAUGHT ME.
I'LL NEVER FORGET THE *DEBT* I OWE YOU.
NO. NO, NOT LIKE THIS.
ARE YOU SURE, KID? NOBODY'LL EVER KNOW. HE'LL DISAPPEAR. HE'LL--
NO, I MEAN NOT WITH THE GUN.
GET ME A ***KNIFE***.

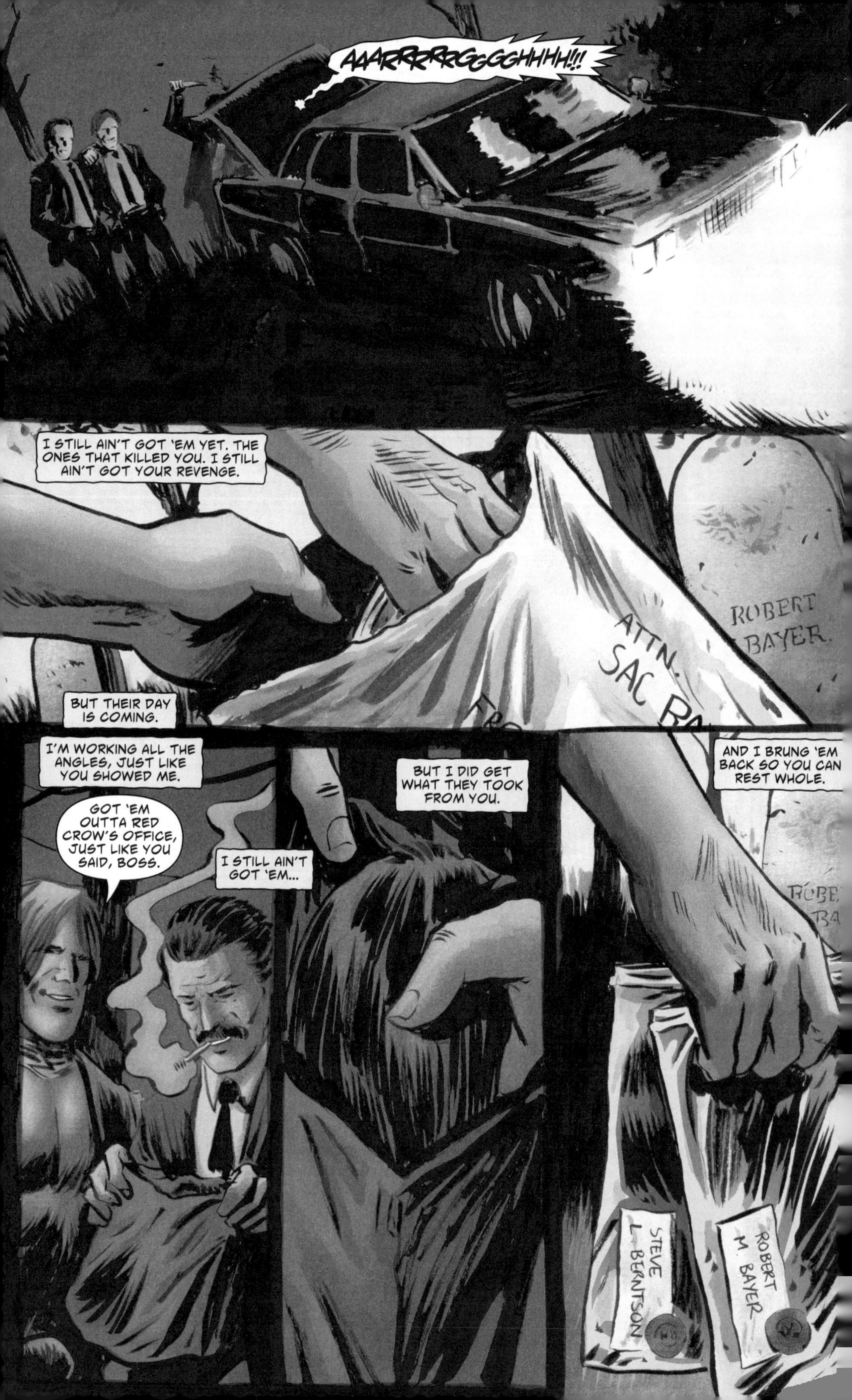
AAARRRRRGGGHHHH!!!
I STILL AIN'T GOT 'EM YET. THE ONES THAT KILLED YOU. I STILL AIN'T GOT YOUR REVENGE.
ROBERT BAYER
ATTN. SAC
BUT THEIR DAY IS COMING.
I'M WORKING ALL THE ANGLES, JUST LIKE YOU SHOWED ME.
GOT 'EM OUTTA RED CROW'S OFFICE, JUST LIKE YOU SAID, BOSS.
I STILL AIN'T GOT 'EM...
BUT I DID GET WHAT THEY TOOK FROM YOU.
AND I BRUNG 'EM BACK SO YOU CAN REST WHOLE.
STEVE L. BERNTSON
ROBERT M. BAYER

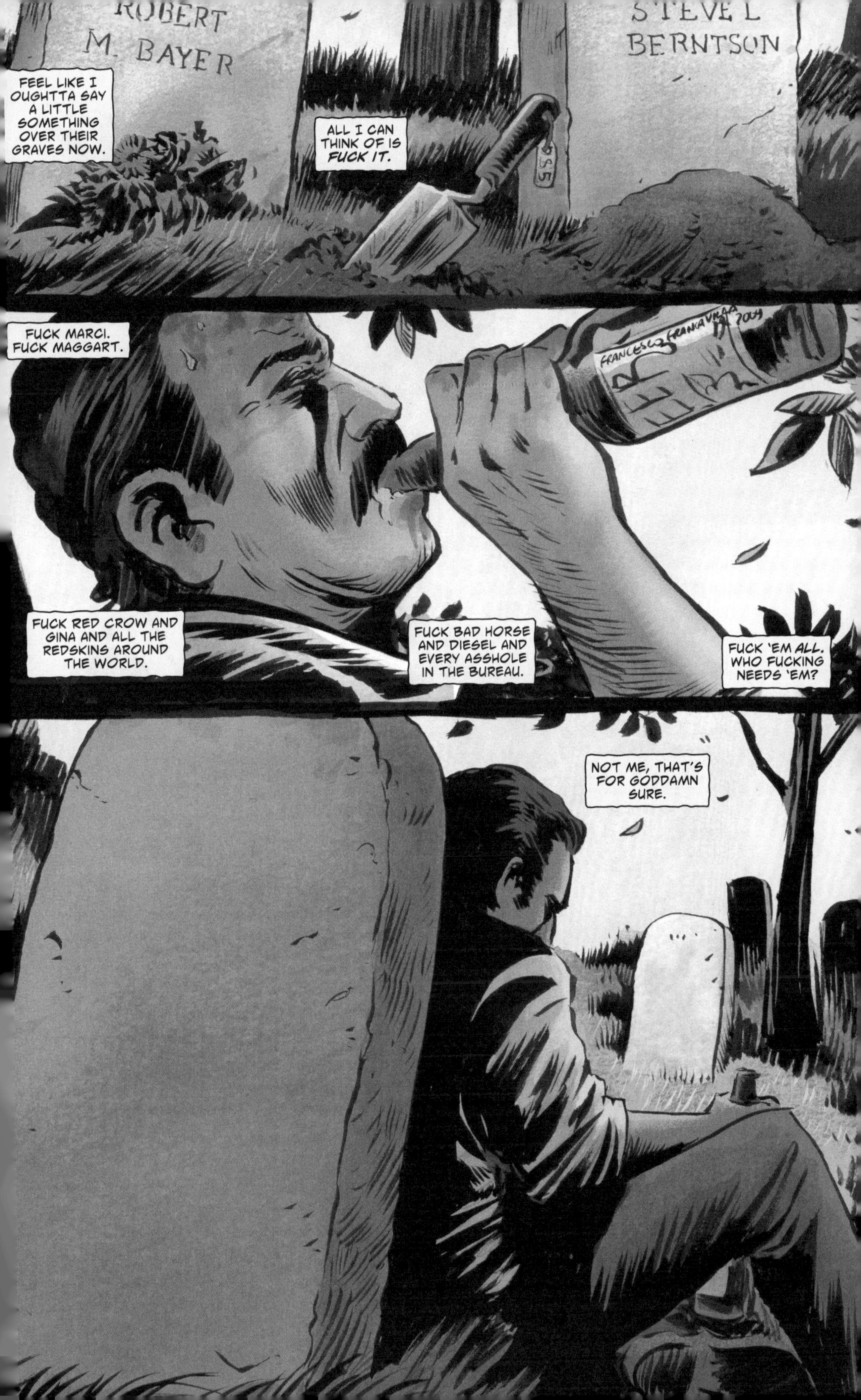
ROBERT
M. BAYER
STEVE L
BERNTSON
FEEL LIKE I OUGHTTA SAY A LITTLE SOMETHING OVER THEIR GRAVES NOW.
ALL I CAN THINK OF IS *FUCK IT*.
FUCK MARCI. FUCK MAGGART.
FUCK RED CROW AND GINA AND ALL THE REDSKINS AROUND THE WORLD.
FUCK BAD HORSE AND DIESEL AND EVERY ASSHOLE IN THE BUREAU.
FUCK 'EM *ALL*. WHO FUCKING NEEDS 'EM?
NOT ME, THAT'S FOR GODDAMN SURE.

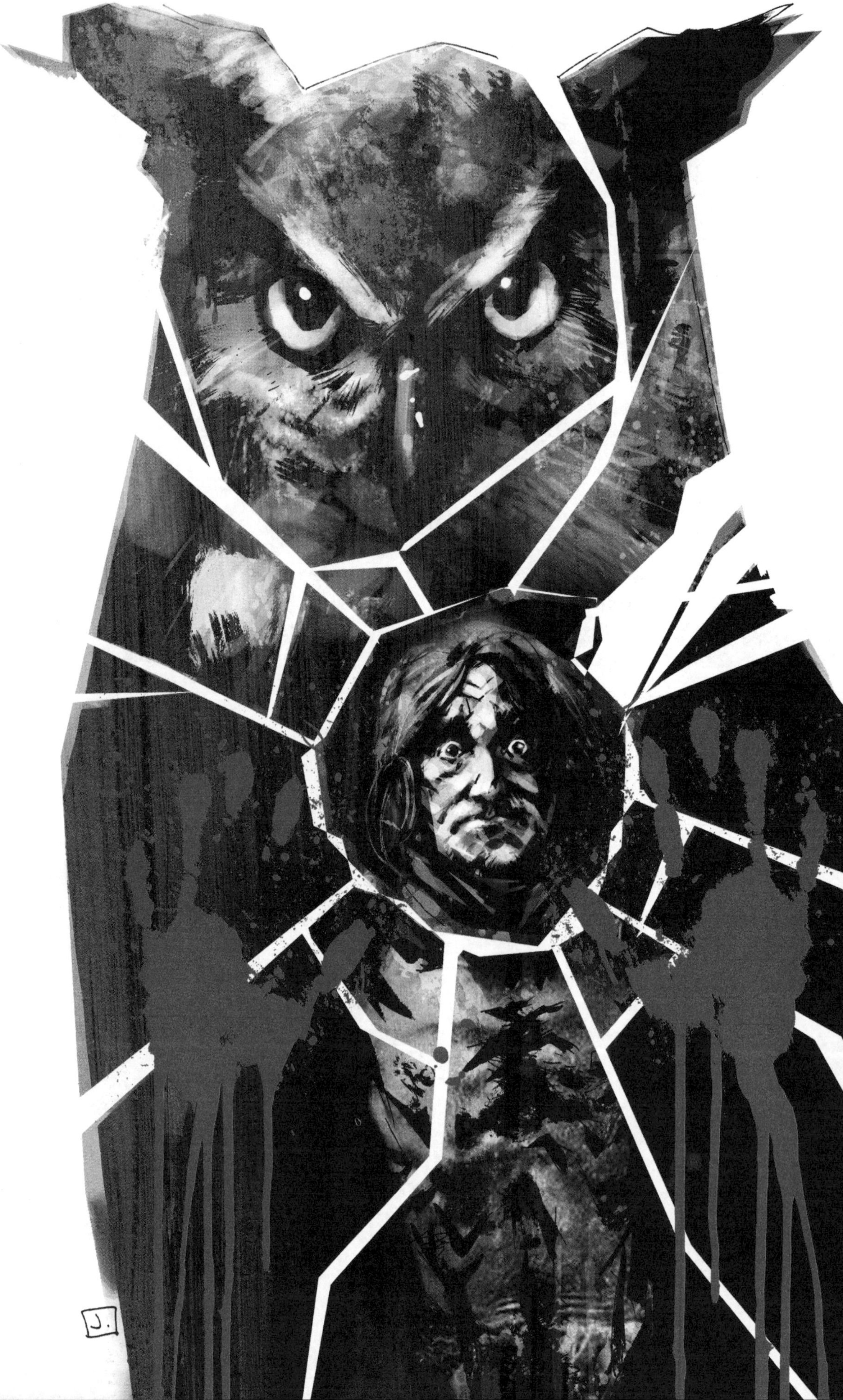
J.

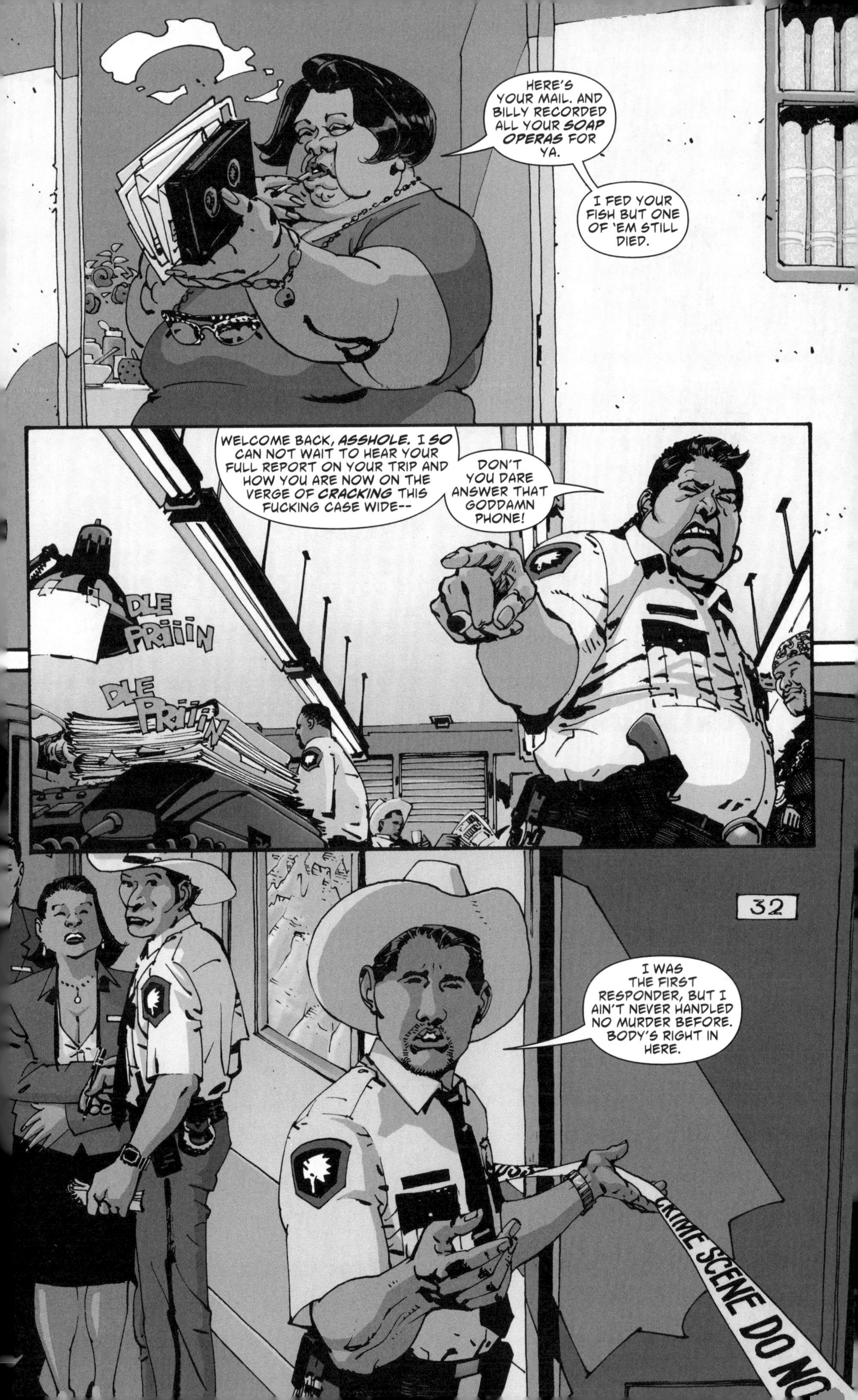
HERE'S YOUR MAIL. AND BILLY RECORDED ALL YOUR SOAP OPERAS FOR YA.
I FED YOUR FISH BUT ONE OF 'EM STILL DIED.
WELCOME BACK, ASSHOLE. I SO CAN NOT WAIT TO HEAR YOUR FULL REPORT ON YOUR TRIP AND HOW YOU ARE NOW ON THE VERGE OF CRACKING THIS FUCKING CASE WIDE--
DON'T YOU DARE ANSWER THAT GODDAMN PHONE!
DLE PRIIIN
DLE PRIIIN
32
I WAS THE FIRST RESPONDER, BUT I AIN'T NEVER HANDLED NO MURDER BEFORE. BODY'S RIGHT IN HERE.
CRIME SCENE DO NO

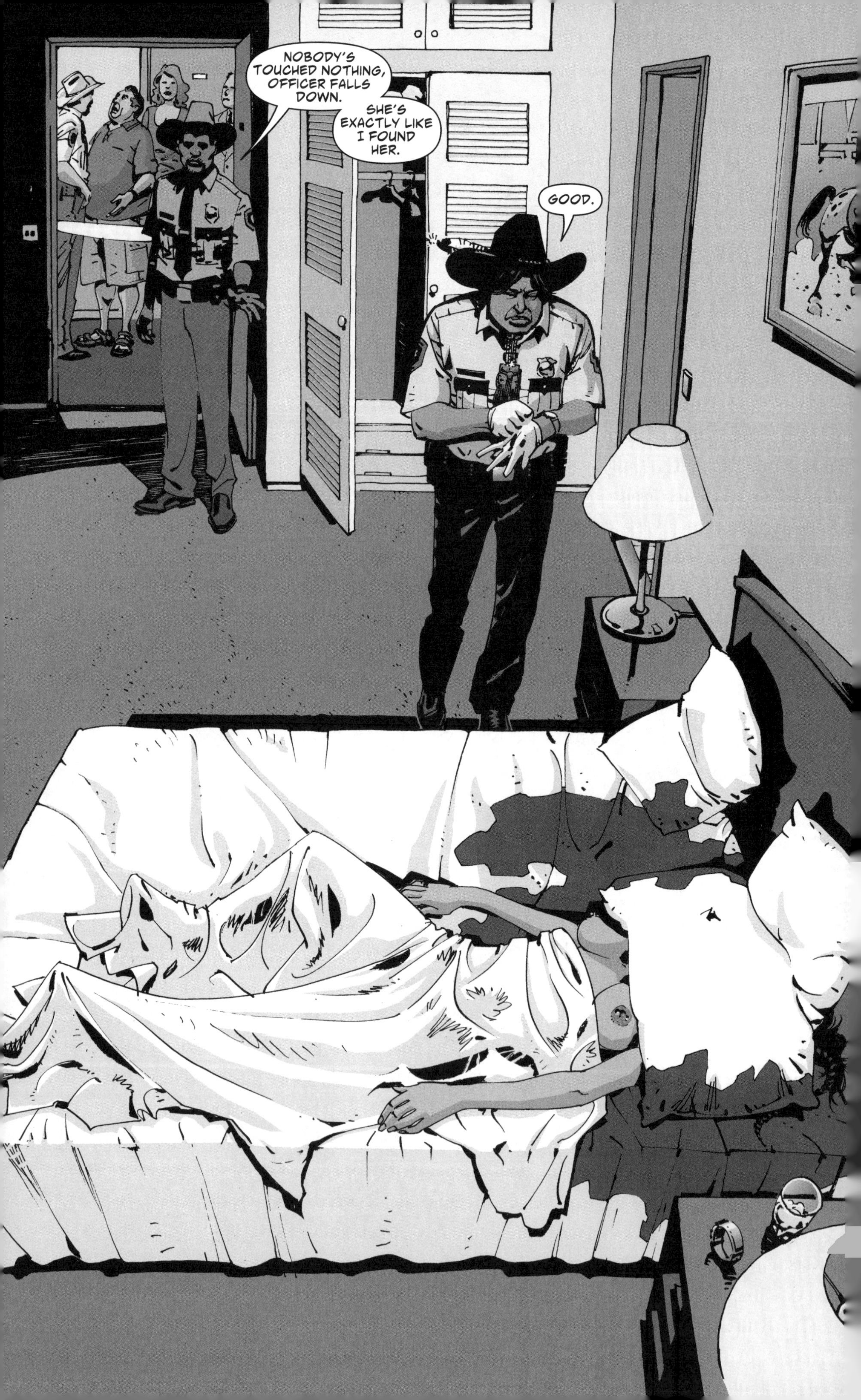
NOBODY'S TOUCHED NOTHING, OFFICER FALLS DOWN.
SHE'S EXACTLY LIKE I FOUND HER.
GOOD.

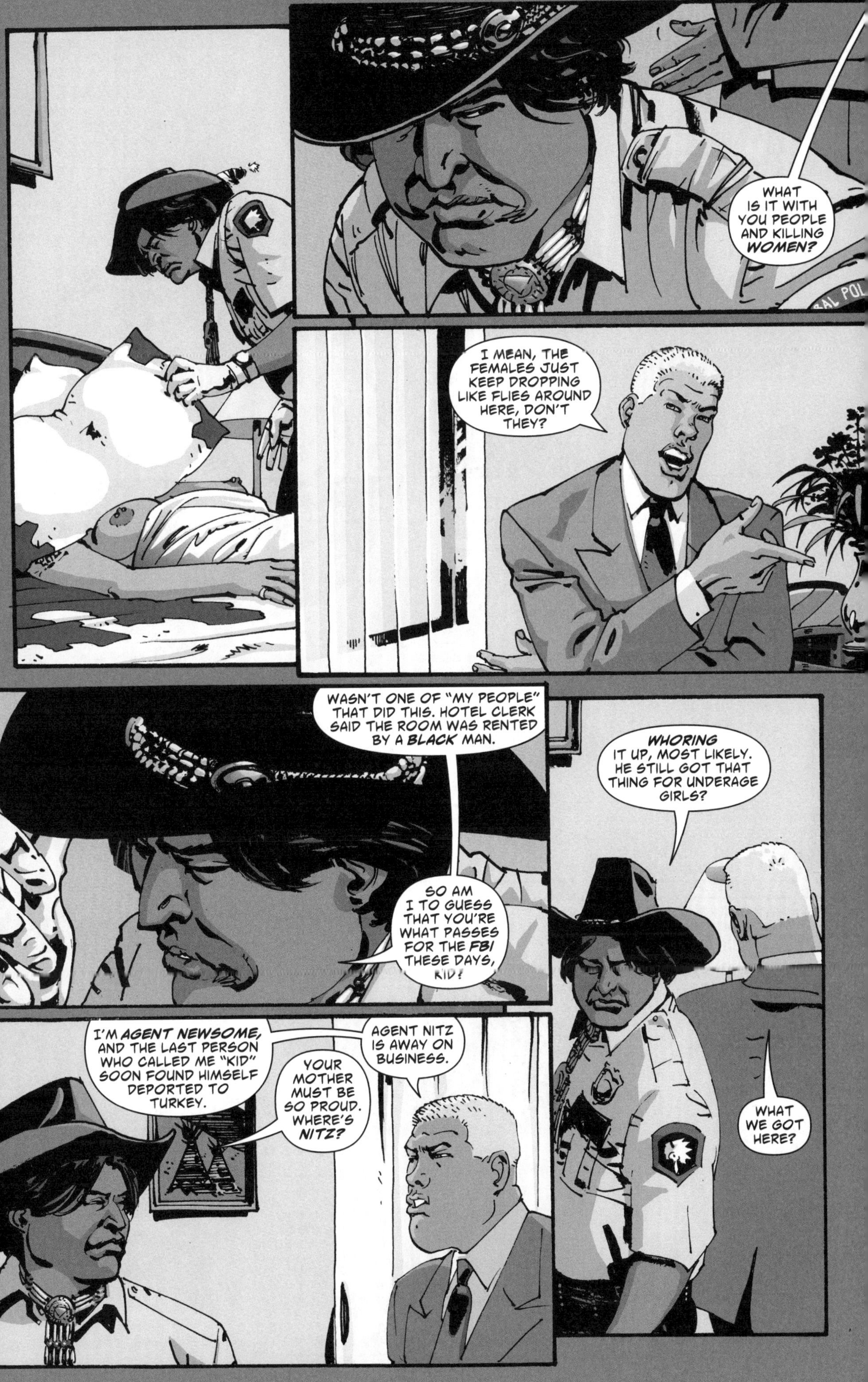
WHAT IS IT WITH YOU PEOPLE AND KILLING WOMEN?
I MEAN, THE FEMALES JUST KEEP DROPPING LIKE FLIES AROUND HERE, DON'T THEY?
WASN'T ONE OF "MY PEOPLE" THAT DID THIS. HOTEL CLERK SAID THE ROOM WAS RENTED BY A BLACK MAN.
SO AM I TO GUESS THAT YOU'RE WHAT PASSES FOR THE FBI THESE DAYS, KID?
WHORING IT UP, MOST LIKELY. HE STILL GOT THAT THING FOR UNDERAGE GIRLS?
WHAT WE GOT HERE?
I'M AGENT NEWSOME, AND THE LAST PERSON WHO CALLED ME "KID" SOON FOUND HIMSELF DEPORTED TO TURKEY.
YOUR MOTHER MUST BE SO PROUD. WHERE'S NITZ?
AGENT NITZ IS AWAY ON BUSINESS.

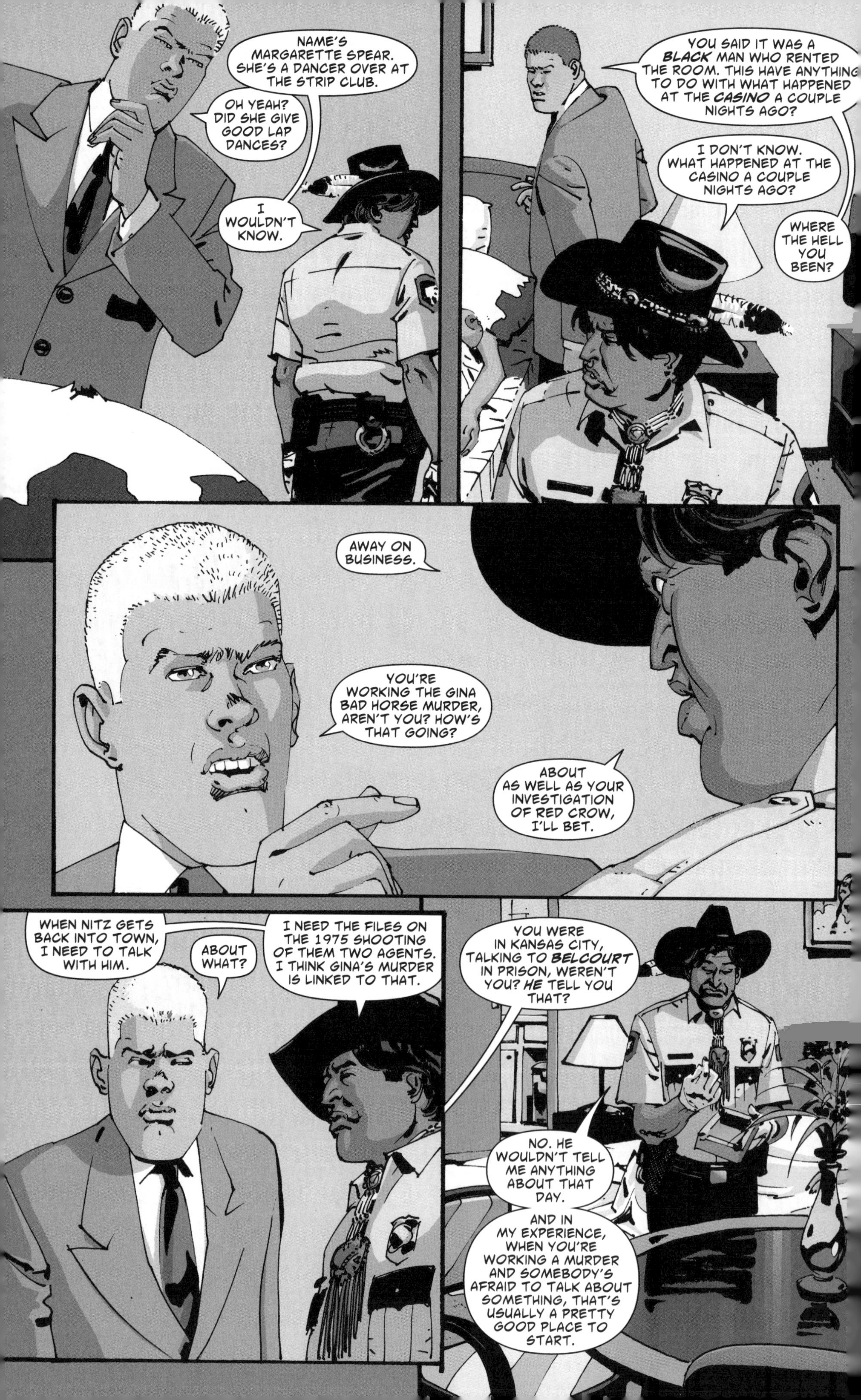
NAME'S MARGARETTE SPEAR. SHE'S A DANCER OVER AT THE STRIP CLUB.
OH YEAH? DID SHE GIVE GOOD LAP DANCES?
I WOULDN'T KNOW.
YOU SAID IT WAS A BLACK MAN WHO RENTED THE ROOM. THIS HAVE ANYTHING TO DO WITH WHAT HAPPENED AT THE CASINO A COUPLE NIGHTS AGO?
I DON'T KNOW. WHAT HAPPENED AT THE CASINO A COUPLE NIGHTS AGO?
WHERE THE HELL YOU BEEN?
AWAY ON BUSINESS.
YOU'RE WORKING THE GINA BAD HORSE MURDER, AREN'T YOU? HOW'S THAT GOING?
ABOUT AS WELL AS YOUR INVESTIGATION OF RED CROW, I'LL BET.
WHEN NITZ GETS BACK INTO TOWN, I NEED TO TALK WITH HIM.
ABOUT WHAT?
I NEED THE FILES ON THE 1975 SHOOTING OF THEM TWO AGENTS. I THINK GINA'S MURDER IS LINKED TO THAT.
YOU WERE IN KANSAS CITY, TALKING TO BELCOURT IN PRISON, WEREN'T YOU? HE TELL YOU THAT?
NO. HE WOULDN'T TELL ME ANYTHING ABOUT THAT DAY.
AND IN MY EXPERIENCE, WHEN YOU'RE WORKING A MURDER AND SOMEBODY'S AFRAID TO TALK ABOUT SOMETHING, THAT'S USUALLY A PRETTY GOOD PLACE TO START.

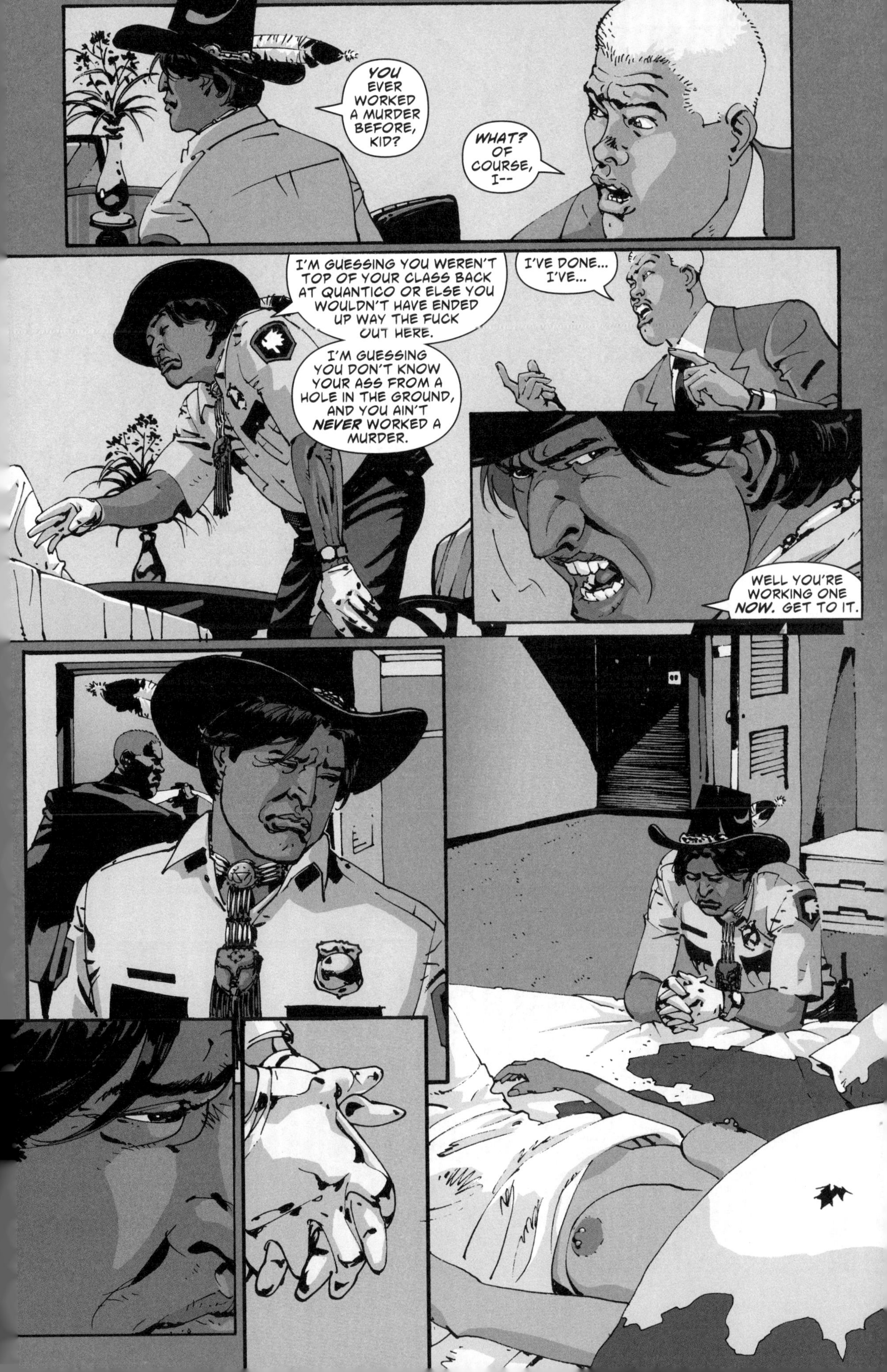

YOU EVER WORKED A MURDER BEFORE, KID?
WHAT? OF COURSE, I--
I'M GUESSING YOU WEREN'T TOP OF YOUR CLASS BACK AT QUANTICO OR ELSE YOU WOULDN'T HAVE ENDED UP WAY THE FUCK OUT HERE.
I'VE DONE... I'VE...
I'M GUESSING YOU DON'T KNOW YOUR ASS FROM A HOLE IN THE GROUND, AND YOU AIN'T NEVER WORKED A MURDER.
WELL YOU'RE WORKING ONE NOW. GET TO IT.

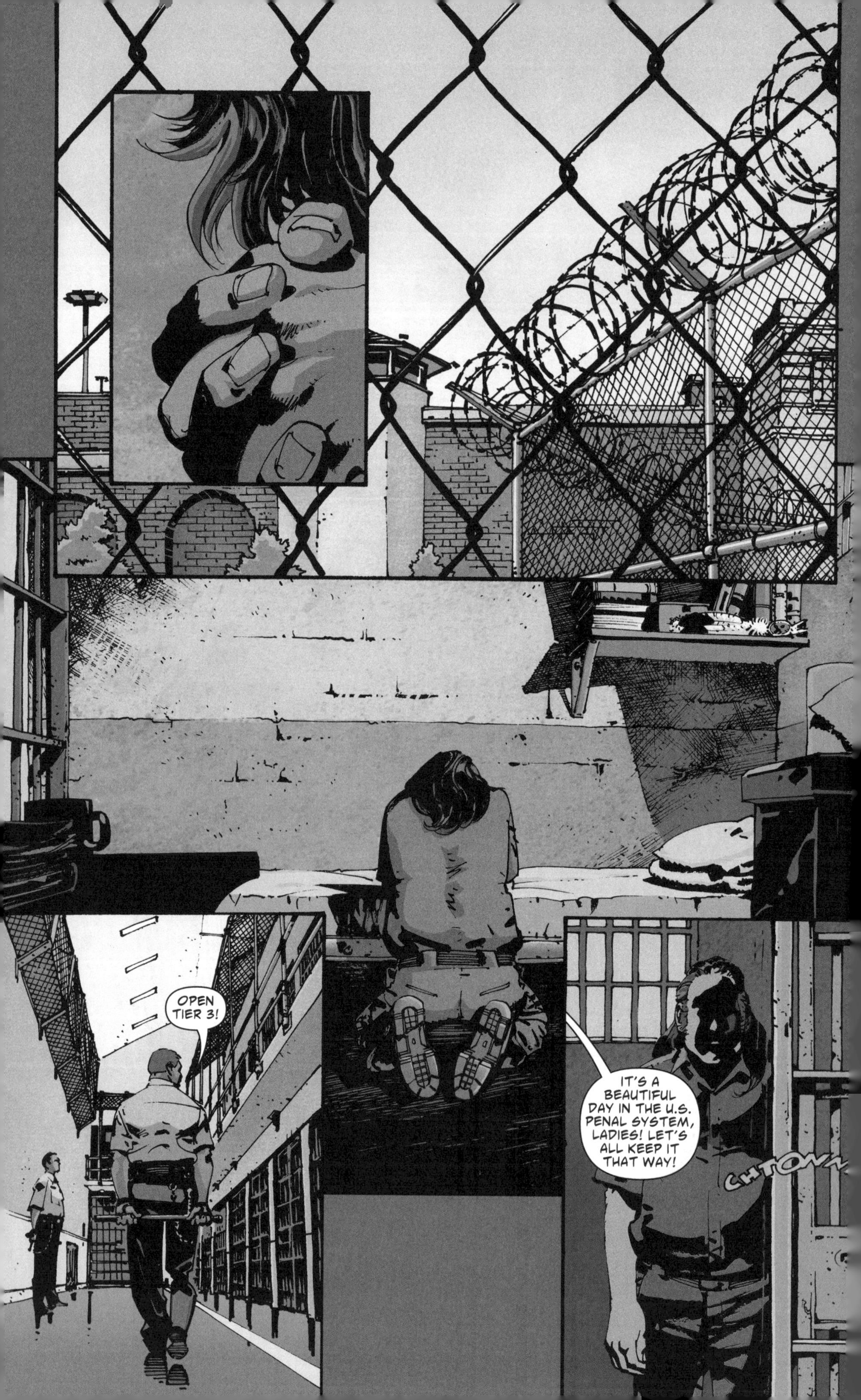
OPEN TIER 3!
IT'S A BEAUTIFUL DAY IN THE U.S. PENAL SYSTEM, LADIES! LET'S ALL KEEP IT THAT WAY!
CHTONN

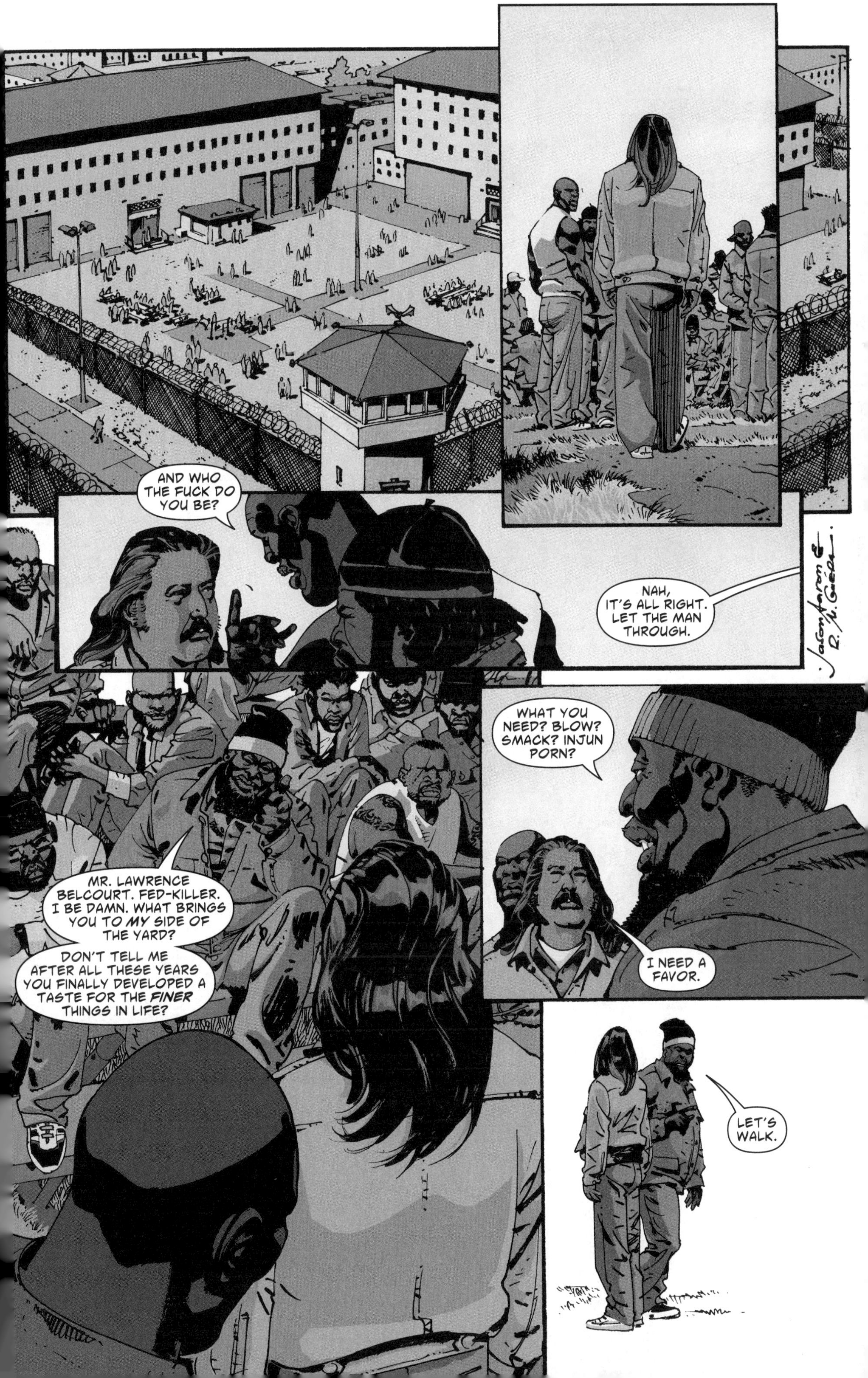
AND WHO THE FUCK DO YOU BE?
NAH, IT'S ALL RIGHT. LET THE MAN THROUGH.
MR. LAWRENCE BELCOURT. FED-KILLER. I BE DAMN. WHAT BRINGS YOU TO MY SIDE OF THE YARD?
DON'T TELL ME AFTER ALL THESE YEARS YOU FINALLY DEVELOPED A TASTE FOR THE FINER THINGS IN LIFE?
WHAT YOU NEED? BLOW? SMACK? INJUN PORN?
I NEED A FAVOR.
LET'S WALK.

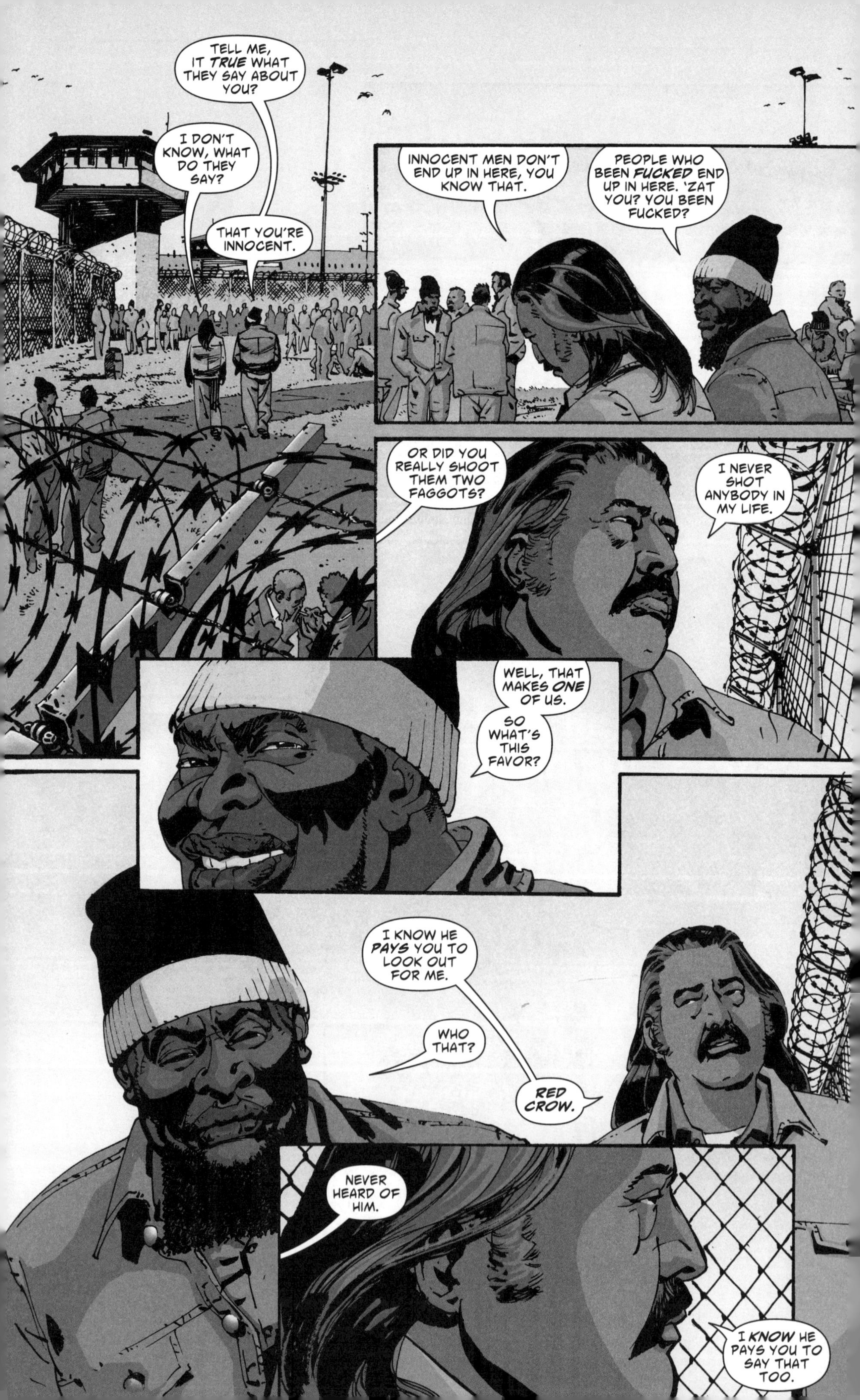
TELL ME, IT TRUE WHAT THEY SAY ABOUT YOU?
I DON'T KNOW, WHAT DO THEY SAY?
THAT YOU'RE INNOCENT.
INNOCENT MEN DON'T END UP IN HERE, YOU KNOW THAT.
PEOPLE WHO BEEN FUCKED END UP IN HERE. 'ZAT YOU? YOU BEEN FUCKED?
OR DID YOU REALLY SHOOT THEM TWO FAGGOTS?
I NEVER SHOT ANYBODY IN MY LIFE.
WELL, THAT MAKES ONE OF US.
SO WHAT'S THIS FAVOR?
I KNOW HE PAYS YOU TO LOOK OUT FOR ME.
WHO THAT?
RED CROW.
NEVER HEARD OF HIM.
I KNOW HE PAYS YOU TO SAY THAT TOO.

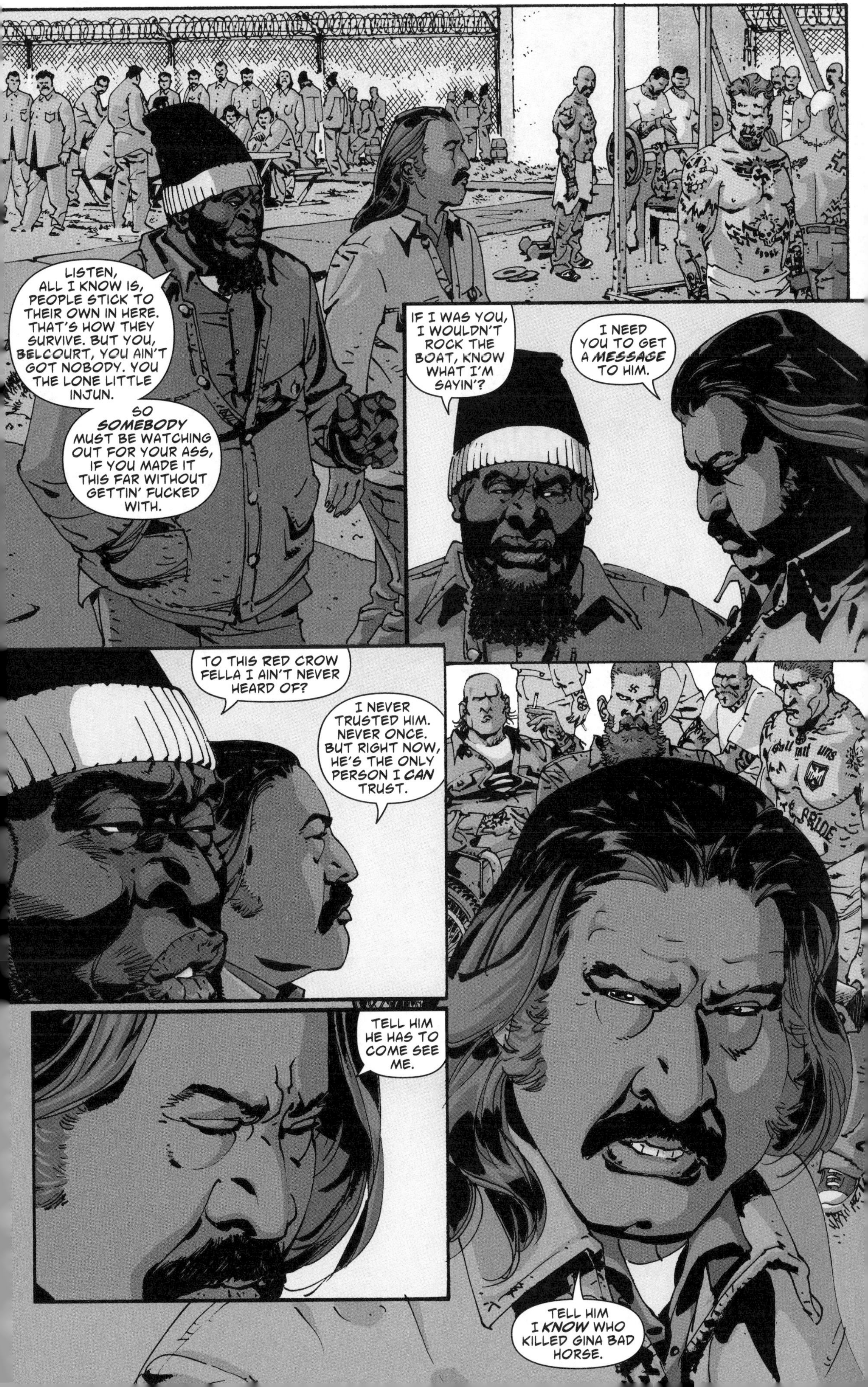
LISTEN, ALL I KNOW IS, PEOPLE STICK TO THEIR OWN IN HERE. THAT'S HOW THEY SURVIVE. BUT YOU, BELCOURT, YOU AIN'T GOT NOBODY. YOU THE LONE LITTLE INJUN.
SO SOMEBODY MUST BE WATCHING OUT FOR YOUR ASS, IF YOU MADE IT THIS FAR WITHOUT GETTIN' FUCKED WITH.
IF I WAS YOU, I WOULDN'T ROCK THE BOAT, KNOW WHAT I'M SAYIN'?
I NEED YOU TO GET A MESSAGE TO HIM.
TO THIS RED CROW FELLA I AIN'T NEVER HEARD OF?
I NEVER TRUSTED HIM. NEVER ONCE. BUT RIGHT NOW, HE'S THE ONLY PERSON I CAN TRUST.
TELL HIM HE HAS TO COME SEE ME.
TELL HIM I KNOW WHO KILLED GINA BAD HORSE.

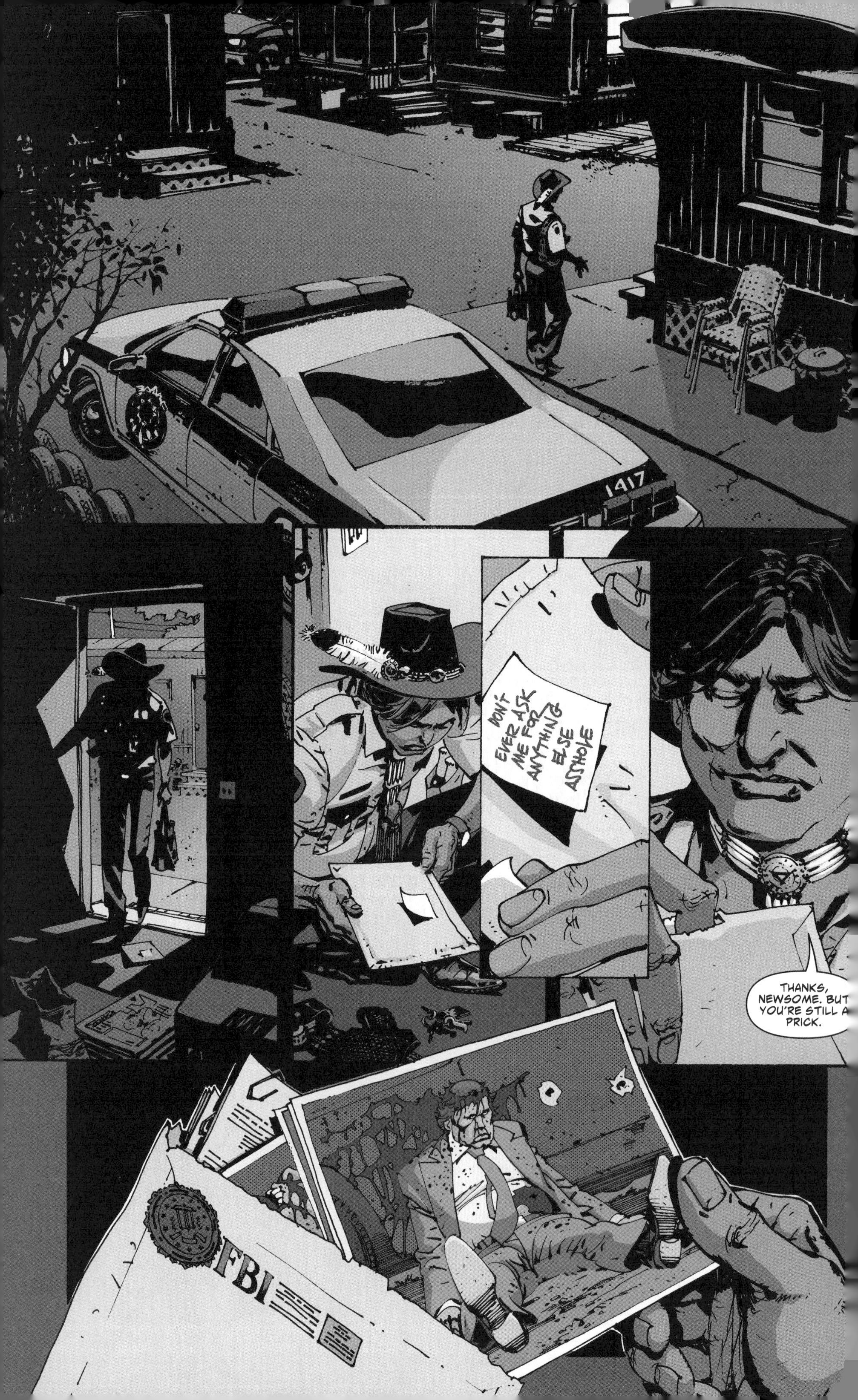

1417
DON'T EVER ASK ME FOR ANYTHING ELSE ASSHOLE
THANKS, NEWSOME. BUT YOU'RE STILL A PRICK.
FBI

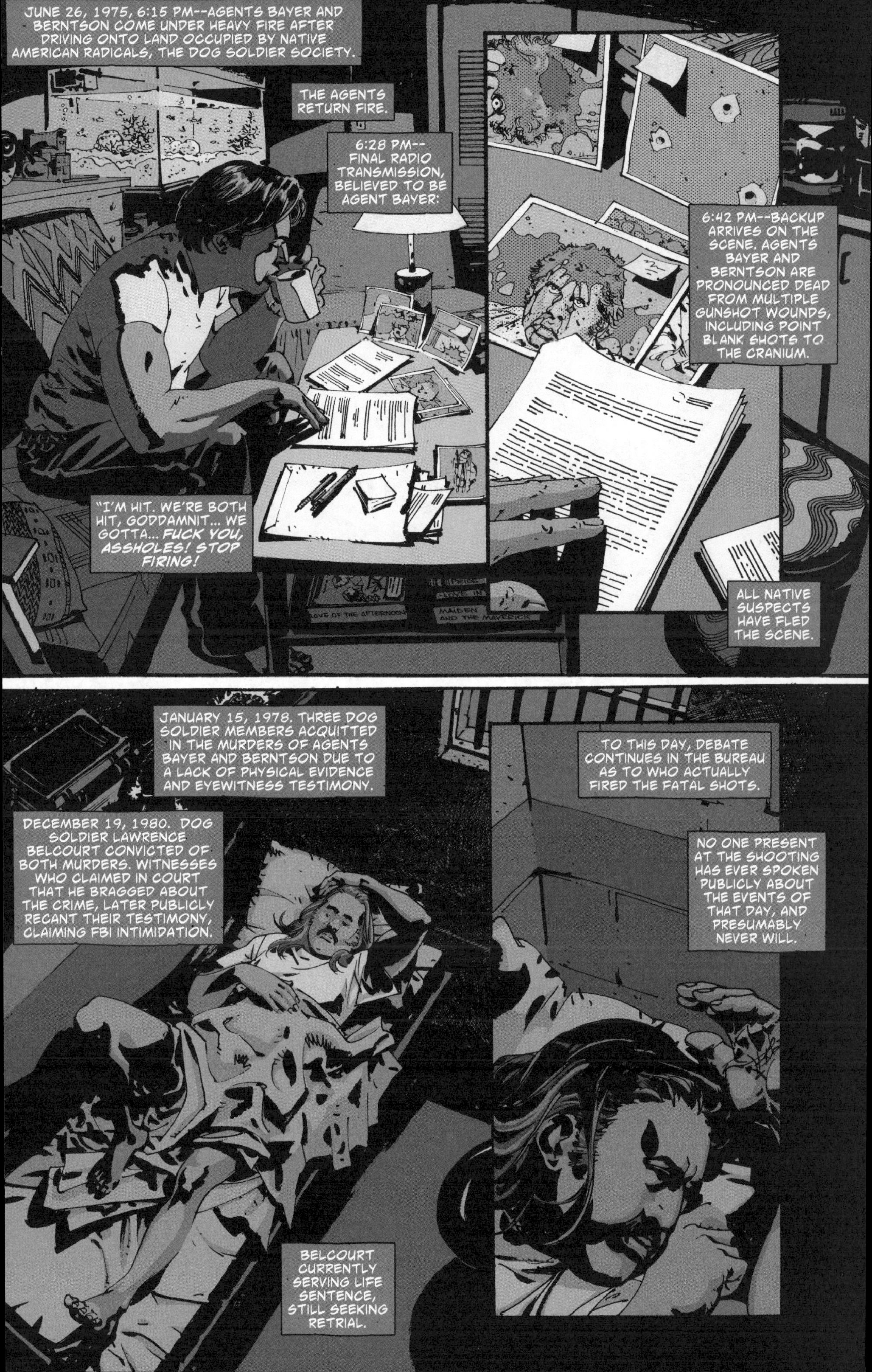
JUNE 26, 1975, 6:15 PM--AGENTS BAYER AND BERNTSON COME UNDER HEAVY FIRE AFTER DRIVING ONTO LAND OCCUPIED BY NATIVE AMERICAN RADICALS, THE DOG SOLDIER SOCIETY.
THE AGENTS RETURN FIRE.
6:28 PM-- FINAL RADIO TRANSMISSION, BELIEVED TO BE AGENT BAYER:
"I'M HIT. WE'RE BOTH HIT, GODDAMNIT... WE GOTTA... *FUCK YOU, ASSHOLES! STOP FIRING!*
6:42 PM--BACKUP ARRIVES ON THE SCENE. AGENTS BAYER AND BERNTSON ARE PRONOUNCED DEAD FROM MULTIPLE GUNSHOT WOUNDS, INCLUDING POINT BLANK SHOTS TO THE CRANIUM.
ALL NATIVE SUSPECTS HAVE FLED THE SCENE.
JANUARY 15, 1978. THREE DOG SOLDIER MEMBERS ACQUITTED IN THE MURDERS OF AGENTS BAYER AND BERNTSON DUE TO A LACK OF PHYSICAL EVIDENCE AND EYEWITNESS TESTIMONY.
DECEMBER 19, 1980. DOG SOLDIER LAWRENCE BELCOURT CONVICTED OF BOTH MURDERS. WITNESSES WHO CLAIMED IN COURT THAT HE BRAGGED ABOUT THE CRIME, LATER PUBLICLY RECANT THEIR TESTIMONY, CLAIMING FBI INTIMIDATION.
BELCOURT CURRENTLY SERVING LIFE SENTENCE, STILL SEEKING RETRIAL.
TO THIS DAY, DEBATE CONTINUES IN THE BUREAU AS TO WHO ACTUALLY FIRED THE FATAL SHOTS.
NO ONE PRESENT AT THE SHOOTING HAS EVER SPOKEN PUBLICLY ABOUT THE EVENTS OF THAT DAY, AND PRESUMABLY NEVER WILL.

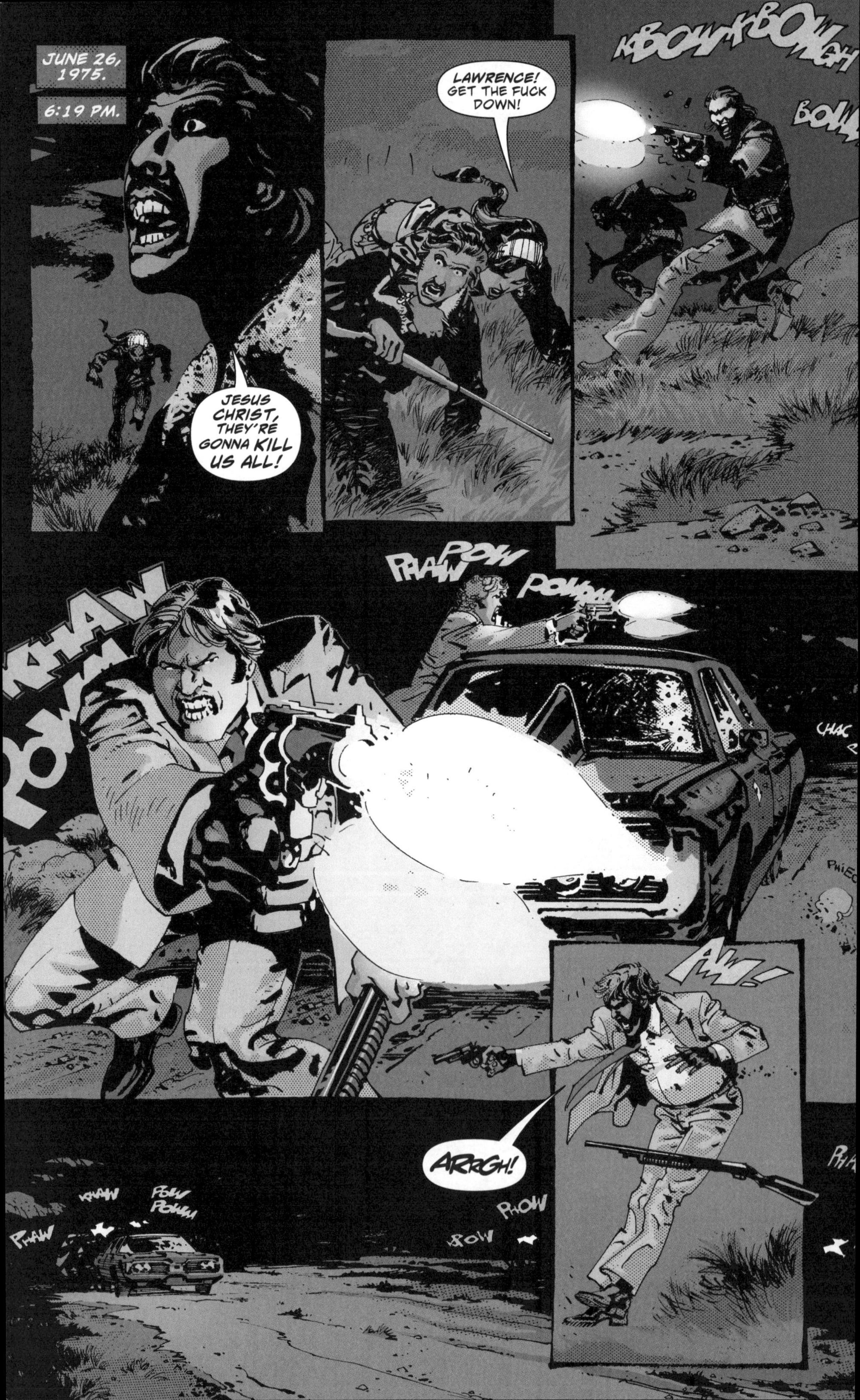

JUNE 26, 1975.
6:19 PM.
JESUS CHRIST, THEY'RE GONNA KILL US ALL!
LAWRENCE! GET THE FUCK DOWN!
BOW
PHAW POW
ARRGH!
PHOW

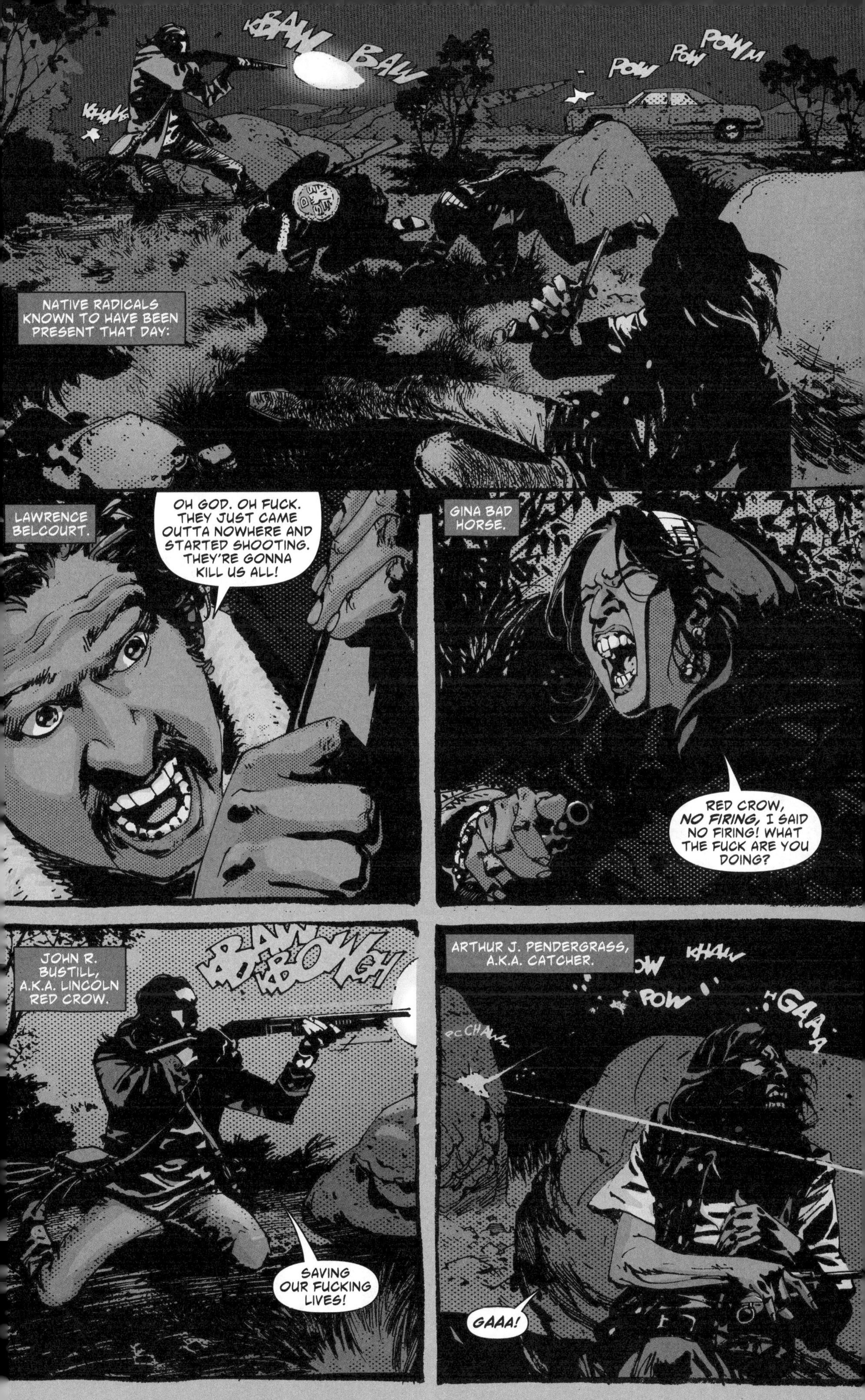
KBAW
BAW
POW
POW
POWM
NATIVE RADICALS KNOWN TO HAVE BEEN PRESENT THAT DAY:
LAWRENCE BELCOURT.
OH GOD. OH FUCK. THEY JUST CAME OUTTA NOWHERE AND STARTED SHOOTING. THEY'RE GONNA KILL US ALL!
GINA BAD HORSE.
RED CROW, *NO FIRING,* I SAID NO FIRING! WHAT THE FUCK ARE YOU DOING?
JOHN R. BUSTILL, A.K.A. LINCOLN RED CROW.
SAVING OUR FUCKING LIVES!
ARTHUR J. PENDERGRASS, A.K.A. CATCHER.
KHAW
POW
GAAA
*GAAA!*

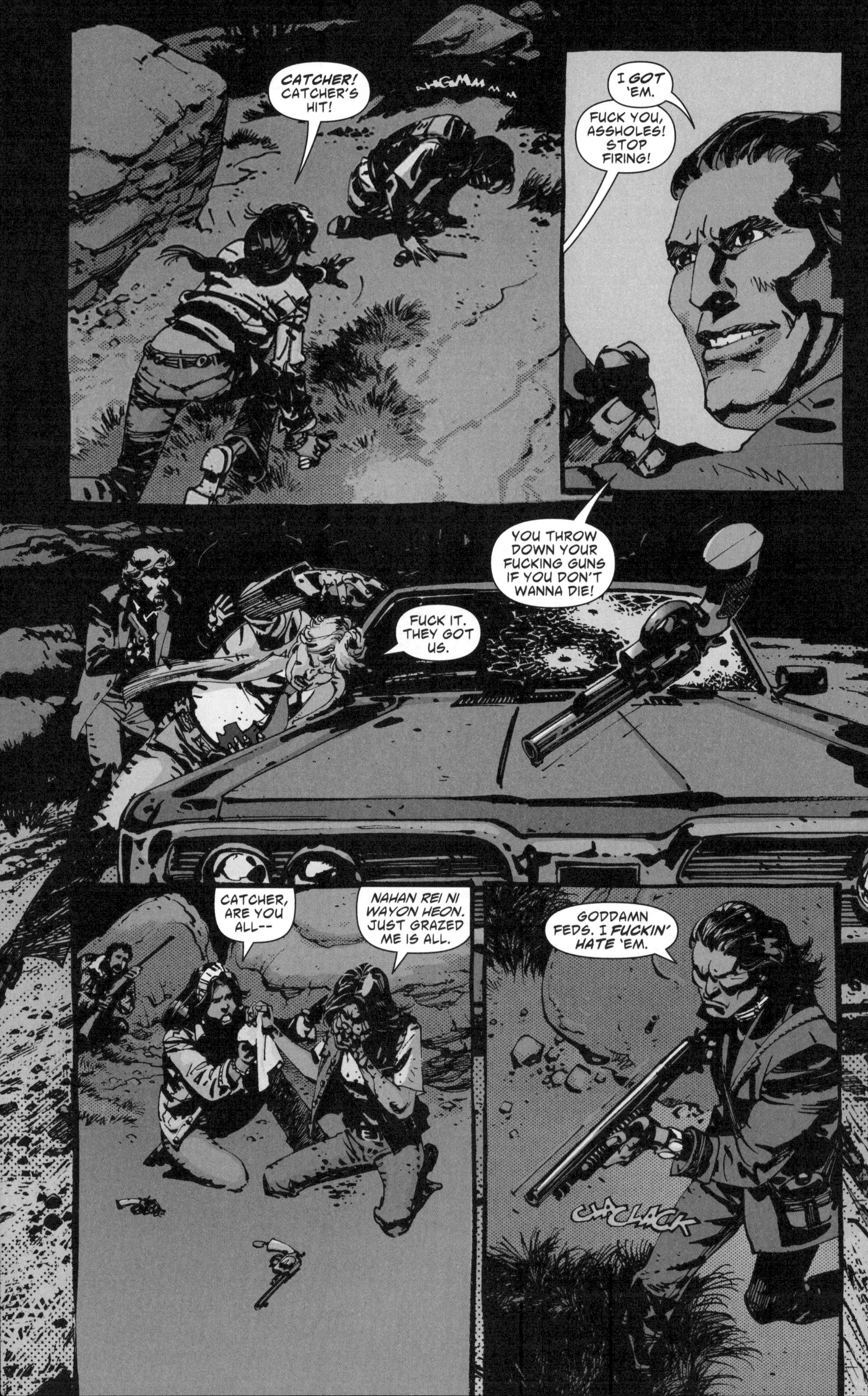

CATCHER! CATCHER'S HIT!
AHGMM
I GOT 'EM.
FUCK YOU, ASSHOLES! STOP FIRING!
YOU THROW DOWN YOUR FUCKING GUNS IF YOU DON'T WANNA DIE!
FUCK IT. THEY GOT US.
CATCHER, ARE YOU ALL--
NAHAN REI NI WAYON HEON. JUST GRAZED ME IS ALL.
GODDAMN FEDS. I FUCKIN' HATE 'EM.
CHACLACK

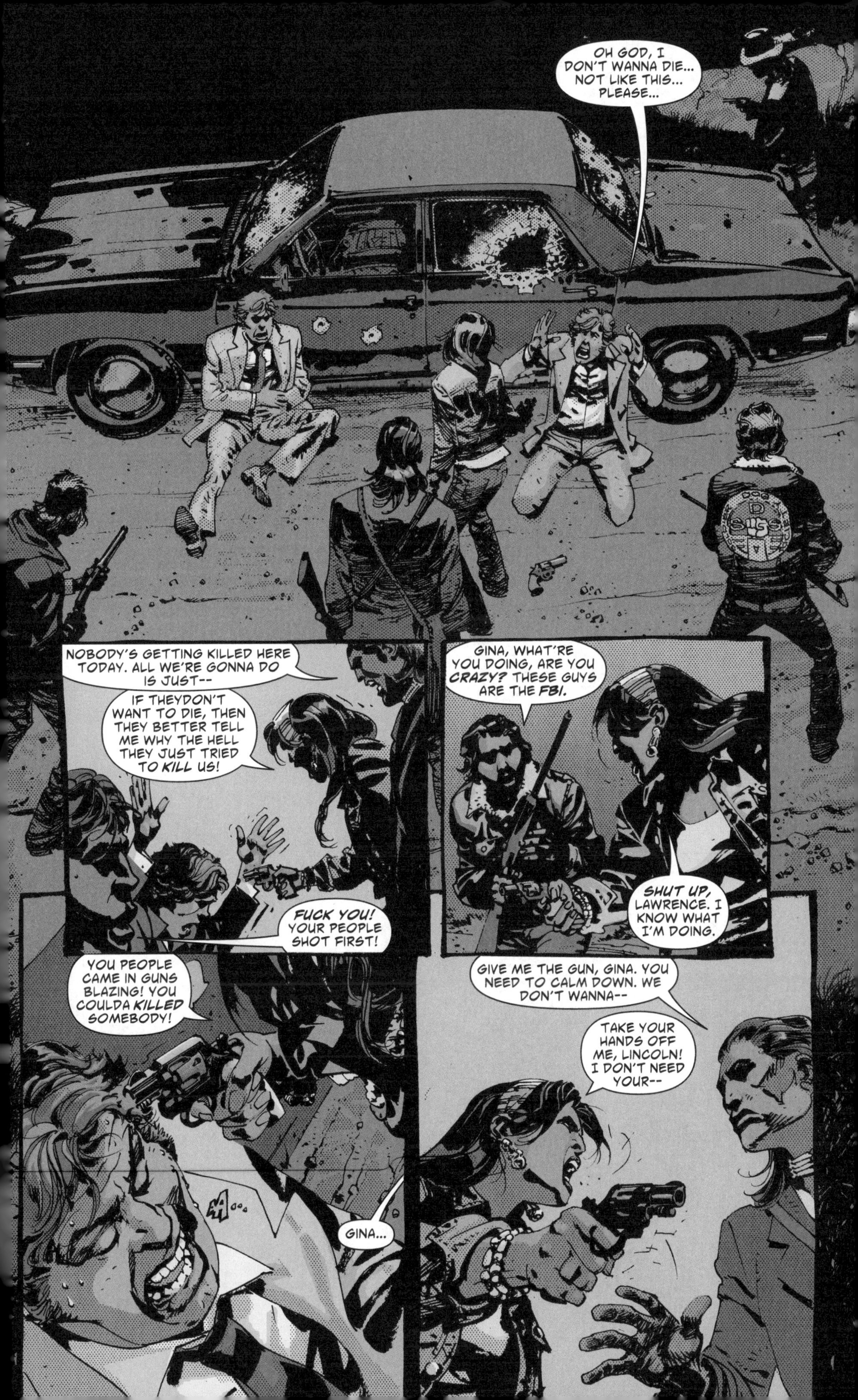
OH GOD, I DON'T WANNA DIE... NOT LIKE THIS... PLEASE...
NOBODY'S GETTING KILLED HERE TODAY. ALL WE'RE GONNA DO IS JUST--
IF THEYDON'T WANT TO DIE, THEN THEY BETTER TELL ME WHY THE HELL THEY JUST TRIED TO KILL US!
FUCK YOU! YOUR PEOPLE SHOT FIRST!
GINA, WHAT'RE YOU DOING, ARE YOU CRAZY? THESE GUYS ARE THE FBI.
SHUT UP, LAWRENCE. I KNOW WHAT I'M DOING.
YOU PEOPLE CAME IN GUNS BLAZING! YOU COULDA KILLED SOMEBODY!
GINA...
GIVE ME THE GUN, GINA. YOU NEED TO CALM DOWN. WE DON'T WANNA--
TAKE YOUR HANDS OFF ME, LINCOLN! I DON'T NEED YOUR--

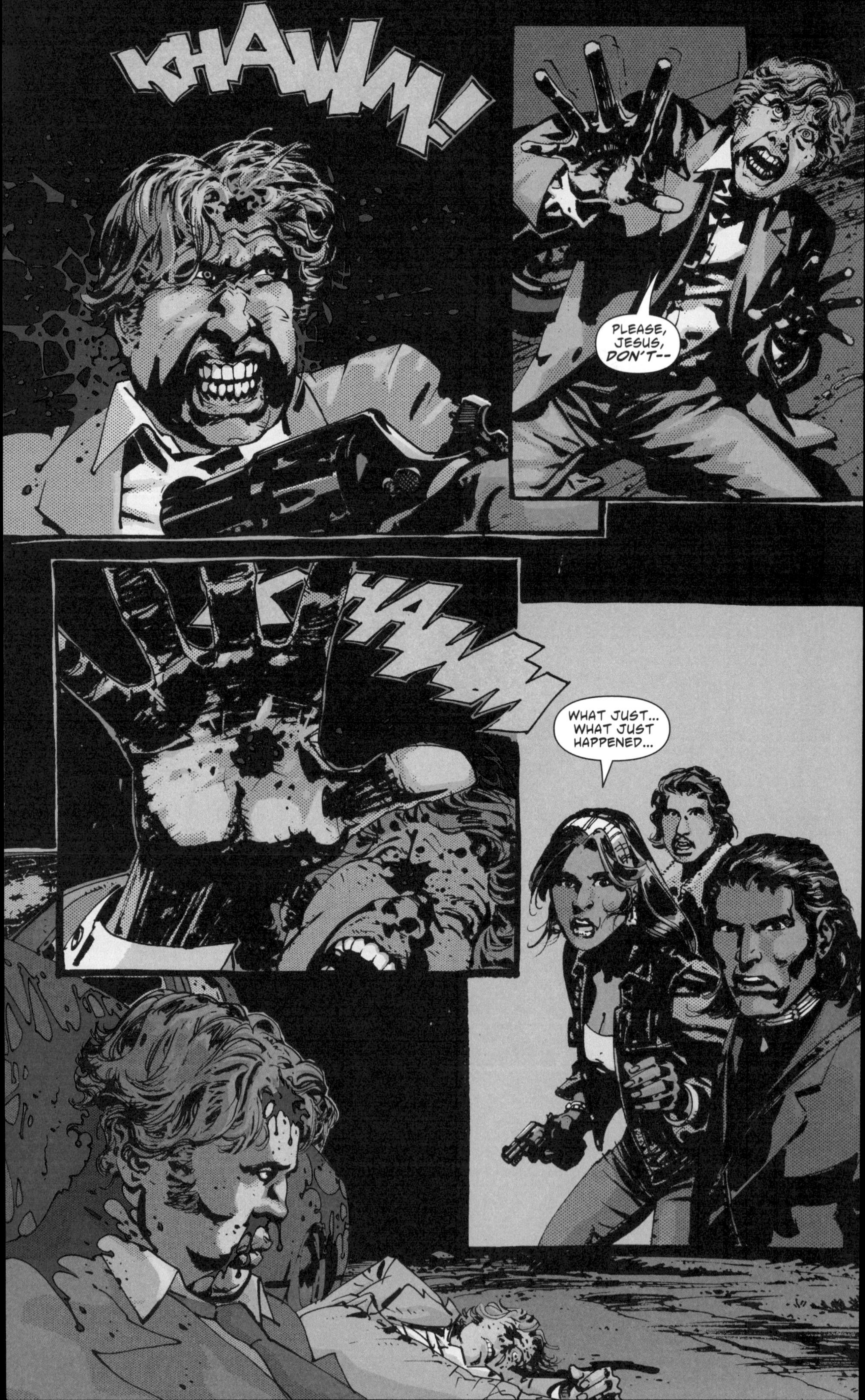
KHAWM!
PLEASE, JESUS, DON'T--
KHAWM
WHAT JUST... WHAT JUST HAPPENED...

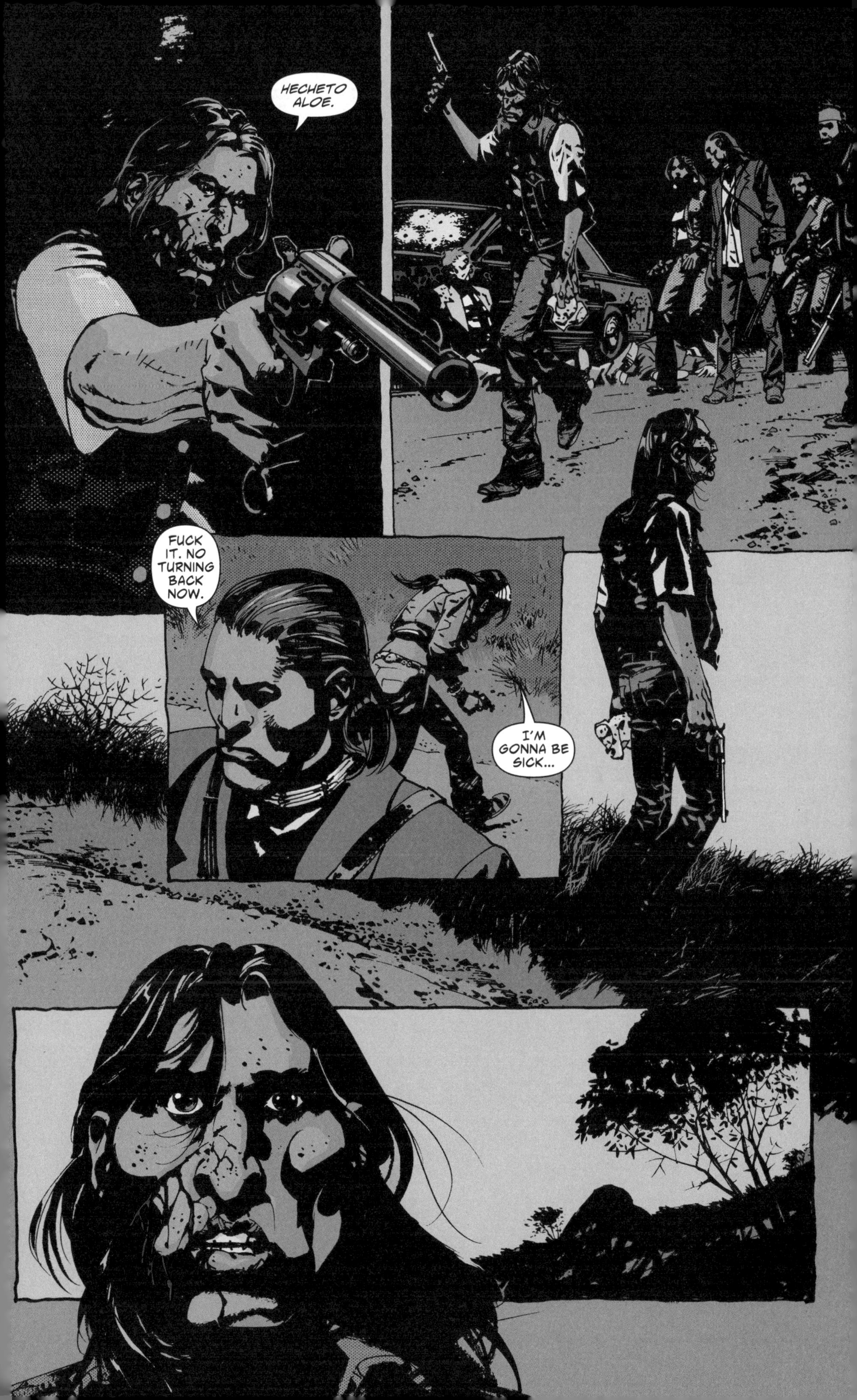
HECHETO ALOE.
FUCK IT. NO TURNING BACK NOW.
I'M GONNA BE SICK...

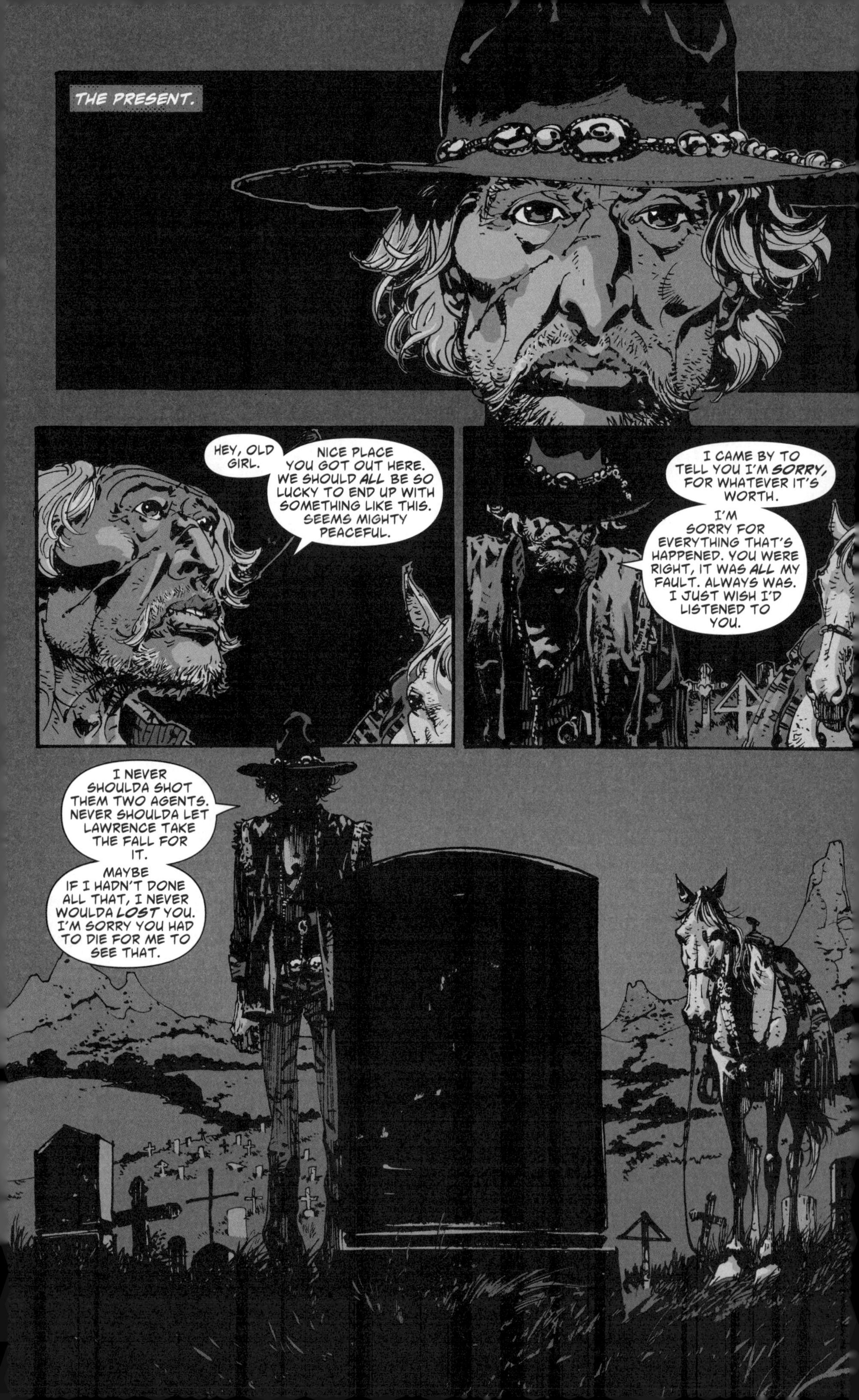
THE PRESENT.
HEY, OLD GIRL.
NICE PLACE YOU GOT OUT HERE. WE SHOULD ALL BE SO LUCKY TO END UP WITH SOMETHING LIKE THIS. SEEMS MIGHTY PEACEFUL.
I CAME BY TO TELL YOU I'M SORRY, FOR WHATEVER IT'S WORTH.
I'M SORRY FOR EVERYTHING THAT'S HAPPENED. YOU WERE RIGHT, IT WAS ALL MY FAULT. ALWAYS WAS. I JUST WISH I'D LISTENED TO YOU.
I NEVER SHOULDA SHOT THEM TWO AGENTS. NEVER SHOULDA LET LAWRENCE TAKE THE FALL FOR IT.
MAYBE IF I HADN'T DONE ALL THAT, I NEVER WOULDA LOST YOU. I'M SORRY YOU HAD TO DIE FOR ME TO SEE THAT.

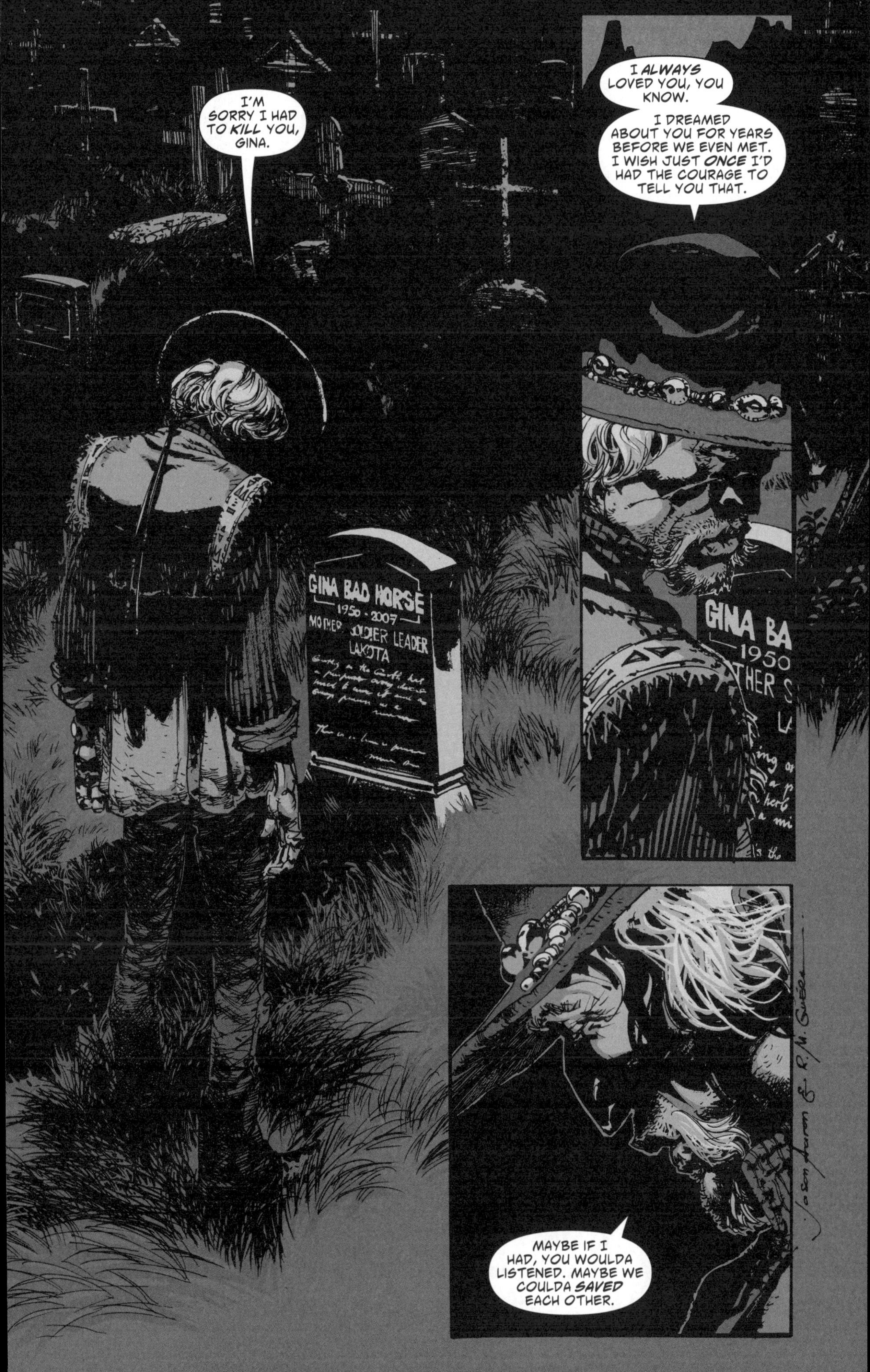
I'M SORRY I HAD TO KILL YOU, GINA.
GINA BAD HORSE
1950 - 2007
MOTHER SOLDIER LEADER
LAKOTA
I ALWAYS LOVED YOU, YOU KNOW.
I DREAMED ABOUT YOU FOR YEARS BEFORE WE EVEN MET. I WISH JUST ONCE I'D HAD THE COURAGE TO TELL YOU THAT.
MAYBE IF I HAD, YOU WOULDA LISTENED. MAYBE WE COULDA SAVED EACH OTHER.

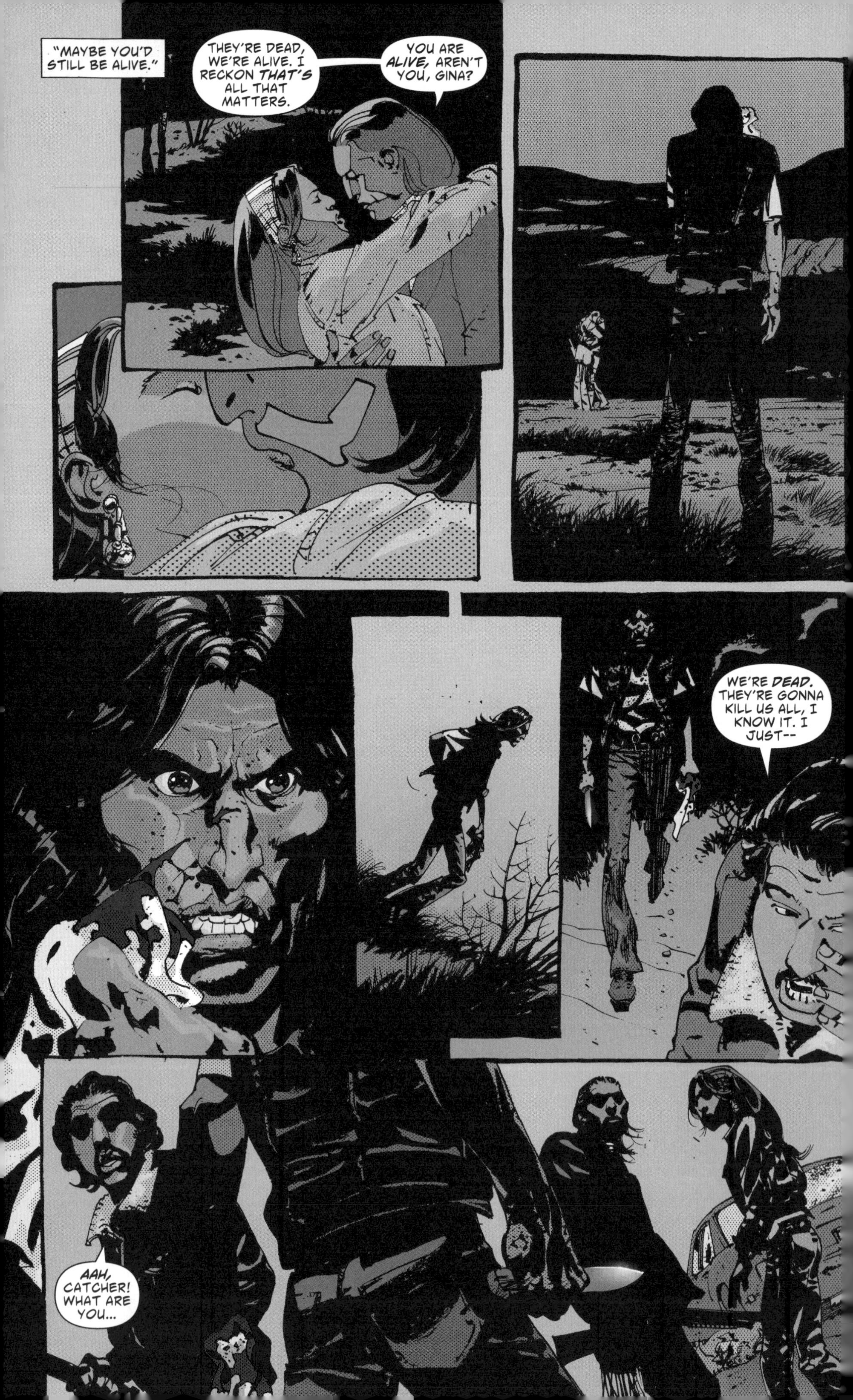
"MAYBE YOU'D STILL BE ALIVE."
THEY'RE DEAD, WE'RE ALIVE. I RECKON THAT'S ALL THAT MATTERS.
YOU ARE ALIVE, AREN'T YOU, GINA?
WE'RE DEAD. THEY'RE GONNA KILL US ALL, I KNOW IT. I JUST--
AAH, CATCHER! WHAT ARE YOU...

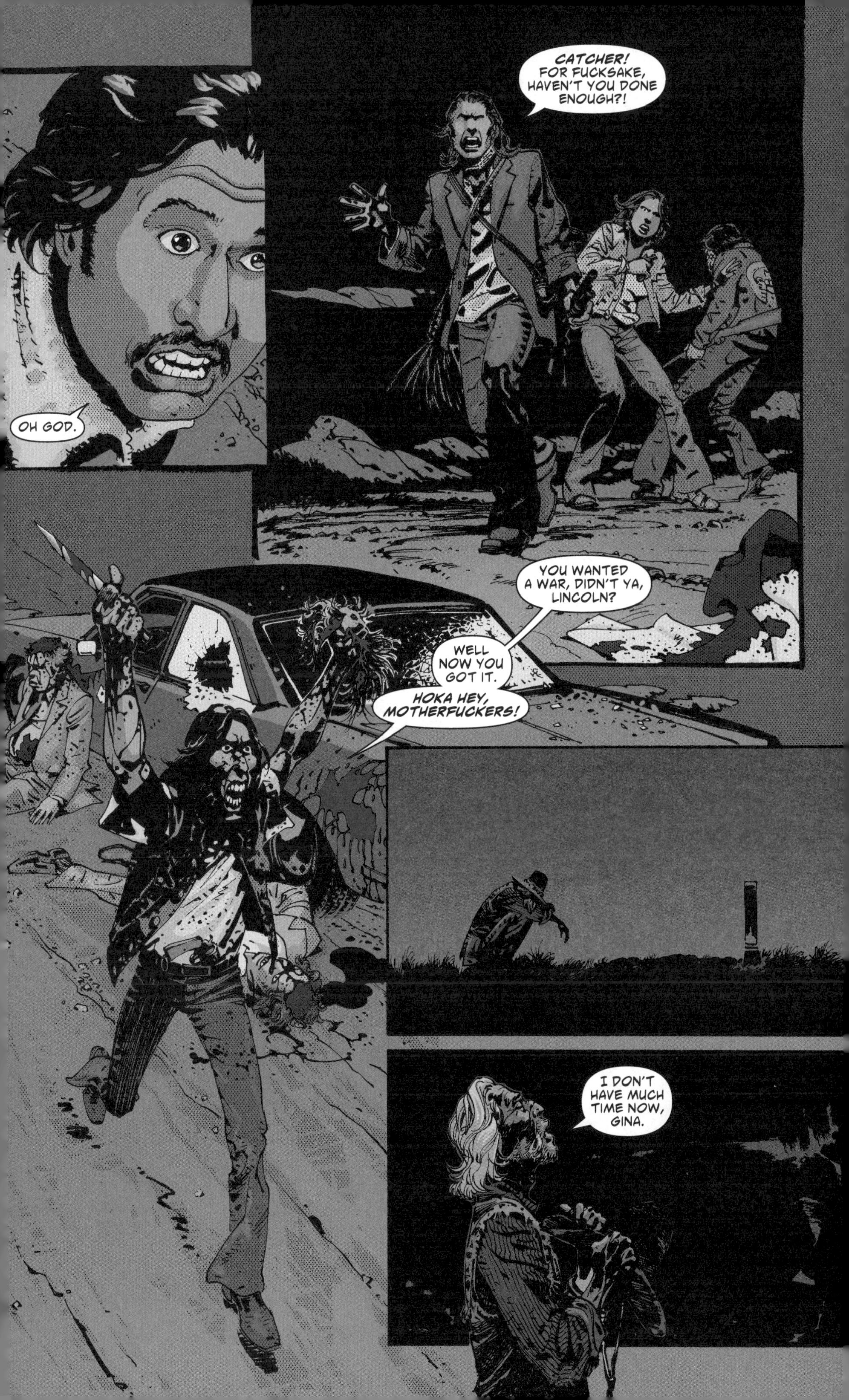
OH GOD.
CATCHER! FOR FUCKSAKE, HAVEN'T YOU DONE ENOUGH?!
YOU WANTED A WAR, DIDN'T YA, LINCOLN?
WELL NOW YOU GOT IT.
HOKA HEY, MOTHERFUCKERS!
I DON'T HAVE MUCH TIME NOW, GINA.

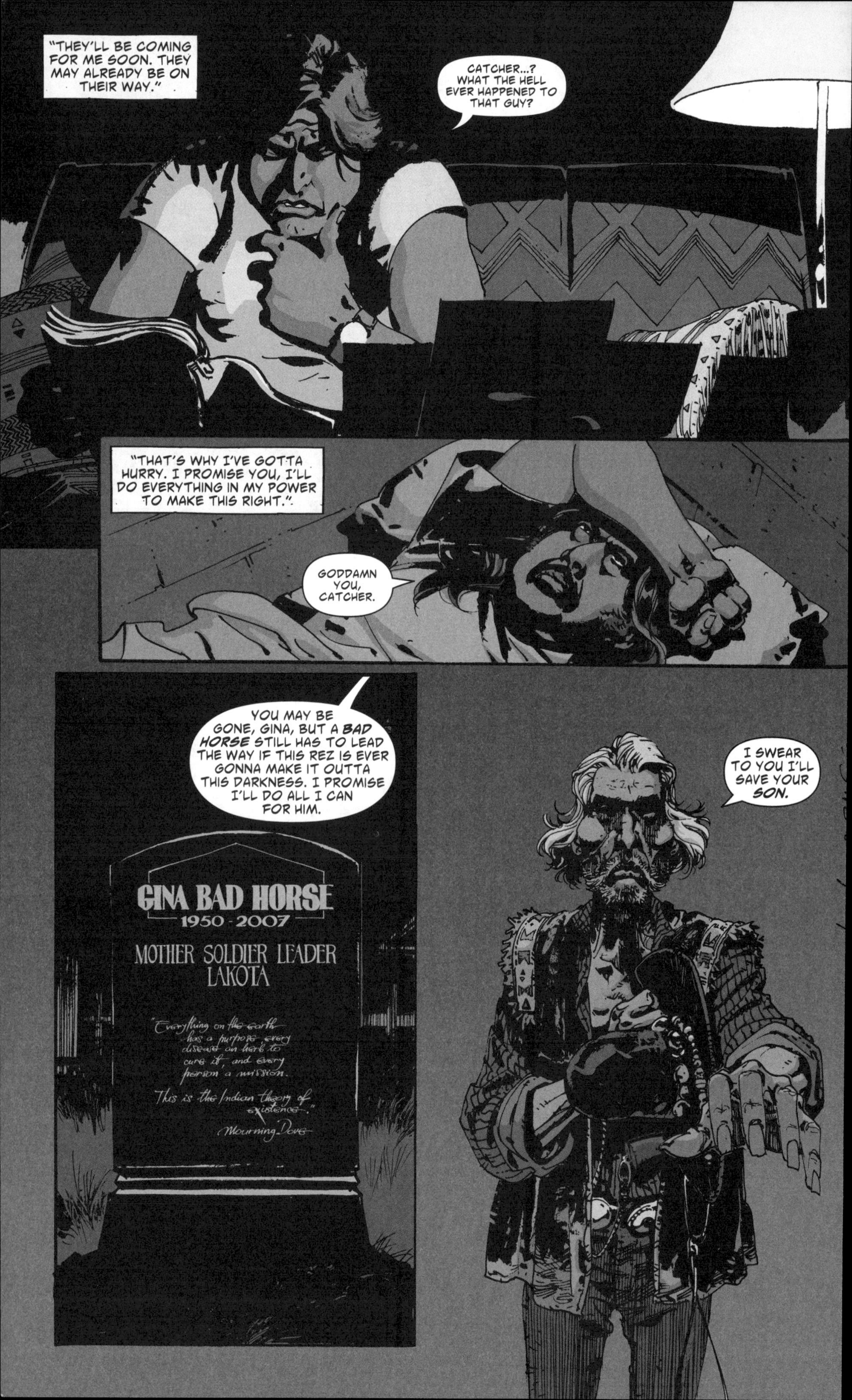
"THEY'LL BE COMING FOR ME SOON. THEY MAY ALREADY BE ON THEIR WAY."
CATCHER...? WHAT THE HELL EVER HAPPENED TO THAT GUY?
"THAT'S WHY I'VE GOTTA HURRY. I PROMISE YOU, I'LL DO EVERYTHING IN MY POWER TO MAKE THIS RIGHT."
GODDAMN YOU, CATCHER.
YOU MAY BE GONE, GINA, BUT A BAD HORSE STILL HAS TO LEAD THE WAY IF THIS REZ IS EVER GONNA MAKE IT OUTTA THIS DARKNESS. I PROMISE I'LL DO ALL I CAN FOR HIM.
I SWEAR TO YOU I'LL SAVE YOUR SON.
GINA BAD HORSE
1950 - 2007
MOTHER SOLDIER LEADER
LAKOTA
"Everything on the earth has a purpose, every disease an herb to cure it, and every person a mission.
This is the Indian theory of existence."
Mourning Dove

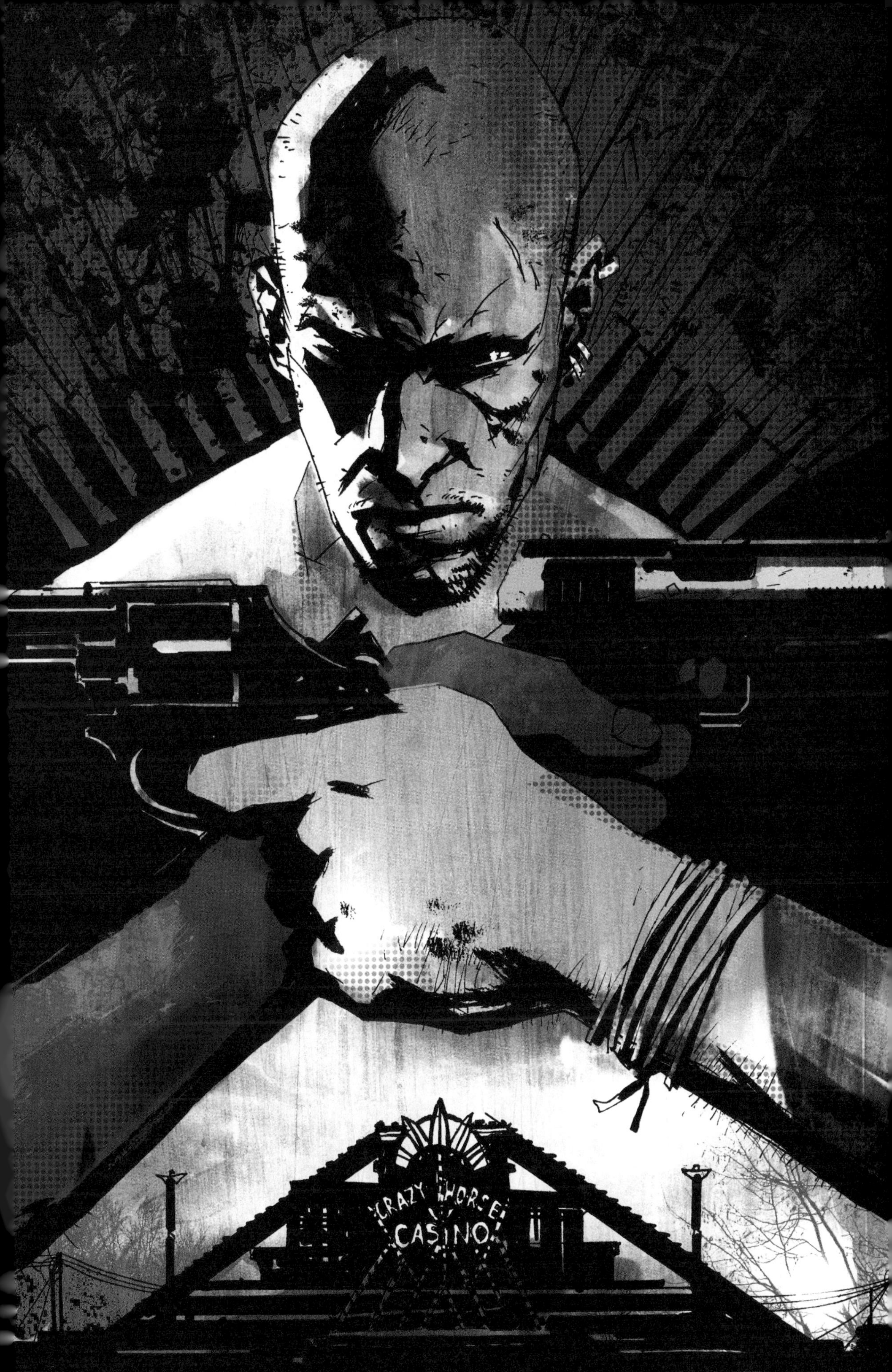
CRAZY HORSE
CASINO

ROCK BOTTOM, POP. 1

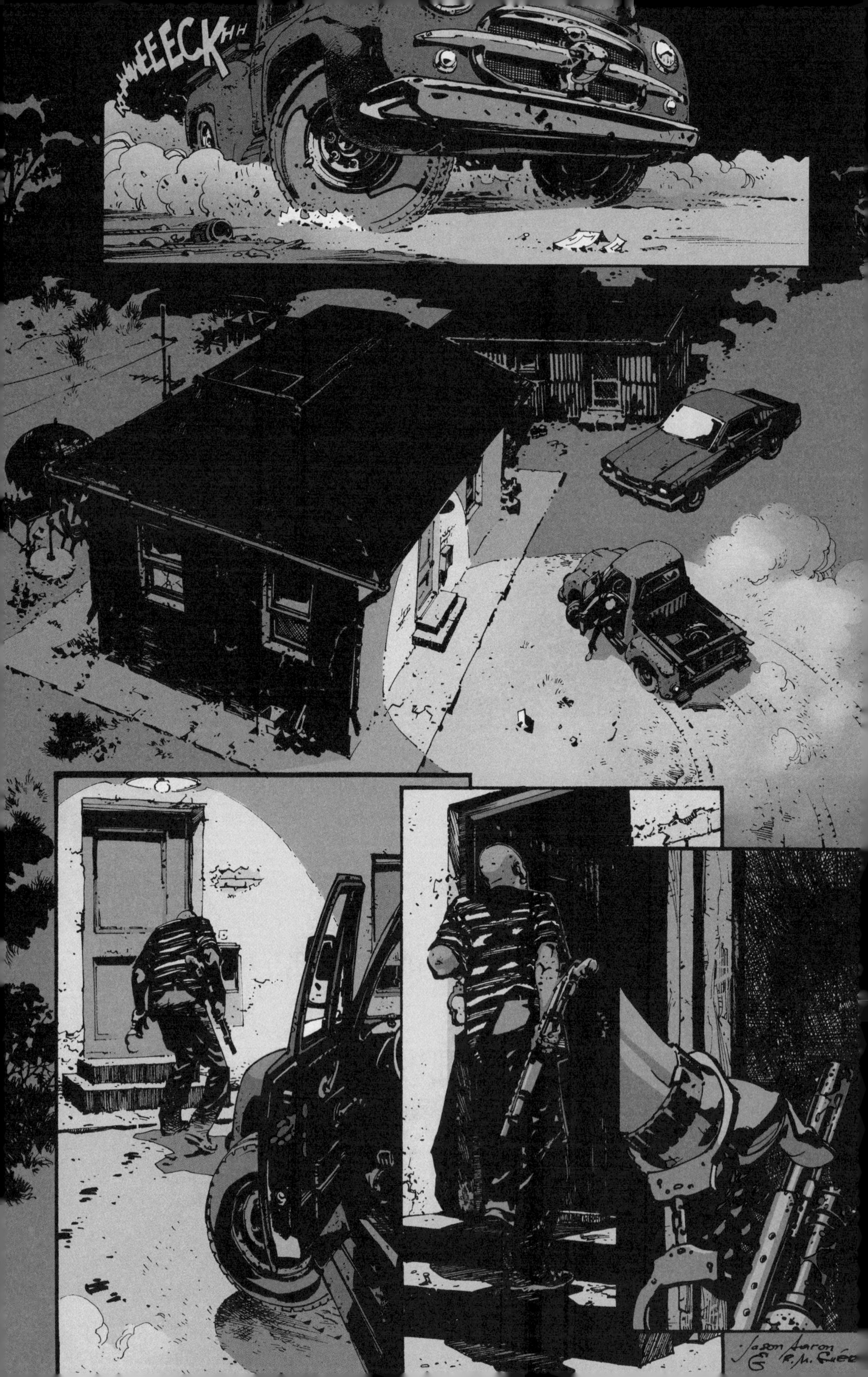

WEEECKHH
Jason Aaron
R.M. Guéra

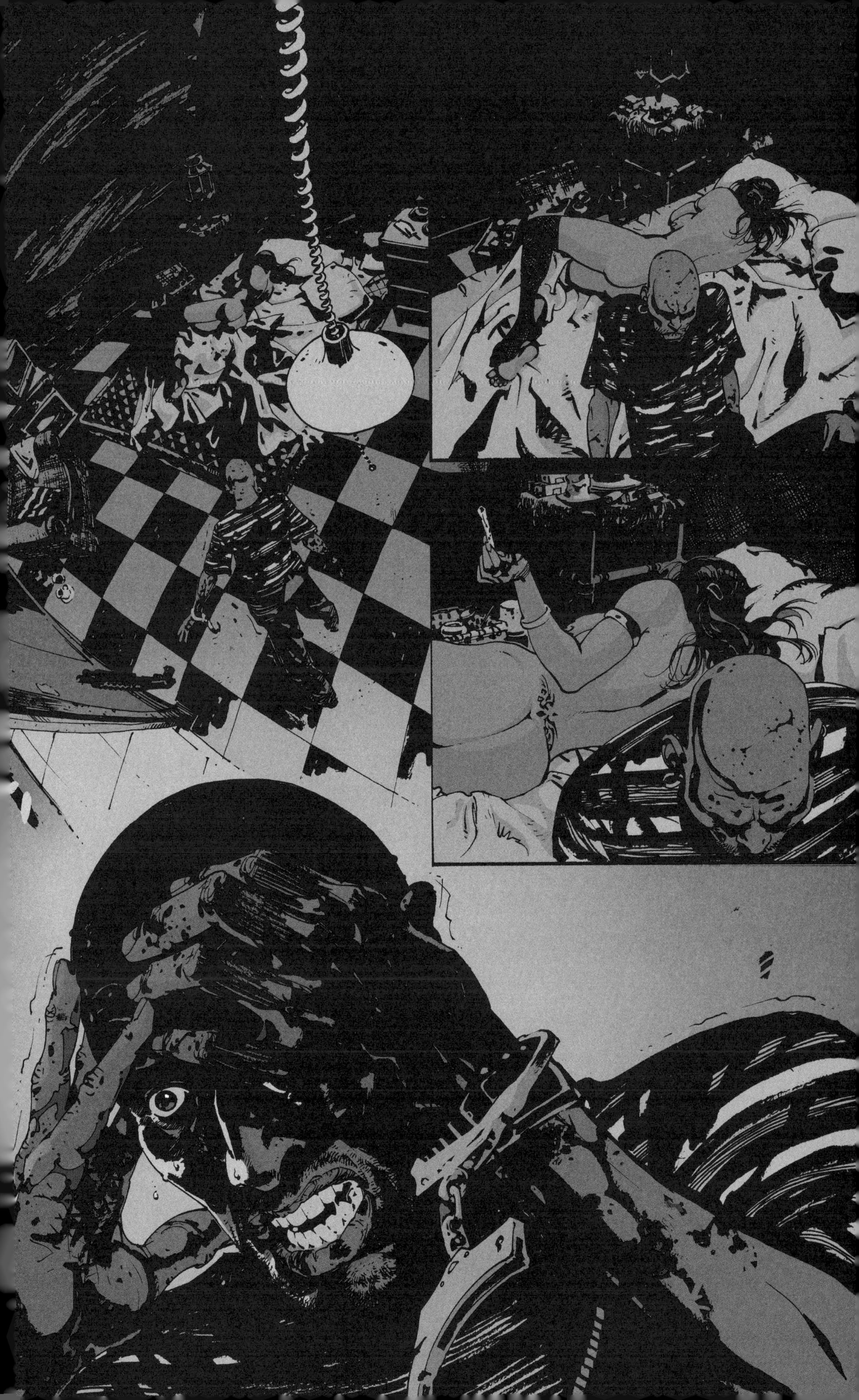

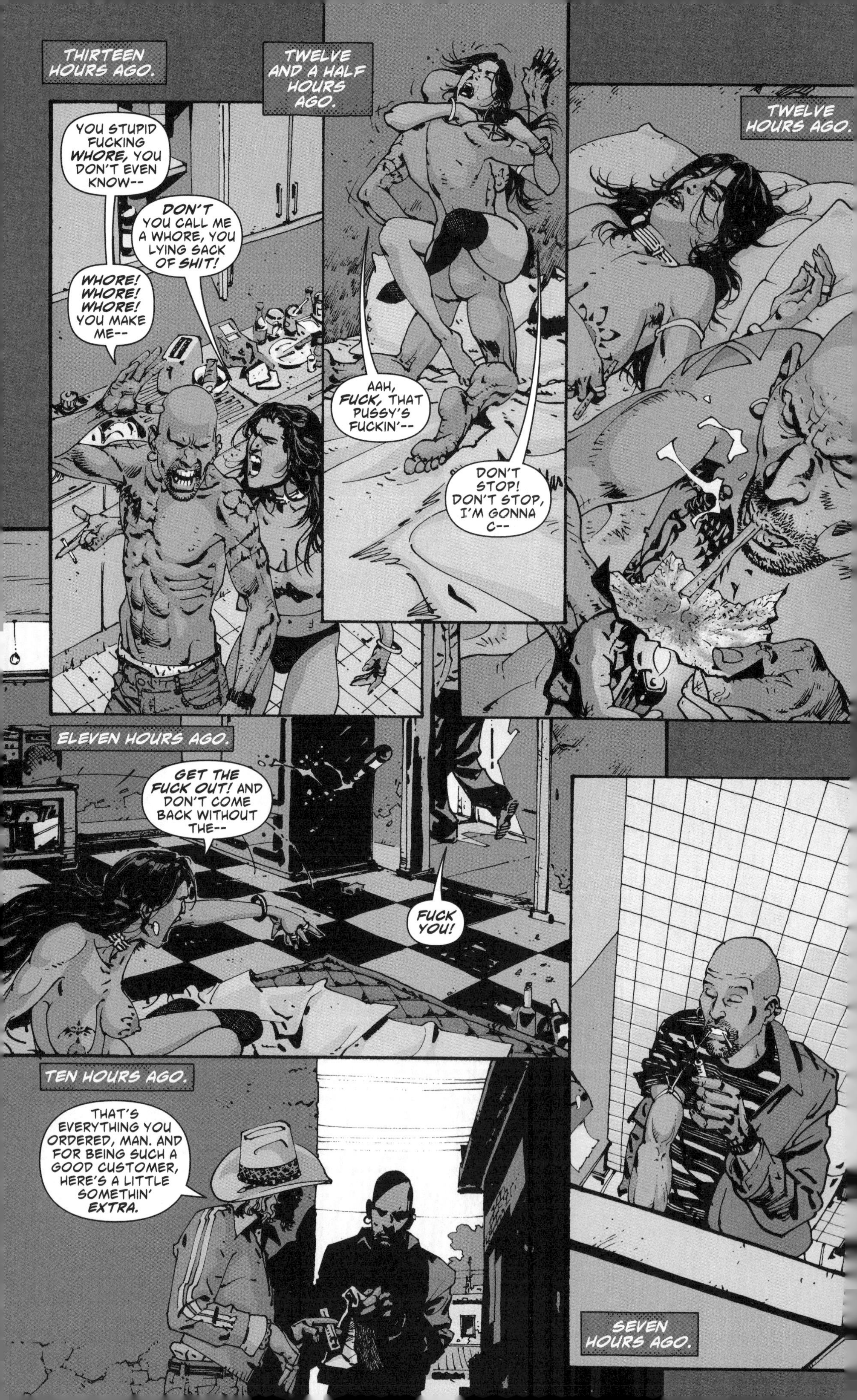

THIRTEEN HOURS AGO.
YOU STUPID FUCKING WHORE, YOU DON'T EVEN KNOW--
DON'T YOU CALL ME A WHORE, YOU LYING SACK OF SHIT!
WHORE! WHORE! WHORE! YOU MAKE ME--
TWELVE AND A HALF HOURS AGO.
AAH, FUCK, THAT PUSSY'S FUCKIN'--
DON'T STOP! DON'T STOP, I'M GONNA C--
TWELVE HOURS AGO.
ELEVEN HOURS AGO.
GET THE FUCK OUT! AND DON'T COME BACK WITHOUT THE--
FUCK YOU!
TEN HOURS AGO.
THAT'S EVERYTHING YOU ORDERED, MAN. AND FOR BEING SUCH A GOOD CUSTOMER, HERE'S A LITTLE SOMETHIN' EXTRA.
SEVEN HOURS AGO.

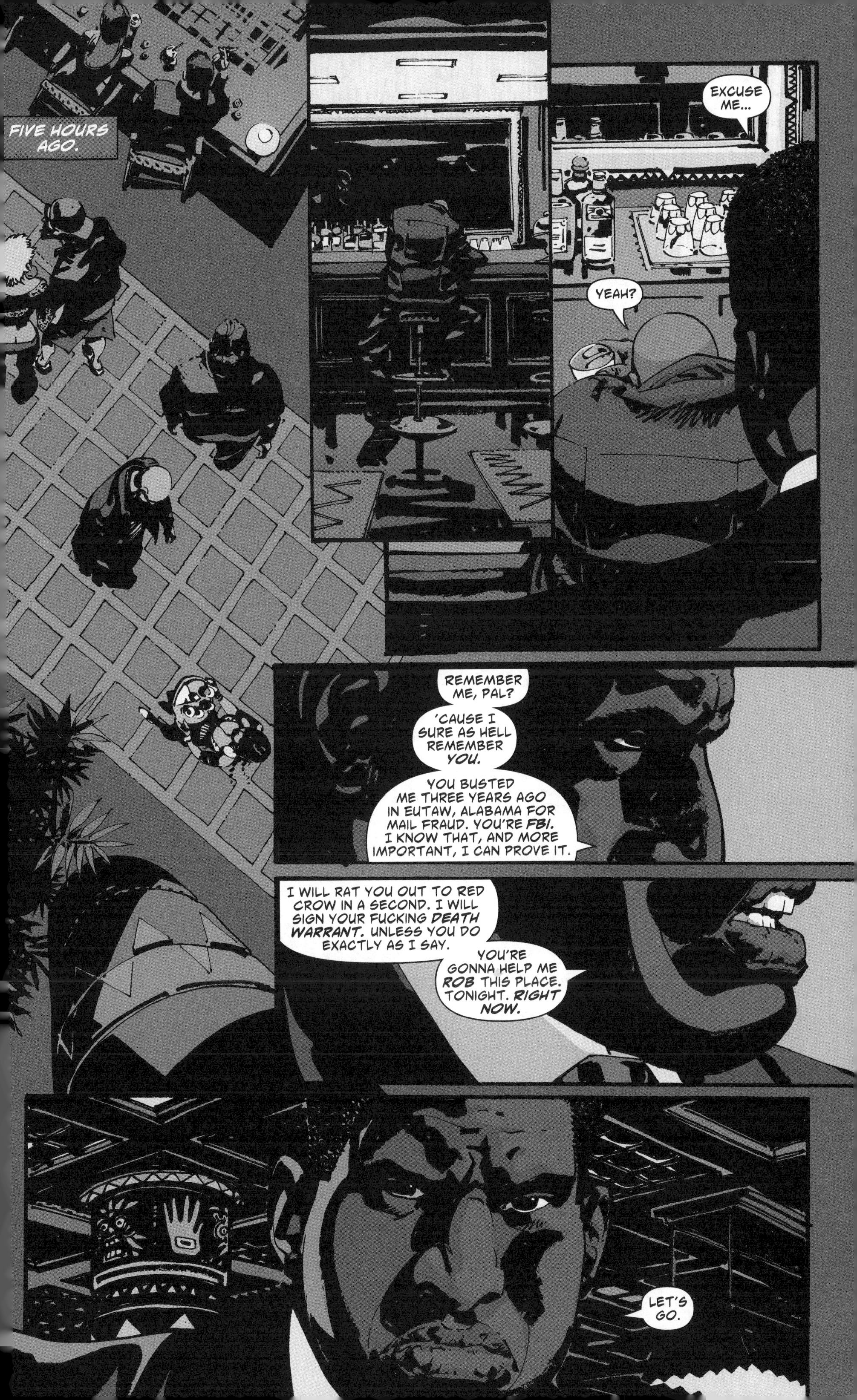
FIVE HOURS AGO.
EXCUSE ME...
YEAH?
REMEMBER ME, PAL?
'CAUSE I SURE AS HELL REMEMBER *YOU.*
YOU BUSTED ME THREE YEARS AGO IN EUTAW, ALABAMA FOR MAIL FRAUD. YOU'RE *FBI.* I KNOW THAT, AND MORE IMPORTANT, I CAN PROVE IT.
I WILL RAT YOU OUT TO RED CROW IN A SECOND. I WILL SIGN YOUR FUCKING *DEATH WARRANT.* UNLESS YOU DO EXACTLY AS I SAY.
YOU'RE GONNA HELP ME *ROB* THIS PLACE. TONIGHT. *RIGHT NOW.*
LET'S GO.

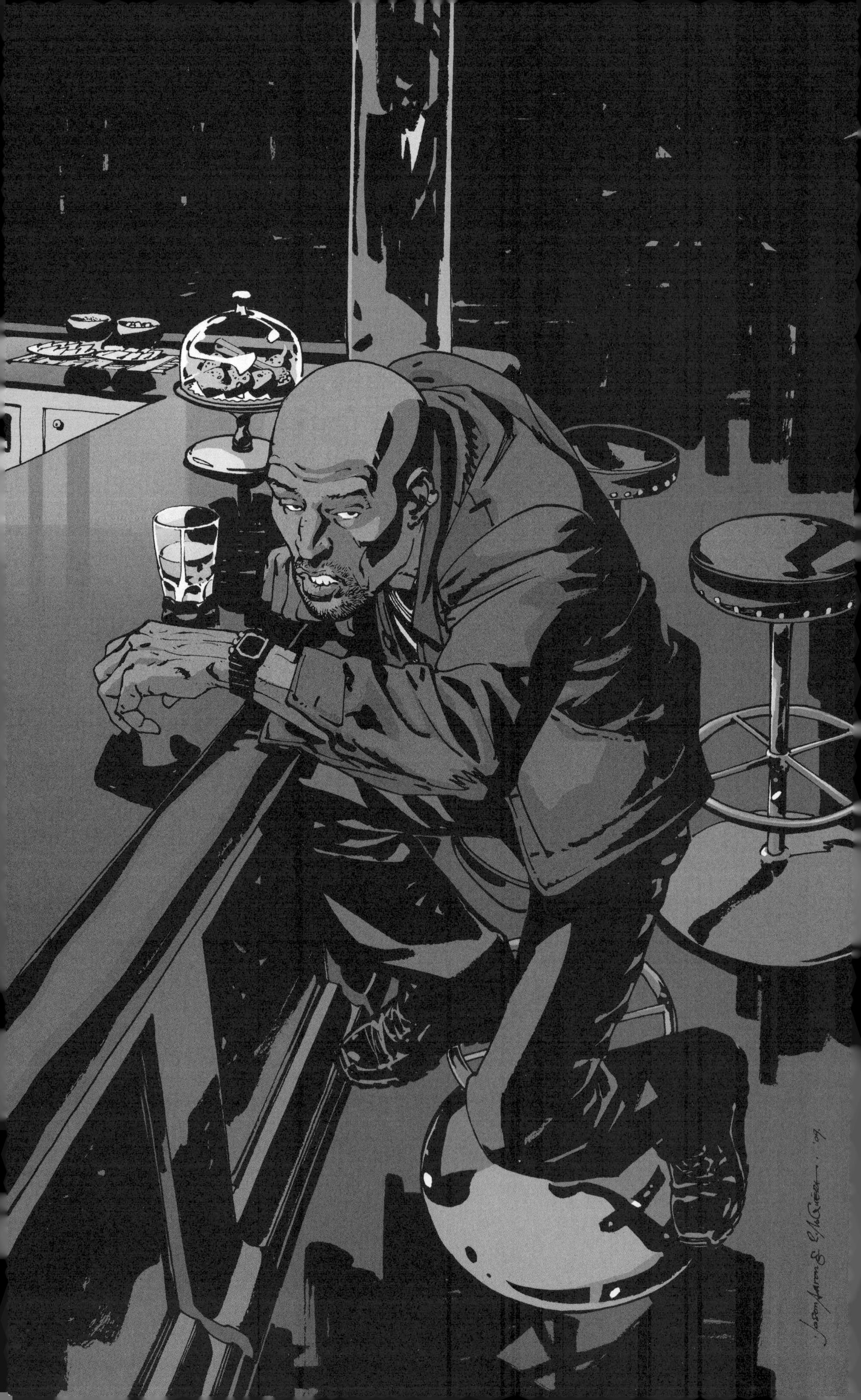

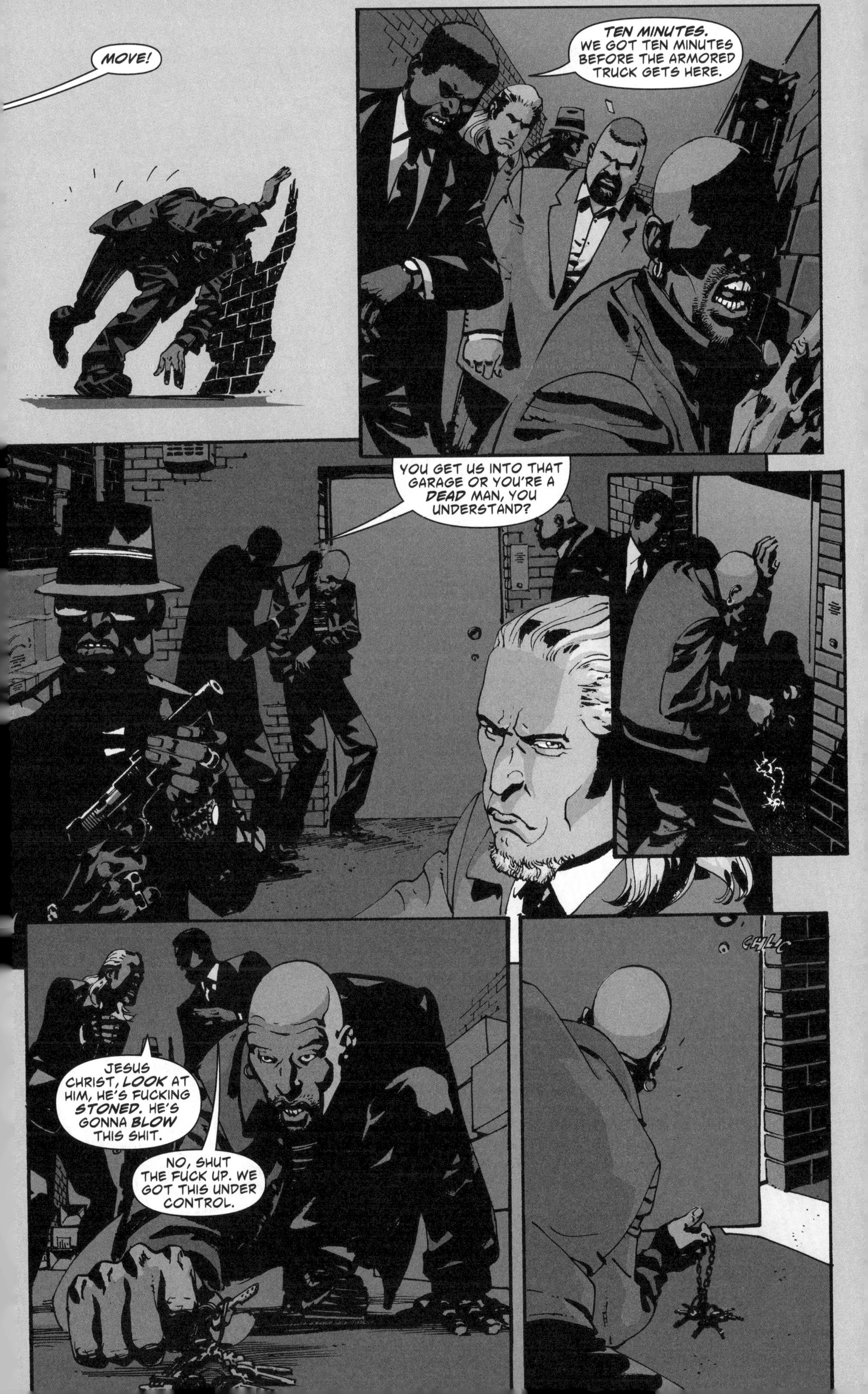
MOVE!
TEN MINUTES. WE GOT TEN MINUTES BEFORE THE ARMORED TRUCK GETS HERE.
YOU GET US INTO THAT GARAGE OR YOU'RE A DEAD MAN, YOU UNDERSTAND?
JESUS CHRIST, LOOK AT HIM, HE'S FUCKING STONED. HE'S GONNA BLOW THIS SHIT.
NO, SHUT THE FUCK UP. WE GOT THIS UNDER CONTROL.
CHLIC

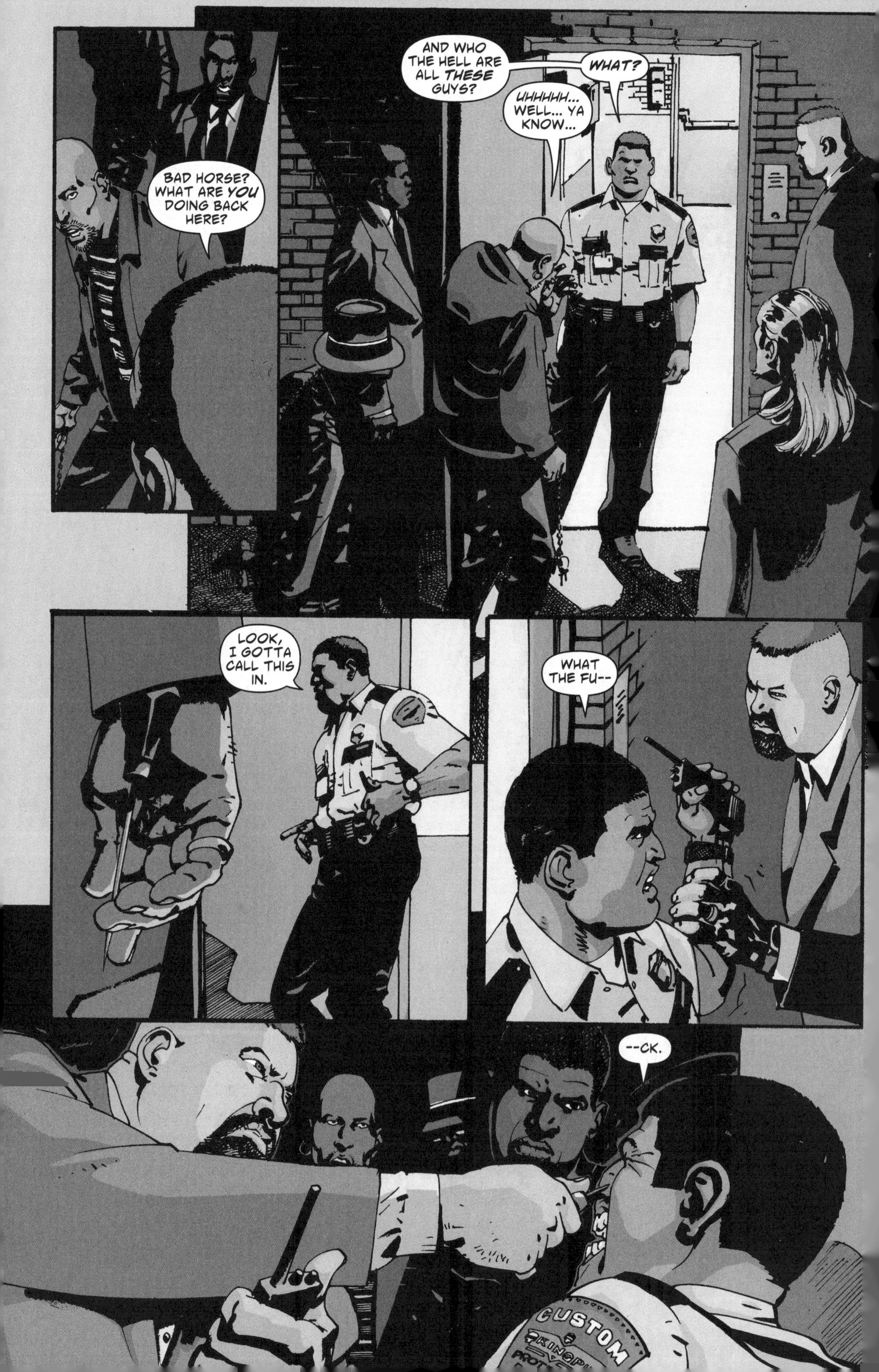
BAD HORSE? WHAT ARE YOU DOING BACK HERE?
AND WHO THE HELL ARE ALL THESE GUYS?
WHAT?
UHHHHH... WELL... YA KNOW...
LOOK, I GOTTA CALL THIS IN.
WHAT THE FU--
--CK.
CUSTOM

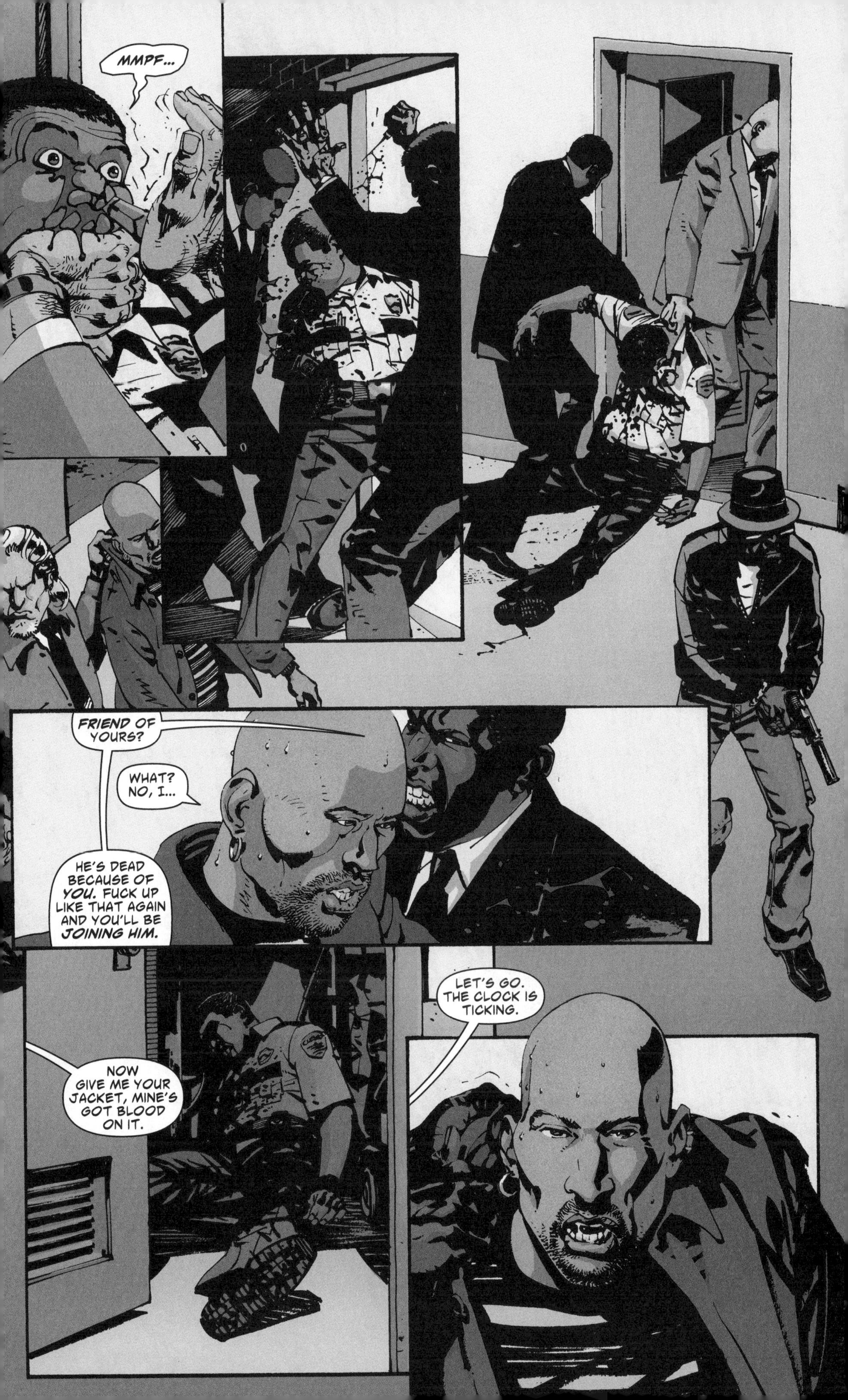
MMPF...
FRIEND OF YOURS?
WHAT? NO, I...
HE'S DEAD BECAUSE OF YOU. FUCK UP LIKE THAT AGAIN AND YOU'LL BE JOINING HIM.
NOW GIVE ME YOUR JACKET, MINE'S GOT BLOOD ON IT.
LET'S GO. THE CLOCK IS TICKING.

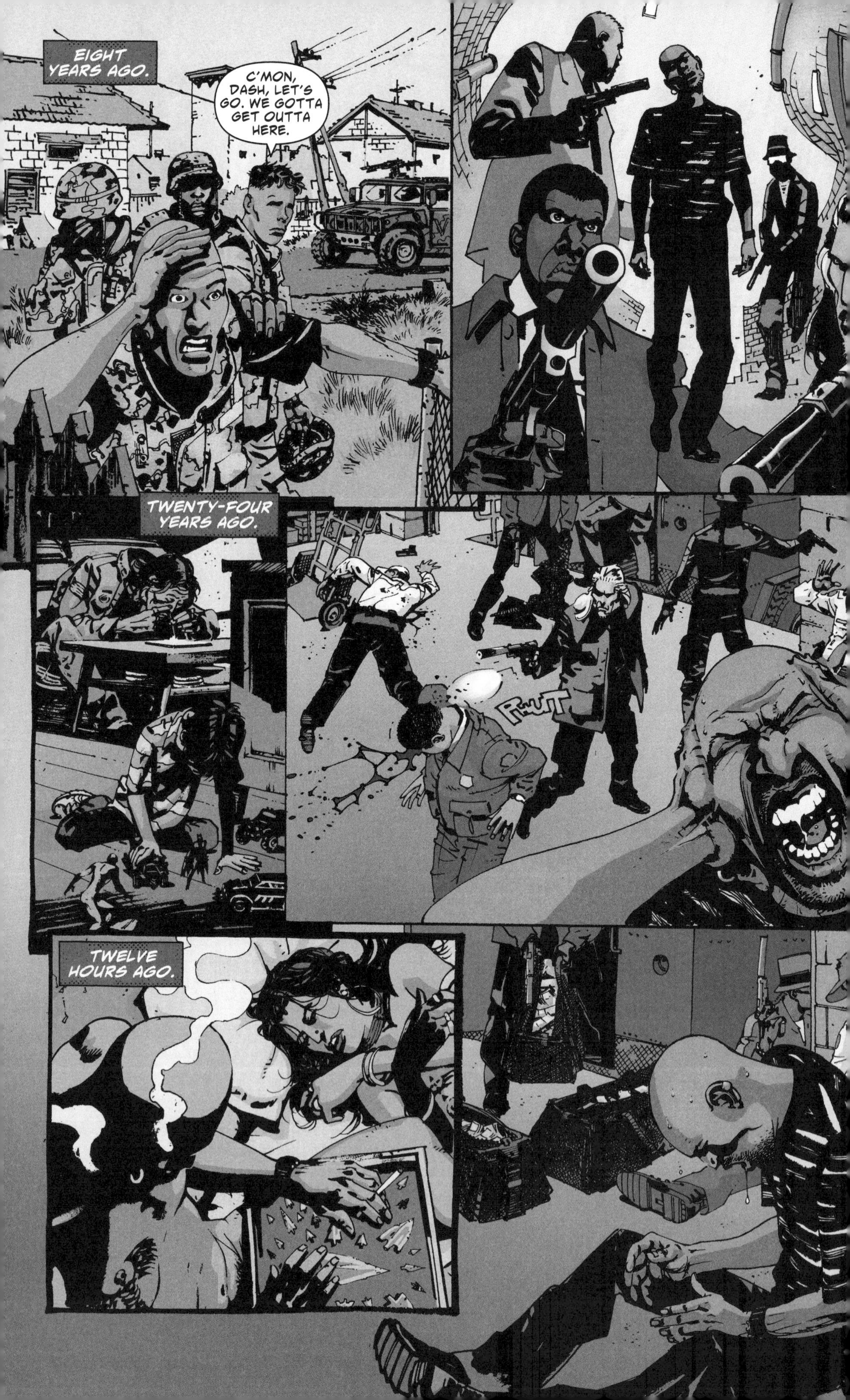
EIGHT YEARS AGO.
C'MON, DASH, LET'S GO. WE GOTTA GET OUTTA HERE.
TWENTY-FOUR YEARS AGO.
PFUT
TWELVE HOURS AGO.

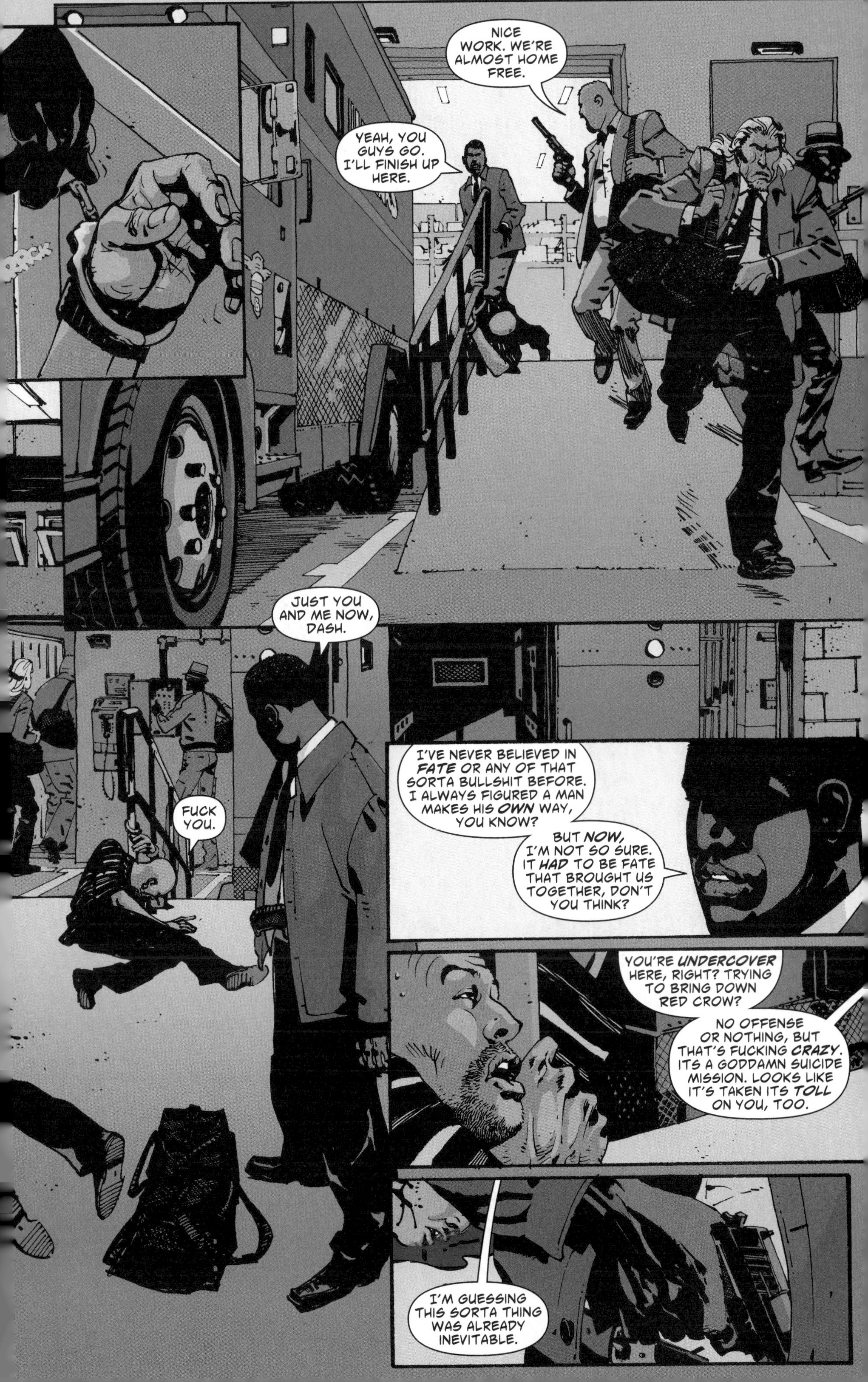
KRACK
NICE WORK. WE'RE ALMOST HOME FREE.
YEAH, YOU GUYS GO. I'LL FINISH UP HERE.
JUST YOU AND ME NOW, DASH.
FUCK YOU.
I'VE NEVER BELIEVED IN FATE OR ANY OF THAT SORTA BULLSHIT BEFORE. I ALWAYS FIGURED A MAN MAKES HIS OWN WAY, YOU KNOW?
BUT NOW, I'M NOT SO SURE. IT HAD TO BE FATE THAT BROUGHT US TOGETHER, DON'T YOU THINK?
YOU'RE UNDERCOVER HERE, RIGHT? TRYING TO BRING DOWN RED CROW?
NO OFFENSE OR NOTHING, BUT THAT'S FUCKING CRAZY. ITS A GODDAMN SUICIDE MISSION. LOOKS LIKE IT'S TAKEN ITS TOLL ON YOU, TOO.
I'M GUESSING THIS SORTA THING WAS ALREADY INEVITABLE.

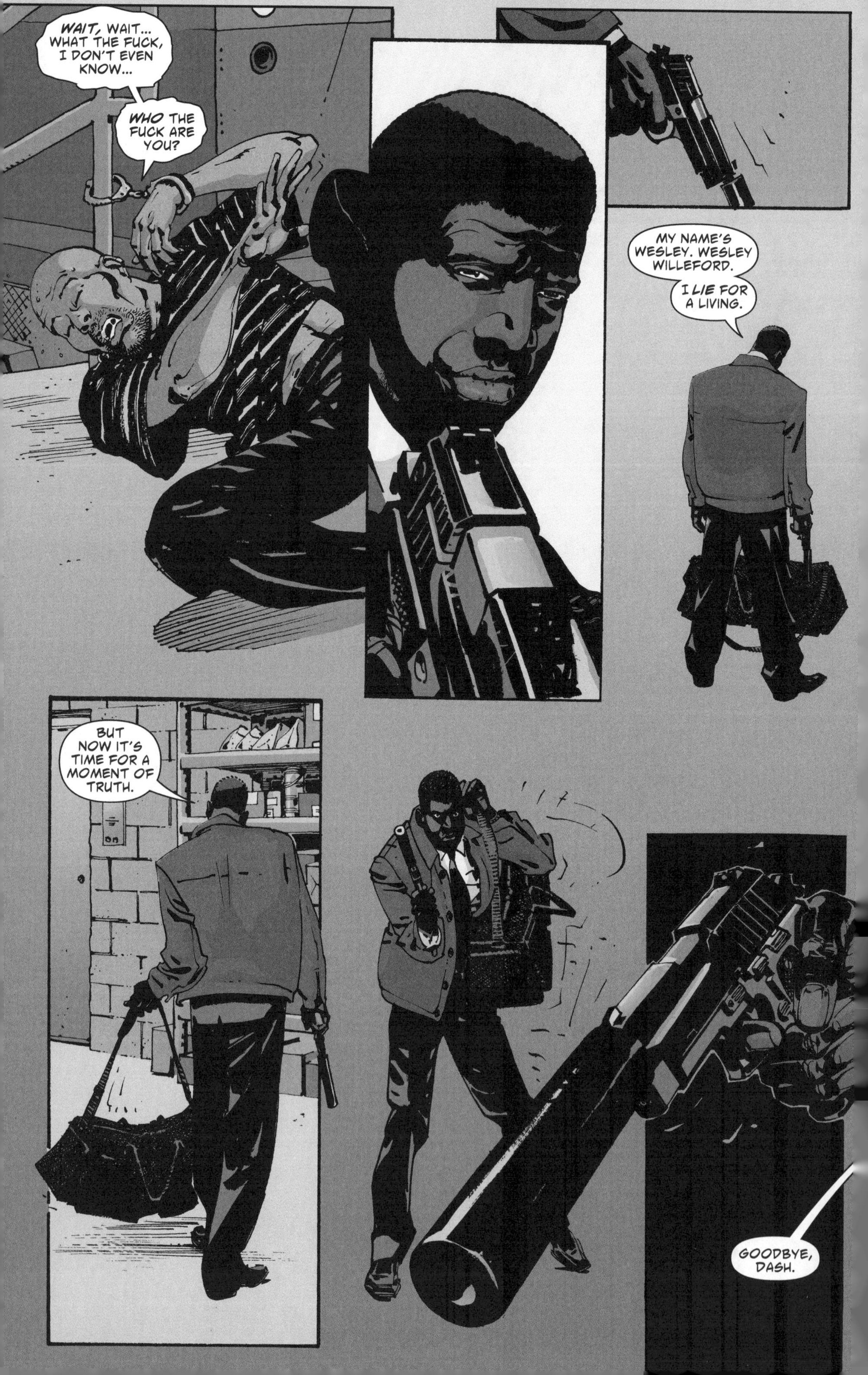
WAIT, WAIT... WHAT THE FUCK, I DON'T EVEN KNOW...
WHO THE FUCK ARE YOU?
MY NAME'S WESLEY. WESLEY WILLEFORD.
I LIE FOR A LIVING.
BUT NOW IT'S TIME FOR A MOMENT OF TRUTH.
GOODBYE, DASH.

UURRRRRᴿ

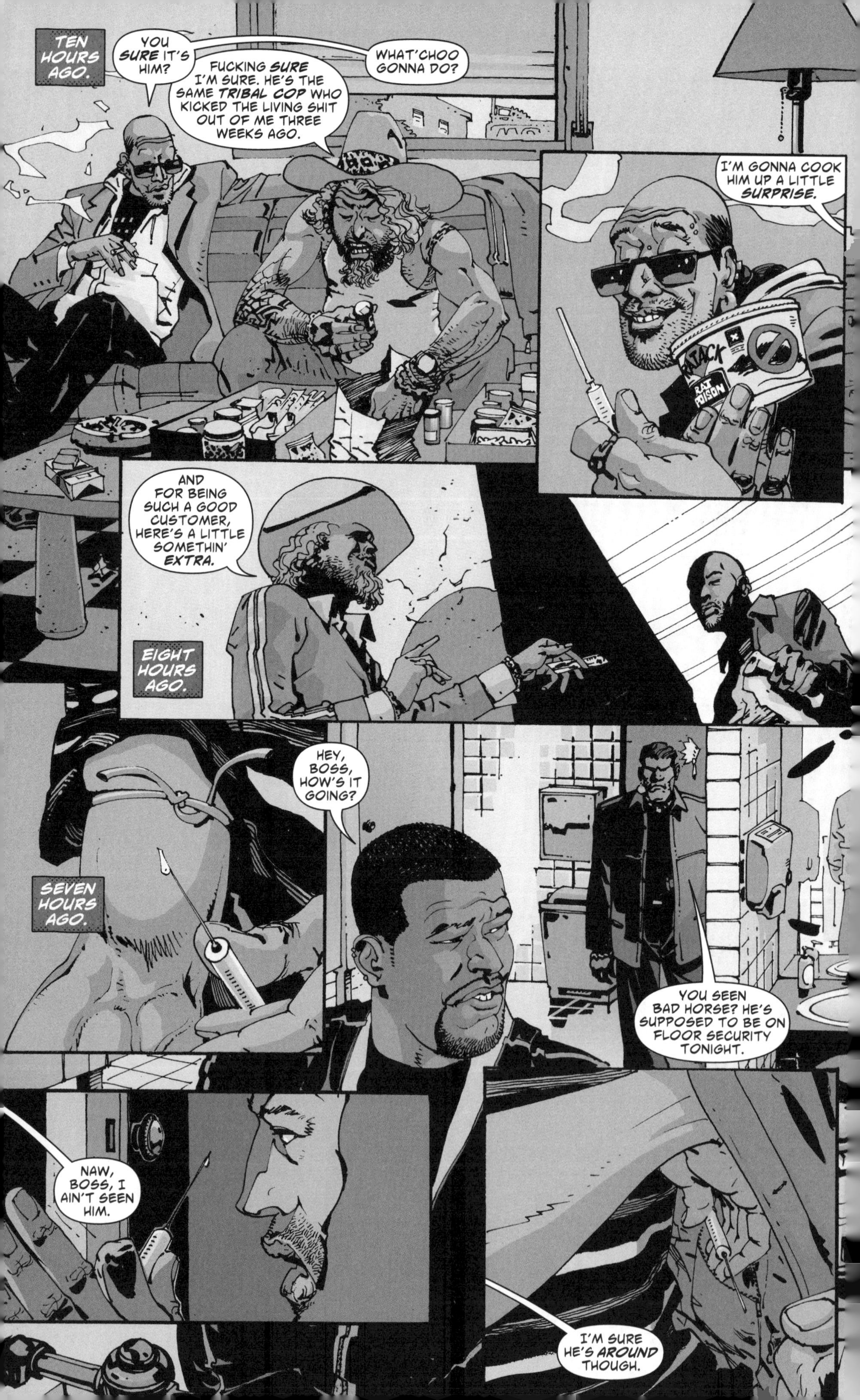
TEN HOURS AGO.
YOU SURE IT'S HIM?
FUCKING SURE I'M SURE. HE'S THE SAME TRIBAL COP WHO KICKED THE LIVING SHIT OUT OF ME THREE WEEKS AGO.
WHAT'CHOO GONNA DO?
I'M GONNA COOK HIM UP A LITTLE SURPRISE.
RAT POISON
AND FOR BEING SUCH A GOOD CUSTOMER, HERE'S A LITTLE SOMETHIN' EXTRA.
EIGHT HOURS AGO.
SEVEN HOURS AGO.
HEY, BOSS, HOW'S IT GOING?
YOU SEEN BAD HORSE? HE'S SUPPOSED TO BE ON FLOOR SECURITY TONIGHT.
NAW, BOSS, I AIN'T SEEN HIM.
I'M SURE HE'S AROUND THOUGH.

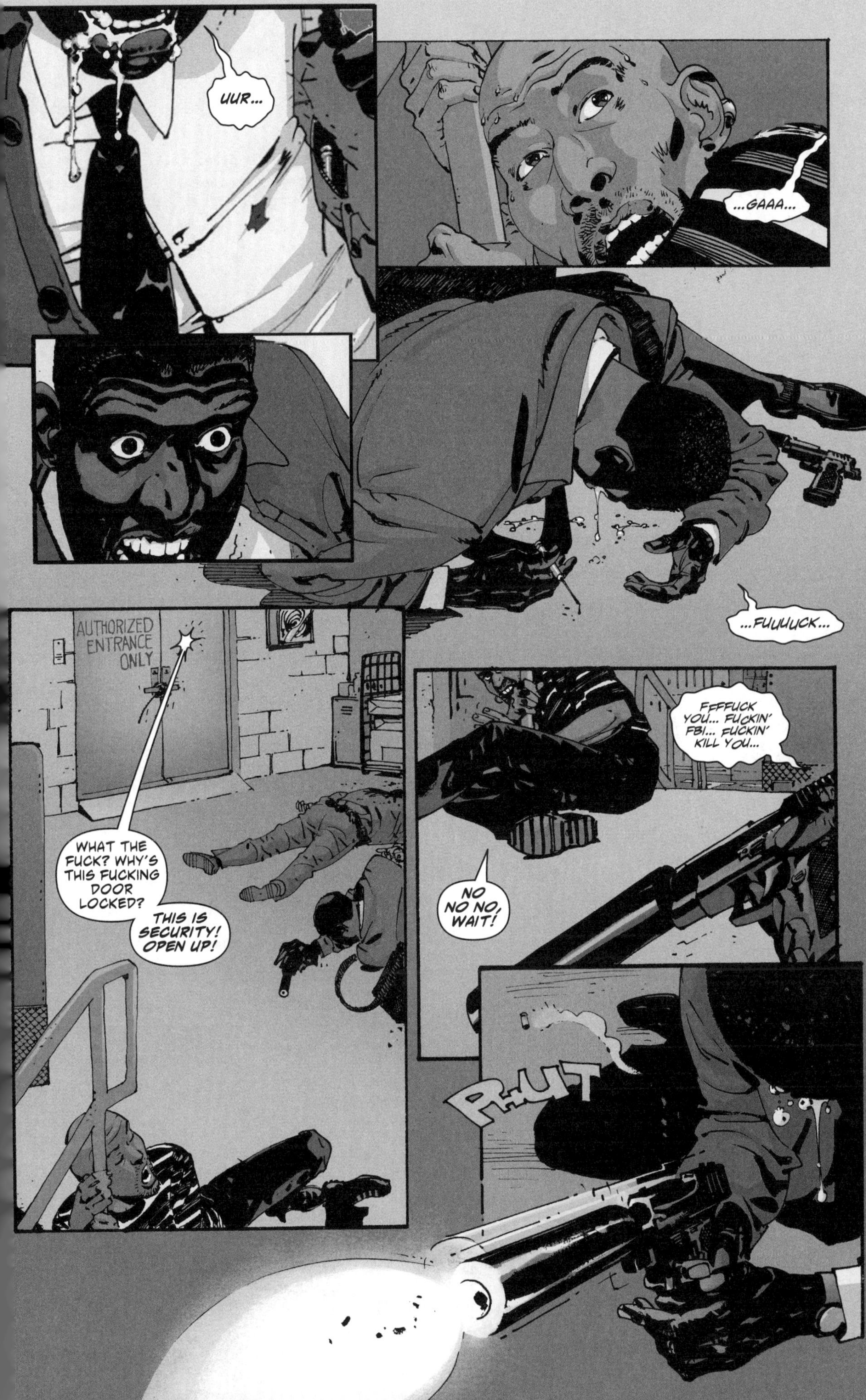
UUR...
...GAAA...
...FUUUUCK...
AUTHORIZED ENTRANCE ONLY
WHAT THE FUCK? WHY'S THIS FUCKING DOOR LOCKED?
THIS IS SECURITY! OPEN UP!
FFFFUCK YOU... FUCKIN' FBI... FUCKIN' KILL YOU...
NO NO NO, WAIT!
P-UT

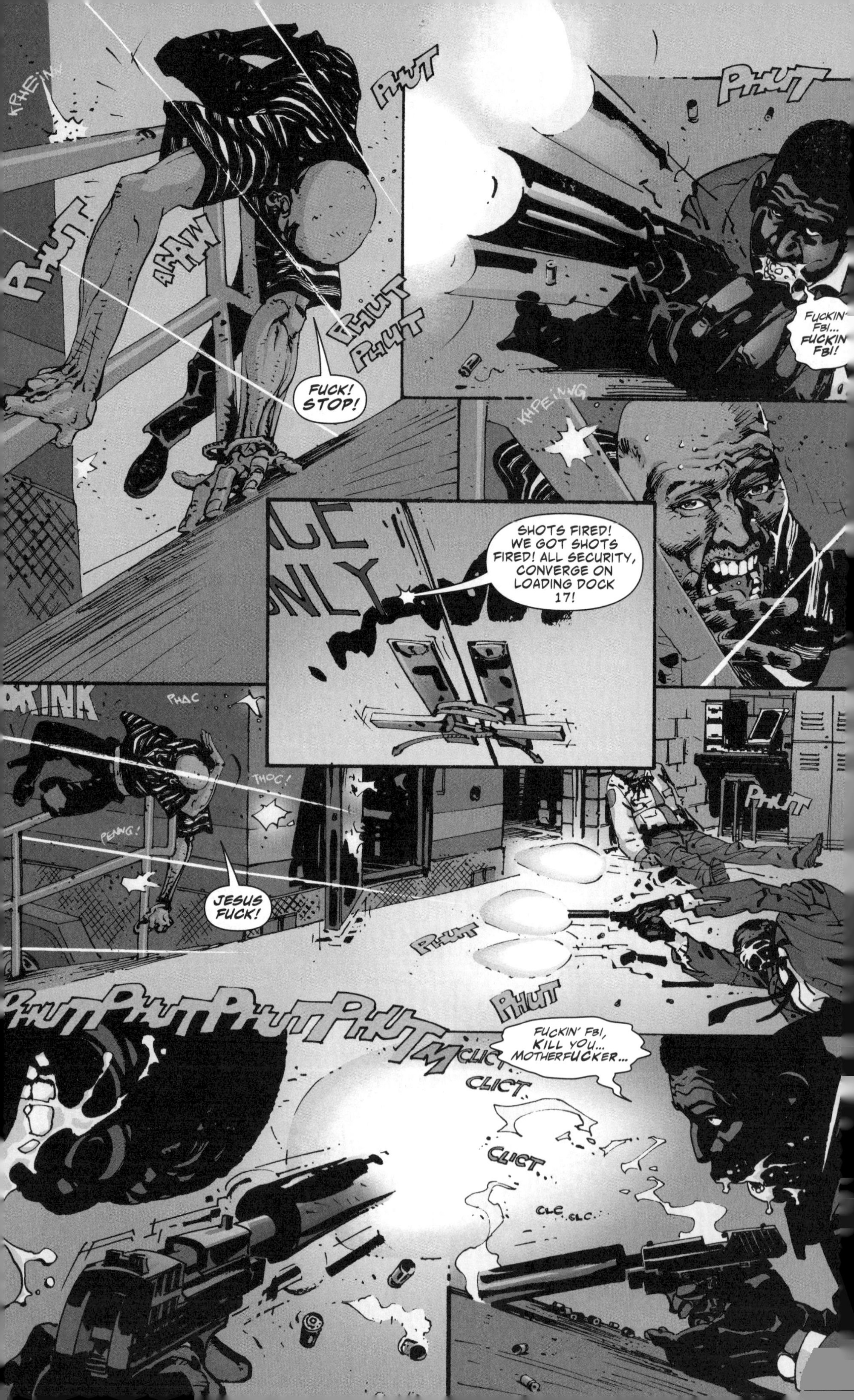
KPHEINN
PHUT
PHUT
AAAAH
PHUT
PHUT
FUCK! STOP!
PHUT
FUCKIN' FBI... FUCKIN' FBI!
KHPEINNG
SHOTS FIRED! WE GOT SHOTS FIRED! ALL SECURITY, CONVERGE ON LOADING DOCK 17!
PHAC
THOC!
PENNG!
JESUS FUCK!
PHUT
PHUT
PHUT
PHUTPHUTPHUTPHUT
FUCKIN' FBI, KILL YOU... MOTHERFUCKER...
CLICT
CLICT
CLICT...
CLC CLC

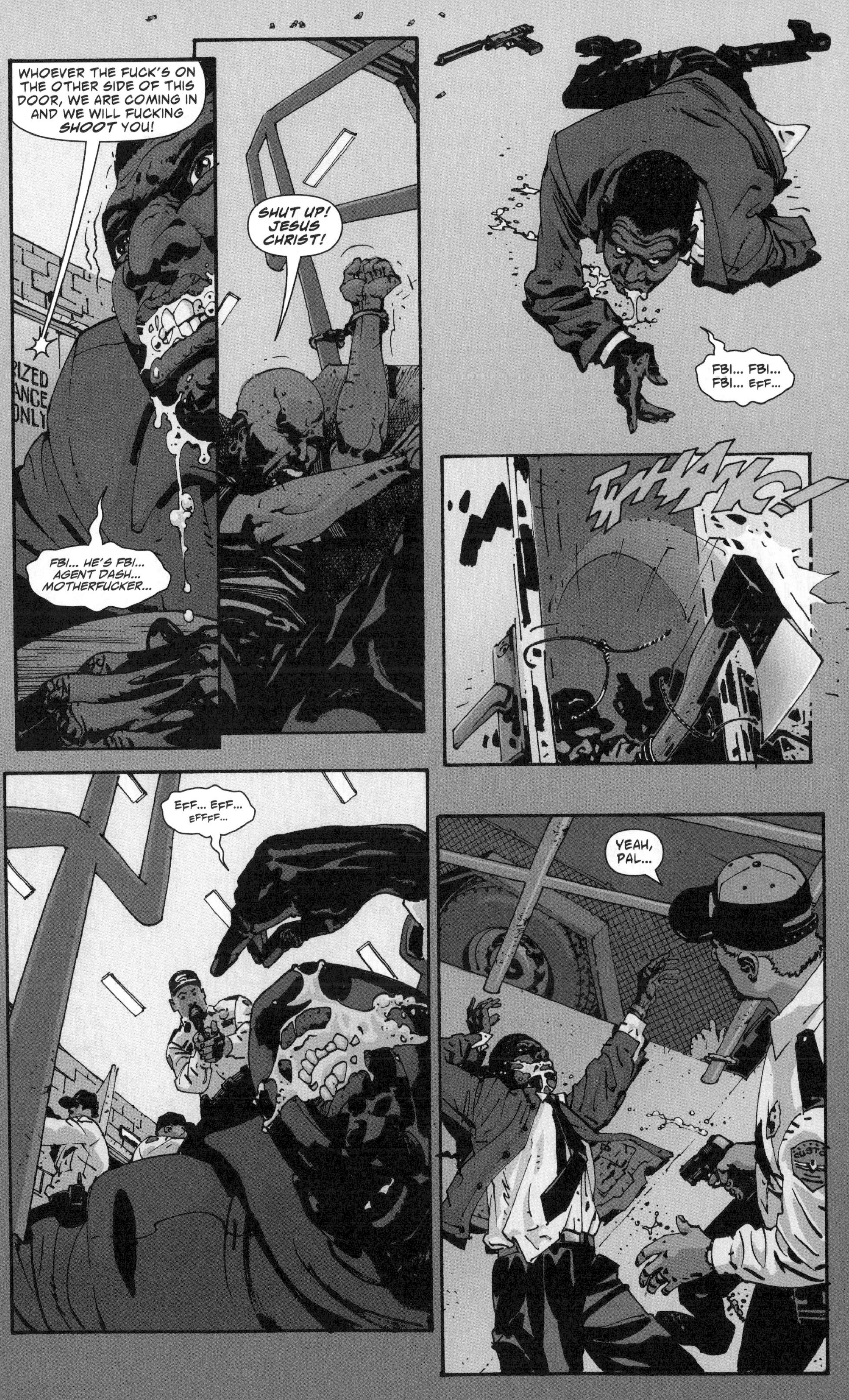

WHOEVER THE FUCK'S ON THE OTHER SIDE OF THIS DOOR, WE ARE COMING IN AND WE WILL FUCKING SHOOT YOU!
SHUT UP! JESUS CHRIST!
FBI... HE'S FBI... AGENT DASH... MOTHERFUCKER...
FBI... FBI... FBI... EFF...
THHANG!!
EFF... EFF... EFFFF...
YEAH, PAL...

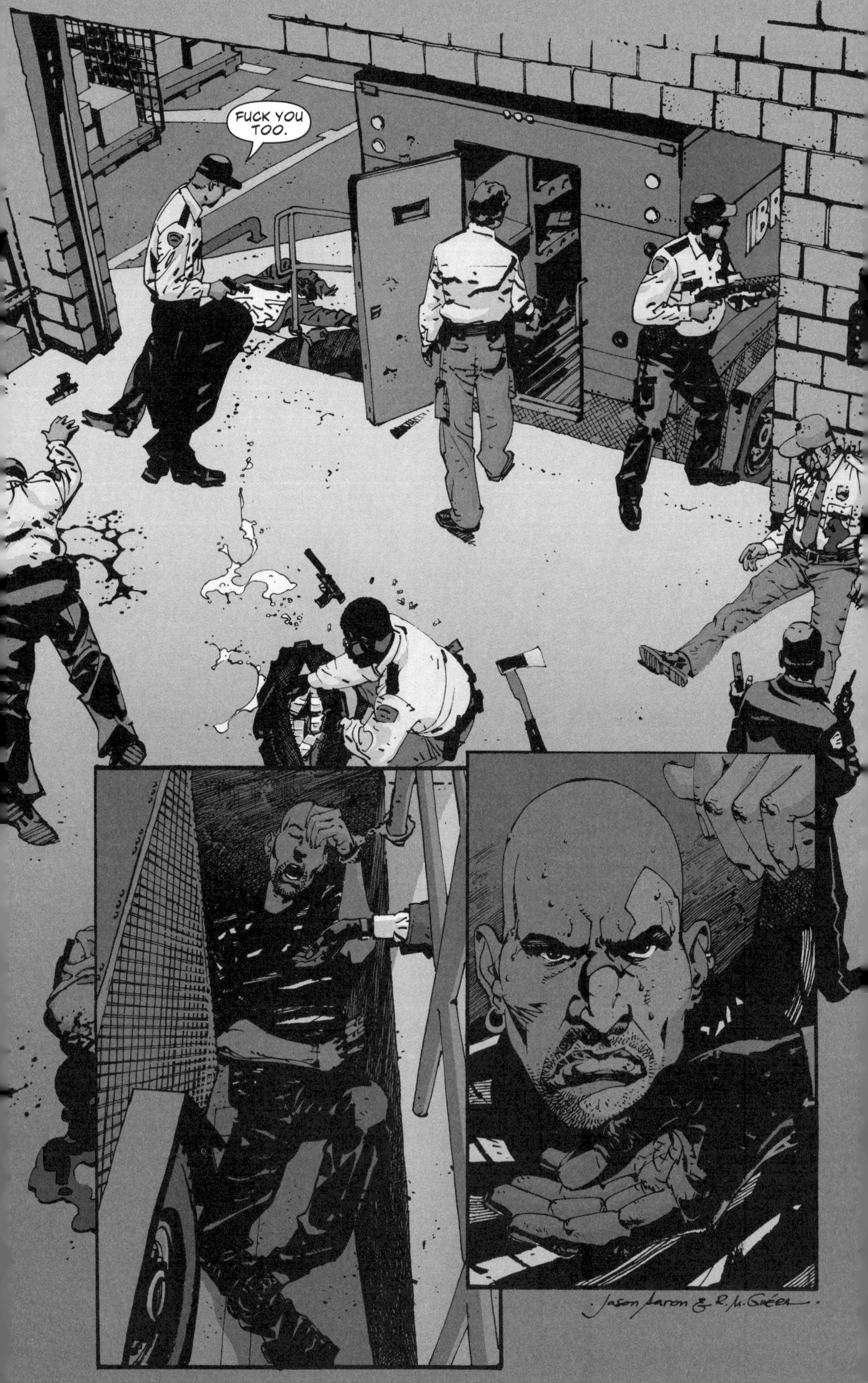
FUCK YOU TOO.
IIBR
Jason Aaron & R.M. Guéra

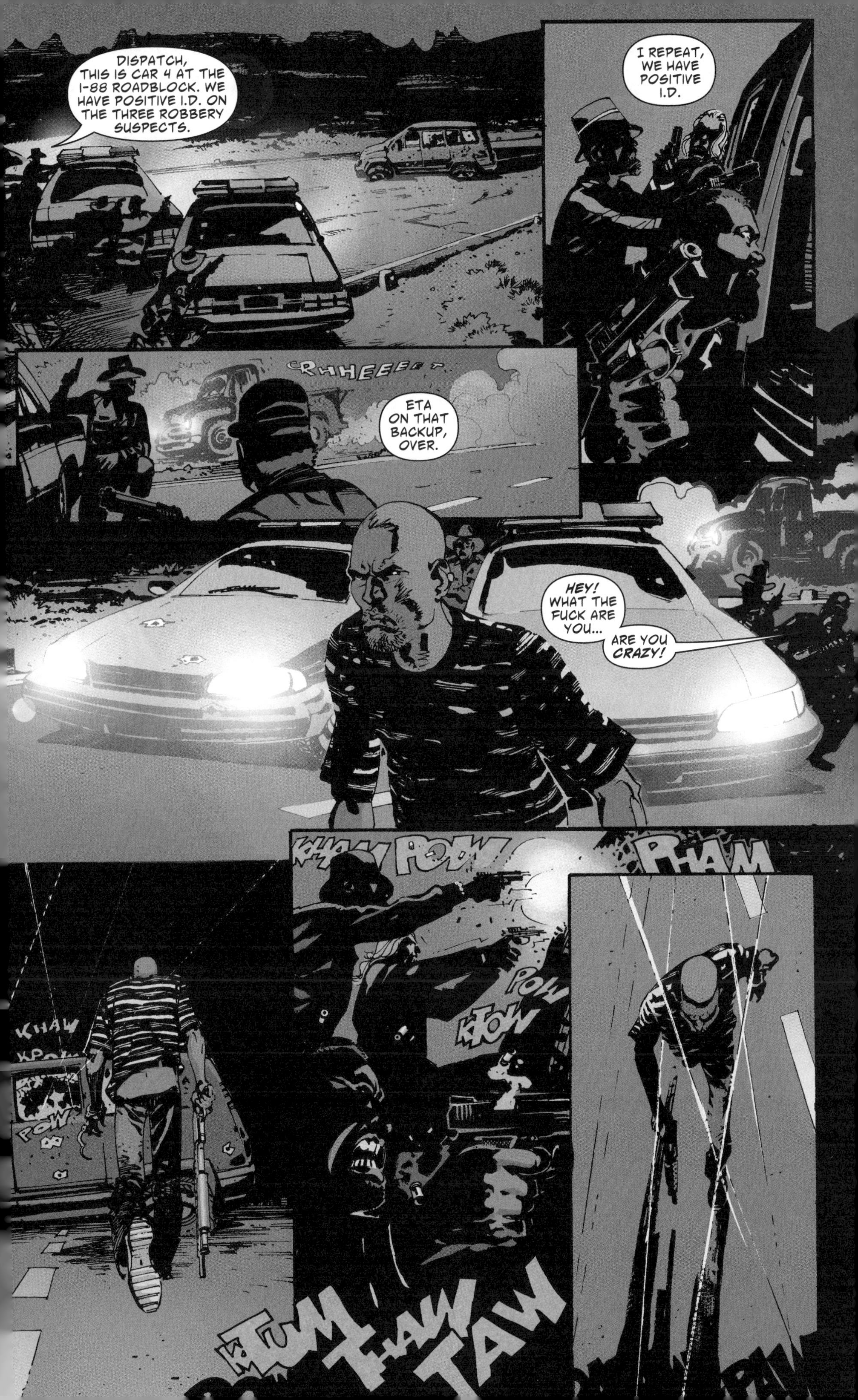
DISPATCH, THIS IS CAR 4 AT THE I-88 ROADBLOCK. WE HAVE POSITIVE I.D. ON THE THREE ROBBERY SUSPECTS.
I REPEAT, WE HAVE POSITIVE I.D.
CRHHEEEEET
ETA ON THAT BACKUP, OVER.
HEY! WHAT THE FUCK ARE YOU...
ARE YOU CRAZY!
KHAW POW
PHAM
POW
KTOW
KHAW
POW
TUM
THAW
TAW

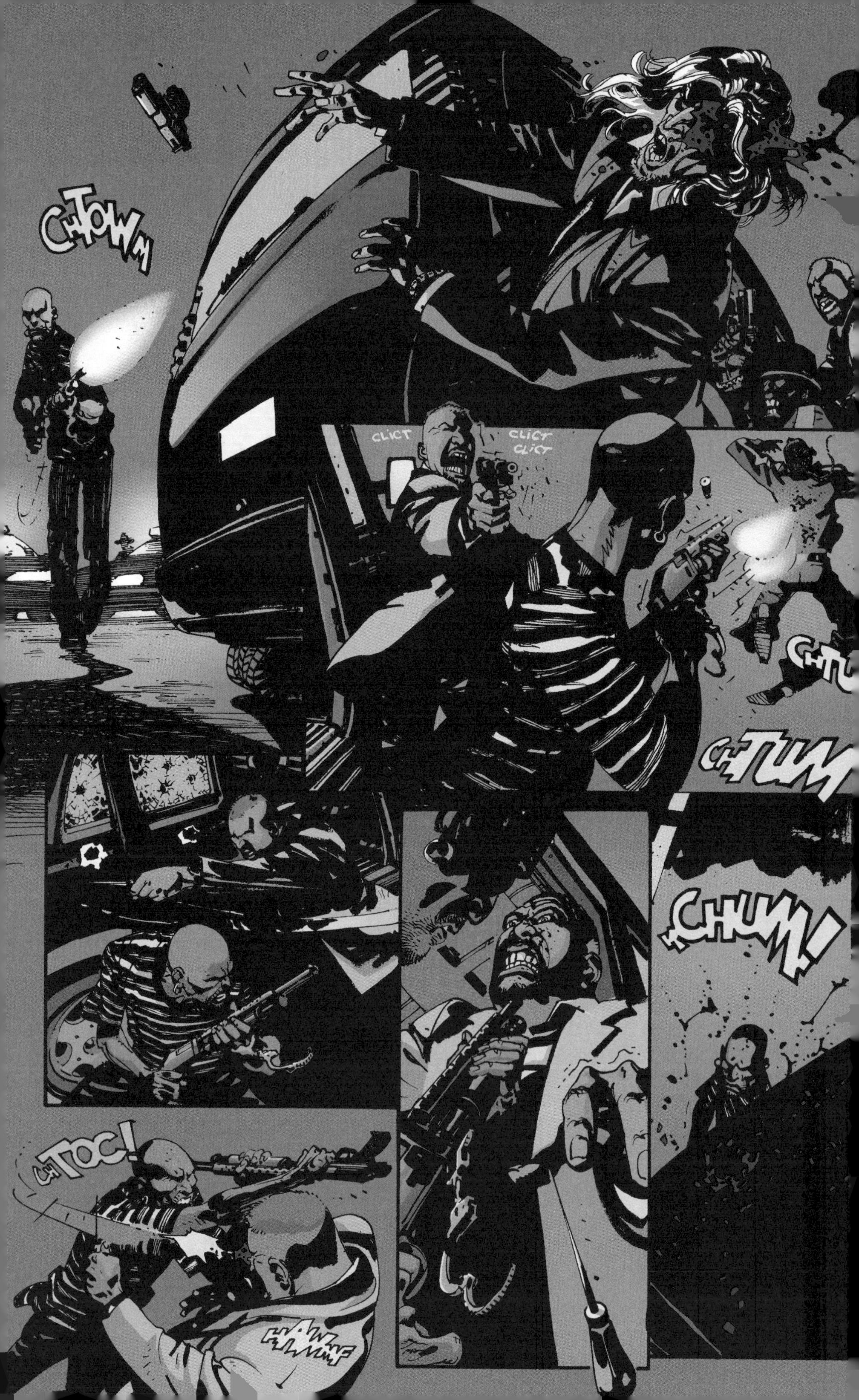
CHTOWM
CLICT
CLICT
CLICT
CHTUM
CHTUM
CHUM!
CHTOC!

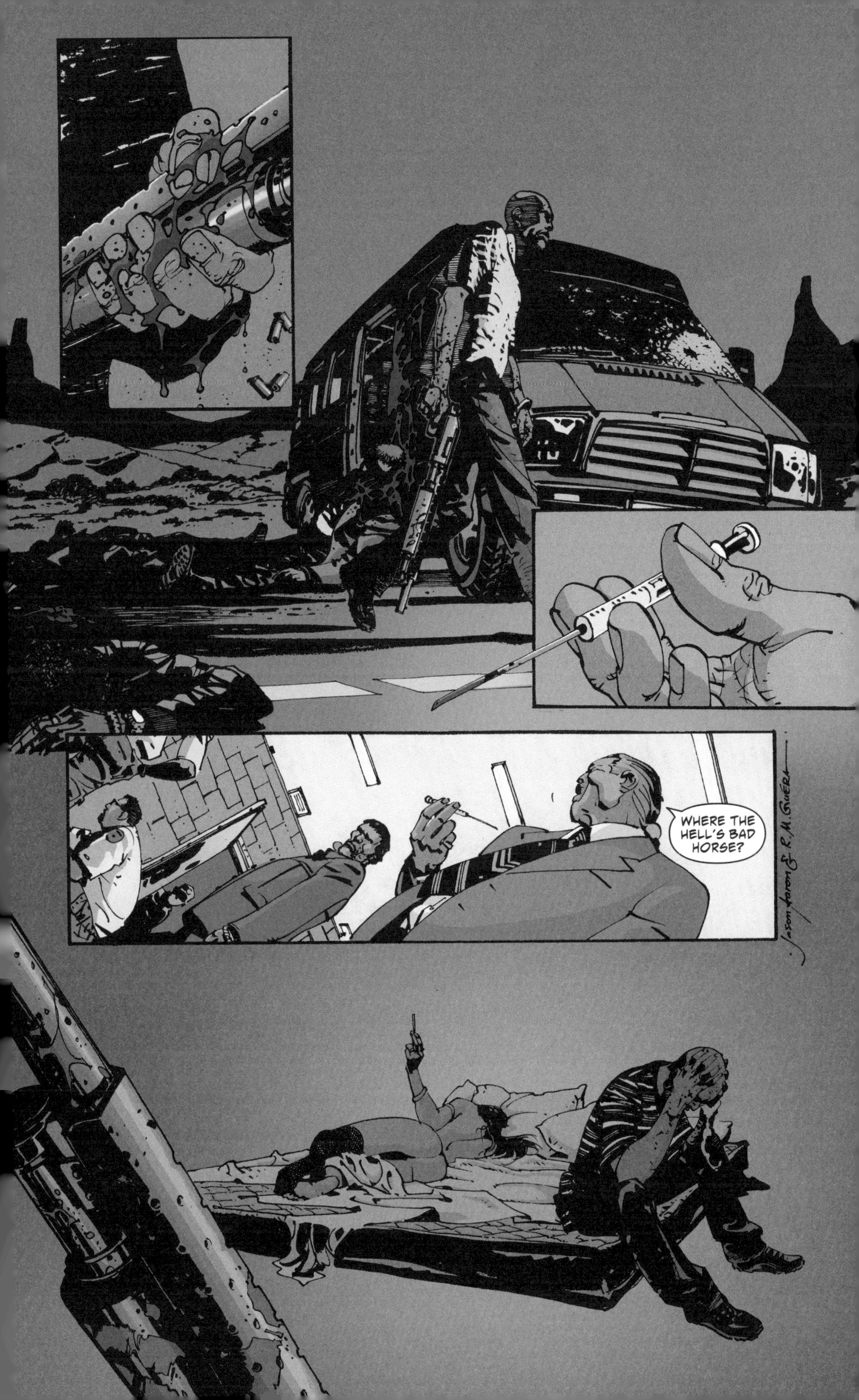
WHERE THE HELL'S BAD HORSE?

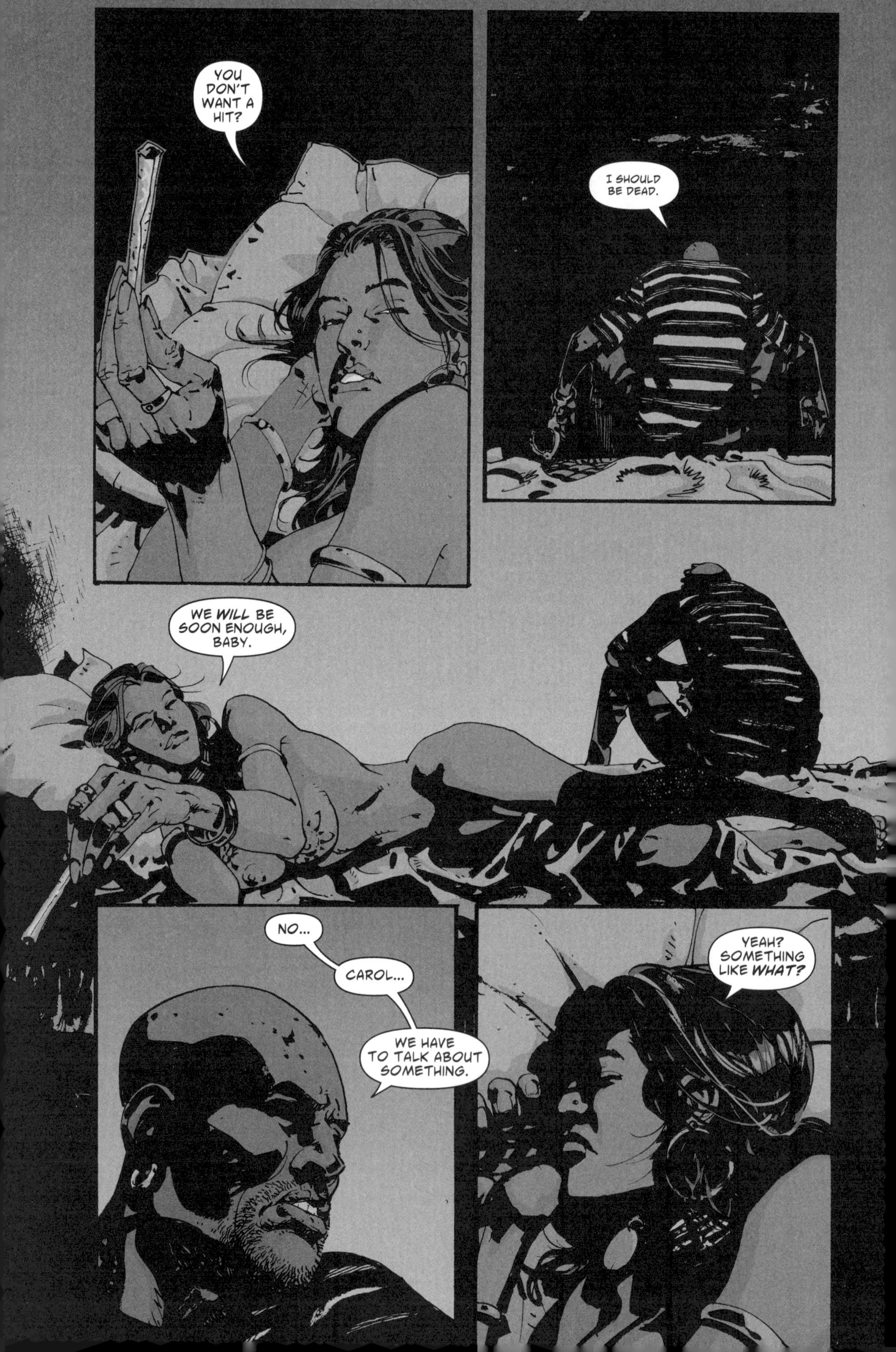
YOU DON'T WANT A HIT?
I SHOULD BE DEAD.
WE *WILL* BE SOON ENOUGH, BABY.
NO...
CAROL...
WE HAVE TO TALK ABOUT SOMETHING.
YEAH? SOMETHING LIKE *WHAT?*

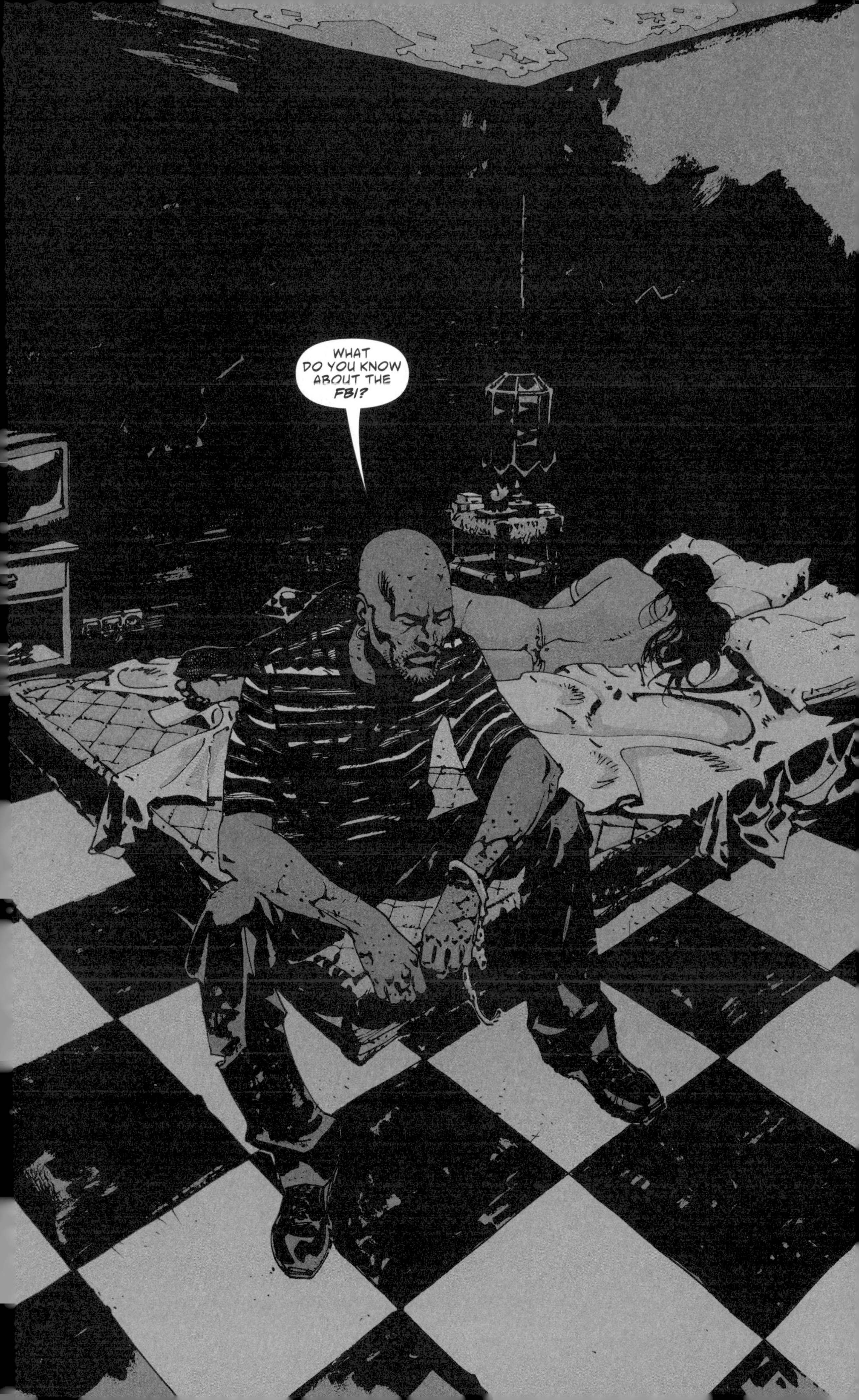
WHAT DO YOU KNOW ABOUT THE FBI?

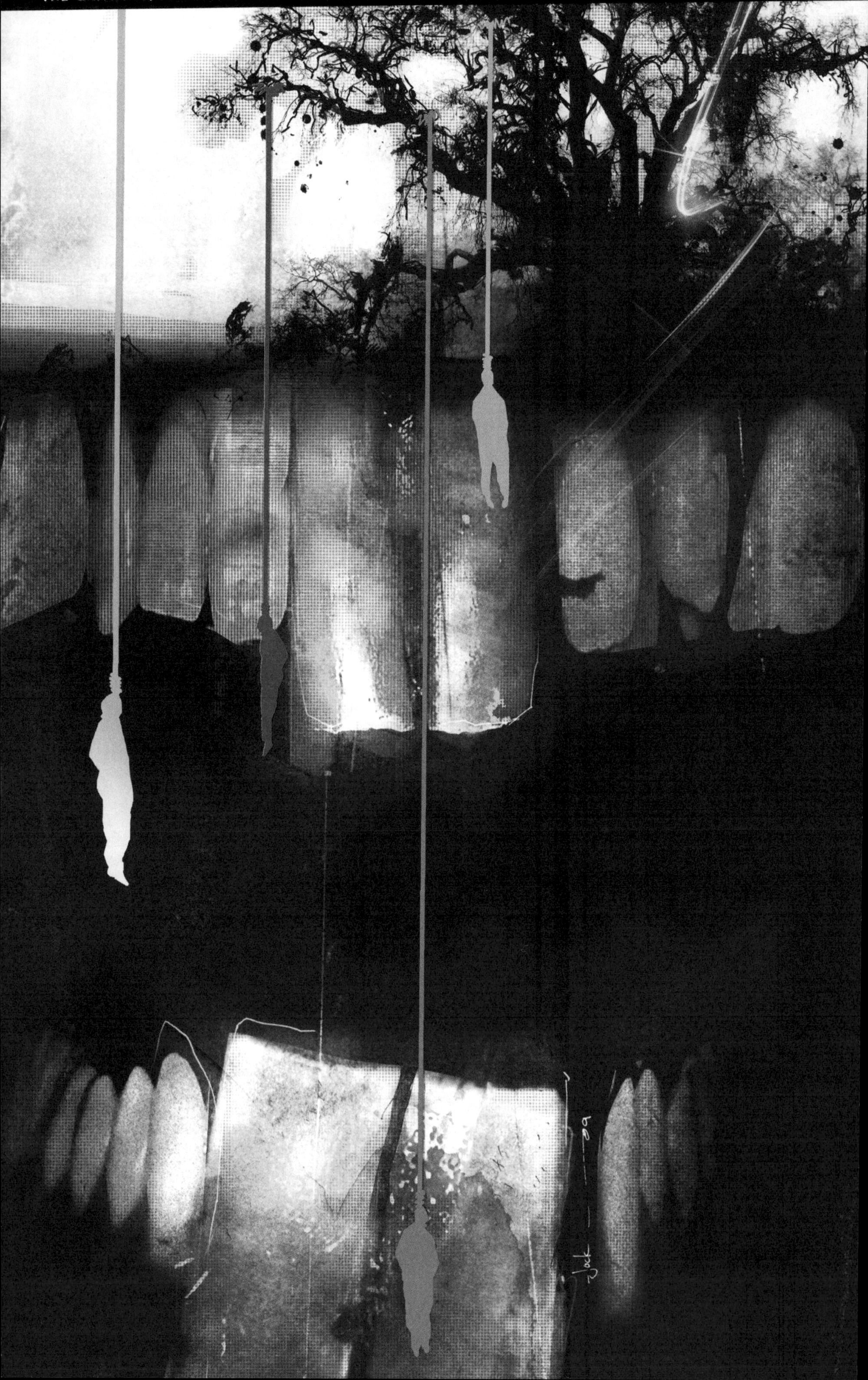
Jock 09

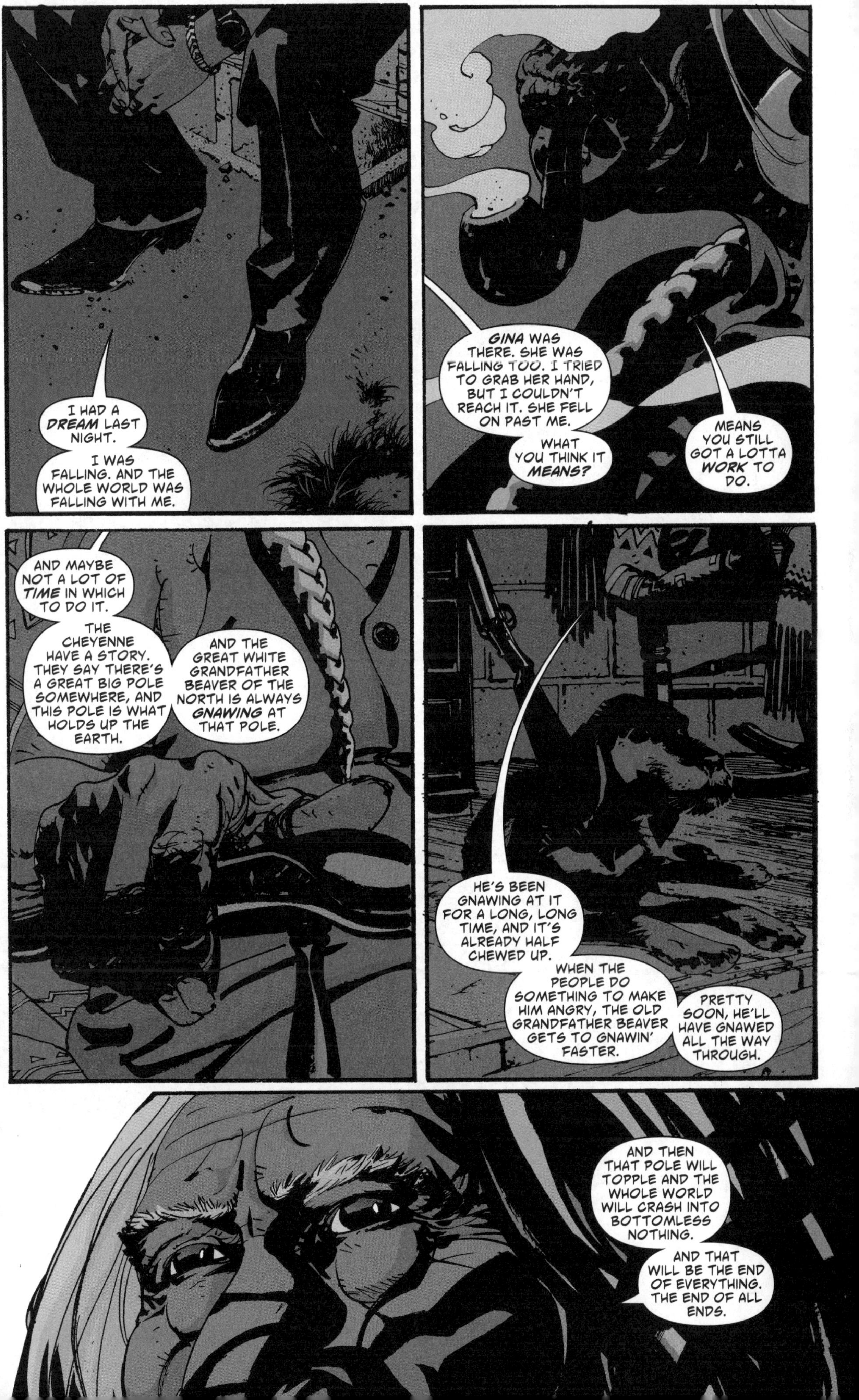
I HAD A DREAM LAST NIGHT.
I WAS FALLING. AND THE WHOLE WORLD WAS FALLING WITH ME.
GINA WAS THERE. SHE WAS FALLING TOO. I TRIED TO GRAB HER HAND, BUT I COULDN'T REACH IT. SHE FELL ON PAST ME.
WHAT YOU THINK IT MEANS?
MEANS YOU STILL GOT A LOTTA WORK TO DO.
AND MAYBE NOT A LOT OF TIME IN WHICH TO DO IT.
THE CHEYENNE HAVE A STORY. THEY SAY THERE'S A GREAT BIG POLE SOMEWHERE, AND THIS POLE IS WHAT HOLDS UP THE EARTH.
AND THE GREAT WHITE GRANDFATHER BEAVER OF THE NORTH IS ALWAYS GNAWING AT THAT POLE.
HE'S BEEN GNAWING AT IT FOR A LONG, LONG TIME, AND IT'S ALREADY HALF CHEWED UP.
WHEN THE PEOPLE DO SOMETHING TO MAKE HIM ANGRY, THE OLD GRANDFATHER BEAVER GETS TO GNAWIN' FASTER.
PRETTY SOON, HE'LL HAVE GNAWED ALL THE WAY THROUGH.
AND THEN THAT POLE WILL TOPPLE AND THE WHOLE WORLD WILL CRASH INTO BOTTOMLESS NOTHING.
AND THAT WILL BE THE END OF EVERYTHING. THE END OF ALL ENDS.

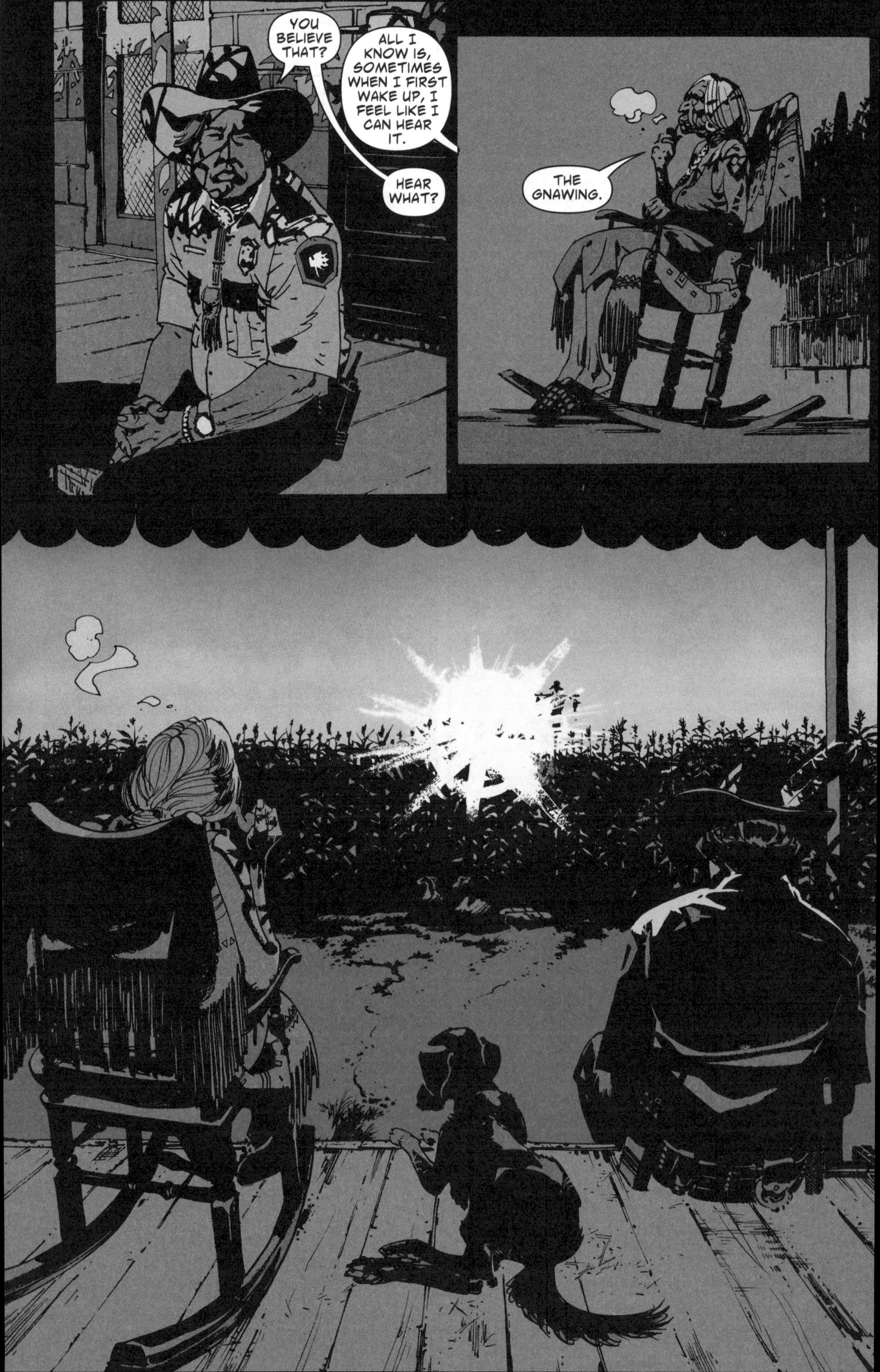
YOU BELIEVE THAT?
ALL I KNOW IS, SOMETIMES WHEN I FIRST WAKE UP, I FEEL LIKE I CAN HEAR IT.
HEAR WHAT?
THE GNAWING.

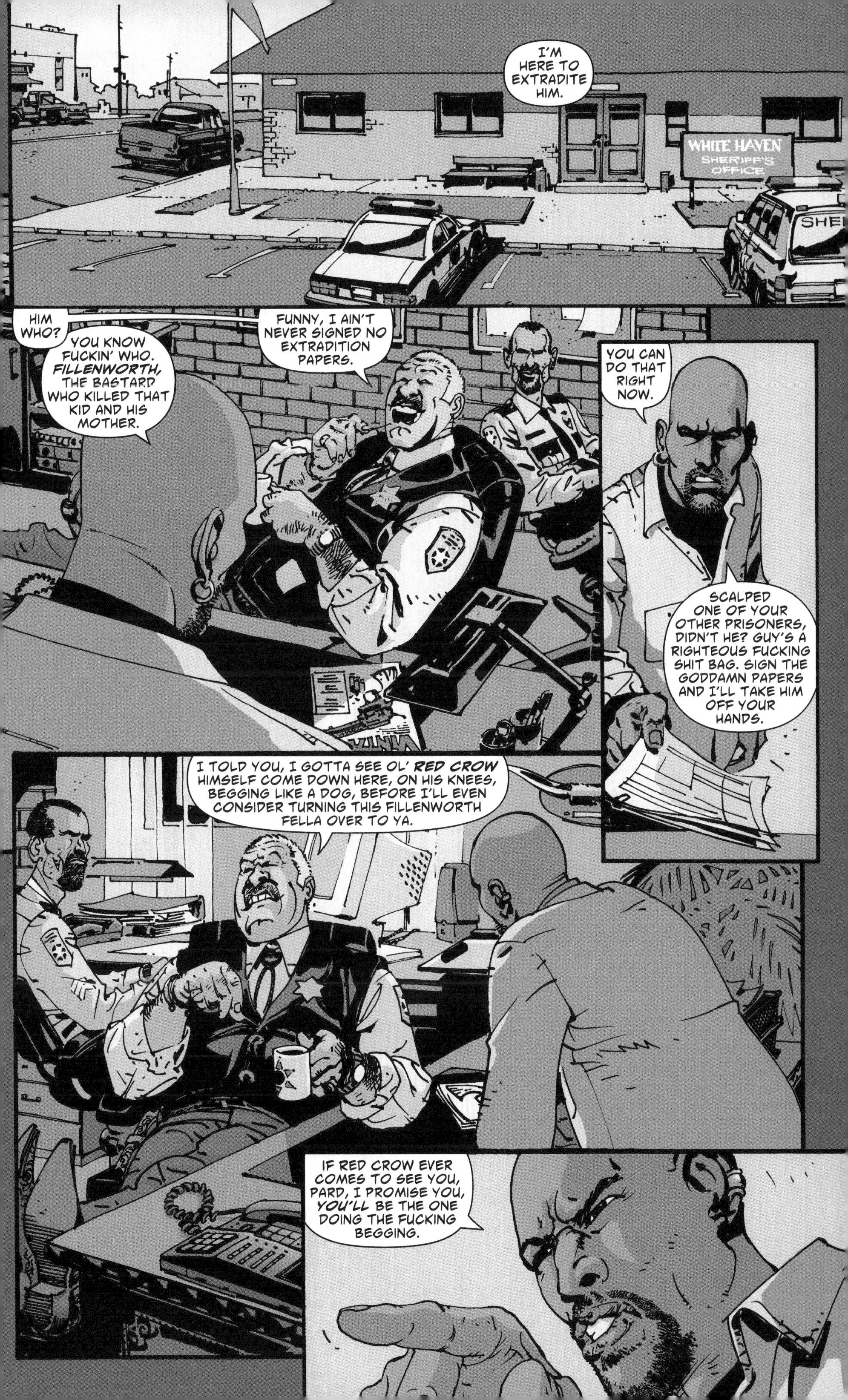
I'M HERE TO EXTRADITE HIM.
WHITE HAVEN SHERIFF'S OFFICE
SHE
HIM WHO?
YOU KNOW FUCKIN' WHO. FILLENWORTH, THE BASTARD WHO KILLED THAT KID AND HIS MOTHER.
FUNNY, I AIN'T NEVER SIGNED NO EXTRADITION PAPERS.
YOU CAN DO THAT RIGHT NOW.
SCALPED ONE OF YOUR OTHER PRISONERS, DIDN'T HE? GUY'S A RIGHTEOUS FUCKING SHIT BAG. SIGN THE GODDAMN PAPERS AND I'LL TAKE HIM OFF YOUR HANDS.
I TOLD YOU, I GOTTA SEE OL' RED CROW HIMSELF COME DOWN HERE, ON HIS KNEES, BEGGING LIKE A DOG, BEFORE I'LL EVEN CONSIDER TURNING THIS FILLENWORTH FELLA OVER TO YA.
IF RED CROW EVER COMES TO SEE YOU, PARD, I PROMISE YOU, YOU'LL BE THE ONE DOING THE FUCKING BEGGING.

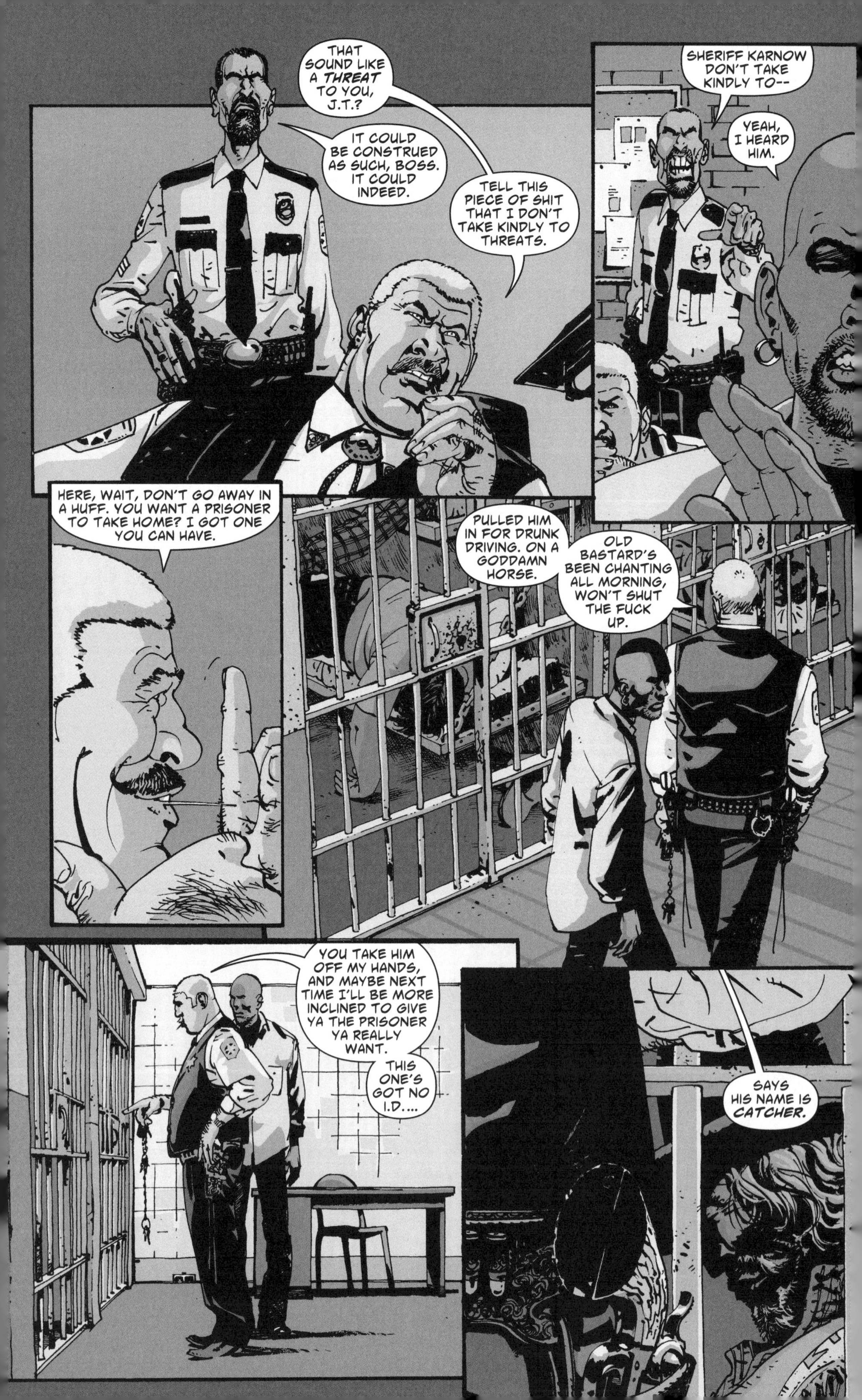
THAT SOUND LIKE A *THREAT* TO YOU, J.T.?
IT COULD BE CONSTRUED AS SUCH, BOSS. IT COULD INDEED.
TELL THIS PIECE OF SHIT THAT I DON'T TAKE KINDLY TO THREATS.
SHERIFF KARNOW DON'T TAKE KINDLY TO--
YEAH, I HEARD HIM.
HERE, WAIT, DON'T GO AWAY IN A HUFF. YOU WANT A PRISONER TO TAKE HOME? I GOT ONE YOU CAN HAVE.
PULLED HIM IN FOR DRUNK DRIVING. ON A GODDAMN HORSE.
OLD BASTARD'S BEEN CHANTING ALL MORNING, WON'T SHUT THE FUCK UP.
YOU TAKE HIM OFF MY HANDS, AND MAYBE NEXT TIME I'LL BE MORE INCLINED TO GIVE YA THE PRISONER YA REALLY WANT.
THIS ONE'S GOT NO I.D....
SAYS HIS NAME IS *CATCHER.*

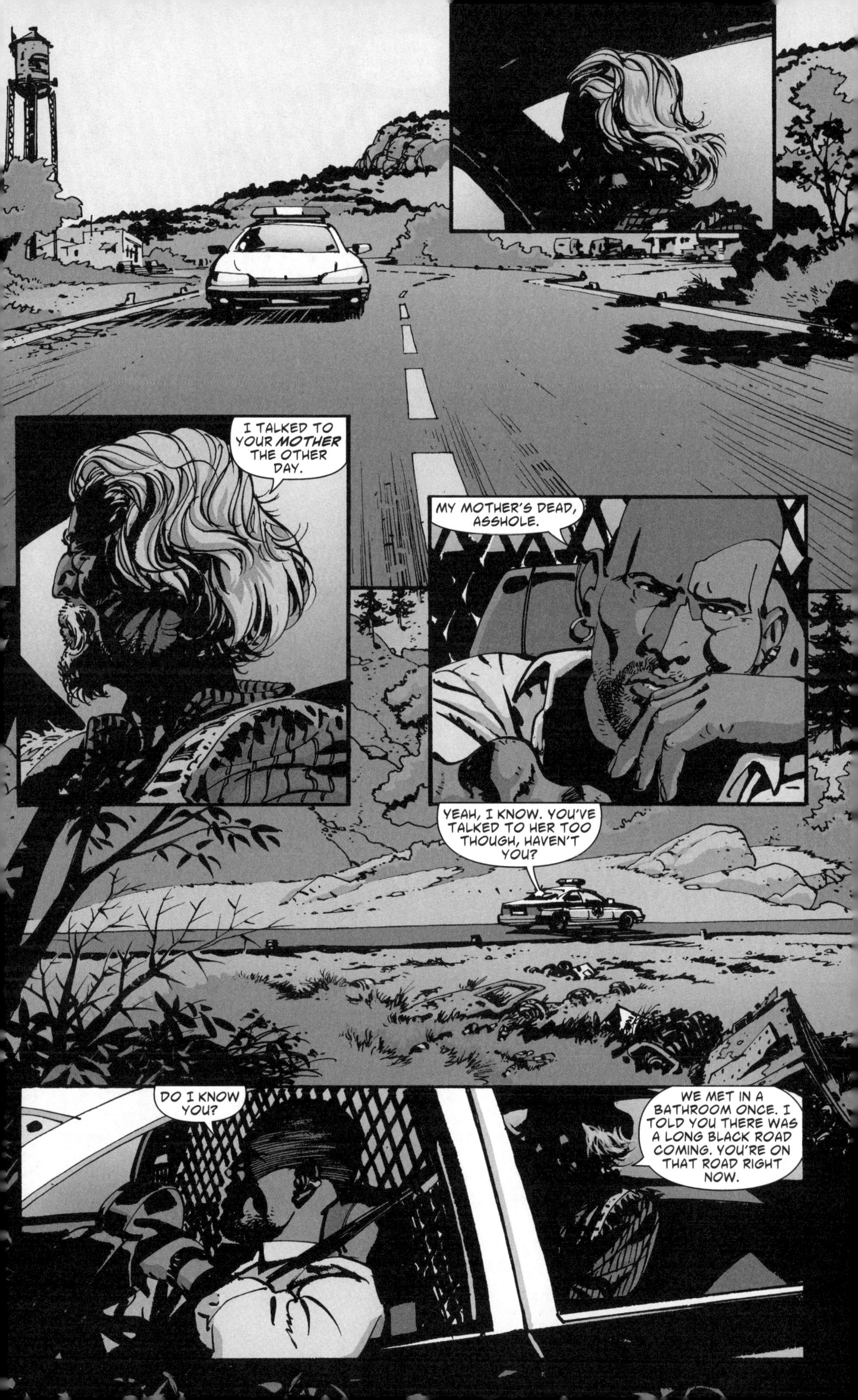
I TALKED TO YOUR MOTHER THE OTHER DAY.
MY MOTHER'S DEAD, ASSHOLE.
YEAH, I KNOW. YOU'VE TALKED TO HER TOO THOUGH, HAVEN'T YOU?
DO I KNOW YOU?
WE MET IN A BATHROOM ONCE. I TOLD YOU THERE WAS A LONG BLACK ROAD COMING. YOU'RE ON THAT ROAD RIGHT NOW.

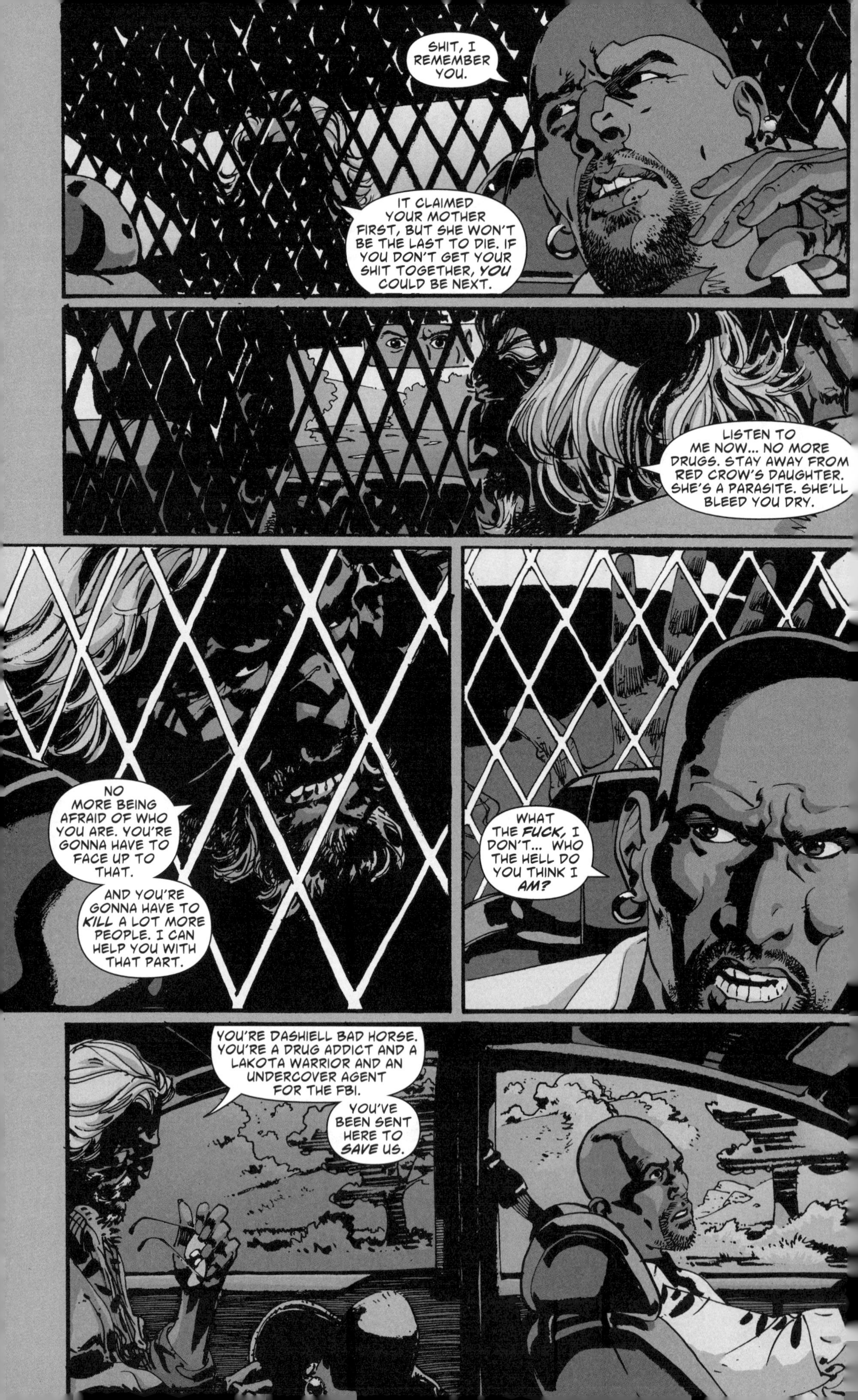
SHIT, I REMEMBER YOU.
IT CLAIMED YOUR MOTHER FIRST, BUT SHE WON'T BE THE LAST TO DIE. IF YOU DON'T GET YOUR SHIT TOGETHER, *YOU* COULD BE NEXT.
LISTEN TO ME NOW... NO MORE DRUGS. STAY AWAY FROM RED CROW'S DAUGHTER. SHE'S A PARASITE. SHE'LL BLEED YOU DRY.
NO MORE BEING AFRAID OF WHO YOU ARE. YOU'RE GONNA HAVE TO FACE UP TO THAT.
AND YOU'RE GONNA HAVE TO *KILL* A LOT MORE PEOPLE. I CAN HELP YOU WITH THAT PART.
WHAT THE *FUCK,* I DON'T... WHO THE HELL DO YOU THINK I *AM?*
YOU'RE DASHIELL BAD HORSE. YOU'RE A DRUG ADDICT AND A LAKOTA WARRIOR AND AN UNDERCOVER AGENT FOR THE FBI.
YOU'VE BEEN SENT HERE TO *SAVE* US.

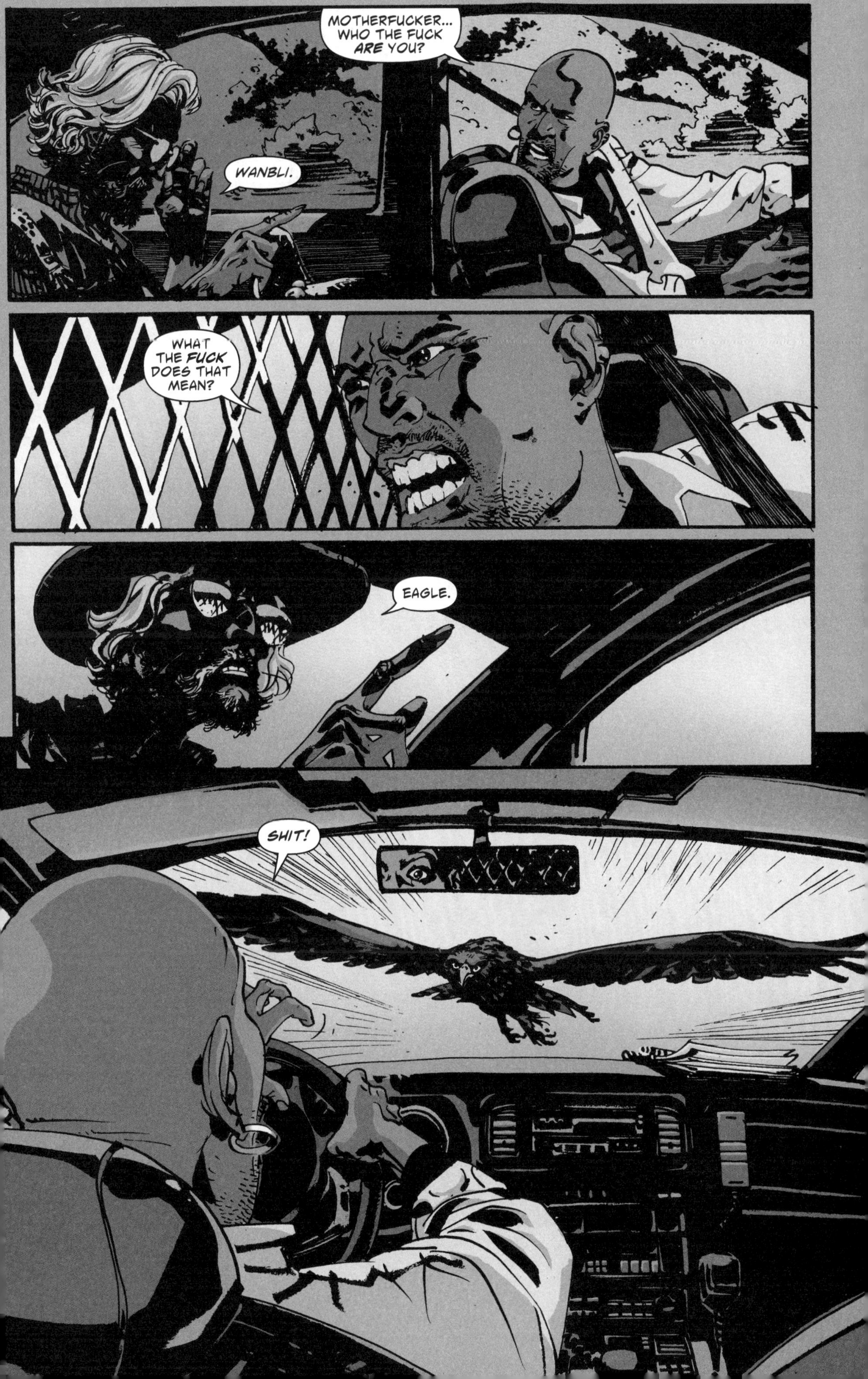
MOTHERFUCKER... WHO THE FUCK ARE YOU?
WANBLI.
WHAT THE FUCK DOES THAT MEAN?
EAGLE.
SHIT!

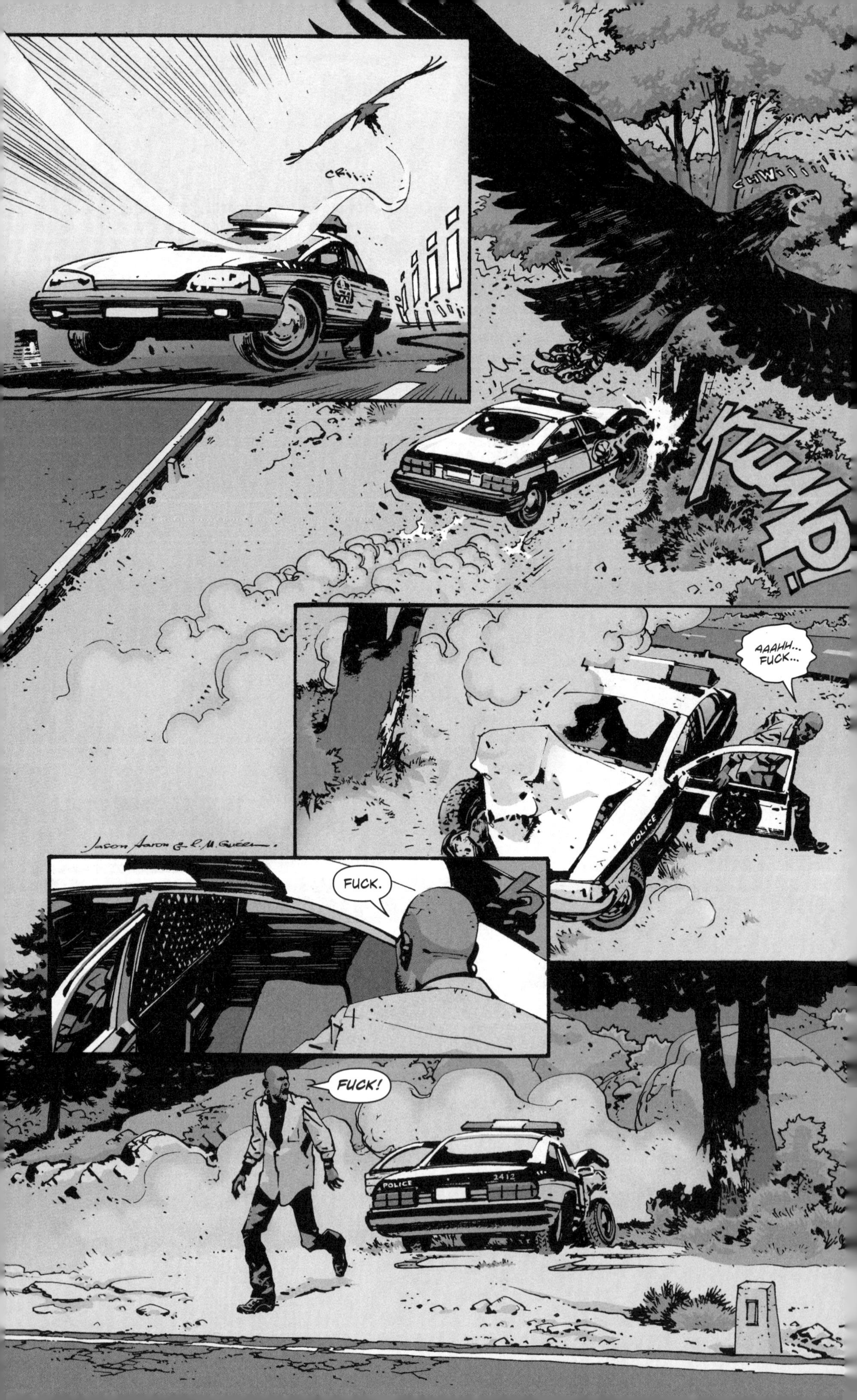
CRIIII...
CHWIIIIII
KRUMP!
AAAHH...
FUCK...
FUCK.
FUCK!

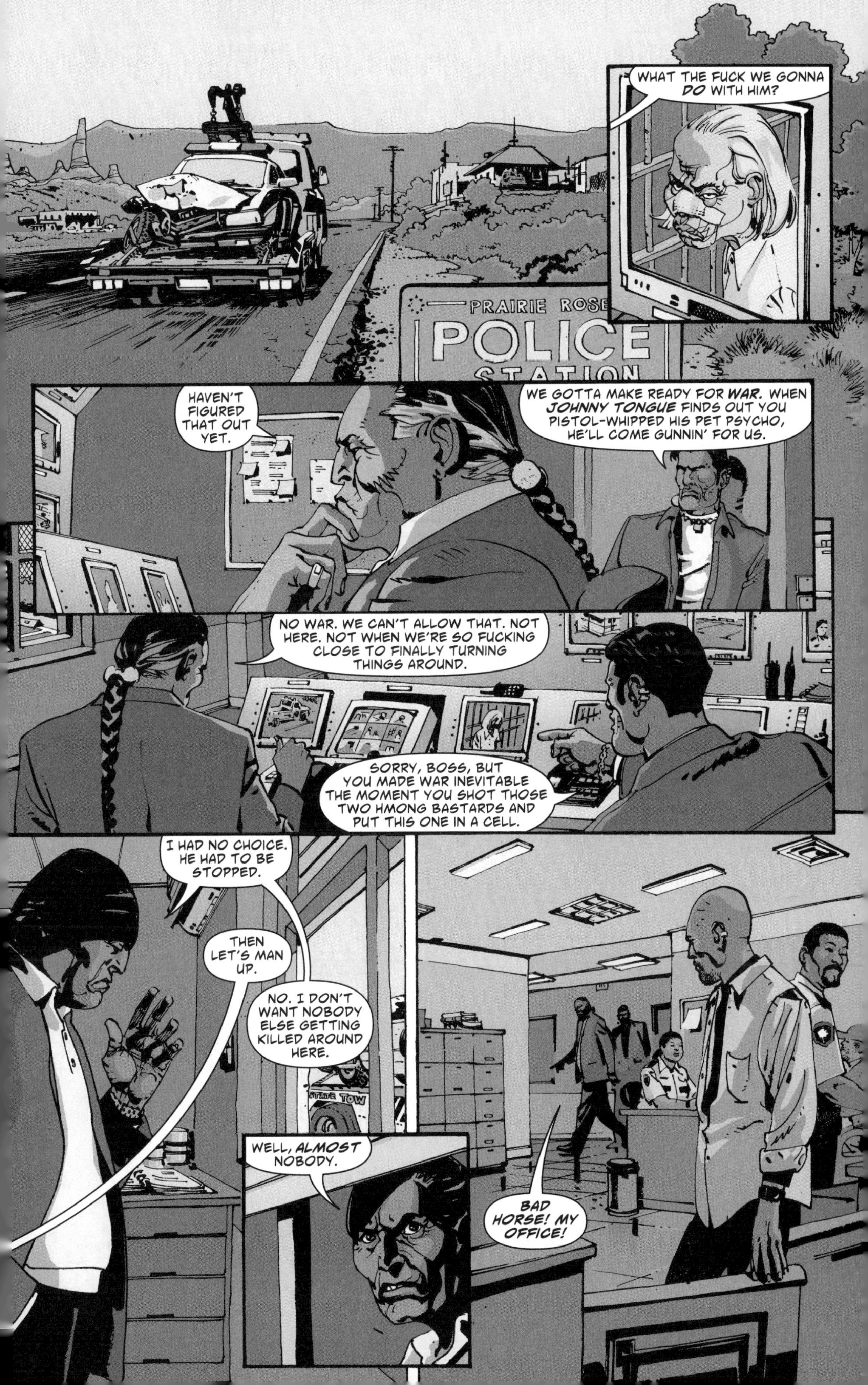
PRAIRIE ROSE
POLICE
STATION
WHAT THE FUCK WE GONNA DO WITH HIM?
HAVEN'T FIGURED THAT OUT YET.
WE GOTTA MAKE READY FOR WAR. WHEN JOHNNY TONGUE FINDS OUT YOU PISTOL-WHIPPED HIS PET PSYCHO, HE'LL COME GUNNIN' FOR US.
NO WAR. WE CAN'T ALLOW THAT. NOT HERE. NOT WHEN WE'RE SO FUCKING CLOSE TO FINALLY TURNING THINGS AROUND.
SORRY, BOSS, BUT YOU MADE WAR INEVITABLE THE MOMENT YOU SHOT THOSE TWO HMONG BASTARDS AND PUT THIS ONE IN A CELL.
I HAD NO CHOICE. HE HAD TO BE STOPPED.
THEN LET'S MAN UP.
NO. I DON'T WANT NOBODY ELSE GETTING KILLED AROUND HERE.
STATE TOW
WELL, ALMOST NOBODY.
BAD HORSE! MY OFFICE!

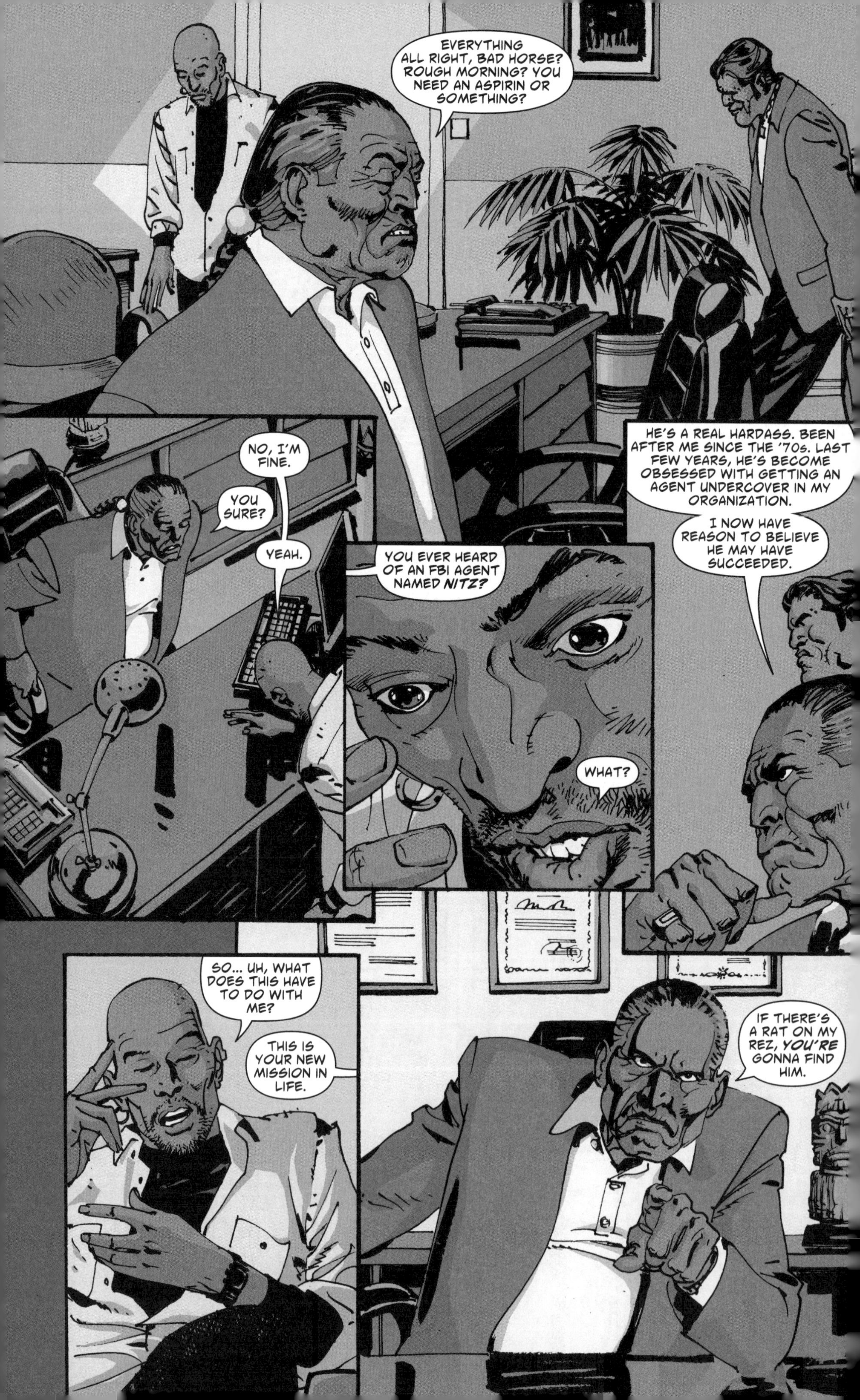
EVERYTHING ALL RIGHT, BAD HORSE? ROUGH MORNING? YOU NEED AN ASPIRIN OR SOMETHING?
NO, I'M FINE.
YOU SURE?
YEAH.
YOU EVER HEARD OF AN FBI AGENT NAMED NITZ?
WHAT?
HE'S A REAL HARDASS. BEEN AFTER ME SINCE THE '70s. LAST FEW YEARS, HE'S BECOME OBSESSED WITH GETTING AN AGENT UNDERCOVER IN MY ORGANIZATION.
I NOW HAVE REASON TO BELIEVE HE MAY HAVE SUCCEEDED.
SO... UH, WHAT DOES THIS HAVE TO DO WITH ME?
THIS IS YOUR NEW MISSION IN LIFE.
IF THERE'S A RAT ON MY REZ, YOU'RE GONNA FIND HIM.

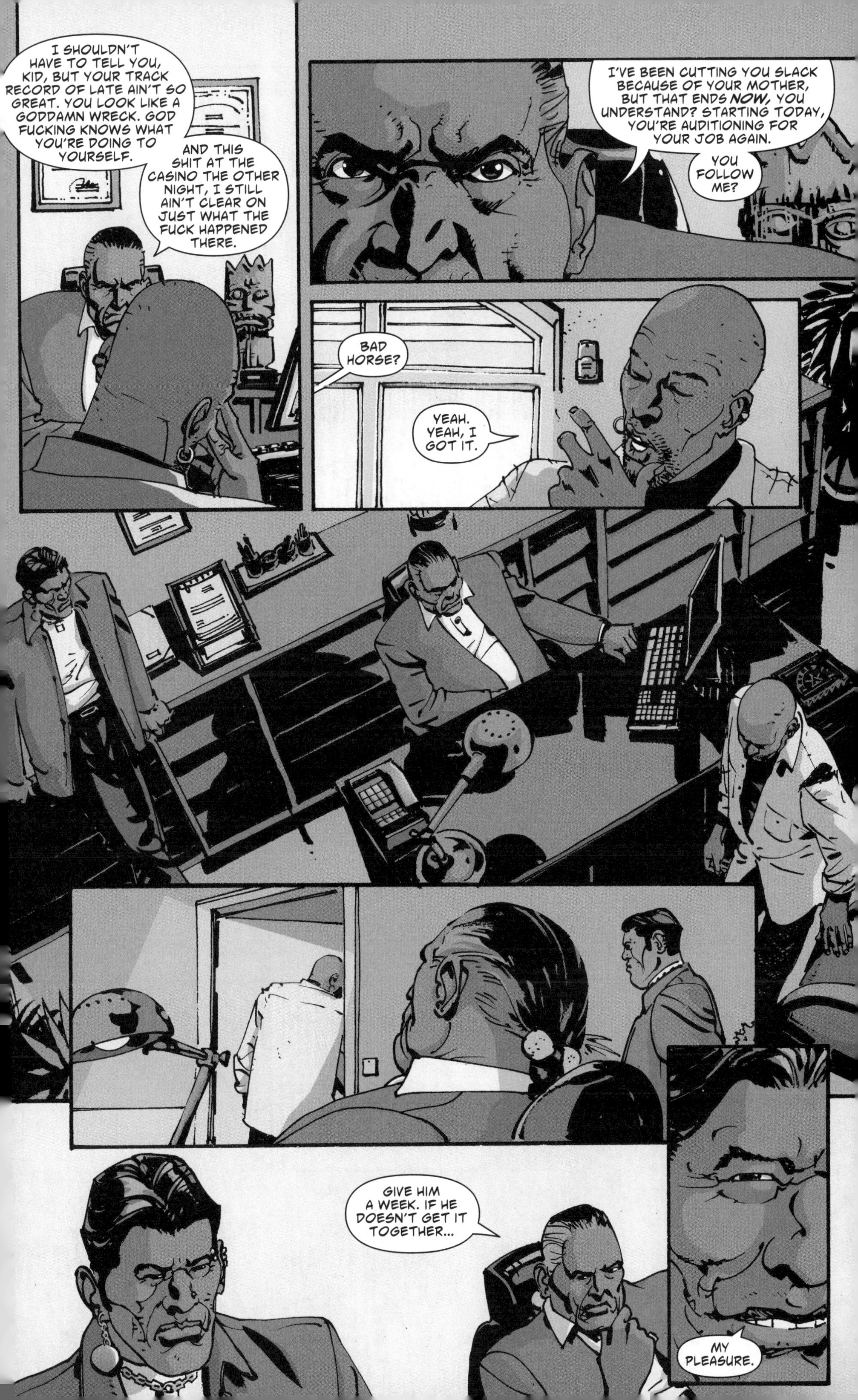
I SHOULDN'T HAVE TO TELL YOU, KID, BUT YOUR TRACK RECORD OF LATE AIN'T SO GREAT. YOU LOOK LIKE A GODDAMN WRECK. GOD FUCKING KNOWS WHAT YOU'RE DOING TO YOURSELF.
AND THIS SHIT AT THE CASINO THE OTHER NIGHT, I STILL AIN'T CLEAR ON JUST WHAT THE FUCK HAPPENED THERE.
I'VE BEEN CUTTING YOU SLACK BECAUSE OF YOUR MOTHER, BUT THAT ENDS *NOW,* YOU UNDERSTAND? STARTING TODAY, YOU'RE AUDITIONING FOR YOUR JOB AGAIN.
YOU FOLLOW ME?
BAD HORSE?
YEAH. YEAH, I GOT IT.
GIVE HIM A WEEK. IF HE DOESN'T GET IT TOGETHER...
MY PLEASURE.

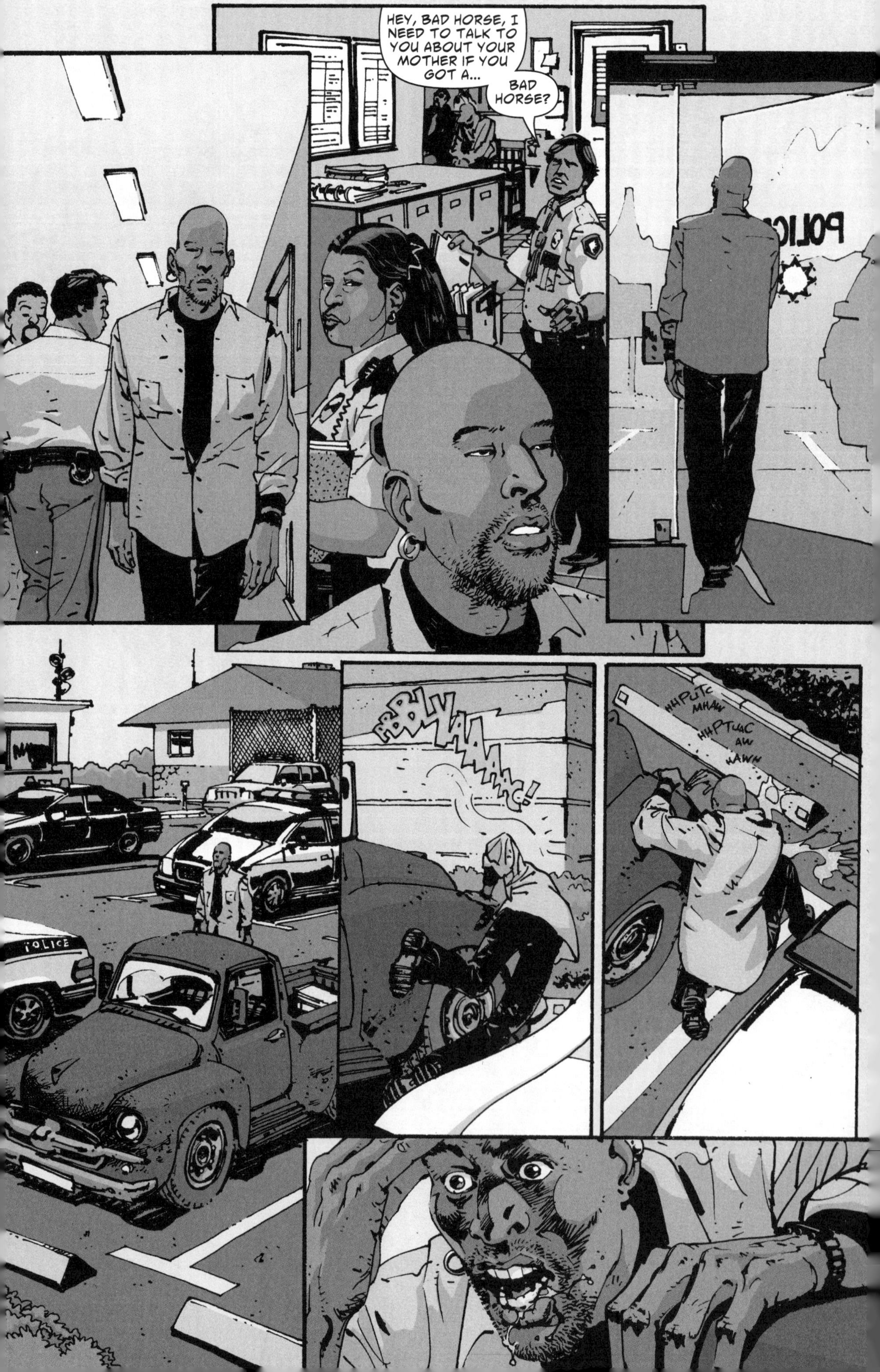
HEY, BAD HORSE, I NEED TO TALK TO YOU ABOUT YOUR MOTHER IF YOU GOT A...
BAD HORSE?
POLICE
HHPUTC MHAW
HHPTUAC AW HAWH

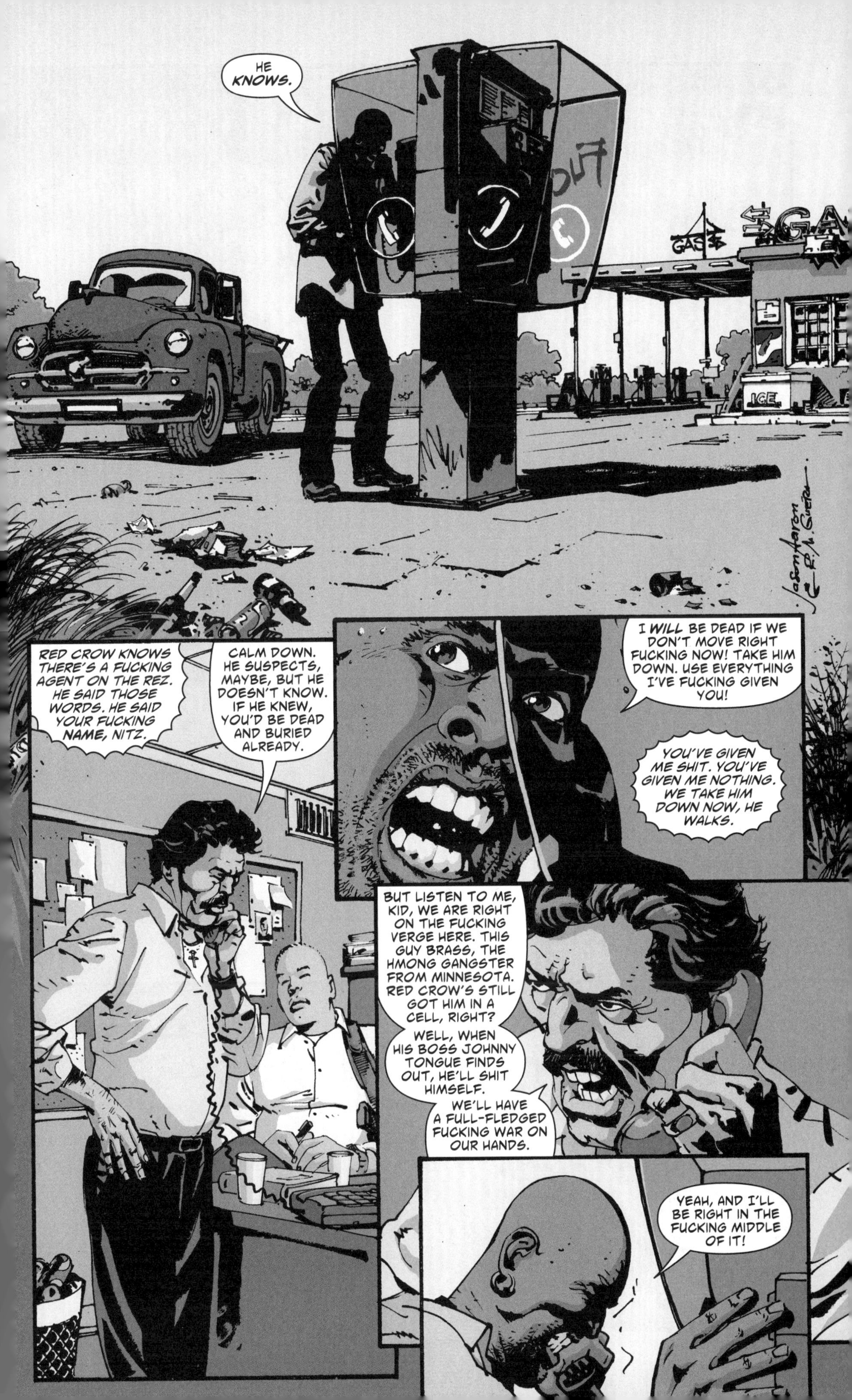
HE KNOWS.
GAS
GA
ICE
RED CROW KNOWS THERE'S A FUCKING AGENT ON THE REZ. HE SAID THOSE WORDS. HE SAID YOUR FUCKING NAME, NITZ.
CALM DOWN. HE SUSPECTS, MAYBE, BUT HE DOESN'T KNOW. IF HE KNEW, YOU'D BE DEAD AND BURIED ALREADY.
I WILL BE DEAD IF WE DON'T MOVE RIGHT FUCKING NOW! TAKE HIM DOWN. USE EVERYTHING I'VE FUCKING GIVEN YOU!
YOU'VE GIVEN ME SHIT. YOU'VE GIVEN ME NOTHING. WE TAKE HIM DOWN NOW, HE WALKS.
BUT LISTEN TO ME, KID, WE ARE RIGHT ON THE FUCKING VERGE HERE. THIS GUY BRASS, THE HMONG GANGSTER FROM MINNESOTA. RED CROW'S STILL GOT HIM IN A CELL, RIGHT?
WELL, WHEN HIS BOSS JOHNNY TONGUE FINDS OUT, HE'LL SHIT HIMSELF.
WE'LL HAVE A FULL-FLEDGED FUCKING WAR ON OUR HANDS.
YEAH, AND I'LL BE RIGHT IN THE FUCKING MIDDLE OF IT!

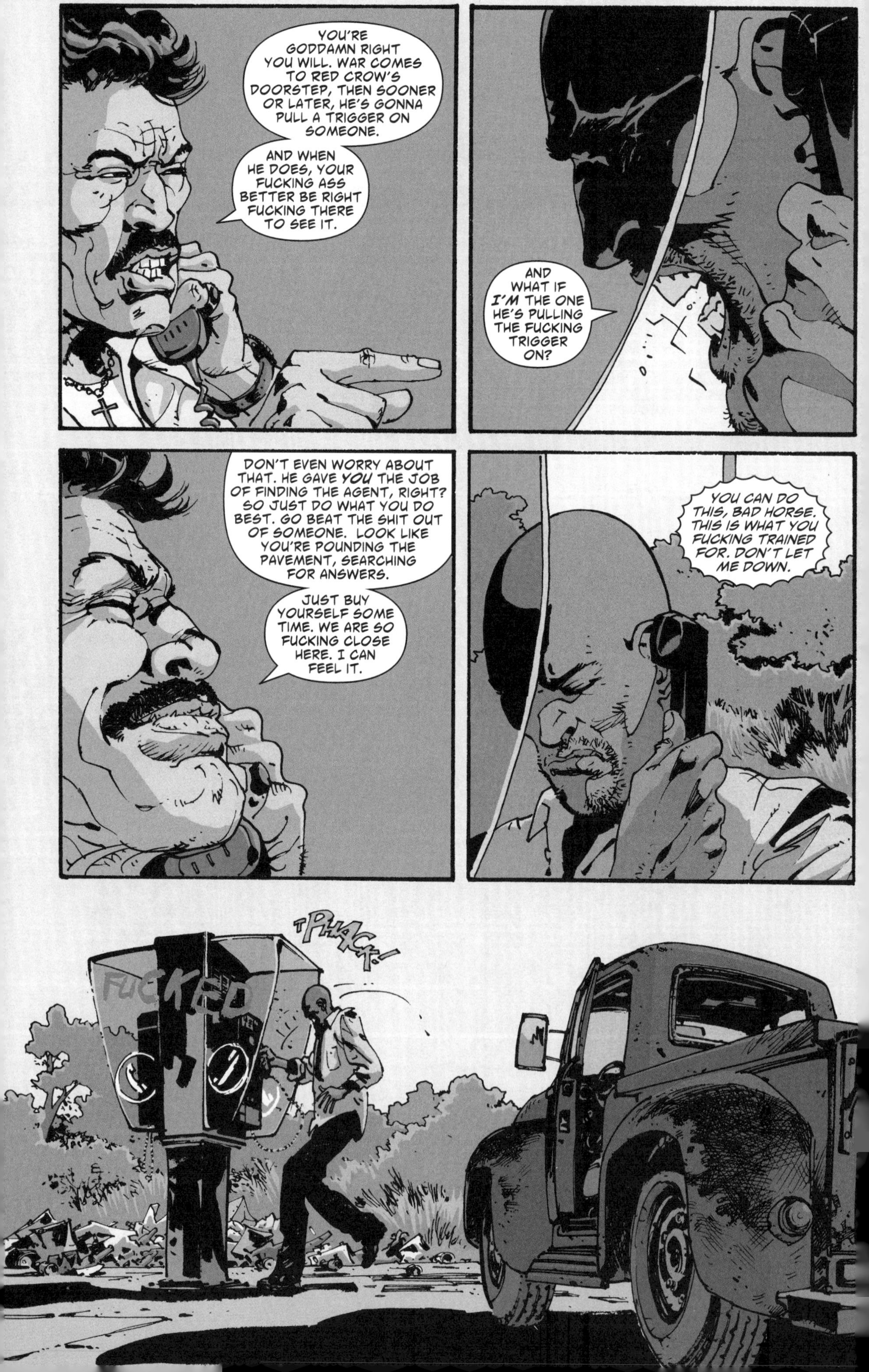
YOU'RE GODDAMN RIGHT YOU WILL. WAR COMES TO RED CROW'S DOORSTEP, THEN SOONER OR LATER, HE'S GONNA PULL A TRIGGER ON SOMEONE.
AND WHEN HE DOES, YOUR FUCKING ASS BETTER BE RIGHT FUCKING THERE TO SEE IT.
AND WHAT IF I'M THE ONE HE'S PULLING THE FUCKING TRIGGER ON?
DON'T EVEN WORRY ABOUT THAT. HE GAVE YOU THE JOB OF FINDING THE AGENT, RIGHT? SO JUST DO WHAT YOU DO BEST. GO BEAT THE SHIT OUT OF SOMEONE. LOOK LIKE YOU'RE POUNDING THE PAVEMENT, SEARCHING FOR ANSWERS.
JUST BUY YOURSELF SOME TIME. WE ARE SO FUCKING CLOSE HERE. I CAN FEEL IT.
YOU CAN DO THIS, BAD HORSE. THIS IS WHAT YOU FUCKING TRAINED FOR. DON'T LET ME DOWN.
FUCKED
TPHACK!

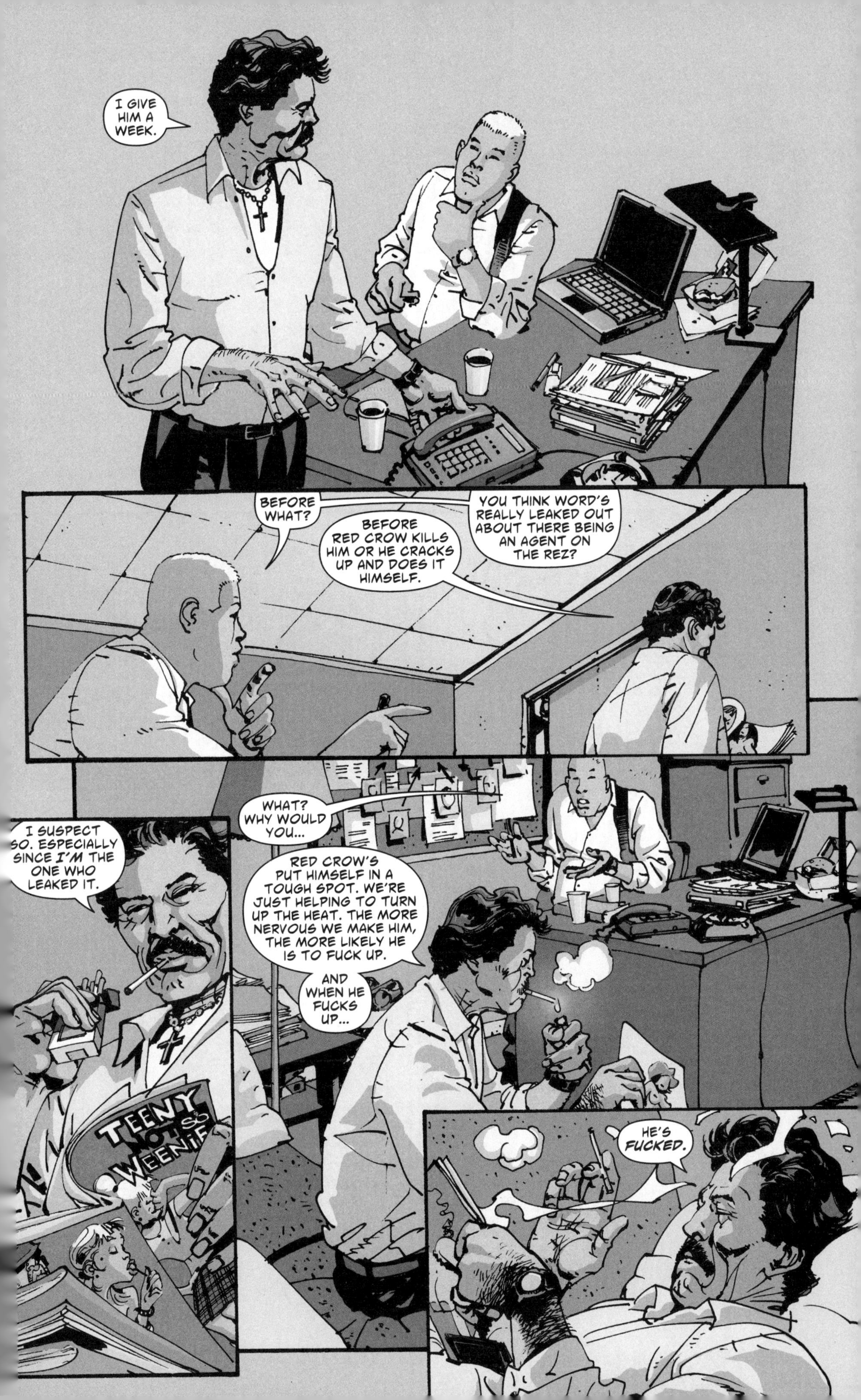
I GIVE HIM A WEEK.
BEFORE WHAT?
BEFORE RED CROW KILLS HIM OR HE CRACKS UP AND DOES IT HIMSELF.
YOU THINK WORD'S REALLY LEAKED OUT ABOUT THERE BEING AN AGENT ON THE REZ?
I SUSPECT SO. ESPECIALLY SINCE I'M THE ONE WHO LEAKED IT.
WHAT? WHY WOULD YOU...
RED CROW'S PUT HIMSELF IN A TOUGH SPOT. WE'RE JUST HELPING TO TURN UP THE HEAT. THE MORE NERVOUS WE MAKE HIM, THE MORE LIKELY HE IS TO FUCK UP.
AND WHEN HE FUCKS UP...
TEENY NOT SO WEENIE
HE'S FUCKED.

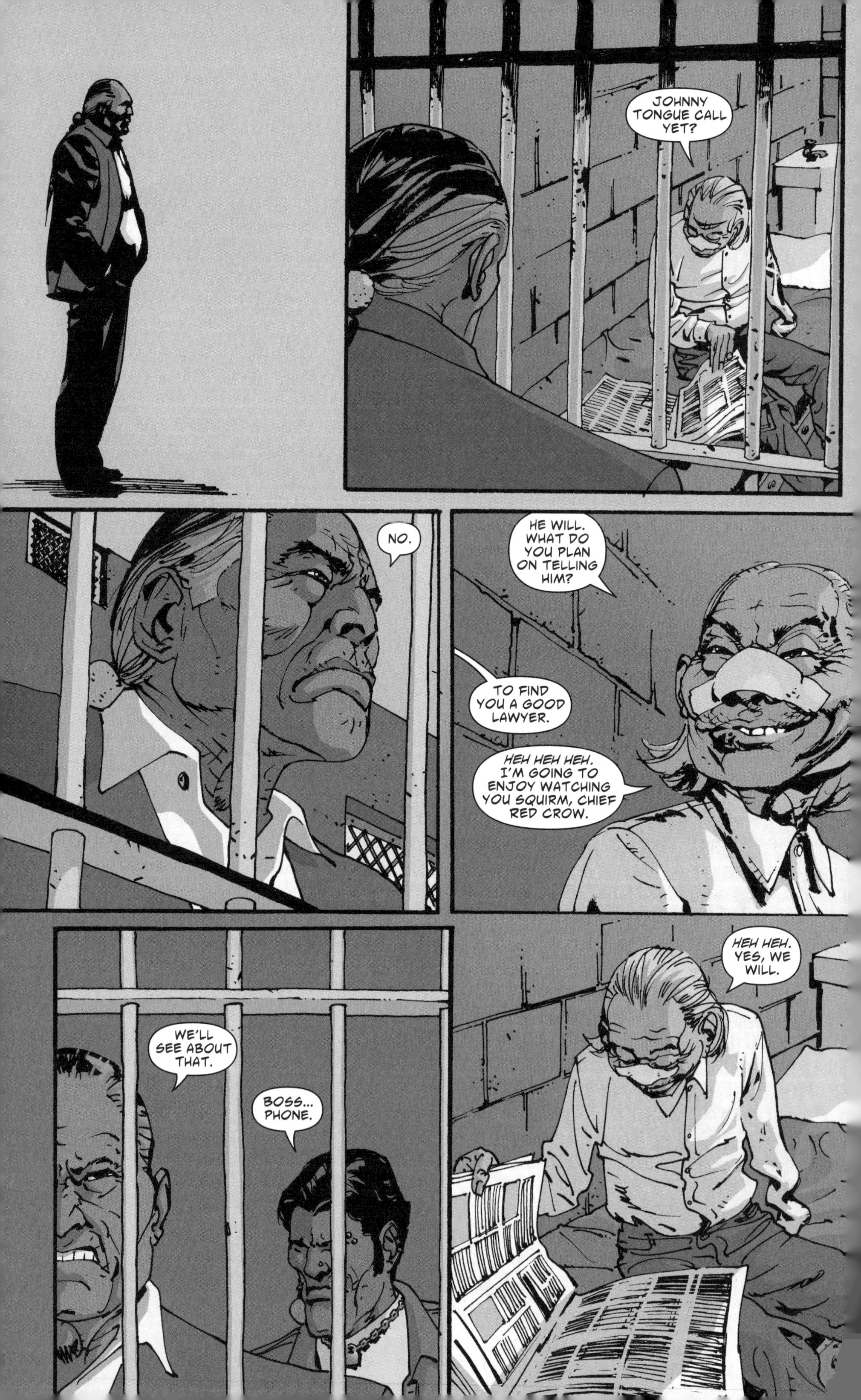
JOHNNY TONGUE CALL YET?
NO.
HE WILL. WHAT DO YOU PLAN ON TELLING HIM?
TO FIND YOU A GOOD LAWYER.
HEH HEH HEH. I'M GOING TO ENJOY WATCHING YOU SQUIRM, CHIEF RED CROW.
WE'LL SEE ABOUT THAT.
BOSS... PHONE.
HEH HEH. YES, WE WILL.

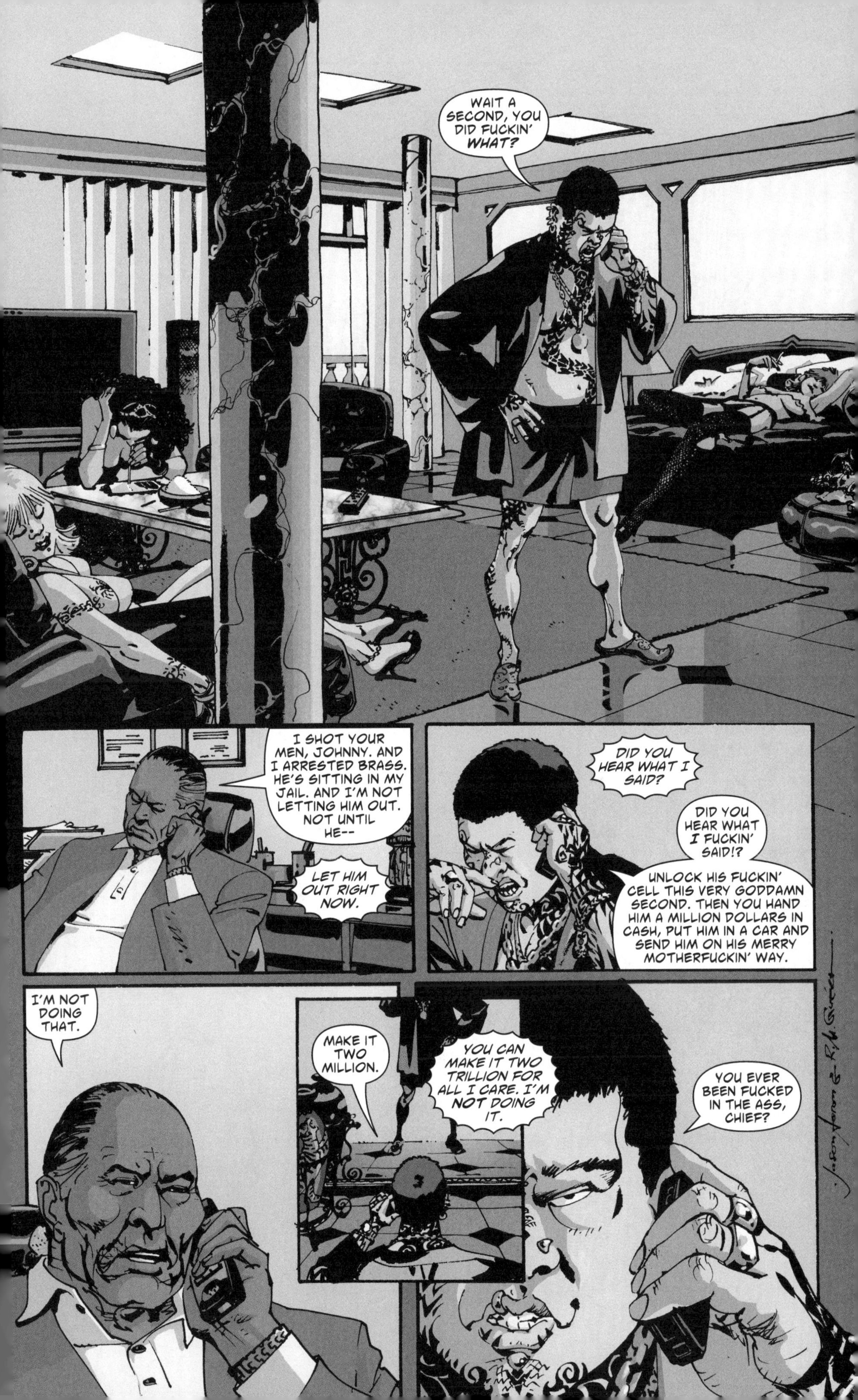
WAIT A SECOND, YOU DID FUCKIN' *WHAT?*
I SHOT YOUR MEN, JOHNNY. AND I ARRESTED BRASS. HE'S SITTING IN MY JAIL. AND I'M NOT LETTING HIM OUT. NOT UNTIL HE--
*LET HIM OUT RIGHT NOW.*
*DID YOU HEAR WHAT I SAID?*
DID YOU HEAR WHAT *I* FUCKIN' SAID!?
UNLOCK HIS FUCKIN' CELL THIS VERY GODDAMN SECOND. THEN YOU HAND HIM A MILLION DOLLARS IN CASH, PUT HIM IN A CAR AND SEND HIM ON HIS MERRY MOTHERFUCKIN' WAY.
I'M NOT DOING THAT.
MAKE IT TWO MILLION.
*YOU CAN MAKE IT TWO TRILLION FOR ALL I CARE. I'M* ***NOT*** *DOING IT.*
YOU EVER BEEN FUCKED IN THE ASS, CHIEF?

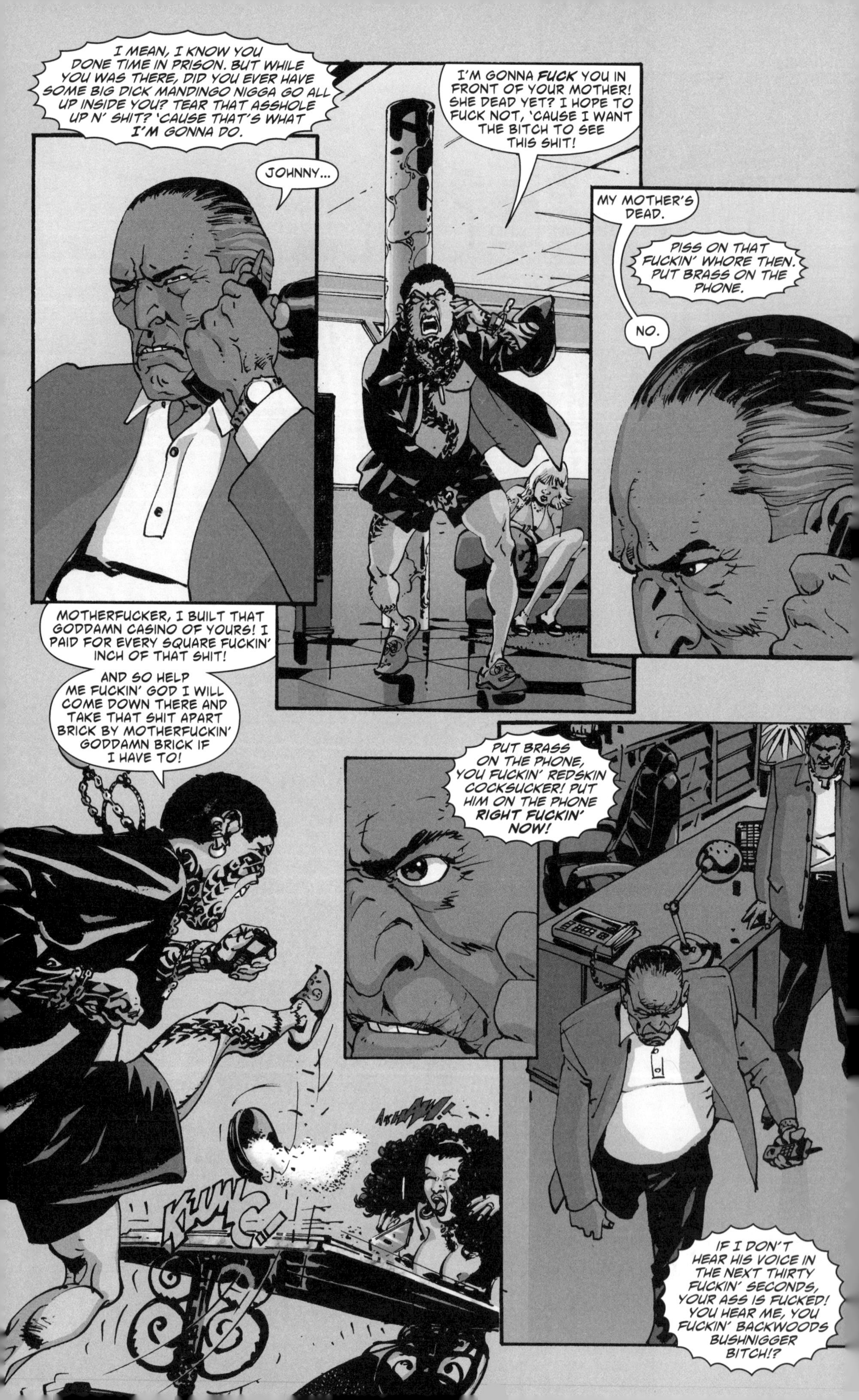
I MEAN, I KNOW YOU DONE TIME IN PRISON. BUT WHILE YOU WAS THERE, DID YOU EVER HAVE SOME BIG DICK MANDINGO NIGGA GO ALL UP INSIDE YOU? TEAR THAT ASSHOLE UP N' SHIT? 'CAUSE THAT'S WHAT I'M GONNA DO.
JOHNNY...
I'M GONNA FUCK YOU IN FRONT OF YOUR MOTHER! SHE DEAD YET? I HOPE TO FUCK NOT, 'CAUSE I WANT THE BITCH TO SEE THIS SHIT!
MY MOTHER'S DEAD.
PISS ON THAT FUCKIN' WHORE THEN. PUT BRASS ON THE PHONE.
NO.
MOTHERFUCKER, I BUILT THAT GODDAMN CASINO OF YOURS! I PAID FOR EVERY SQUARE FUCKIN' INCH OF THAT SHIT!
AND SO HELP ME FUCKIN' GOD I WILL COME DOWN THERE AND TAKE THAT SHIT APART BRICK BY MOTHERFUCKIN' GODDAMN BRICK IF I HAVE TO!
PUT BRASS ON THE PHONE, YOU FUCKIN' REDSKIN COCKSUCKER! PUT HIM ON THE PHONE RIGHT FUCKIN' NOW!
AHHAW!
KRUNCH!
IF I DON'T HEAR HIS VOICE IN THE NEXT THIRTY FUCKIN' SECONDS, YOUR ASS IS FUCKED! YOU HEAR ME, YOU FUCKIN' BACKWOODS BUSHNIGGER BITCH!?

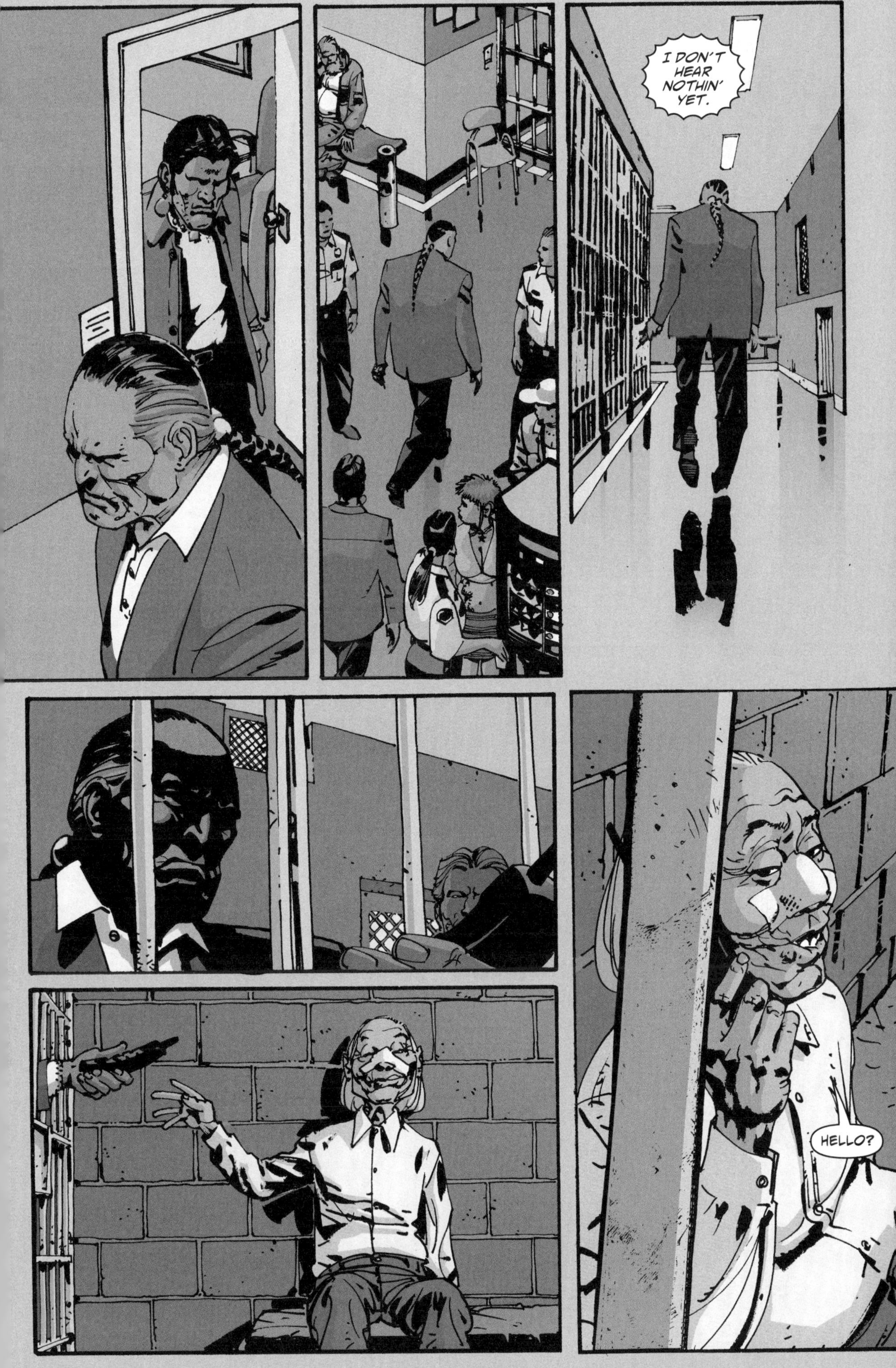
I DON'T HEAR NOTHIN' YET.
HELLO?

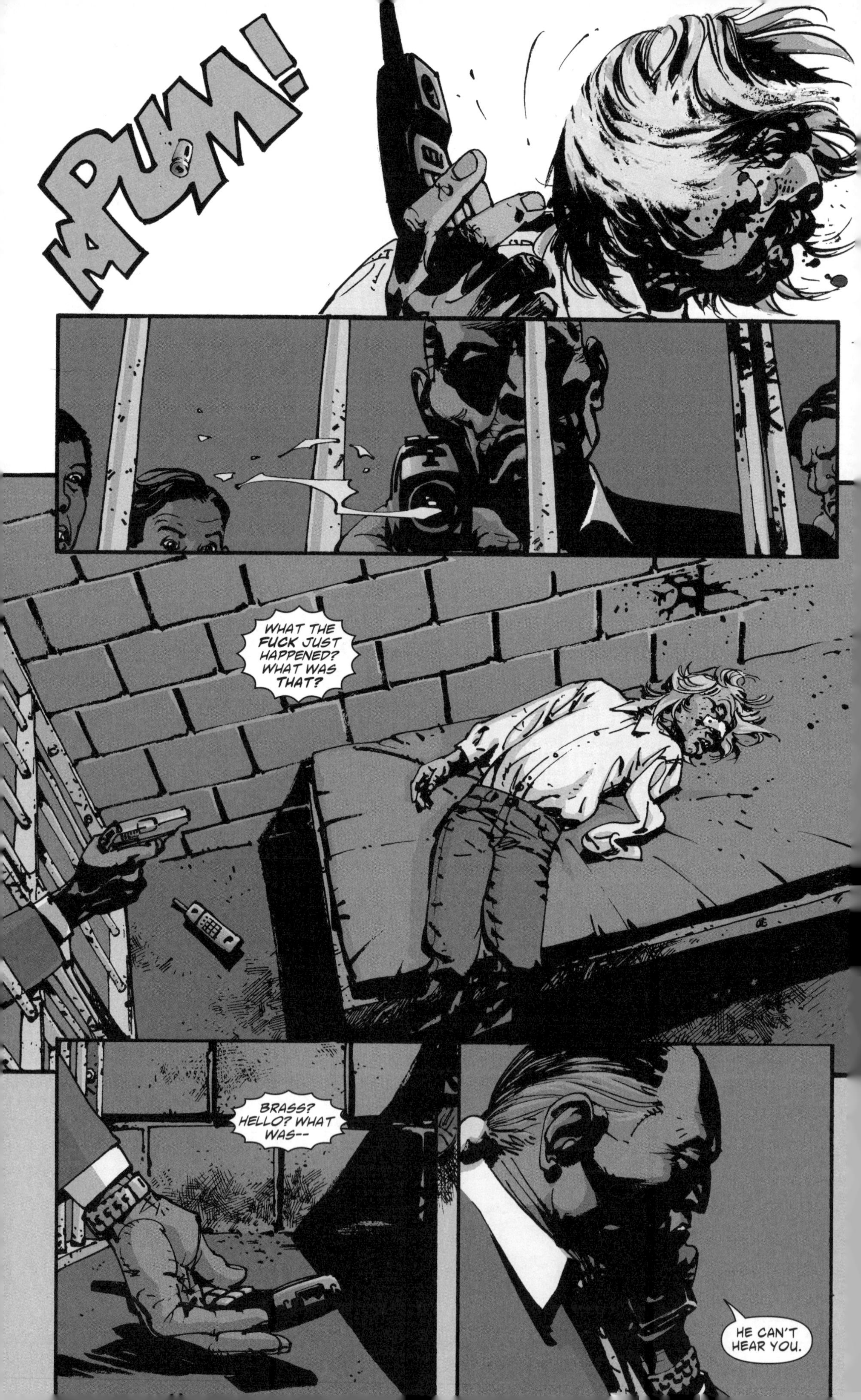
KA-BLAM!
WHAT THE FUCK JUST HAPPENED? WHAT WAS THAT?
BRASS? HELLO? WHAT WAS--
HE CAN'T HEAR YOU.

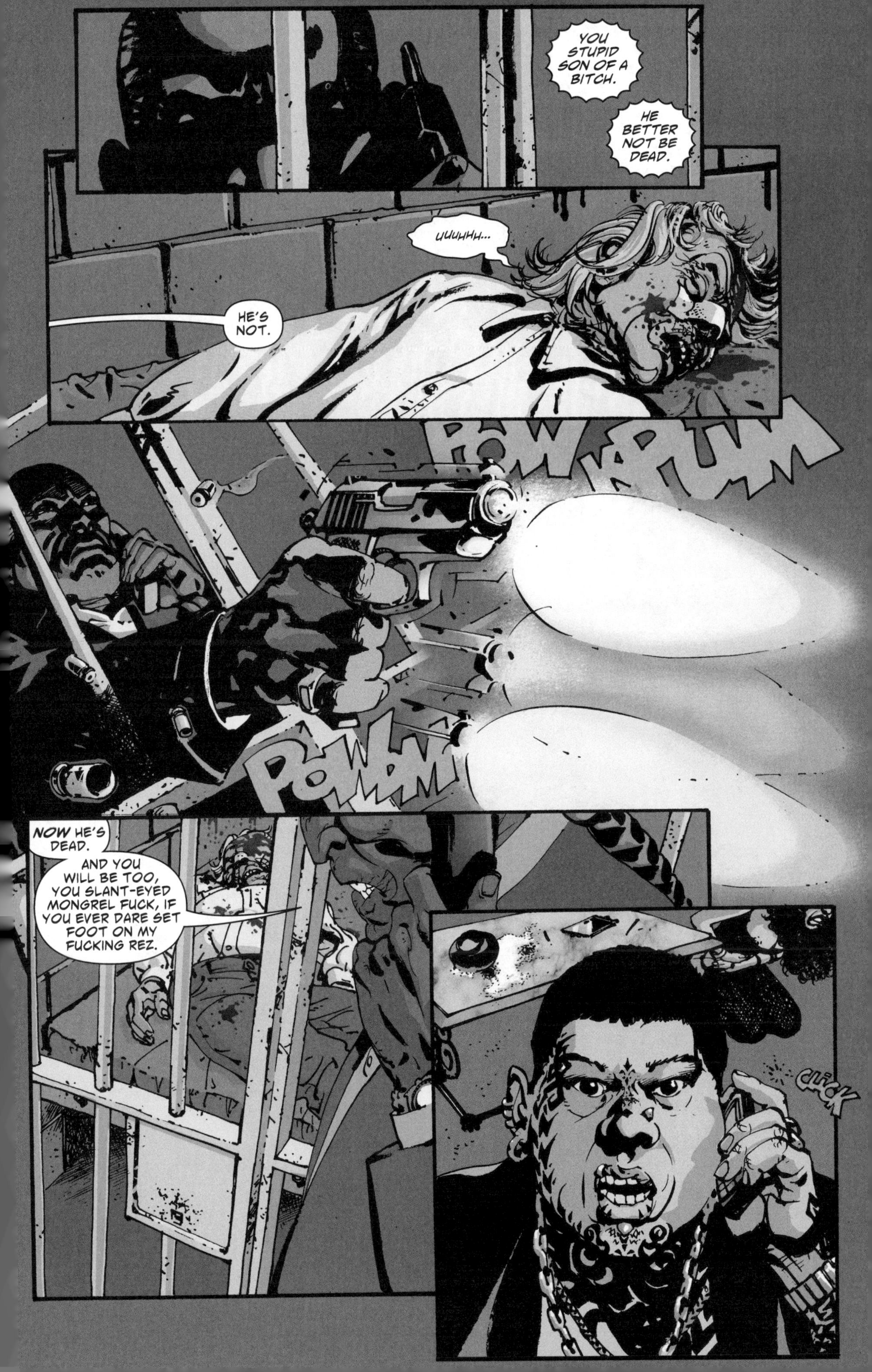
YOU STUPID SON OF A BITCH.
HE BETTER NOT BE DEAD.
UUUHHH...
HE'S NOT.
POW
KA-BLAM
POW
NOW HE'S DEAD.
AND YOU WILL BE TOO, YOU SLANT-EYED MONGREL FUCK, IF YOU EVER DARE SET FOOT ON MY FUCKING REZ.
CLICK

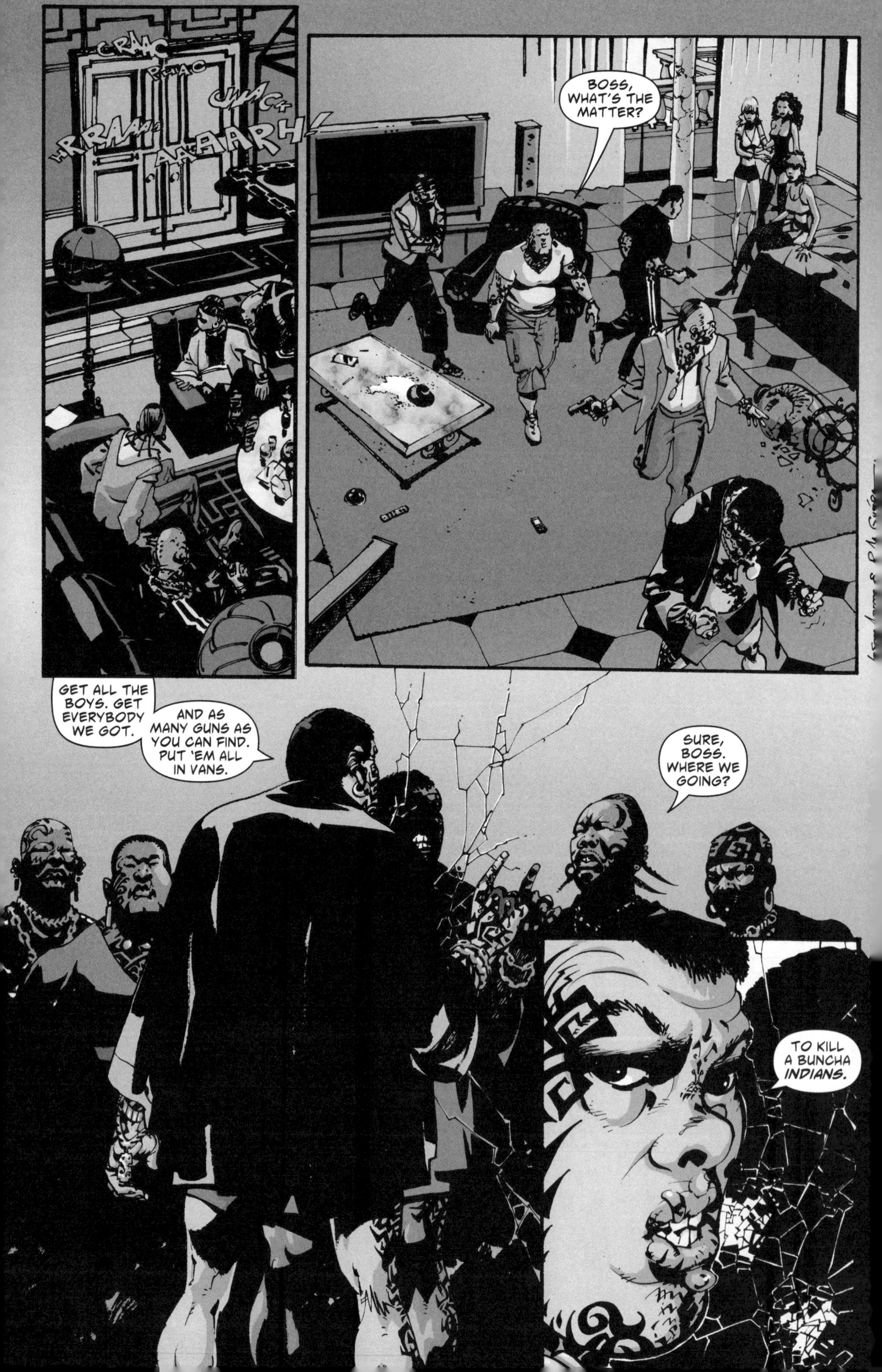
CRAAC
PHAC
CWACK
HRRAAAAAAAARH!
BOSS, WHAT'S THE MATTER?
GET ALL THE BOYS. GET EVERYBODY WE GOT.
AND AS MANY GUNS AS YOU CAN FIND. PUT 'EM ALL IN VANS.
SURE, BOSS. WHERE WE GOING?
TO KILL A BUNCHA *INDIANS.*

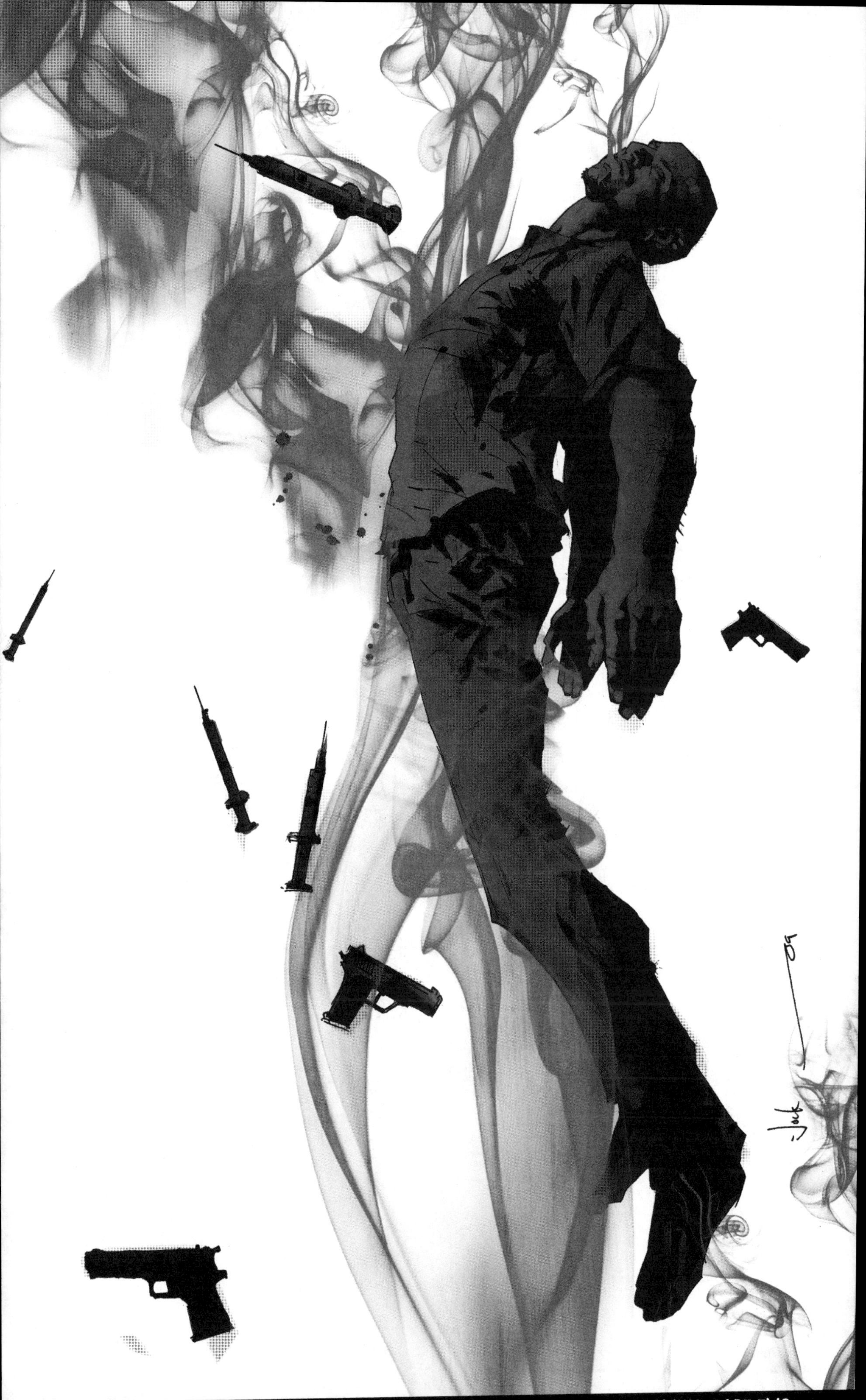

THE GNAWING, PART TWO

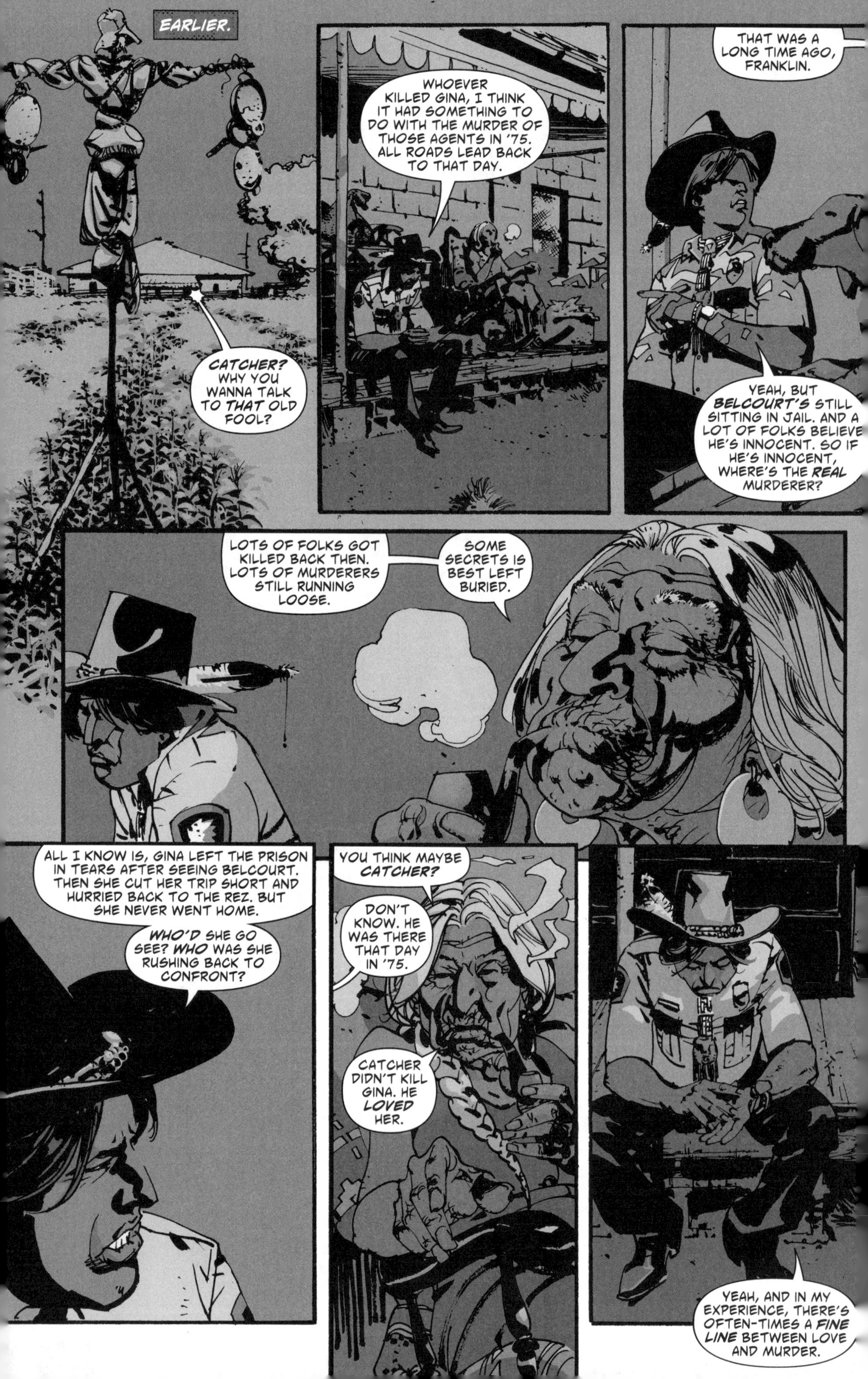
EARLIER.
CATCHER? WHY YOU WANNA TALK TO THAT OLD FOOL?
WHOEVER KILLED GINA, I THINK IT HAD SOMETHING TO DO WITH THE MURDER OF THOSE AGENTS IN '75. ALL ROADS LEAD BACK TO THAT DAY.
THAT WAS A LONG TIME AGO, FRANKLIN.
YEAH, BUT BELCOURT'S STILL SITTING IN JAIL. AND A LOT OF FOLKS BELIEVE HE'S INNOCENT. SO IF HE'S INNOCENT, WHERE'S THE REAL MURDERER?
LOTS OF FOLKS GOT KILLED BACK THEN. LOTS OF MURDERERS STILL RUNNING LOOSE.
SOME SECRETS IS BEST LEFT BURIED.
ALL I KNOW IS, GINA LEFT THE PRISON IN TEARS AFTER SEEING BELCOURT. THEN SHE CUT HER TRIP SHORT AND HURRIED BACK TO THE REZ. BUT SHE NEVER WENT HOME.
WHO'D SHE GO SEE? WHO WAS SHE RUSHING BACK TO CONFRONT?
YOU THINK MAYBE CATCHER?
DON'T KNOW. HE WAS THERE THAT DAY IN '75.
CATCHER DIDN'T KILL GINA. HE LOVED HER.
YEAH, AND IN MY EXPERIENCE, THERE'S OFTEN-TIMES A FINE LINE BETWEEN LOVE AND MURDER.

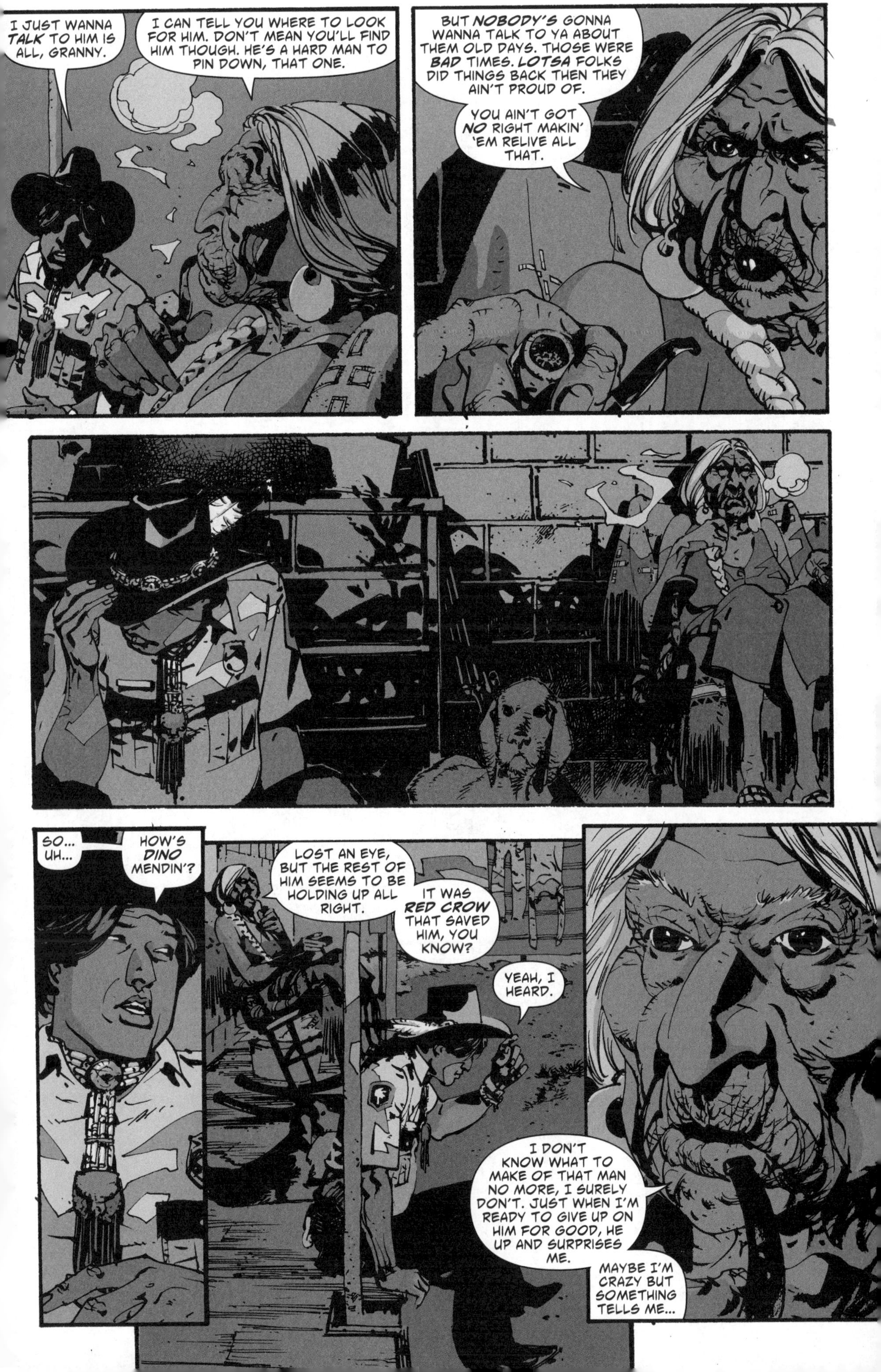
I JUST WANNA TALK TO HIM IS ALL, GRANNY.
I CAN TELL YOU WHERE TO LOOK FOR HIM. DON'T MEAN YOU'LL FIND HIM THOUGH. HE'S A HARD MAN TO PIN DOWN, THAT ONE.
BUT NOBODY'S GONNA WANNA TALK TO YA ABOUT THEM OLD DAYS. THOSE WERE BAD TIMES. LOTSA FOLKS DID THINGS BACK THEN THEY AIN'T PROUD OF.
YOU AIN'T GOT NO RIGHT MAKIN' 'EM RELIVE ALL THAT.
SO... UH...
HOW'S DINO MENDIN'?
LOST AN EYE, BUT THE REST OF HIM SEEMS TO BE HOLDING UP ALL RIGHT.
IT WAS RED CROW THAT SAVED HIM, YOU KNOW?
YEAH, I HEARD.
I DON'T KNOW WHAT TO MAKE OF THAT MAN NO MORE, I SURELY DON'T. JUST WHEN I'M READY TO GIVE UP ON HIM FOR GOOD, HE UP AND SURPRISES ME.
MAYBE I'M CRAZY BUT SOMETHING TELLS ME...

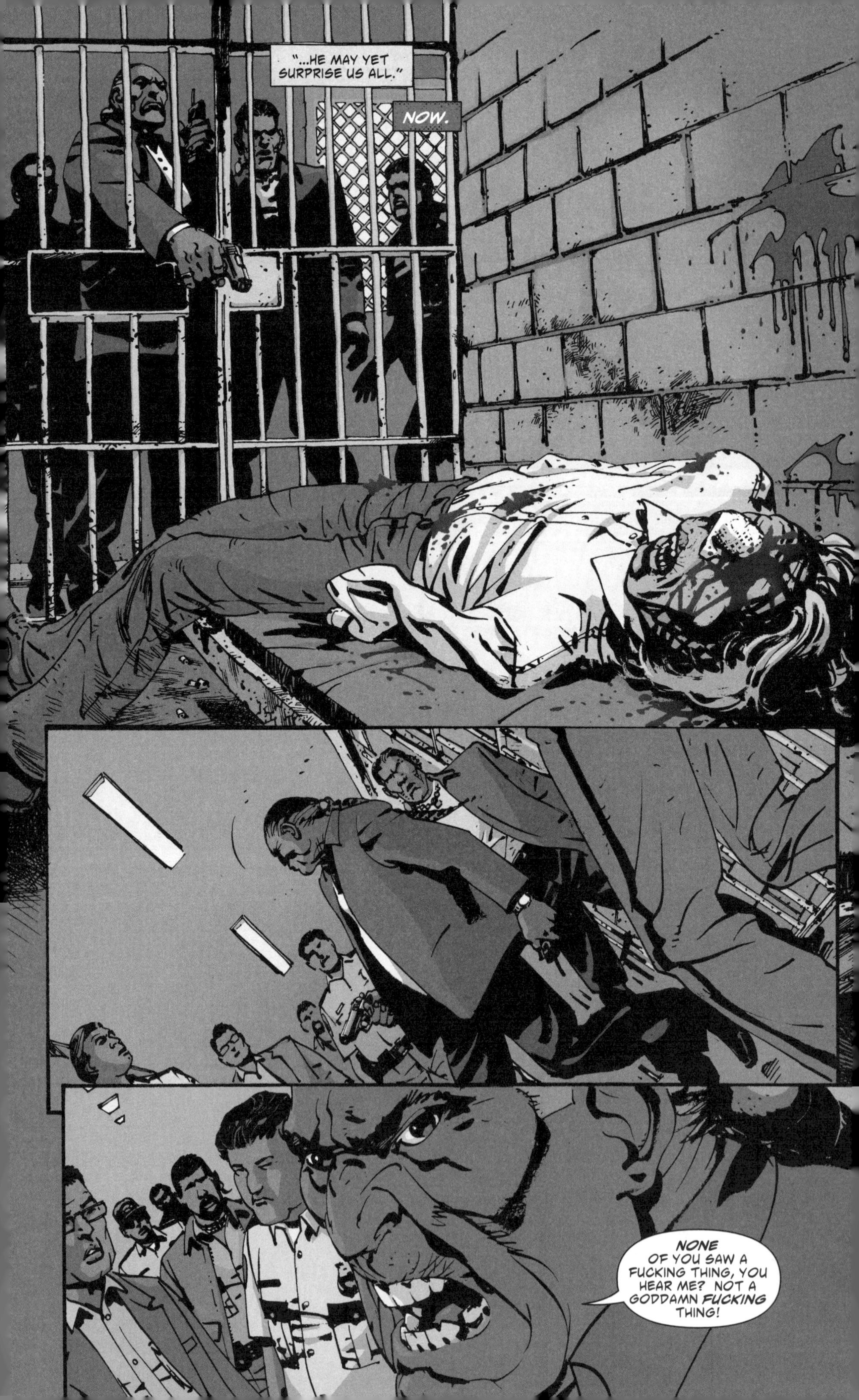
"...HE MAY YET SURPRISE US ALL."
NOW.
NONE OF YOU SAW A FUCKING THING, YOU HEAR ME? NOT A GODDAMN FUCKING THING!

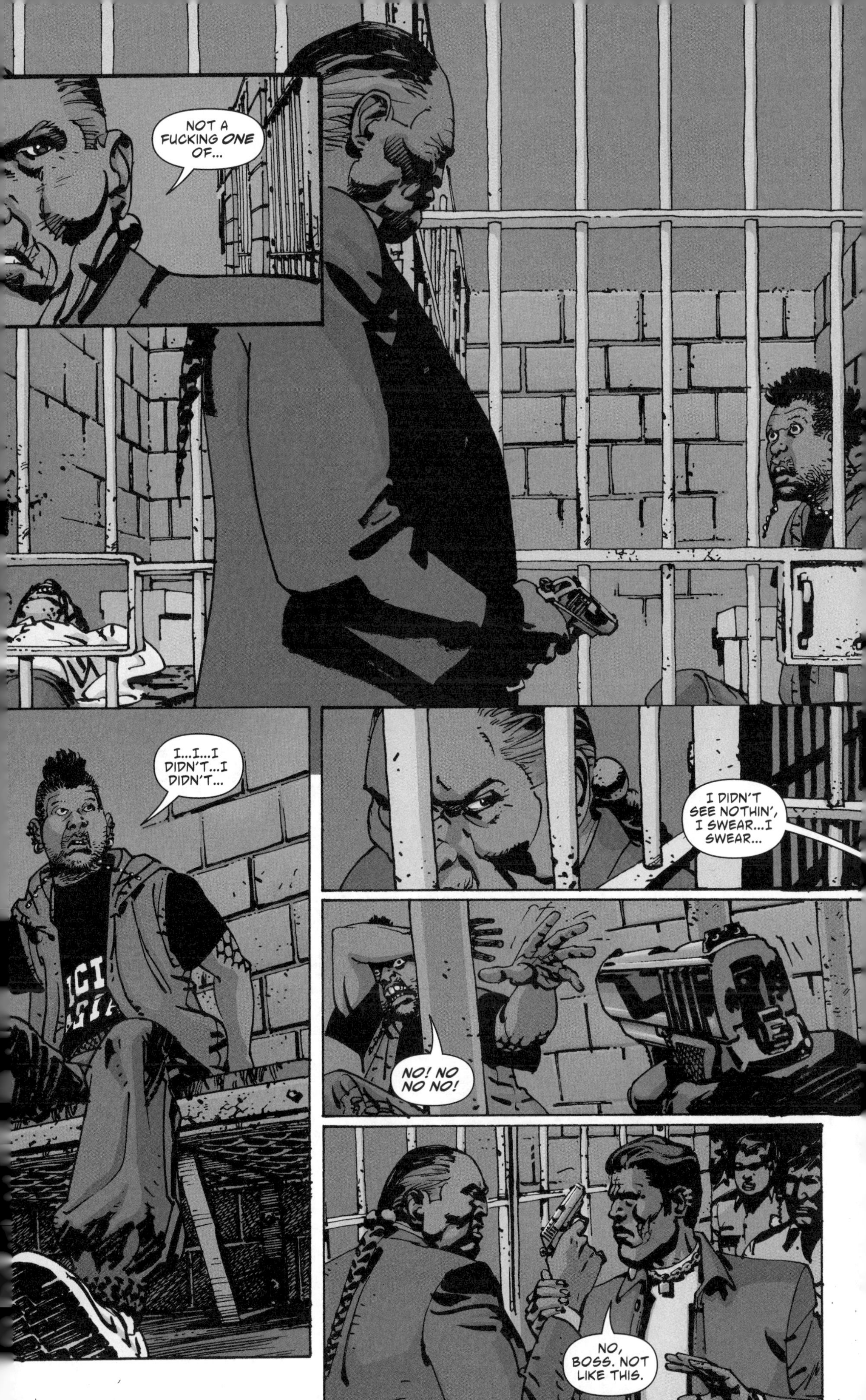
NOT A FUCKING ONE OF...
I...I...I DIDN'T...I DIDN'T...
I DIDN'T SEE NOTHIN', I SWEAR...I SWEAR...
NO! NO NO NO!
NO, BOSS. NOT LIKE THIS.

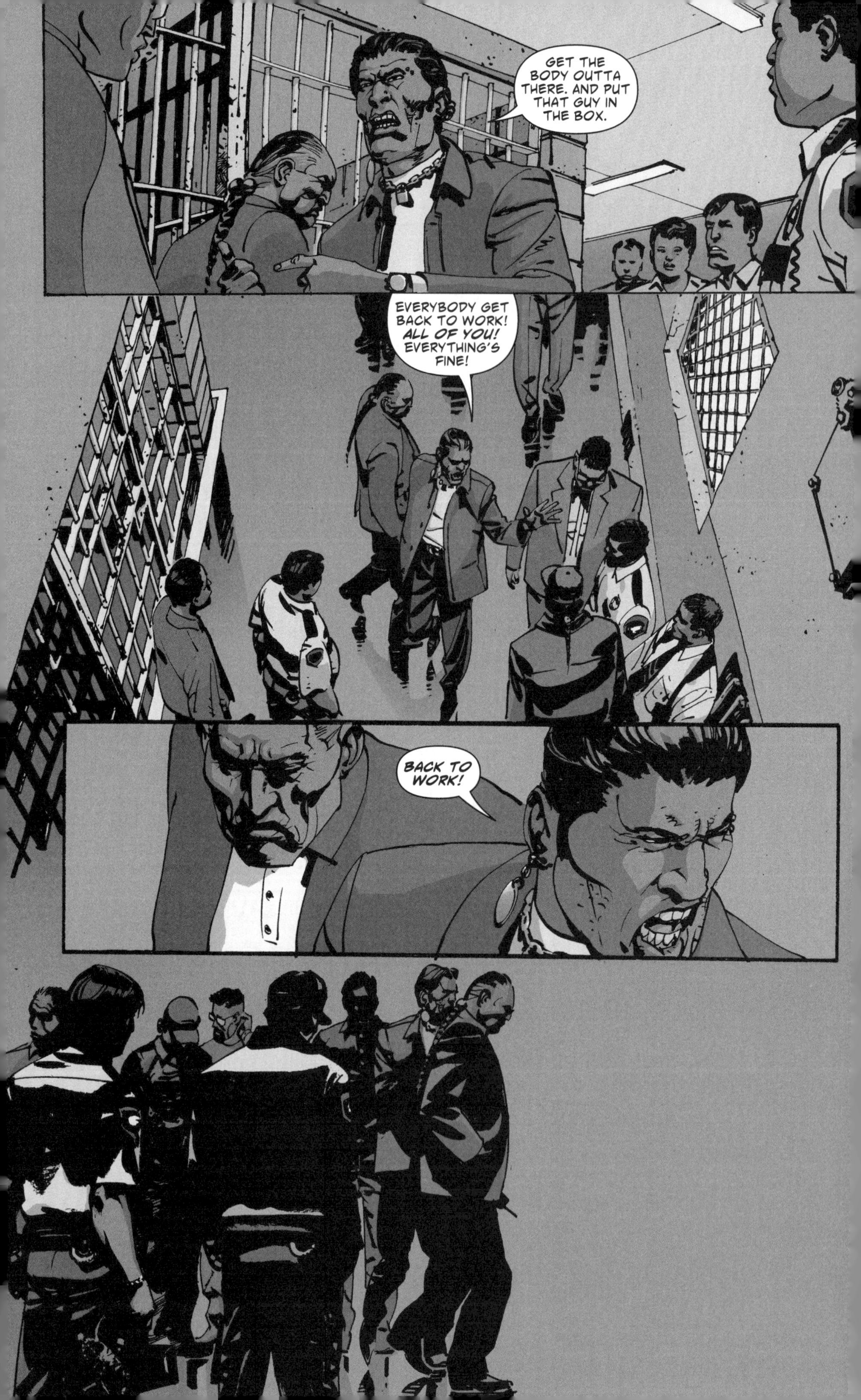
GET THE BODY OUTTA THERE. AND PUT THAT GUY IN THE BOX.
EVERYBODY GET BACK TO WORK! ALL OF YOU! EVERYTHING'S FINE!
BACK TO WORK!

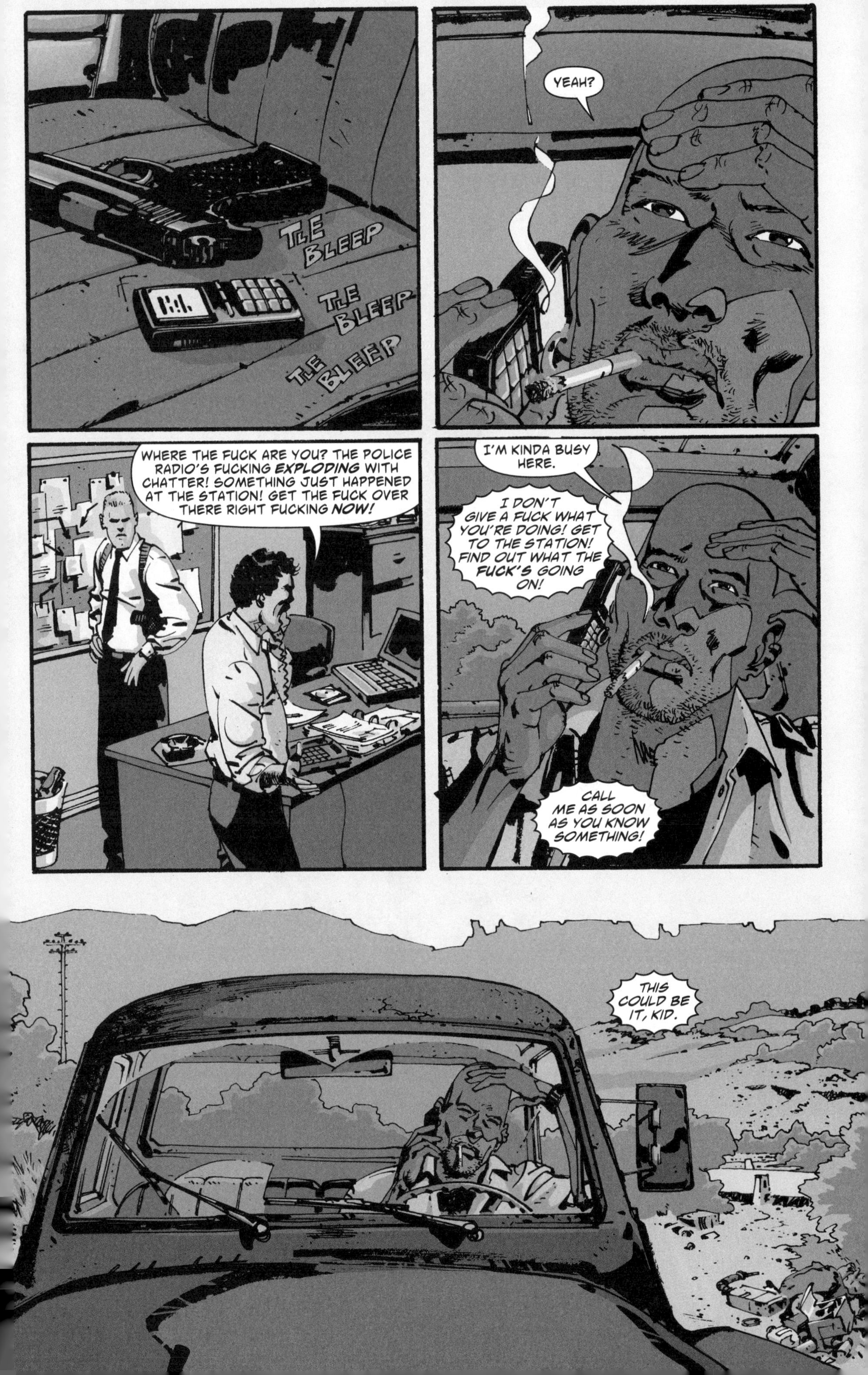
TLE BLEEP
TLE BLEEP
TLE BLEEP
YEAH?
WHERE THE FUCK ARE YOU? THE POLICE RADIO'S FUCKING EXPLODING WITH CHATTER! SOMETHING JUST HAPPENED AT THE STATION! GET THE FUCK OVER THERE RIGHT FUCKING NOW!
I'M KINDA BUSY HERE.
I DON'T GIVE A FUCK WHAT YOU'RE DOING! GET TO THE STATION! FIND OUT WHAT THE FUCK'S GOING ON!
CALL ME AS SOON AS YOU KNOW SOMETHING!
THIS COULD BE IT, KID.

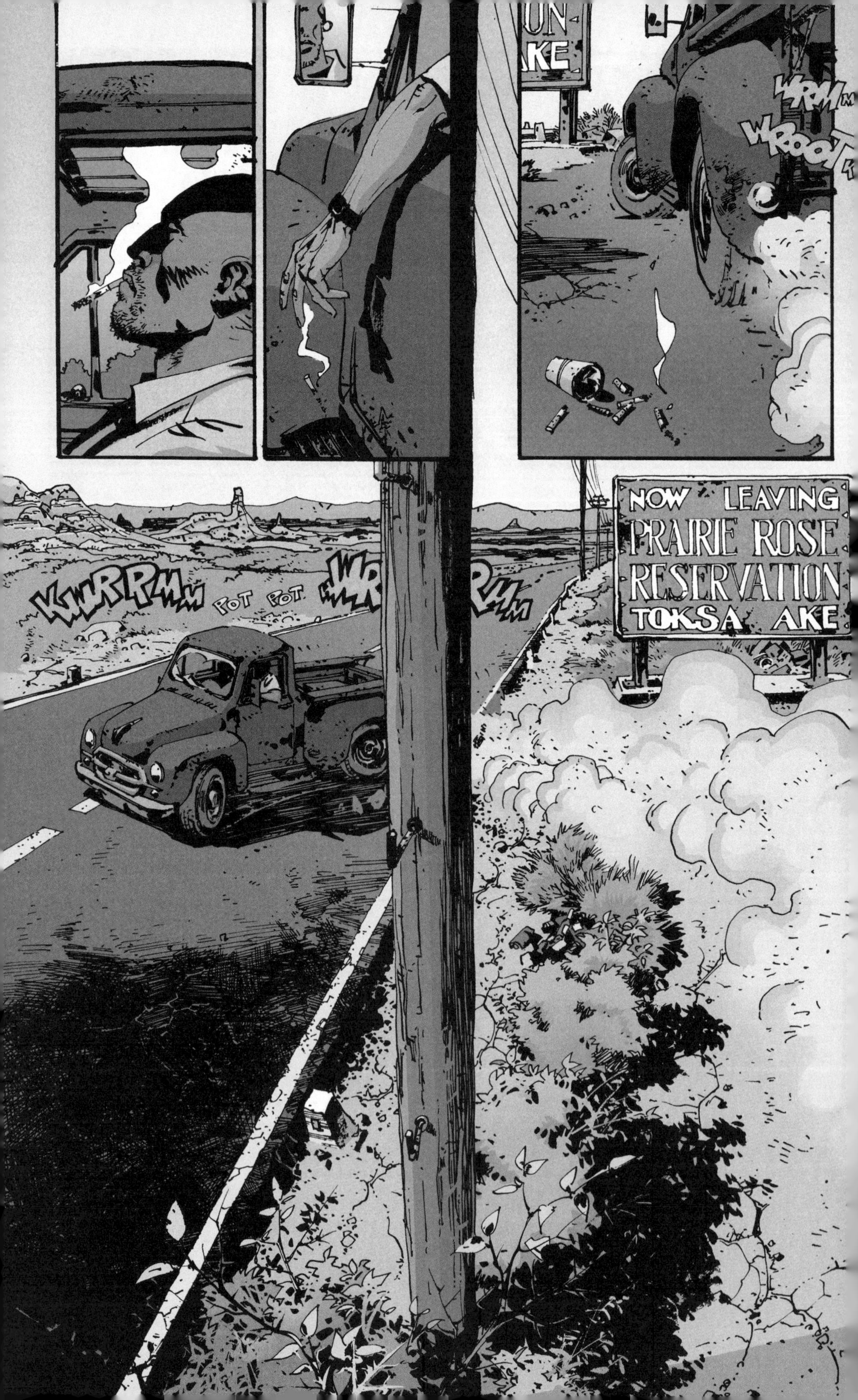
KWRRPMM
POT POT
NOW LEAVING
PRAIRIE ROSE
RESERVATION
TOKSA AKE

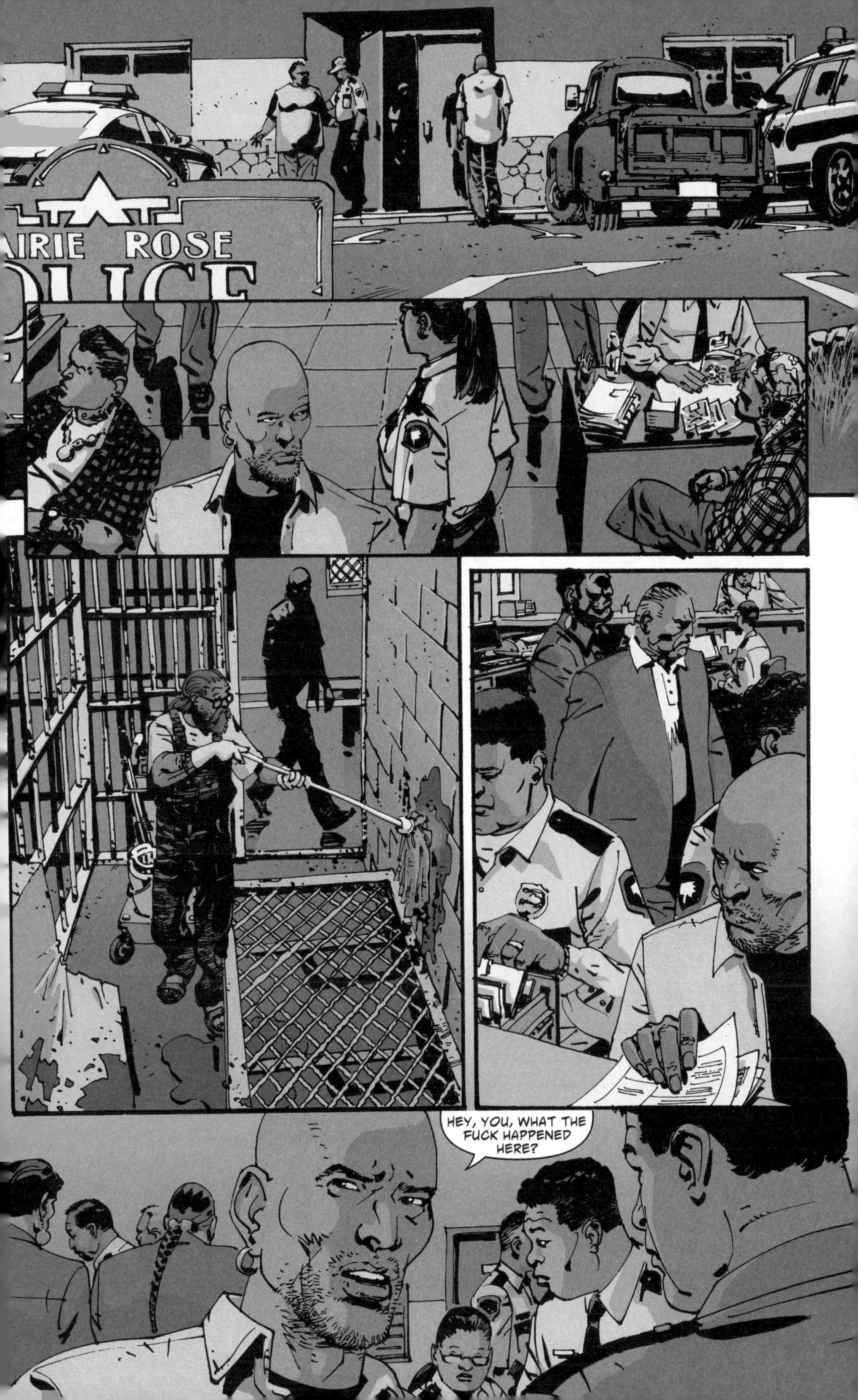
AIRIE ROSE
OLICE
HEY, YOU, WHAT THE FUCK HAPPENED HERE?

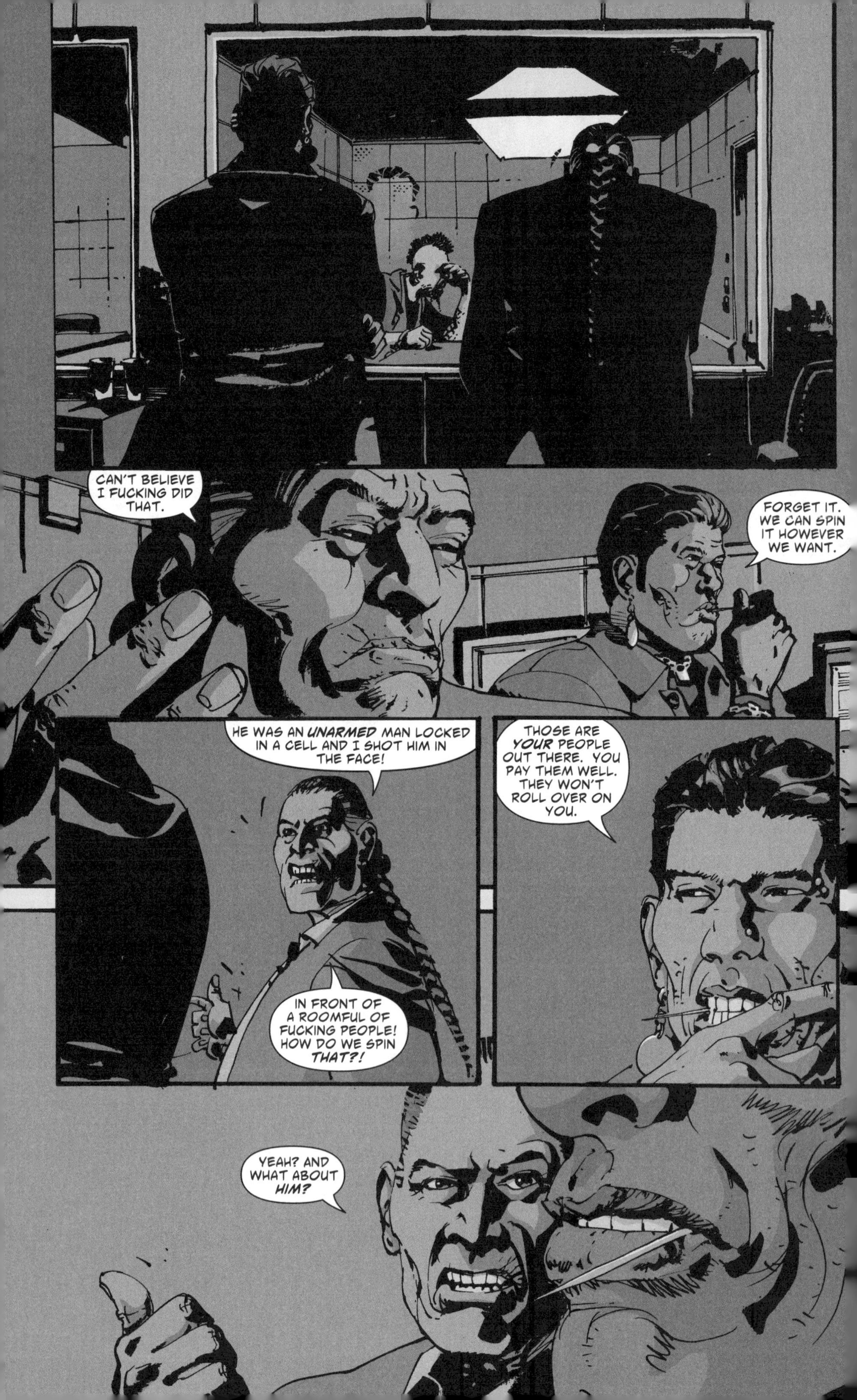
CAN'T BELIEVE I FUCKING DID THAT.
FORGET IT. WE CAN SPIN IT HOWEVER WE WANT.
HE WAS AN UNARMED MAN LOCKED IN A CELL AND I SHOT HIM IN THE FACE!
IN FRONT OF A ROOMFUL OF FUCKING PEOPLE! HOW DO WE SPIN THAT?!
THOSE ARE YOUR PEOPLE OUT THERE. YOU PAY THEM WELL. THEY WON'T ROLL OVER ON YOU.
YEAH? AND WHAT ABOUT HIM?

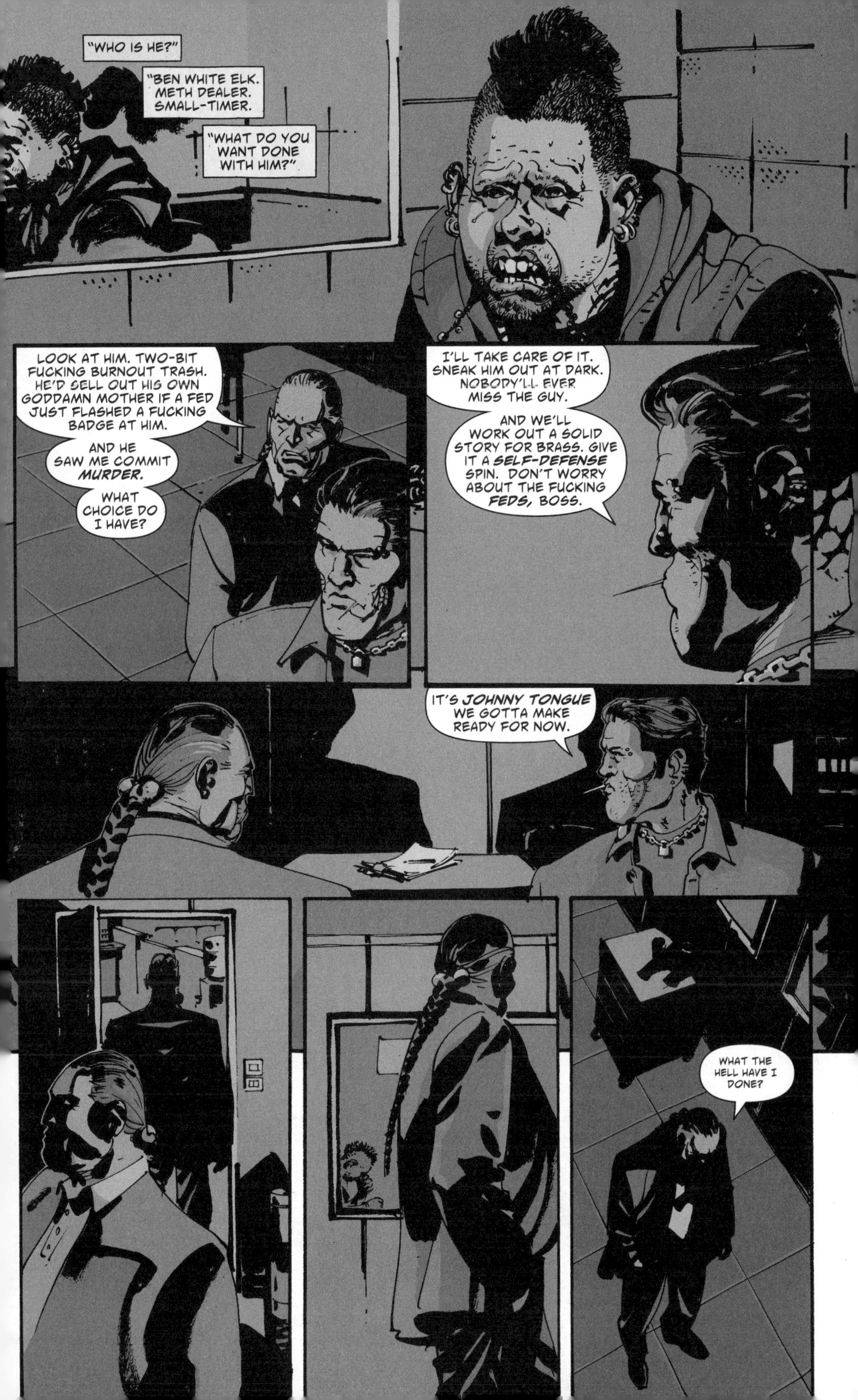
"WHO IS HE?"
"BEN WHITE ELK. METH DEALER. SMALL-TIMER.
"WHAT DO YOU WANT DONE WITH HIM?"
LOOK AT HIM. TWO-BIT FUCKING BURNOUT TRASH. HE'D SELL OUT HIS OWN GODDAMN MOTHER IF A FED JUST FLASHED A FUCKING BADGE AT HIM.
AND HE SAW ME COMMIT *MURDER.*
WHAT CHOICE DO I HAVE?
I'LL TAKE CARE OF IT. SNEAK HIM OUT AT DARK. NOBODY'LL EVER MISS THE GUY.
AND WE'LL WORK OUT A SOLID STORY FOR BRASS. GIVE IT A *SELF-DEFENSE* SPIN. DON'T WORRY ABOUT THE FUCKING *FEDS,* BOSS.
IT'S *JOHNNY TONGUE* WE GOTTA MAKE READY FOR NOW.
WHAT THE HELL HAVE I DONE?

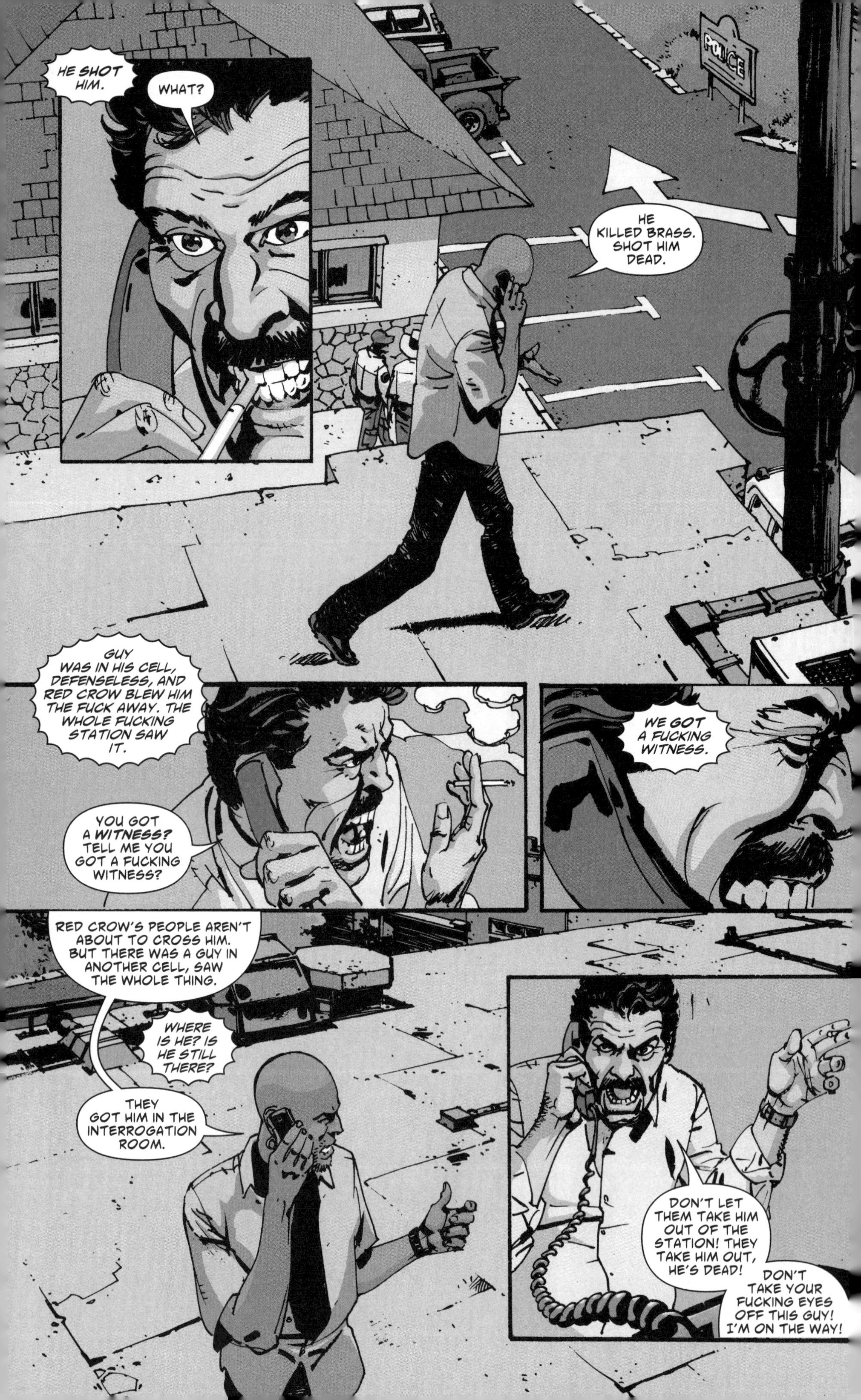
POLICE
HE SHOT HIM.
WHAT?
HE KILLED BRASS. SHOT HIM DEAD.
GUY WAS IN HIS CELL, DEFENSELESS, AND RED CROW BLEW HIM THE FUCK AWAY. THE WHOLE FUCKING STATION SAW IT.
YOU GOT A WITNESS? TELL ME YOU GOT A FUCKING WITNESS?
WE GOT A FUCKING WITNESS.
RED CROW'S PEOPLE AREN'T ABOUT TO CROSS HIM. BUT THERE WAS A GUY IN ANOTHER CELL, SAW THE WHOLE THING.
WHERE IS HE? IS HE STILL THERE?
THEY GOT HIM IN THE INTERROGATION ROOM.
DON'T LET THEM TAKE HIM OUT OF THE STATION! THEY TAKE HIM OUT, HE'S DEAD!
DON'T TAKE YOUR FUCKING EYES OFF THIS GUY! I'M ON THE WAY!

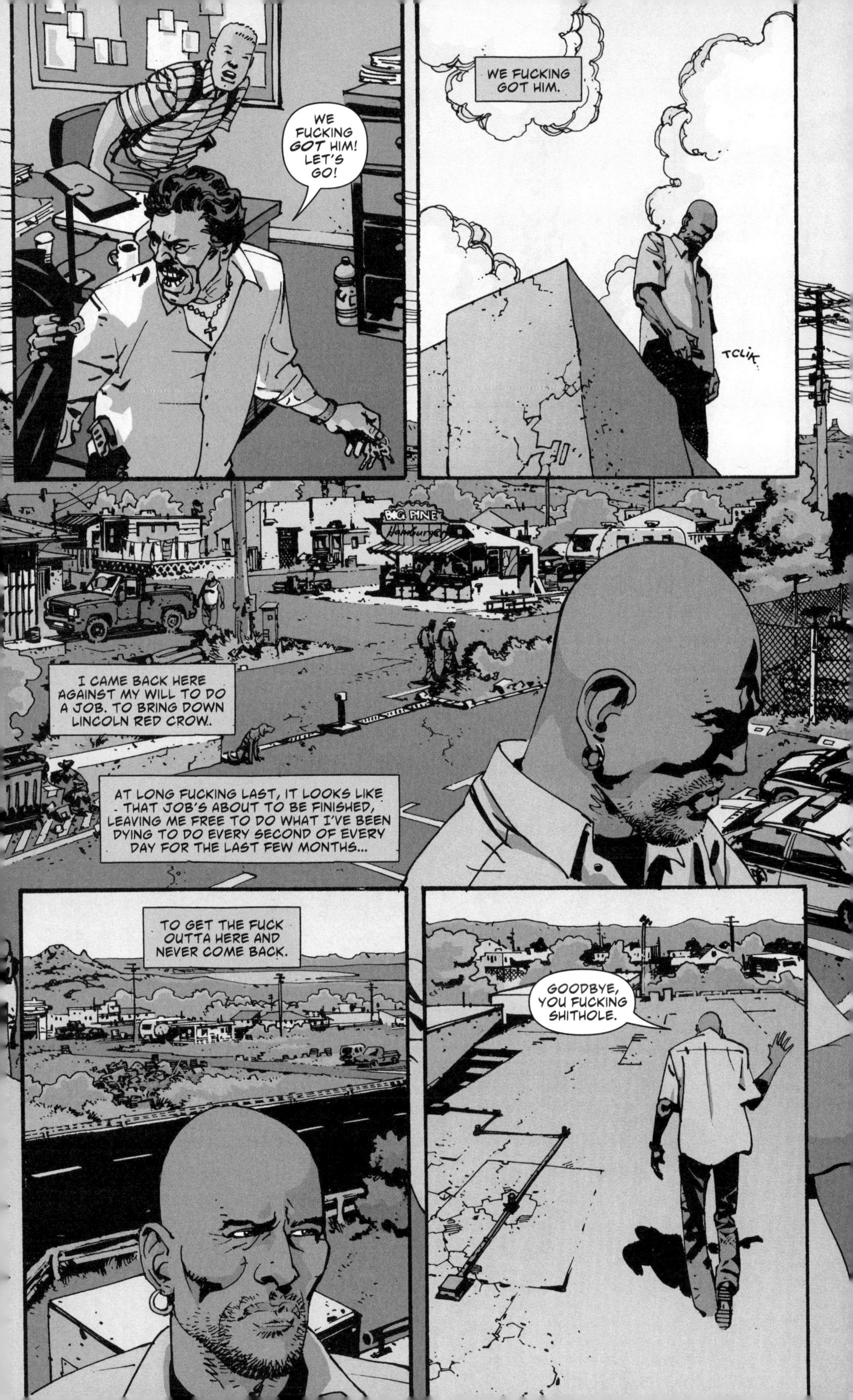
WE FUCKING GOT HIM! LET'S GO!
WE FUCKING GOT HIM.
TCLIK
I CAME BACK HERE AGAINST MY WILL TO DO A JOB. TO BRING DOWN LINCOLN RED CROW..
AT LONG FUCKING LAST, IT LOOKS LIKE THAT JOB'S ABOUT TO BE FINISHED, LEAVING ME FREE TO DO WHAT I'VE BEEN DYING TO DO EVERY SECOND OF EVERY DAY FOR THE LAST FEW MONTHS...
TO GET THE FUCK OUTTA HERE AND NEVER COME BACK.
GOODBYE, YOU FUCKING SHITHOLE.

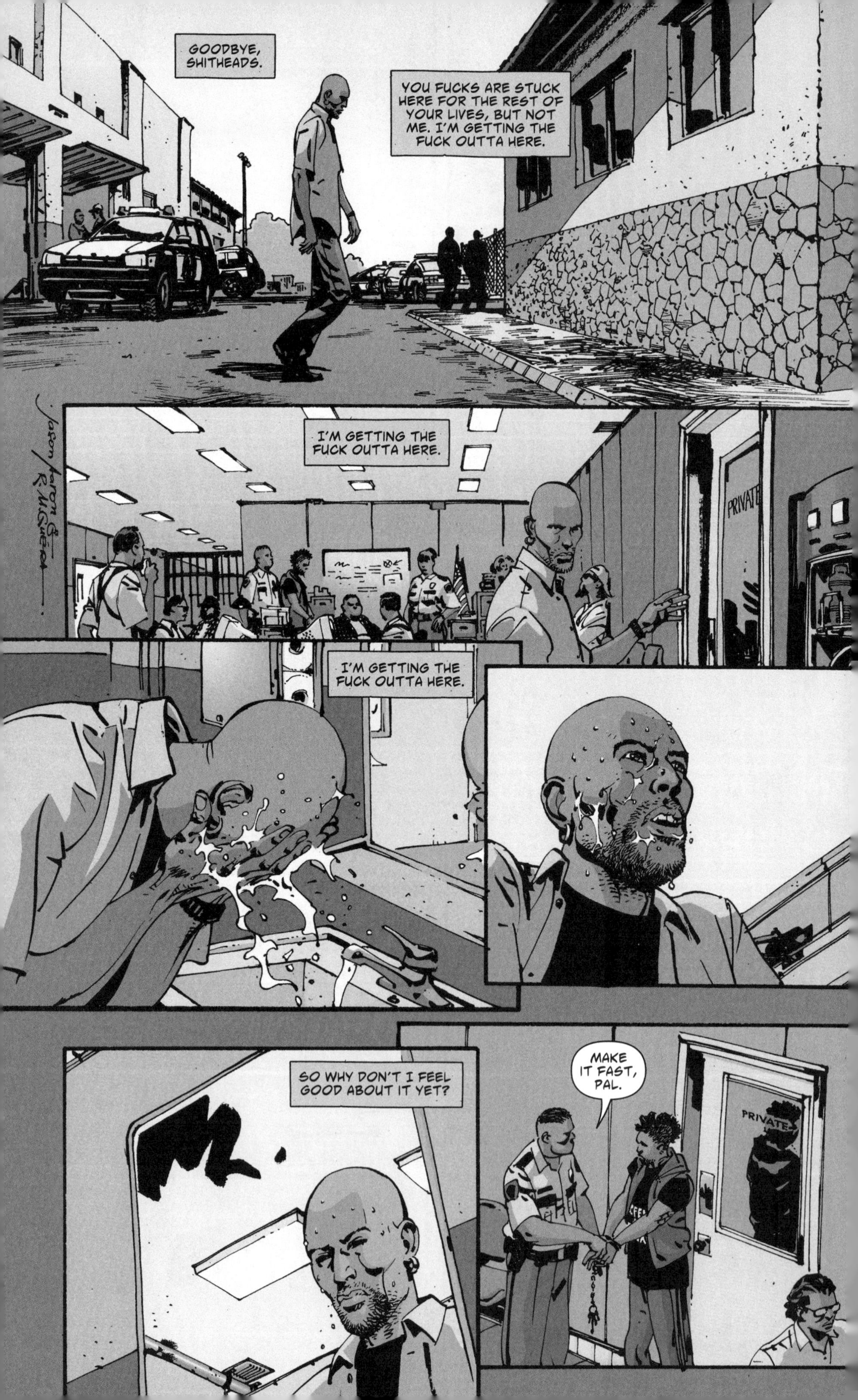
GOODBYE, SHITHEADS.
YOU FUCKS ARE STUCK HERE FOR THE REST OF YOUR LIVES, BUT NOT ME. I'M GETTING THE FUCK OUTTA HERE.
I'M GETTING THE FUCK OUTTA HERE.
PRIVATE
I'M GETTING THE FUCK OUTTA HERE.
SO WHY DON'T I FEEL GOOD ABOUT IT YET?
MAKE IT FAST, PAL.
PRIVATE

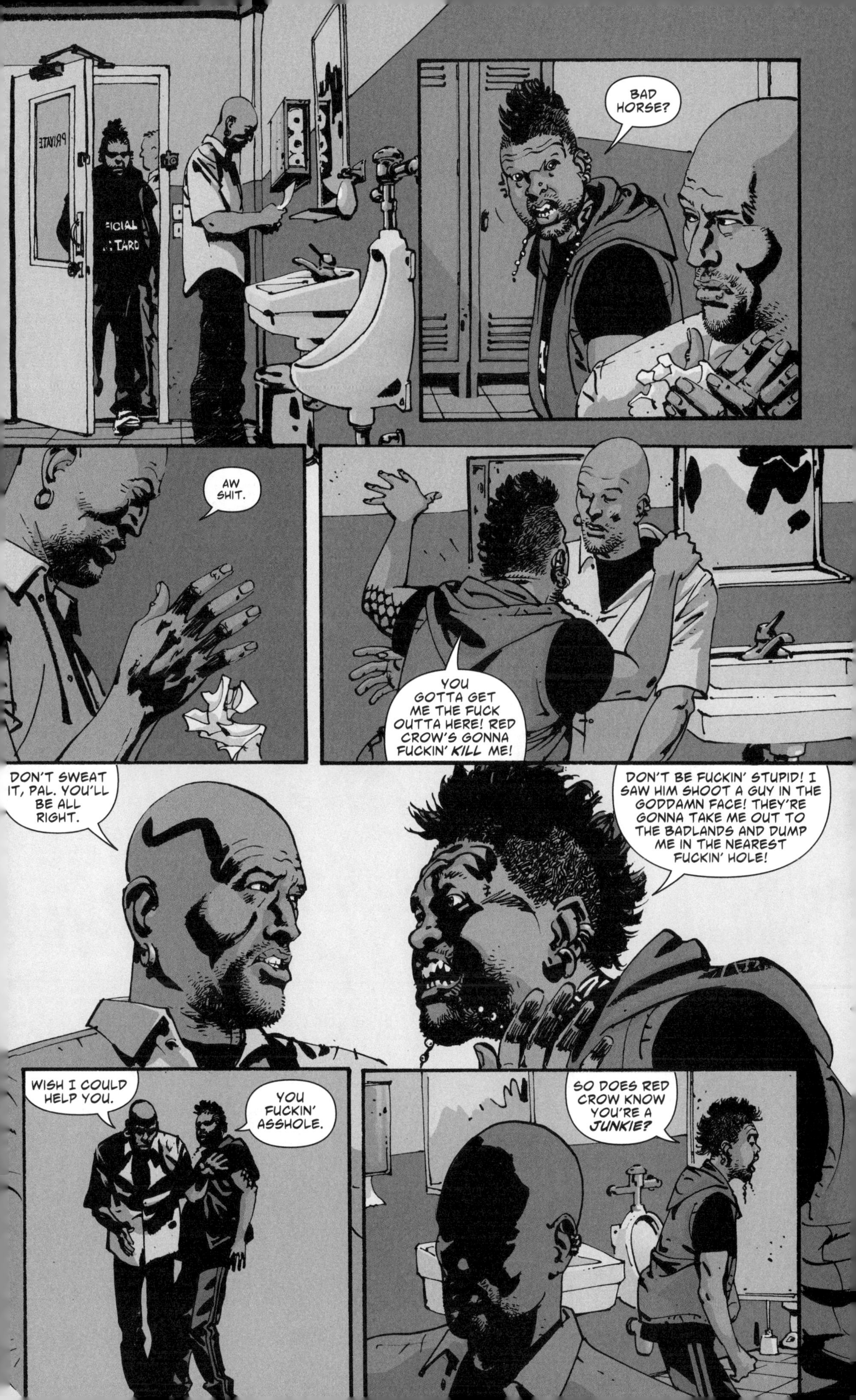
PRIVATE
BAD HORSE?
AW SHIT.
YOU GOTTA GET ME THE FUCK OUTTA HERE! RED CROW'S GONNA FUCKIN' KILL ME!
DON'T SWEAT IT, PAL. YOU'LL BE ALL RIGHT.
DON'T BE FUCKIN' STUPID! I SAW HIM SHOOT A GUY IN THE GODDAMN FACE! THEY'RE GONNA TAKE ME OUT TO THE BADLANDS AND DUMP ME IN THE NEAREST FUCKIN' HOLE!
WISH I COULD HELP YOU.
YOU FUCKIN' ASSHOLE.
SO DOES RED CROW KNOW YOU'RE A JUNKIE?

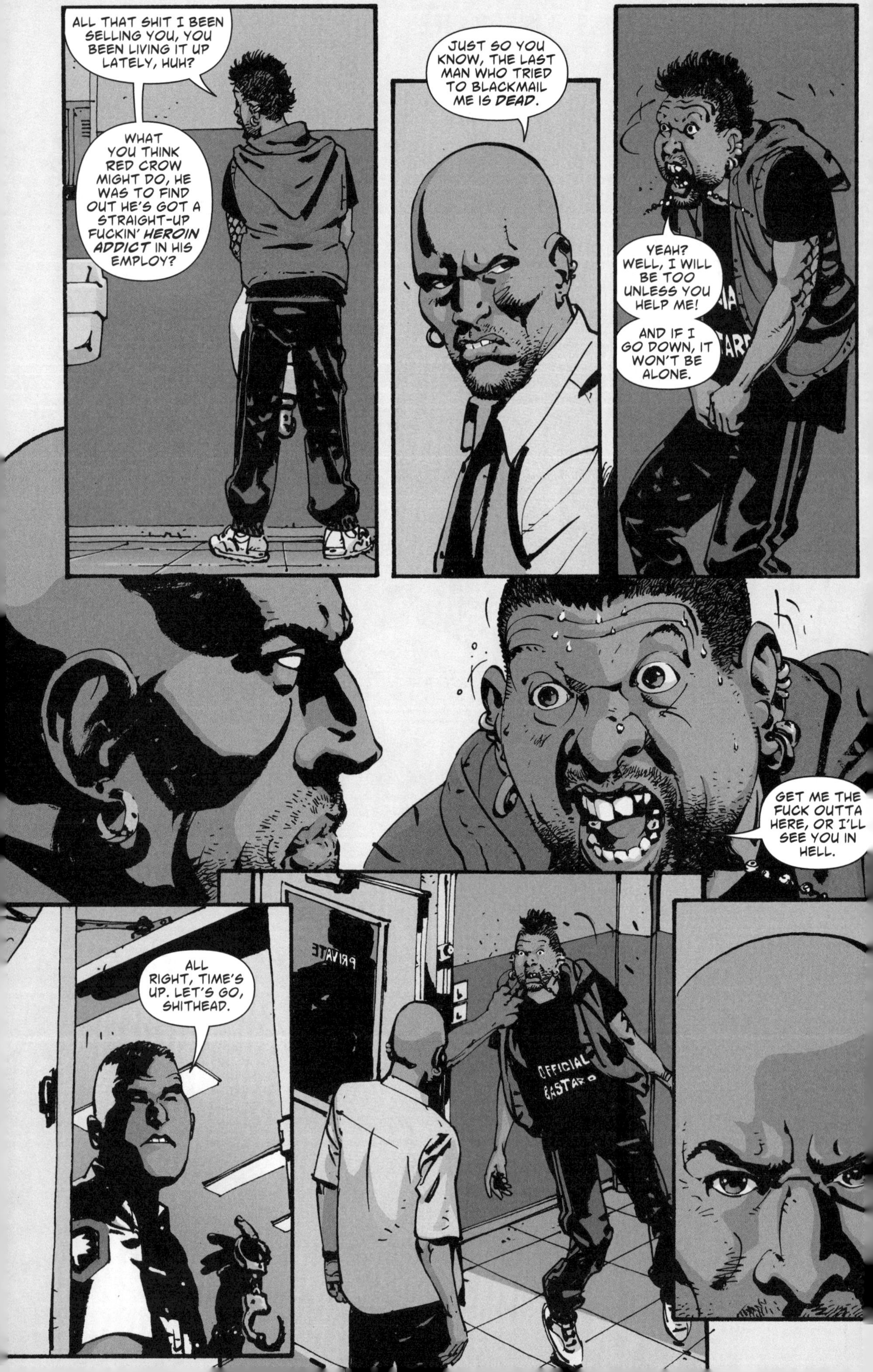
ALL THAT SHIT I BEEN SELLING YOU, YOU BEEN LIVING IT UP LATELY, HUH?
WHAT YOU THINK RED CROW MIGHT DO, HE WAS TO FIND OUT HE'S GOT A STRAIGHT-UP FUCKIN' HEROIN ADDICT IN HIS EMPLOY?
JUST SO YOU KNOW, THE LAST MAN WHO TRIED TO BLACKMAIL ME IS DEAD.
YEAH? WELL, I WILL BE TOO UNLESS YOU HELP ME!
AND IF I GO DOWN, IT WON'T BE ALONE.
GET ME THE FUCK OUTTA HERE, OR I'LL SEE YOU IN HELL.
ALL RIGHT, TIME'S UP. LET'S GO, SHITHEAD.
PRIVATE
OFFICIAL BASTARD

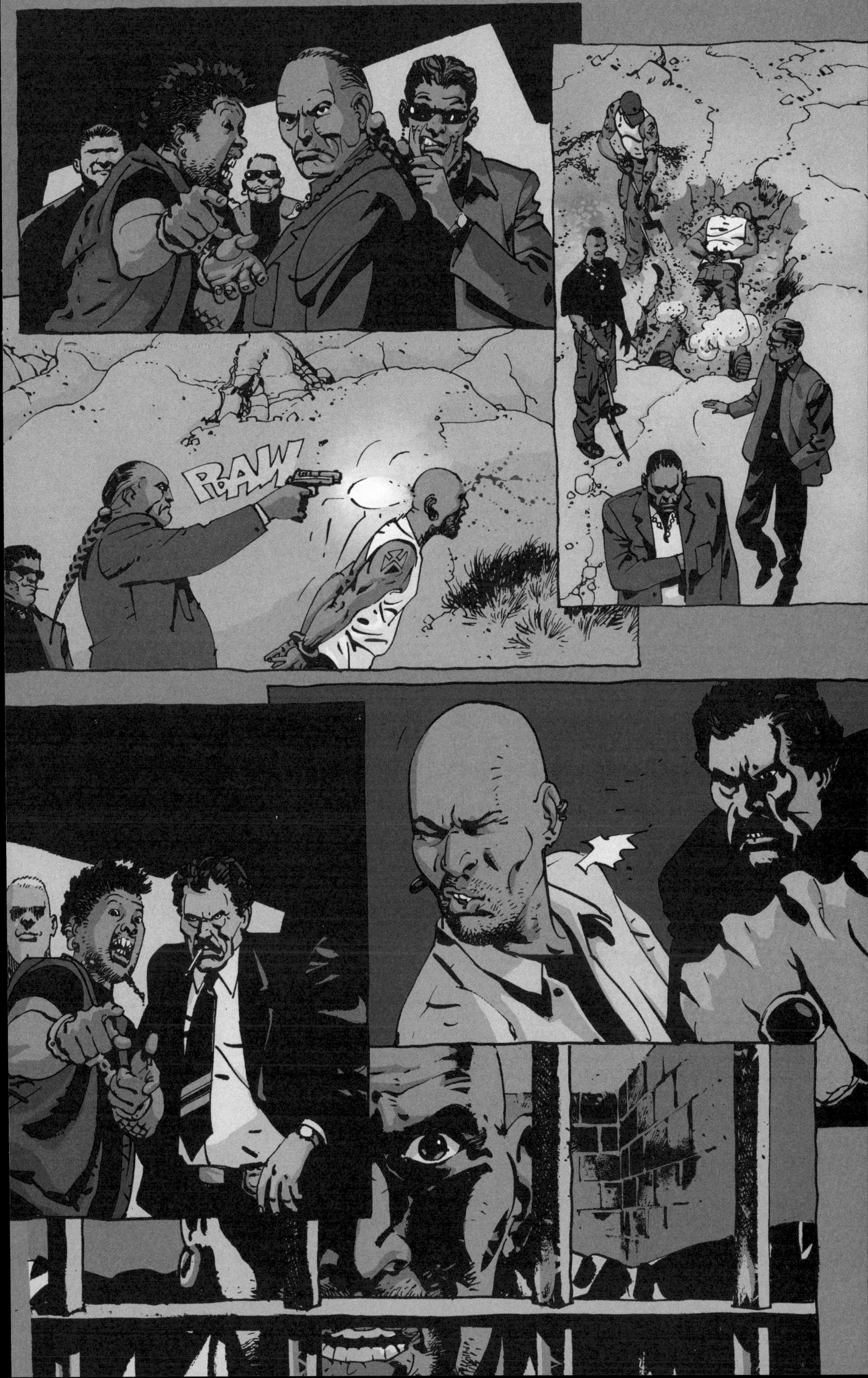
RAW

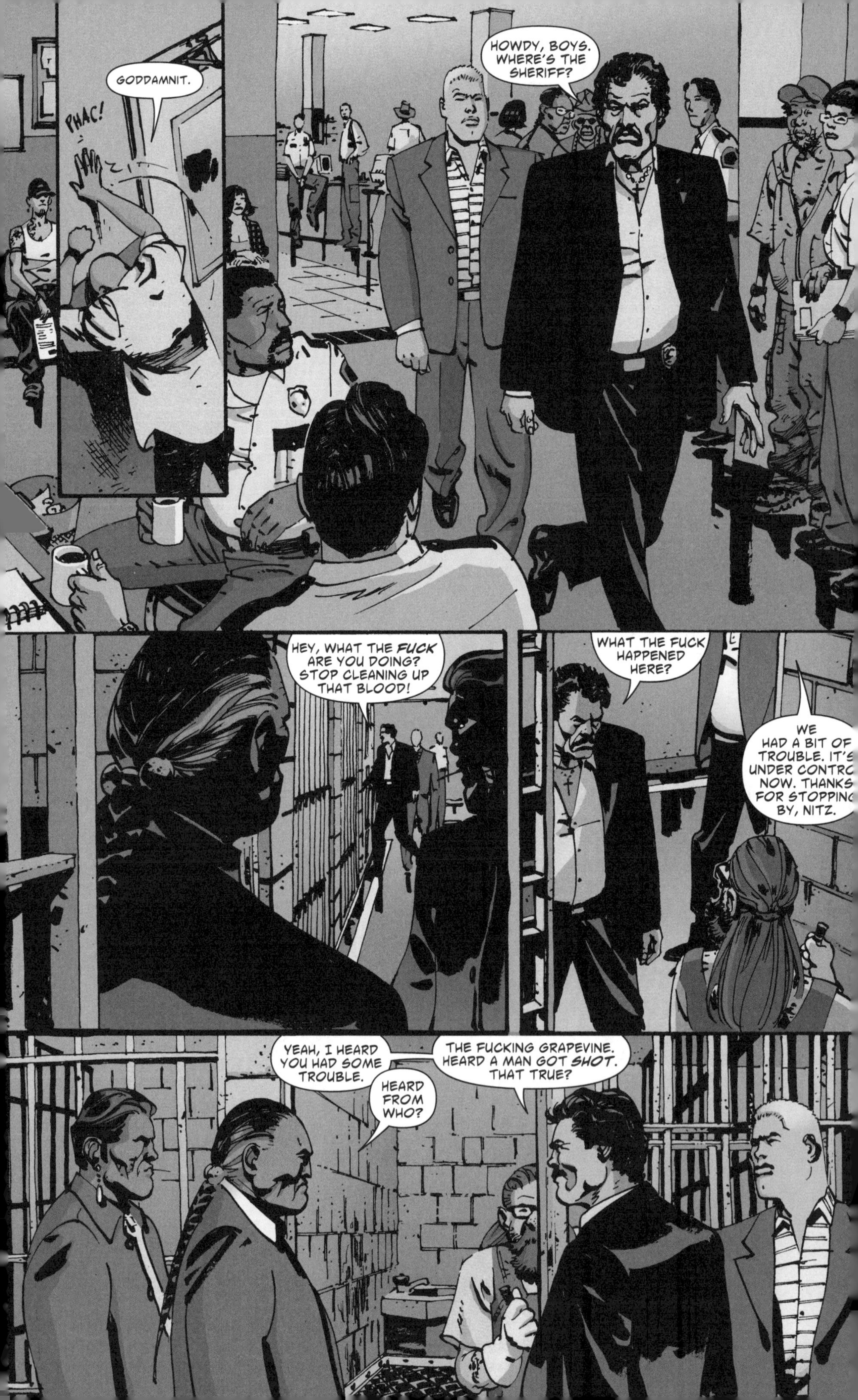
GODDAMNIT.
PHAC!
HOWDY, BOYS. WHERE'S THE SHERIFF?
HEY, WHAT THE FUCK ARE YOU DOING? STOP CLEANING UP THAT BLOOD!
WHAT THE FUCK HAPPENED HERE?
WE HAD A BIT OF TROUBLE. IT'S UNDER CONTRO NOW. THANKS FOR STOPPING BY, NITZ.
YEAH, I HEARD YOU HAD SOME TROUBLE.
HEARD FROM WHO?
THE FUCKING GRAPEVINE. HEARD A MAN GOT SHOT. THAT TRUE?

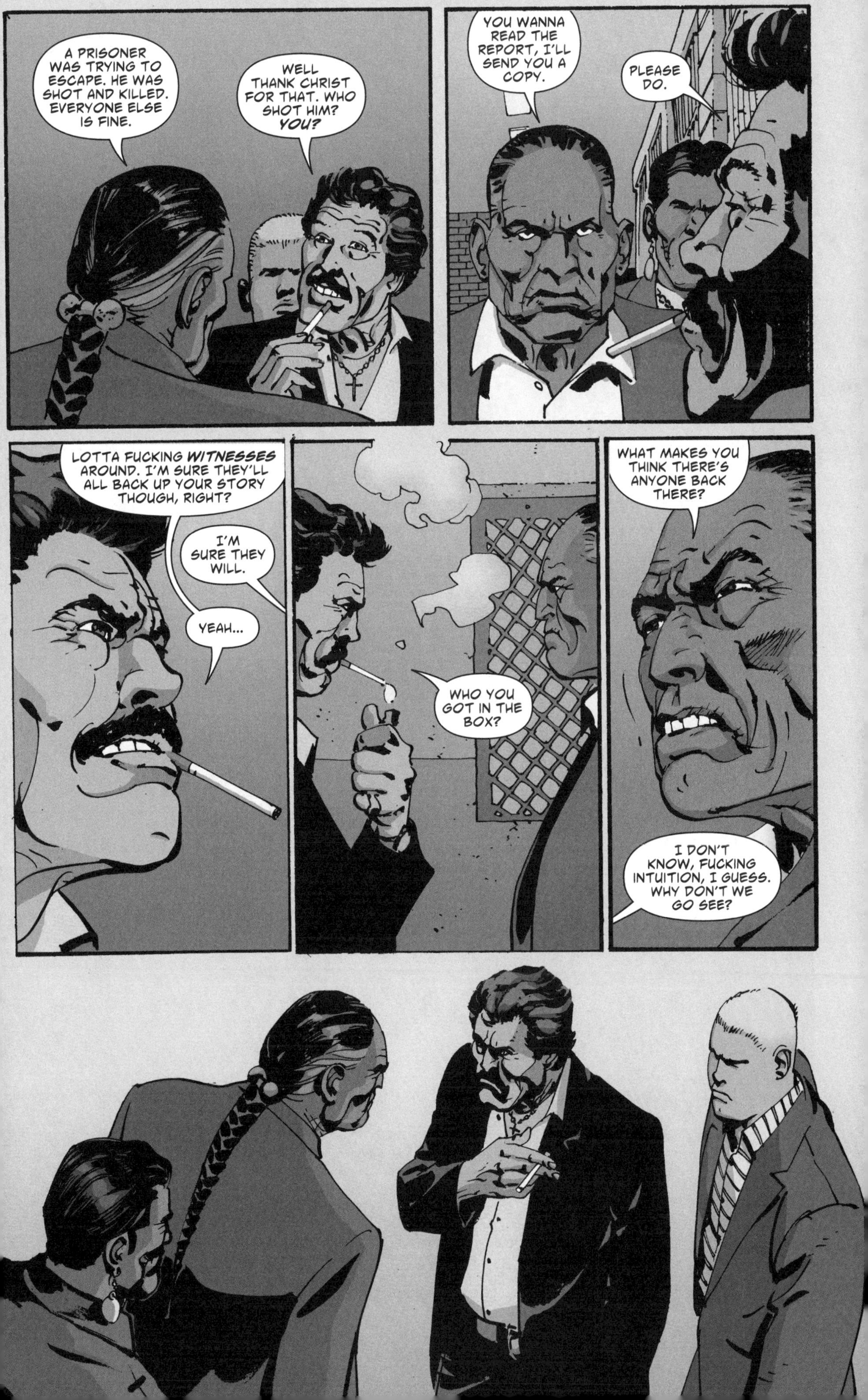
A PRISONER WAS TRYING TO ESCAPE. HE WAS SHOT AND KILLED. EVERYONE ELSE IS FINE.
WELL THANK CHRIST FOR THAT. WHO SHOT HIM? *YOU?*
YOU WANNA READ THE REPORT, I'LL SEND YOU A COPY.
PLEASE DO.
LOTTA FUCKING *WITNESSES* AROUND. I'M SURE THEY'LL ALL BACK UP YOUR STORY THOUGH, RIGHT?
I'M SURE THEY WILL.
YEAH...
WHO YOU GOT IN THE BOX?
WHAT MAKES YOU THINK THERE'S ANYONE BACK THERE?
I DON'T KNOW, FUCKING INTUITION, I GUESS. WHY DON'T WE GO SEE?

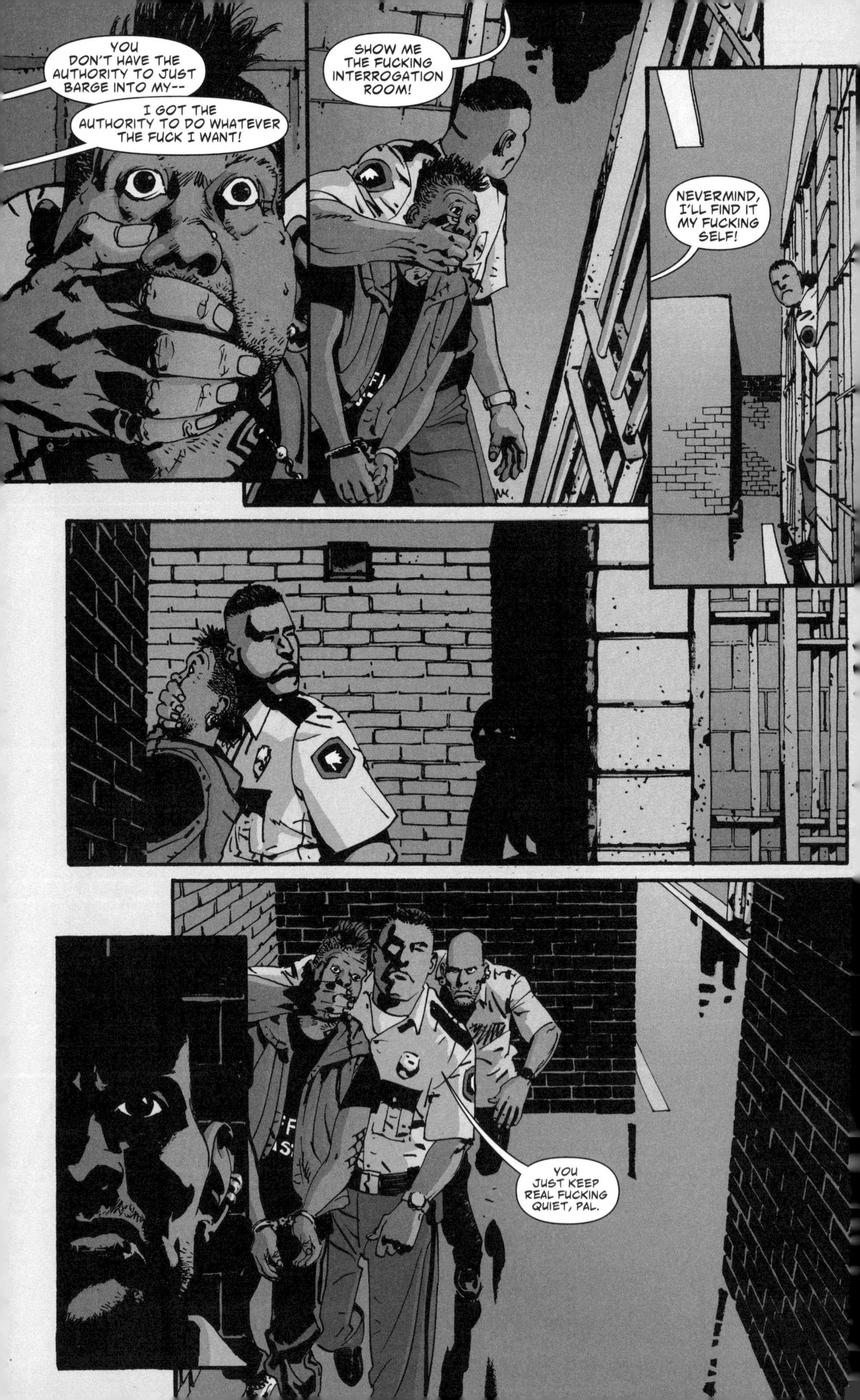
YOU DON'T HAVE THE AUTHORITY TO JUST BARGE INTO MY--
I GOT THE AUTHORITY TO DO WHATEVER THE FUCK I WANT!
SHOW ME THE FUCKING INTERROGATION ROOM!
NEVERMIND, I'LL FIND IT MY FUCKING SELF!
YOU JUST KEEP REAL FUCKING QUIET, PAL.

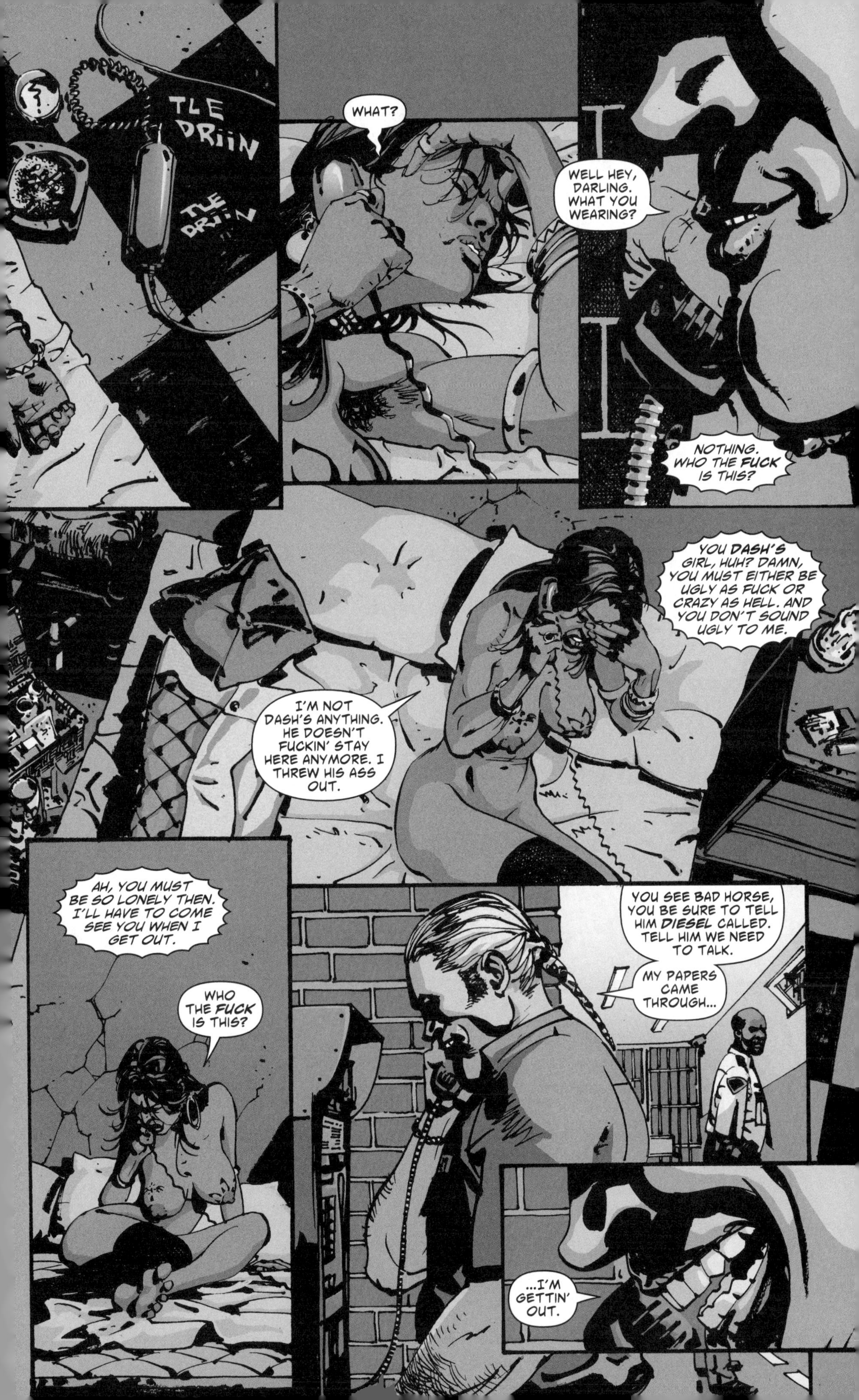
TLE DRIIN
TLE DRIIN
WHAT?
WELL HEY, DARLING. WHAT YOU WEARING?
NOTHING. WHO THE FUCK IS THIS?
YOU DASH'S GIRL, HUH? DAMN, YOU MUST EITHER BE UGLY AS FUCK OR CRAZY AS HELL. AND YOU DON'T SOUND UGLY TO ME.
I'M NOT DASH'S ANYTHING. HE DOESN'T FUCKIN' STAY HERE ANYMORE. I THREW HIS ASS OUT.
AH, YOU MUST BE SO LONELY THEN. I'LL HAVE TO COME SEE YOU WHEN I GET OUT.
WHO THE FUCK IS THIS?
YOU SEE BAD HORSE, YOU BE SURE TO TELL HIM DIESEL CALLED. TELL HIM WE NEED TO TALK.
MY PAPERS CAME THROUGH...
...I'M GETTIN' OUT.

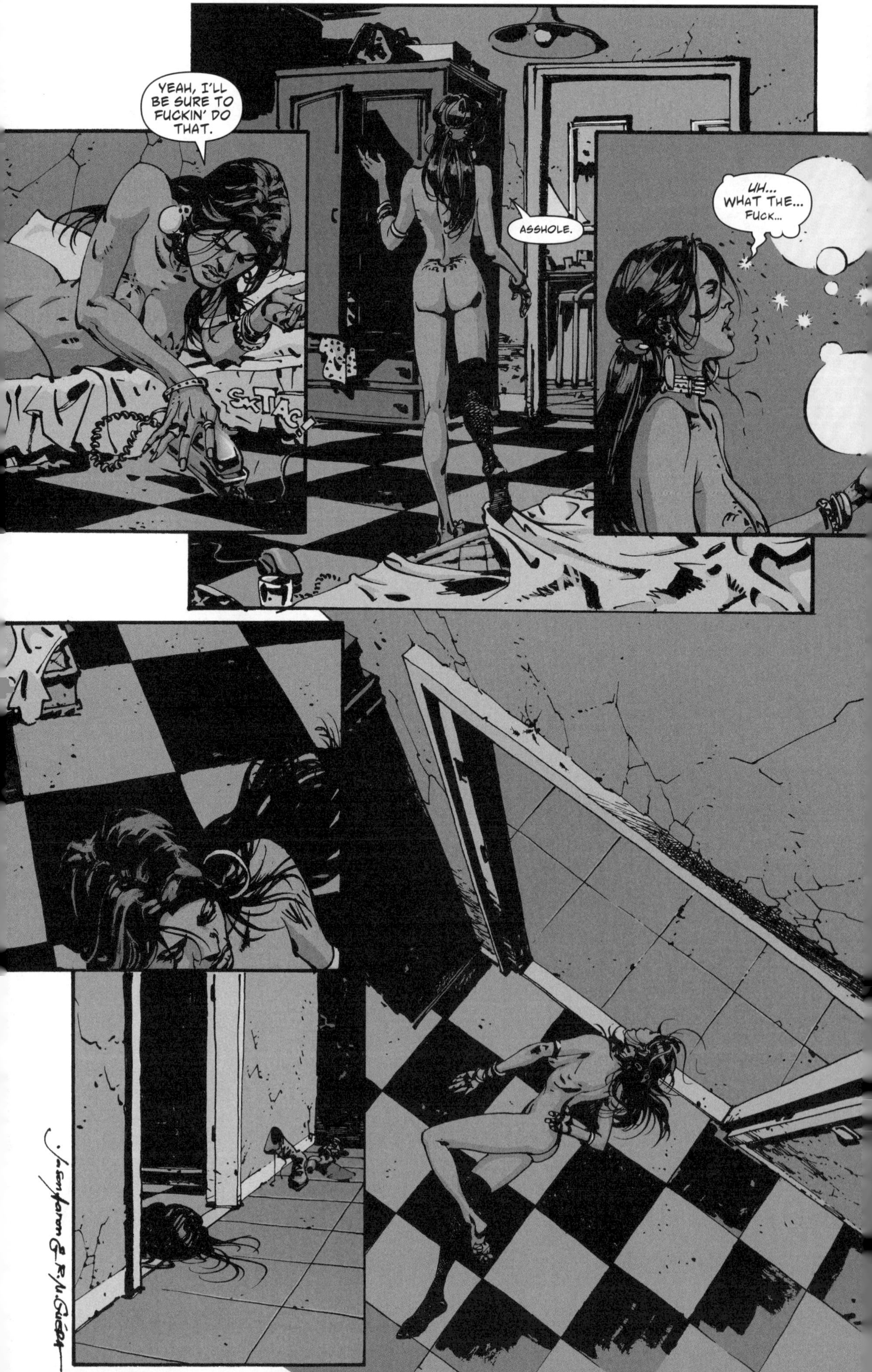
YEAH, I'LL BE SURE TO FUCKIN' DO THAT.
SKTAC!
ASSHOLE.
UH... WHAT THE... FUCK...

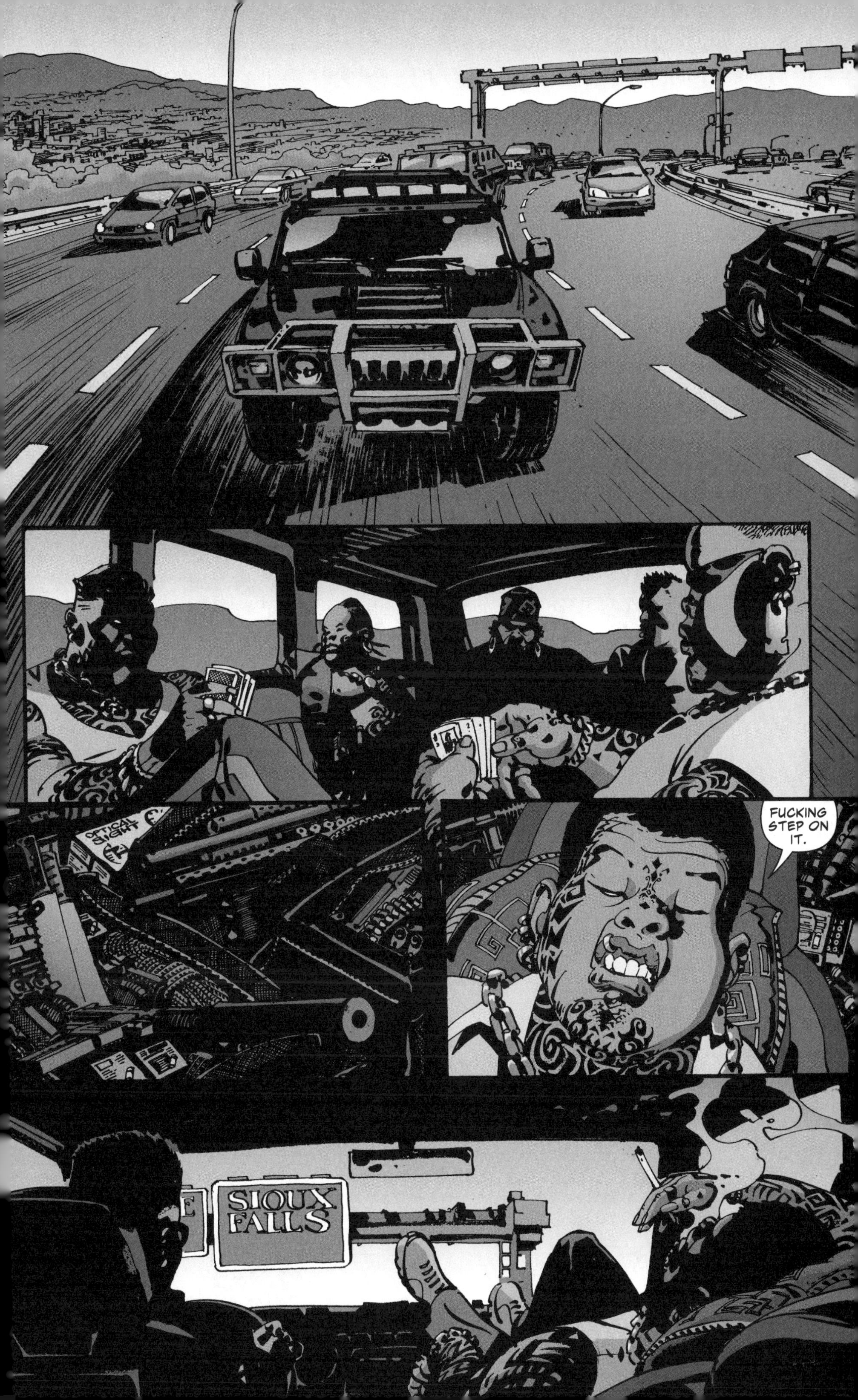
OPTICAL SIGHT
FUCKING STEP ON IT.
SIOUX FALLS

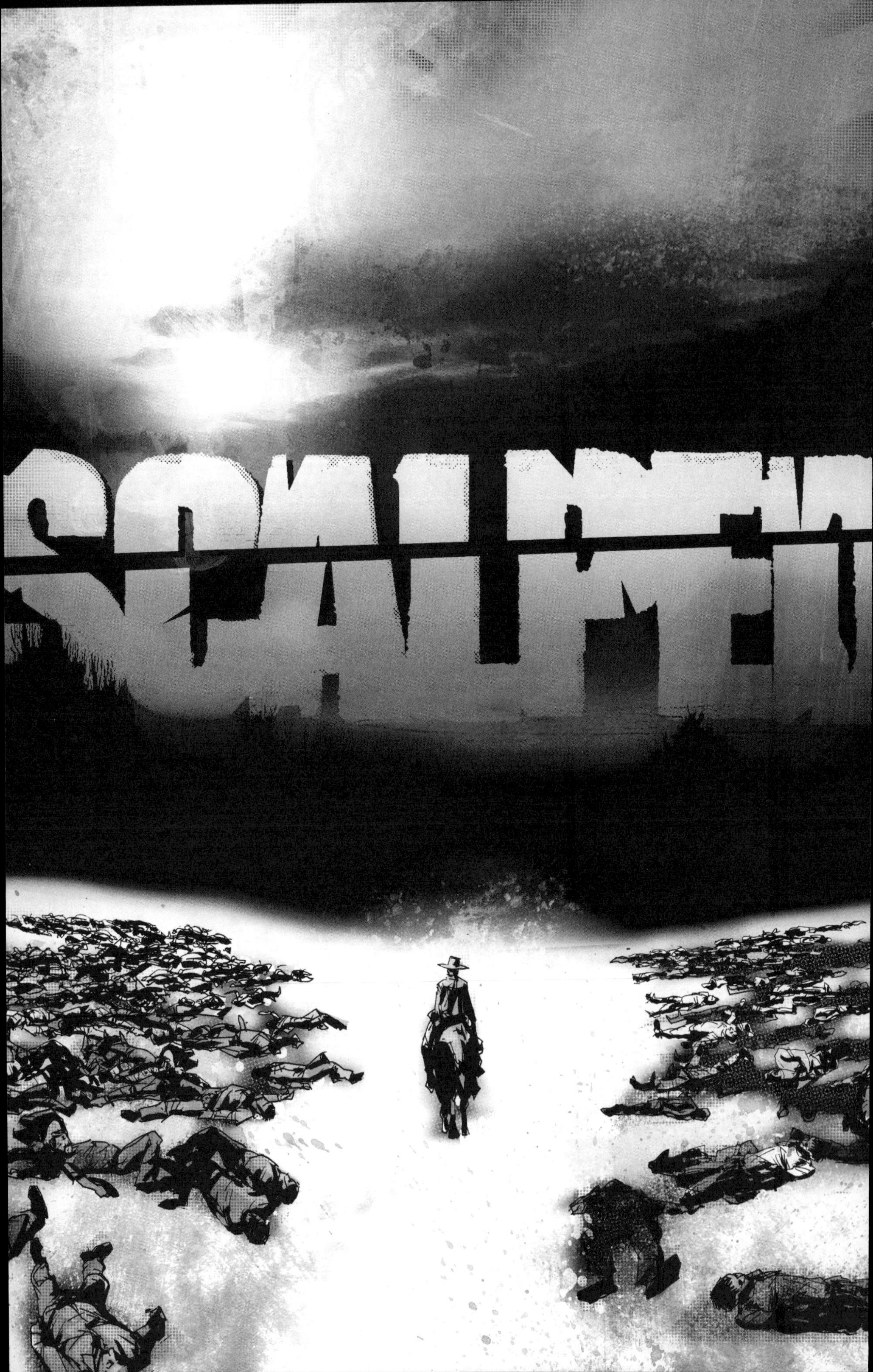
SCALPED

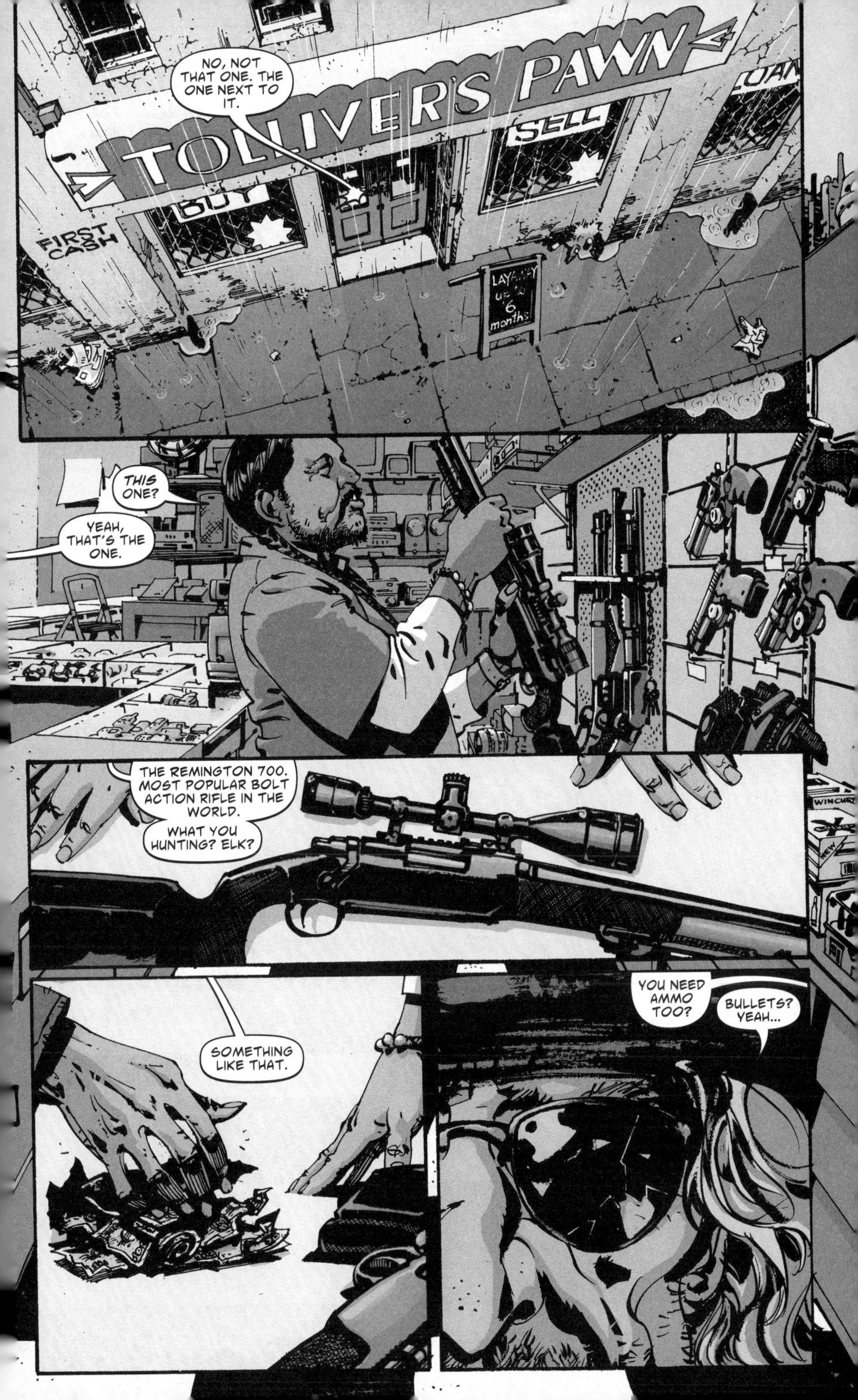
TOLLIVER'S PAWN
LOAN
SELL
BUY
FIRST CASH
NO, NOT THAT ONE. THE ONE NEXT TO IT.
LAYAWAY up to 6 months
THIS ONE?
YEAH, THAT'S THE ONE.
THE REMINGTON 700. MOST POPULAR BOLT ACTION RIFLE IN THE WORLD.
WHAT YOU HUNTING? ELK?
SOMETHING LIKE THAT.
YOU NEED AMMO TOO?
BULLETS? YEAH...

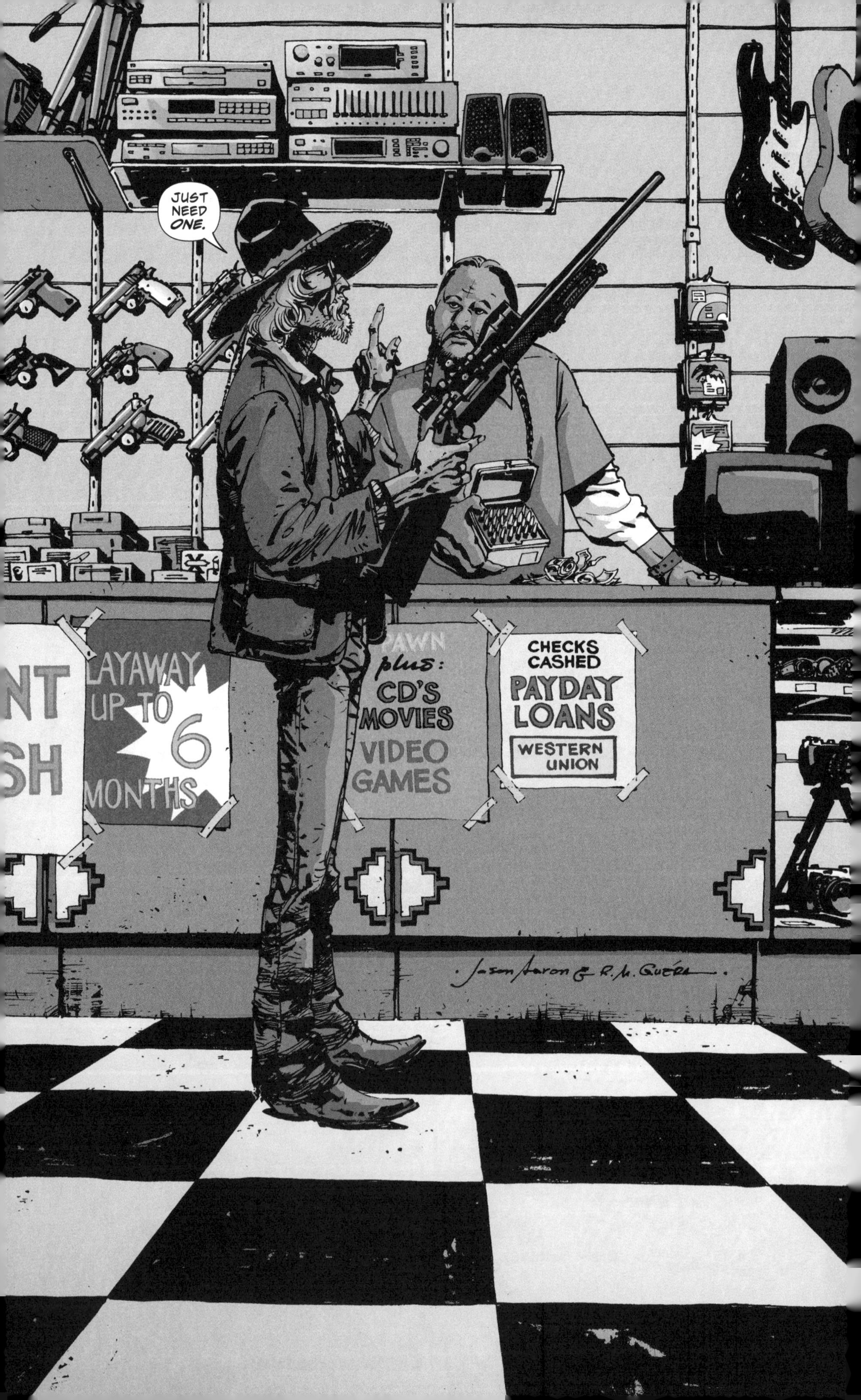
JUST NEED ONE.
LAYAWAY UP TO 6 MONTHS
PAWN plus: CD'S MOVIES VIDEO GAMES
CHECKS CASHED
PAYDAY LOANS
WESTERN UNION
Jason Aaron & R.M. Guéra

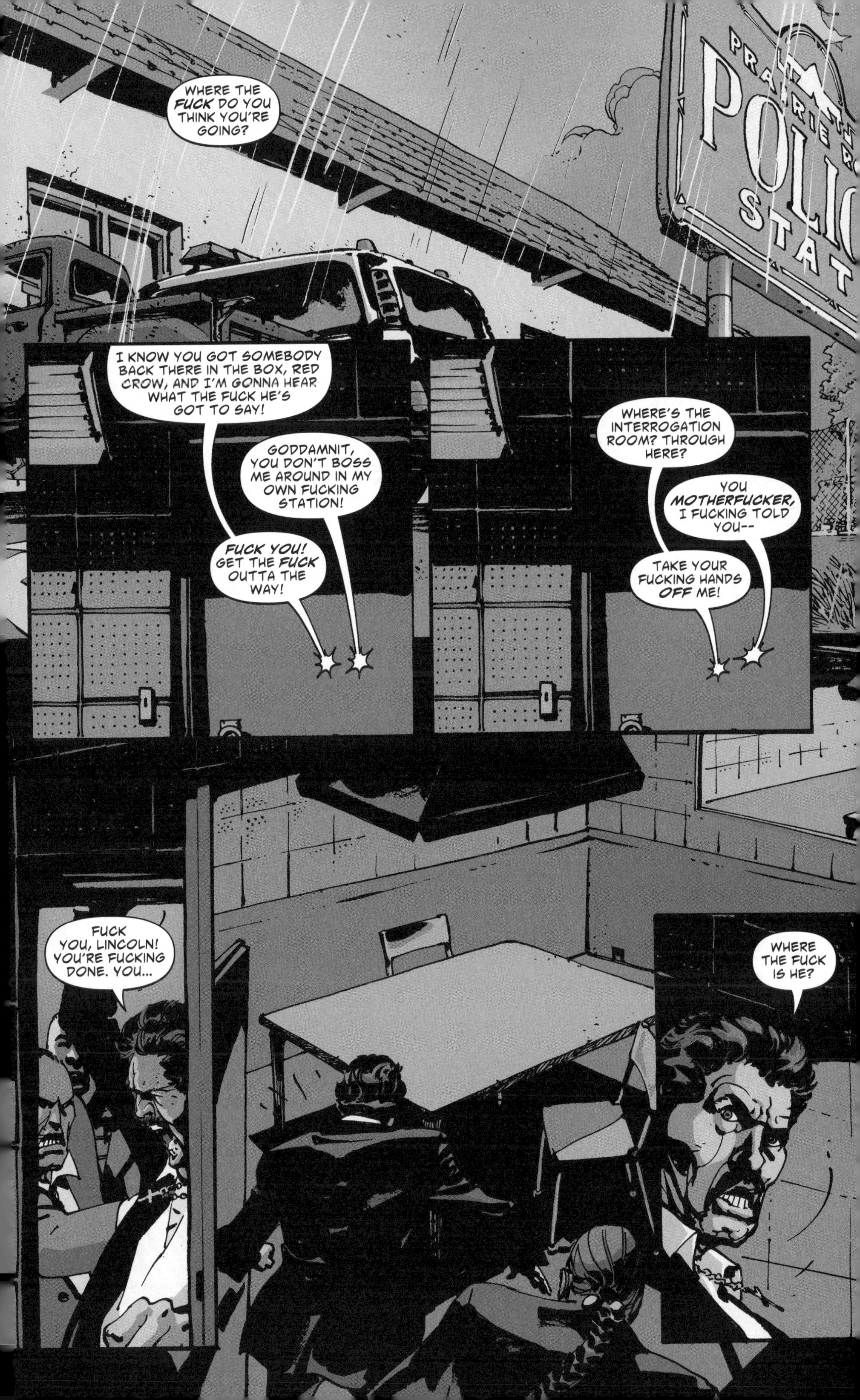
PRAIRIE ROSE POLICE STATION
WHERE THE FUCK DO YOU THINK YOU'RE GOING?
I KNOW YOU GOT SOMEBODY BACK THERE IN THE BOX, RED CROW, AND I'M GONNA HEAR WHAT THE FUCK HE'S GOT TO SAY!
GODDAMNIT, YOU DON'T BOSS ME AROUND IN MY OWN FUCKING STATION!
FUCK YOU! GET THE FUCK OUTTA THE WAY!
WHERE'S THE INTERROGATION ROOM? THROUGH HERE?
YOU MOTHERFUCKER, I FUCKING TOLD YOU--
TAKE YOUR FUCKING HANDS OFF ME!
FUCK YOU, LINCOLN! YOU'RE FUCKING DONE. YOU...
WHERE THE FUCK IS HE?

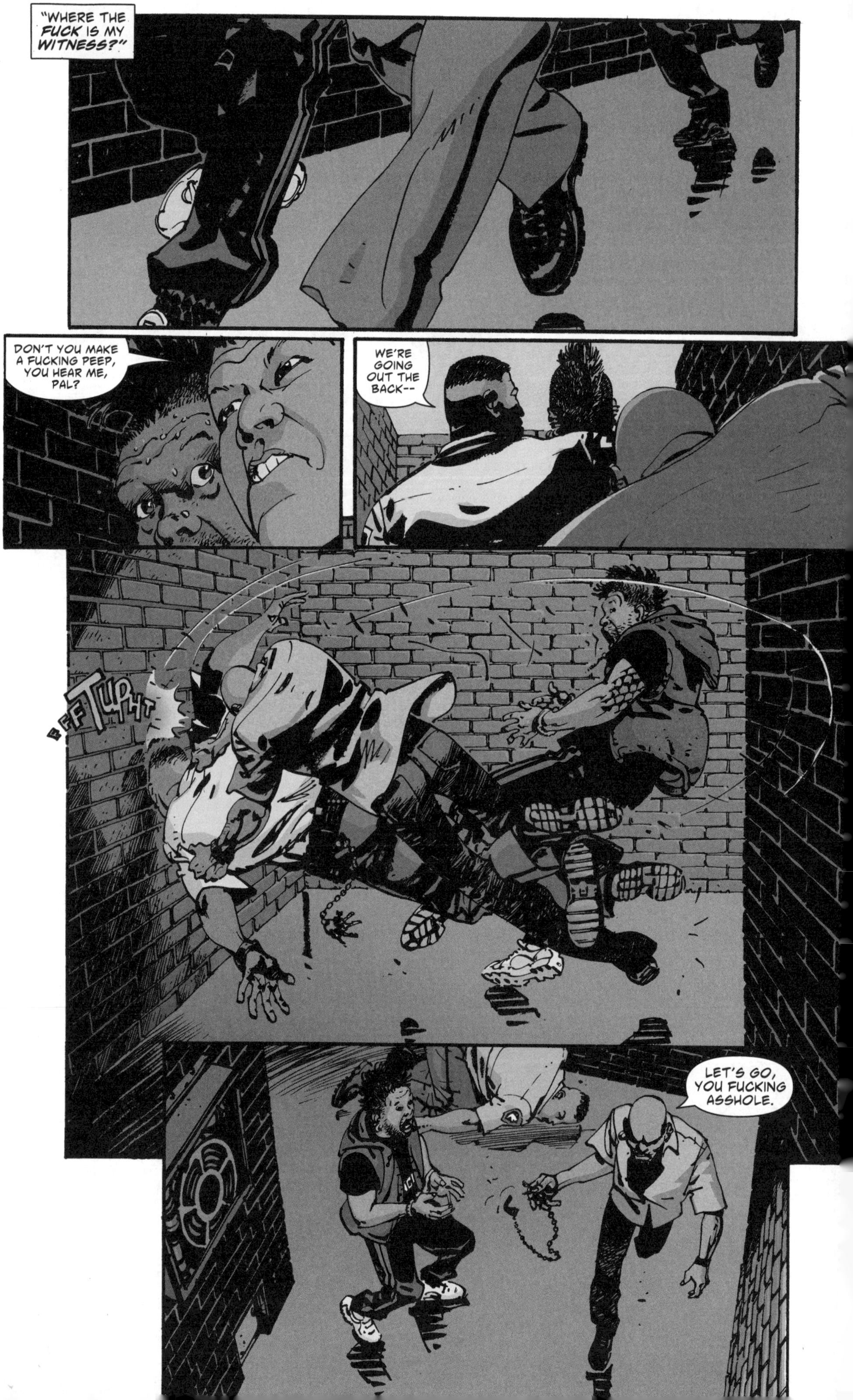
"WHERE THE FUCK IS MY WITNESS?"
DON'T YOU MAKE A FUCKING PEEP, YOU HEAR ME, PAL?
WE'RE GOING OUT THE BACK--
FFTUPHT
LET'S GO, YOU FUCKING ASSHOLE.

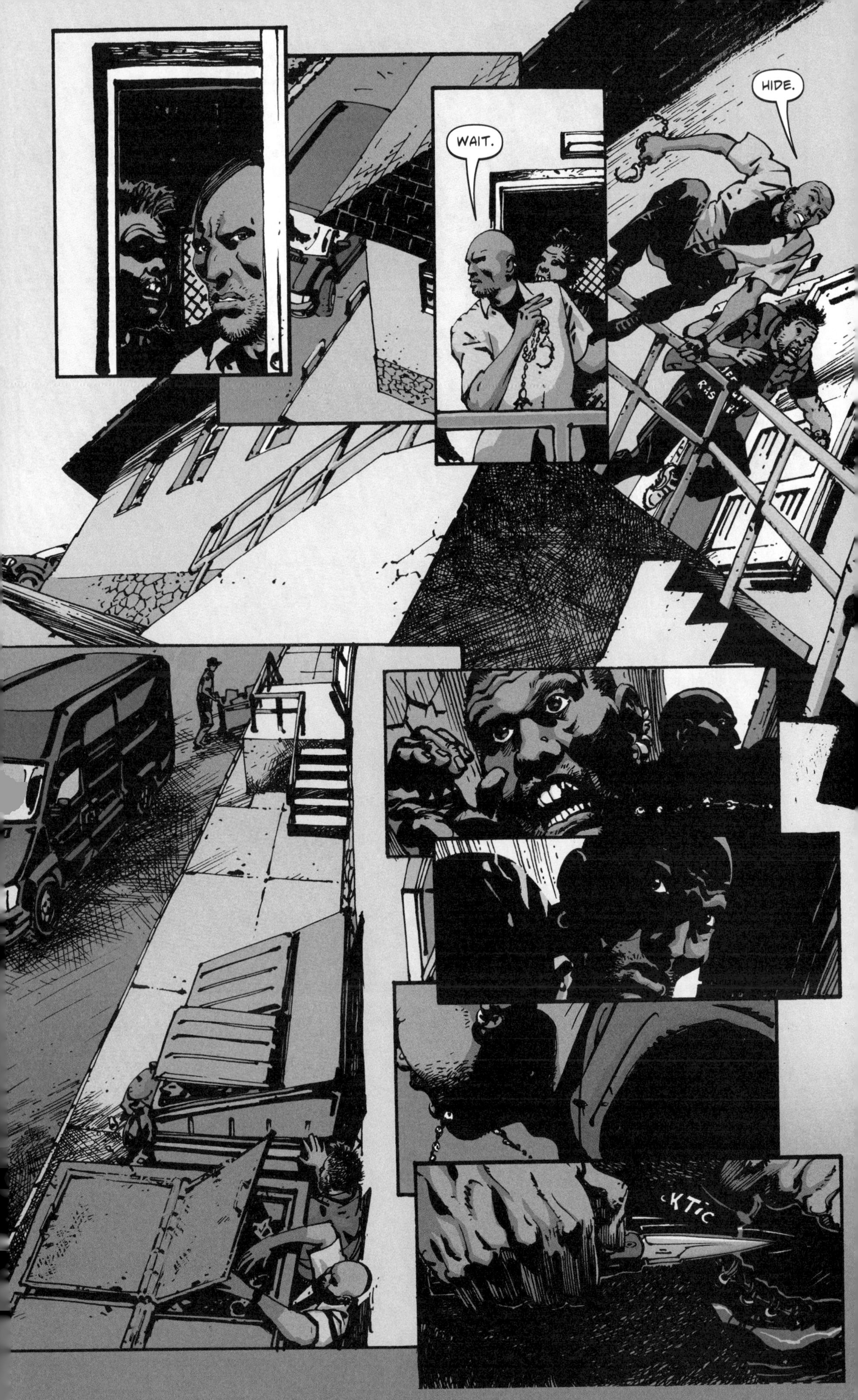
WAIT.
HIDE.
cKTic

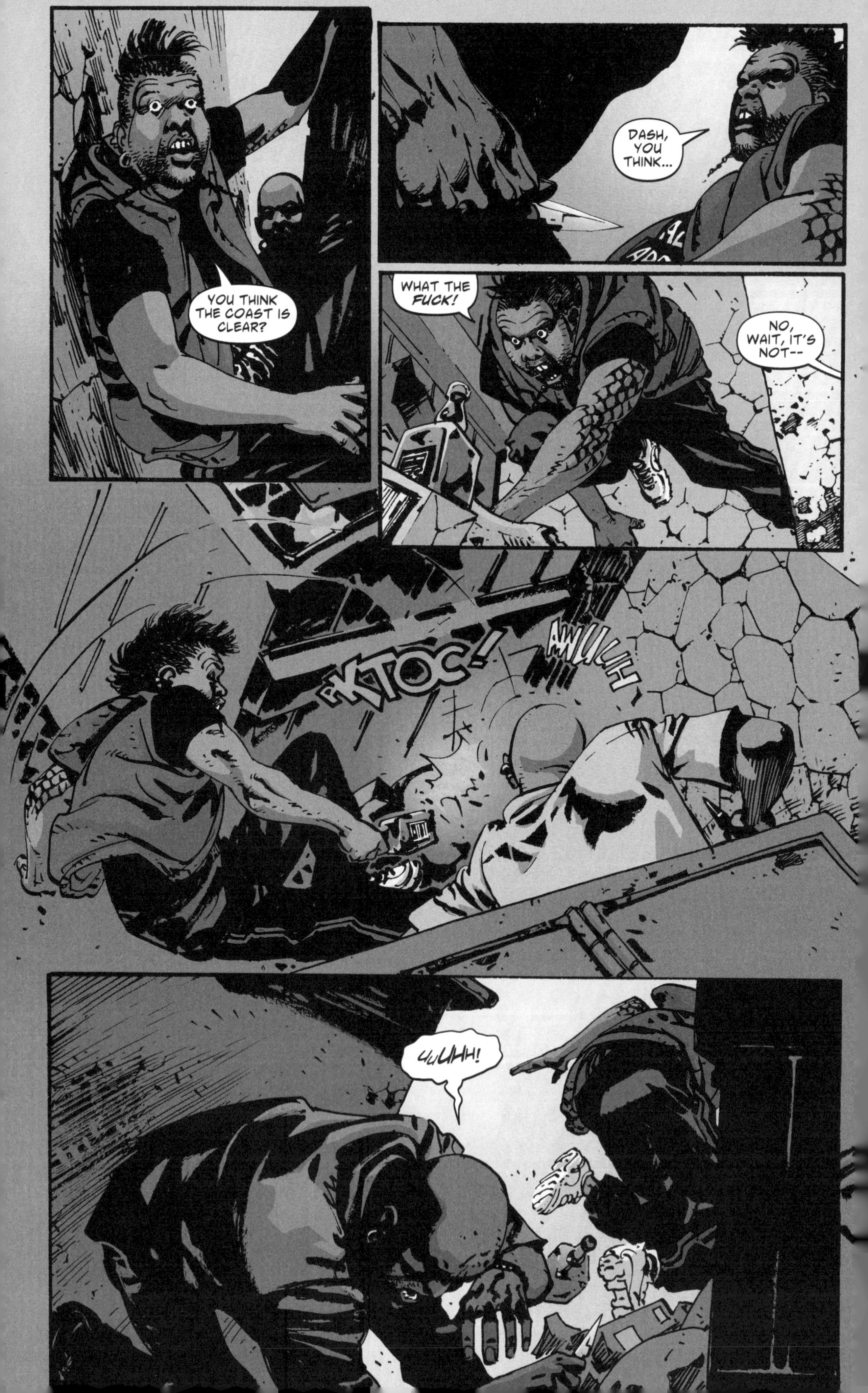
YOU THINK THE COAST IS CLEAR?
DASH, YOU THINK...
WHAT THE FUCK!
NO, WAIT, IT'S NOT--
KTOC!
AWUUH
UUUHH!

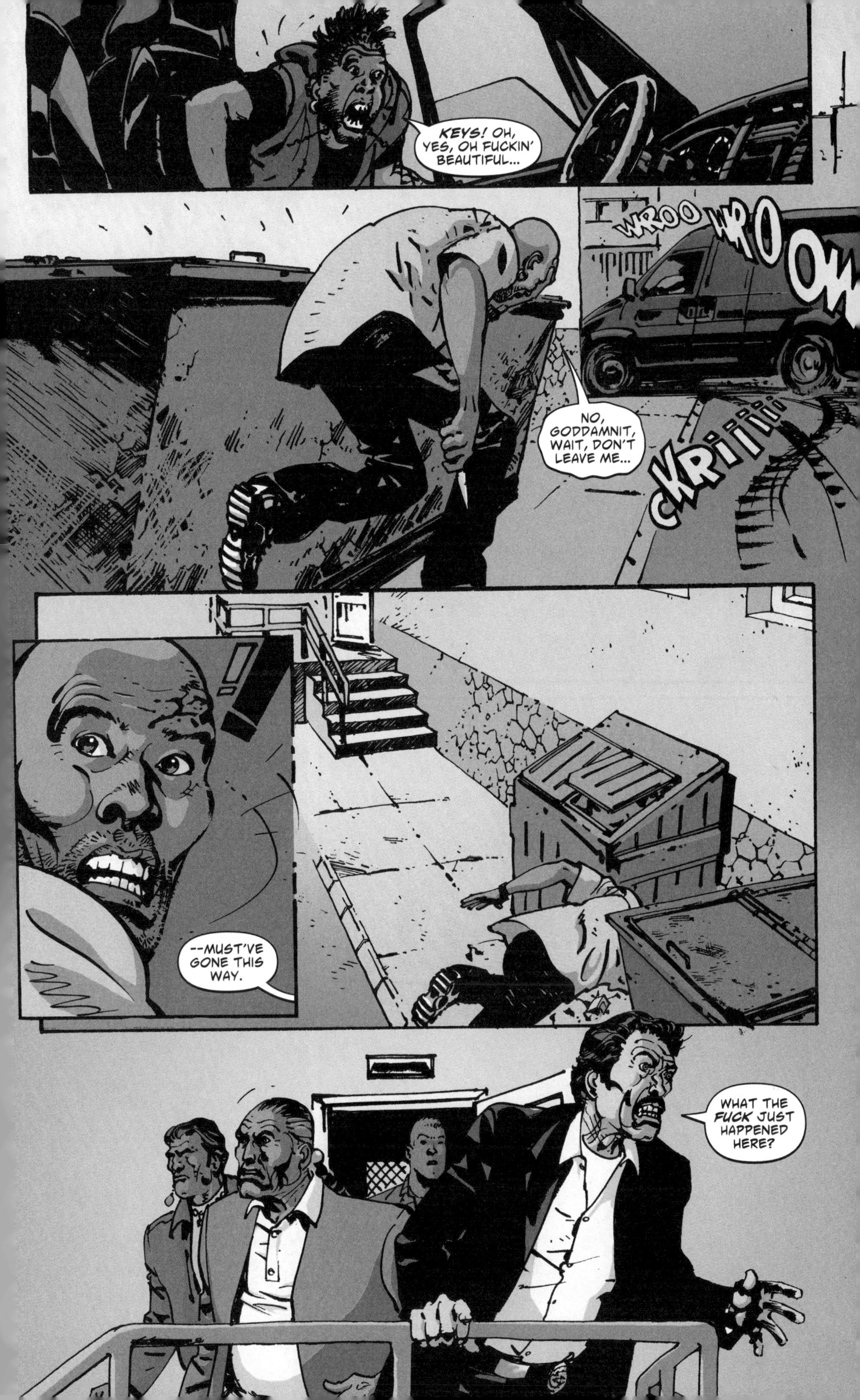
KEYS! OH, YES, OH FUCKIN' BEAUTIFUL...
WROO WROOOM
NO, GODDAMNIT, WAIT, DON'T LEAVE ME...
cKRiiiiii
--MUST'VE GONE THIS WAY.
WHAT THE FUCK JUST HAPPENED HERE?

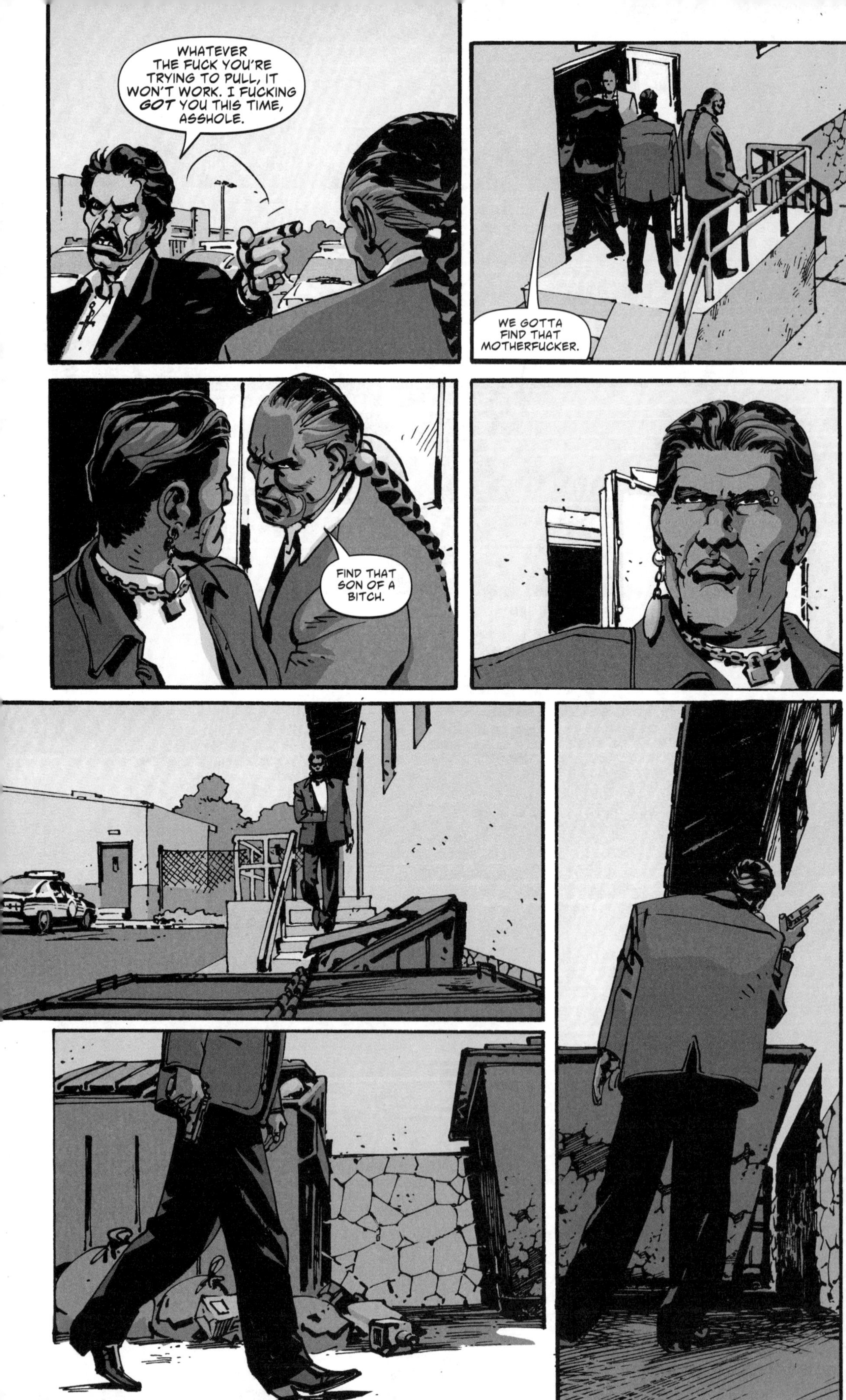
WHATEVER THE FUCK YOU'RE TRYING TO PULL, IT WON'T WORK. I FUCKING *GOT* YOU THIS TIME, ASSHOLE.
WE GOTTA FIND THAT MOTHERFUCKER.
FIND THAT SON OF A BITCH.

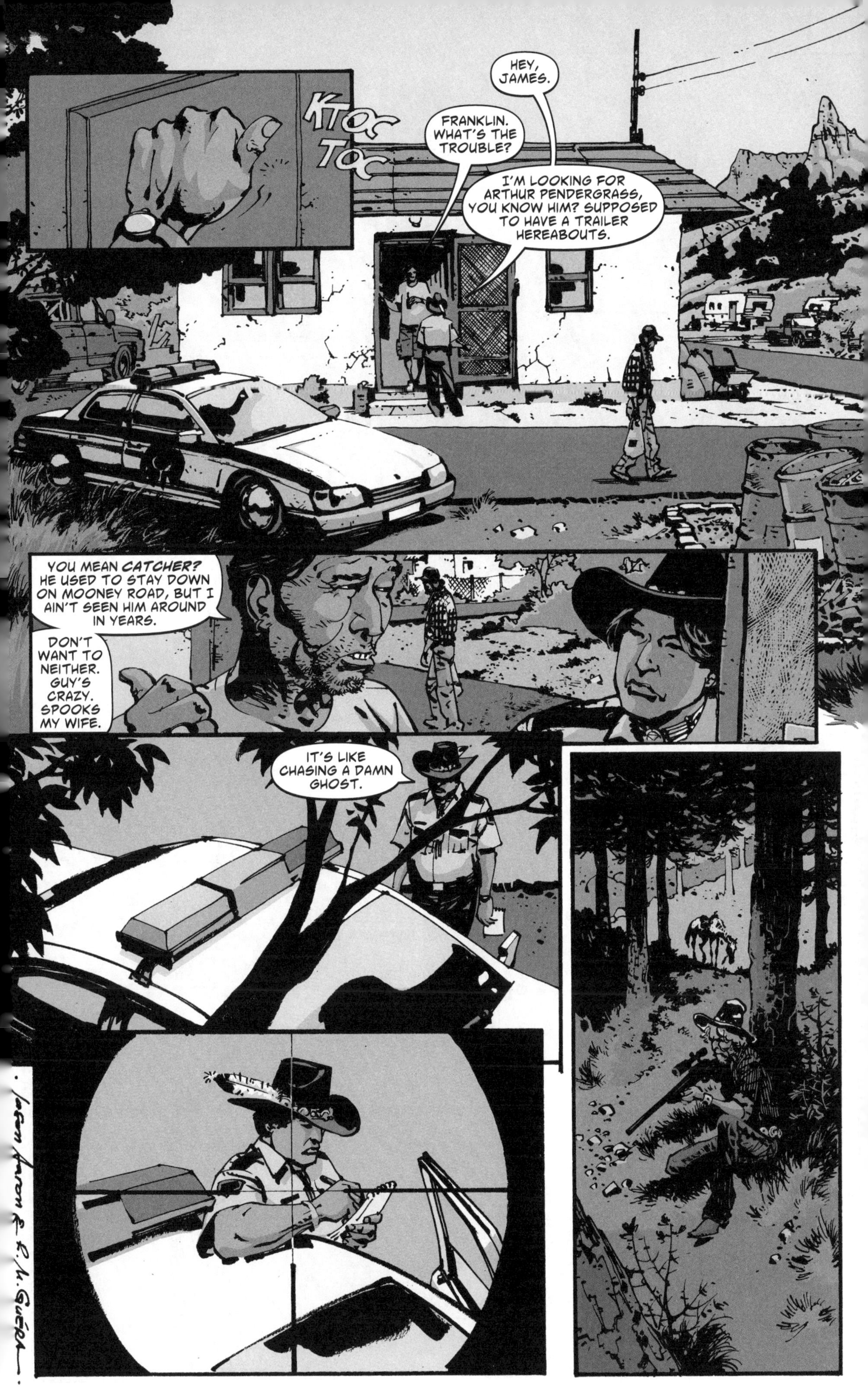
KTOC TOC
HEY, JAMES.
FRANKLIN. WHAT'S THE TROUBLE?
I'M LOOKING FOR ARTHUR PENDERGRASS, YOU KNOW HIM? SUPPOSED TO HAVE A TRAILER HEREABOUTS.
YOU MEAN *CATCHER?* HE USED TO STAY DOWN ON MOONEY ROAD, BUT I AIN'T SEEN HIM AROUND IN YEARS.
DON'T WANT TO NEITHER. GUY'S CRAZY. SPOOKS MY WIFE.
IT'S LIKE CHASING A DAMN GHOST.

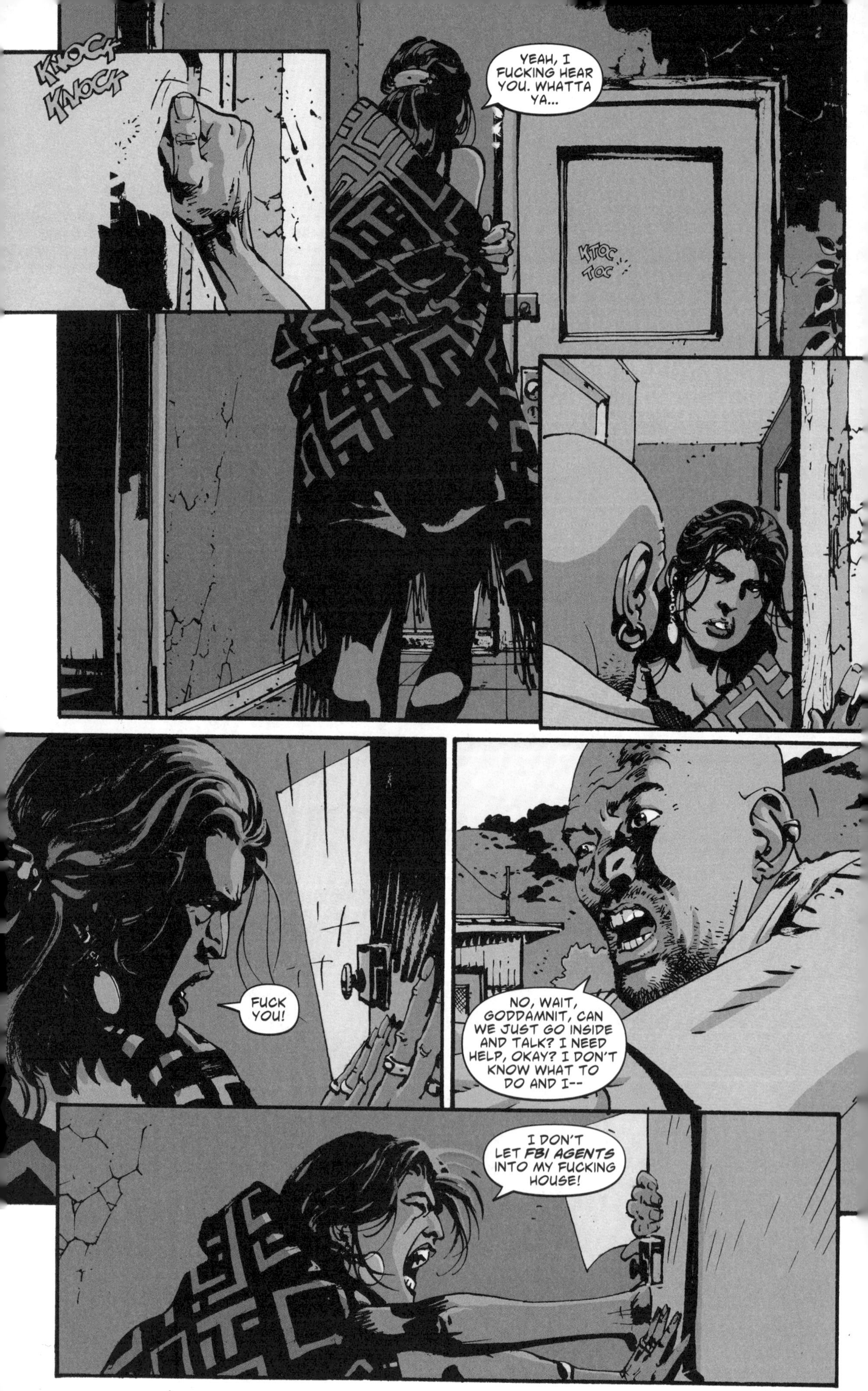
KNOCK KNOCK
YEAH, I FUCKING HEAR YOU. WHATTA YA...
KTOC TOC
FUCK YOU!
NO, WAIT, GODDAMNIT, CAN WE JUST GO INSIDE AND TALK? I NEED HELP, OKAY? I DON'T KNOW WHAT TO DO AND I--
I DON'T LET *FBI AGENTS* INTO MY FUCKING HOUSE!

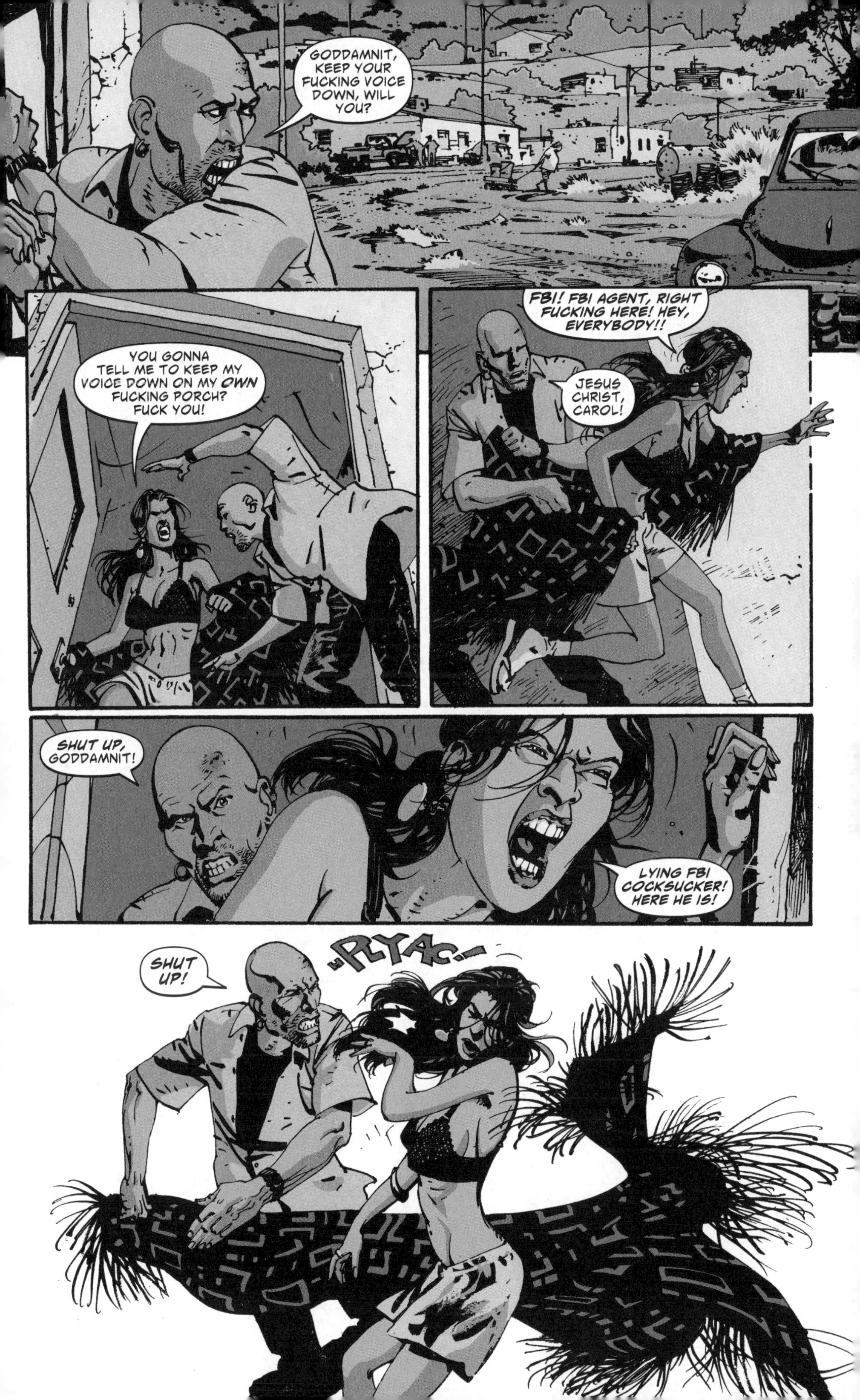
GODDAMNIT, KEEP YOUR FUCKING VOICE DOWN, WILL YOU?
YOU GONNA TELL ME TO KEEP MY VOICE DOWN ON MY OWN FUCKING PORCH? FUCK YOU!
FBI! FBI AGENT, RIGHT FUCKING HERE! HEY, EVERYBODY!!
JESUS CHRIST, CAROL!
SHUT UP, GODDAMNIT!
LYING FBI COCKSUCKER! HERE HE IS!
SHUT UP!
-PLYAC-

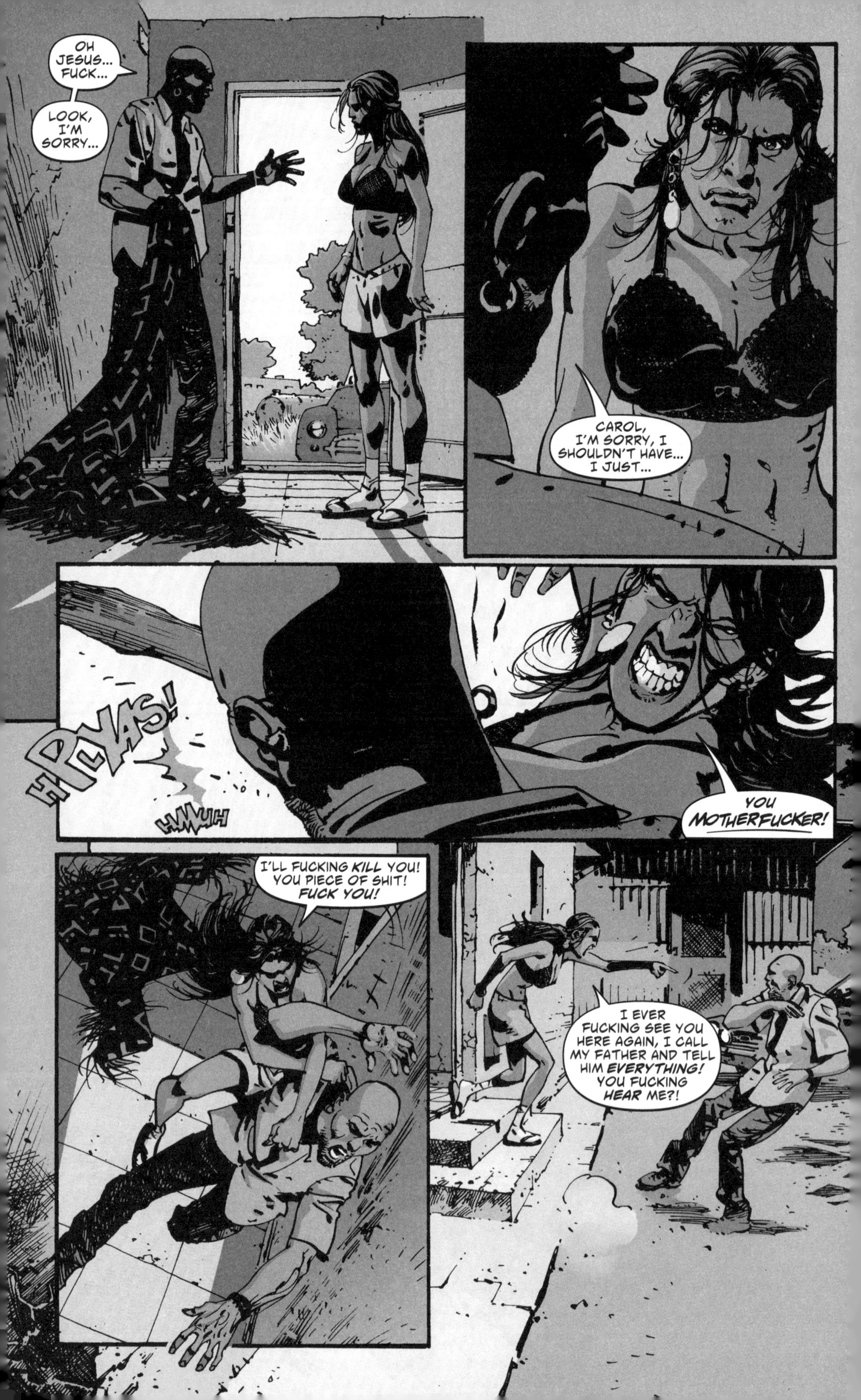
OH JESUS... FUCK...
LOOK, I'M SORRY...
CAROL, I'M SORRY, I SHOULDN'T HAVE... I JUST...
YOU MOTHERFUCKER!
I'LL FUCKING KILL YOU! YOU PIECE OF SHIT! FUCK YOU!
I EVER FUCKING SEE YOU HERE AGAIN, I CALL MY FATHER AND TELL HIM EVERYTHING! YOU FUCKING HEAR ME?!

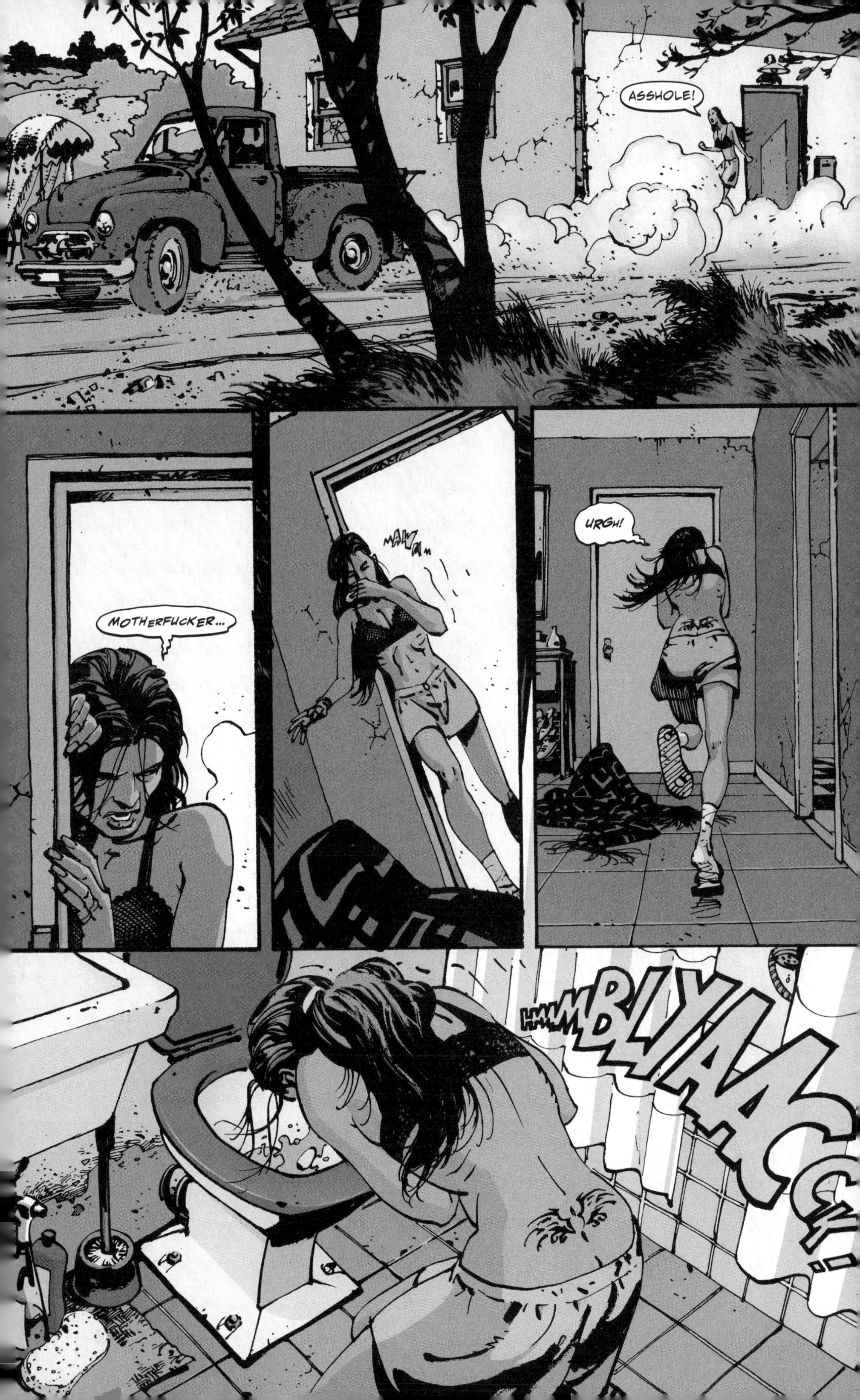
ASSHOLE!
MOTHERFUCKER...
URGH!

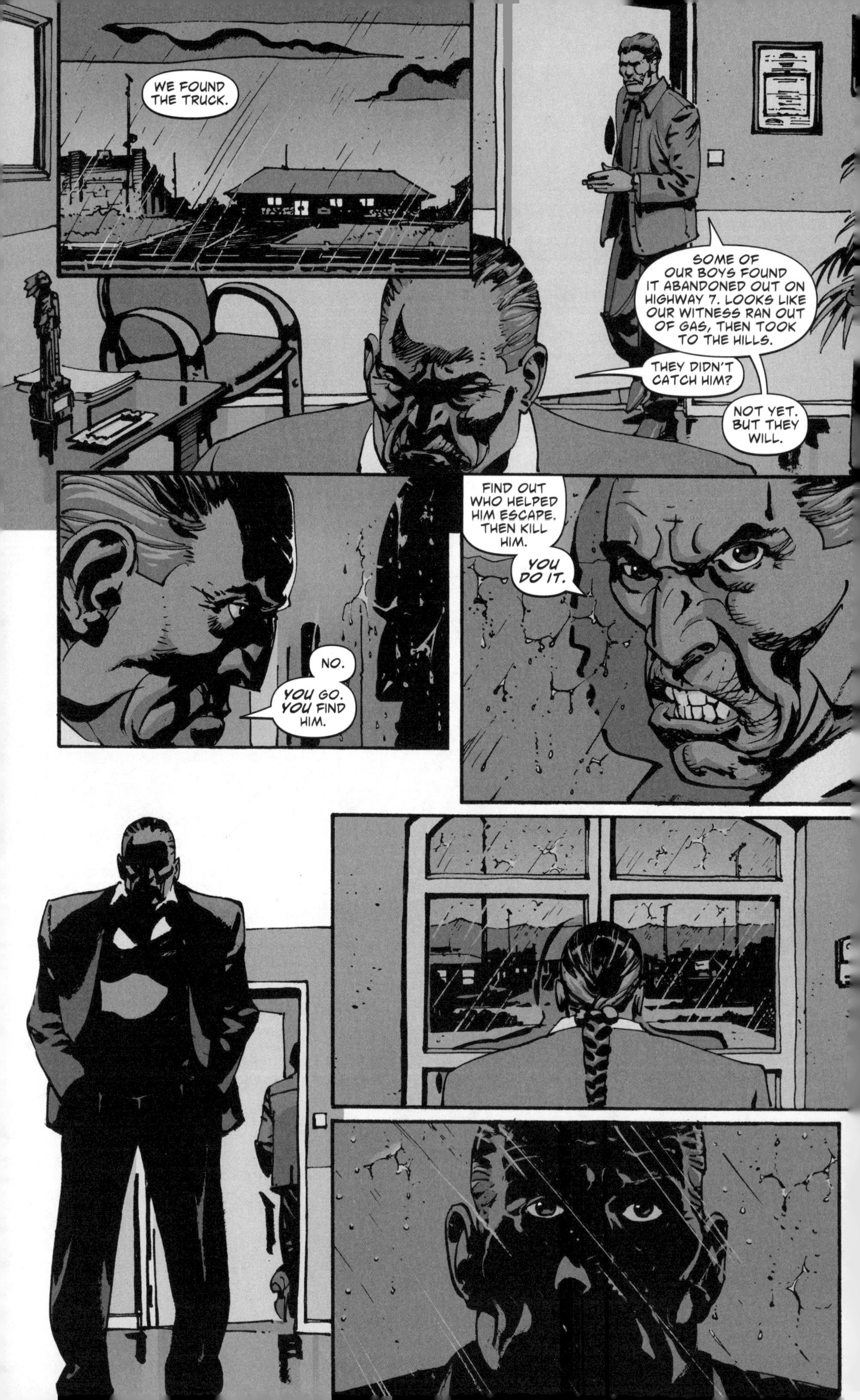
WE FOUND THE TRUCK.
SOME OF OUR BOYS FOUND IT ABANDONED OUT ON HIGHWAY 7. LOOKS LIKE OUR WITNESS RAN OUT OF GAS, THEN TOOK TO THE HILLS.
THEY DIDN'T CATCH HIM?
NOT YET. BUT THEY WILL.
FIND OUT WHO HELPED HIM ESCAPE. THEN KILL HIM.
YOU DO IT.
NO.
YOU GO. YOU FIND HIM.

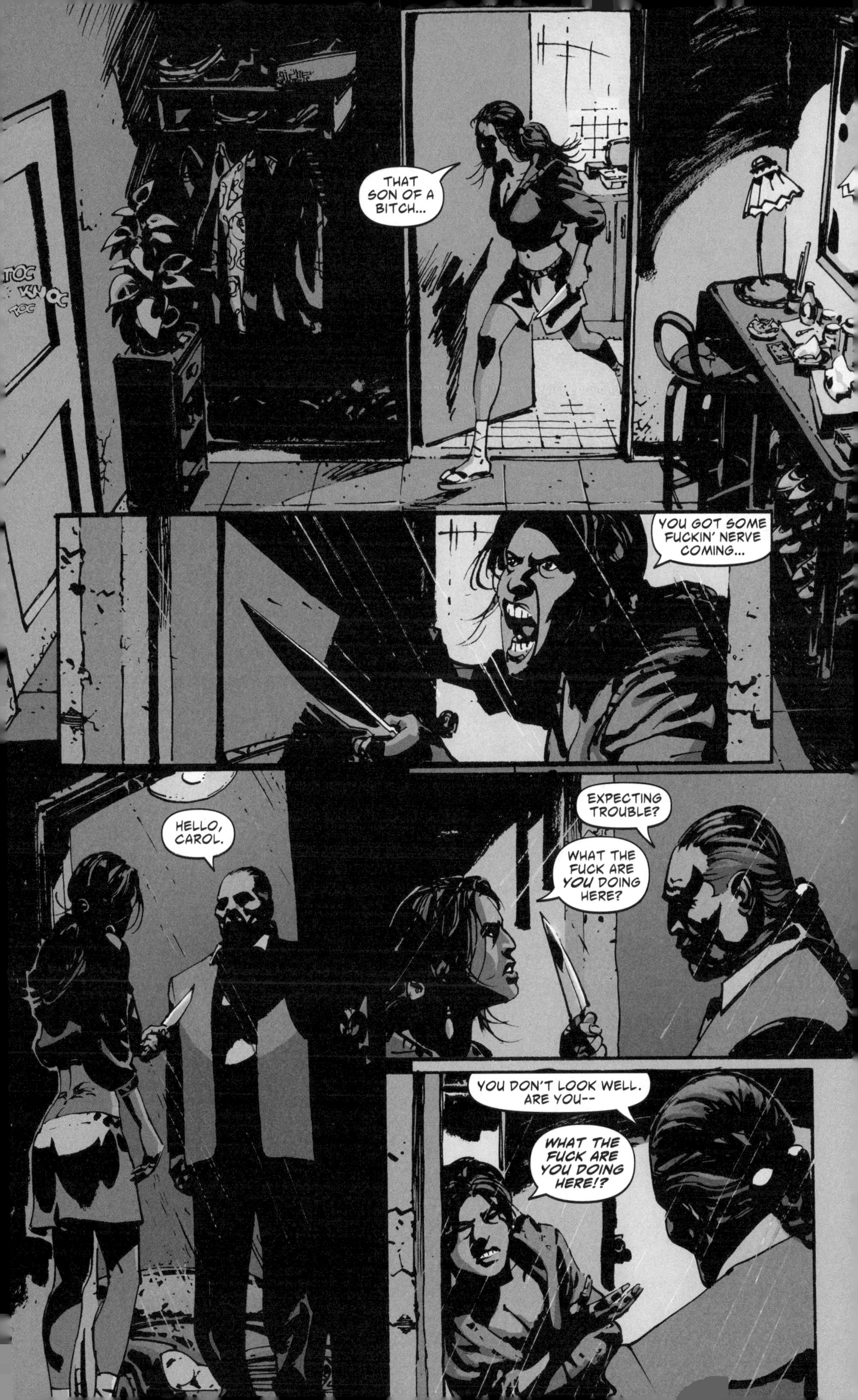
TOC
KNOC
TOC
THAT SON OF A BITCH...
YOU GOT SOME FUCKIN' NERVE COMING...
HELLO, CAROL.
EXPECTING TROUBLE?
WHAT THE FUCK ARE *YOU* DOING HERE?
YOU DON'T LOOK WELL. ARE YOU--
*WHAT THE FUCK ARE YOU DOING HERE!?*

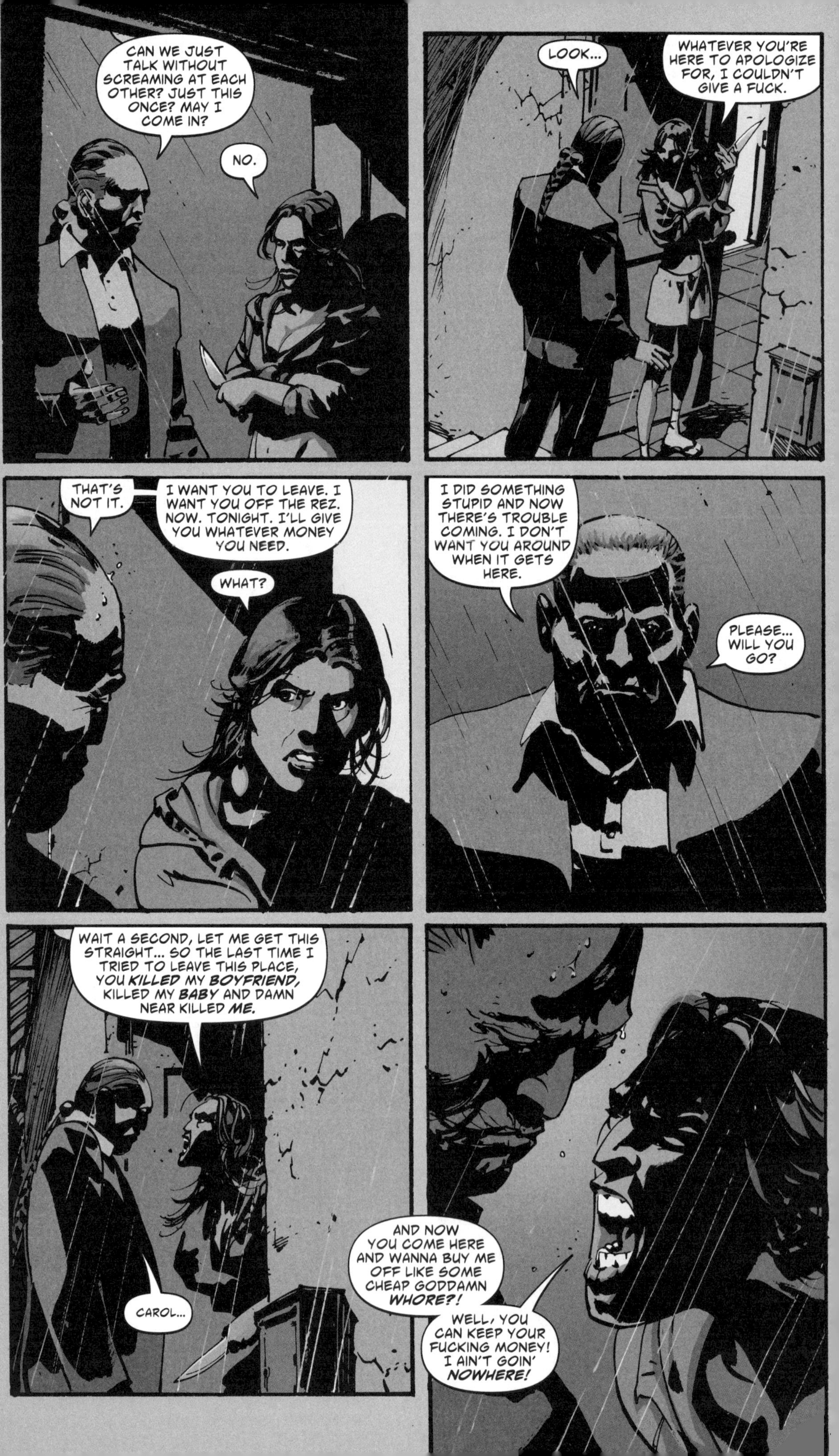
CAN WE JUST TALK WITHOUT SCREAMING AT EACH OTHER? JUST THIS ONCE? MAY I COME IN?
NO.
LOOK...
WHATEVER YOU'RE HERE TO APOLOGIZE FOR, I COULDN'T GIVE A FUCK.
THAT'S NOT IT.
I WANT YOU TO LEAVE. I WANT YOU OFF THE REZ. NOW. TONIGHT. I'LL GIVE YOU WHATEVER MONEY YOU NEED.
WHAT?
I DID SOMETHING STUPID AND NOW THERE'S TROUBLE COMING. I DON'T WANT YOU AROUND WHEN IT GETS HERE.
PLEASE... WILL YOU GO?
WAIT A SECOND, LET ME GET THIS STRAIGHT... SO THE LAST TIME I TRIED TO LEAVE THIS PLACE, YOU KILLED MY BOYFRIEND, KILLED MY BABY AND DAMN NEAR KILLED ME.
CAROL...
AND NOW YOU COME HERE AND WANNA BUY ME OFF LIKE SOME CHEAP GODDAMN WHORE?!
WELL, YOU CAN KEEP YOUR FUCKING MONEY! I AIN'T GOIN' NOWHERE!

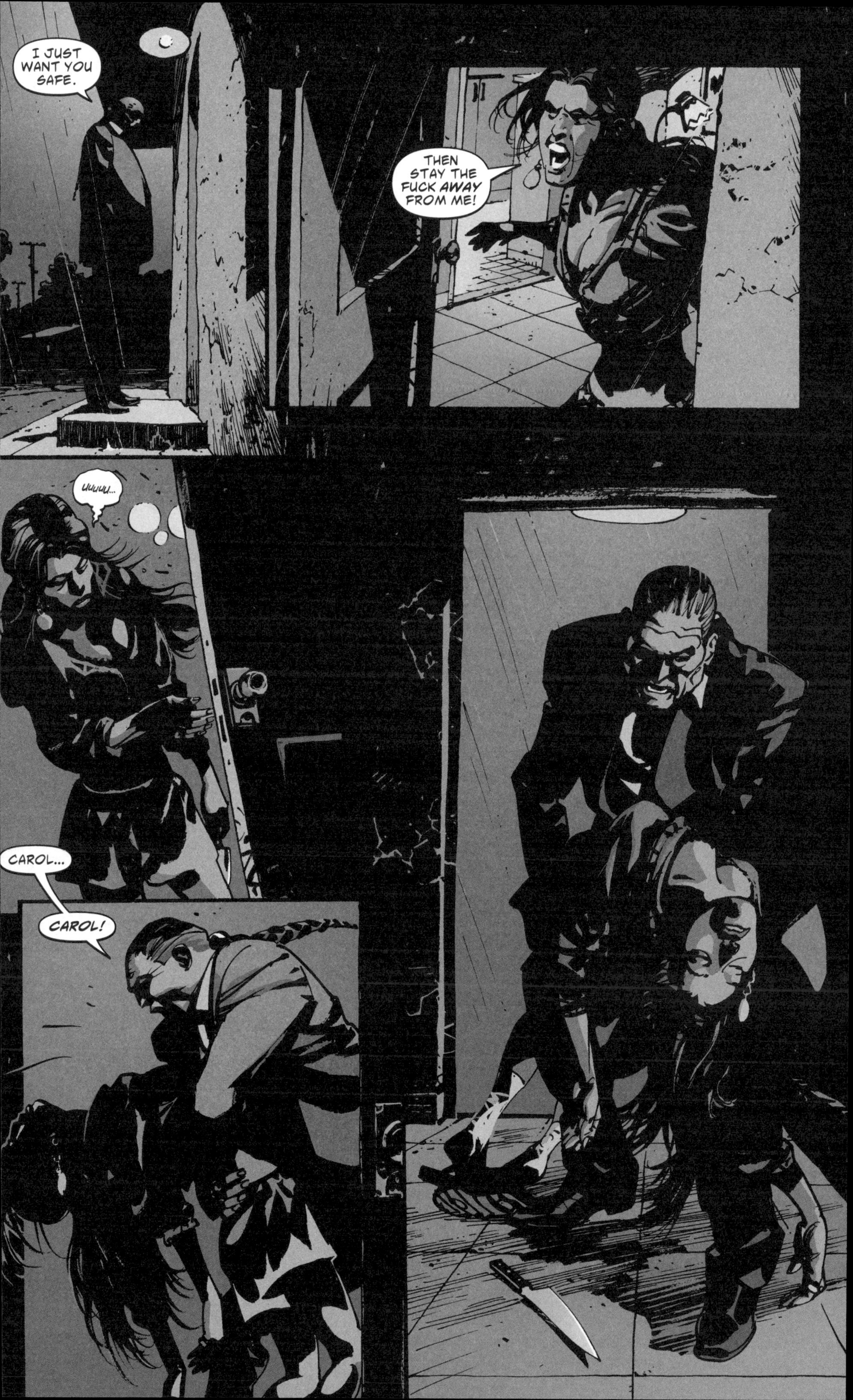
I JUST WANT YOU SAFE.
THEN STAY THE FUCK AWAY FROM ME!
uuuuu...
CAROL...
CAROL!

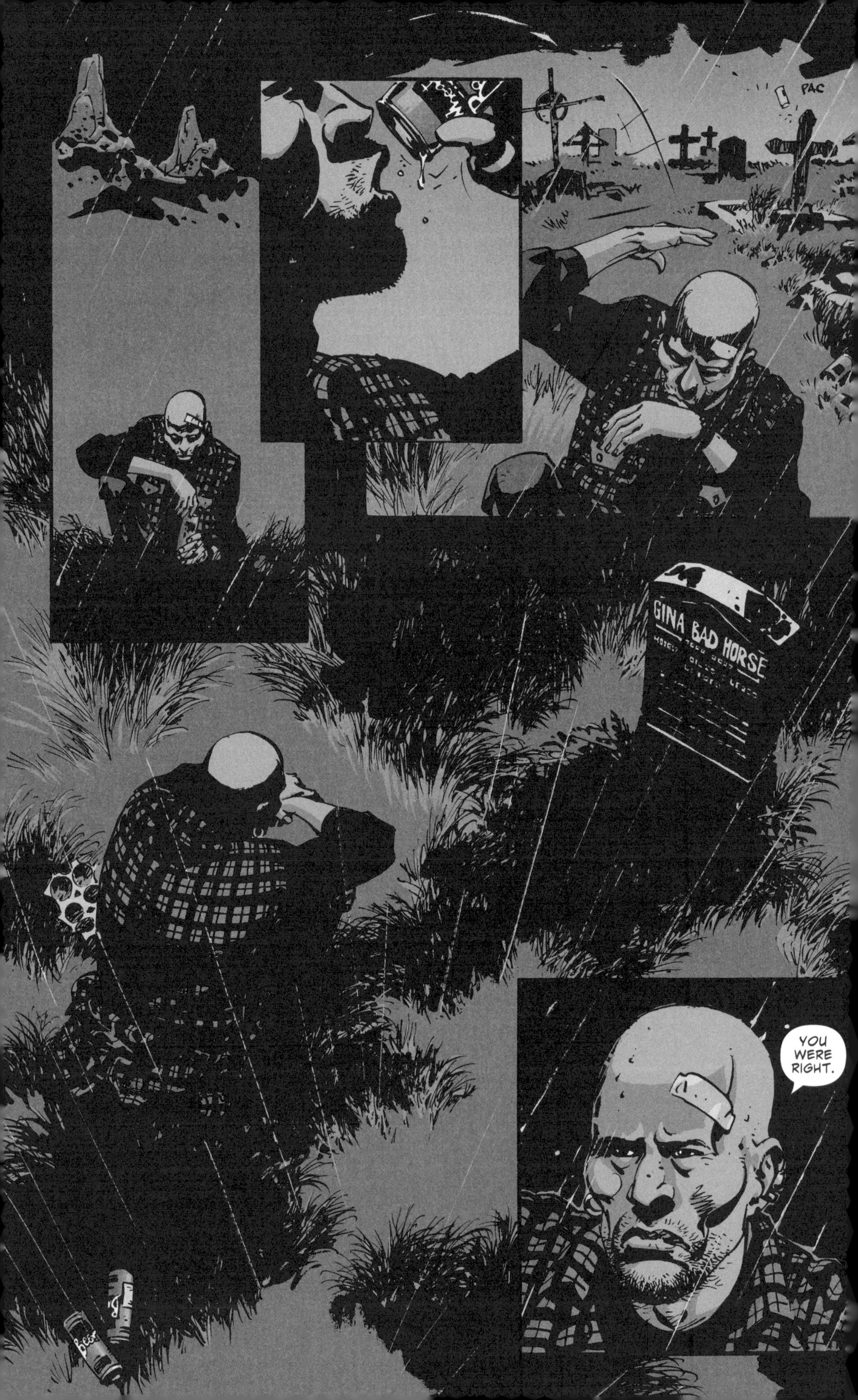
PAC
GINA BAD HORSE
YOU WERE RIGHT.

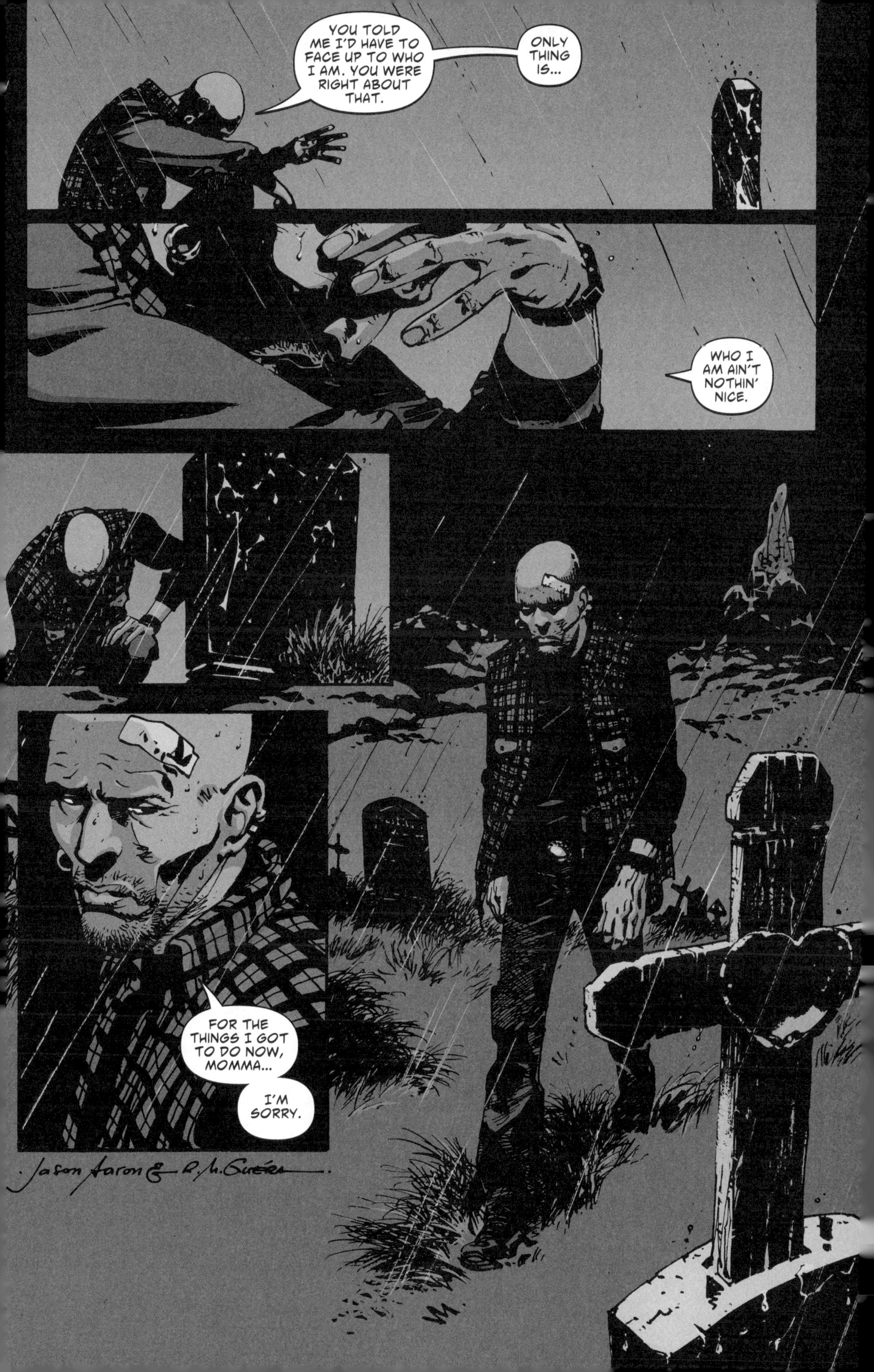
YOU TOLD ME I'D HAVE TO FACE UP TO WHO I AM. YOU WERE RIGHT ABOUT THAT.
ONLY THING IS...
WHO I AM AIN'T NOTHIN' NICE.
FOR THE THINGS I GOT TO DO NOW, MOMMA...
I'M SORRY.
Jason Aaron & R.M. Guéra

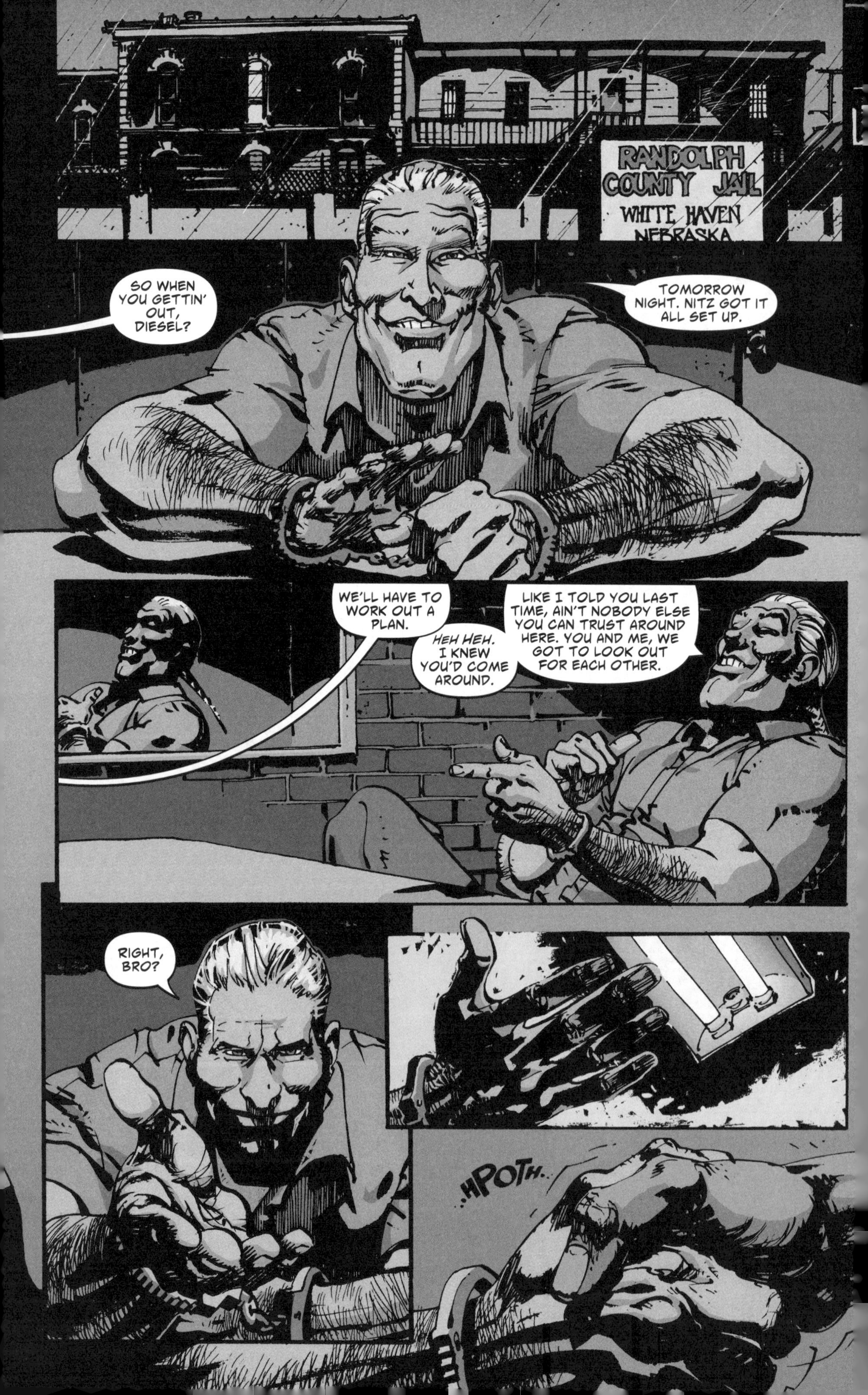
RANDOLPH COUNTY JAIL
WHITE HAVEN NEBRASKA
SO WHEN YOU GETTIN' OUT, DIESEL?
TOMORROW NIGHT. NITZ GOT IT ALL SET UP.
WE'LL HAVE TO WORK OUT A PLAN.
HEH HEH. I KNEW YOU'D COME AROUND.
LIKE I TOLD YOU LAST TIME, AIN'T NOBODY ELSE YOU CAN TRUST AROUND HERE. YOU AND ME, WE GOT TO LOOK OUT FOR EACH OTHER.
RIGHT, BRO?
HPOTH..

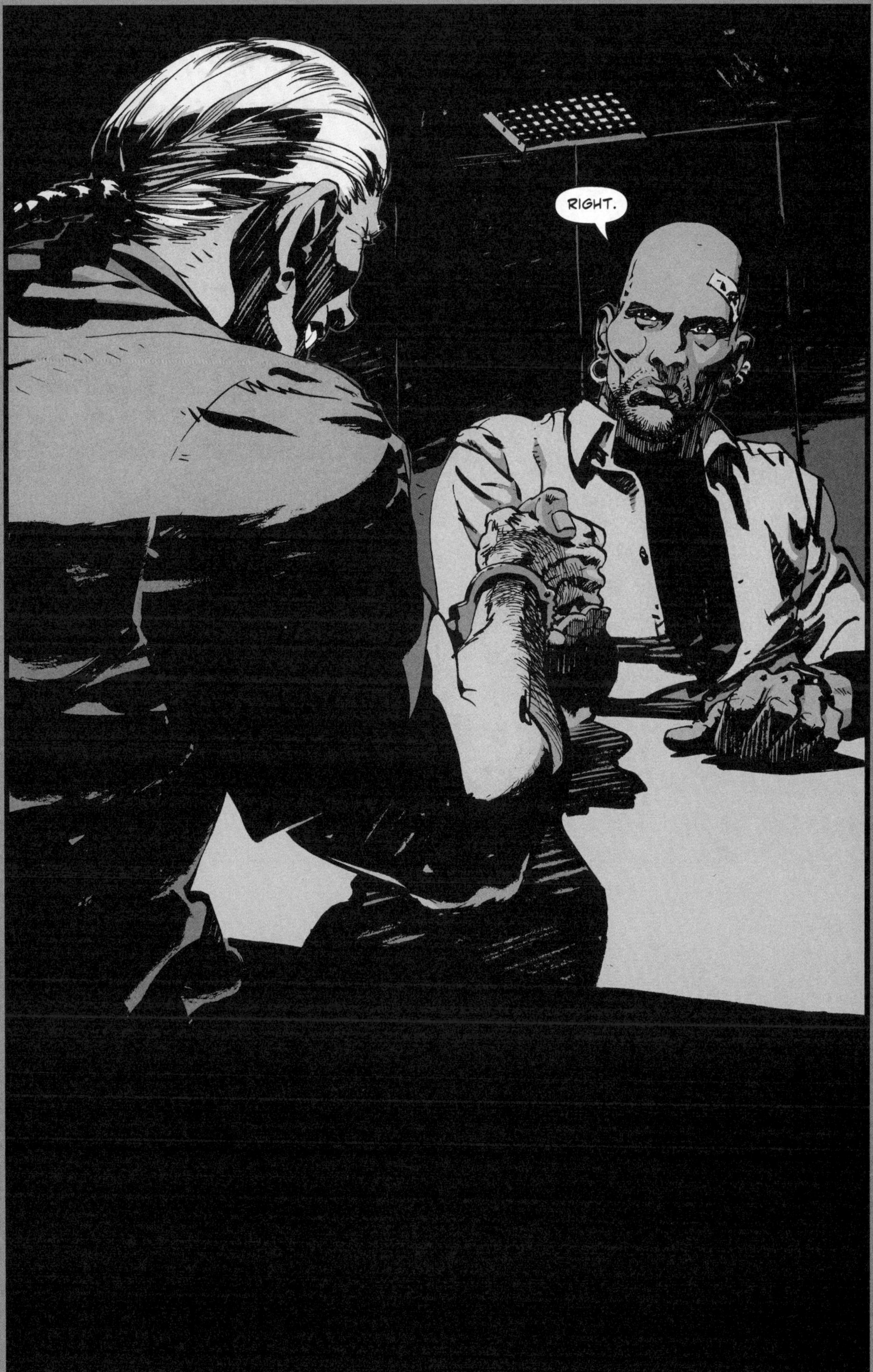
RIGHT.

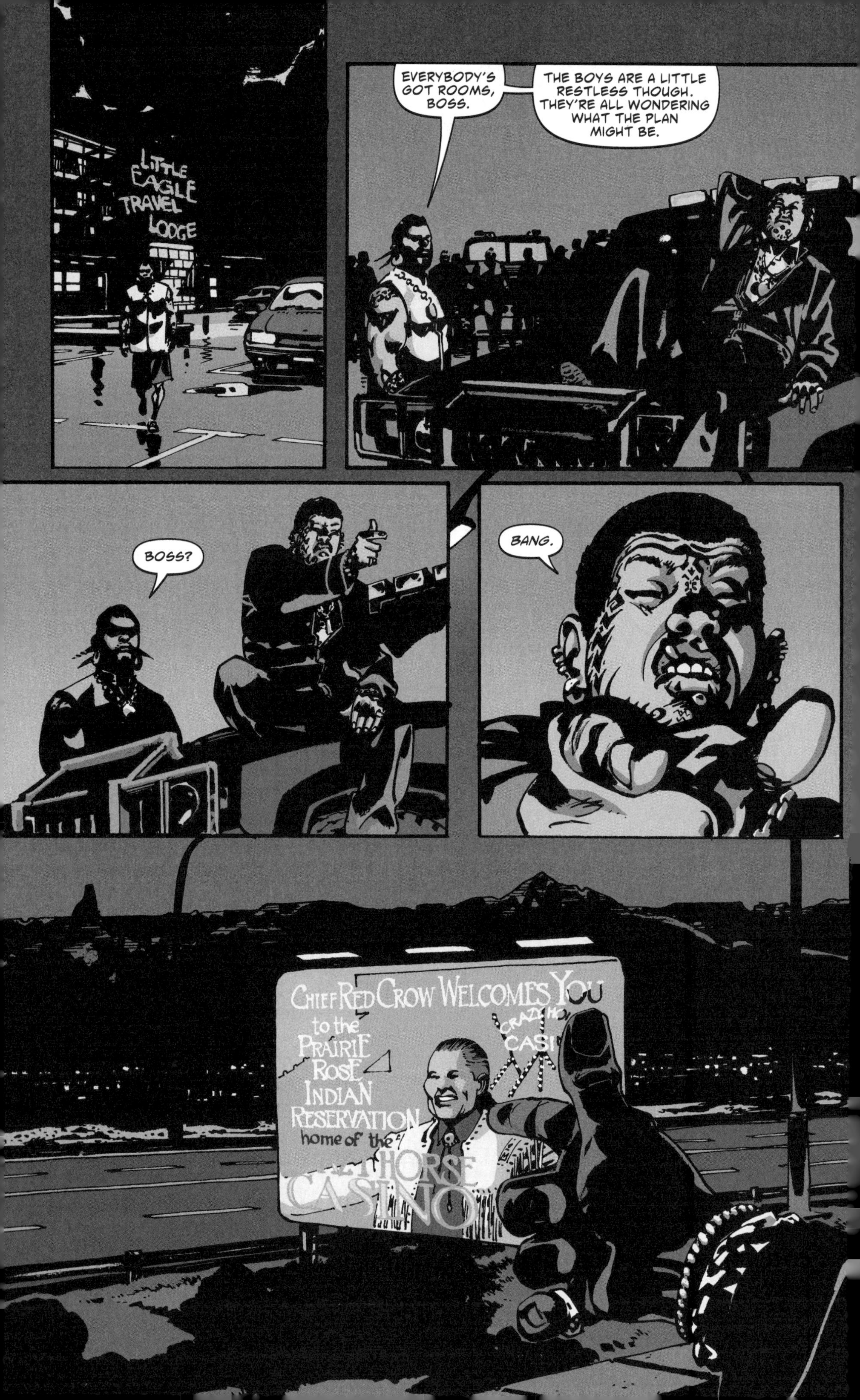
LITTLE EAGLE TRAVEL LODGE
EVERYBODY'S GOT ROOMS, BOSS.
THE BOYS ARE A LITTLE RESTLESS THOUGH. THEY'RE ALL WONDERING WHAT THE PLAN MIGHT BE.
BOSS?
BANG.
CHIEF RED CROW WELCOMES YOU
to the PRAIRIE ROSE INDIAN RESERVATION
home of the
HORSE CASINO

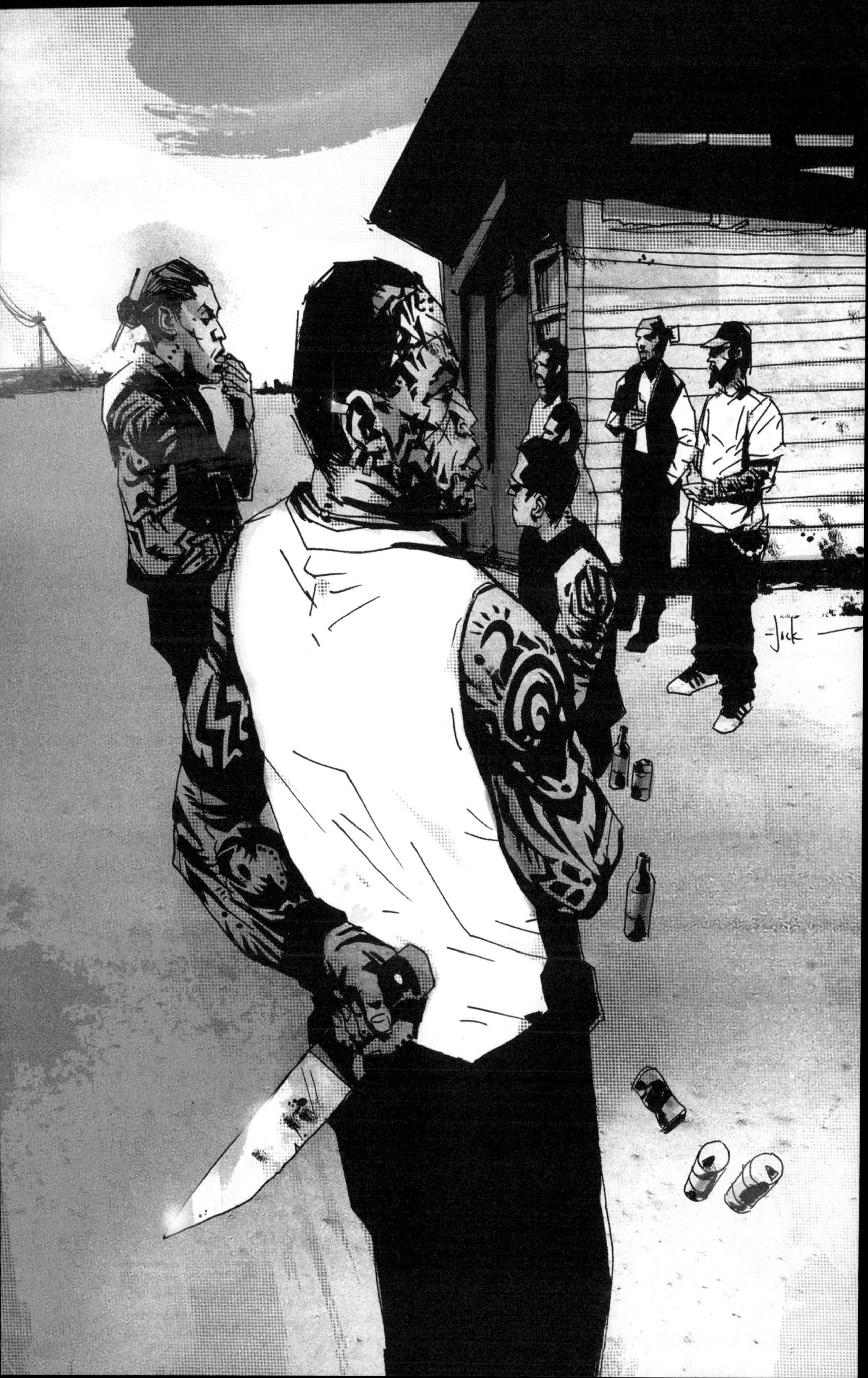

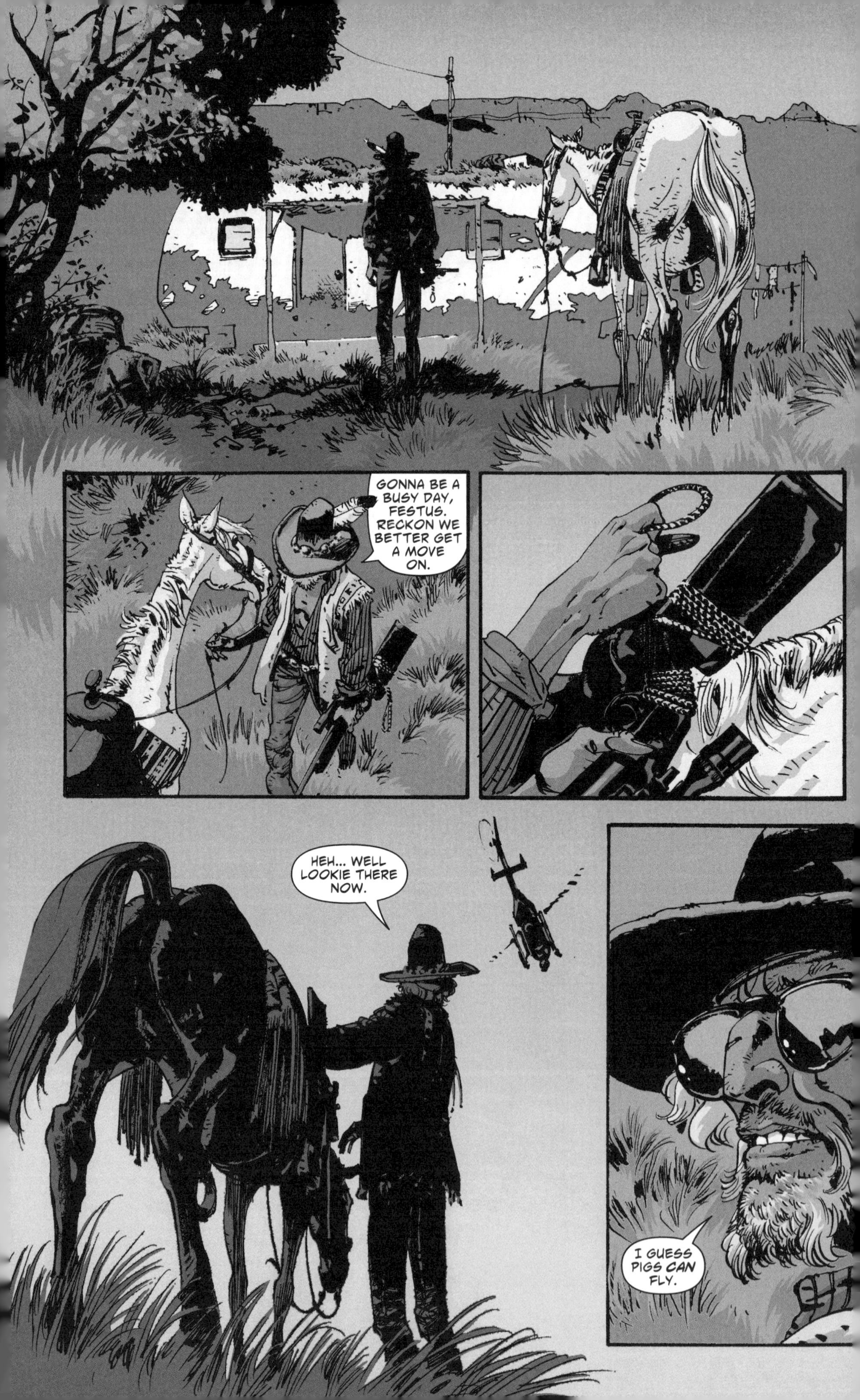
GONNA BE A BUSY DAY, FESTUS. RECKON WE BETTER GET A MOVE ON.
HEH... WELL LOOKIE THERE NOW.
I GUESS PIGS CAN FLY.

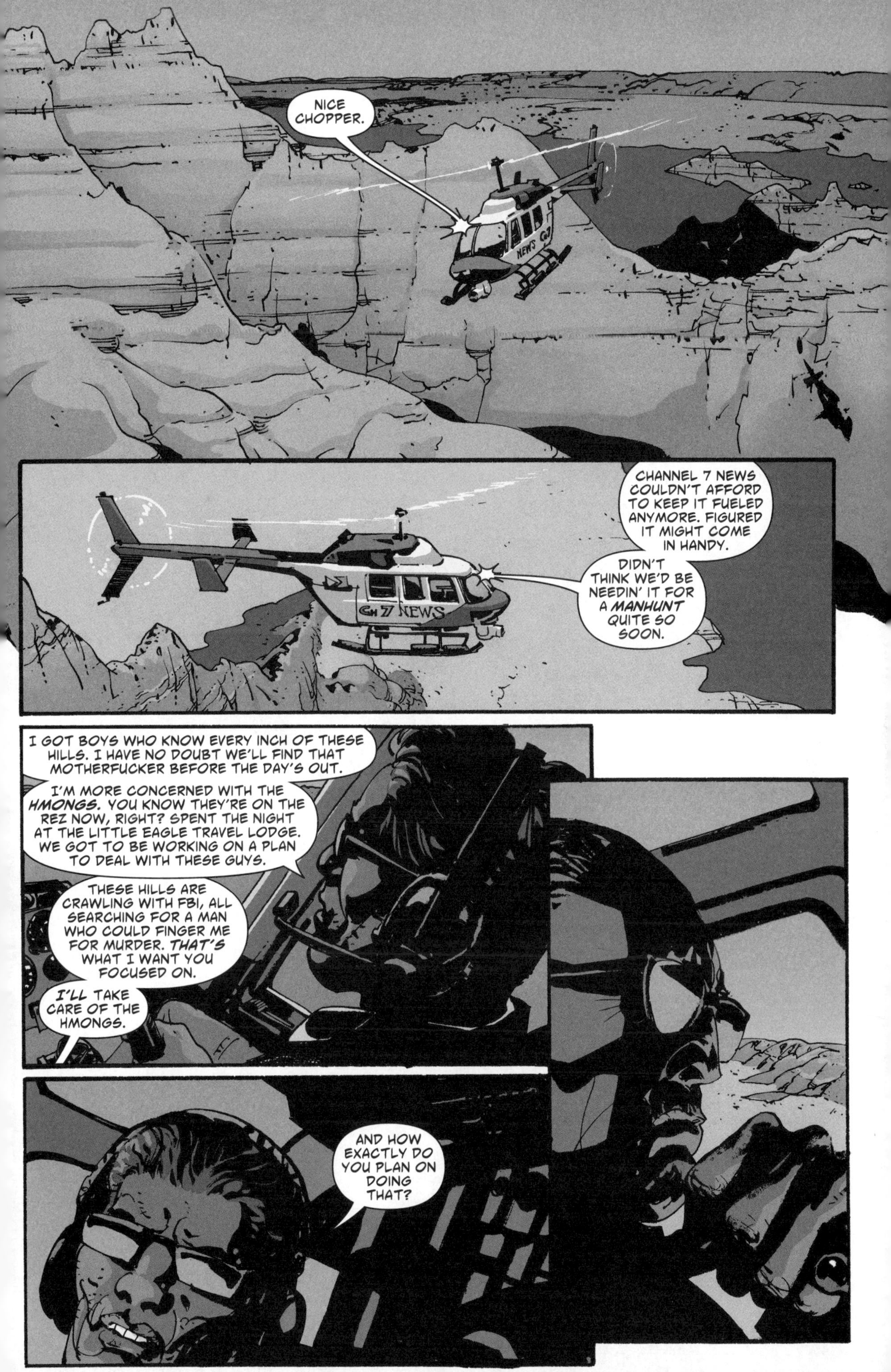
NICE CHOPPER.
CHANNEL 7 NEWS COULDN'T AFFORD TO KEEP IT FUELED ANYMORE. FIGURED IT MIGHT COME IN HANDY.
DIDN'T THINK WE'D BE NEEDIN' IT FOR A *MANHUNT* QUITE SO SOON.
CH 7 NEWS
I GOT BOYS WHO KNOW EVERY INCH OF THESE HILLS. I HAVE NO DOUBT WE'LL FIND THAT MOTHERFUCKER BEFORE THE DAY'S OUT.
I'M MORE CONCERNED WITH THE *HMONGS.* YOU KNOW THEY'RE ON THE REZ NOW, RIGHT? SPENT THE NIGHT AT THE LITTLE EAGLE TRAVEL LODGE. WE GOT TO BE WORKING ON A PLAN TO DEAL WITH THESE GUYS.
THESE HILLS ARE CRAWLING WITH FBI, ALL SEARCHING FOR A MAN WHO COULD FINGER ME FOR MURDER. *THAT'S* WHAT I WANT YOU FOCUSED ON.
*I'LL* TAKE CARE OF THE HMONGS.
AND HOW EXACTLY DO YOU PLAN ON DOING THAT?

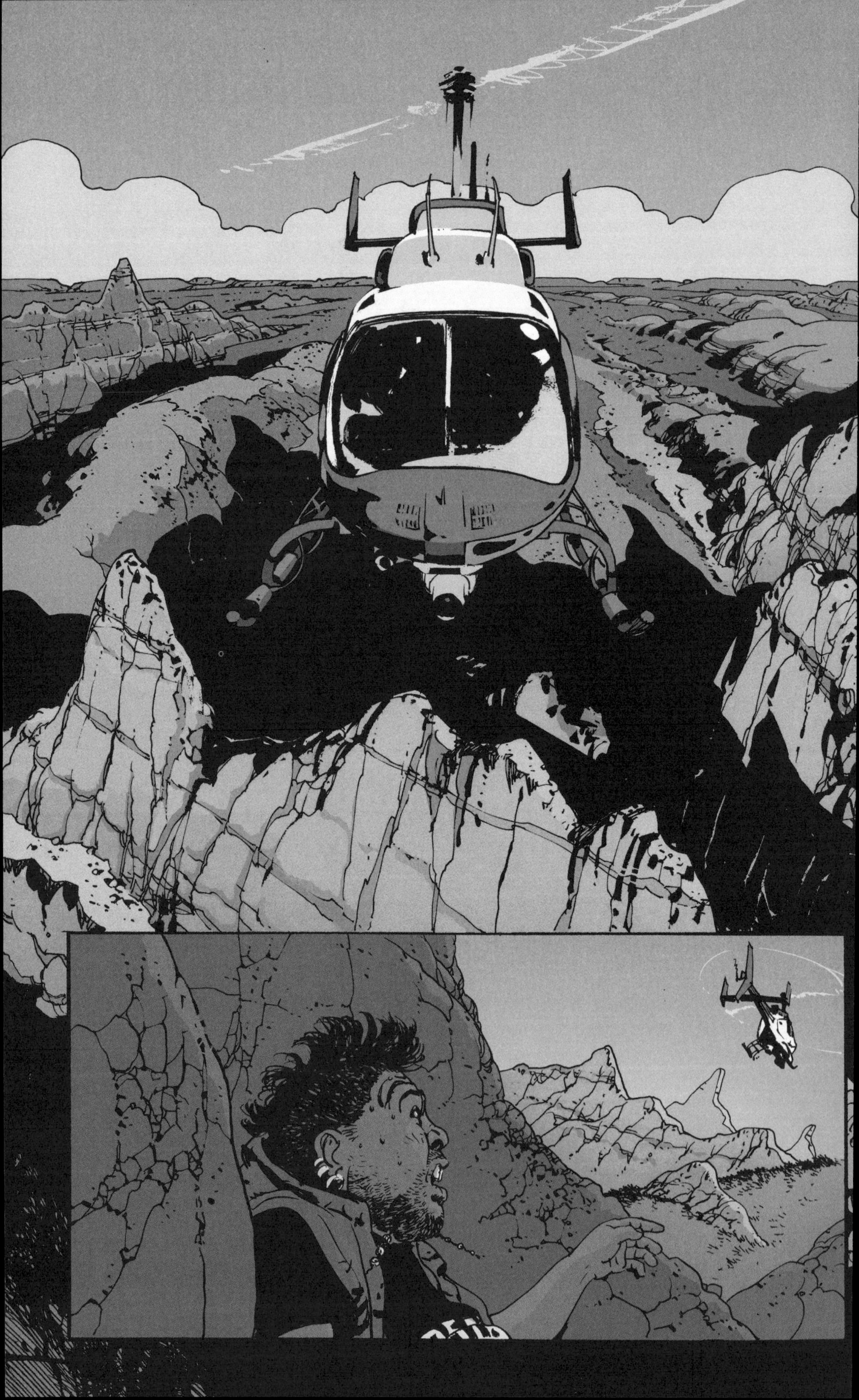

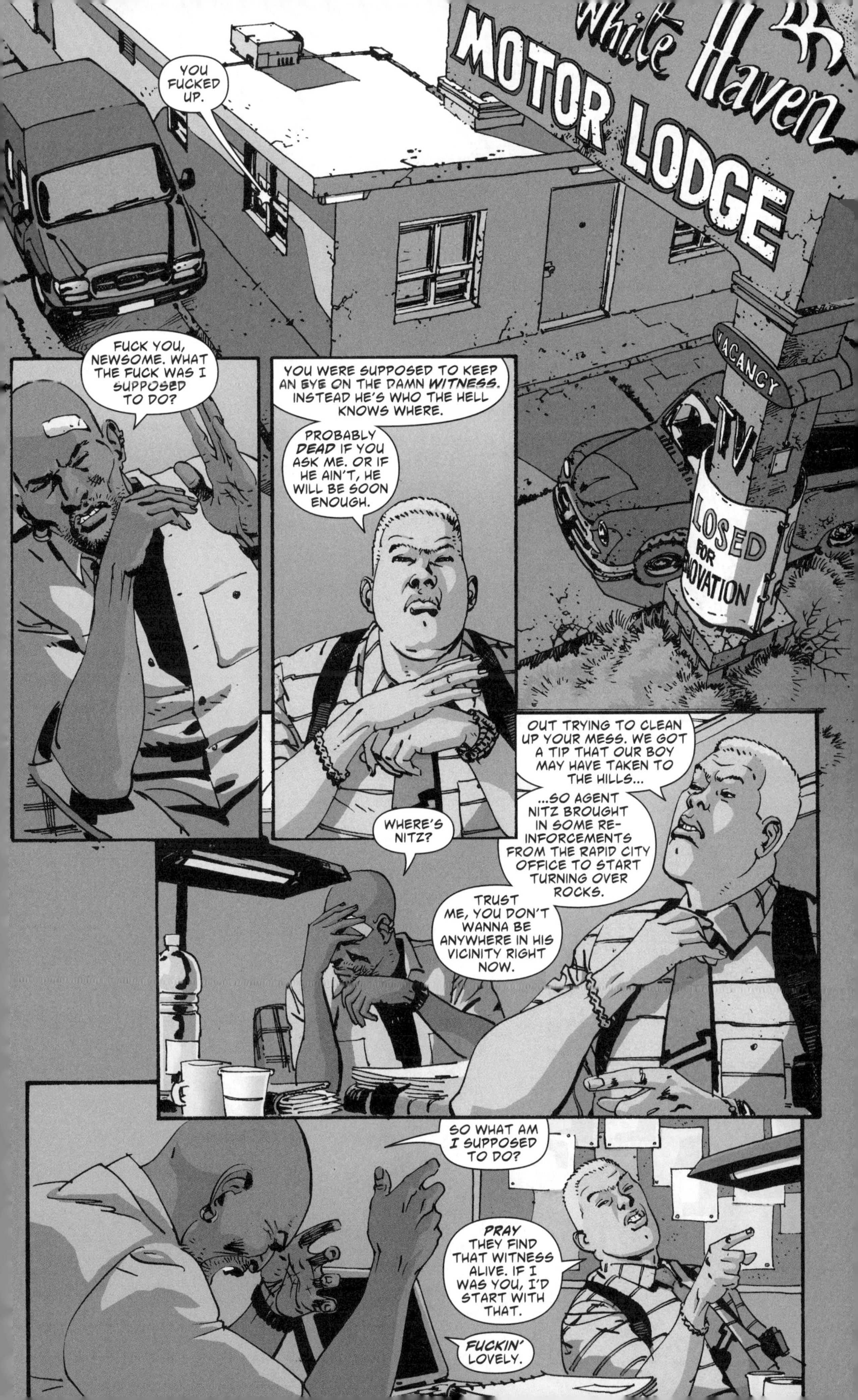
White Haven
MOTOR LODGE
YOU FUCKED UP.
FUCK YOU, NEWSOME. WHAT THE FUCK WAS I SUPPOSED TO DO?
YOU WERE SUPPOSED TO KEEP AN EYE ON THE DAMN WITNESS. INSTEAD HE'S WHO THE HELL KNOWS WHERE.
PROBABLY DEAD IF YOU ASK ME. OR IF HE AIN'T, HE WILL BE SOON ENOUGH.
VACANCY
TV
LOSED FOR NOVATION
WHERE'S NITZ?
OUT TRYING TO CLEAN UP YOUR MESS. WE GOT A TIP THAT OUR BOY MAY HAVE TAKEN TO THE HILLS...
...SO AGENT NITZ BROUGHT IN SOME RE-INFORCEMENTS FROM THE RAPID CITY OFFICE TO START TURNING OVER ROCKS.
TRUST ME, YOU DON'T WANNA BE ANYWHERE IN HIS VICINITY RIGHT NOW.
SO WHAT AM I SUPPOSED TO DO?
PRAY THEY FIND THAT WITNESS ALIVE. IF I WAS YOU, I'D START WITH THAT.
FUCKIN' LOVELY.

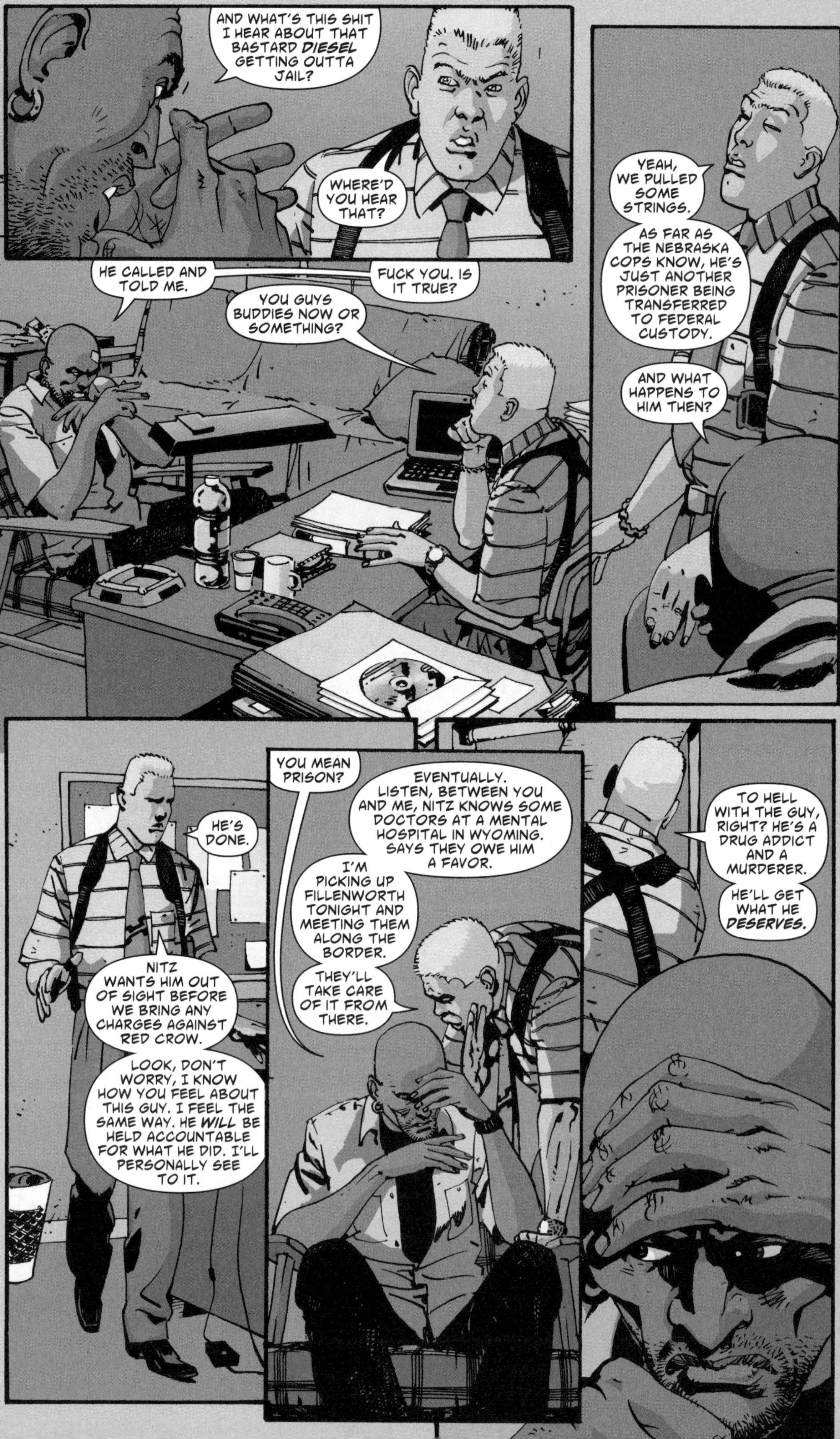
AND WHAT'S THIS SHIT I HEAR ABOUT THAT BASTARD DIESEL GETTING OUTTA JAIL?
WHERE'D YOU HEAR THAT?
HE CALLED AND TOLD ME.
FUCK YOU. IS IT TRUE?
YOU GUYS BUDDIES NOW OR SOMETHING?
YEAH, WE PULLED SOME STRINGS.
AS FAR AS THE NEBRASKA COPS KNOW, HE'S JUST ANOTHER PRISONER BEING TRANSFERRED TO FEDERAL CUSTODY.
AND WHAT HAPPENS TO HIM THEN?
HE'S DONE.
NITZ WANTS HIM OUT OF SIGHT BEFORE WE BRING ANY CHARGES AGAINST RED CROW.
LOOK, DON'T WORRY, I KNOW HOW YOU FEEL ABOUT THIS GUY. I FEEL THE SAME WAY. HE WILL BE HELD ACCOUNTABLE FOR WHAT HE DID. I'LL PERSONALLY SEE TO IT.
YOU MEAN PRISON?
EVENTUALLY. LISTEN, BETWEEN YOU AND ME, NITZ KNOWS SOME DOCTORS AT A MENTAL HOSPITAL IN WYOMING. SAYS THEY OWE HIM A FAVOR.
I'M PICKING UP FILLENWORTH TONIGHT AND MEETING THEM ALONG THE BORDER.
THEY'LL TAKE CARE OF IT FROM THERE.
TO HELL WITH THE GUY, RIGHT? HE'S A DRUG ADDICT AND A MURDERER.
HE'LL GET WHAT HE DESERVES.

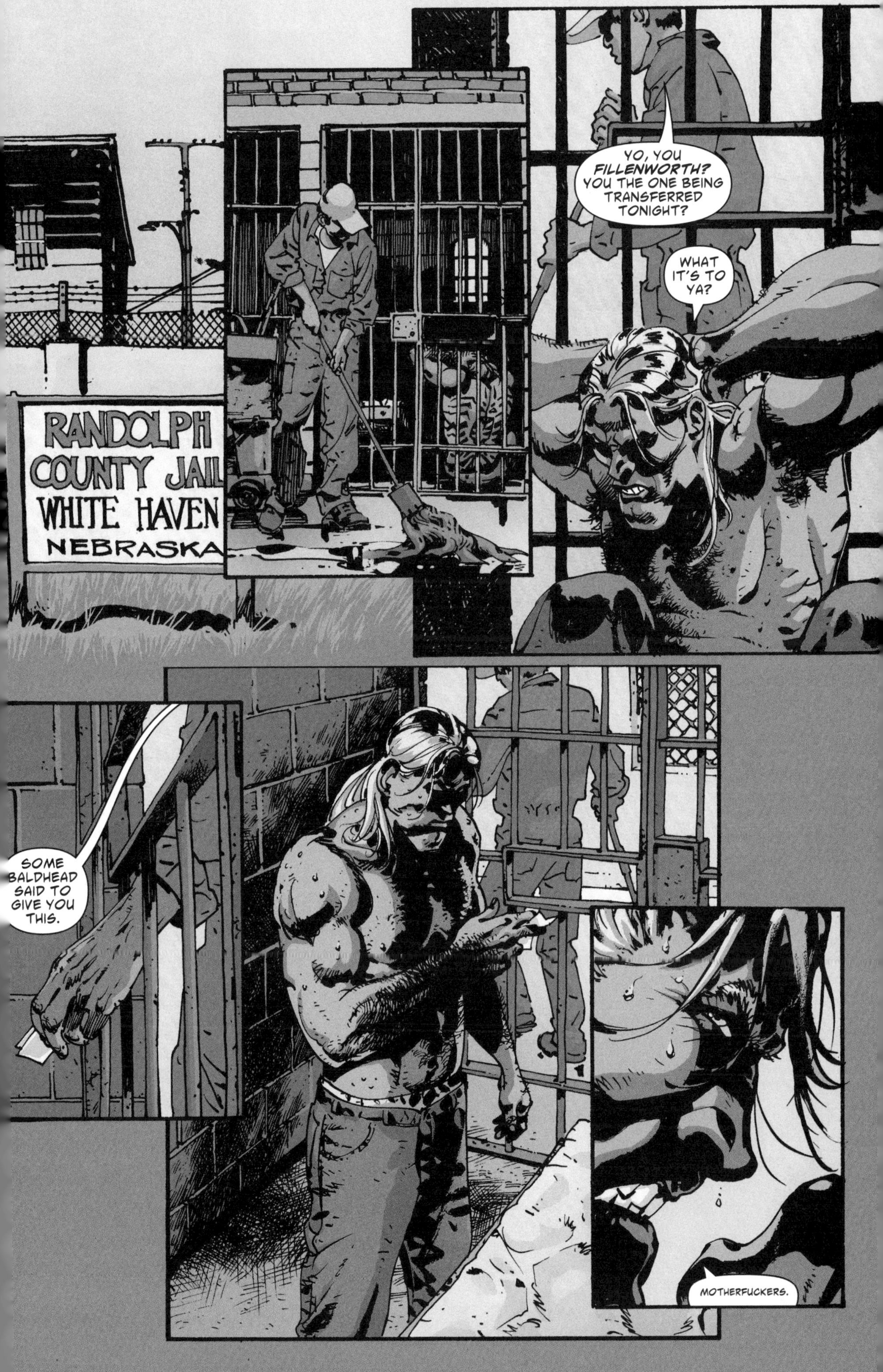
RANDOLPH
COUNTY JAIL
WHITE HAVEN
NEBRASKA
YO, YOU FILLENWORTH? YOU THE ONE BEING TRANSFERRED TONIGHT?
WHAT IT'S TO YA?
SOME BALDHEAD SAID TO GIVE YOU THIS.
MOTHERFUCKERS.

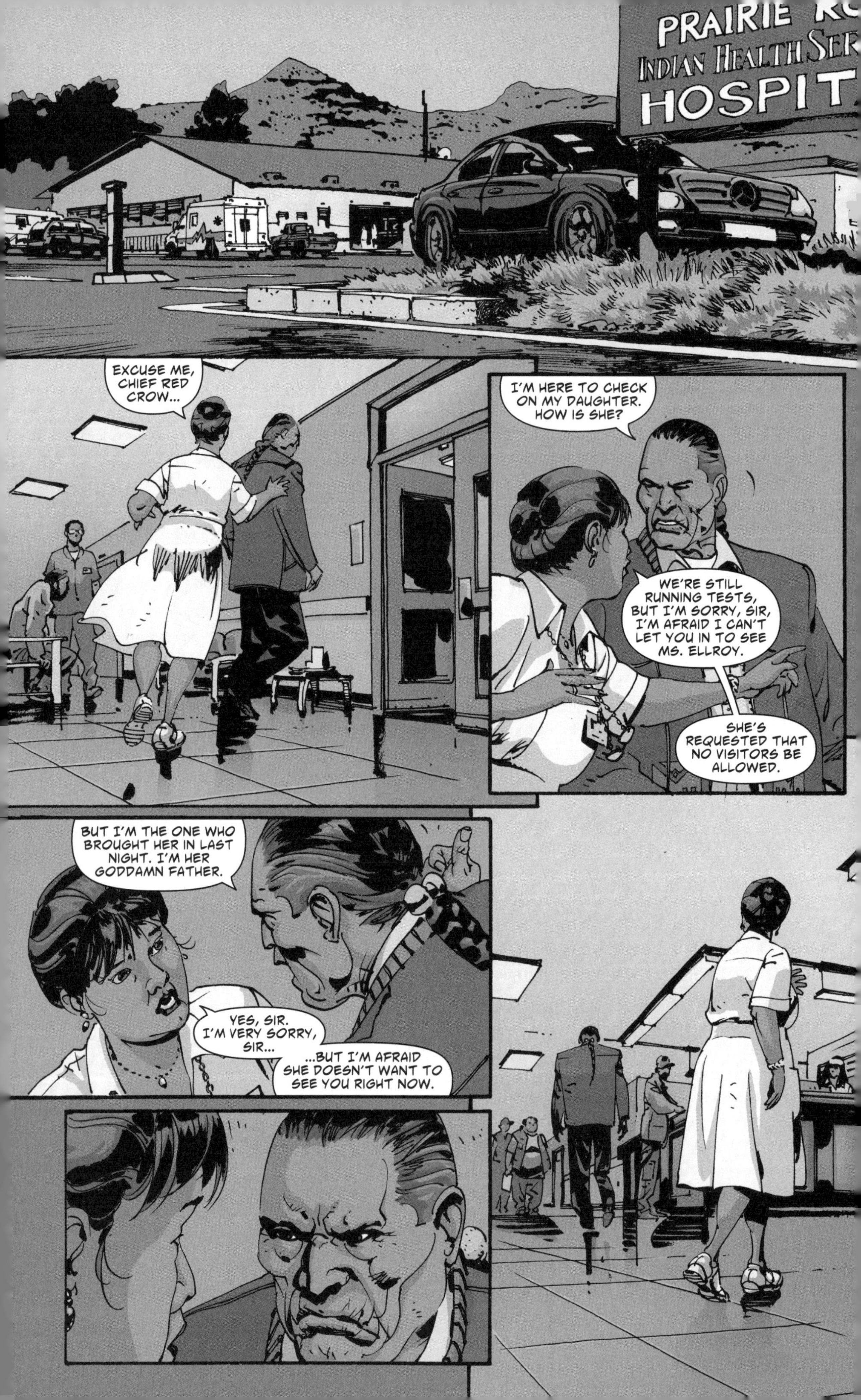
PRAIRIE R
INDIAN HEALTH SER
HOSPIT
EXCUSE ME, CHIEF RED CROW...
I'M HERE TO CHECK ON MY DAUGHTER. HOW IS SHE?
WE'RE STILL RUNNING TESTS, BUT I'M SORRY, SIR, I'M AFRAID I CAN'T LET YOU IN TO SEE MS. ELLROY.
SHE'S REQUESTED THAT NO VISITORS BE ALLOWED.
BUT I'M THE ONE WHO BROUGHT HER IN LAST NIGHT. I'M HER GODDAMN FATHER.
YES, SIR. I'M VERY SORRY, SIR...
...BUT I'M AFRAID SHE DOESN'T WANT TO SEE YOU RIGHT NOW.

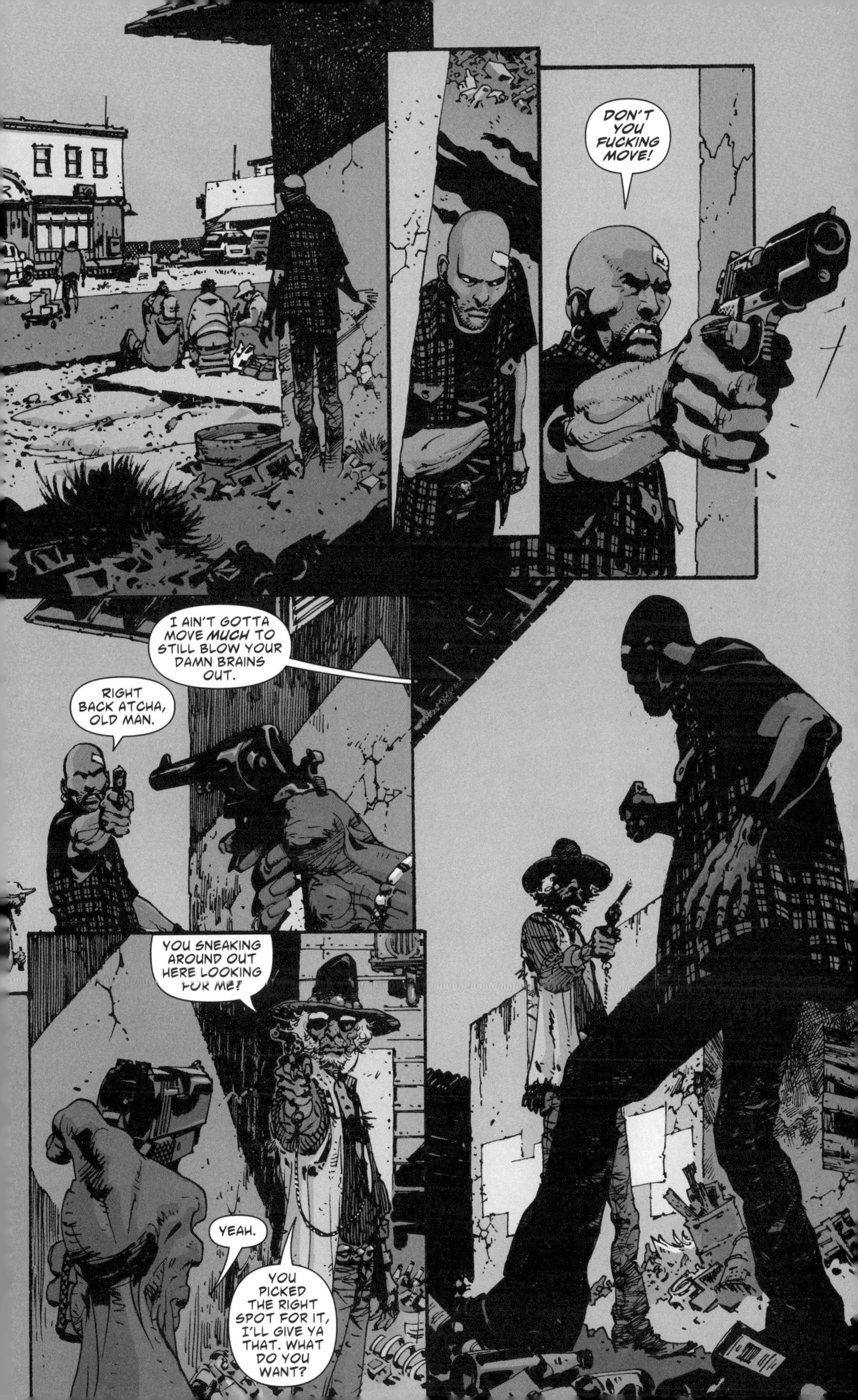
DON'T YOU FUCKING MOVE!
I AIN'T GOTTA MOVE MUCH TO STILL BLOW YOUR DAMN BRAINS OUT.
RIGHT BACK ATCHA, OLD MAN.
YOU SNEAKING AROUND OUT HERE LOOKING FOR ME?
YEAH.
YOU PICKED THE RIGHT SPOT FOR IT, I'LL GIVE YA THAT. WHAT DO YOU WANT?

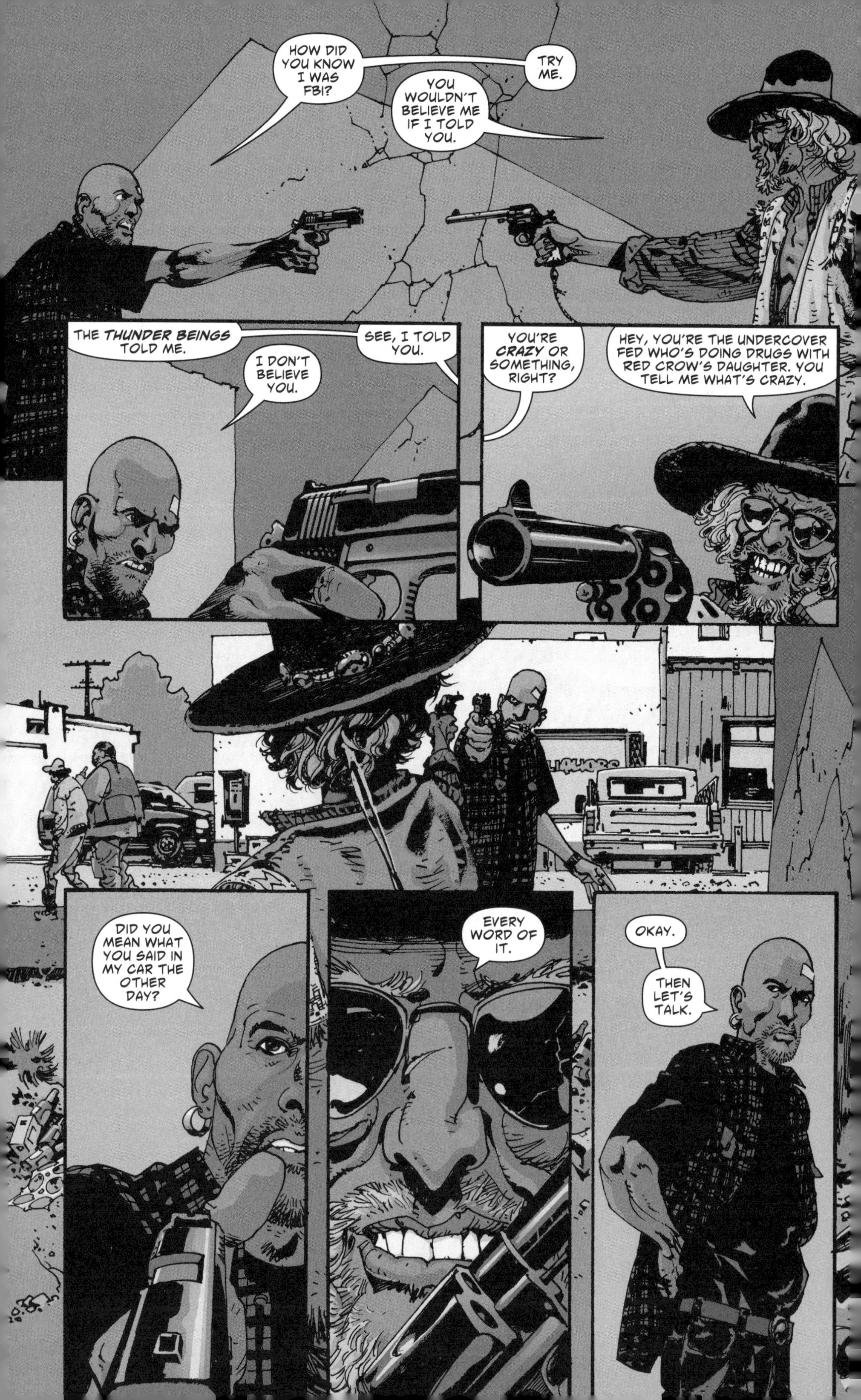
HOW DID YOU KNOW I WAS FBI?
YOU WOULDN'T BELIEVE ME IF I TOLD YOU.
TRY ME.
THE *THUNDER BEINGS* TOLD ME.
I DON'T BELIEVE YOU.
SEE, I TOLD YOU.
YOU'RE *CRAZY* OR SOMETHING, RIGHT?
HEY, YOU'RE THE UNDERCOVER FED WHO'S DOING DRUGS WITH RED CROW'S DAUGHTER. YOU TELL ME WHAT'S CRAZY.
DID YOU MEAN WHAT YOU SAID IN MY CAR THE OTHER DAY?
EVERY WORD OF IT.
OKAY.
THEN LET'S TALK.

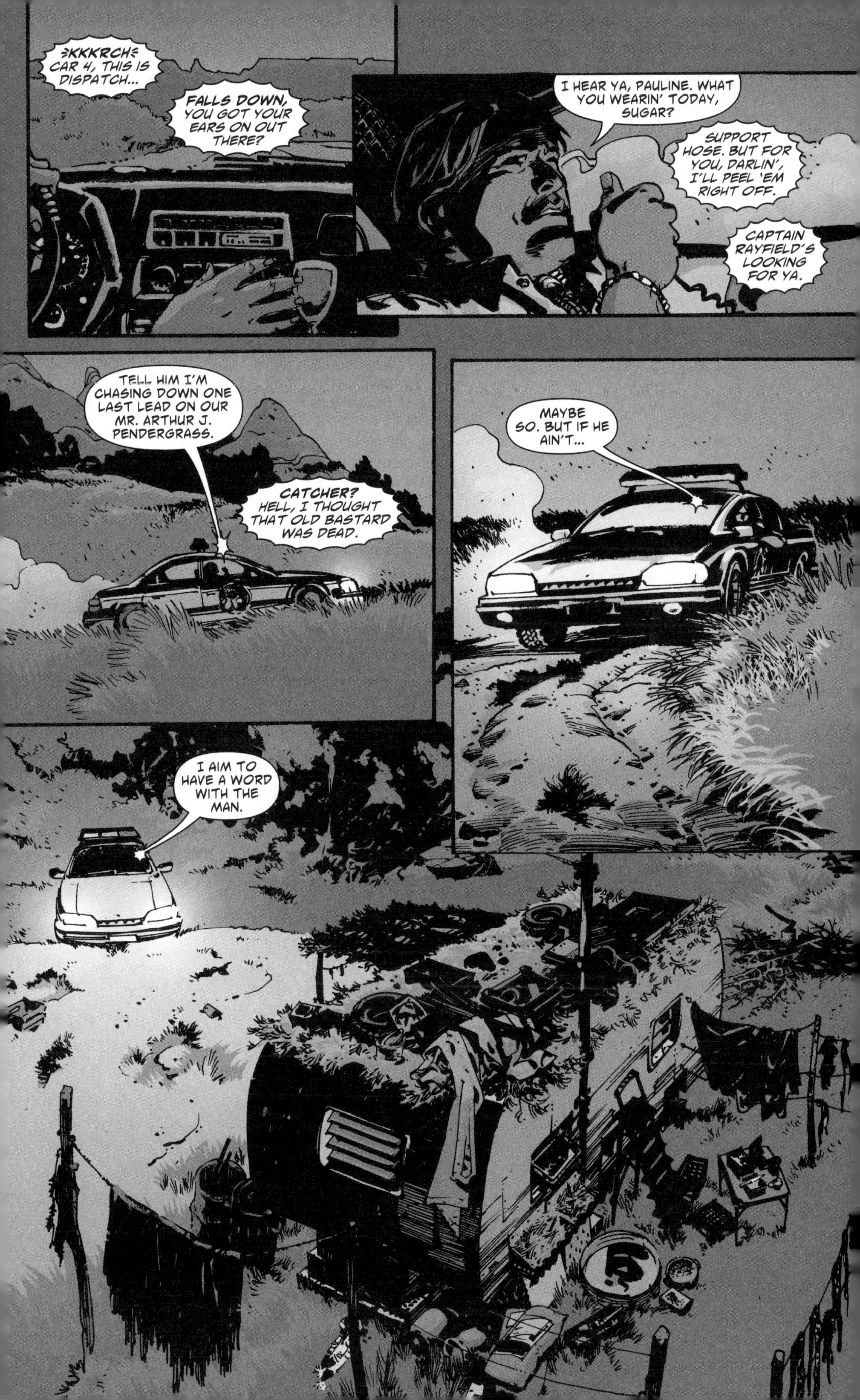

≈KKKRCH≈ CAR 4, THIS IS DISPATCH...
FALLS DOWN, YOU GOT YOUR EARS ON OUT THERE?
I HEAR YA, PAULINE. WHAT YOU WEARIN' TODAY, SUGAR?
SUPPORT HOSE. BUT FOR YOU, DARLIN', I'LL PEEL 'EM RIGHT OFF.
CAPTAIN RAYFIELD'S LOOKING FOR YA.
TELL HIM I'M CHASING DOWN ONE LAST LEAD ON OUR MR. ARTHUR J. PENDERGRASS.
CATCHER? HELL, I THOUGHT THAT OLD BASTARD WAS DEAD.
MAYBE SO. BUT IF HE AIN'T...
I AIM TO HAVE A WORD WITH THE MAN.

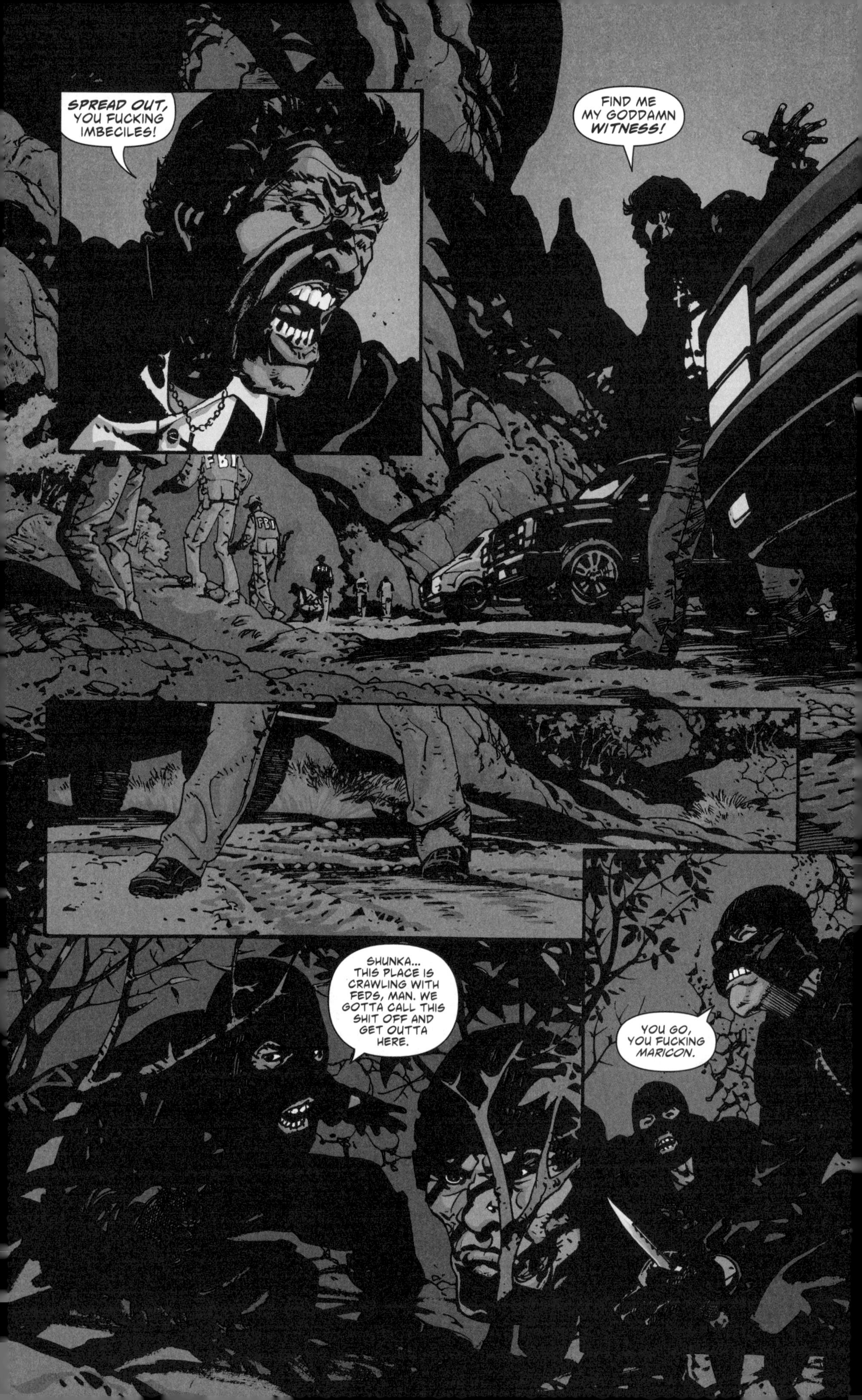
SPREAD OUT, YOU FUCKING IMBECILES!
FIND ME MY GODDAMN WITNESS!
SHUNKA... THIS PLACE IS CRAWLING WITH FEDS, MAN. WE GOTTA CALL THIS SHIT OFF AND GET OUTTA HERE.
YOU GO, YOU FUCKING MARICON.
FBI
FBI
FBI

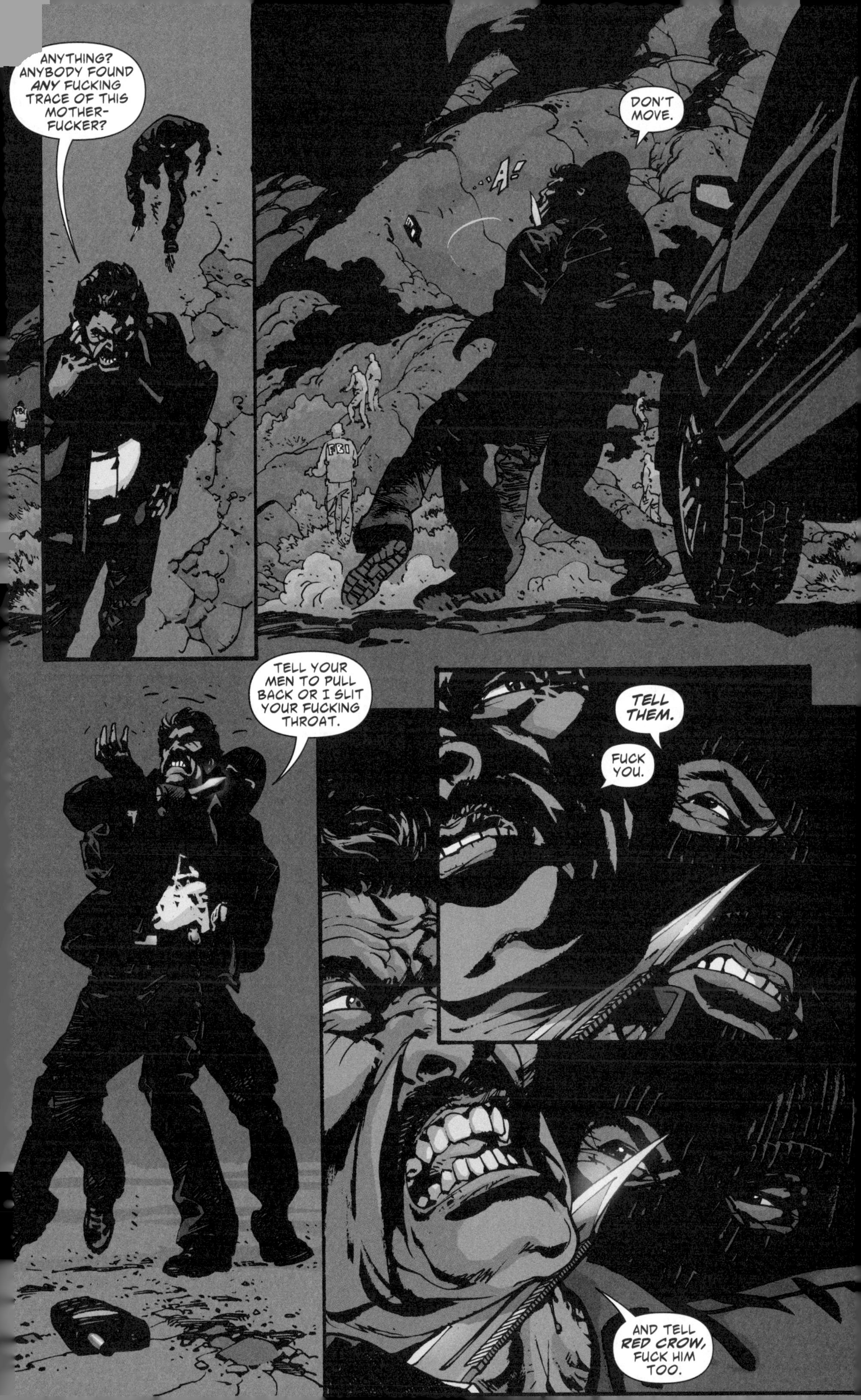
ANYTHING? ANYBODY FOUND *ANY* FUCKING TRACE OF THIS MOTHER-FUCKER?
DON'T MOVE.
A!
FBI
TELL YOUR MEN TO PULL BACK OR I SLIT YOUR FUCKING THROAT.
**TELL THEM.**
FUCK YOU.
AND TELL **RED CROW,** FUCK HIM TOO.

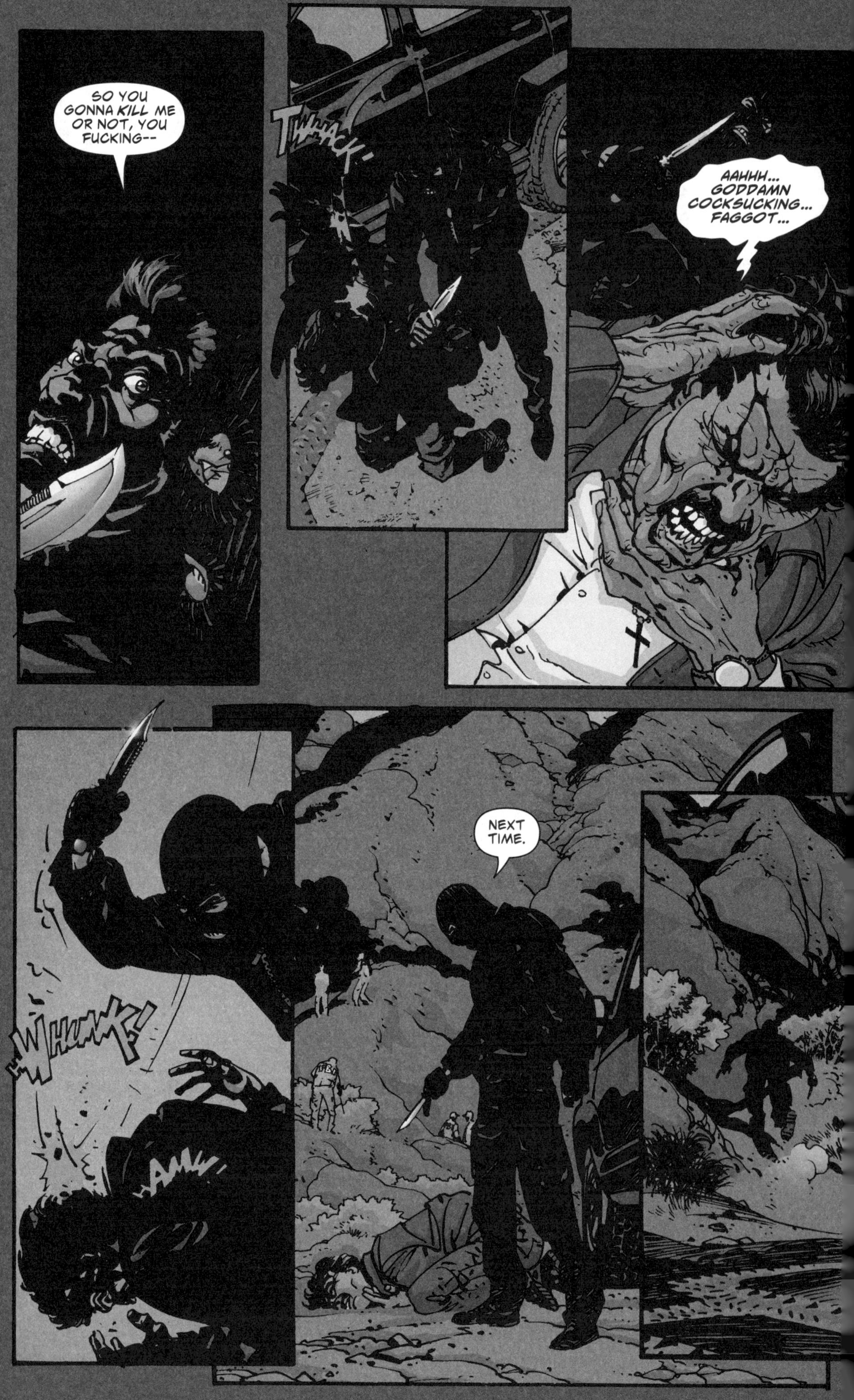
SO YOU GONNA KILL ME OR NOT, YOU FUCKING--
TWHACK
AAHHH... GODDAMN COCKSUCKING... FAGGOT...
WHUNK!
NEXT TIME.

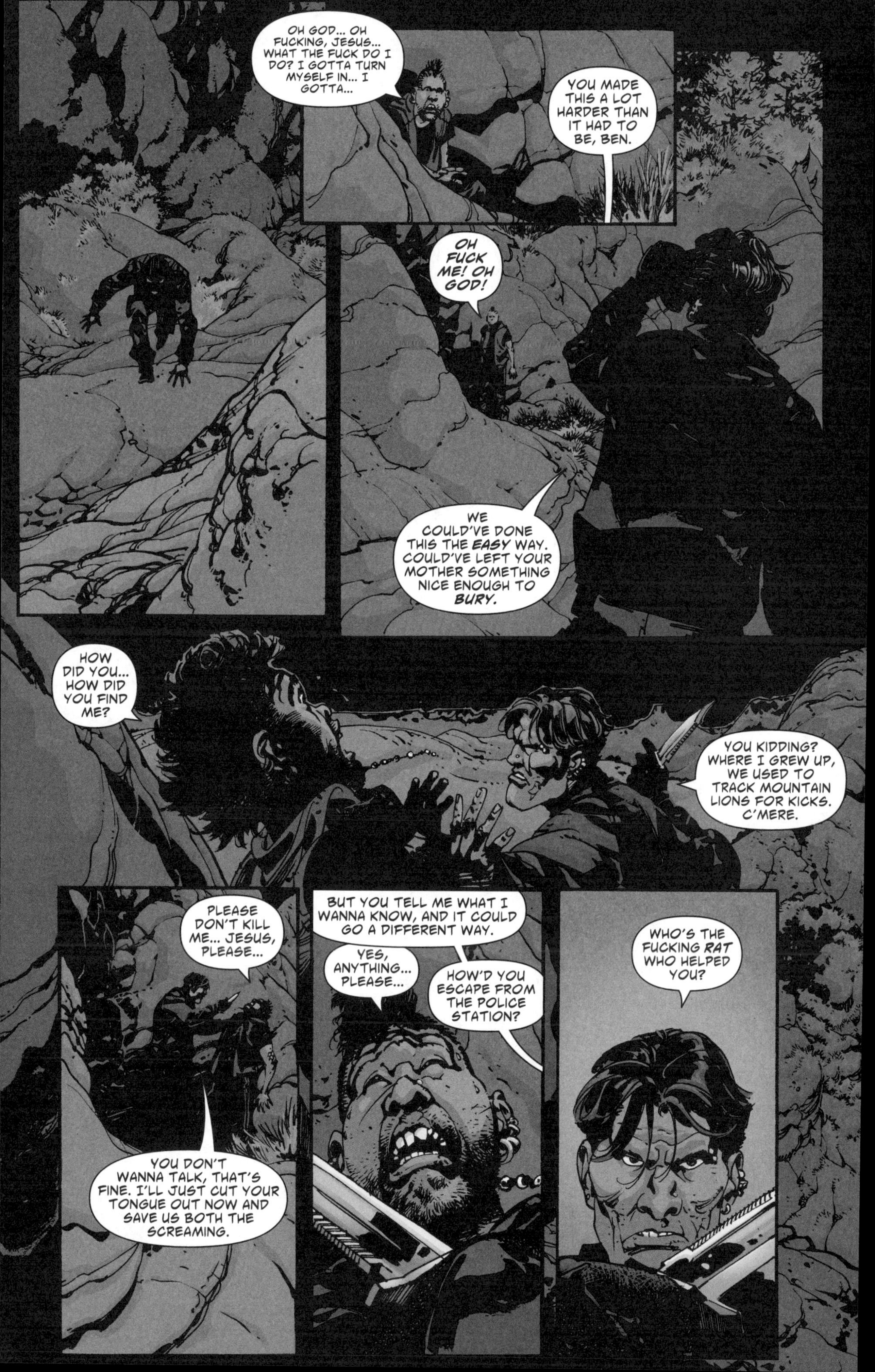

OH GOD... OH FUCKING, JESUS... WHAT THE FUCK DO I DO? I GOTTA TURN MYSELF IN... I GOTTA...
YOU MADE THIS A LOT HARDER THAN IT HAD TO BE, BEN.
OH FUCK ME! OH GOD!
WE COULD'VE DONE THIS THE EASY WAY. COULD'VE LEFT YOUR MOTHER SOMETHING NICE ENOUGH TO BURY.
HOW DID YOU... HOW DID YOU FIND ME?
YOU KIDDING? WHERE I GREW UP, WE USED TO TRACK MOUNTAIN LIONS FOR KICKS. C'MERE.
PLEASE DON'T KILL ME... JESUS, PLEASE...
YOU DON'T WANNA TALK, THAT'S FINE. I'LL JUST CUT YOUR TONGUE OUT NOW AND SAVE US BOTH THE SCREAMING.
BUT YOU TELL ME WHAT I WANNA KNOW, AND IT COULD GO A DIFFERENT WAY.
YES, ANYTHING... PLEASE...
HOW'D YOU ESCAPE FROM THE POLICE STATION?
WHO'S THE FUCKING RAT WHO HELPED YOU?

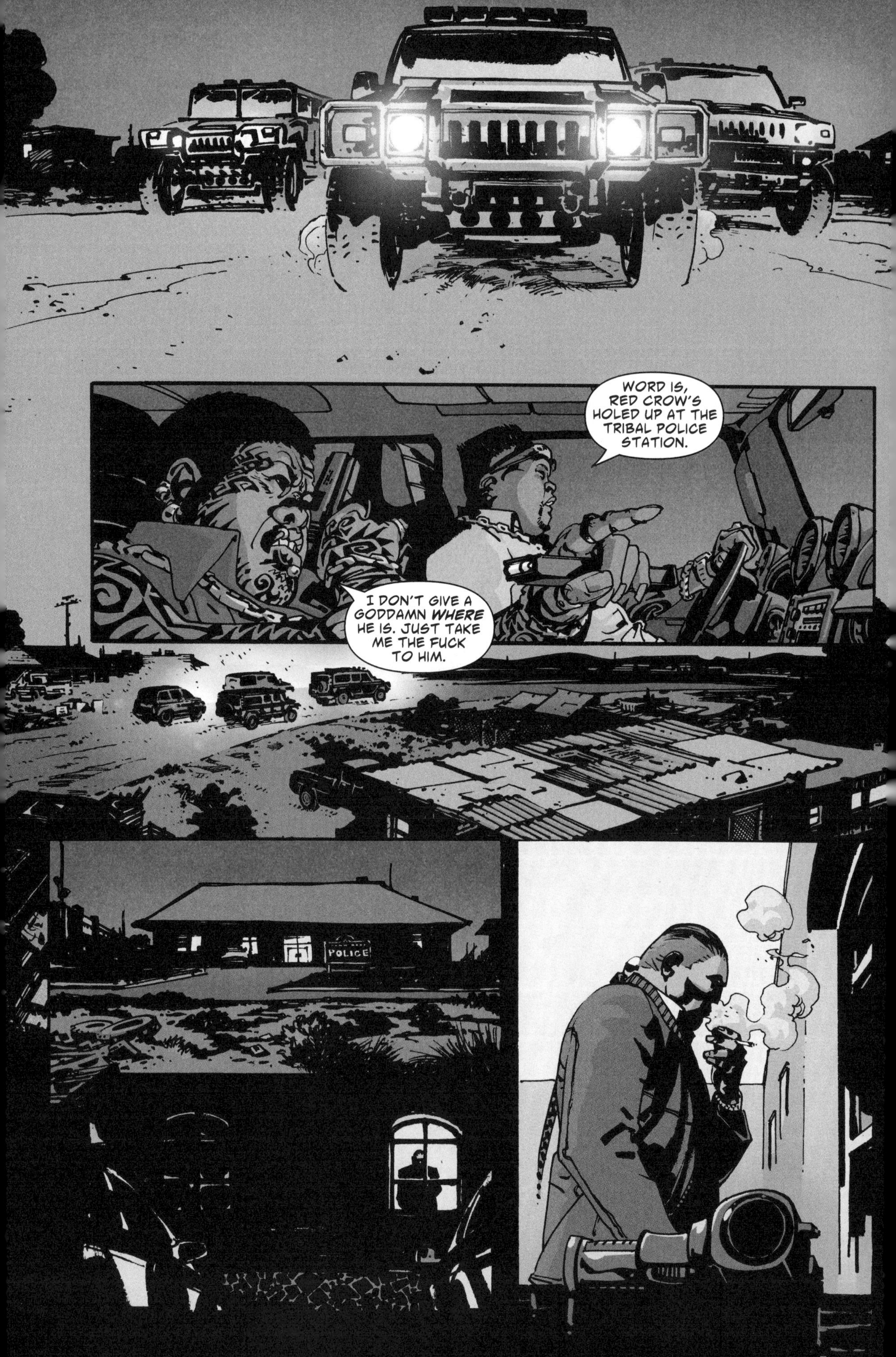
WORD IS, RED CROW'S HOLED UP AT THE TRIBAL POLICE STATION.
I DON'T GIVE A GODDAMN *WHERE* HE IS. JUST TAKE ME THE FUCK TO HIM.
POLICE

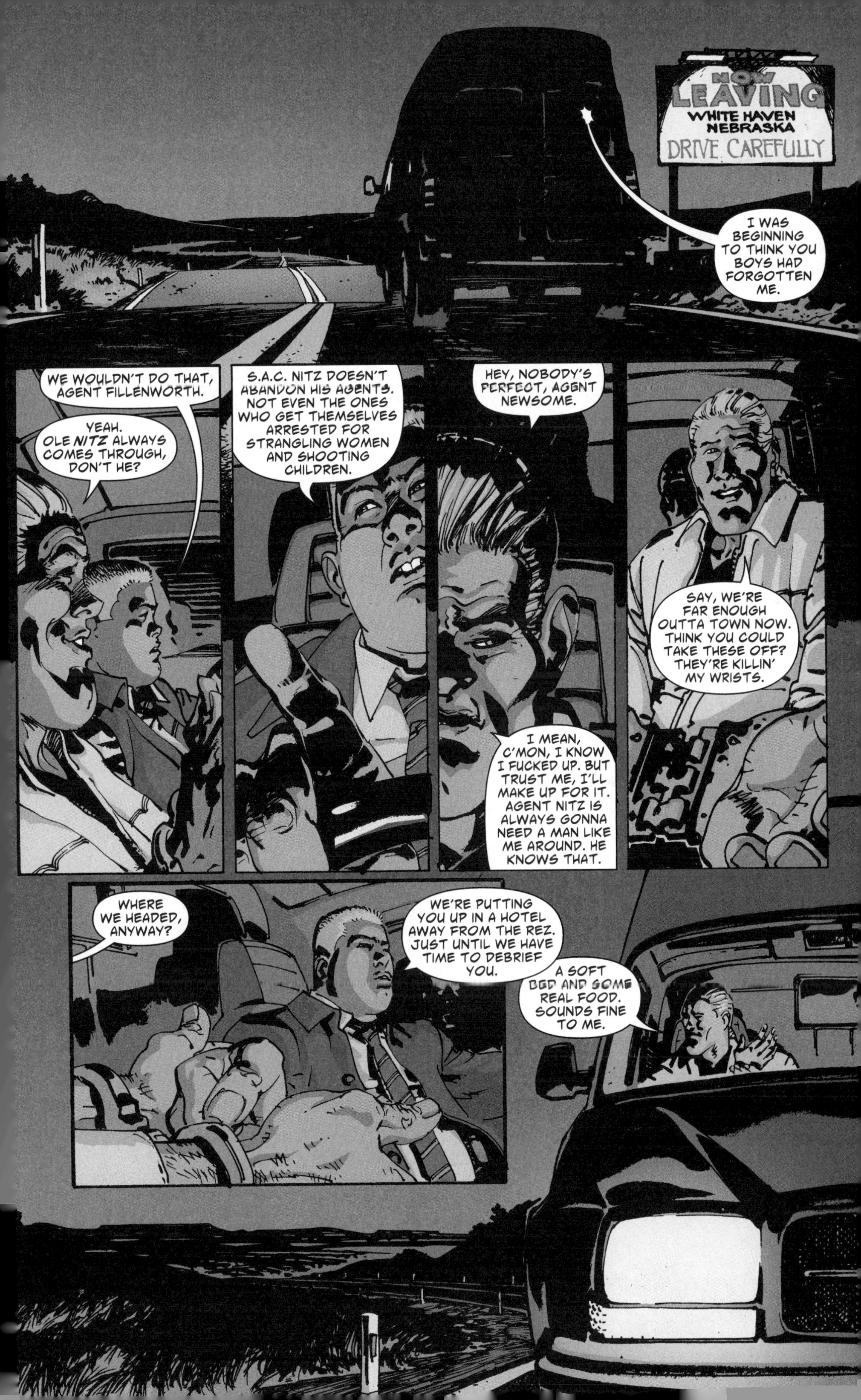
NOW LEAVING
WHITE HAVEN NEBRASKA
DRIVE CAREFULLY
I WAS BEGINNING TO THINK YOU BOYS HAD FORGOTTEN ME.
WE WOULDN'T DO THAT, AGENT FILLENWORTH.
YEAH. OLE *NITZ* ALWAYS COMES THROUGH, DON'T HE?
S.A.C. NITZ DOESN'T ABANDON HIS AGENTS. NOT EVEN THE ONES WHO GET THEMSELVES ARRESTED FOR STRANGLING WOMEN AND SHOOTING CHILDREN.
HEY, NOBODY'S PERFECT, AGENT NEWSOME.
I MEAN, C'MON, I KNOW I FUCKED UP. BUT TRUST ME, I'LL MAKE UP FOR IT. AGENT NITZ IS ALWAYS GONNA NEED A MAN LIKE ME AROUND. HE KNOWS THAT.
SAY, WE'RE FAR ENOUGH OUTTA TOWN NOW. THINK YOU COULD TAKE THESE OFF? THEY'RE KILLIN' MY WRISTS.
WHERE WE HEADED, ANYWAY?
WE'RE PUTTING YOU UP IN A HOTEL AWAY FROM THE REZ. JUST UNTIL WE HAVE TIME TO DEBRIEF YOU.
A SOFT BED AND SOME REAL FOOD. SOUNDS FINE TO ME.

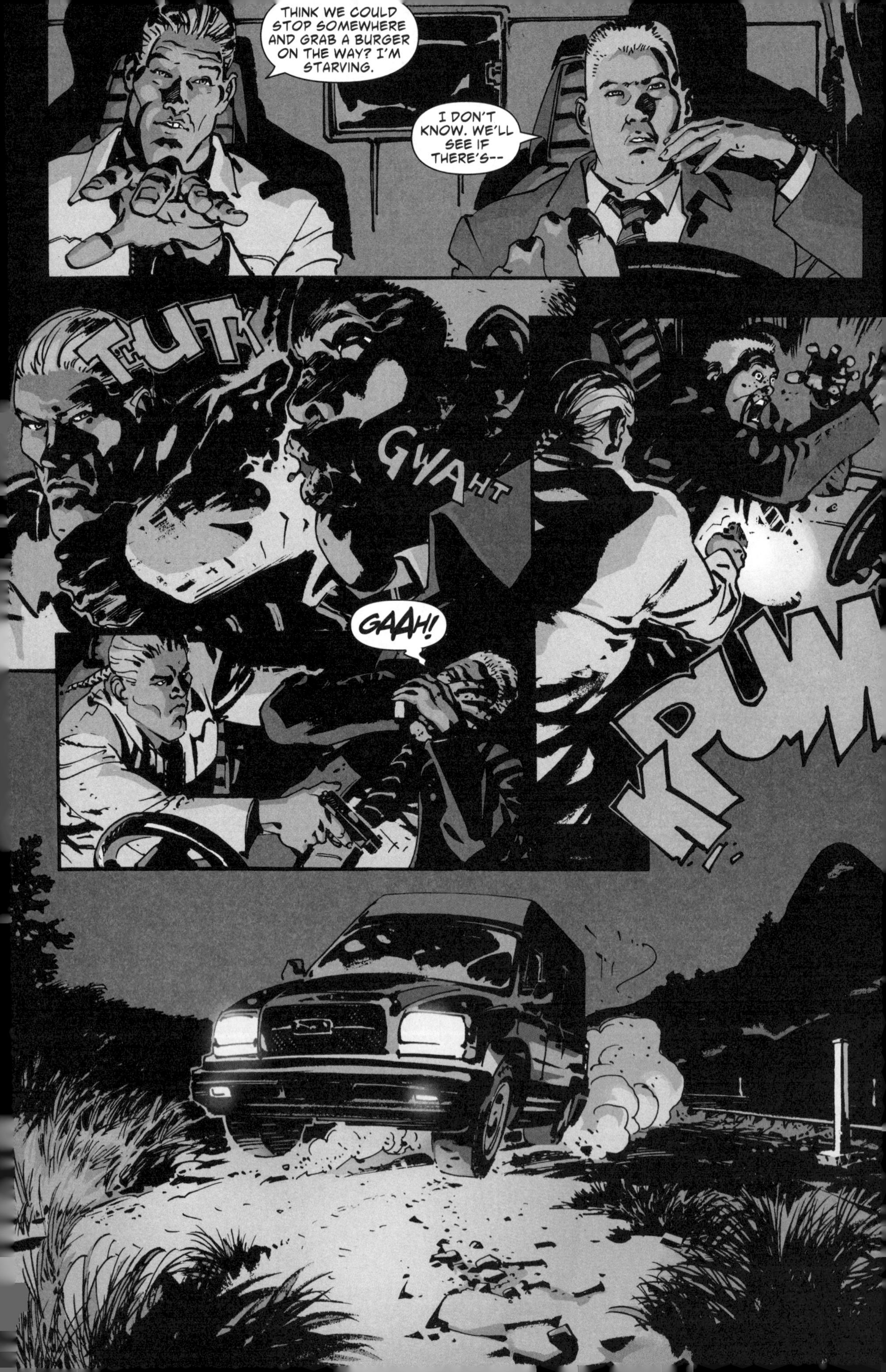
THINK WE COULD STOP SOMEWHERE AND GRAB A BURGER ON THE WAY? I'M STARVING.
I DON'T KNOW. WE'LL SEE IF THERE'S--
TUK
GWAHT
GAAH!
KRUMM

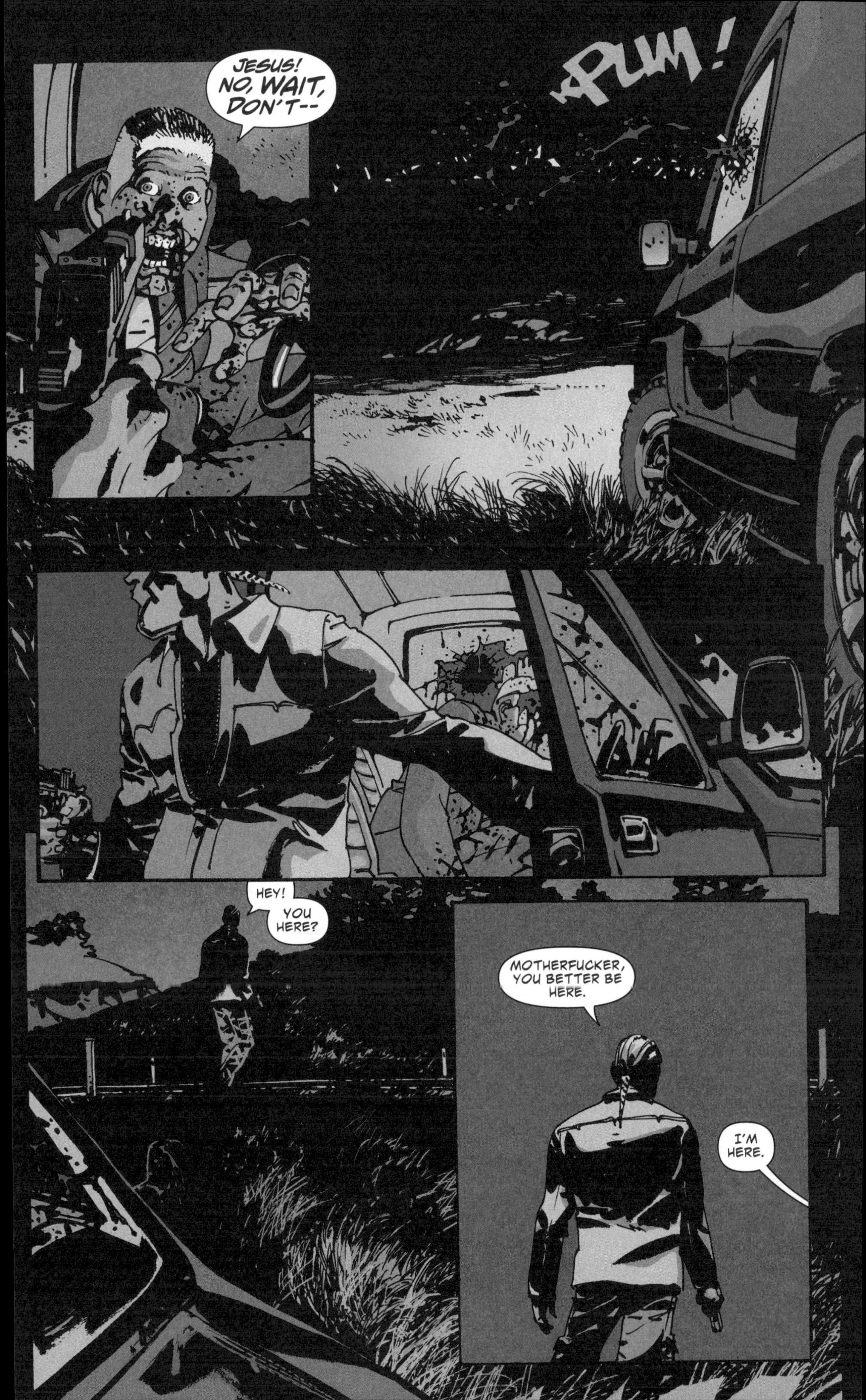
JESUS! NO, WAIT, DON'T--
PUM!
HEY!
YOU HERE?
MOTHERFUCKER, YOU BETTER BE HERE.
I'M HERE.

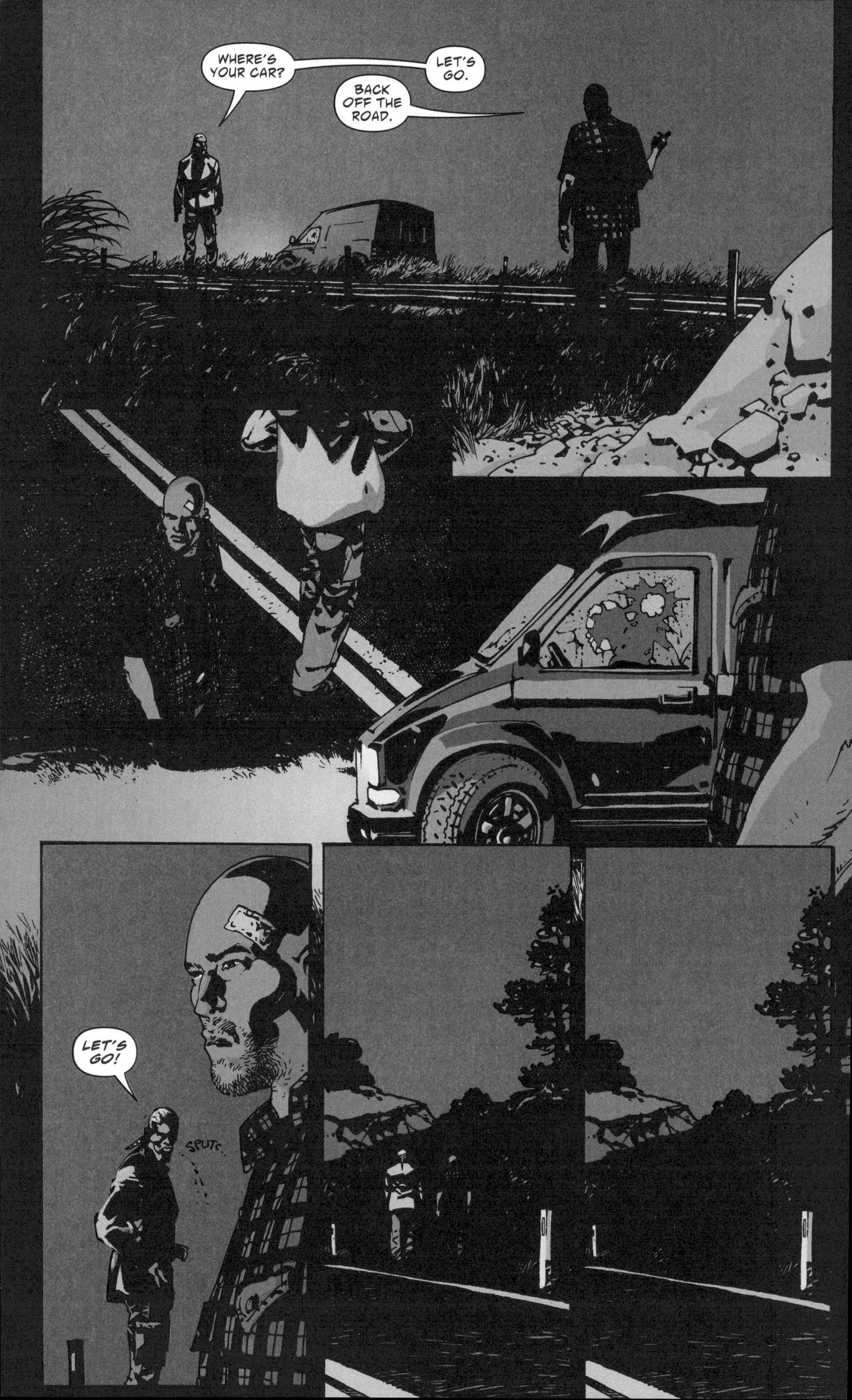
WHERE'S YOUR CAR?
LET'S GO.
BACK OFF THE ROAD.
LET'S GO!
SPUTC..

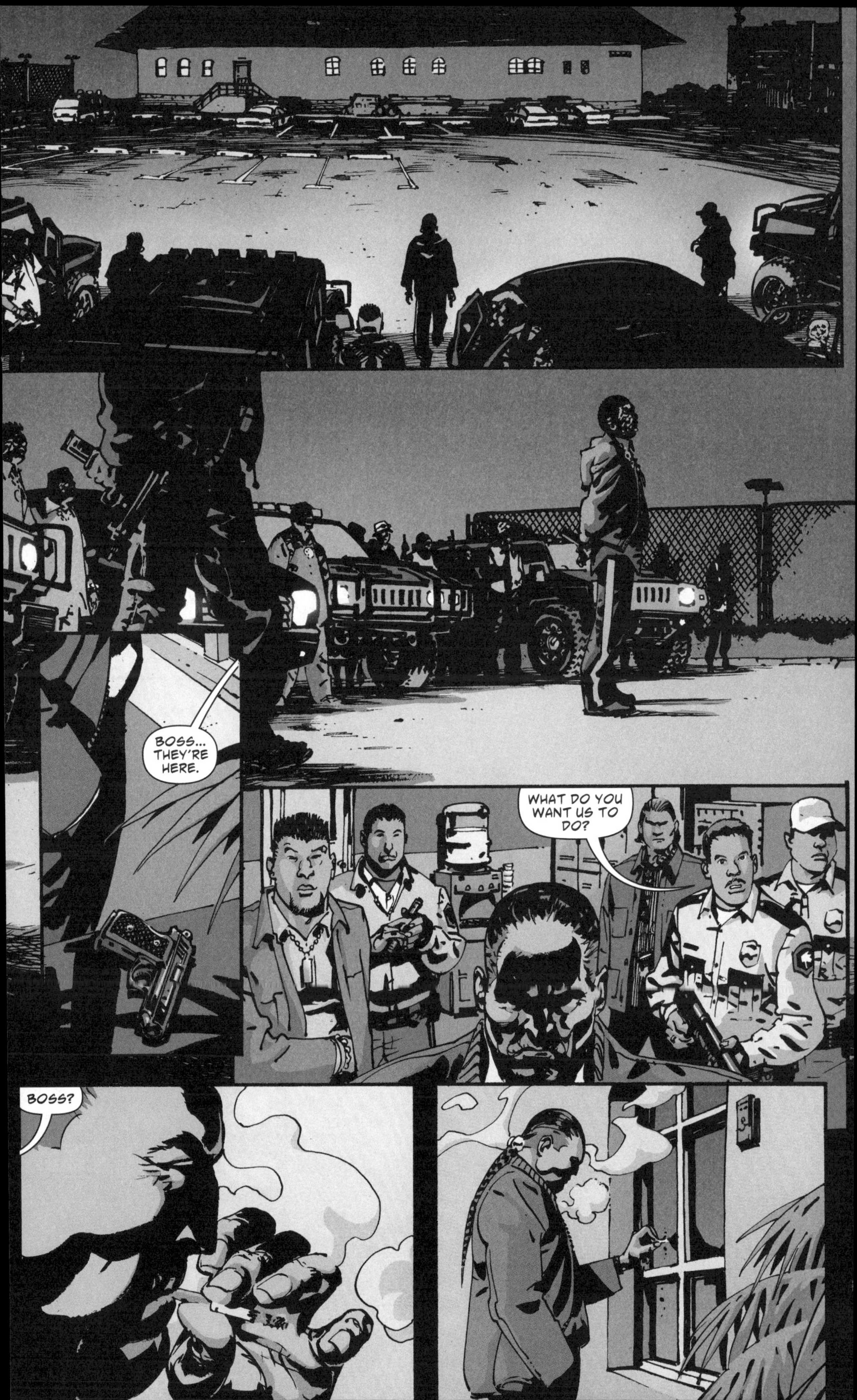
BOSS... THEY'RE HERE.
WHAT DO YOU WANT US TO DO?
BOSS?

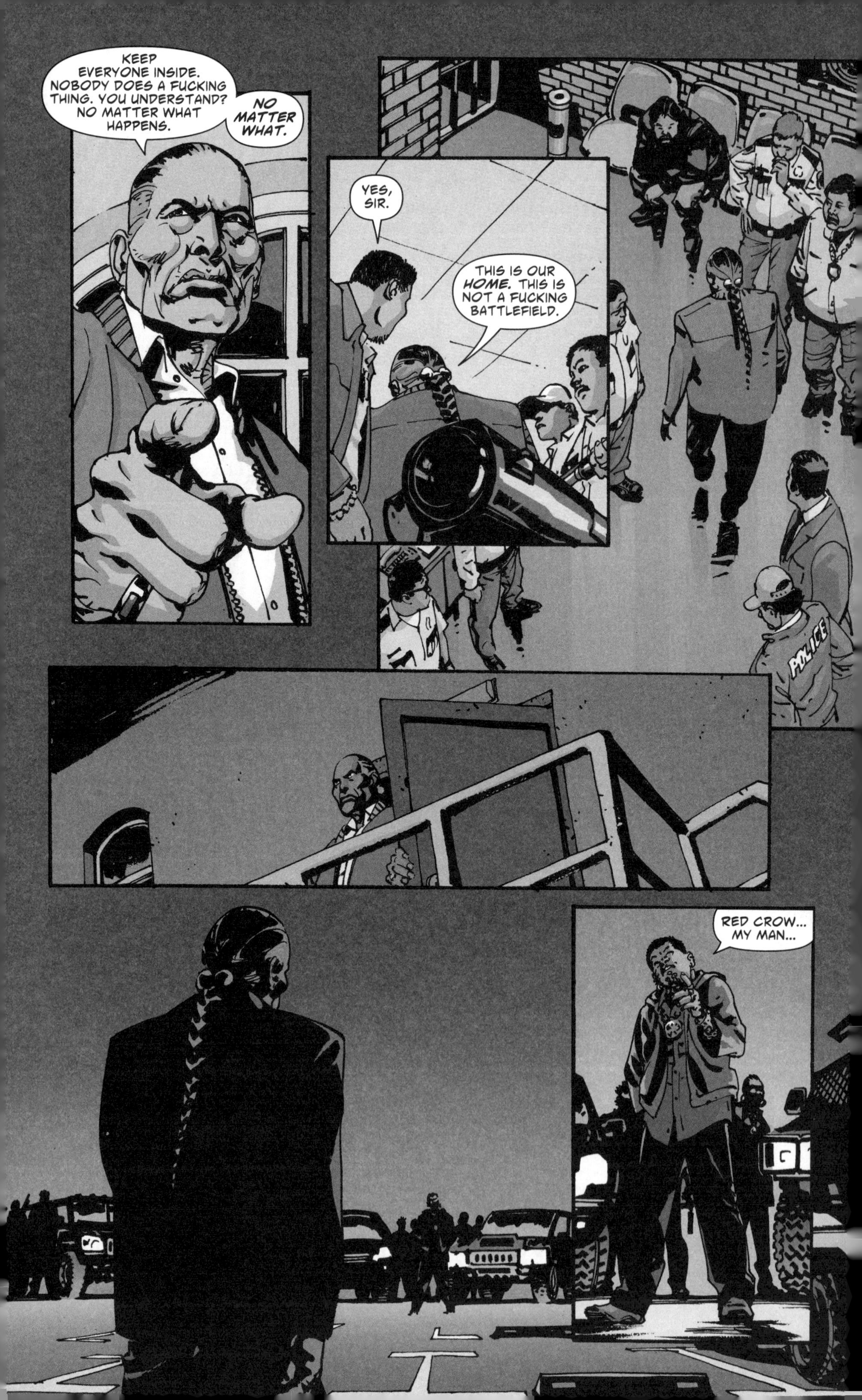
KEEP EVERYONE INSIDE. NOBODY DOES A FUCKING THING. YOU UNDERSTAND? NO MATTER WHAT HAPPENS.
NO MATTER WHAT.
YES, SIR.
THIS IS OUR HOME. THIS IS NOT A FUCKING BATTLEFIELD.
POLICE
RED CROW... MY MAN...

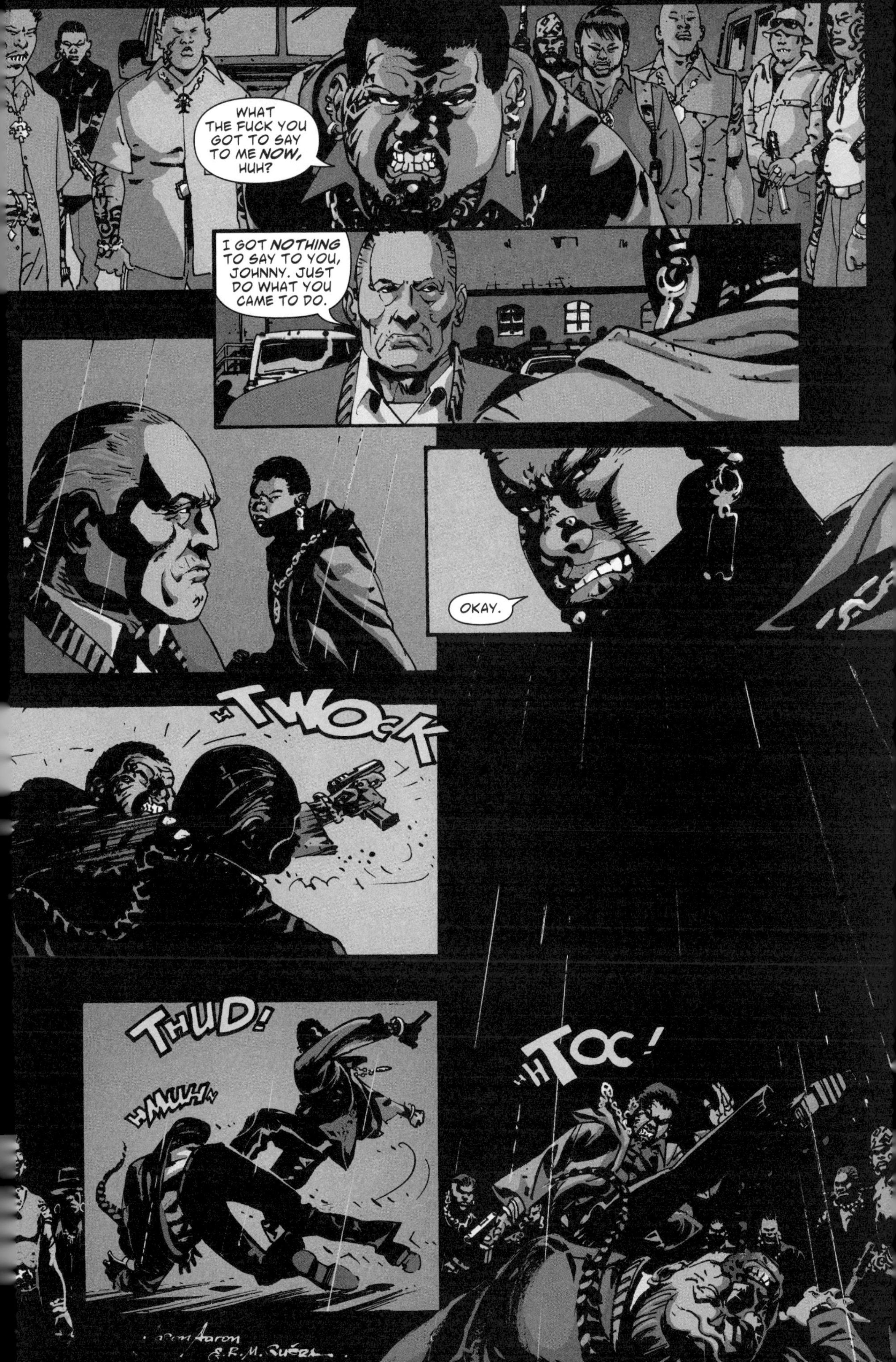
WHAT THE FUCK YOU GOT TO SAY TO ME *NOW,* HUH?
I GOT *NOTHING* TO SAY TO YOU, JOHNNY. JUST DO WHAT YOU CAME TO DO.
OKAY.
TWOCK
THUD!
MUH
TOC!

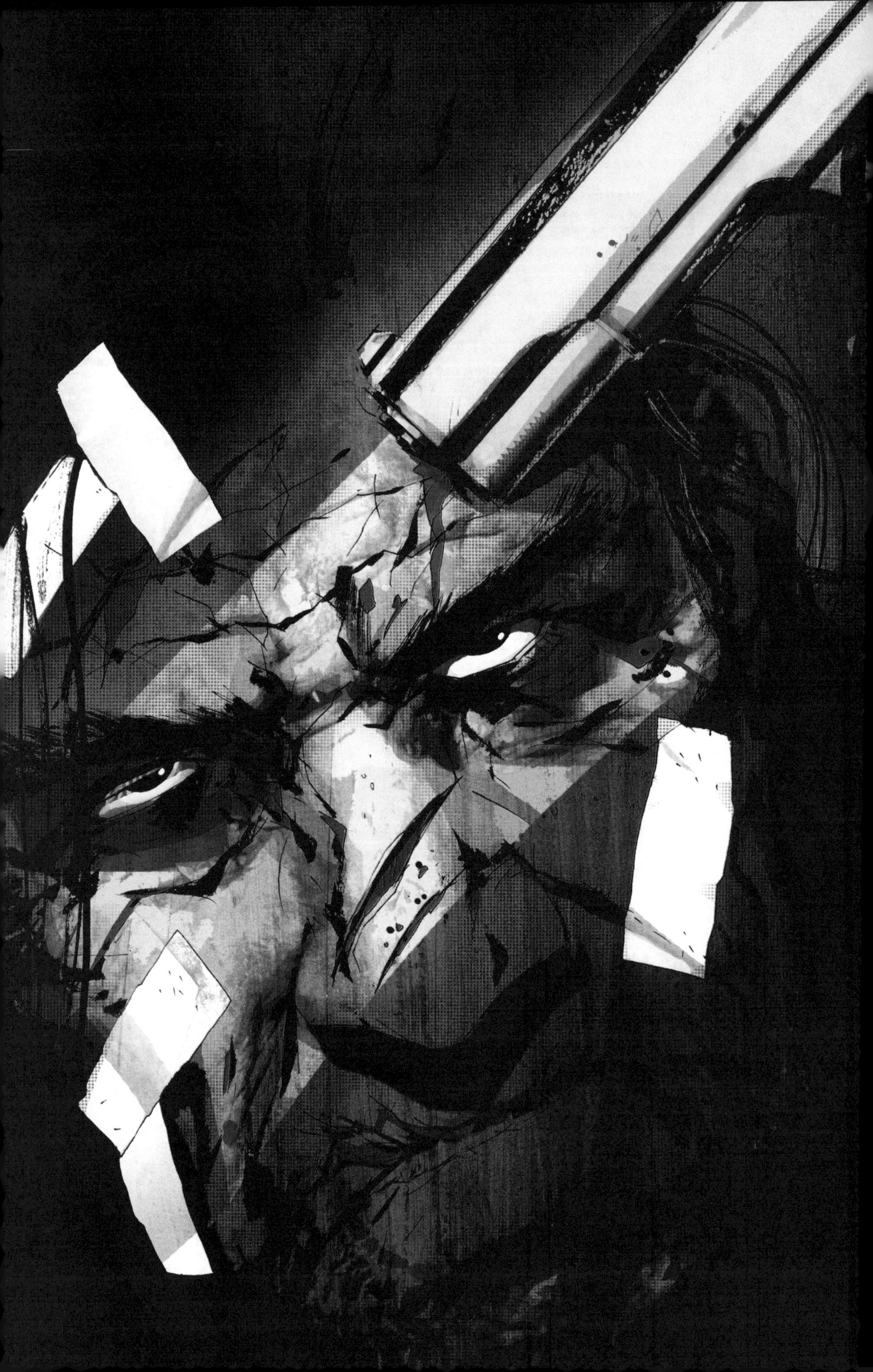

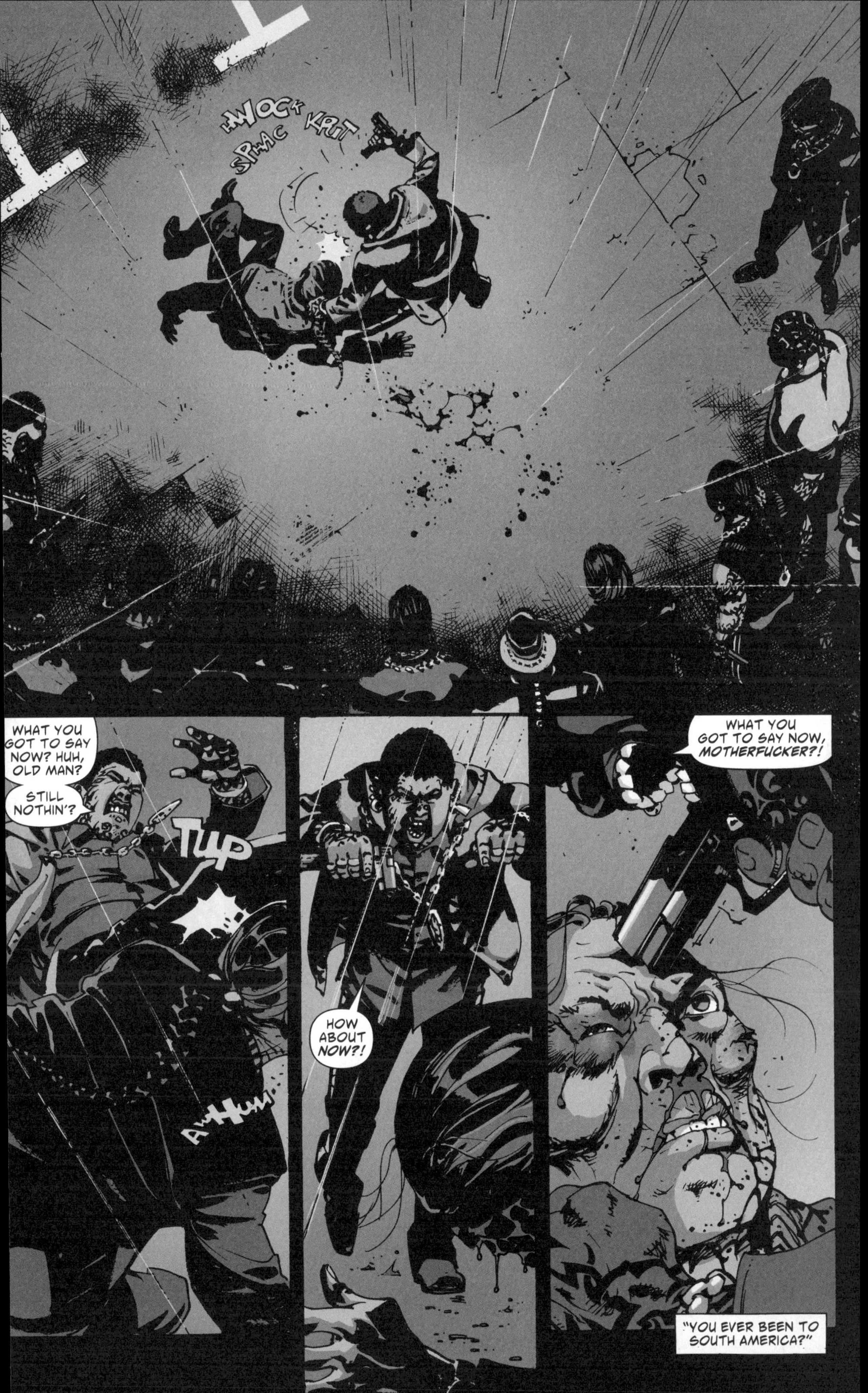

KNOCK
SPAAC KRUT
WHAT YOU GOT TO SAY NOW? HUH, OLD MAN?
STILL NOTHIN'?
TUP
AWHUM
HOW ABOUT NOW?!
WHAT YOU GOT TO SAY NOW, MOTHERFUCKER?!
"YOU EVER BEEN TO SOUTH AMERICA?"

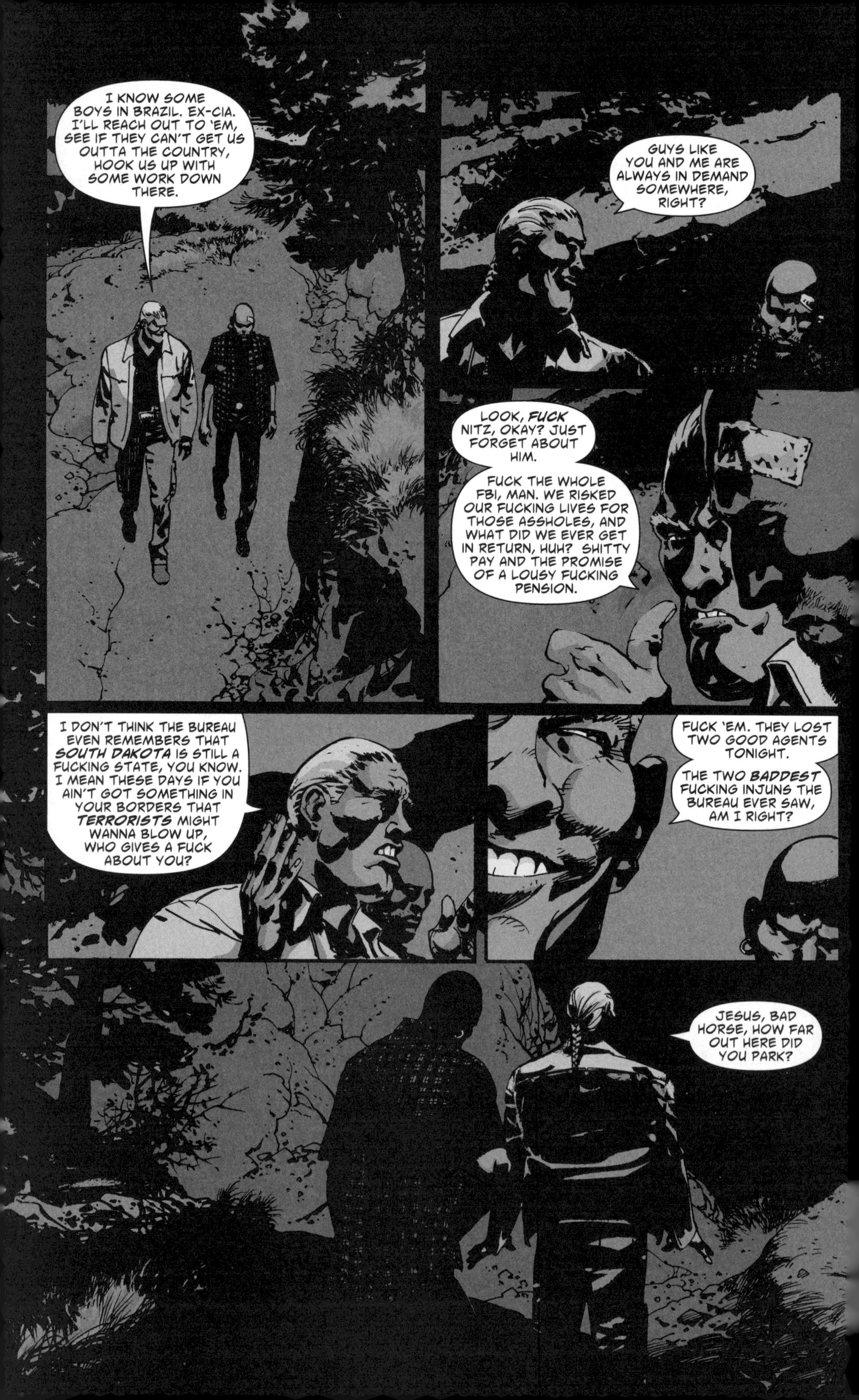

I KNOW SOME BOYS IN BRAZIL. EX-CIA. I'LL REACH OUT TO 'EM, SEE IF THEY CAN'T GET US OUTTA THE COUNTRY, HOOK US UP WITH SOME WORK DOWN THERE.
GUYS LIKE YOU AND ME ARE ALWAYS IN DEMAND SOMEWHERE, RIGHT?
LOOK, FUCK NITZ, OKAY? JUST FORGET ABOUT HIM.
FUCK THE WHOLE FBI, MAN. WE RISKED OUR FUCKING LIVES FOR THOSE ASSHOLES, AND WHAT DID WE EVER GET IN RETURN, HUH? SHITTY PAY AND THE PROMISE OF A LOUSY FUCKING PENSION.
I DON'T THINK THE BUREAU EVEN REMEMBERS THAT SOUTH DAKOTA IS STILL A FUCKING STATE, YOU KNOW. I MEAN THESE DAYS IF YOU AIN'T GOT SOMETHING IN YOUR BORDERS THAT TERRORISTS MIGHT WANNA BLOW UP, WHO GIVES A FUCK ABOUT YOU?
FUCK 'EM. THEY LOST TWO GOOD AGENTS TONIGHT.
THE TWO BADDEST FUCKING INJUNS THE BUREAU EVER SAW, AM I RIGHT?
JESUS, BAD HORSE, HOW FAR OUT HERE DID YOU PARK?

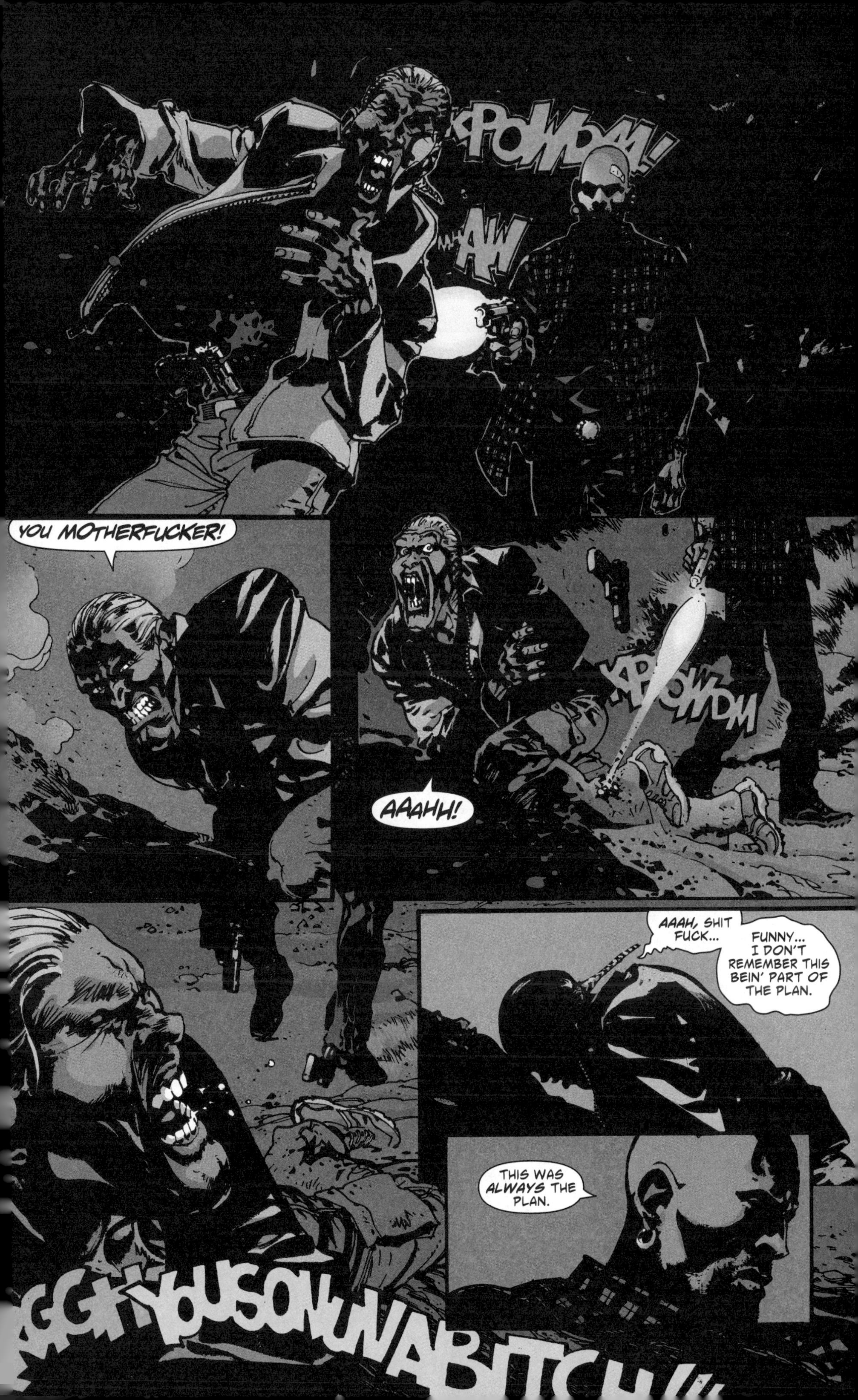
KPOWBAM!
AW
YOU MOTHERFUCKER!
AAAHH!
KAPOWDM
AAAH, SHIT FUCK...
FUNNY... I DON'T REMEMBER THIS BEIN' PART OF THE PLAN.
THIS WAS ALWAYS THE PLAN.
GGHYOUSONUVABITCH!

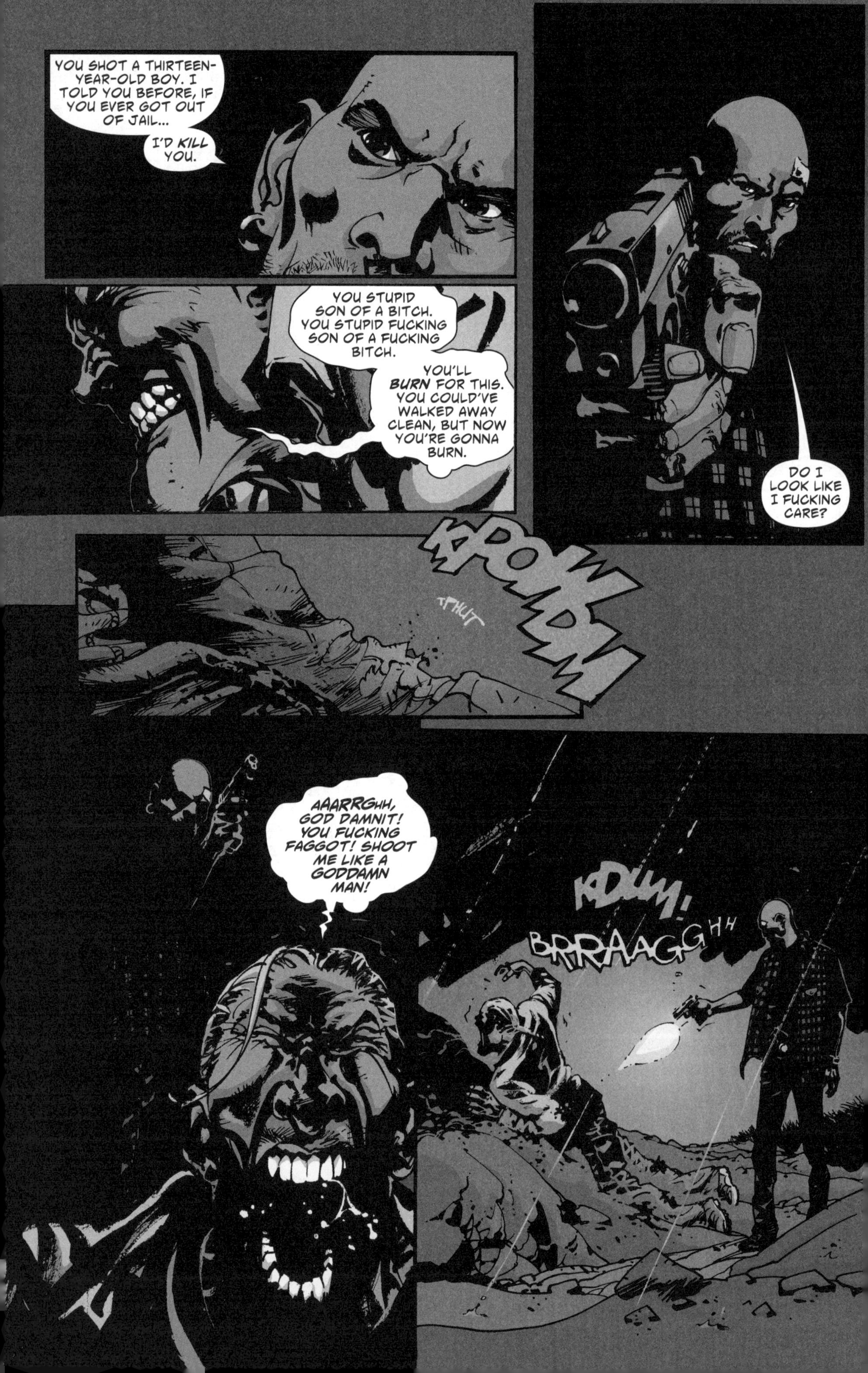

YOU SHOT A THIRTEEN-YEAR-OLD BOY. I TOLD YOU BEFORE, IF YOU EVER GOT OUT OF JAIL...
I'D KILL YOU.
YOU STUPID SON OF A BITCH. YOU STUPID FUCKING SON OF A FUCKING BITCH.
YOU'LL BURN FOR THIS. YOU COULD'VE WALKED AWAY CLEAN, BUT NOW YOU'RE GONNA BURN.
DO I LOOK LIKE I FUCKING CARE?
KPOWWW
THUT
AAARRGHH, GOD DAMNIT! YOU FUCKING FAGGOT! SHOOT ME LIKE A GODDAMN MAN!
KDUM!
BRRAAGGHH

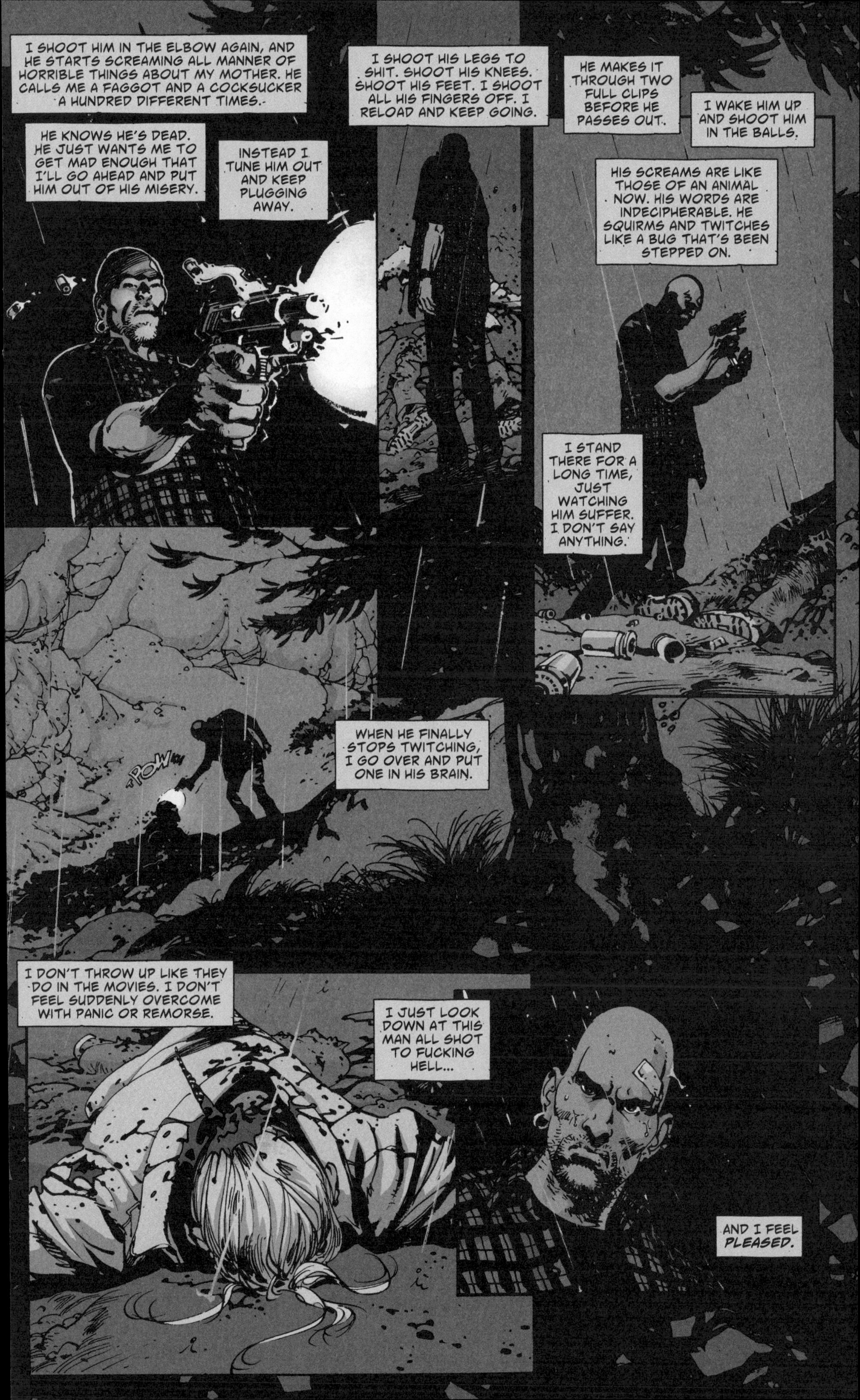
I SHOOT HIM IN THE ELBOW AGAIN, AND HE STARTS SCREAMING ALL MANNER OF HORRIBLE THINGS ABOUT MY MOTHER. HE CALLS ME A FAGGOT AND A COCKSUCKER A HUNDRED DIFFERENT TIMES.
HE KNOWS HE'S DEAD. HE JUST WANTS ME TO GET MAD ENOUGH THAT I'LL GO AHEAD AND PUT HIM OUT OF HIS MISERY.
INSTEAD I TUNE HIM OUT AND KEEP PLUGGING AWAY.
I SHOOT HIS LEGS TO SHIT. SHOOT HIS KNEES. SHOOT HIS FEET. I SHOOT ALL HIS FINGERS OFF. I RELOAD AND KEEP GOING.
HE MAKES IT THROUGH TWO FULL CLIPS BEFORE HE PASSES OUT.
I WAKE HIM UP AND SHOOT HIM IN THE BALLS.
HIS SCREAMS ARE LIKE THOSE OF AN ANIMAL NOW. HIS WORDS ARE INDECIPHERABLE. HE SQUIRMS AND TWITCHES LIKE A BUG THAT'S BEEN STEPPED ON.
I STAND THERE FOR A LONG TIME, JUST WATCHING HIM SUFFER. I DON'T SAY ANYTHING.
POW
WHEN HE FINALLY STOPS TWITCHING, I GO OVER AND PUT ONE IN HIS BRAIN.
I DON'T THROW UP LIKE THEY DO IN THE MOVIES. I DON'T FEEL SUDDENLY OVERCOME WITH PANIC OR REMORSE.
I JUST LOOK DOWN AT THIS MAN ALL SHOT TO FUCKING HELL...
AND I FEEL *PLEASED.*

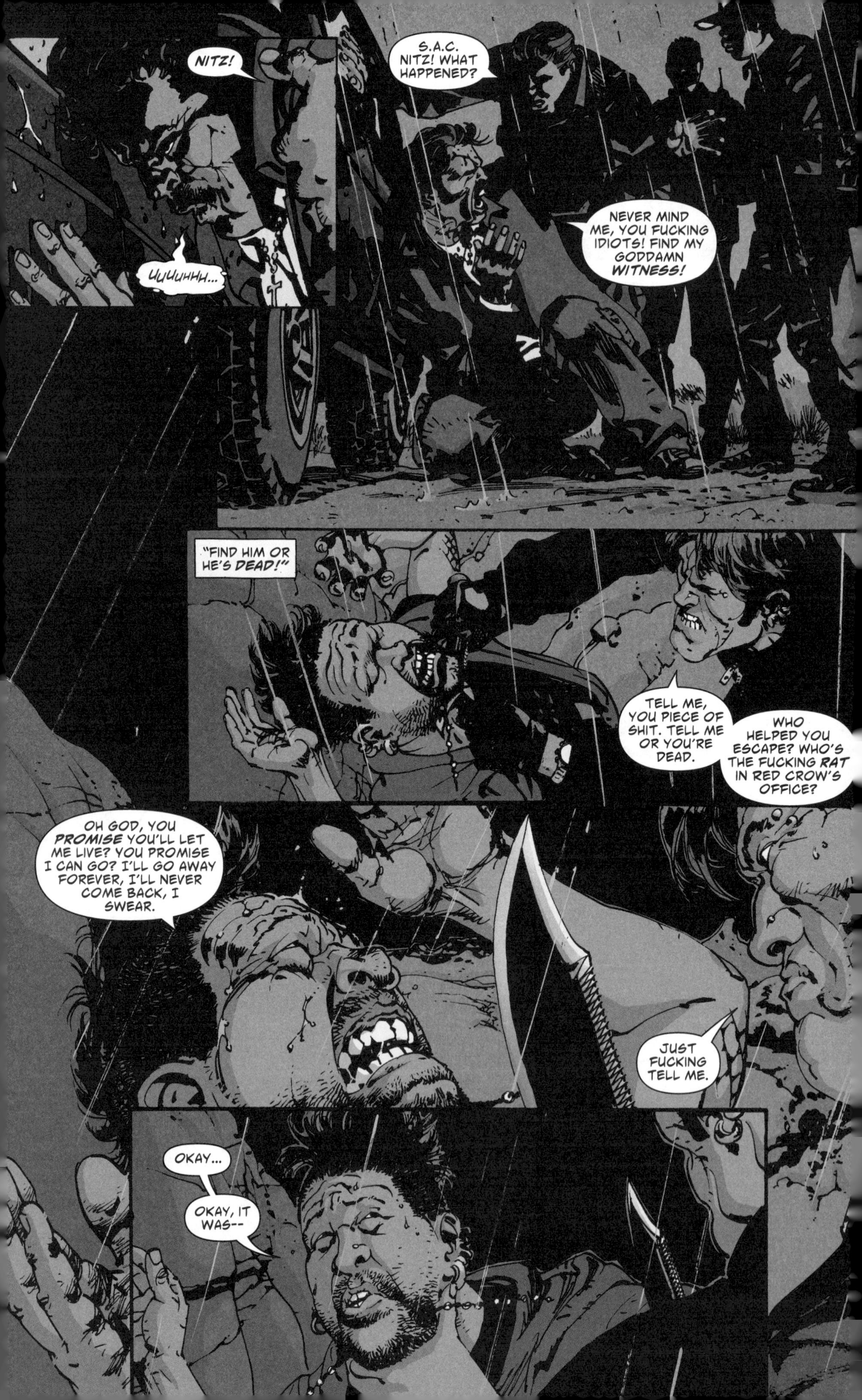
NITZ!
UUUUHHH...
S.A.C. NITZ! WHAT HAPPENED?
NEVER MIND ME, YOU FUCKING IDIOTS! FIND MY GODDAMN WITNESS!
"FIND HIM OR HE'S DEAD!"
TELL ME, YOU PIECE OF SHIT. TELL ME OR YOU'RE DEAD.
WHO HELPED YOU ESCAPE? WHO'S THE FUCKING RAT IN RED CROW'S OFFICE?
OH GOD, YOU PROMISE YOU'LL LET ME LIVE? YOU PROMISE I CAN GO? I'LL GO AWAY FOREVER, I'LL NEVER COME BACK, I SWEAR.
JUST FUCKING TELL ME.
OKAY...
OKAY, IT WAS--

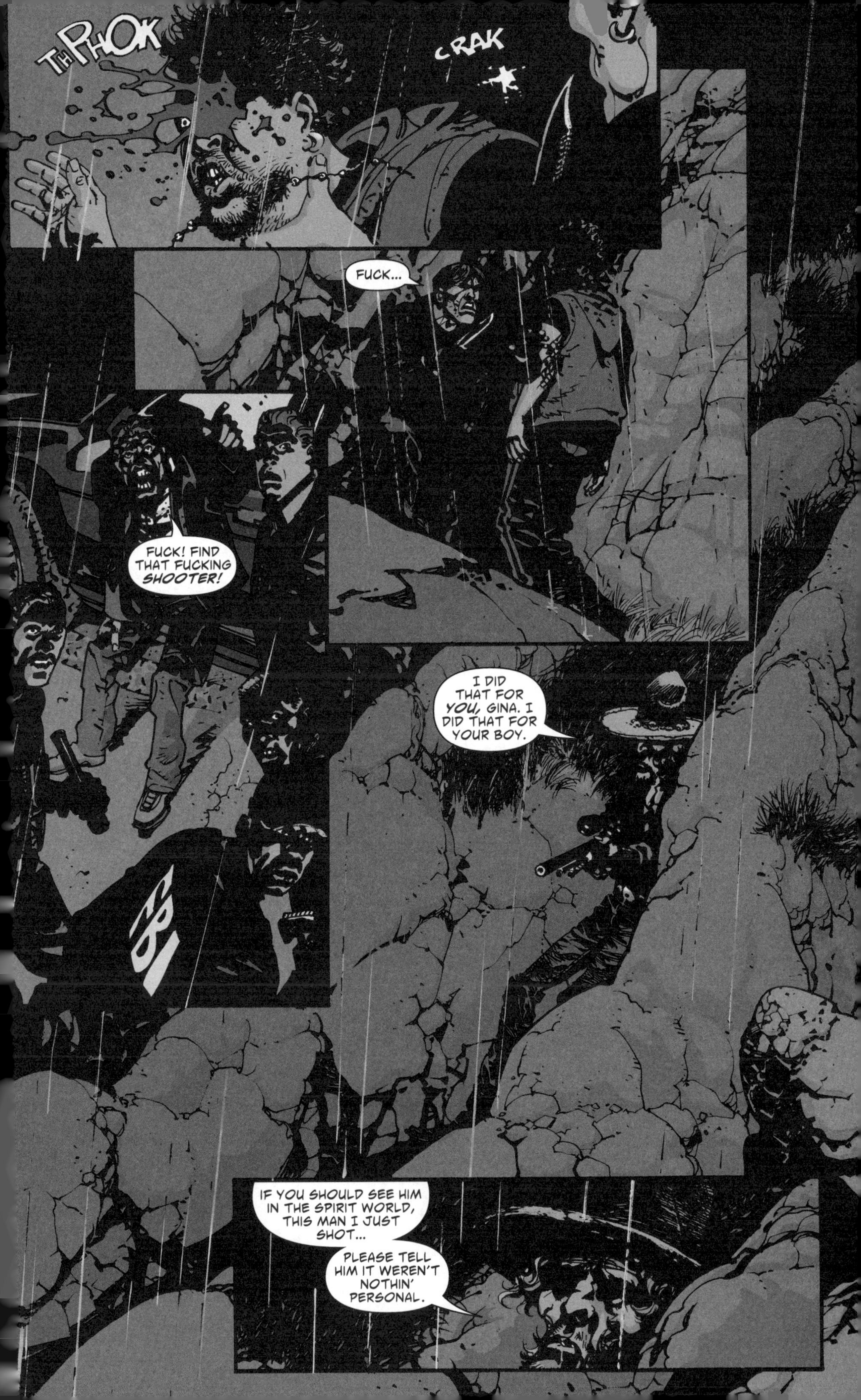
THPHOK
CRAK
FUCK...
FUCK! FIND THAT FUCKING SHOOTER!
FBI
I DID THAT FOR YOU, GINA. I DID THAT FOR YOUR BOY.
IF YOU SHOULD SEE HIM IN THE SPIRIT WORLD, THIS MAN I JUST SHOT...
PLEASE TELL HIM IT WEREN'T NOTHIN' PERSONAL.

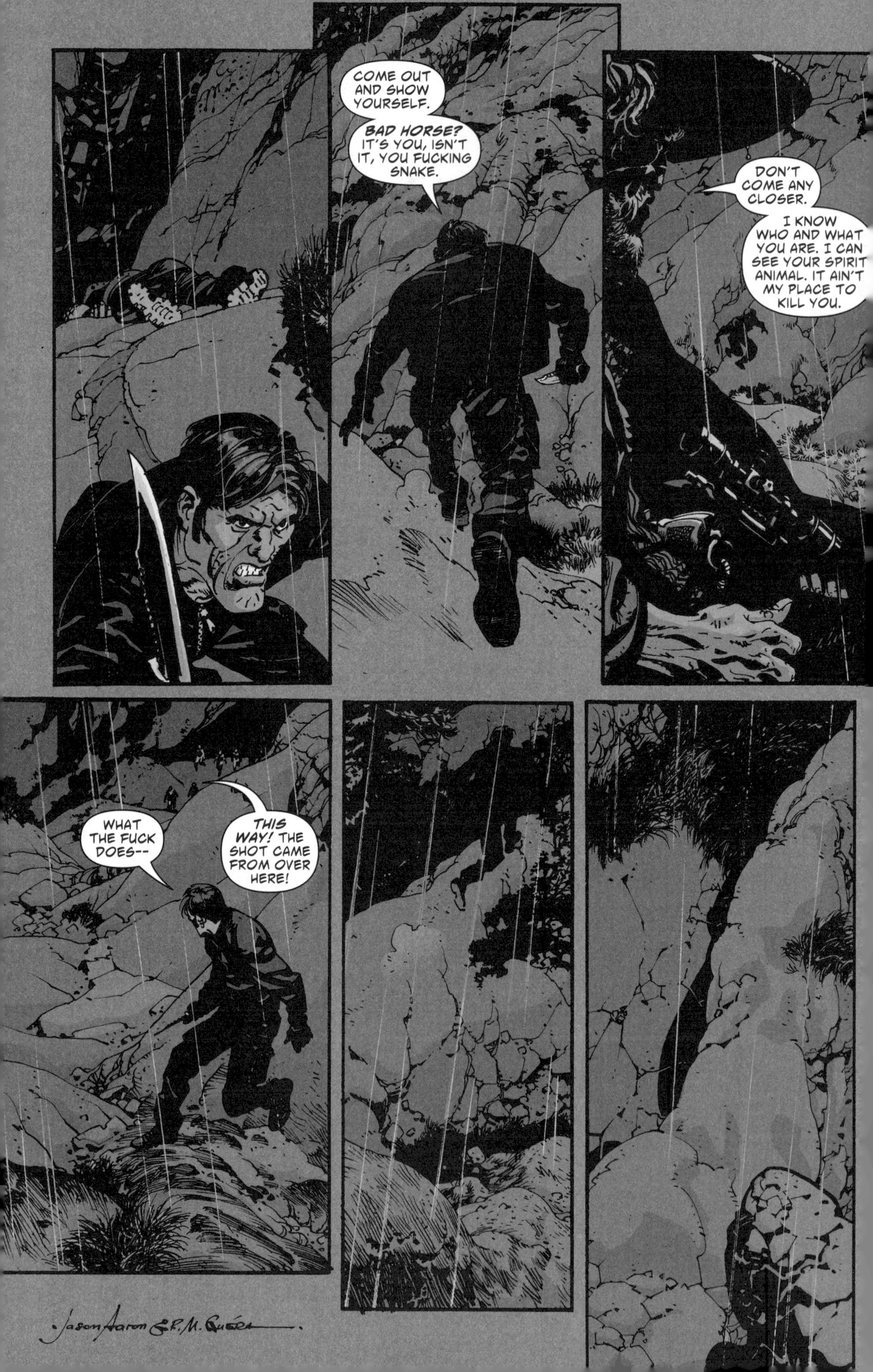
COME OUT AND SHOW YOURSELF.
BAD HORSE? IT'S YOU, ISN'T IT, YOU FUCKING SNAKE.
DON'T COME ANY CLOSER.
I KNOW WHO AND WHAT YOU ARE. I CAN SEE YOUR SPIRIT ANIMAL. IT AIN'T MY PLACE TO KILL YOU.
WHAT THE FUCK DOES--
THIS WAY! THE SHOT CAME FROM OVER HERE!
Jason Aaron & R.M. Guéra

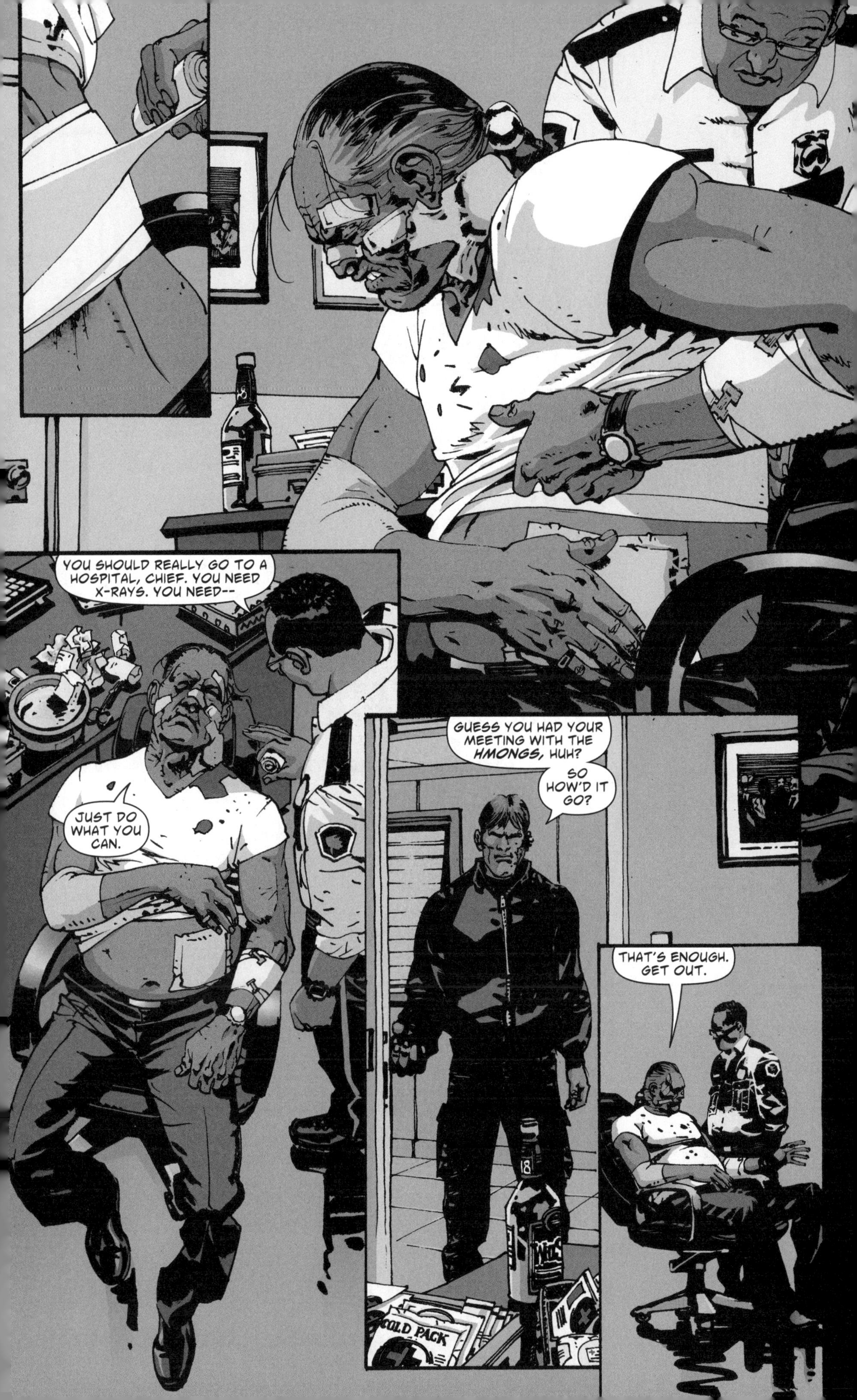
YOU SHOULD REALLY GO TO A HOSPITAL, CHIEF. YOU NEED X-RAYS. YOU NEED--
JUST DO WHAT YOU CAN.
GUESS YOU HAD YOUR MEETING WITH THE HMONGS, HUH?
SO HOW'D IT GO?
THAT'S ENOUGH. GET OUT.
COLD PACK

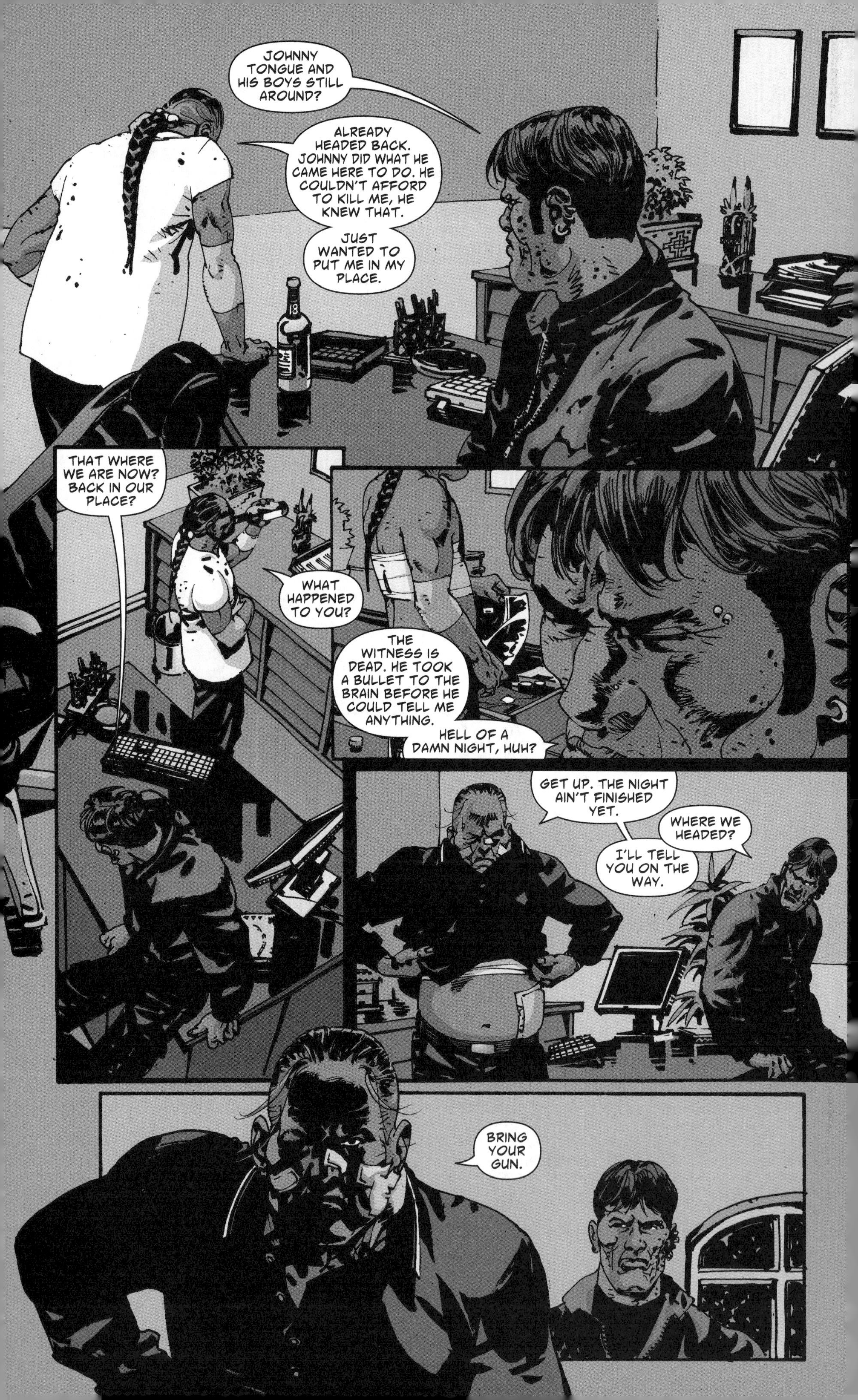
JOHNNY TONGUE AND HIS BOYS STILL AROUND?
ALREADY HEADED BACK. JOHNNY DID WHAT HE CAME HERE TO DO. HE COULDN'T AFFORD TO KILL ME, HE KNEW THAT.
JUST WANTED TO PUT ME IN MY PLACE.
THAT WHERE WE ARE NOW? BACK IN OUR PLACE?
WHAT HAPPENED TO YOU?
THE WITNESS IS DEAD. HE TOOK A BULLET TO THE BRAIN BEFORE HE COULD TELL ME ANYTHING.
HELL OF A DAMN NIGHT, HUH?
GET UP. THE NIGHT AIN'T FINISHED YET.
WHERE WE HEADED?
I'LL TELL YOU ON THE WAY.
BRING YOUR GUN.

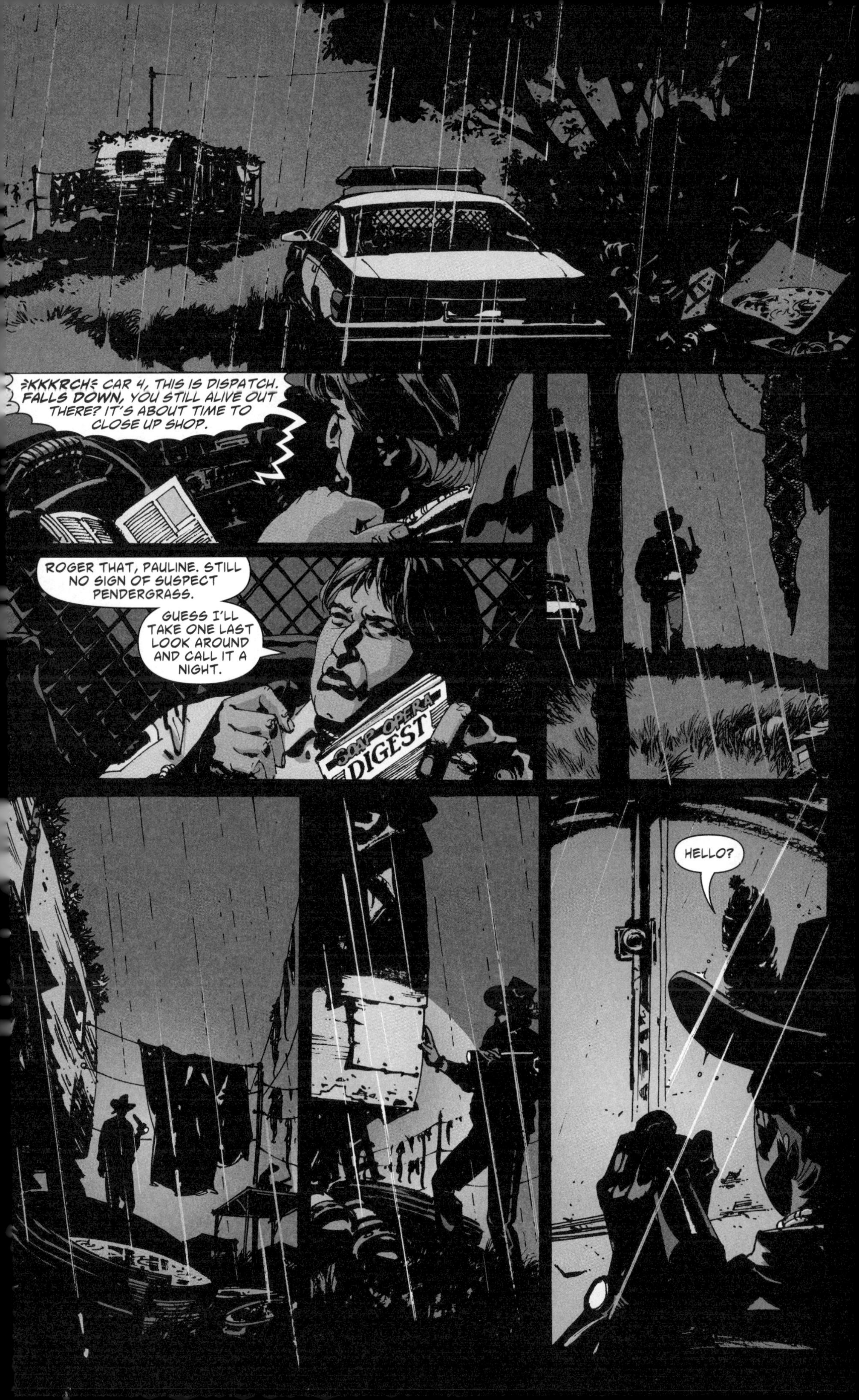

≠KKKRCH≠ CAR 4, THIS IS DISPATCH. FALLS DOWN, YOU STILL ALIVE OUT THERE? IT'S ABOUT TIME TO CLOSE UP SHOP.
ROGER THAT, PAULINE. STILL NO SIGN OF SUSPECT PENDERGRASS.
GUESS I'LL TAKE ONE LAST LOOK AROUND AND CALL IT A NIGHT.
SOAP OPERA DIGEST
HELLO?

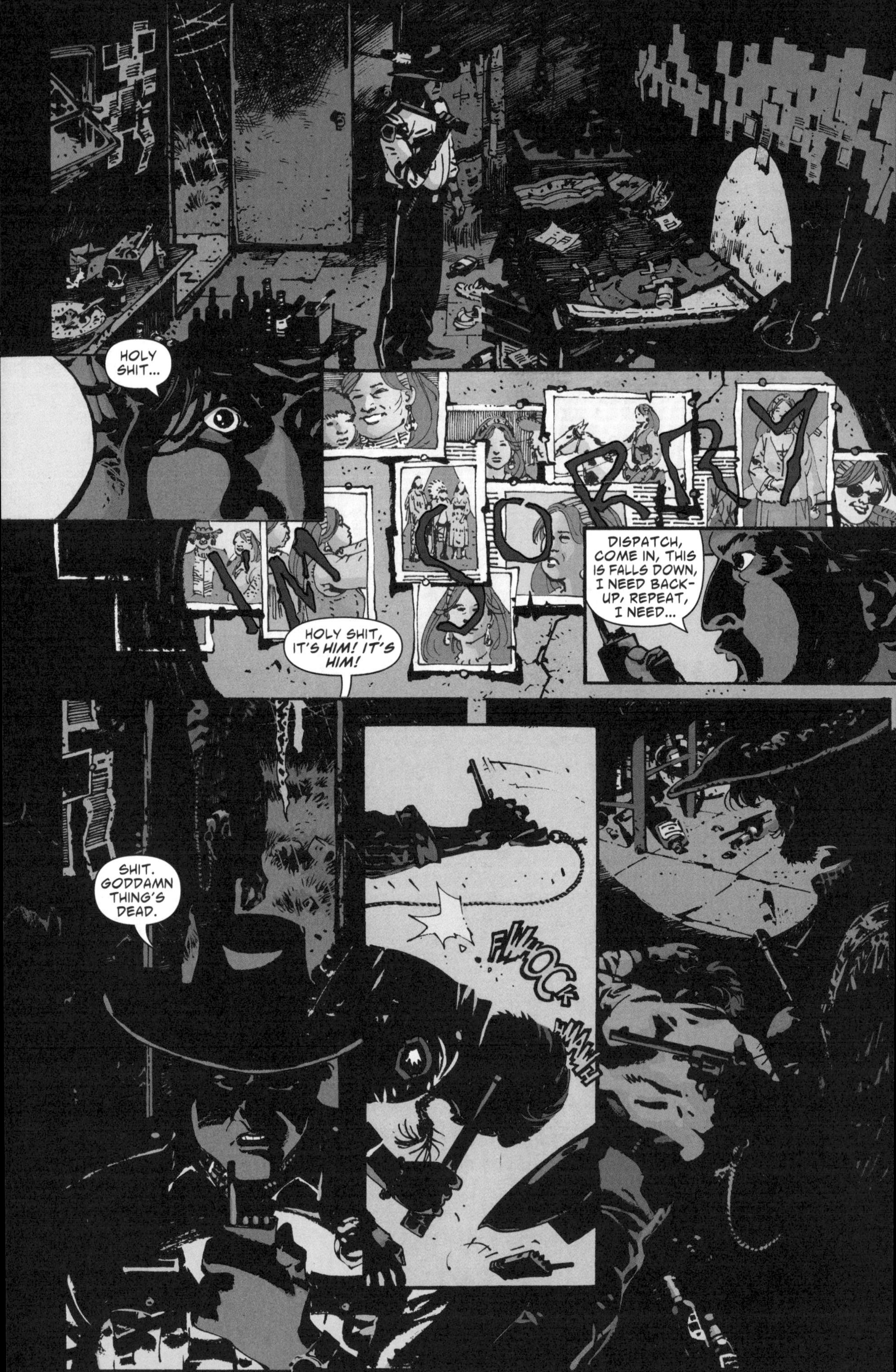
HOLY SHIT...
I'M SORRY
HOLY SHIT, IT'S *HIM!* IT'S *HIM!*
DISPATCH, COME IN, THIS IS FALLS DOWN, I NEED BACK-UP, REPEAT, I NEED...
SHIT. GODDAMN THING'S DEAD.
FWOCK

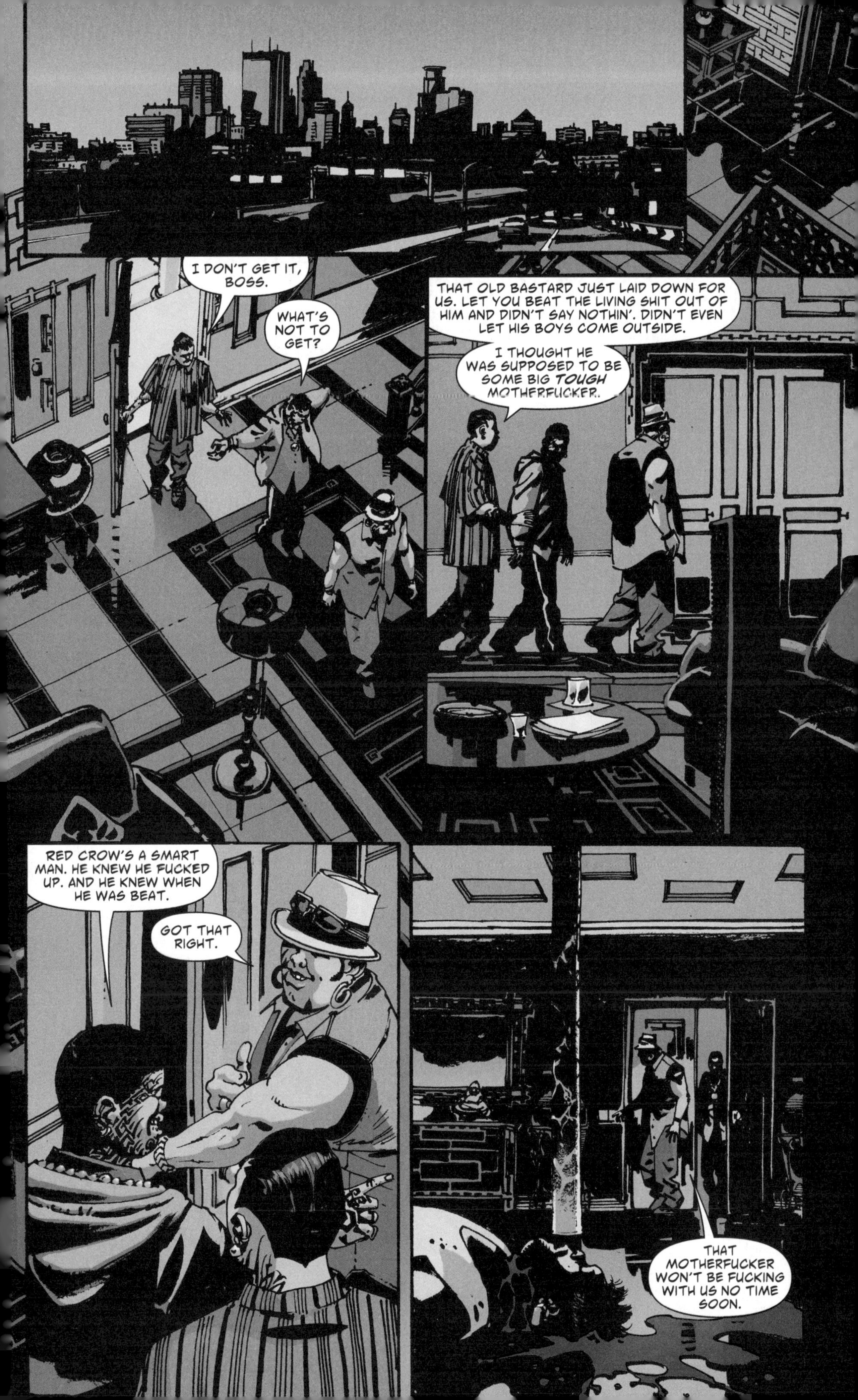

I DON'T GET IT, BOSS.
WHAT'S NOT TO GET?
THAT OLD BASTARD JUST LAID DOWN FOR US. LET YOU BEAT THE LIVING SHIT OUT OF HIM AND DIDN'T SAY NOTHIN'. DIDN'T EVEN LET HIS BOYS COME OUTSIDE.
I THOUGHT HE WAS SUPPOSED TO BE SOME BIG *TOUGH* MOTHERFUCKER.
RED CROW'S A SMART MAN. HE KNEW HE FUCKED UP. AND HE KNEW WHEN HE WAS BEAT.
GOT THAT RIGHT.
THAT MOTHERFUCKER WON'T BE FUCKING WITH US NO TIME SOON.

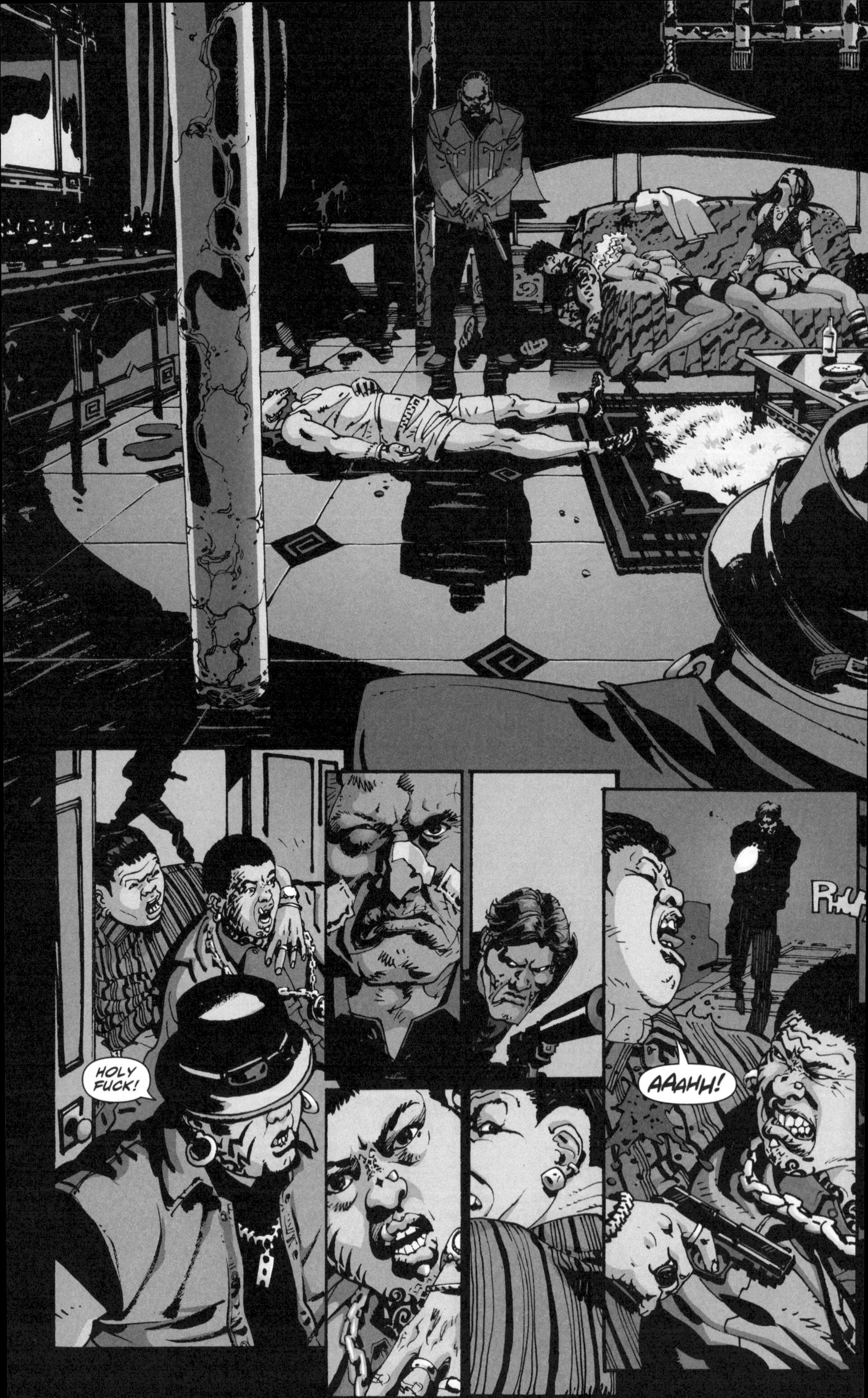
HOLY FUCK!
AAAHH!

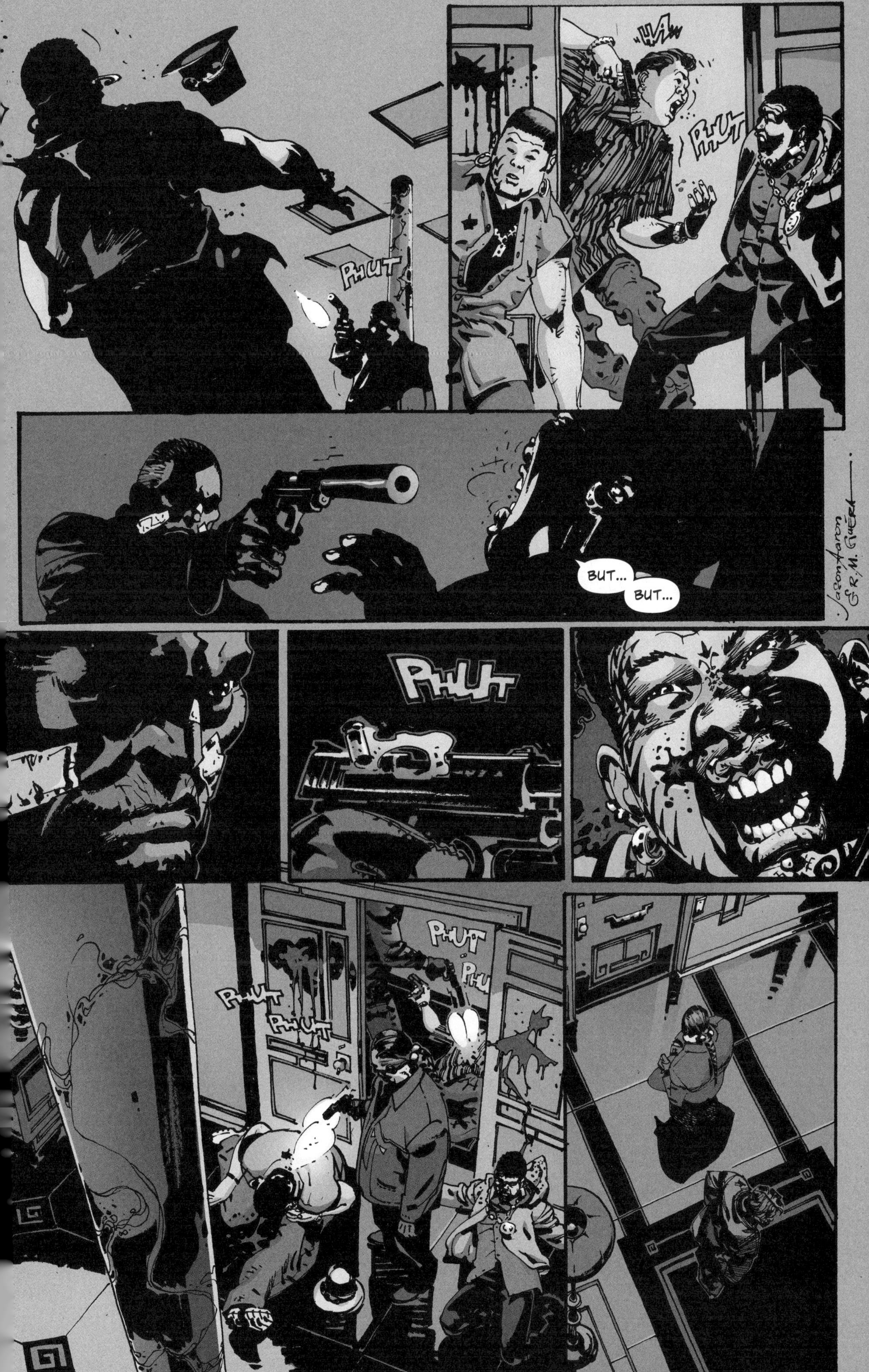

HA
PHUT
PHUT
BUT...
BUT...
PHUT
PHUT
PHUT
PHU
PHUT
Jason Aaron & R.M. Guéra

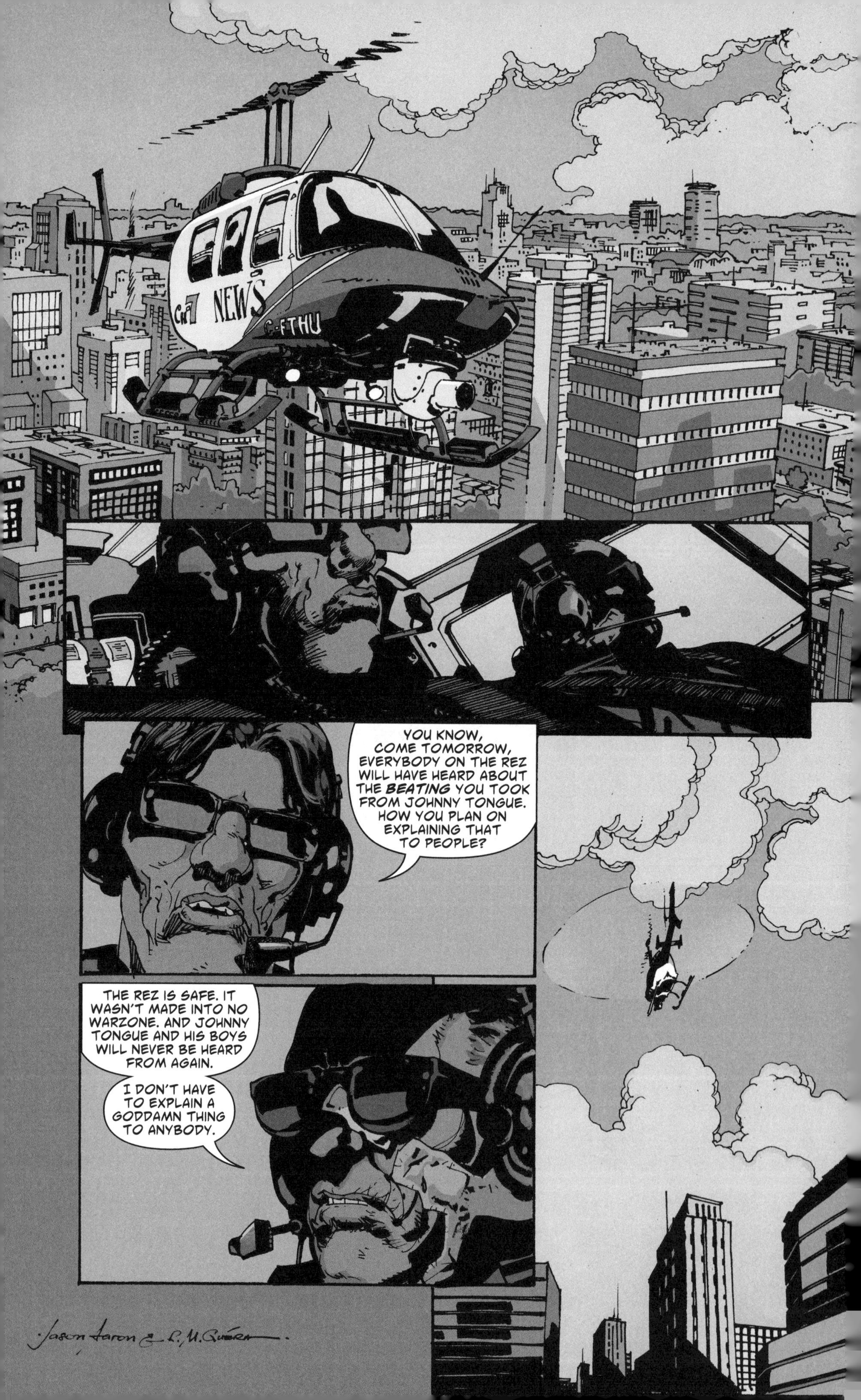

C-FTHU
YOU KNOW, COME TOMORROW, EVERYBODY ON THE REZ WILL HAVE HEARD ABOUT THE BEATING YOU TOOK FROM JOHNNY TONGUE. HOW YOU PLAN ON EXPLAINING THAT TO PEOPLE?
THE REZ IS SAFE. IT WASN'T MADE INTO NO WARZONE. AND JOHNNY TONGUE AND HIS BOYS WILL NEVER BE HEARD FROM AGAIN.
I DON'T HAVE TO EXPLAIN A GODDAMN THING TO ANYBODY.

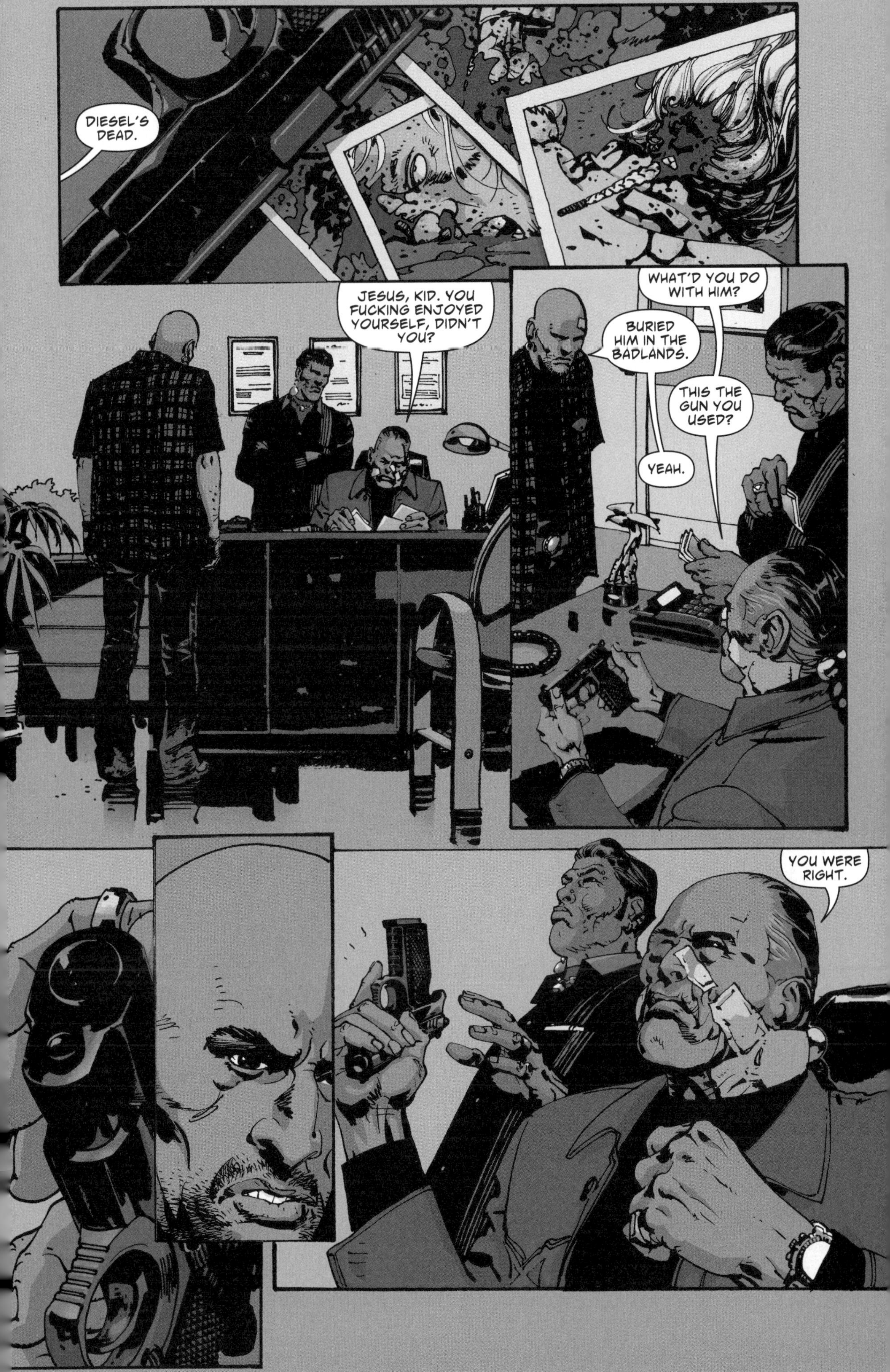
DIESEL'S DEAD.
JESUS, KID. YOU FUCKING ENJOYED YOURSELF, DIDN'T YOU?
WHAT'D YOU DO WITH HIM?
BURIED HIM IN THE BADLANDS.
THIS THE GUN YOU USED?
YEAH.
YOU WERE RIGHT.

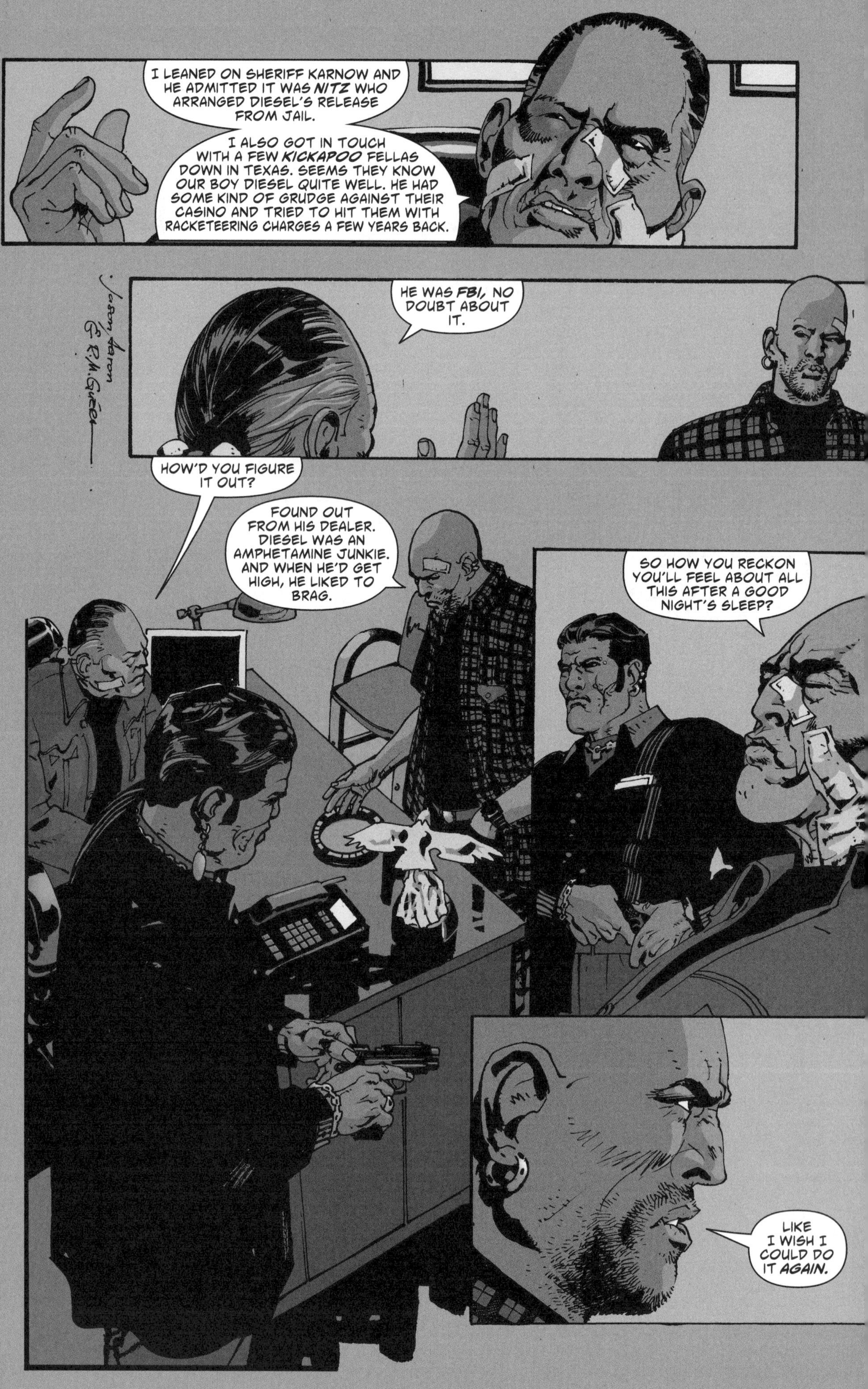
I LEANED ON SHERIFF KARNOW AND HE ADMITTED IT WAS NITZ WHO ARRANGED DIESEL'S RELEASE FROM JAIL.
I ALSO GOT IN TOUCH WITH A FEW KICKAPOO FELLAS DOWN IN TEXAS. SEEMS THEY KNOW OUR BOY DIESEL QUITE WELL. HE HAD SOME KIND OF GRUDGE AGAINST THEIR CASINO AND TRIED TO HIT THEM WITH RACKETEERING CHARGES A FEW YEARS BACK.
HE WAS FBI, NO DOUBT ABOUT IT.
HOW'D YOU FIGURE IT OUT?
FOUND OUT FROM HIS DEALER. DIESEL WAS AN AMPHETAMINE JUNKIE. AND WHEN HE'D GET HIGH, HE LIKED TO BRAG.
SO HOW YOU RECKON YOU'LL FEEL ABOUT ALL THIS AFTER A GOOD NIGHT'S SLEEP?
LIKE I WISH I COULD DO IT AGAIN.

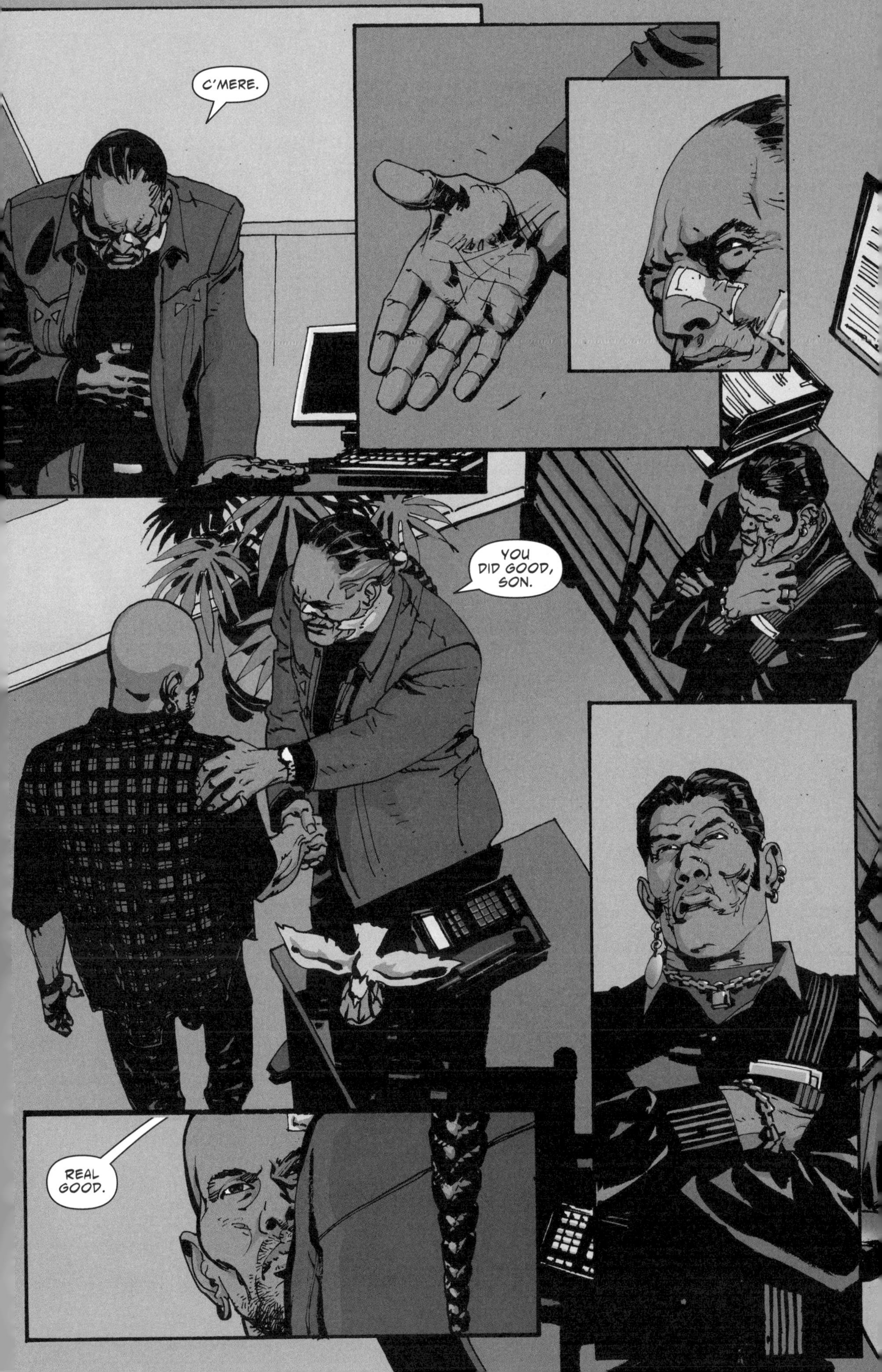
C'MERE.
YOU DID GOOD, SON.
REAL GOOD.

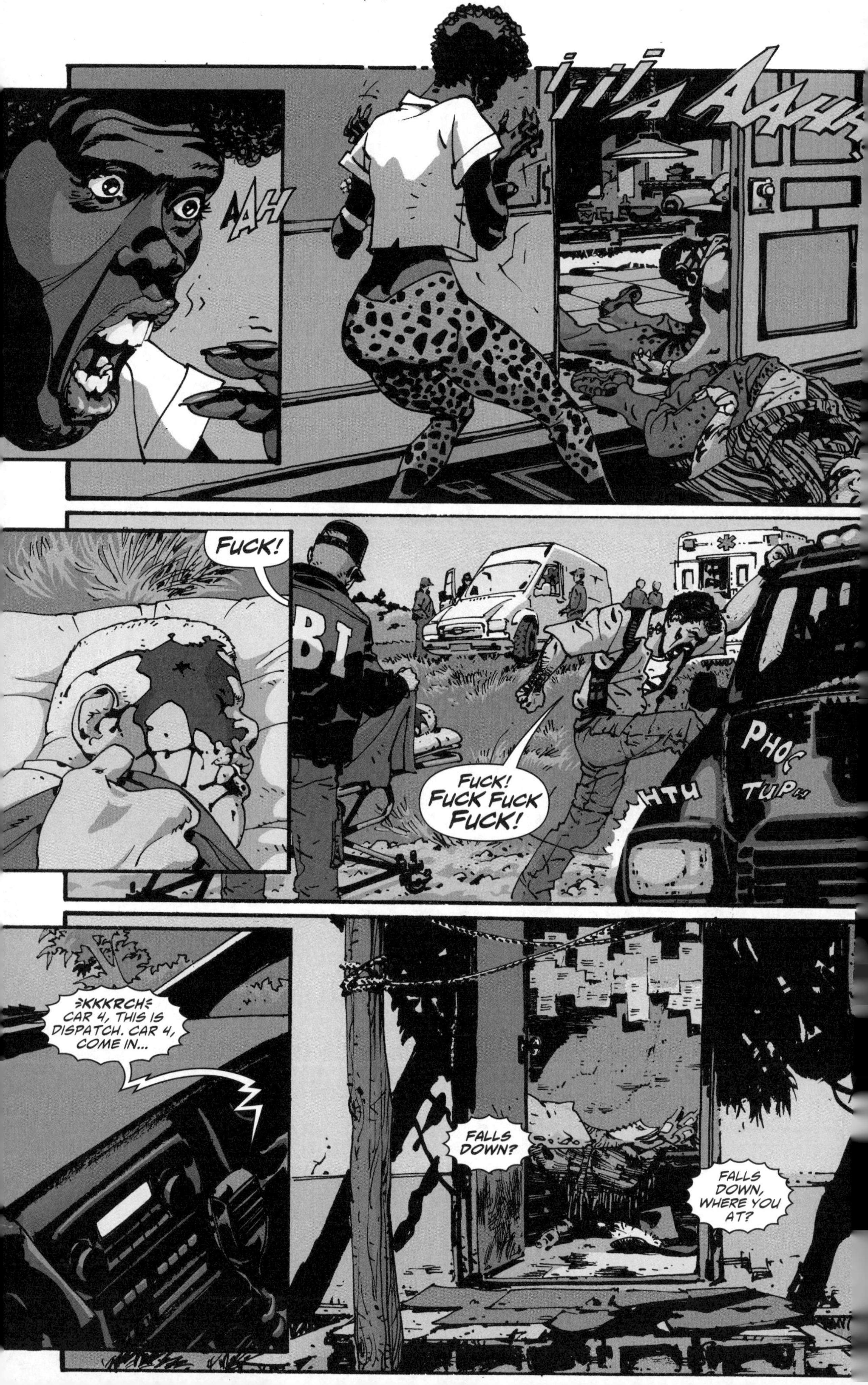
AAH
I-I-I AAAH
FUCK!
FUCK! FUCK FUCK FUCK!
PHOC
TUP
HTU
KKKRCH
CAR 4, THIS IS DISPATCH. CAR 4, COME IN...
FALLS DOWN?
FALLS DOWN, WHERE YOU AT?

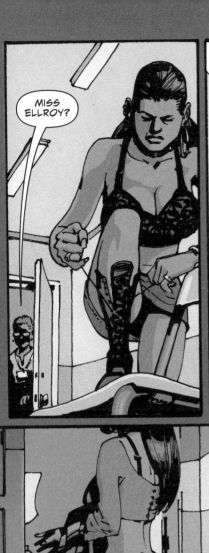

MISS ELLROY?

I'M CHECKING OUT.

MA'AM, I NEED YOU TO SIT DOWN FOR A MOMENT AND LISTEN TO ME. WE'VE GOT THE RESULTS OF YOUR TESTS BACK.

I DON'T CARE WHAT YOUR GODDAMN TESTS SAY. I FEEL FINE. I'M GOING HOME.

YOU'VE GOT A DRUG PROBLEM. WE CAN HELP YOU WITH THAT.

YEAH? THAT WHAT YOU LEARNED FROM YOUR FUCKING TESTS? GO TO HELL, LADY.

YOU'RE PREGNANT.

CONGRATULATIONS.

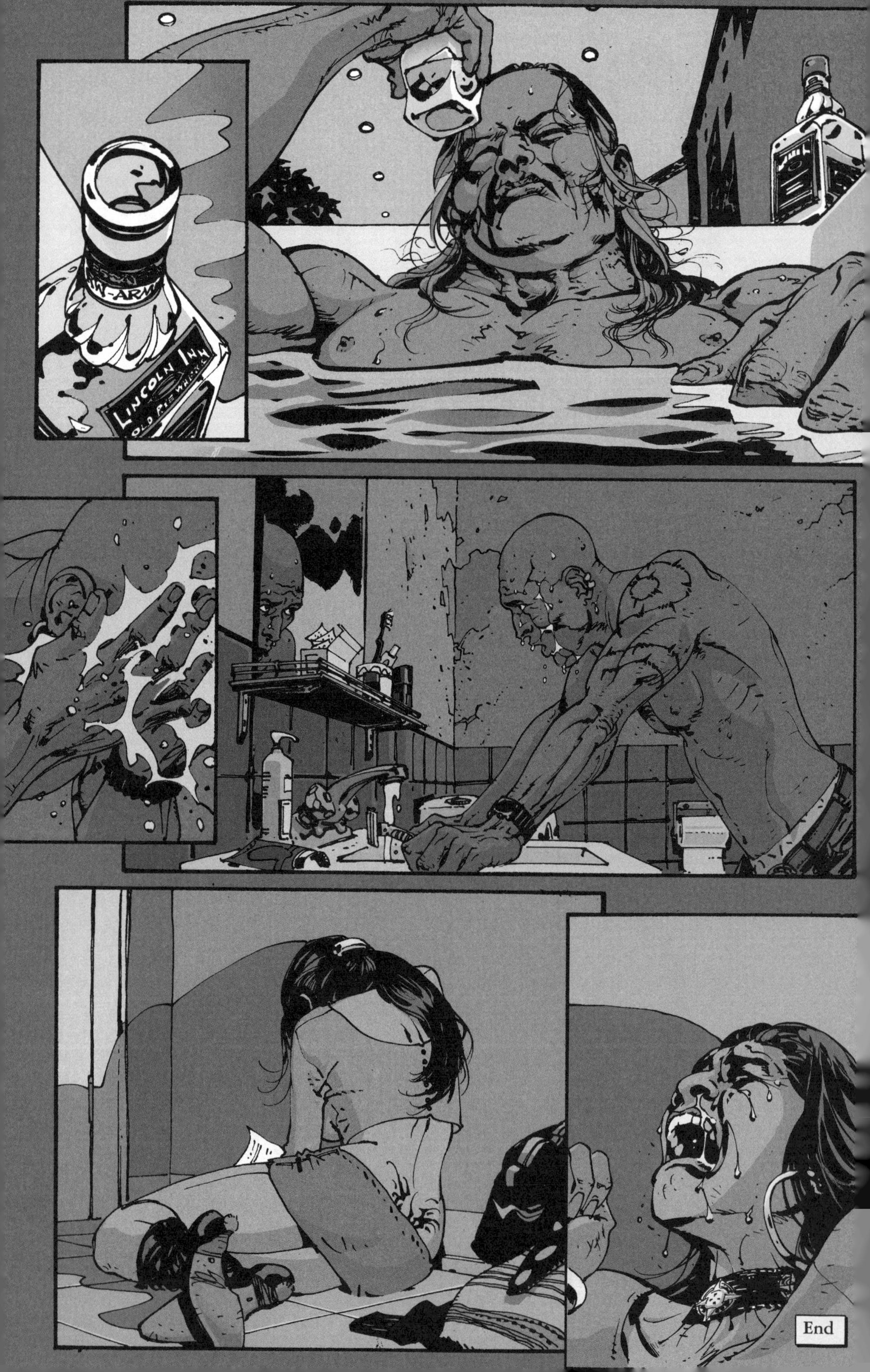

LINCOLN INN
OLD PIE WHISKY
End

# SCALPED SKETCHBOOK by R.M. GUÉRA

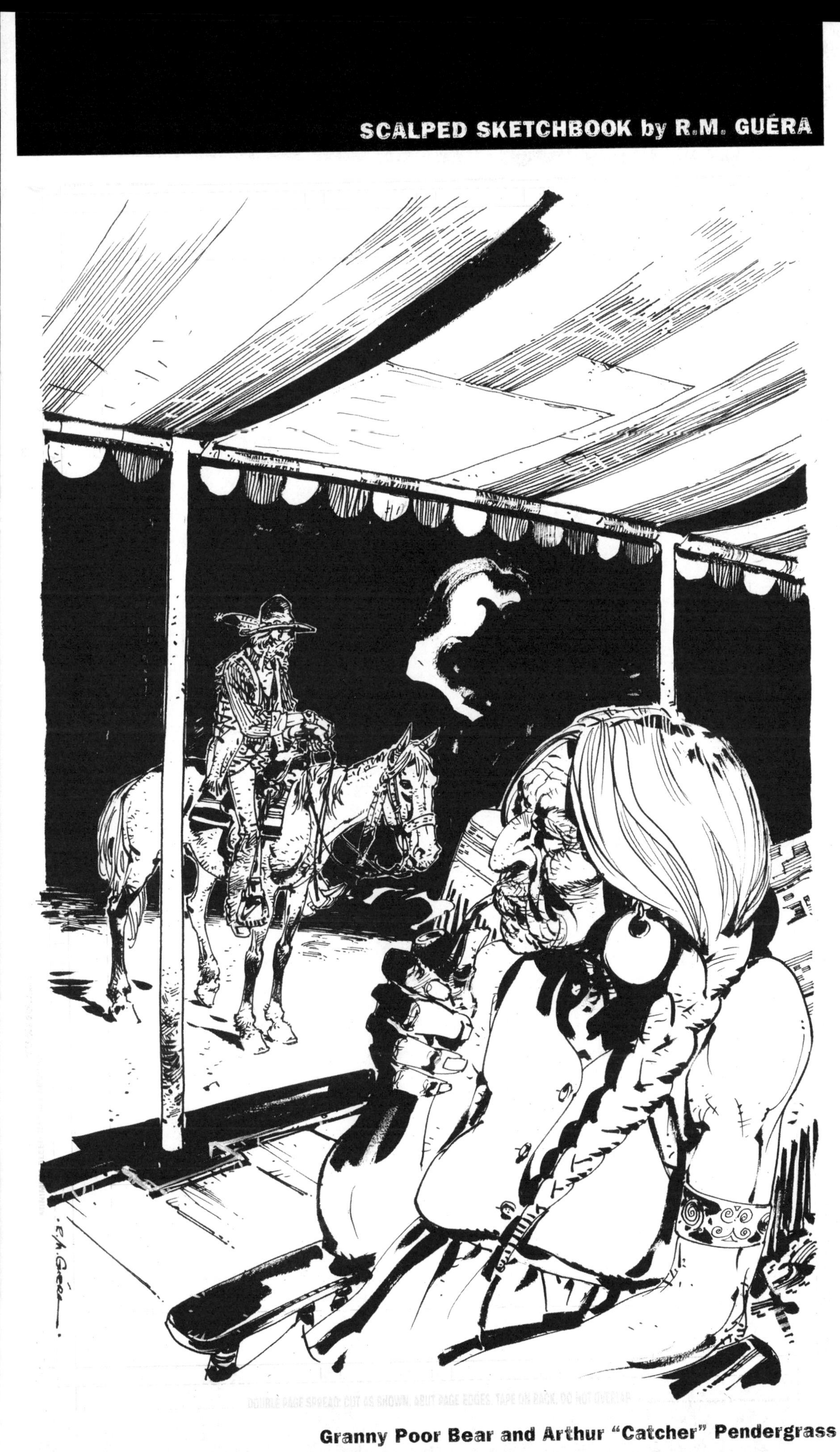

**Granny Poor Bear and Arthur "Catcher" Pendergrass**

## Pencil roughs: Relations and mood

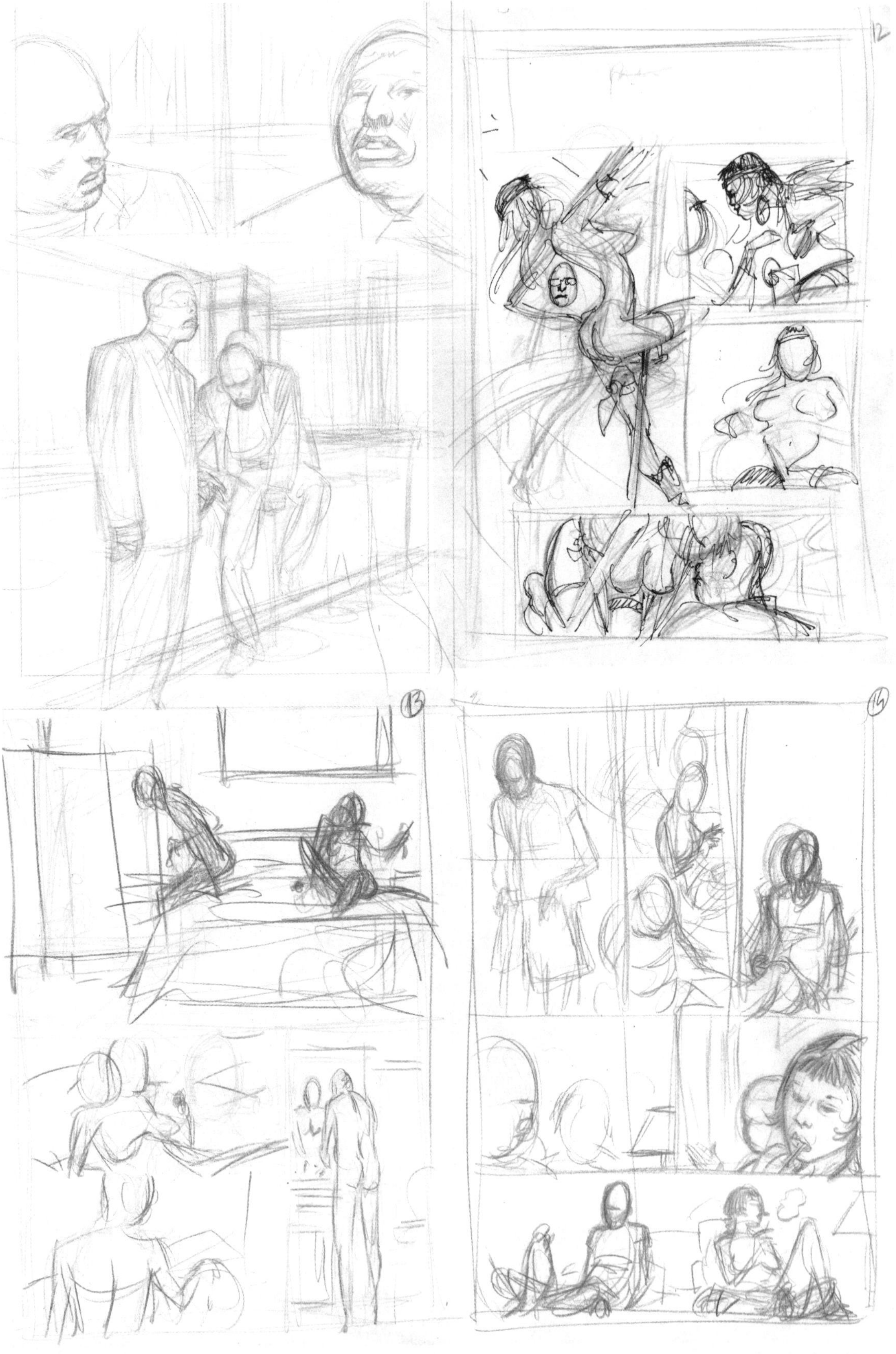

## Pencil roughs: Not today

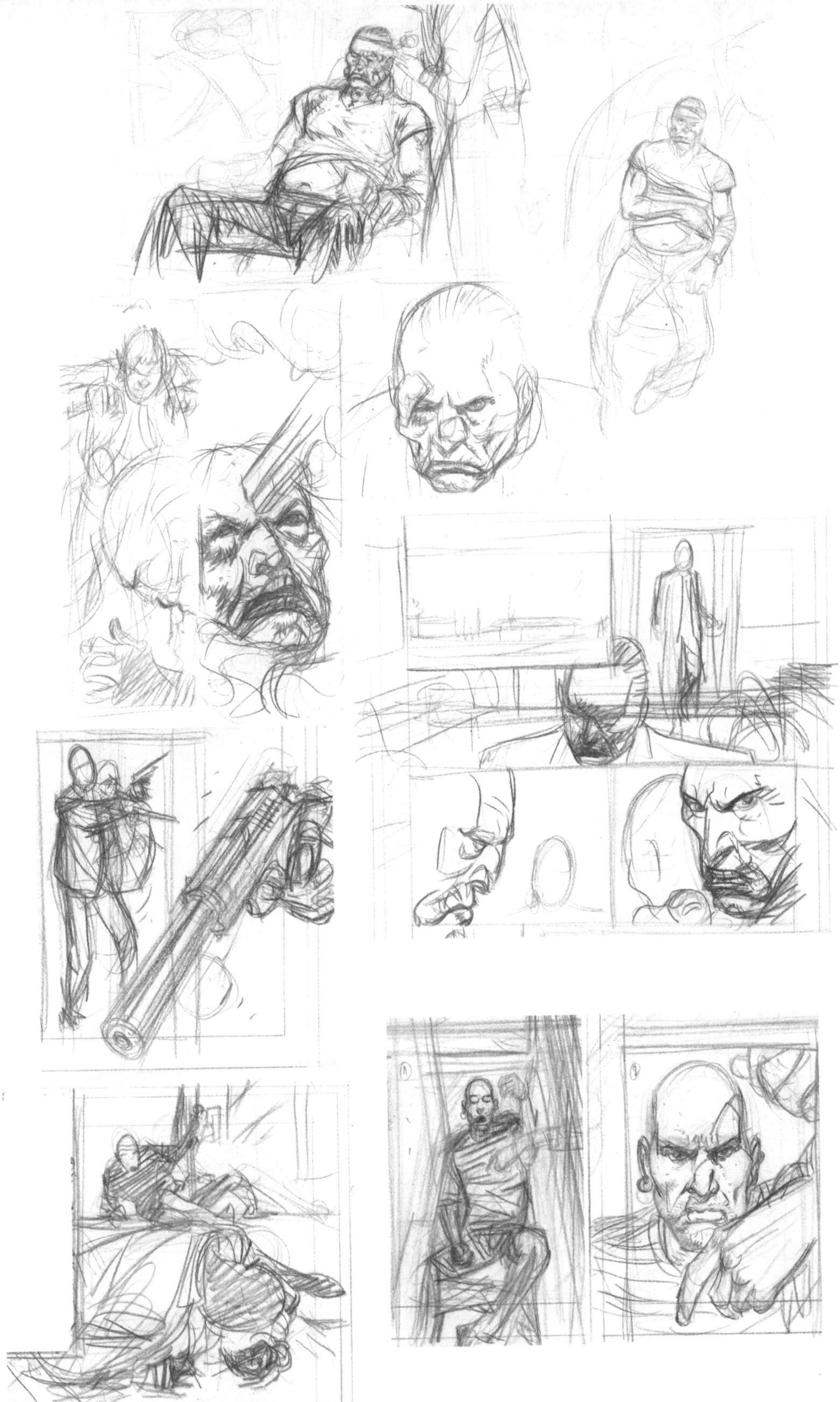

## Pencil roughs: Dilemmas and decisions

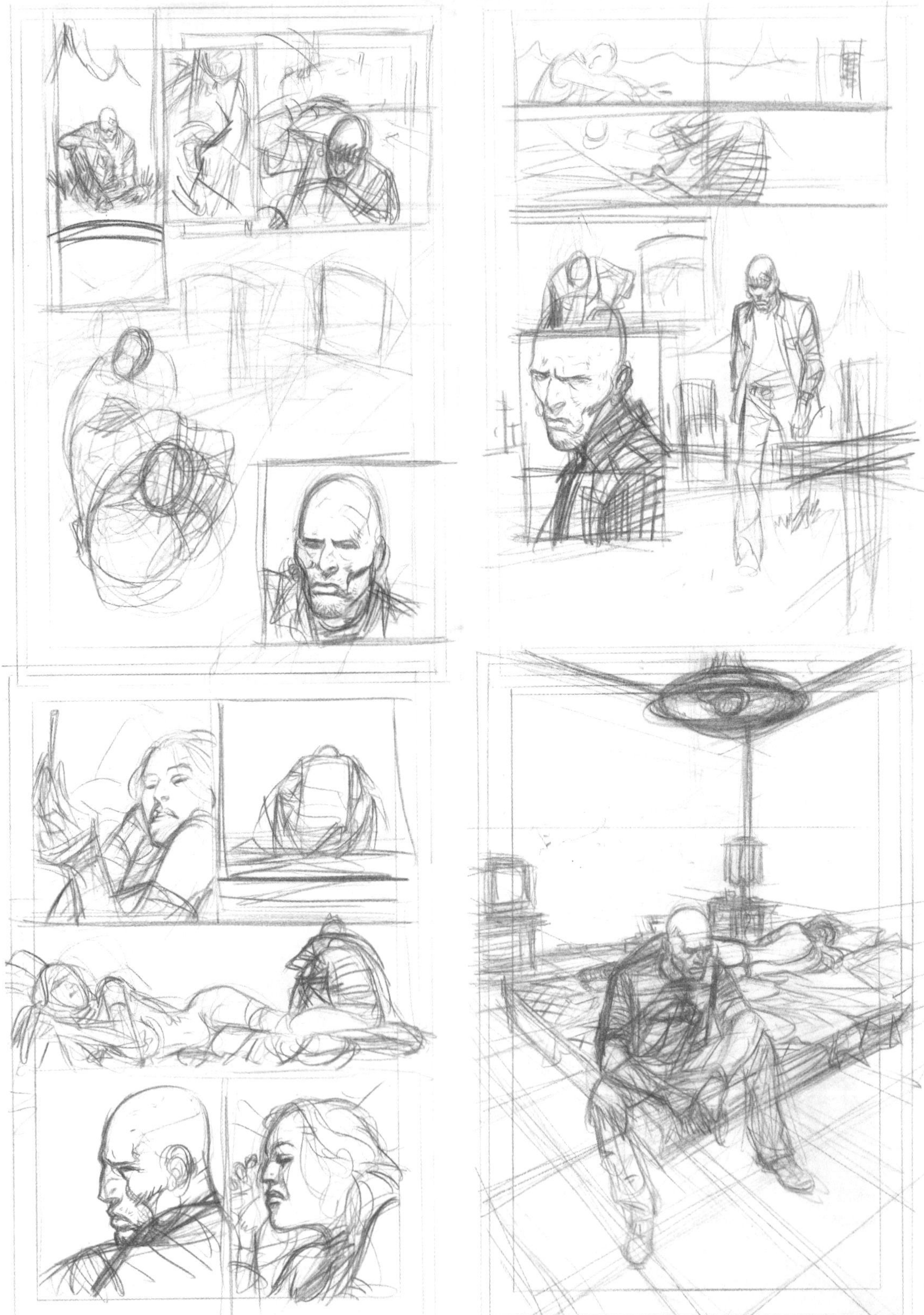

**Cover layout for the French edition of HIGH LONESOME**

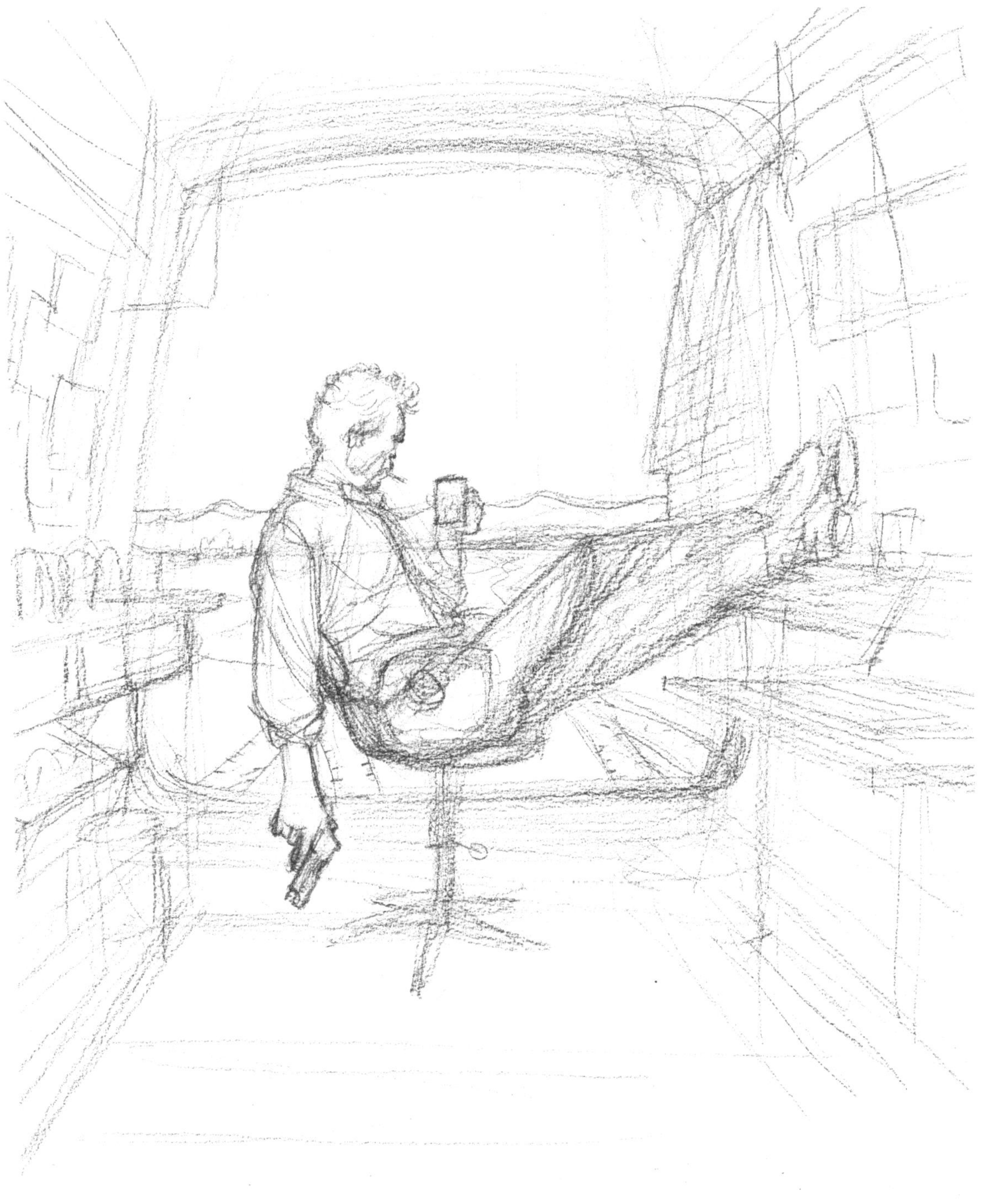

## Pencil roughs: Traces of the past

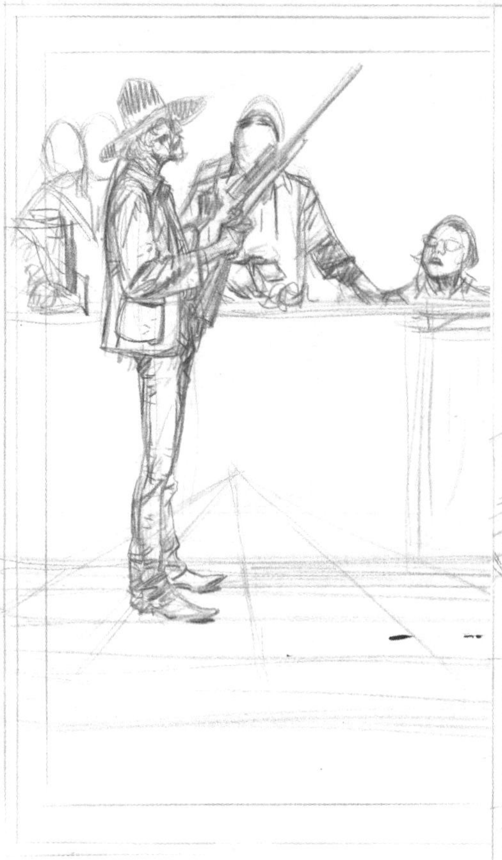

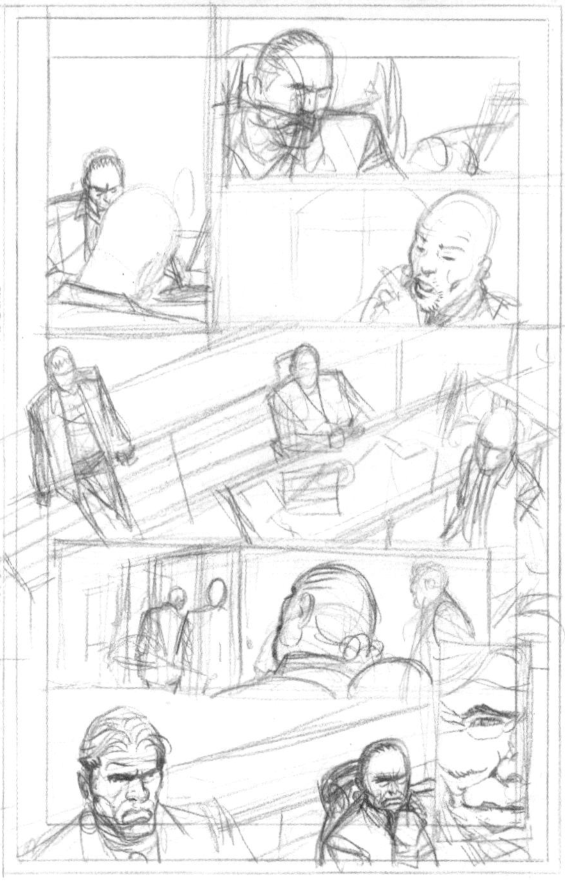

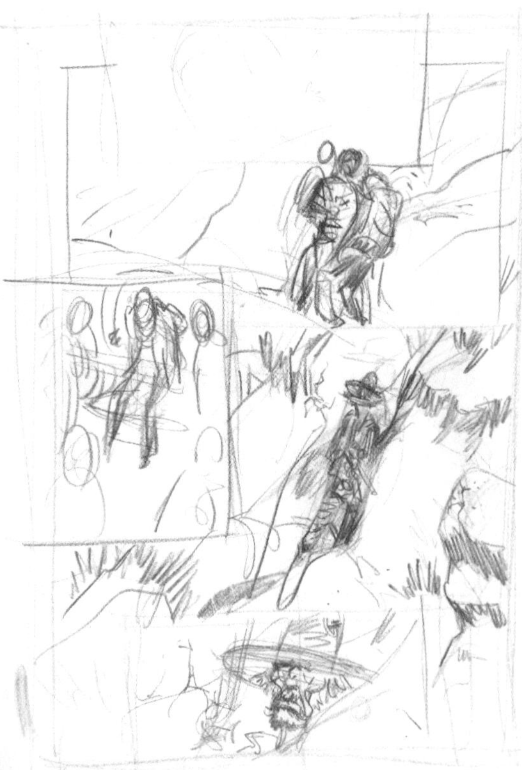

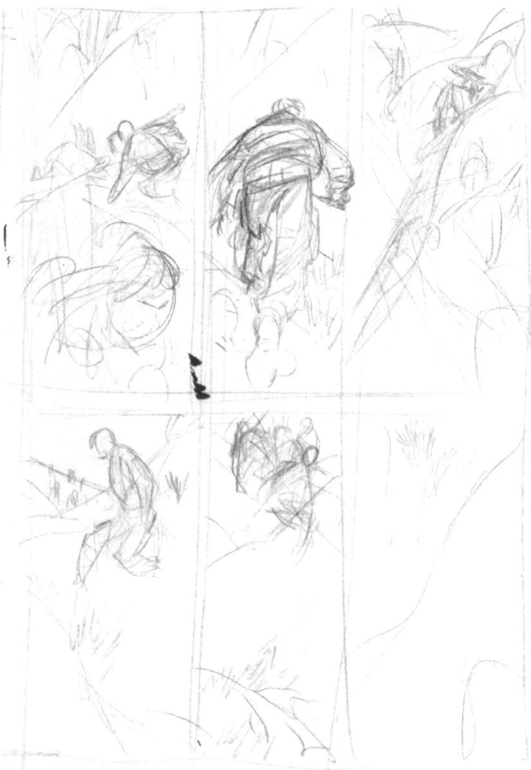

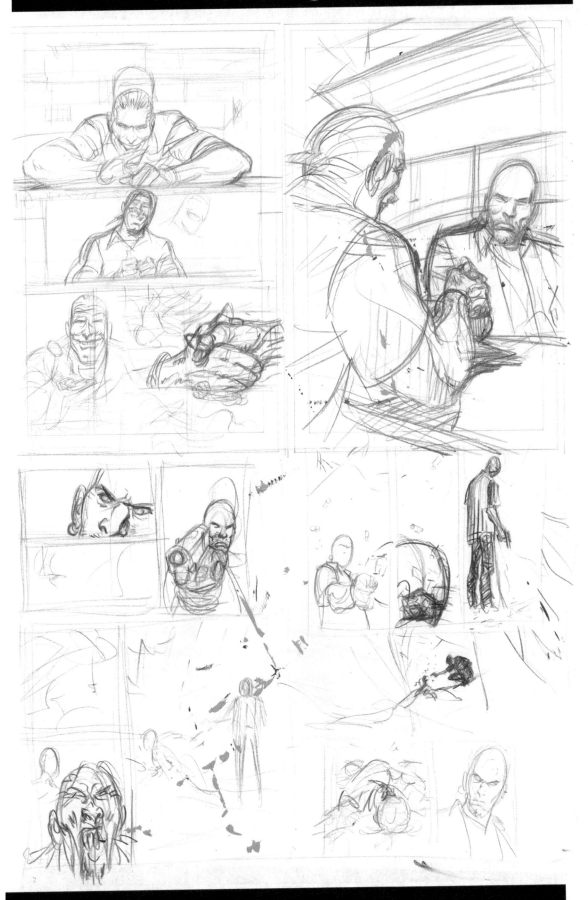

## Pencil roughs: Doomed

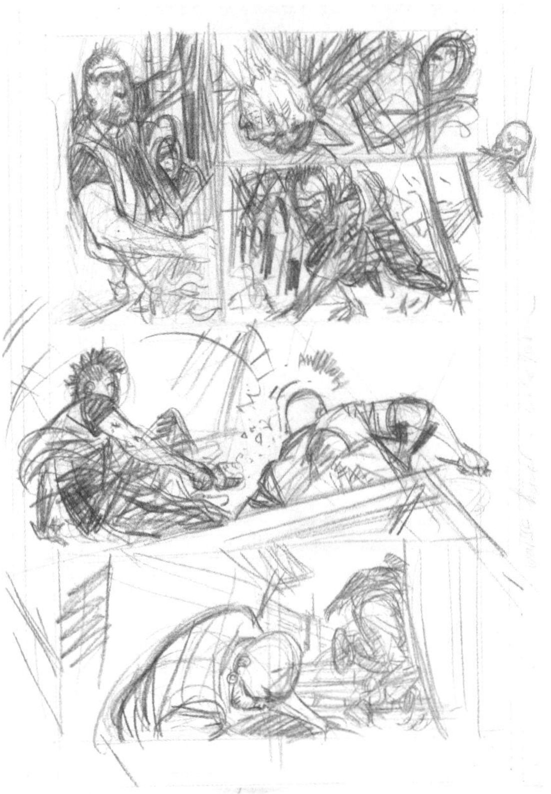

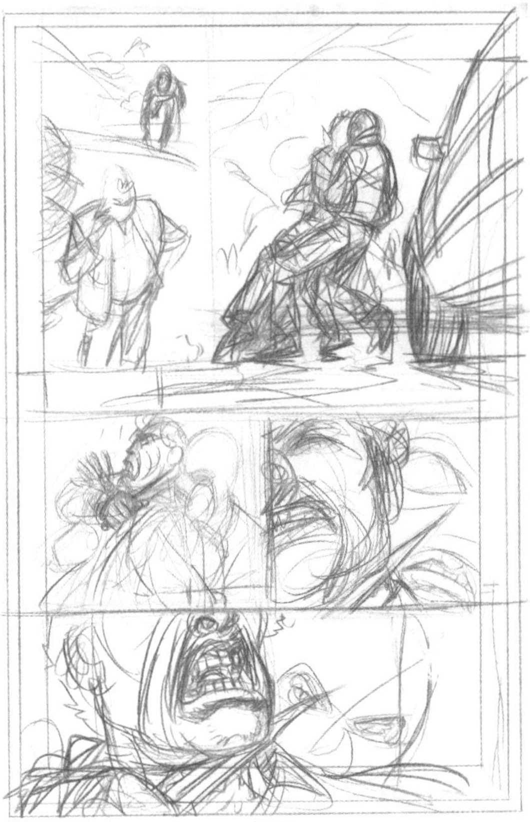

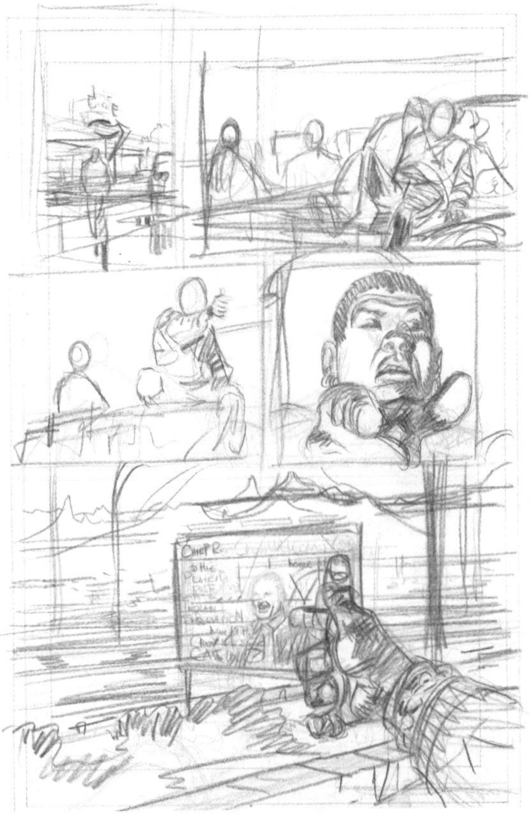

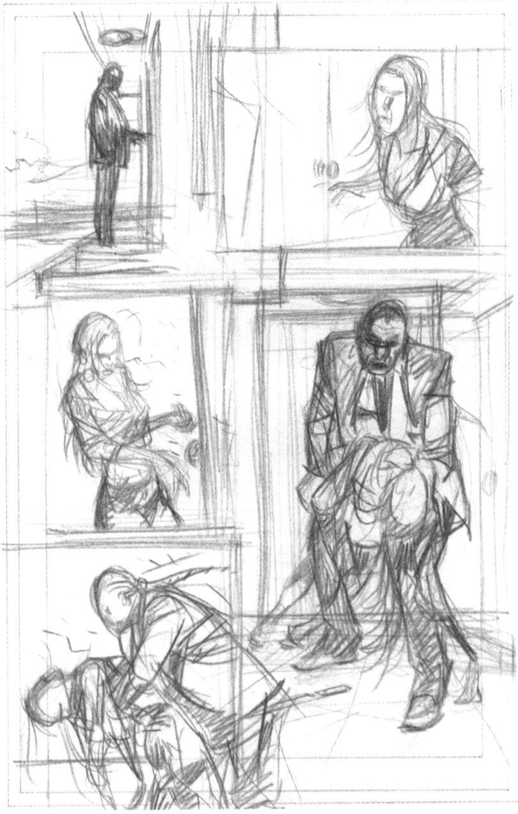

Cover layout for the French edition of THE GNAWING

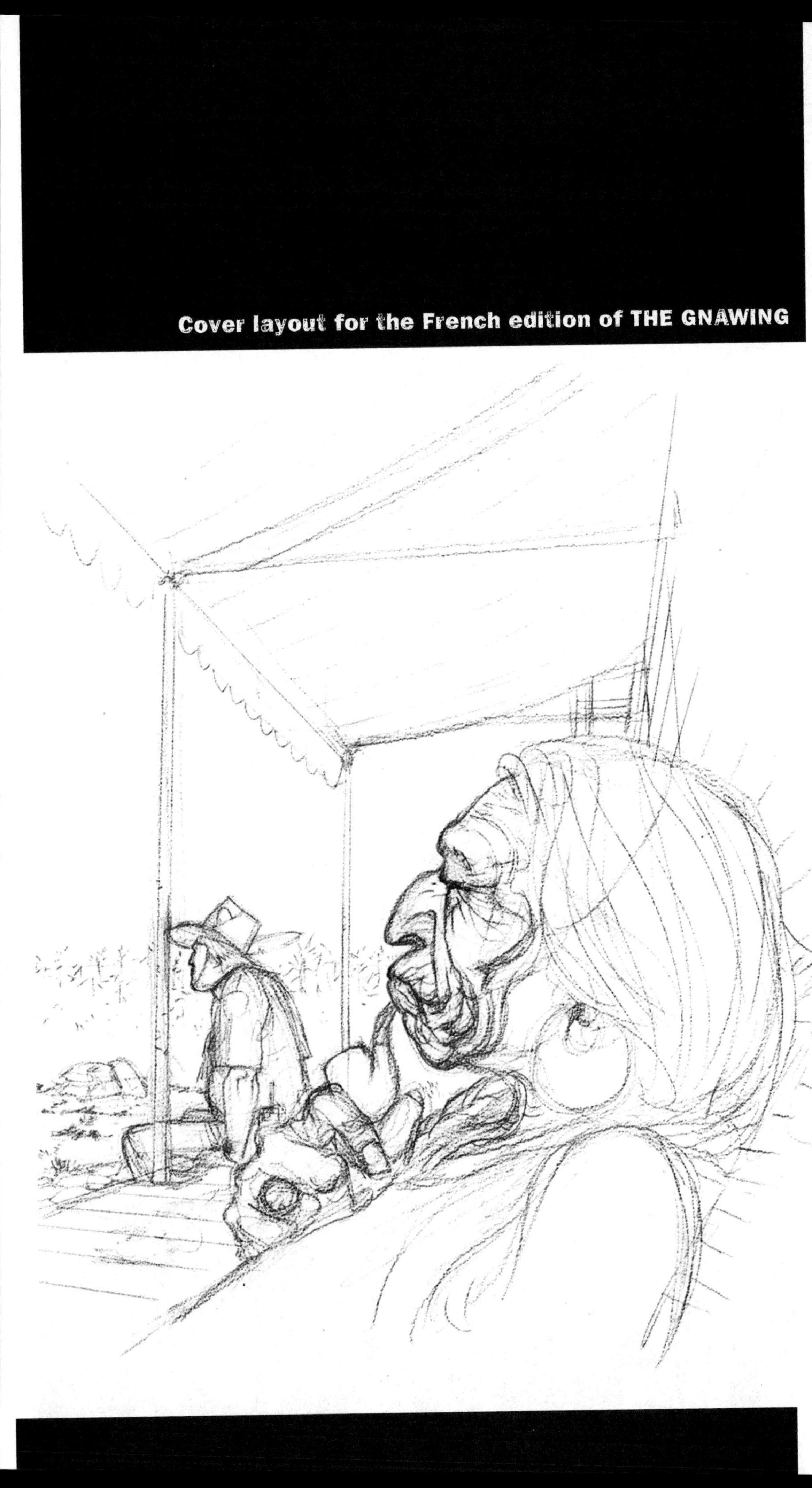

## Final cover art for the French edition of THE GNAWING

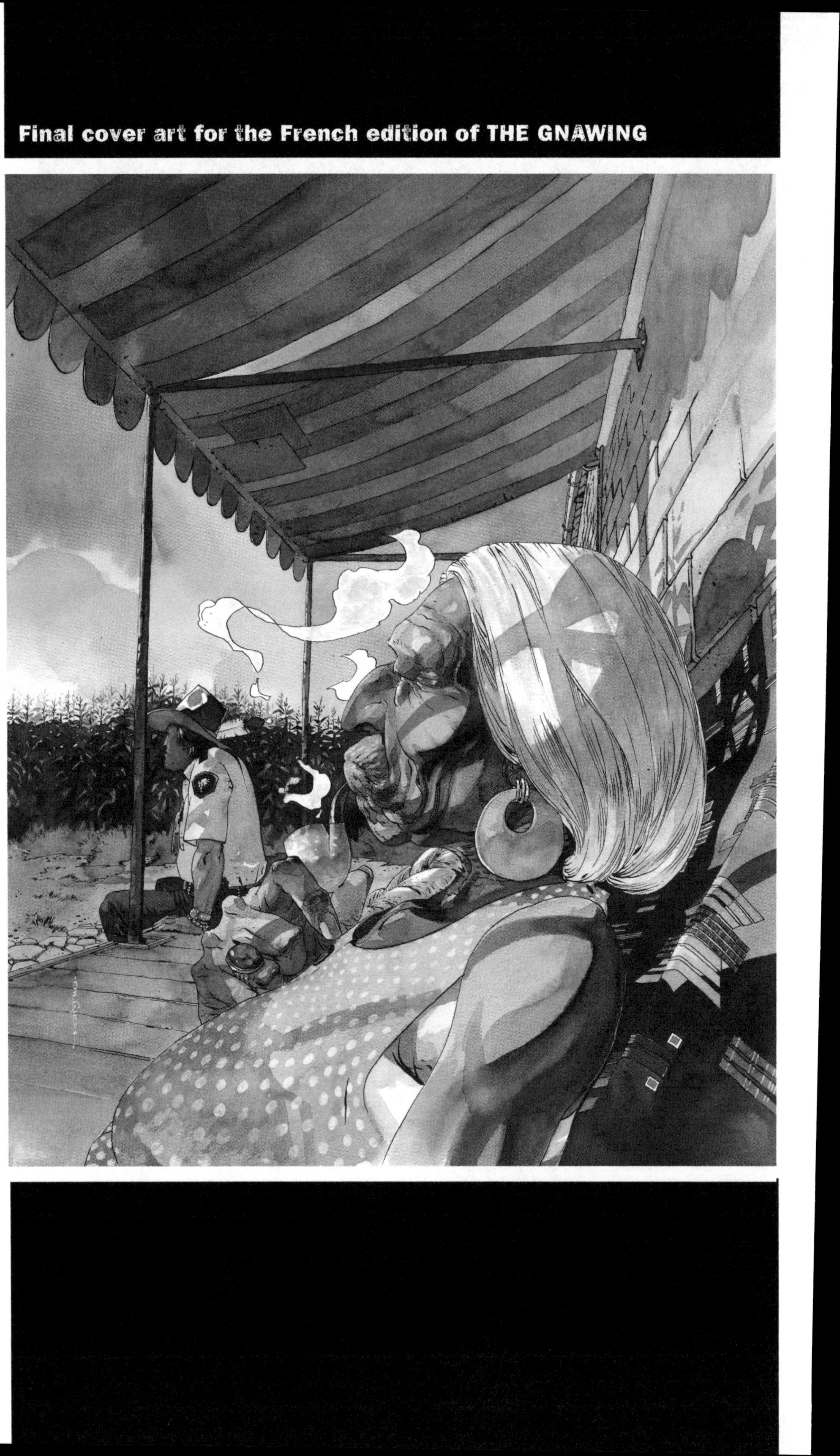

## SCALPED SKETCHBOOK BY DAVIDE FURNÒ

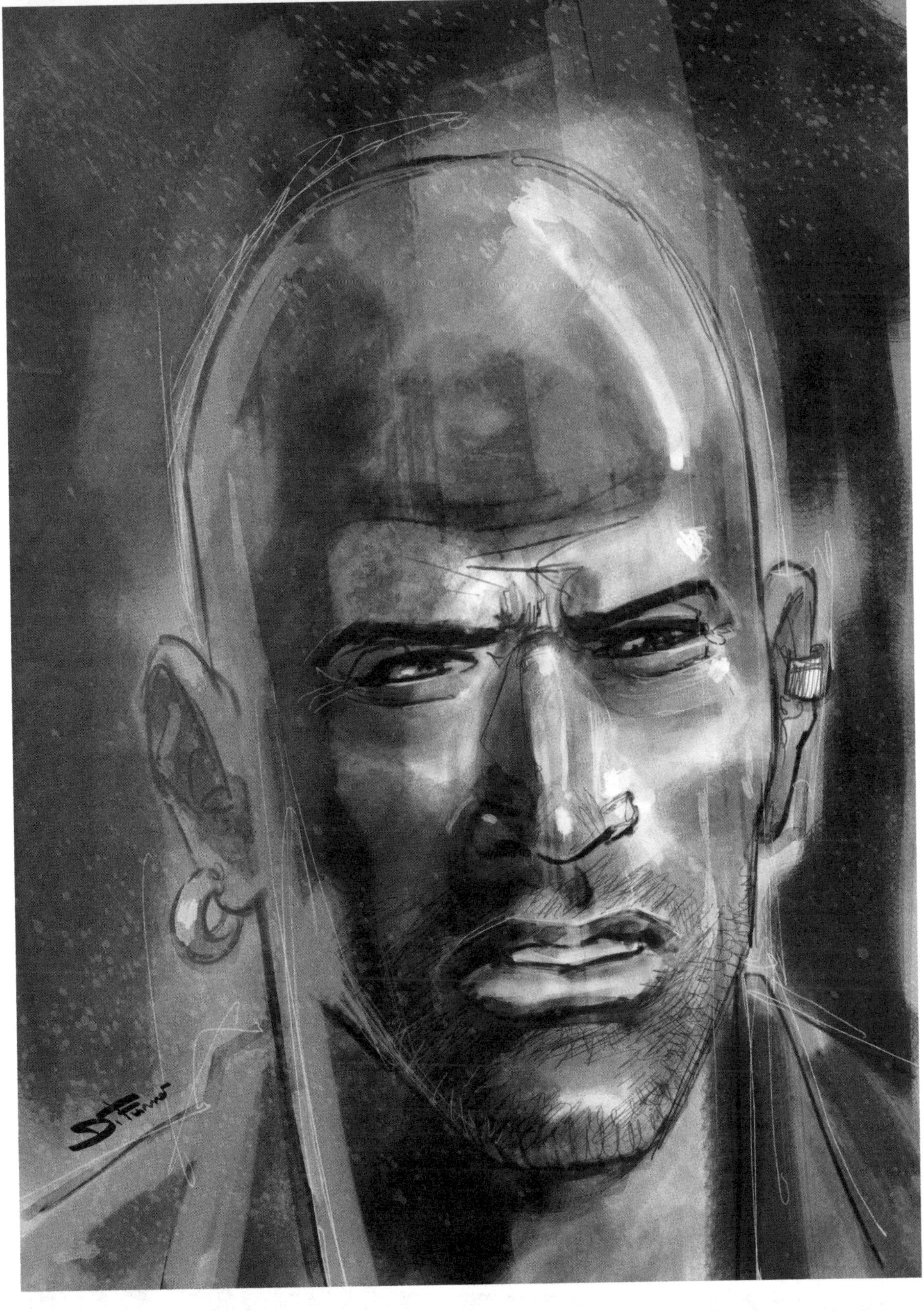

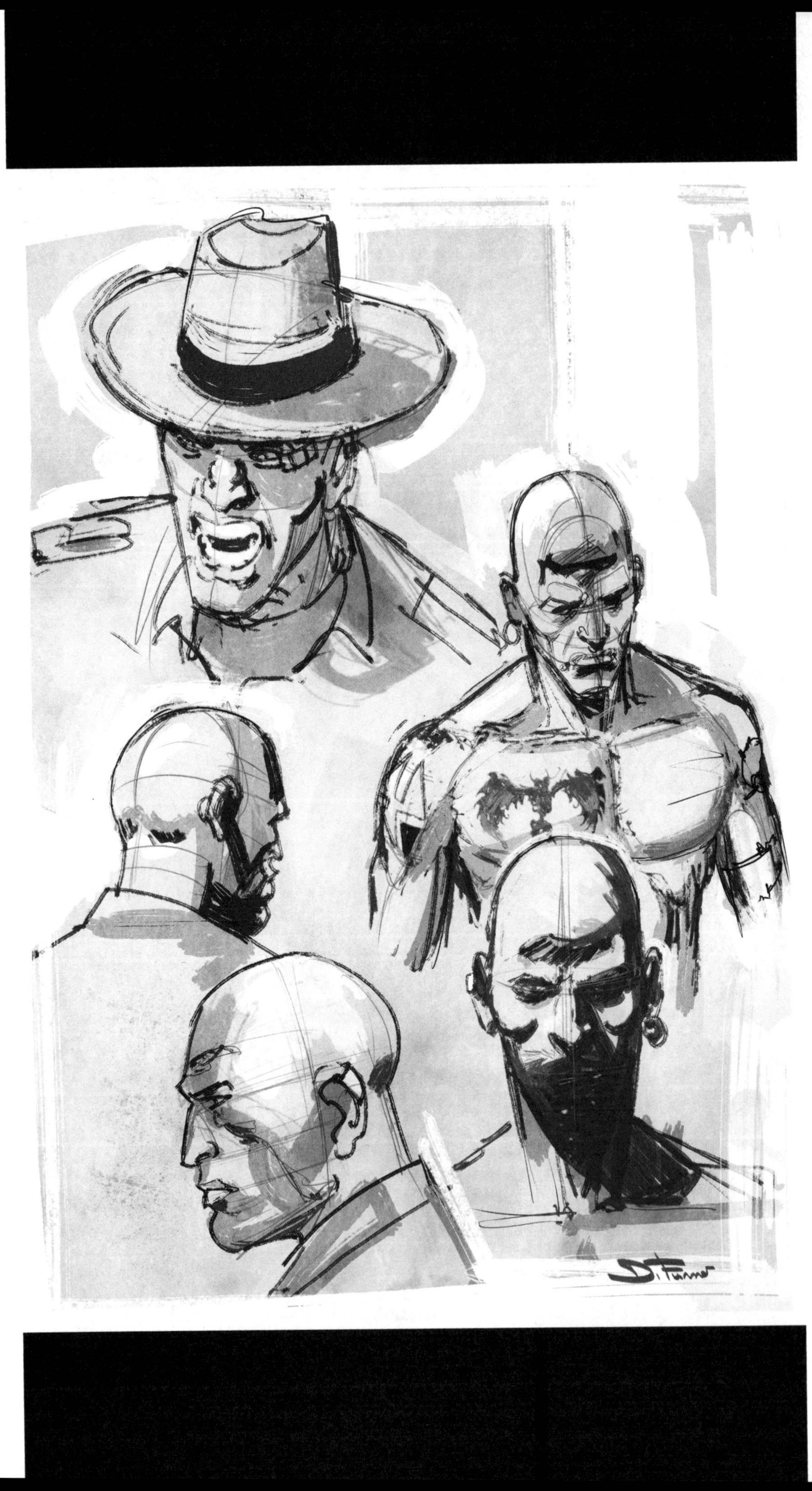

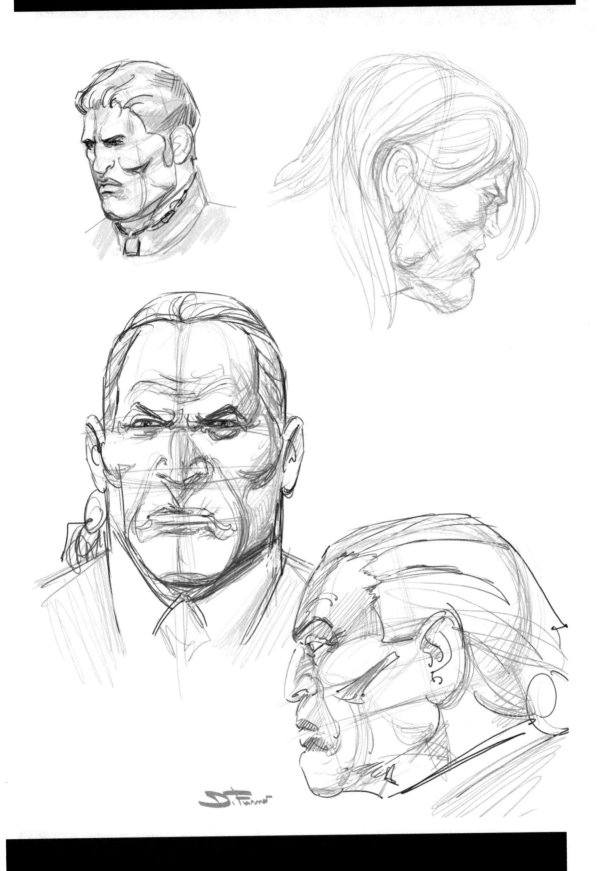

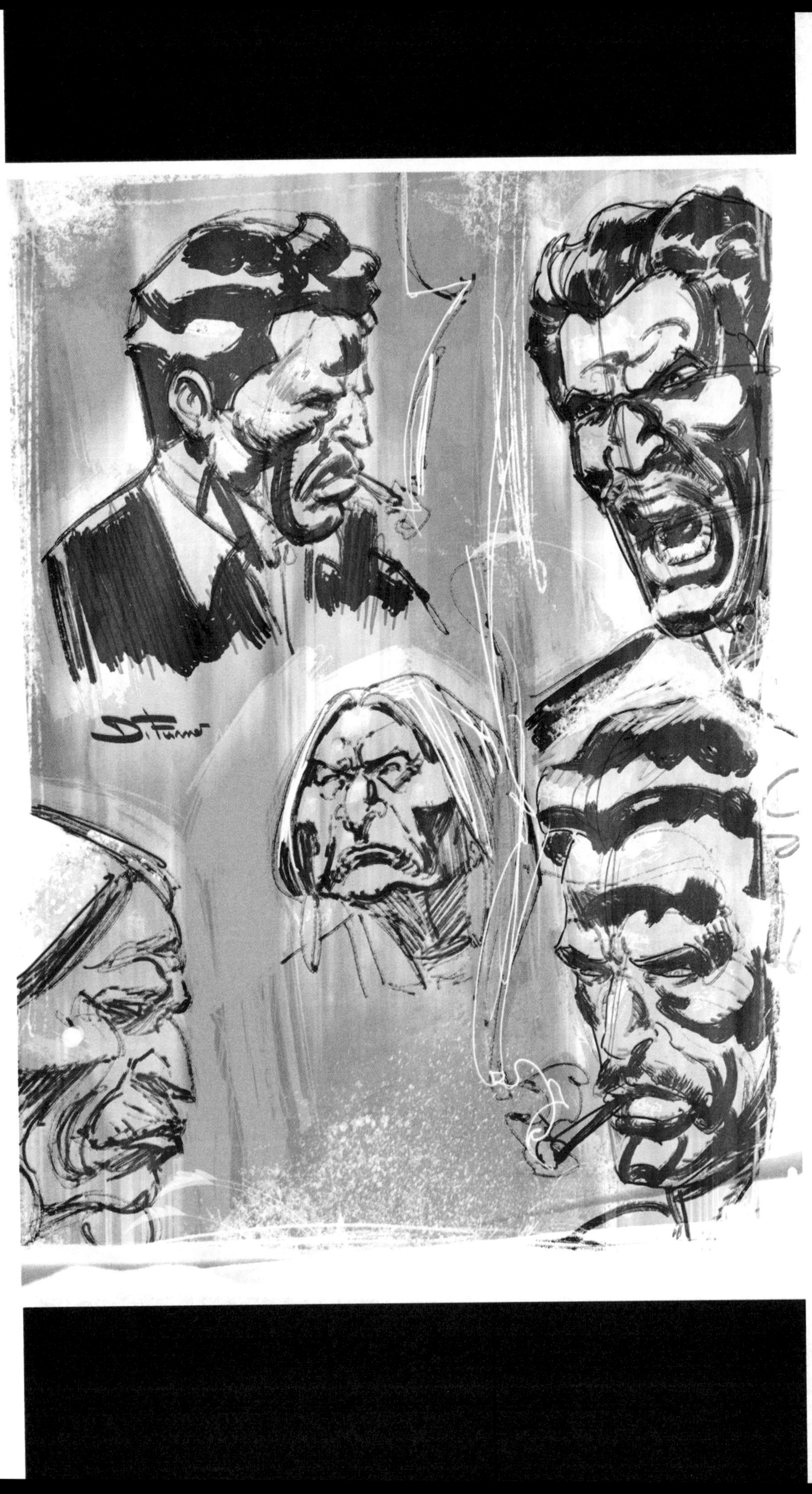

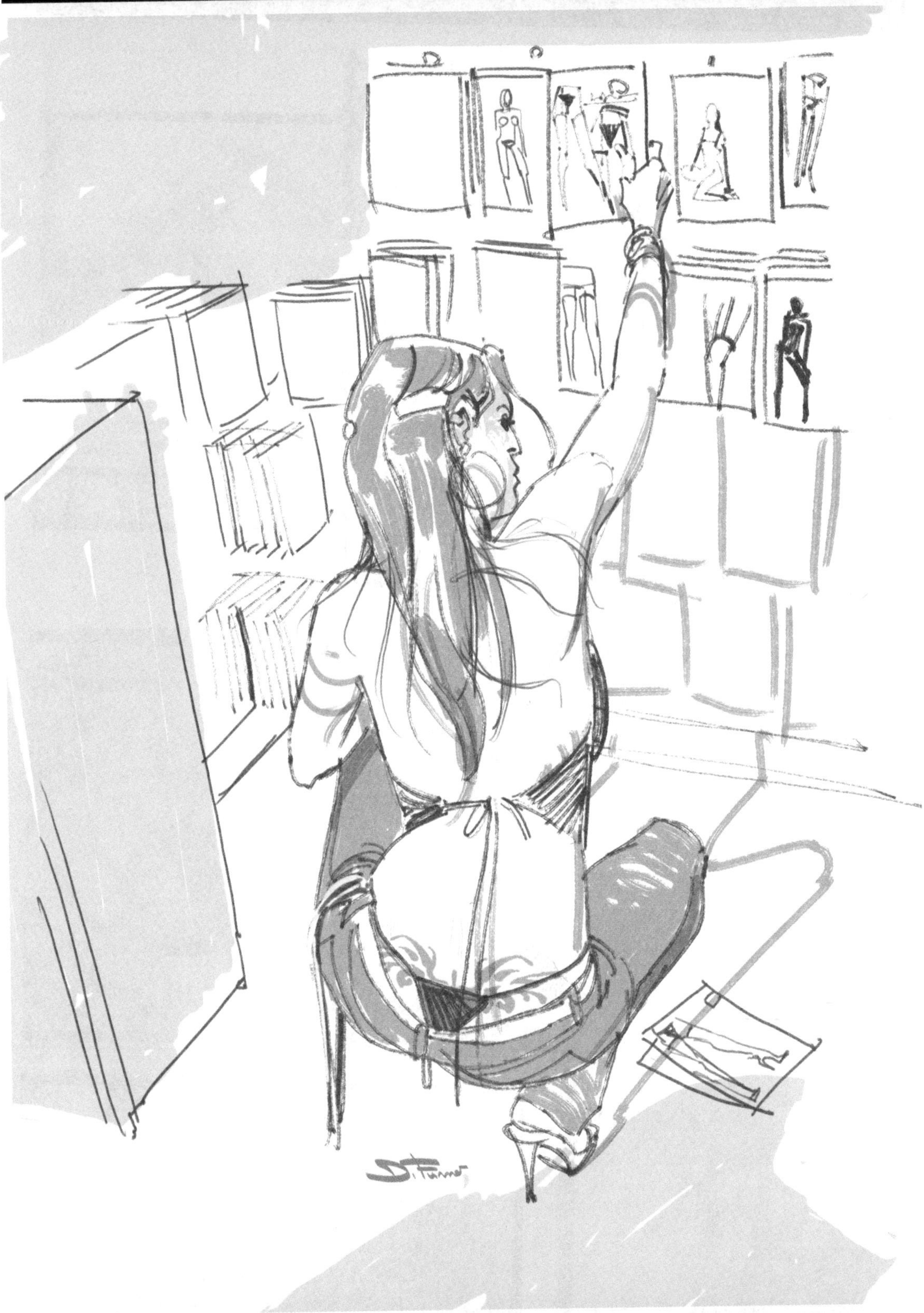

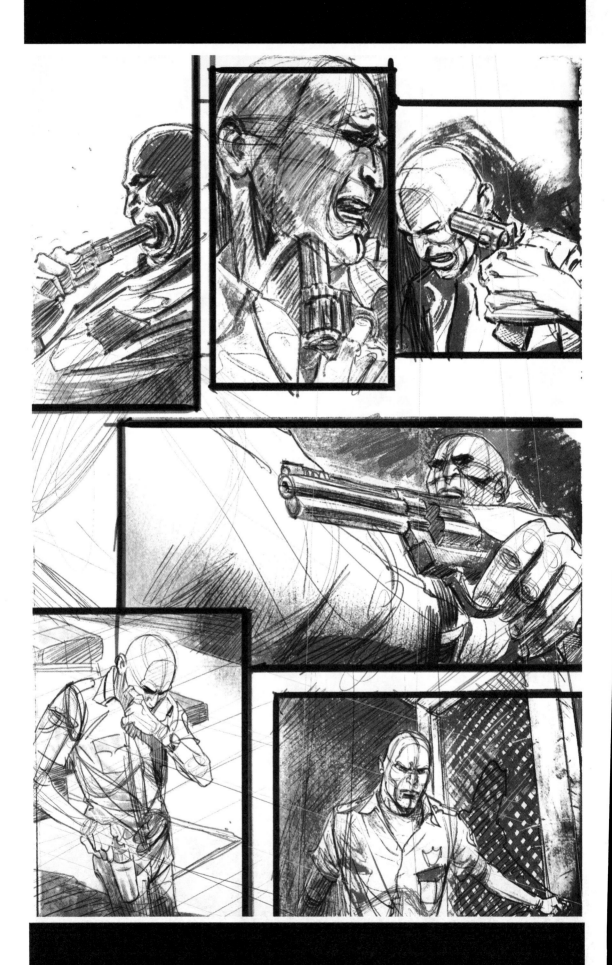

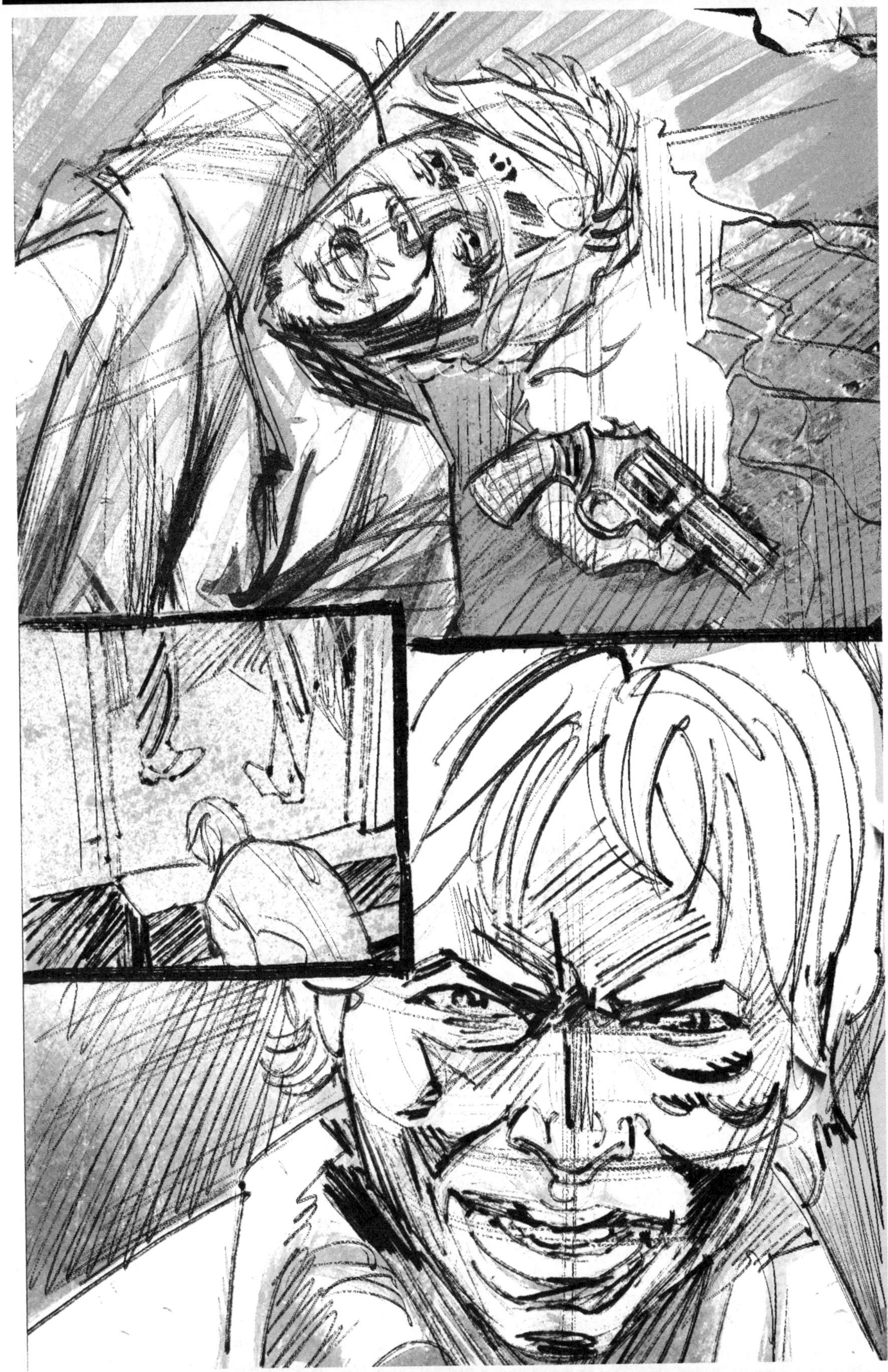

## JASON AARON

Jason Aaron is an Eisner and Harvey Award-nominated comic book writer whose best-known work includes the Native American crime drama SCALPED for DC Comics' Vertigo imprint. He also wrote several well-regarded runs on a number of titles for Marvel Comics, including *Wolverine*, *Ghost Rider* and *Thor*. Jason was born in Alabama and currently resides in Kansas City. He enjoys many things, but shaving is not one of them.

## R. M. GUÉRA

Born in Yugoslavia, comic book artist R.M. Guéra has lived in Spain since 1991. His internationally published work includes two volumes of the French series *Le Lièvre de Mars*, written by Patrick Cothias and published by Glénat, and the critically acclaimed Native American crime series SCALPED, written by Jason Aaron and published by Vertigo. He has also illustrated BATMAN ETERNAL for DC Comics, as well as the comics adaptation of Quentin Tarantino's DJANGO UNCHAINED for Vertigo.

## DAVIDE FURNÒ

Davide Furnò is an Italian artist known in the U.S. for his work on the Vertigo series SCALPED and GREEK STREET, as well as IDW's *30 Days of Night*, *24* and *Infestation*. In Italy, Furnò's art has appeared in such series as *Dylan Dog* and *Saguaro* for publisher Sergio Bonelli Editore and on the covers of a line of *noir* titles for publisher Edizioni BD. Furnò also teaches at the International School of Comics in Rome, and he recently illustrated the Caped Crusader for an issue of BATMAN: ETERNAL.

## FRANCESCO FRANCAVILLA

A native of Italy, Francesco Francavilla is known for his moody, pulpy brushwork and brilliant colors. His artistic talent has graced the covers of many well-known comics titles, including DETECTIVE COMICS, *Hellboy*, *Zorro*, *Dark Shadows* and *Archie*. He has also provided sequential art for writer Scott Snyder on DETECTIVE COMICS and SWAMP THING and illustrated acclaimed runs on Marvel's *Black Panther* and *Captain America*. When not busy creating comics, Francavilla illustrates children's books and works as a storyboard artist for a variety of animated series. Fans can check out his work, including his creator-owned series *The Black Beetle*, at francescofrancavilla.com.